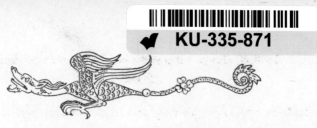

A note from the author:

INKDEATH came to life in my new home in Los Angeles. For the first time, I had enough room to put up all the photographs and paintings that inspired me to write. Hundreds of notes with ideas and plot points covered my bookshelves (yes, I also had room for my books!), and in front of the windows my son played.

When I sat down to write the first chapter, it felt like meeting up with very old friends. In the story, only two months have passed since Dustfinger's death and so it felt for me. But once again, I was surprised. Mo had become the Bluejay, much more than I had expected, and INKDEATH soon became as great a writing adventure as INKHEART and INKSPELL. As an author, I especially enjoyed the Fenoglio chapters (and I hope you'll like that he has two more glassmen to help him).

Some of you may know that Rolf, my husband of twenty-six years, became sick and died shortly before I finished this book. You may wonder if the loss and the grief my children and I felt made me write a story that deals so much with death. But it's not true. The story was told already, and only a few lines felt wrong and had to be rewritten.

I am the song that sings the bird.
I am the leaf that grows the land.
I am the tide that moves the moon.
I am the stream that halts the sand.
I am the cloud that drives the storm.
I am the earth that lights the sun.
I am the fire that strikes the stone.
I am the clay that shapes the hand.
I am the word that speaks the man.

Charles Causley, *I Am the Song*

Inkheart

Mortimer Folchart (Mo), a bookbinder, has such a beautiful voice that it can bring characters out of books when he reads aloud. He discovered his dangerous gift by accident when he was reading a story called *Inkheart* to his wife Resa and daughter Meggie. Several characters, including the evil Capricorn and some of his followers, came out of it into our world – and Resa vanished into the world of the book. Meggie, only three at the time, can't even remember her mother.

Nine years later the fire-eater Dustfinger, one of the Inkheart characters and desperately homesick for his own world, visits Mo and Meggie (now twelve years old) to warn them that Capricorn is looking for all copies of the book to destroy them, so that no one can ever move between the two worlds again by reading from it. He is after the copy that Mo still has, and he also wants to force Mo to read treasure out of books for him.

Capricorn and his criminal gang have made an Italian village their headquarters, and when Dustfinger treacherously tells them where to find Mo, he is kidnapped and taken there. Meggie, her great-aunt Elinor (a book collector with a fine library) and the repentant Dustfinger join forces to rescue him. But they no longer have the book that might help Dustfinger to get home and Mo to find his wife at last. With a new friend – Farid, a boy read accidentally out of the Arabian Nights by Mo – they track down the author of *Inkheart*, old Fenoglio, but his own copies have also

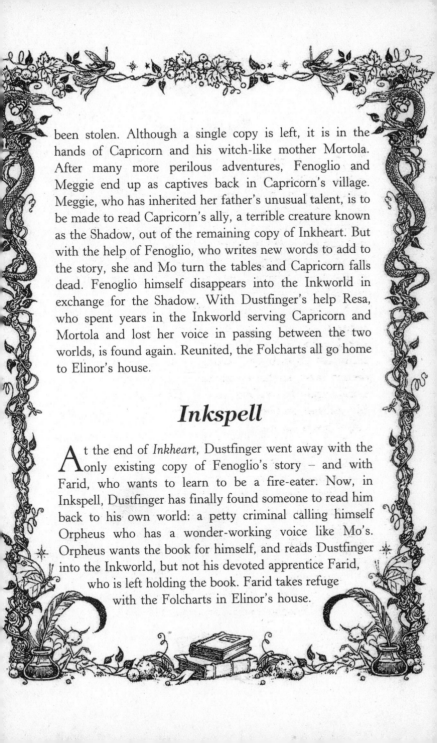

been stolen. Although a single copy is left, it is in the hands of Capricorn and his witch-like mother Mortola. After many more perilous adventures, Fenoglio and Meggie end up as captives back in Capricorn's village. Meggie, who has inherited her father's unusual talent, is to be made to read Capricorn's ally, a terrible creature known as the Shadow, out of the remaining copy of Inkheart. But with the help of Fenoglio, who writes new words to add to the story, she and Mo turn the tables and Capricorn falls dead. Fenoglio himself disappears into the Inkworld in exchange for the Shadow. With Dustfinger's help Resa, who spent years in the Inkworld serving Capricorn and Mortola and lost her voice in passing between the two worlds, is found again. Reunited, the Folcharts all go home to Elinor's house.

Inkspell

At the end of *Inkheart*, Dustfinger went away with the only existing copy of Fenoglio's story – and with Farid, who wants to learn to be a fire-eater. Now, in Inkspell, Dustfinger has finally found someone to read him back to his own world: a petty criminal calling himself Orpheus who has a wonder-working voice like Mo's. Orpheus wants the book for himself, and reads Dustfinger into the Inkworld, but not his devoted apprentice Farid, who is left holding the book. Farid takes refuge with the Folcharts in Elinor's house.

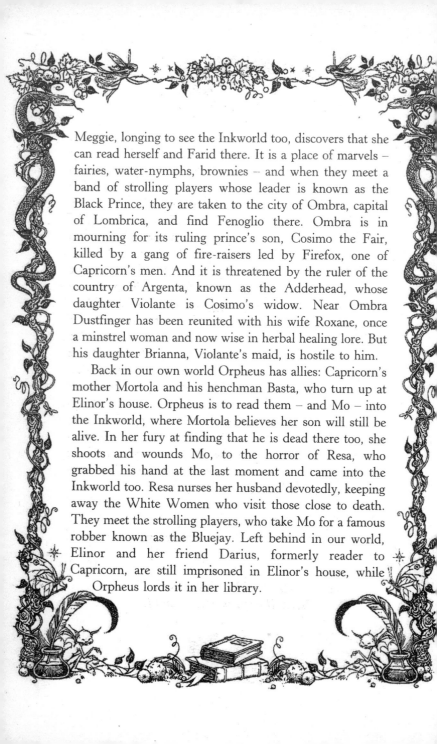

Meggie, longing to see the Inkworld too, discovers that she can read herself and Farid there. It is a place of marvels – fairies, water-nymphs, brownies – and when they meet a band of strolling players whose leader is known as the Black Prince, they are taken to the city of Ombra, capital of Lombrica, and find Fenoglio there. Ombra is in mourning for its ruling prince's son, Cosimo the Fair, killed by a gang of fire-raisers led by Firefox, one of Capricorn's men. And it is threatened by the ruler of the country of Argenta, known as the Adderhead, whose daughter Violante is Cosimo's widow. Near Ombra Dustfinger has been reunited with his wife Roxane, once a minstrel woman and now wise in herbal healing lore. But his daughter Brianna, Violante's maid, is hostile to him.

Back in our own world Orpheus has allies: Capricorn's mother Mortola and his henchman Basta, who turn up at Elinor's house. Orpheus is to read them – and Mo – into the Inkworld, where Mortola believes her son will still be alive. In her fury at finding that he is dead there too, she shoots and wounds Mo, to the horror of Resa, who grabbed his hand at the last moment and came into the Inkworld too. Resa nurses her husband devotedly, keeping away the White Women who visit those close to death. They meet the strolling players, who take Mo for a famous robber known as the Bluejay. Left behind in our world, Elinor and her friend Darius, formerly reader to Capricorn, are still imprisoned in Elinor's house, while Orpheus lords it in her library.

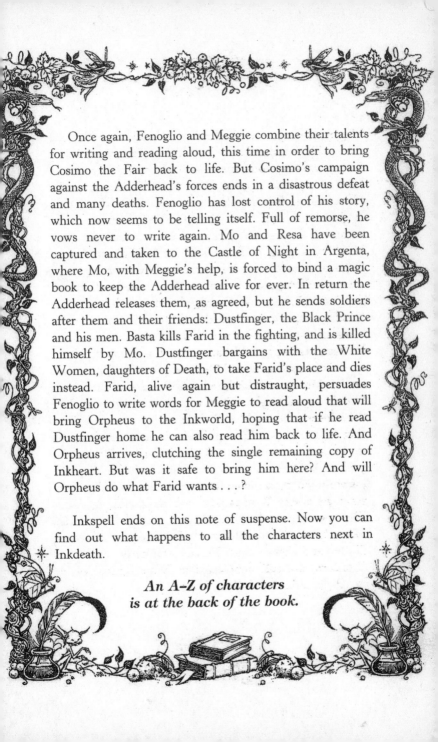

Once again, Fenoglio and Meggie combine their talents for writing and reading aloud, this time in order to bring Cosimo the Fair back to life. But Cosimo's campaign against the Adderhead's forces ends in a disastrous defeat and many deaths. Fenoglio has lost control of his story, which now seems to be telling itself. Full of remorse, he vows never to write again. Mo and Resa have been captured and taken to the Castle of Night in Argenta, where Mo, with Meggie's help, is forced to bind a magic book to keep the Adderhead alive for ever. In return the Adderhead releases them, as agreed, but he sends soldiers after them and their friends: Dustfinger, the Black Prince and his men. Basta kills Farid in the fighting, and is killed himself by Mo. Dustfinger bargains with the White Women, daughters of Death, to take Farid's place and dies instead. Farid, alive again but distraught, persuades Fenoglio to write words for Meggie to read aloud that will bring Orpheus to the Inkworld, hoping that if he read Dustfinger home he can also read him back to life. And Orpheus arrives, clutching the single remaining copy of Inkheart. But was it safe to bring him here? And will Orpheus do what Farid wants . . . ?

Inkspell ends on this note of suspense. Now you can find out what happens to all the characters next in Inkdeath.

**An A–Z of characters
is at the back of the book.**

1
Nothing But a Dog and a Sheet of Paper

Hark, the footsteps of the night
Fade in silence long.
Quiet chirps my reading light
Like a cricket's song.

Books inviting us to read
On the bookshelves stand.
Piers for bridges that will lead
Into fairyland.

Rilke, *Sacrifice to the Lares,* **from** *Vigils III*

Moonlight fell on Elinor's dressing gown, her nightdress, her bare feet, and the dog lying in front of them. Orpheus's dog. Oh, the way he looked at her with his eternally sad eyes! As if asking himself why, in the name of all the exciting smells in the world, she was sitting in her library in the middle of the night, surrounded by silent books, just staring into space.

'Why?' said Elinor in the silence. 'Because I can't sleep, you stupid animal.' But she patted his head all the same. This is what you've come to, Elinor, she thought as she hauled herself out of her armchair. Spending your nights talking to a dog. You don't even like dogs, least of all this one, with his heavy breathing that always reminds you of his appalling master!

Still, she had kept the dog in spite of the painful memories he brought back. She'd kept the chair too, even though the Magpie had sat in it. Mortola . . . how often Elinor thought she heard the old woman's voice when she went into the quiet library, how often she seemed to see Mortimer and Resa standing among the bookshelves, or Meggie sitting by the window with a book on her lap, face hidden behind her smooth, bright hair . . .

Memories. They were all she had left. No more tangible than the pictures conjured up by books. But what would be left if she lost those memories too? Then she'd be alone again for ever – with the silence and the emptiness in her heart. And an ugly dog.

Her feet looked so old in the pale moonlight. Moonlight! she thought, wiggling her toes in it. In many stories moonlight had magical powers. All lies. Her whole head was full of printed lies. She couldn't even look at the moon with eyes unclouded by veils of letters. Couldn't she wipe all those words out of her head and heart, and see the world through her own eyes again, at least once?

Heavens, Elinor, what a fabulous mood you're in, she thought as she made her way over to the glass case where she kept everything that Orpheus had left behind, apart from his dog. Wallowing in self-pity, like that stupid dog rolling over in every puddle.

The sheet of paper that lay behind the glass looked nothing

special, just an ordinary piece of lined paper densely written in pale-blue ink. Not to be compared with the magnificently illuminated books in the other display cases – even though the tracing of every letter showed how very impressed Orpheus was with himself. I hope the fire-elves have burnt that self-satisfied smile off his lips, thought Elinor as she opened the glass case. I hope the men-at-arms have skewered him – or, even better, I hope he's starved to death in the Wayless Wood, miserably and very, very slowly. It wasn't the first time she had pictured Orpheus's wretched end in the Inkworld to herself. These images gave her lonely heart more pleasure than almost anything.

The sheet of paper was already yellowing. To add insult to injury, it was cheap stuff. And the words on it really didn't look as though they could have spirited their writer away to another world right before Elinor's eyes. Three photographs lay beside the sheet of paper – one of Meggie and two of Resa – a photo of her as a child and another taken only a few months ago, with Mortimer beside her, both of them smiling so happily! Hardly a night went by when Elinor didn't look at those photographs. By now, at least, the tears had stopped running down her cheeks when she did so, but they were still there in her heart. Bitter tears. Her heart was full to the brim with them, a horrible feeling.

Lost.

Meggie.

Resa.

Mortimer.

Almost three months had passed since their disappearance. In fact, Meggie had even been gone a few days longer than her parents . . .

3

The dog stretched and came trotting drowsily over to her. He pushed his nose into her dressing-gown pocket, knowing there were always a few dog biscuits in it for him.

'Yes, all right, all right,' she murmured, shoving one of the smelly little things into his broad muzzle. 'Where's your master, then?' She held the sheet of paper in front of his nose, and the stupid creature sniffed it as if he really could catch Orpheus's scent behind the words on the page.

Elinor stared at the words, shaping them with her lips. *In the streets of Ombra* . . . She'd stood here so often over the last few weeks, surrounded by books that meant nothing to her; now she was once again alone with them. They didn't speak to her, just as if they knew that she'd have exchanged them all on the spot for the three people she had lost. Lost in a book.

'I *will* learn how, damn it!' Her voice sounded defiant, like a child's. 'I'll learn how to read them so that they'll swallow me up too, I will, I will!'

The dog was looking at her as if he believed every word of it, but Elinor didn't, not a single one. No, she was no Silvertongue. Even if she tried for a dozen years or more, the words wouldn't make music when she spoke them. She'd loved words so much all her life. Although they didn't sing for her the way they sang for Meggie or Mortimer – or Orpheus, damn him three times over.

The piece of paper shook in her fingers as she started to cry. Here came the tears again. She'd held them back for so long, all the tears in her heart, until it was simply overflowing with them. Elinor's sobs were so loud that the dog cowered in alarm. How ridiculous that water ran out of your eyes when your heart hurt. Tragic heroines in books tended to be amazingly beautiful. Not a word about swollen eyes or a red nose.

4

Crying always gives me a red nose, thought Elinor. I expect that's why I'll never be in any book.

'Elinor?'

She spun round, hastily wiping her tears away.

Darius stood in the open doorway, wearing the dressing gown that she had given him for his last birthday. It was much too large for him.

'What is it?' she snapped. Where had that handkerchief gone this time? Sniffing, she pulled it from her sleeve and blew her nose. 'Three months, they've been gone three months now, Darius! Isn't that a good reason to cry? Yes, it is. Don't look at me so pityingly with your owlish eyes. Never mind how many books we buy,' she said, with a wide sweep of her arm towards her well-filled shelves, 'never mind how many we get at auctions, swap or steal – not one of them tells me what I want to know! Thousands of pages, and not a word on any of them with news of the only people I want to know about. Why would I be interested in anything else? Theirs is the only story I want to hear! How is Meggie now, do you think? How are Resa and Mortimer? Are they happy, Darius? Are they still alive? Will I ever see them again?'

Darius looked along the books, as if the answer might after all be found in one of them. But then, like all those printed pages, he gave her no answer.

'I'll make you some hot milk and honey,' he said at last, disappearing into the kitchen.

And Elinor was alone again with the books, the moonlight and Orpheus's ugly dog.

2

Only a Village

The wind was a torrent of darkness among the gusty trees,
The moon was a ghostly galleon tossed upon cloudy seas,
The road was a ribbon of moonlight over the purple moor,
And the highwayman came riding –
Riding – riding –
The highwayman came riding, up to the old inn-door.

Alfred Noyes, *The Highwayman*

The fairies were already beginning to dance among the trees, swarms of tiny blue bodies. Their wings caught the starlight, and Mo saw the Black Prince glancing anxiously at the sky. It was still as dark as the hills all around, but the fairies were never wrong. On a cold night like this, only the coming of dawn could lure them from their nests, and the village whose harvest the robbers were trying to save this time lay dangerously close to Ombra. As soon as daybreak came they must be gone.

A village like many others: only a dozen poor huts, a few barren, stony fields, and a wall that would hardly keep out a child, let alone a soldier. Thirty women without their menfolk, three dozen fatherless children. Two days ago the new governor's men had carried off almost the entire harvest of the neighbouring village. The robbers had reached the place too late, but something could still be salvaged here. They'd spent hours digging, showing the women how to hide livestock and provisions underground . . .

The Strong Man was carrying the last hastily-dug sackful of potatoes, his rough-hewn face red with effort. It went the same colour when he was fighting or drunk. Between them all, they lowered the sack into the hiding place they had made just beyond the fields, and Mo covered the entrance with a network of twigs to hide the storage pit from soldiers and tax gatherers. By now, toads were croaking in the surrounding hills, as if to entice the day out, and the men on watch among the huts were getting restless. They'd seen the fairies too. High time to get away, back into the forest where a hiding place could always be found, even though the new governor was sending more and more patrols out to the hills. The Milksop, the widows of Ombra called him. A good nickname for the Adderhead's puny brother-in-law. But the Milksop's greed for what few possessions his new subjects had was insatiable.

Mo rubbed his eyes. Heavens, he was tired. He'd hardly slept for days. There were just too many villages that they might yet be able to reach ahead of the soldiers.

'You look worn out,' Resa had said only yesterday when she woke up beside him, unaware that he hadn't come to bed beside her until the first light of dawn. He had said something about bad dreams, told her he'd been passing the sleepless hours by working on the book he was binding, a collection of her drawings of fairies and glass men. He hoped Resa and Meggie would be asleep again now when he came back to the lonely farmhouse that the Black Prince had found for them. It was east of Ombra, an hour's journey from the city on foot, and far from the land where the Adderhead still ruled, made immortal by a book that Mo had bound with his own hands.

Soon, thought Mo. Soon the book won't protect him any more. But how often had he told himself that before? And the Adderhead was still immortal.

A girl hesitantly approached Mo. How old would she be? Six? Seven? Her hair was as blonde as Meggie's, but it was a long time since Meggie had been so small. Shyly, she stopped a pace away from him.

Snapper emerged from the darkness and went over to the child. 'Yes, go on, take a good look!' he whispered to the little girl. 'That's really him – the Bluejay! He eats children like you for supper.'

Snapper loved such jokes. Mo bit back the words on the tip of his tongue. 'Don't believe a word he says!' he said, in a low voice. 'Why aren't you asleep like everyone else?'

The child looked at him. Then she pushed up his sleeve with her small hands until the scar showed. The scar of which the songs told tales . . .

She looked at him, wide-eyed, with the same mixture of awe and fear he had now seen in so many faces. The Bluejay. The girl ran back to her mother, and Mo straightened up. Whenever his chest hurt where Mortola had wounded him, it felt as if he had slipped in there to join him – the robber to whom Fenoglio had given Mo's face and voice. Or had the Bluejay always been a part of him, merely sleeping until Fenoglio's world brought him to life?

8

Sometimes when they were taking meat to one of the starving villages, or a few sacks of grain stolen from the Milksop's bailiffs, women would come up to him and kiss his hand. 'Go and thank the Black Prince, not me,' he always told them, but the Prince just laughed. 'Get yourself a bear,' he said. 'Then they'll leave you alone.'

A child began crying in one of the huts. A tinge of red was showing in the night sky, and Mo thought he heard hoof beats. Horsemen, at least a dozen of them, maybe more. How fast the ears learnt to tell what sounds meant, much faster than it took the eyes to decipher written words.

The fairies scattered. Women cried out, and ran to the huts where their children slept. Mo's hand drew his sword as if of its own accord. As if it had never done anything else. It was the sword he had taken from the Castle of Night, the sword that once belonged to Firefox.

The first light of dawn.

Wasn't it said that they always came at first light because they loved the red of the sky? With any luck they'd be drunk after one of their master's endless banquets.

The Prince signalled to the robbers to take up their positions surrounding the village. It was only a couple of courses of flat stones, and the huts wouldn't offer much protection either. The bear was snorting and grunting, and here they came now out of the darkness: horsemen, more than a dozen of them with the new crest of Ombra on their breasts, a basilisk on a red background. They had not, of course, been expecting to find men here. Weeping women, crying children, yes, but not men, and armed men at that. Taken aback, they reined in their horses. They were drunk. Good – that would slow them down.

9

They didn't hesitate for long, seeing at once that they were far better armed than the ragged robbers. And they had horses.

Fools. They'd die before they realized that weapons and horses weren't all that counted.

'Every last one of them!' Snapper whispered hoarsely to Mo. 'We have to kill them all, Bluejay. I hope your soft heart understands that. If a single man gets back to Ombra, this village will burn tomorrow.'

Mo merely nodded. As if he didn't know.

The horses neighed shrilly as their riders urged them towards the robbers, and Mo felt it again, just as he had on Mount Adder when he had killed Basta – that coldness of the blood. Cold as the hoarfrost at his feet. The only fear he felt was fear of himself.

But then came the screams. The groans. The blood. His own heartbeat, loud and much too fast. Striking and thrusting, pulling his sword out of the bodies of strangers, the blood of strangers wet on his clothes, faces distorted by hatred – or was it fear? Fortunately you couldn't see much under their helmets. They were so young! Smashed limbs, smashed human beings. Careful, watch out behind you. Kill. Fast. Not one of them must get away.

'Bluejay.'

One of the soldiers whispered the name before Mo struck him down. Perhaps he had been thinking, with his last breath, of all the silver he'd get for bringing the Bluejay's body back to Ombra Castle – more silver than he could ever take as loot in a whole lifetime as a soldier. Mo pulled his sword out of the man's chest. They had come without their body armour. Who needed armour against women and children? How cold

10

killing made you, very cold, although your own skin was burning and your blood was flowing fever-hot.

They did indeed kill them all. It was quiet in the huts as they threw the bodies over the precipice. Two were their own men, whose bones would now mingle with those of their enemies. There was no time to bury them.

The Black Prince had a nasty cut on his shoulder. Mo bandaged it as best he could. The bear sat beside them, looking anxious. The child came out of one of the huts, the little girl who had pushed his sleeve up. From a distance she really did look like Meggie. Meggie, Resa . . . he hoped they'd still be asleep when he got back. How was he going to explain all the blood if they weren't? So much blood . . .

Sometime, Mortimer, he thought, the nights will overshadow the days. Nights of blood. Peaceful days – days when Meggie showed him everything she had only been able to tell him about in the tower of the Castle of Night. Nymphs with scaly skins dwelling in blossom-covered pools, footprints of giants long gone, flowers that whispered when you touched them, trees growing right up to the sky, moss-women who appeared between their roots as if they had peeled away from the bark . . . Peaceful days. Nights of blood.

They did what they could to cover up the traces of the fight and left, taking the horses with them. There was a note of fear in the stammered thanks of the village women as they left. They'd seen with their own eyes that their allies knew as much about killing as their enemies did.

Snapper rode back to the robbers' camp with the horses and most of the men. The camp was moved almost daily. At present it was in a dark ravine that became hardly any lighter even by day. They would send for Roxane to tend the wounded, while Mo went back to where Resa and Meggie were sleeping at the deserted farm. The Prince had found it for them, because Resa didn't want to stay in the robbers' camp and Meggie too longed for a house to live in after all those homeless weeks.

The Black Prince accompanied Mo, as he so often did. 'Of course. The Bluejay never travels without a retinue,' mocked Snapper before they parted company. Mo, whose heart was still racing from all the killing, could have dragged him off his horse for that, but the Prince restrained him.

They travelled on foot. It meant a painfully long walk for their tired limbs, but their footprints were harder to follow than a trail left by horses' hooves. And the farm must be kept safe, for everything Mo loved was waiting there.

The house, and the dilapidated farm buildings, always appeared among the trees as unexpectedly as if someone had dropped and lost them there. There was no trace now of the fields where food for the farm had once been grown, and the path that used to lead to the nearest village had disappeared long ago. The forest had swallowed everything up. Here it was no longer called the Wayless Wood, the name it bore south of Ombra. Here the forest had as many names as there were local villages: the Fairy Forest, the Dark Wood, the Moss-Women's Wood. If the Strong Man was to be believed, the place where the Bluejay's hide-out lay was called Larkwood. 'Larkwood? Nonsense,' was Meggie's response to that. 'The Strong Man calls everything after birds! He even gives birds' names to the fairies, although they can't stand the birds. Battista says it's called the Wood of Lights, which suits it much better. Did you ever see so many glow-worms and fire-elves in a wood? And all those fireflies that sit in the treetops at night . . .'

Whatever the name of the wood, Mo was always captivated afresh by the peace and quiet under its trees. It reminded him that this, too, was a part of the Inkworld, as much a part of it as the Milksop's soldiers. The first of the morning sun was filtering through the branches, dappling the trees with pale gold, and the fairies were dancing as if intoxicated in the cold autumn sunlight. They fluttered into the bear's furry face until he hit out at them, and the Black Prince held one of the little creatures to his ear, smiling as if he could understand what its cross, shrill little voice was saying.

Had the other world been like this? Why could he hardly remember? Had life there been the same beguiling mixture of darkness and light, cruelty and beauty . . . so much beauty that it sometimes almost made you drunk?

The Black Prince had the farm guarded by his men day and night.

Gecko was one of the guards today. As Mo and the Prince came through the trees he emerged from the ruined pigsty, a morose expression on his face. Gecko was always on the move. He was a small man whose slightly protuberant eyes had earned him his name. One of his tame crows was perched on his shoulder. The Prince used the crows as messengers, but most of the time they stole for Gecko from the markets; the amount they could carry away in their beaks always amazed Mo.

When he saw the blood on their clothes Gecko turned pale. But the shadows of the Inkworld had obviously left the isolated farm untouched again last night.

Mo almost fell over his own feet with weariness as he walked towards the well. The Prince reached for his arm,

13

although he too was swaying with exhaustion.

'It was a close shave this time,' he said quietly, as if the peace were an illusion that could be shattered by his voice. 'If we're not more careful the soldiers will be waiting for us in the next village. The price the Adderhead has set on your head is high enough to buy all of Ombra. I can hardly trust my own men any more, and by this time even the children recognize you in the villages. Perhaps you ought to lie low here for a while.'

Mo shooed away the fairies whirring in the air above the well, then let the wooden bucket down. 'Nonsense. They recognize you too.'

The water in the depths below shone as if the moon were hiding from morning there. Like the well outside Merlin's cottage, thought Mo, as he cooled his face with the clear water and cleaned the cut that a soldier had given him on his forearm. All we need now is for Archimedes to fly up on my shoulder, while Wart comes stumbling out of the wood . . .

'What are you smiling at?' The Black Prince leant on the edge of the well beside Mo, while his bear lumbered around, snuffling, on ground that was wet with dew.

'A story I once read.' Mo put the bucket of water down for the bear. 'I'll tell it to you sometime. It's a good story, even though it has a sad ending.'

But the Prince shook his head, and passed his hand over his tired face. 'If it ends sadly I don't want to hear it.'

Gecko wasn't the only man who had been guarding the sleeping farm. Mo smiled when Battista stepped out of the tumbledown barn. Battista had no great opinion of fighting, but Mo liked him and the Strong Man best of all the robbers, and he found it easier to go out at night if one of them was watching over Resa and Meggie. Battista still did his clown act at fairs, even when his audience had hardly a penny to spare. 'We don't want them forgetting how to laugh altogether!' he said when Snapper mocked him for it. He liked to hide his pockmarked face behind the masks he made for himself: laughing masks, weeping masks, whatever he felt like at the time. But when he joined Mo at the well he handed him not a mask, but a bundle of black clothes.

'A very good morning to you, Bluejay,' he said, with the same deep bow that he made to his audience. 'Sorry I took rather a long time with your order, but I ran out of thread. Like everything else, it's hard to get in Ombra. But luckily Gecko here,' he added, bowing in the man's direction, 'sent one of his black-feathered friends off to steal me a few reels from one of the market traders. Thanks to our new governor, they're still rich.'

'Black clothes?' The Prince looked enquiringly at Mo. 'What for?'

'A bookbinder's garments. Binding books is still my trade, or have you forgotten? What's more, black is good camouflage by night. As for this,' said Mo, stripping off his bloodstained shirt, 'I'd better dye it black too, or I can't very well wear it again.'

The Prince looked at him thoughtfully. 'I'll say it again, even though you don't want to listen. Lie low here for a few days. Forget the outside world, just as the world has forgotten this farm.'

The anxiety in his dark face touched Mo, and for a moment he was almost tempted to give the bundle back to Battista. But only almost.

When the Prince had gone, Mo hid the shirt and his

bloodstained trousers in the former bakehouse, now converted into his workshop, and put on the black clothes. They fitted perfectly, and he was wearing them as he slipped back into the house just as the morning made its way in through the unglazed windows.

Meggie and Resa were still asleep. A fairy had lost her way in the gloom of Meggie's room. Mo lured her to his hand with a few quiet words. 'Will you look at that?' Snapper always used to say. 'Even the damn fairies love his voice. Looks like I'm the only person not to fall under its spell.'

Mo carried the fairy over to the window and let her flutter out. He pulled Meggie's blanket up over her shoulders, the way he used to on all those nights when he and she had only each other, and he glanced at her face. How young she still looked when she was asleep. Awake, she seemed so much more grown-up. She whispered a name in her sleep. Farid. Was it when you fell in love for the first time that you grew up?

'Where have you been?'

Mo spun round. Resa was standing in the open doorway, rubbing sleep from her eyes.

'Watching the fairies' morning dance. The nights are getting colder now. Soon they'll hardly leave their nests at all.'

It wasn't exactly a lie. And the sleeves of the black tunic were long enough to hide the cut on his forearm. 'Come with me, or we'll wake this big daughter of ours.'

He drew her with him into the bedroom where they slept.

'What kind of clothes are those?'

'A bookbinder's outfit. Battista made them for me. Black as ink. Suitable, don't you think? I've asked him to make you and Meggie something too. You'll be needing another dress soon.'

16

He put his hand on her belly. You couldn't see it yet. A new child brought with them from the old world, although they had found out only in this one. It was barely a week since Resa had told him. 'Which would you like,' she'd asked, 'a daughter or a son?'

'Can I choose?' he had replied, trying to imagine what it would be like to hold tiny fingers in his hand again, so tiny that they could scarcely grasp his thumb. It was just the right time – before Meggie was so grown-up that he could hardly call her a child at all.

'The sickness is getting worse. I'll ride over to see Roxane tomorrow. She's sure to know what to do for it.'

'Yes, she's sure to know.' Mo took her in his arms.

Peaceful days. Nights of blood.

3

Written Silver

To what was sombre he was most disposed
When, in his bare room with its shutters closed,
High-ceilinged, blue, he read his story, thinking,
And in his mind's eye picturing forests sinking
Under the water, seeing ochre skies,
Fleshy flowers in woods of stars before his eyes . . .

Arthur Rimbaud, *The Poet at Seven Years Old*

Of course Orpheus did none of the digging himself. He
stood there in his fine clothes watching Farid sweat. He
had made him dig in two places already, and the hole Farid
was excavating now was already deep enough to come up to
his chest. The earth was moist and heavy. It had rained a great
deal these last few days, and the spade was useless. In addition, there was a hanged man dangling right above Farid's
head. The cold wind swung the body back and forth on its
rotting rope. Suppose it fell, and buried him under its decay-
ing bones?

Three more sombre figures swung from the gallows on

Farid's right. Milksop, the new governor, liked hanging people. Folk said that he had his wigs made from the hair of executed men and women – and the widows in Ombra whispered that this was the reason why so many women had been condemned to hang.

'How much longer are you going to take? It's getting light! Go on, dig faster!' Orpheus snapped, kicking a skull down into the pit. Skulls lay beneath the gallows like terrible fruits.

It was true that day was beginning to dawn. Damn that Cheeseface! He'd had Farid digging almost all night long. If only he could wring the man's pale neck!

'Faster? Get your fine bodyguard to do some digging for a change!' Farid shouted up to him. 'Then his muscles would at least be some use!'

The Chunk folded his bulky arms and smiled down with derision. Orpheus had found the giant working for a physician in the marketplace, holding down the man's customers while he pulled out their rotten teeth. 'What on earth are you going on about now?' was all Orpheus had said, condescendingly, when Farid asked why he needed *another* servant. 'Even the rag-and-bone men in Ombra have bodyguards to protect them from the riffraff roaming the streets. And I'm a good deal richer than they are!' In this he was certainly right – and as Orpheus offered better pay than the physician, and the Chunk's ears hurt from listening to all those screams of agony, he went with them without a word. He called himself Oss, a very short name for such a large fellow, but it suited a man who spoke so seldom that at first Farid could have sworn he had no tongue in his ugly mouth. However, that mouth worked overtime at eating, and more and more frequently the Chunk would devour what Orpheus's maids put in front of

Farid too. At first Farid had complained, but after Oss lay in wait for him on the cellar steps one night he preferred to sleep on an empty stomach, or steal something from the market-place. The Chunk had made life in Orpheus's service even worse. A handful of pieces of broken glass inside Farid's straw mattress, a leg stuck out to trip him up at the bottom of a staircase, a sudden rough hand grasping his hair . . . he had to be on his guard against Oss all the time. There was no peace from him except at night, when the man slept outside Orpheus's bedroom, docile as a dog.

'Bodyguards don't dig!' Orpheus explained in a weary tone, pacing impatiently up and down between the holes Farid had dug. 'And if you go on dawdling like that we really will need a bodyguard. They're bringing two poachers here to hang before noon!'

'Well, there you are, then! I keep telling you: let's just look for buried treasure behind your house!' The hills where gallows stood, graveyards, burnt-out farms . . . Orpheus loved places that sent a shiver down Farid's spine. Cheeseface certainly wasn't afraid of ghosts, you had to give him that. Farid wiped the sweat out of his eyes. 'You might at least write a more detailed description of *which* damn gallows the treasure's under. And why does it have to be buried so deep, for heaven's sake?'

'Why buried so deep? Why not behind my house?' Orpheus pursed his girlishly soft lips scornfully. 'What an original idea! Does that sound as if it belongs in this story? Even Fenoglio wouldn't fall for such nonsense. But why do I bother to keep explaining? You wouldn't understand anyway.'

'Oh no?' Farid drove his spade so deep into the damp soil that it stuck. 'Well, there's one thing I understand very well.

While you're writing yourself treasure after treasure, acting the rich merchant and chasing every maid in Ombra, Dustfinger still lies among the dead!'

Farid felt tears come to his eyes yet again. The pain was as fresh now as it had been on the night when Dustfinger died for him. If he could only forget that still face! If he could only remember Dustfinger as he was in life! But he kept seeing him lying in the disused mine, cold and silent, his heart frozen.

'I'm sick and tired of being your servant!' he shouted up at Orpheus. In his fury he even forgot the hanged men, whose ghosts certainly wouldn't like so much shouting in the place where they had died. 'You haven't kept your side of the bargain! Instead of bringing him back, you've made yourself as comfortable in this world as a maggot in a side of bacon. You've buried him, like all the others! Fenoglio's right, you're about as much use as a perfumed pig's bladder! I'm going to tell Meggie to send you back again. And she'll do it, just you wait and see!'

Oss looked enquiringly at Orpheus, his eyes asking permission to seize Farid and beat him black and blue, but Orpheus ignored him. 'Ah, so we're back to that subject!' he said, barely able to control his voice. 'The amazing, wonderful Meggie, daughter of an equally fabulous father who answers to the name of a bird these days, hiding out in the forest with a band of verminous robbers while ragged minstrels make up song after song about him.'

Orpheus adjusted his glasses and looked up at the sky, as if complaining to the powers above of Mo's unearned fame. He liked the nickname those glasses had earned him: Four-Eyes. It was whispered with fear and horror in Ombra, which pleased Orpheus even more. And the glasses were regarded as evidence that all the lies he told about his origins were the plain truth: he came from beyond the sea, he said, from a distant land ruled by princes who all had two sets of eyes, which allowed them to read their subjects' thoughts. He claimed to be a son of the king of that country, born out of wedlock, and said he'd had to flee after his own brother's wife had fallen madly in love with him. 'By the god of books, what a wretched story!' Fenoglio had cried, when Farid told Minerva's children about it. 'The slushy notions churning around in that fellow's mind! He hasn't a single fresh idea in his slimy brain – all he can do is mess about with other people's stories!'

But while Fenoglio was spending his days and nights feeling sorry for himself, Orpheus had leisure to put his own stamp on this story – and he seemed to know more about it than the man who had originally made it up.

'When you love a book so much that you read it again and again, do you know what it makes you wish?' Orpheus had asked Farid, as they had stood outside the city gate of Ombra for the first time. 'No, of course you don't. How could you? I'm sure a book only makes *you* think how well it would burn on a cold night. But I'll tell you the answer all the same: you want to be in the book yourself. Although certainly not as a poor court poet. I'm happy to leave that role to Fenoglio – though even there he cuts a sorry figure!'

Orpheus had set to work the third night after he arrived, in a dirty inn near the city walls. He had told Farid to steal him some wine and a candle, and had produced a grubby piece of paper and a pencil from under his cloak – and the book, the thrice-accursed book, *Inkheart*. His fingers had wandered over the pages collecting words, more and more words, like magpies in search of glittering baubles. And Farid had been fool enough to believe that the words Orpheus was so busily writing on his sheet of paper would heal the pain in his heart and bring Dustfinger back.

But Orpheus had very different ideas in mind. He sent Farid away before reading aloud what he had written, and before dawn the next morning ordered him to dig up his first treasure from the soil of Ombra, in the graveyard just beyond the infirmary. The sight of the coins had made Orpheus as happy as a child. But Farid had stared at the graves, tasting his own tears in his mouth.

Orpheus had spent the silver on new clothes for himself, hired two maids and a cook, and bought a silk merchant's magnificent house. Its previous owner had gone away in search of his son, who had ridden with Cosimo to Argenta and never came back.

Orpheus made out that he himself was a merchant, one who sold the granting of unusual wishes – and soon it had reached the Milksop's ears that this stranger with the thin fair hair and skin as pale as a prince's could supply bizarre things: spotted brownies, fairies as brightly coloured as butterflies, jewellery made of fire-elves' wings, belts set with the scales of river-nymphs, gold and white piebald horses to draw princely coaches, and other creatures previously known in Ombra only from fairy tales. The right words for all sorts of things could be found in Fenoglio's original book of *Inkheart* – Orpheus just had to fit them together in a slightly different way. Now and then one of his creations would die after taking only a few breaths, or would turn out vicious (the Chunk often had bandaged hands), but that didn't bother Orpheus. Why would he mind if a few dozen fire-elves died of starvation in the forest because they had no wings, or a handful of river-nymphs drifted dead in the water without their scales? He pulled thread after thread out of the fine fabric that Fenoglio had spun and wove patterns of his own, adding them to the old man's tapestry like brightly coloured patches, and growing rich on what his voice could entice out of another man's words.

Curses on him. A thousand and one curses. This was too much.

'I won't do anything for you any more! I won't do anything at all!' Farid wiped the moist earth from his hands and tried to climb out of the hole, but at a gesture from Orpheus Oss pushed him roughly back again.

'Dig!' he grunted.

'Dig yourself!' Farid was trembling in his sweaty tunic, though whether with cold or rage he couldn't have said. 'Your fine master is just a fraud! He's already been in jail for his lies, and that's where he'll end up again!'

Orpheus narrowed his eyes. He didn't like to have that chapter in his life mentioned at all.

'I bet you were the sort who cons money out of old ladies' pockets. And here you are all puffed up like a bullfrog, just because your lies are suddenly coming true. You suck up to the Milksop, because he's Adderhead's brother-in-law, and think yourself cleverer than anyone else! But what can you really do? Write fairies here who look like they've fallen into a vat of dye, chests full of treasure, and jewellery made of elves' wings for him. But you can't do what we brought you here for, you can't do that. Dustfinger is dead. He's dead. He – is – still – dead!'

And now here came those wretched tears again. Farid wiped them away with his dirty fingers, while the Chunk stared down at him as blankly as only someone can who doesn't understand a word of what's being said. And how could he? What did Oss know about the words Orpheus was collecting on the sly, what did he know about the book and Orpheus's voice?

'No one *brought* me here for anything!' Orpheus leant over the edge of the pit as if to spit the words into Farid's face. 'And I certainly don't have to listen to any lectures about Dustfinger from the boy who caused his death! Have you forgotten how he sacrificed himself for you? Why, I knew his name before you were even born, and I and no one else will bring him back, after you so drastically removed him from this story . . . but how and when I do it will be my own decision. Now dig. Or do you think, you brilliant example of the wisdom of Arabia –' Farid thought he felt the words slicing through him – 'do you think I'll be more likely to write if I can't pay my maids and I have to wash my own clothes?'

Damn him. Damn him to hell. Farid bowed his head so that Orpheus wouldn't see his tears. *The boy who caused his death . . .*

'Tell me why I keep paying minstrels good silver for their pitiful songs. Because I've forgotten Dustfinger? No. It's because you still haven't managed to find out how and where in this world I can speak to the White Women who have him now! So I go on listening to bad songs, I stand beside dying beggars, I bribe the healers in the infirmaries to call me when a patient is at death's door. Of course, it would be much easier if you could summon the White Women with fire, like your master, but we've tried that often enough and got nowhere, right? If at least they'd visit you, as it seems they like to visit those they've touched once with death already – but no! The fresh chicken blood I put outside the door was no use either, and nor were the children's bones I bought from a gravedigger for a bag of silver after the guards at the gate told you that was sure to raise a dozen White Women at once!'

Yes, yes! Farid wanted to put his hands over his ears. Orpheus was right. They'd tried everything, but the White Women simply didn't appear to them, and who else was to tell Orpheus how to bring Dustfinger back from the dead?

Without a word, Farid pulled his spade out of the ground and began digging again.

He had blisters on his hands by the time he finally struck wood. The chest he pulled out of the ground wasn't very large, but like the last one it was filled to the brim with silver coins. Farid had been listening when Orpheus read it there: *Under the gallows on the Dark Hill, long before the Prince of Sighs had the oaks there felled for his son's coffin, a band of highwaymen had buried a casket of silver in the ground. Then they killed each other in a quarrel, but the silver still lay there in the earth with their bones bleaching above it.*

The wood of the chest was rotten and, as with the other treasures he had dug up, Farid wondered whether the silver might not have been lying under the gallows even *before* Orpheus wrote his words. If asked such questions Cheeseface would only smile knowingly, but Farid doubted whether he really knew the answer.

'There you are! Now who's talking? That ought to last another month.' Orpheus's smile was so self-satisfied that Farid would have liked to wipe it off his face with a spadeful of earth. Another month! The silver he and the Chunk were putting into leather bags would have filled the hungry bellies of everyone in Ombra for months to come.

'How much longer is this going to take? The hangman's probably already on his way with fresh gallows fodder.' When Orpheus was nervous his voice sounded less impressive.

Without a word Farid tied up another bag full to bursting, kicked the empty chest back into the pit, and gave the hanged men one last glance. There had been a gallows on the Dark Hill before, but it was the Milksop who had declared it the main place of execution again. The stink of corpses drifted up to the castle too often from the gallows outside the city gate, and the stench didn't go well with the fine dishes that the Adderhead's brother-in-law ate while Ombra went hungry.

'Have you found me some minstrels for this afternoon?'

Farid just nodded as he followed Orpheus, carrying the heavy bags.

'The one you got me yesterday was ugly as sin!' Orpheus got Oss to help him up on to his horse. 'Like a scarecrow come to life! And most of what came out of his toothless mouth was the usual old stuff: beautiful princess loves poor strolling player, tralalala, handsome prince's son falls in love with peasant's daughter, tralalalee . . . not a word about the White Women for me to use.'

Farid was only half listening. He didn't think much of the strolling players any more. Most of them sang and danced for the Milksop these days, and they had voted the Black Prince out of his position as their king because he was openly hostile to the occupying army.

'All the same,' Orpheus went on, 'the scarecrow did know a couple of new songs about the Bluejay. It cost me a pretty penny to worm them out of him, and he sang them as quietly as if the Milksop in person were standing under my window, but one of them I'd really never heard before. Are you still sure Fenoglio isn't writing again?'

'Perfectly sure.' Farid slung his rucksack on his back and whistled softly through his teeth, as Dustfinger always used to. Jink shot out from under the gallows with a dead mouse in his jaws. Only the younger marten had stayed with Farid. Gwin was with Roxane, Dustfinger's wife – as if he wanted to be where his master was most likely to go if Death's pale fingers really did give him up.

'Just why are you so sure?' Orpheus twisted his mouth in distaste as Jink jumped up on Farid's shoulder and disappeared inside the rucksack. Cheeseface disliked the marten, but tolerated him, presumably because he had once belonged to Dustfinger.

'Rosenquartz says he isn't writing any more, and as Fenoglio's glass man he should know, right?'

In fact, Rosenquartz was always complaining of his hard life now that Fenoglio was back in Minerva's attic room, and Farid himself cursed the steep wooden staircase every time Orpheus sent him to question Fenoglio about things that Orpheus couldn't find in his original book. *What lands lay south of the sea bordering Argenta? Is the prince who rules northern Lombrica related to the Adderhead's wife? Where exactly do the giants live, or have they died out now? Do the predatory fish in the rivers eat river-nymphs?*

Sometimes Fenoglio wouldn't even let Farid in after he'd toiled up all those stairs, but now and then he would have drunk so much that he was in a talkative mood. On those days the old man overwhelmed him with such a torrent of information that Farid's head was spinning by the time he came back to Orpheus – who then questioned him all over again. It was enough to drive you crazy. But every time Orpheus and

Fenoglio tried communicating with each other directly they started to quarrel within a few minutes.

'Good. Excellent! It would complicate matters if the old man took to liking words better than wine again! His last notions led to nothing but hopeless confusion . . .' Orpheus picked up the reins and looked at the sky. It was going to be another rainy day, grey and dismal as the faces of the people of Ombra. 'Masked robbers, books of immortality, a prince returning from the dead!' Shaking his head, he rode his horse towards the path to Ombra. 'Who knows what he'd have thought up next! Better for Fenoglio to drink away what few wits he has left. I'll see to his story myself. After all, I understand it a great deal better than he does.'

Farid had stopped listening as he dragged his donkey out of the bushes. Let Cheeseface talk away. Farid didn't care who wrote the words to bring Dustfinger back, just so long as he did come back in the end! Even if the whole wretched story went to hell in the process.

As usual, the donkey tried to bite Farid when he swung himself up on to its bony back. Cheeseface was riding one of the finest horses in Ombra. Despite his podgy figure, he was a good horseman – but of course, mean as he was, he'd bought only a donkey for Farid, a vicious animal so old that its head was bald. Even two donkeys couldn't have carried the Chunk, so Oss trotted along beside Orpheus like an overgrown dog, his face sweating with the effort of running up and down the narrow paths through the hills around Ombra.

'Good. So Fenoglio isn't writing any more.' Orpheus liked to think out loud. It sometimes seemed as if he couldn't put his ideas in order unless he heard his own voice at the same time. 'But where do all the stories about the Bluejay come from, then? The widows he protects, silver left on poor folk's doorsteps, poached meat on the plates of fatherless children . . . is all that really Mo's own doing, or did Fenoglio write a few words by way of giving him a helping hand?'

A cart came towards them. Cursing, Orpheus turned his horse towards the thorny bushes, and the Chunk stared up with a silly grin at the two boys kneeling in the cart, hands tied behind their backs, faces pinched with fear. One of them had eyes even brighter than Meggie's, and neither of them was older than Farid. Of course not. If they'd been older they would have gone with Cosimo on the disastrous expedition against the Adderhead that got all the men killed, and they'd be dead by now too. But presumably that was no comfort to them this morning. Their bodies would be visible from Ombra, a dreadful example to all who were tempted by hunger to go poaching.

Did people die on the gallows too quickly for the White Women to come? Farid instinctively put his hand to his back, where Basta's knife had gone in. They hadn't come to him, had they? He didn't remember. He didn't even remember the pain, only Meggie's face when he regained consciousness, and how he had turned to see Dustfinger lying there . . . 'Why don't you just write that they come and take me away instead of him?' he had asked Orpheus, who merely laughed out loud. 'You? Do you seriously think the White Women would exchange the Fire-Dancer for a rascally thief like you? No, we'll have to offer them tastier bait than that.'

The bags of silver jogged up and down beside Orpheus's saddle as he spurred his horse on, and Oss's face was so red with effort that it looked as if it would explode on his fleshy neck any moment now.

Curses on Cheeseface! Yes, Meggie had better send him back to his own world, thought Farid as he dug his heels into the donkey's sides. And the sooner the better! But who was going to write the words for her? And who but Orpheus could bring Dustfinger back from the dead?

He'll never come back, a voice whispered inside him. Dustfinger is dead, Farid. Dead.

So? he snapped back at the quiet voice. What does that mean in this world? I came back, didn't I?

If only he could remember the way.

4

Ink-Clothes

It seems only yesterday I used to believe
there was nothing under my skin but light.
If you cut me I would shine.
But now when I fall upon the sidewalks of life,
I skin my knees. I bleed.

Billy Collins, *On Turning Ten*

A new morning woke Meggie, with pale light that fell on her face, and air as fresh as if no one had ever breathed it before. The fairies were twittering outside her window like birds that had learned to talk, and a bluejay screeched somewhere – if it really was a bluejay. The Strong Man could imitate any bird's call so well that it sounded as if the real thing were nesting in his broad chest. And they all answered him: larks, mockingbirds, woodpeckers, nightingales, and Gecko's tame crows.

Mo was awake too. She heard his voice outside – and her mother's. Could Farid have come at last? She quickly rose from the straw mattress she slept on (what had sleeping in a bed felt like? She could hardly remember) and went to the window. She'd been waiting for Farid for days. He had promised to come. However, she saw no one out in the yard but her parents and the Strong Man, who smiled at her when he saw her standing at the window.

Mo was helping Resa to saddle one of the horses that had been waiting in the stables when they first came here. The horses were so beautiful that they must once have belonged to one of the Milksop's high-born friends, but as with many of the things the Black Prince brought, Meggie tried not to think too much about how they fell into the robbers' hands. She loved the Black Prince, Battista and the Strong Man, but some of the others sent a shudder down her spine. Men like Snapper and Gecko, for instance, although the same men had rescued her and her parents on Mount Adder. 'Robbers are robbers, Meggie,' Farid often said. 'The Prince does what he does for other people, but several of his men just want to fill their pockets without having to toil in the fields or in a workshop.' Farid . . . she missed him so much that she felt ashamed of it.

Her mother was looking pale. Resa had often been sick over the last few days. That must be why she wanted to ride over and see Roxane. No one knew what to do in such cases better than Dustfinger's widow, except perhaps for the Barn Owl, but he himself hadn't been particularly well since the death of Dustfinger, and especially since the Adderhead had burnt down the infirmary he'd run for so many years on the other side of the forest. No one knew what had become of Bella and all the other healers there.

A mouse, horned like Dustfinger's marten, scurried past as Meggie went outside, and a fairy whirred towards her and snatched at her hair, but by now Meggie knew just how to shoo them away. The colder the weather, the fewer fairies ventured out of their nests, but they were still on the hunt for human hair. 'Nothing keeps them warmer,' Battista always said. 'Except for bears' hair, and it's dangerous to pull that out.'

The morning was so cool that Meggie wrapped her arms around herself, shivering. The clothes the robbers had found for them weren't as warm as the sweaters she'd have worn on a day like this in the other world, and she thought almost wistfully of the warm socks waiting for her in Elinor's cupboards.

Mo turned and smiled as she came towards him. He looked tired but happy to see her. He wasn't sleeping much. Often he would work late into the night in his makeshift workshop, using the few tools that Fenoglio had found him. And he was always going out into the forest, either alone or with the Prince. He thought Meggie didn't know, but several times when she had been standing by the window unable to sleep, waiting for Farid, she had seen the robbers come for him. They called to Mo with the bluejay's cry. Meggie heard it almost every night.

'Are you feeling any better?' She looked at her mother anxiously. 'Perhaps it was those mushrooms we found the other day.'

'No, it definitely wasn't the mushrooms.' Resa looked at Mo and smiled. 'Roxane is sure to know a herb that will help. Would you like to come with me? Brianna might be there, she doesn't work for Orpheus every day.'

Brianna. Why would Meggie want to see *her*? Because they were almost the same age? After Cosimo's death and the massacre of Ombra's menfolk, Her Ugliness had thrown Brianna out as a belated punishment for having favoured Cosimo's company over hers. So Brianna had come home to help Roxane in the fields at first, but now she was working for Orpheus. Just like Farid. By this time Orpheus had half a dozen maids. Farid said sarcastically that Cheeseface didn't even have to comb his own thin hair any more. Orpheus hired only beautiful girls, and Brianna was very beautiful, so beautiful that beside her Meggie felt like a duck next to a swan. To make it even worse, Brianna was Dustfinger's daughter. 'So? I don't even speak to her,' Farid had said when Meggie asked about her. 'She hates me, just like her mother.' Still, he saw Brianna almost every day . . . and all the others. And it was almost two weeks since he had been to see Meggie.

'Well, are you coming with me?' Resa was still looking enquiringly at her, and Meggie felt herself blushing as if her mother had overheard all her thoughts.

'No,' she said, 'no, I think I'd rather stay here. The Strong Man will be riding with you, won't he?'

'Of course.' The Strong Man had made it his business to protect Meggie and Resa. Meggie wasn't sure whether Mo had asked him to, or whether he simply did it to show his devotion to the Bluejay.

Resa let him help her up on to the horse. She often complained of the difficulty of riding in a dress, and how much rather she'd have worn men's clothes in this world. 'I'll be back before dark,' she told Mo. 'And maybe Roxane will have something to help you sleep better at night, too.'

Then she disappeared among the trees with the Strong Man, and Meggie was alone with Mo, just as she had been in the old days when there were only the two of them.

'She really isn't well!'

'Don't worry, Roxane will know what to do.' Mo glanced at the old bakehouse that he had made into his workshop. What were those black clothes he was wearing? Meggie wondered. 'I have to go out myself, but I'll be back this evening. Gecko and Battista are in the stables, and the Prince is going to send Woodenfoot to be here too while the Strong Man's gone. Those three will look after you better than I can.'

What was it she heard in his voice? A lie? He'd changed since Mortola all but killed him. He was more reserved, and often as abstracted as if part of him had been left behind in the cave where he almost died, or in the tower prison in the Castle of Night.

'Where are you going? I'll come with you.' Meggie felt him start nervously as she put her arm through his. 'What's the matter?'

'Nothing, nothing at all.' He picked at his black sleeve and avoided her eyes.

'You've been out with the Prince again. I saw him in the farmyard last night. What happened?'

'It's nothing, Meggie. Really it isn't.' He stroked her hair, an absent expression on his face, then turned and made for the bakehouse.

'Nothing at all?' Meggie followed him. The doorway was so low that Mo had to bend his head. 'Where did you get those black clothes?'

'It's a bookbinder's outfit. Battista made it for me.'

He went over to the table where he worked. Some leather lay on it, a few sheets of parchment, some thread, a knife, and the slim volume into which he had bound Resa's drawings over the last few weeks: pictures of fairies, fire-elves and glass men, of the Black Prince and the Strong Man, Battista and

Roxane. There was one of Farid too. The book was tied up as if Mo were taking it with him. The book, the black clothes . . .

Oh, she knew him so well.

'No, Mo!' Meggie snatched the book away and hid it behind her back. He might be able to deceive Resa but he couldn't deceive her.

'What is it?' He was trying really hard to look as if he had no idea what she meant. He was better at pretending than he used to be.

'You're planning to go to Ombra to see Balbulus. Are you out of your mind? It's far too dangerous!'

For a moment Mo actually considered telling her more lies, but then he sighed. 'All right, I still can't fool you! I thought it might be easier now you're almost grown up. Stupid of me.'

He put his arms round her and gently removed the book from her hands. 'Yes, I want to see Balbulus. Before the books you've told me so much about are sold. Fenoglio will smuggle me into the castle as a bookbinder. How many casks of wine do you think the Milksop can buy for a book? They say half the library's gone already to pay for his banquets!'

'Mo, it's too dangerous! Suppose someone recognizes you?'

'Who? No one in Ombra has ever seen me.'

'One of the soldiers could remember you from the dungeon in the Castle of Night. And they say Sootbird's in Ombra too! A few black clothes aren't likely to deceive him.'

'Oh, come on! When Sootbird last saw me I was half dead. And another encounter with me will be the worse for him.' His face, more familiar to her than any other, suddenly became the face of a stranger – and not for the first time. Cold, chilly.

'Don't look at me like that!' he said, smiling the chill away. But the smile didn't linger. 'Do you know, my own hands seem strange to me, Meggie.' He held them out to her as if she could see the change in them. 'They do things I didn't even know they *could* do – and they do those things well.'

Meggie looked at his hands as if they were another man's. She had so often seen them cutting paper, stitching pages together, stretching leather – or putting a plaster on her knee when she had cut it. But she knew only too well what Mo meant. She'd watched him often enough practising behind the farm outbuildings with Battista or the Strong Man – with the sword he had carried ever since they were in the Castle of Night. Firefox's sword. Now he could make it dance as if his hands knew it as well as a paperknife or a bone folder for the pages in a book.

The Bluejay.

'I think I ought to remind my hands of their real trade, Meggie. I'd like to remind myself of it too. Fenoglio has told Balbulus that he's found someone to repair and present his books as they deserve. But Balbulus wants to see this book-binder before entrusting his works to him. That's why I'm going to ride to the castle and prove that I know my craft as well as he knows his. It's your own fault I can't wait to see his workshop with my own eyes at last! Do you remember all you told me about Balbulus and his brushes and pens, up in the tower of the Castle of Night?' He imitated her voice. *He's an illuminator, Mo! In Ombra Castle! The best of them all. You should see his brushes, and his paints.*

'Yes,' she whispered. 'Yes, I remember.' She even remembered what he had replied: *I'd really like to see those brushes*. But she also remembered how afraid she had been for him back then.

'Does Resa know where you're going?' She put her hand on his chest, where there was only a scar now as a reminder that he had almost died.

He didn't need to answer. His guilty look said clearly enough that he hadn't told her mother anything about his plans. Meggie looked at the tools lying on the table. Maybe he was right. Maybe it was time to remind his hands of their trade. Maybe he could also play that part in this world, the part that he'd loved so much in the other one, even if it was said that the Milksop considered books even more unnecessary than boils on the face. But Ombra belonged to the Adderhead. His soldiers were everywhere. Suppose one of them recognized the man who had been their dark lord's prisoner a few months ago?

'Mo . . .' The words were on the tip of Meggie's tongue. She had often thought them over these last few days but never ventured to speak them aloud, because she wasn't sure whether she really meant them. 'Don't you sometimes think we ought to go back? I do. Back to Elinor and Darius. I know I persuaded you to stay, but . . . but the Adderhead is still looking for you, and you go out at night with the robbers. Maybe Resa doesn't notice, but I do! We've seen it all, the fairies and nymphs, the Wayless Wood and the glass men . . .' It was so difficult to find the right words, words which could also explain to her what she herself was feeling. 'Perhaps . . . perhaps it's time. I know Fenoglio isn't writing any more, but we could ask Orpheus. He's jealous of you anyway. I'm sure he'd be glad if we went away and left him the only reader in this story!'

Mo just looked at her, and Meggie knew his answer. They had changed places. Now he was the one who didn't want to go back. On the table, with the coarsely-made paper and the knives provided by Fenoglio, lay a bluejay's tail feather.

'Come here!' Mo perched on the edge of the table and drew her to his side, the way he had done countless times when she was a little girl. That was long ago, so long ago! As if it were in another story, and the Meggie in it was a different Meggie. But when Mo put his arm around her shoulders she was back in that story for a moment, feeling safe, protected, without the longing that now felt as if it had always lived in her heart . . . the longing for a boy with black hair and soot on his fingers.

'I know why you want to go back,' said Mo quietly. He might have changed, but he could still read her thoughts as easily as his own. 'How long since Farid was last here? Five days? Six?'

'Twelve,' said Meggie in a miserable voice, and buried her face against his shoulder.

'Twelve? What a faithless fellow. Shall we ask the Strong Man to tie a few knots in his skinny arms?'

Meggie had to laugh. What would she do if someday Mo wasn't there any more to make her laugh?

'I haven't seen it all yet, Meggie,' he said. 'I still haven't seen Balbulus's books, and they matter the most. Handwritten books, Meggie, illuminated books, not stained by the dust of endless years, not yellowing and trimmed again and again . . . no, the paint has only just dried on their pages, the bindings are supple. Who knows, maybe Balbulus will even let me watch him at work for a while. Imagine it! I've so often wished that I could see one of those tiny faces being painted on the parchment, just once, and the tendrils beginning to twine around an initial, and . . .'

Meggie couldn't help it, she had to smile. 'All right, all right,' she said, and put her hand over his mouth. 'All right,' she repeated. 'We'll ride to see Balbulus, but together.'

As we used to, she added in her thoughts. Just you and me. And when Mo was about to protest she closed his mouth again. 'You said it yourself! Back in the disused mine.' The mine where Dustfinger had died . . . Meggie repeated Mo's words in a soft voice. She seemed to remember every word that had been spoken in those days, as if someone had written them on her heart. 'Show me the fairies, Meggie. And the water-nymphs. And the book illuminator in Ombra Castle. Let's find out how fine his brushes really are.'

Mo straightened up and began sorting out the tools lying on the table, as he always used to in his workshop in Elinor's garden.

'Yes. Yes, I expect those were my words,' he said, without looking at her. 'But the Adderhead's brother-in-law rules Ombra now. What do you think your mother would say if I put you in such danger?'

Her mother. Yes . . .

'Resa doesn't have to know. Please, Mo! You must take me with you! Or . . . or I'll tell Gecko to tell the Black Prince what you're planning. Then you'll never get to Ombra!'

He turned his face away, but Meggie heard him laughing softly. 'That's blackmail. Did I teach you how to be a black-mailer?'

With a sigh, he turned back and looked at her for a long time. 'Oh, very well,' he said at last. 'Let's go to see the pens and brushes together. After all, we were together in the

Adderhead's Castle of Night. Ombra Castle can't be so very dark by comparison, can it – although his brother-in-law rules it now?'

He stroked his black sleeve. 'I'm glad bookbinders here don't wear a costume as yellow as glue,' he said, as he put the book of Resa's drawings into a saddlebag. 'As for your mother – I'll fetch her from Roxane's after we've been to the castle, but don't tell her anything about our expedition. I expect you've guessed why she feels sick in the mornings, haven't you?'

Meggie looked at him blankly – and then suddenly seemed to herself very, very stupid.

'A brother or a sister? Which would you rather have?' Mo looked so happy. 'Poor Elinor. Did you know she's been waiting for that news ever since we moved in with her? And now we've taken the baby away to another world with us.'

A brother or a sister. For a while, when Meggie was little, she had pretended she had an invisible sister. She used to make her daisy tea and bake sand cakes.

'But . . . how long have you two known?'

'The baby comes from the same story as you do, if that's what you mean. From Elinor's house, to be precise. A flesh and blood child, not made of words, not made of ink and paper. Although . . . who knows? Perhaps we've only slipped out of one story and into another. What do you think?'

Meggie looked around, saw the table, the tools, the feather – and Mo's black clothes. Wasn't all this made of words? Fenoglio's words. The house, the farmyard, the sky above them, the trees, the rocks, the rain, the sun and the moon. Yes, what about us? Meggie thought. What are we made of? Resa, me, Mo and the baby on its way. She didn't know the

42

answer any more. Had she ever known it?

It seemed as if the things around her were whispering of all that would be and all that had been, and when Meggie looked at her hands she felt as if she could read letters there, letters saying: *and then a new child was born.*

5
Fenoglio Feels Sorry for Himself

'What is it?' Harry asked shakily.
'This? This is called a Pensieve,' said Dumbledore. 'I sometimes find, and I am sure you know the feeling, that I simply have too many thoughts and memories crammed into my mind.'

J.K. Rowling, *Harry Potter and the Goblet of Fire*

Fenoglio was lying in bed, as he had so often in these last few weeks. Or was it months? It didn't matter. Morosely, he looked up at the fairies' nests above his head. They had all been abandoned except one, which poured out a constant stream of chattering and giggling. It shimmered in iridescent colours like a patch of oil on water. Orpheus's doing! The fairies in this world were blue, for heaven's sake! It said so in black and white in his book. What did that idiot think he was doing, creating fairies in all the colours of the rainbow? And to make it even worse, the rainbow-coloured fairies drove away the blue ones wherever they went. Rainbow-coloured fairies, spotted brownies, and apparently there were some four-armed glass men around the place too. Fenoglio's head ached at the mere thought of it. And not an hour passed when he didn't think of it, and wonder what Orpheus was writing now in his fine big house, where he held court as if he were the most important man in Ombra!

Fenoglio sent Rosenquartz to spy on the place almost every day, but it couldn't be said that the glass man showed much talent for the job. Far from it. Fenoglio also suspected that Rosenquartz sometimes stole off to Seamstresses' Alley to chase glass women instead of going to Orpheus's house. Your fault, Fenoglio, he told himself grumpily, you should have written a little more sense of duty into their glass heads. Which is not, I am afraid, the only thing you omitted to do . . .

He was reaching for the jug of red wine standing by his bed to comfort himself for this depressing fact when a small, rather breathless figure appeared at the skylight above. At last. Rosenquartz's limbs, usually pale pink, had turned carmine. Glass men couldn't sweat. They just changed colour if they'd been making a strenuous effort, another rule that Fenoglio himself had made, although with the best will in the world he couldn't now say why. But what did the foolish fellow think he was doing, clambering over the roof tops like that, with limbs that would smash if the stupid creature so much as fell off a table? A glass man certainly wasn't the ideal spy, but then again their small size made them very inconspicuous – and, fragile as their limbs were, their transparency undoubtedly came in useful on secret reconnaissance missions.

'Well, what's he writing? Come on, out with it!' Fenoglio picked up the jug and made his way over to the glass man barefoot. Rosenquartz demanded a thimbleful of red wine in return for his spying activities, which – as he never tired of emphasizing– were not among the standard duties of a glass man, and thus called for extra payment. The thimble of wine wasn't too high a price, Fenoglio had to admit, but then so far Rosenquartz hadn't found out very much, and in addition the wine disagreed with him. It made him even more contrary than usual – and had him belching for hours on end.

'Can't I even get my breath back before making my report?' he snapped.

That was Rosenquartz for you: contrary. And always so quick to take offence!

'You're breathing now, aren't you? And you can obviously talk as well!' Fenoglio plucked the glass man off the thread that he had fastened to the skylight so that Rosenquartz could let himself down from it, and carried him over to the table. He'd exchanged his writing desk for it in the marketplace.

'I repeat,' he said, giving Rosenquartz his thimbleful from the wine jug, 'what is he writing?'

Rosenquartz sniffed the wine and wrinkled his nose, which was now dark red. 'Your wine is getting worse and worse!' he observed in injured tones. 'I ought to ask for some other kind of fee!'

Annoyed, Fenoglio removed the thimble from his glass hands. 'You haven't even earned this one yet!' he thundered. 'Admit it, once again you haven't found anything out. Not the least little thing.'

The glass man folded his arms. 'Oh, haven't I?'

It was enough to drive a man crazy. And you couldn't even shake him for fear of breaking off an arm, or even his head.

Looking grim, Fenoglio put the thimble back on the table.

Rosenquartz dipped his finger in and licked the wine off it. 'He's written himself another treasure.'

'What, yet again? For heaven's sake, he gets through more silver than the Milksop!' It always annoyed Fenoglio that he hadn't thought of that idea himself. On the other hand, he'd have needed someone to read his words aloud and turn them into jingling coins, and he wasn't sure whether Meggie or her father would have lent their tongues to something so prosaic. 'Right. A treasure. What else?'

'Oh, he's certainly writing something, but he doesn't seem very pleased with it. Did I tell you before that he has two glass men working for him now? You remember the four-armed one he was boasting of all over town?' Rosenquartz lowered his voice as if his next words were too terrible to be spoken. 'They say he threw him at the wall in a rage! Everyone in Ombra's heard about it, but Orpheus pays well – ' Fenoglio ignored the glass man's reproachful gaze as he made this remark – 'so now he has these two brothers working for him, Jasper and Ironstone. The elder brother's a monster! He—'

'Two? What does that fool want two glass men for? Is he so busy mucking about with my story that one isn't enough to sharpen his quills for him?' Fenoglio felt anger turning his stomach, although it was good news that the four-armed glass man had come to grief. Perhaps it was beginning to dawn on Orpheus that his creations weren't worth the paper he wrote them on.

'Good. Tell me more.'

Rosenquartz said nothing. He had folded his arms with an injured expression. He didn't like being interrupted.

'Good God, don't be so coy about it!' Fenoglio pushed the wine a little closer to him. 'What else is he writing? Exotic

new prey for the Milksop to hunt? Horned lapdogs for the
ladies at court? Or maybe he's decided my world could do
with some spotted dwarves?'

Rosenquartz dipped his finger in the wine again. 'You'll
have to buy me new trousers,' he remarked. 'I tore these with
all that horrible climbing about. They're worn out anyway.
It's all right for you to go around however you please, but I
didn't come to live with humans just to be worse dressed than
my cousins in the forest.'

There were days when Fenoglio would gladly have snapped
the glass man in half. 'Trousers? Why would I be interested
in your trousers?' he asked tartly.

Rosenquartz took a deep draught from the thimble – and
spat the wine out on to his glass feet. 'Pure vinegar!' he said
crossly. 'Did I get bones thrown at me for this? Did I make
my way through pigeon droppings and over broken tiles for
this? Don't look so sceptical. That Ironstone threw chicken
bones at me when he caught me looking at Orpheus's papers!
He tried to push me out of the window!'

Sighing, he wiped the wine off his feet. 'Very well. There
was something about horned wild boar, but I could hardly
decipher it, and then something else about singing fish –
pretty silly stuff, if you ask me – and quite a lot about the
White Women. Four-Eyes is obviously collecting everything
the strolling players sing about them . . .'

'Yes, yes, all Ombra knows! Did it take you so long just to
find that out?' Fenoglio buried his face in his hands. The wine
really wasn't much good. His head seemed heavier every day.
Damn it!

Rosenquartz took another mouthful, even though he made
a face as he swallowed it. That glass idiot! He'd have another

bellyache by tomorrow, if not sooner. 'Well, never mind that. This is my last report!' he announced between belches. 'I'm never going spying again! Not as long as that Ironstone works there. He's as strong as a brownie, and they say he's already broken the arms off at least two glass men!'

'Yes, yes, all right. You're a terrible spy anyway,' muttered Fenoglio as he staggered back to his bed. 'Admit it, you're far keener to chase the glass women in Seamstresses' Alley. Just don't think I don't know about it!'

With a groan, he lay down on his straw mattress and stared up at the empty fairies' nests. Was there any more wretched existence than the life of a writer who had run out of words? Was there a worse fate than having to watch someone else twist your own words, adding colourful touches – in very bad taste – to the world you'd made? No room in the castle for him now as court poet, no chest full of fine clothes, no horse of his own – no, he was back in the little room in Minerva's attic. And it was a marvel that she'd taken him in again, considering that his words and songs had made sure she had no husband now, and no father for her children. All Ombra knew what part Fenoglio had played in Cosimo's war. It was amazing they hadn't hauled him out of bed yet and killed him, but no doubt the women of Ombra had their hands too full keeping starvation at bay. 'Where else would you go?' was all Minerva had said when she opened her door to find him standing there. 'They don't need a poet up at the castle now. I suppose they'll be singing the Piper's songs in future.' And there, of course, she was right. The Milksop loved the silver-nosed man's bloodthirsty verses – when he wasn't composing a few poorly rhymed lines himself, all about his hunting prowess.

Luckily, at least Violante sent for Fenoglio now and then, never guessing, of course, that he brought her words stolen from poets in another world. But Her Ugliness didn't pay particularly well. The Adderhead's own daughter was poorer than the new governor's court ladies, so Fenoglio also worked as a scribe in the marketplace, which naturally had Rosenquartz telling anyone who would listen how low his master had sunk. But who paid any attention to a glass man's chirping little voice? Let the silly transparent fellow talk! Fenoglio had forsworn words for ever, no matter how invitingly Rosenquartz laid a blank piece of parchment on the table every evening. He was never going to write a single word again – except those he stole from others, and the dry, bloodless twaddle he had to put down on paper or parchment for wills, sales agreements and similar stuff. The time for living words was over. They were deceitful, murderous, bloodsucking monsters black as ink and bringing nothing but misfortune. He wasn't going to help them do it any more, not he. A walk through the streets of Ombra, empty of men these days, and he needed a whole jug of wine to keep off the gloom that had deprived him of any zest for life since Cosimo's defeat.

Beardless boys, decrepit old men, cripples and beggars, travelling merchants who hadn't yet heard that there wasn't a copper coin to be made in Ombra now, or who did business with those leeches up in the castle – that was what you saw these days in the once lively streets. Women with eyes reddened from weeping, fatherless children, men from beyond the forest hoping to find a young widow or an abandoned workshop here . . . and soldiers. Yes, there were plenty of soldiers in Ombra. They took what they wanted, day after day, night after night. No house was safe from them. They called it compensation for war crimes, and they had a point. After all, Cosimo had been the attacker – Cosimo, his most beautiful and innocent creation (or so, at least, Fenoglio had thought). Now he lay dead in a sarcophagus in the crypt beneath the castle. Minerva claimed that Violante went down there every day, officially to mourn her dead husband but really – so people whispered – to meet her informers. They said Her Ugliness didn't even have to pay her spies. Hatred of the Milksop brought them to her by the dozen. Of course. You had only to look at the fellow – that perfumed, pigeon-breasted hangman, governor only by the grace of his brother-in-law, the Adderhead. If you painted a face on an egg it would bear a striking resemblance to him. And no, Fenoglio hadn't made him up. Once again, the story had produced the Milksop entirely by itself.

As his first official act, he had ordered a document to be hung up by the castle gates, listing the punishments that would be meted out in Ombra for various crimes from now on – with pictures, so that those who couldn't read would know what threatened them too. The loss of an eye for this offence, the loss of a hand for that one, whippings, the pillory, branding, blinding. Fenoglio looked away whenever he passed that notice, and when he was out with Minerva's children he put his hand over their eyes if they had to cross the marketplace, where most of the punishments were inflicted (although Ivo always wanted to peek). Of course they could still hear the screams.

Luckily there weren't too many offenders left to be punished in this city without men. Many of the women had left with their children, travelling far away from the Wayless Wood that no longer protected them from the prince who ruled on the other side of it, the immortal Adderhead.

And yes, Fenoglio thought, that had undoubtedly been his idea. But more and more rumours were being heard all the time, whispering that the Adderhead took little pleasure in his immortality.

There was a knock at the door. Who could that be? Oh, the devil, was he forgetting everything these days? Of course! Where was the damn note that crow had brought yesterday evening? Rosenquartz had been scared to death when he'd suddenly seen the bird perching on the skylight. Mortimer was coming to Ombra. Today! And wasn't he, Fenoglio, supposed to meet him outside the castle gates? This visit was a reckless notion. There were 'Wanted' posters up for the Bluejay on every street corner. Luckily the picture on them wasn't in the least like Mortimer, but all the same . . . Another knock.

Rosenquartz stayed where he was, beside his thimble. A glass man wasn't even any good at opening doors! Fenoglio felt sure Orpheus didn't have to open his door for himself. Apparently his new bodyguard was so large he could hardly get through the city gate. Bodyguard! If I ever do write again, thought Fenoglio, I'll get Meggie to read me a giant here, and we'll see what the calf's-head has to say about that.

The knocking was getting rather impatient.

'Coming, coming!' Fenoglio stumbled over an empty wine jug as he looked for his trousers. Laboriously he climbed into them. How his bones ached! The hell with old age. Why hadn't he written a story in which people were young for ever? Because it would be boring, he thought as he hopped over to the door, one leg in the scratchy trousers. Deadly boring.

'Sorry, Mortimer!' he called. 'The glass man forgot to wake me up at the right time!'

Behind him, Rosenquartz began protesting, but the voice that replied to him outside wasn't Mortimer's – even if it was almost as beautiful as his. Orpheus. Talk of the devil! What did he want here? Come to complain that Rosenquartz had been in his house spying? If anyone has a reason to complain, I do, thought Fenoglio. After all, it's my story he's plundering and distorting! Miserable calf's-head, milkface, bullfrog, whippersnapper . . . Fenoglio had many names for Orpheus, none of them flattering.

Wasn't it bad enough that he kept sending Farid to bother him? Did he have to come himself? He was sure to ask thousands of stupid questions again. Your own fault, Fenoglio! How often he'd cursed himself for the words he'd written in the mine at Meggie's urging: *So he called on another, younger man, Orpheus by name – skilled in letters, even if he could not yet handle them with the mastery of Fenoglio himself – and decided to instruct him in his art, as every master does at some time. For a while Orpheus should play with words in his place, seduce and lie with them, create and destroy, banish and restore – while Fenoglio waited for his weariness to pass, for his pleasure in words to reawaken, and then he would send Orpheus back to the world from which he had summoned him, to keep his story alive with new words never used before.*

'I ought to write him back where he came from!' Fenoglio growled as he kicked the empty jug out of his way. 'Right now!'

'Write? Did I hear you say write?' Rosenquartz asked ironically behind him. He was back to his normal colour. Fenoglio threw a dry crust of bread at him, but it missed Rosenquartz's pale pink head by more than a hand's breadth, and the glass man gave a sympathetic sigh.

'Fenoglio? Fenoglio, I know you're in there! Open the door.' God, how he hated that voice. Planting words in his story like weeds. His own words!

'No, I'm not here!' growled Fenoglio. 'Not for you, calf's-head!'

Fenoglio, is Death a man or a woman? Were the White Women once living human beings? Fenoglio, how am I to bring Dustfinger back if you can't even tell me the simplest rules of this world? Enough of his questions. For God's sake, who had asked him to bring Dustfinger back? If everything had gone the way Fenoglio had originally written it, the man would have been dead long ago in any case. And as for 'the simplest rules', since when, might he ask, were life and death simple? Hang it all (and there was more than enough hanging in Ombra these days anyway), how was he supposed to know how *everything* worked, in this or any other world? He'd never thought much about death, or what came after it. Why bother? While you were alive, why would death interest you? And once you were dead – well, presumably you weren't interested in anything any more.

'Of course he's there! Fenoglio?' That was Minerva's voice. Damn it, the calf's-head had roped her in to help him. Cunning. At least Orpheus was far from stupid.

Fenoglio hid the empty wine jugs under the bed, forced his other leg into his trousers, and unbolted the door.

'So there you are!' Minerva inspected him disapprovingly from his uncombed head to his bare feet. 'I told your visitor you were at home.' How sad she looked. Weary too. These days she was working in the castle kitchen, where Fenoglio had asked Violante to find her a job. But the Milksop had a preference for feasting by night, so Minerva often didn't get

home until the early hours of the morning. Very likely she'd
drop dead of exhaustion some day and leave her poor children
orphans. It was a wretched situation. What had become of his
wonderful Ombra?

'Fenoglio!' Orpheus pushed past Minerva with that ghastly, innocent smile he always had ready as camouflage. Of
course he'd brought notes with him again, notes full of questions. How did he pay for the fine clothes he wore? Fenoglio
himself had never worn such clothes, not even in his days of
glory as court poet. Ah, he thought, but you forgot the treasures he's writing for himself, didn't you, Fenoglio?

Without a word Minerva went down the steep staircase
again, and a man made his way through Fenoglio's door
behind Orpheus. Even ducking his head, he almost got stuck
in the doorway. Aha, the legendary bodyguard. There was
even less space in Fenoglio's modest little room with this huge
meatball inside it.

Farid, on the other hand, didn't take up much space,
although so far he had played a big part in the story. Farid,
Dustfinger's angel of death . . . he followed his new master
through the door hesitantly, as if ashamed to be keeping such
company.

'Well now, Fenoglio, I'm truly sorry,' said Orpheus, his
supercilious smile giving the lie to his words, 'but I'm afraid
I've found a few more inconsistencies.'

Inconsistencies!

'I've sent Farid here before with my questions, but you
gave him some very strange answers.' Looking portentous, he
straightened his glasses and brought the book out from under
his heavy velvet coat. Yes, that calf's-head had brought
Fenoglio's book with him into the world of the story it told:

the very last copy of *Inkheart*. But had he given it back to him, the author? Oh no. 'I'm sorry, Fenoglio,' was all he had said, with the arrogant expression that he had mastered so perfectly. (Orpheus had been quick to abandon the mask of a diligent student.) 'I'm sorry, but this book is mine. Or do you seriously claim that an author is the rightful owner of every copy of his books?' Puffed-up, milk-faced young upstart! What a way to speak to him, Fenoglio, the creator of everything around Orpheus himself, even the air he breathed!

'Are you after me again for information on death?' Fenoglio squeezed his feet into his worn old boots. 'Why? So that you can go telling this poor boy you'll bring Dustfinger back from the White Women, just to keep him in your service?'

Farid tightened his lips. Dustfinger's marten blinked sleepily on his shoulder – or was this a different animal?

'What nonsense you talk!' Orpheus sounded distinctly peeved – he took offence very easily. 'Do I look as if I have any trouble finding servants? I have six maids, a bodyguard, a cook and the boy. You know very well it's not just for the boy I want to bring Dustfinger back. He belongs in this story. It's not half as good without him, it's a flower without petals, a night without stars—'

'A forest without trees?' Fenoglio muttered.

Orpheus turned as red as beetroot. It was so amusing to make fun of the arrogant fop – one of the few pleasures Fenoglio still had left.

'You're drunk, old man!' Orpheus spat. His voice could sound very unpleasant.

'Drunk or not, I still know a hundred times more about words than you do. You trade at second-hand. You unravel whatever you can find and knit it up again as if a story were

56

a pair of old socks! So don't you tell me what part Dustfinger ought to play in this one. Perhaps you remember I had him dead once already, before he decided to go with the White Women! What do you think you're doing, coming here to lecture me about my own story? Take a look at that, why don't you?' Furiously, he pointed to the shimmering fairies' nest above his bed. 'Rainbow-coloured fairies! Ever since they built their horrible nest up there I've had the most appalling dreams! And they steal the blue fairies' stocks of winter provisions!'

'So?' Orpheus shrugged his plump shoulders. 'They look pretty, all the same, don't they? I thought it was so tedious for all fairies to be blue.'

'Did you, indeed?' Fenoglio's voice rose to such volume that one of the colourful fairies interrupted her constant chatter and peered out of her gaudy nest. 'Then write your own world! This one's mine, understand? Mine! I'm sick and tired of your meddling with it. I admit I've made some mistakes in my life, but writing you here was far and away the worst of them!'

Bored, Orpheus inspected his fingernails. They were bitten to the quick. 'I'm not listening to any more of this!' he said in a menacingly soft voice. 'All that stuff about "you wrote me here", "she read me here" – nonsense! I'm the one who does the reading and writing around here now. The only one. The words don't obey you any more, old man, it's a long time since they did, and you know it!'

'They'll obey me again! And the first thing I'll write will be a return ticket for you!'

'Oh yes? And who's going to read these fabulous words? As far as I'm aware, you need someone to read them aloud *for* you. Unlike me.'

'Well?' Fenoglio came so close that Orpheus's long-sighted eyes blinked at him in annoyance. 'I'll ask Mortimer! They don't call him Silvertongue for nothing, even if he goes by another name these days. Ask the boy! If it weren't for Mortimer, he'd still be in the desert shovelling camel dung.'

'Mortimer!' Orpheus produced a derisive smile, although with some difficulty. 'Is your head buried so deep in your wine jug that you don't know what's going on in this world of yours? He's not doing any reading now. The bookbinder prefers to play the outlaw these days – the role you created especially for him.'

The bodyguard uttered a grunt, probably meant to be something like laughter. What a ghastly fellow! Had Fenoglio himself written him into the story, or had Orpheus? Fenoglio scrutinized the muscleman for a moment, irritated, and then turned back to his master.

'I did not make it especially for him!' he said. 'It's the other way round: I used Mortimer as my pattern for the character . . . and from all I hear, he plays his part well. But that doesn't mean the Bluejay no longer has a silver tongue. Not to mention his gifted daughter.'

'Oh yes? And do you know where he is?' Orpheus asked almost casually. He was staring at his fingernails again, while his bodyguard had set to work on what was left of Fenoglio's breakfast.

'Indeed I do. He's coming—' Fenoglio fell abruptly silent as the boy suddenly came up and clapped his hand over the old man's mouth. Why did he keep forgetting the lad's name? Because you're going senile, Fenoglio, he said to himself, that's why.

'No one knows where the Bluejay is!' How reproachfully Farid's black eyes were looking at Fenoglio! 'No one!'

Of course. Damn drunken old fool that he was! How could he have forgotten that Orpheus turned green with jealousy whenever he heard Mortimer's name, or that he went in and out of the Milksop's castle all the time? Fenoglio could have bitten his tongue off.

But Orpheus smiled. 'Don't look so alarmed, old man! So the bookbinder's coming here. Bold of him. Does he want to make the songs that sing of his daring come true before they hang him? Because that's how he'll meet his end, like all heroes. We both know that, don't we? Don't worry, I don't intend to hand him over ripe for the gallows. Others will do that. No, I just want to talk to him about the White Women. There aren't many who have survived a meeting with them, that's why I really would like a word with him. There are some very interesting rumours about such survivors.'

'I'll tell him if I see him,' replied Fenoglio brusquely. 'But I can't think that he will want to talk to you. After all, I don't suppose he'd ever have met the White Women at all if you hadn't been so willing to read him here for Mortola. Rosenquartz!' He strode to the door with as much dignity as was possible in his shabby boots. 'I have some errands to run. See our guests out, and mind you keep away from that marten!'

Fenoglio stumbled down the staircase to the yard almost as fast as he had on the day when Basta had paid him a visit. Mortimer would be waiting outside the castle gates already! Suppose Orpheus found him there when he went to the castle to tell the Milksop what he had heard? The Bluejay was the Governor's mortal enemy.

The boy caught up with him halfway downstairs. Farid. Yes, that was the name. Of course. Going senile, for sure

'Is Silvertongue really coming here?' he whispered breathlessly. 'Don't worry, Orpheus won't give him away. Not yet! But Ombra is far too dangerous for him! Is he bringing Meggie with him?'

'Farid!' Orpheus was looking down at them from the top of the stairs as if he were the king of the Inkworld. 'If the old fool doesn't tell Mortimer I want to speak to him, then you do it. Understand?'

Old fool, thought Fenoglio. Oh, ye gods of words, give them back to me so that I can get this damned calf's-head out of my story!

He wanted to give Orpheus a suitably cutting answer, but not even his tongue could find the right words now, and the boy impatiently hauled him away.

6

Sad Ombra

My courtiers called me the happy prince, and happy indeed
I was, if pleasure be happiness. So I lived and so I died. And
now that I am dead they have set me high that I can see all
the ugliness and all the misery in the city, and though my
heart is made of lead yet I cannot choose but weep.

Oscar Wilde, *The Happy Prince*

Farid had told Meggie how difficult it was to get into
Ombra now, and she had passed on everything he said to
Mo. 'The guards aren't the harmless fools who used to stand
there. If they ask you what you are doing in Ombra, think
hard before you answer. Whatever they demand, you must
stay humble and submissive. They don't search many people.
Sometimes you may even be lucky and they'll just wave you
through!'

They weren't lucky. The guards stopped them, and Meggie
felt like clinging to Mo when one of the soldiers gestured to
him to dismount and brusquely asked to see a sample of his
craft. While the guard looked at the book of her mother's

drawings, Meggie wondered in alarm whether she already knew the face under the open helmet from her imprisonment in the Castle of Night, and whether he would find the knife hidden in Mo's belt. They might kill him just for that knife. No one was allowed to carry weapons except the occupiers from Argenta, but Battista had made the belt so well that even the suspicious hands of the guard at the gate could find nothing wrong with it.

Meggie was glad Mo had the knife with him as they rode through the ironbound gates, past the lances of the guards, and into the city that now belonged to the Adderhead.

She hadn't been in Ombra since she and Dustfinger first set out for the secret camp of the Motley Folk. It seemed an eternity ago that she had run through the streets with Resa's letter telling her that Mortola had shot her father. For a moment she pressed her face against Mo's back, so happy that he was back with her, alive and well. At last she would be able to show him what she'd told him so much about: Balbulus's workshop and the Laughing Prince's books. For one precious moment she forgot all her fears, and it seemed as if the Inkworld belonged only to him and her.

Mo liked Ombra. Meggie could see it in his face, from the way he looked around, reining in his horse again and again to look down the streets. Although it was impossible to ignore the mark left on the city by the occupying forces, Ombra was still what the stonemasons had made of it when they first carved its gates, columns and arches. Their works of art couldn't be carried away and broken up – for then they'd be worth no more than the paving stones in the street. So stone flowers still grew under the windows and balconies of Ombra, tendrils twined around columns and cornices, and faces stuck tongues out of grotesquely distorted mouths from the sand-coloured walls, weeping stony tears. But the Laughing Prince's coat of arms was defaced everywhere, and you could recognize the lion on it only from what was left of its mane.

'The street on the right leads to the marketplace!' Meggie whispered to Mo, and he nodded like a sleepwalker. Very likely he was hearing, in his mind, the words that had once told him about the scene now surrounding him as he rode on. Meggie had heard about the Inkworld only from her mother, but Mo had read Fenoglio's book countless times as he tried again and again to find Resa among the words.

'Is it the way you imagined it?' she asked him quietly.

'Yes,' Mo whispered back. 'Yes – and no.'

There was a crowd of people in the marketplace, just as if the peace-loving Laughing Prince still ruled Ombra – except that there were hardly any men to be seen, and you could stop and watch entertainers again. For the Milksop allowed strolling players into the city, although only – it was whispered – if they were prepared to spy for him. Mo rode his horse past a crowd of children. There were many children in Ombra, even though their fathers were dead. Meggie saw a torch whirling through the air above the small heads – two, three, four torches – and sparks fading and going out in the cold air. Farid? she wondered, although she knew he'd done no more fire-eating since Dustfinger's death. But Mo suddenly pulled his hood down over his forehead, and then she too saw the familiar well-oiled face with its constant smile.

Sootbird.

Meggie's fingers closed on Mo's cloak, but her father rode on, as if the man who had betrayed him once already wasn't there at all. More than a dozen strolling players had lost their lives because Sootbird had revealed the whereabouts of the secret camp, and Mo himself had almost been among the dead. Everyone in Lombrica knew that Sootbird went in and out of the Castle of Night, that he'd been paid for his treachery in silver by the Piper himself and was now also on excellent terms with the Milksop, yet there he stood in Ombra marketplace, smiling, unrivalled now that Dustfinger was dead and Farid had lost his enthusiasm for fire-eating.

Oh yes, Ombra certainly had new masters. Nothing could have made that clearer to Meggie than Sootbird's smug, mask-like face. It was said that the Adderhead's alchemists had taught him certain things, and that what he played with now was dark fire, wily and deadly like the powders he used to tame it. The Strong Man had told Meggie that its smoke beguiled the senses, making Sootbird's spectators think they were watching the greatest fire-eater on earth.

Whatever the truth of that was, the children of Ombra clapped. The torches didn't fly half as high in the air as they had for Dustfinger or Farid, but for a while the show made them forget their sad mothers, and the work waiting at home.

'Mo, please!' Meggie quickly turned her face away as Sootbird looked in her direction. 'Let's turn back! Suppose he recognizes you?'

They were going to close the gates, then the two of them would be hunted through the streets like rats in a trap!

But Mo just shook his head very slightly as he reined in his horse behind one of the market stalls. 'Don't worry, Sootbird is far too busy keeping the fire away from his pretty face!' he whispered to Meggie. 'But let's dismount. We won't be so conspicuous on foot.'

The horse shied when Mo led it into the crowd, but he

soothed it in a quiet voice. Meggie saw a juggler who had once followed the Black Prince among the stalls. Many of the strolling players had changed sides now that the Milksop was filling their pockets. These were not bad times for them, and the market traders did good business too. The women of Ombra couldn't afford any of the wares for sale, but with the money they had extorted the Milksop and his friends bought costly fabrics, jewellery, weapons, and delicacies with names that Fenoglio himself might not know. You could even buy horses here.

Mo looked around at the bustling, colourful throng as if he didn't want to miss a single face or any of the wares offered for sale, but finally his gaze turned to the towers rising high above the tiled roof tops, and lingered there. Meggie's heart constricted. He was still determined to go to the castle, and she cursed herself for ever telling him about Balbulus and his art.

She almost stopped breathing when they passed a 'Wanted' poster for the Bluejay, but Mo just cast a glance of amusement at the picture and ran his hand through his dark hair, which he now wore short like a peasant. Perhaps he thought his carefree attitude would soothe Meggie, but it didn't. It frightened her. When he acted like that he *was* the Bluejay, a stranger with her father's face.

Suppose one of the soldiers who had guarded him in the Castle of Night was here? Wasn't that one staring at them? And the minstrel woman over there – didn't she look like one of the women who had gone out through the gates of the Castle of Night with them? *Move away, Mo!* she thought, willing him to walk on with her through one of the arches, into a street – any street – just to be out of sight of all those eyes.

Two children clutched her skirt and held out their dirty hands, begging. Meggie smiled at them helplessly. She didn't have any money, not a coin. How hungry they looked! A soldier made his way through the crush and roughly pushed the beggar children aside. If only we were in there with Balbulus, thought Meggie – and stumbled into Mo as he abruptly stopped.

Beside the stall of a physician who was praising his miracle medicine at the top of his voice, a few boys were standing around a pillory. There was a woman in it, her hands and head wedged in the wood, helpless as a doll. Rotting vegetables stuck to her face and hands, fresh dung, anything the children could find among the stalls.

Meggie had seen such things before, in Fenoglio's company, but Mo stood there as if he had forgotten what he'd come to Ombra for. He was almost as pale as the woman, whose tears mingled with the dirt on her face, and for a moment Meggie was afraid he was going to reach for the knife hidden in his belt.

'Mo!' She took his arm and quickly led him on, away from the gawping children who were already turning to look at him, and into the street going up to the castle.

'Have you seen anything like that before?' The way he was looking at her! As if he couldn't believe she had been able to control herself so well at such a sight.

His glance made Meggie feel ashamed. 'Yes,' she said awkwardly. 'Yes, a few times. They put people in the pillory during the Laughing Prince's rule too.'

Mo was still looking at her. 'Don't tell me you can get used to such sights.'

Meggie bent her head. The answer was yes. Yes, you could.

Mo took a deep breath, as if he had forgotten about breathing when he saw the weeping woman. Then he walked on in silence. He didn't say a word until they reached the castle forecourt.

There was another pillory right beside the castle gates, with a boy in it. Fire-elves had settled on his bare skin. Mo handed Meggie the horse's reins before she could stop him, and went over to the boy. Ignoring the guards at the gateway, who were staring at him, and the women passing by who turned their heads away in alarm, he shooed the fire-elves off the boy's skinny arms. The boy just looked at him incredulously. There was nothing to be seen on his face but fear, fear and shame. And Meggie remembered a story that Farid had told her, of how Dustfinger and the Black Prince had once been in the pillory together, side by side, when they were not much older than the lad now looking at his protector in such alarm.

'Mortimer!'

Meggie recognized the old man dragging Mo away from the pillory only after a second glance. Fenoglio's grey hair came almost down to his shoulders; his eyes were bloodshot, his face unshaven. He looked old – Meggie had never considered Fenoglio old before, but now it was all she could think of.

'Are you out of your mind?' he snapped at her father in a low voice. 'Hello, Meggie,' he added abstractedly, and Meggie felt the blood shoot into her face as Farid appeared behind him.

Farid.

Keep very cool, she thought, but a smile had already stolen to her lips. Make it go away! But how, when it was so good to see his face? Jink was sitting on his shoulder, and sleepily flicked his tail when he saw her.

'Hello, Meggie. How are you?' Farid stroked the marten's bushy coat.

Twelve days. Not a sign of life from him for twelve whole days. Hadn't she firmly resolved not to say a word when she saw him again? But she just couldn't be angry with him. He still looked so sad. Not a sign of the laughter that once used to be as much a part of his face as his black eyes. The smile he gave her now was only a sad shadow of it.

'I've been wanting to come and see you so often, but Orpheus just wouldn't let me go out!' He was hardly listening to his own words. He had eyes only for Meggie's father. The Bluejay.

Farid had led Mo away with him – away from the pillory, away from the soldiers. Meggie followed them. The horse was restless, but Farid calmed it. Dustfinger had taught him how to talk to animals. He was close beside Meggie, so near and yet so far away.

'What was the idea of that?' Fenoglio was still holding Mo firmly, as if afraid he might go back to the pillory. 'Do you want to put your own head in that thing too? Or – no, very likely they'd impale it on a pike right away!'

'Those are fire-elves, Fenoglio! They'll burn his skin.' Mo's voice was husky with rage.

'You think I don't know that? I invented the little brutes. The boy will survive. I imagine he's a thief. I don't want to know any more.'

Mo moved away, turning his back on Fenoglio as abruptly as if to keep himself from striking the old man. He scrutinized the guards and their weapons, the castle walls and the pillory, as if trying to think of a way to make them all disappear.

Don't look at the guards, Mo! Meggie thought. That was the first thing Fenoglio had taught her in this world: not to look any soldier in the eye – any soldier, any nobleman – anyone who was allowed to carry a weapon.

'Shall I spoil their appetite for his skin, Silvertongue?' Farid came up between Mo and Fenoglio.

Jink spat at the old man, as if detecting him as the cause of all that was wrong in his world. Without waiting for Mo's answer Farid went up to the pillory, where the elves had settled on the boy's skin again. With a snap of his fingers he sent sparks flying to singe their shimmering wings and send them swirling through the air and away, with an angry buzz. One of the guards picked up his lance, but before he could move Farid painted a fiery basilisk on the castle wall with his finger, bowed to the guards – who were staring incredulously at their master's burning emblem – and strolled back casually to Mo's side.

'Very audacious, dear boy!' growled Fenoglio disapprovingly, but Farid took no notice of him.

'Why did you come here, Silvertongue?' he asked, lowering his voice. 'This is dangerous!' But his eyes were shining. Farid loved dangerous ventures, and he loved Mo for being the Bluejay.

'I want to look at some books.'

'Books?' Farid was so bewildered that Mo couldn't help smiling.

'Yes, books. Very special books.' He looked up at the tallest of the castle towers. Meggie had told him exactly where Balbulus had his workshop.

'What's Orpheus up to?' Mo glanced at the guards. At this moment they were searching a butcher's deliveries – though what for they didn't seem to know. 'I've heard he's growing richer and richer.'

'Yes, he is.' Farid's hand stroked Meggie's back. When Mo was with them he always confined himself to caresses that weren't too obvious. Farid felt great respect for fathers. But Meggie's rosy blush certainly didn't escape Mo's attention. 'He's growing richer, but he hasn't written anything to rescue Dustfinger yet! He thinks of nothing but his treasures, and what he can sell to the Milksop: wild boar with horns, golden lapdogs, spider moths, leaf men, anything else he can dream up.'

'Spider moths? Leaf men?' Fenoglio looked at Farid in alarm, but Farid didn't seem to notice.

'Orpheus wants to talk to you!' he whispered to Mo. 'About the White Women. Please do meet him! Maybe you know something that could help him to bring Dustfinger back!'

Meggie saw the pity in Mo's face. He didn't believe Dustfinger would ever come back, any more than she did. 'Nonsense,' he said as his hand instinctively went to the place where Mortola had wounded him. 'I don't know anything. Anything more than everyone knows.'

The guards had let the butcher pass, and one of them was staring at Mo again. The basilisk painted by Farid on the stones was still burning on the castle walls.

Mo turned his back on the soldier. 'Listen!' he whispered to Meggie. 'I ought not to have brought you here. Suppose you stay with Farid while I go to see Balbulus? He can take you to Roxane's, and I'll meet you and Resa there.'

Farid put his arm round Meggie's shoulders. 'Yes, you go. I'll look after her.'

But Meggie pushed his arm roughly away. She didn't like the idea of Mo going on his own – although she had to admit she'd have been only too happy to stay with Farid. She'd missed his face so much.

'Look after me? You don't have to look after me!' she snapped at him, more sharply than she had intended. Being in love made you so stupid!

'She's right about that. No one has to look after Meggie.' Mo gently took the horse's reins from her hand. 'Now that I come to think of it, she's looked after me more often than the other way round. I'll soon be back,' he told her. 'I promise. And not a word to your mother, all right?'

Meggie just nodded.

'Stop looking at me so anxiously!' Mo whispered in a conspiratorial tone. 'Don't the songs say the Bluejay hardly ever does anything without his beautiful daughter? So I'm much less of a suspicious character without you!'

'Yes, but the songs are lying,' Meggie whispered back. 'The Bluejay doesn't have a daughter at all. He's not my father, he's a robber.'

Mo looked at her for a long moment. Then he kissed her on the forehead as if obliterating what she had said, and went slowly towards the castle with Fenoglio.

Meggie never took her eyes off him as he reached the guards and stopped. In his black clothes he really did look like a stranger – the bookbinder from a foreign land who had come all this way to see the famous Balbulus's pictures and give them proper clothes to wear at last. Who cared that he'd also become a robber on his long journey?

Farid took Meggie's hand as soon as Mo had turned his back to them. 'Your father's as brave as a lion,' he whispered to her, 'but a little crazy too, if you ask me. If I were the Bluejay I'd never go through that gate, certainly not to see a few books!'

'You don't understand,' replied Meggie quietly. 'He wouldn't do it for anything *except* the books.'

She was wrong about that, but she wouldn't know it until later.

The soldiers let the writer and the bookbinder pass. Mo looked back at Meggie once more before he disappeared through the great gateway with its pointed iron portcullis. Ever since the Milksop had come to the castle it was lowered as soon as darkness fell, or whenever an alarm bell rang inside the building. Meggie had heard the sound once, and she instinctively expected to hear it again as Mo disappeared inside those mighty walls: the ringing of bells, the rattle of chains as the portcullis dropped, the sound of the iron spikes meeting the ground . . .

'Meggie?' Farid put one hand under her chin and turned her face to his. 'You must believe me – I'd have come to see you ages ago, but Orpheus makes me work hard all day, and at night I steal out to Roxane's farm. I know she goes to the place where she's hidden Dustfinger almost every night! But she always catches me before I can follow her. Her stupid goose lets me bribe it with raisin bread, but if the linchetto in her stable doesn't bite me then Gwin gives me away. Roxane even lets him into the house now, though she always used to throw stones at him before!'

What was he going on about? She didn't want to talk about Dustfinger or Gwin. If you really missed me, she kept thinking, then why didn't you come to see me at least once instead of going to Roxane's? Just once. There was only one answer:

because he hadn't been missing her half as much as she'd missed him. He loved Dustfinger more than her. He would always love Dustfinger, even now he was dead. All the same, she let him kiss her, only a few paces from where the boy was still in the pillory with fire-elves on his skin. *Don't tell me you can get used to such sights* . . .

Meggie didn't see Sootbird until he had reached the guards.

'What is it?' Farid asked, as she stared over his shoulder. 'Ah, Sootbird. Yes. He's always going in and out of the castle. Whenever I see him I feel I could slit his throat!'

'We must warn Mo!'

The guards let the fire-eater pass through like an old acquaintance. Meggie took a step towards them, but Farid kept her back.

'Where do you think you're going? Don't worry, he won't see your father! The castle is large, and Silvertongue is going to see Balbulus. Sootbird won't lose his way and end up there too, you can bet! He has three lovers among the court ladies, he's off to see them – if Jacopo doesn't nab him first. He has to perform for the boy twice a day, and he's still a terrible fire-eater in spite of all they say about him. Miserable informer! I really wonder why the Black Prince hasn't killed him yet – or your father. Why are you looking at me like that?' he added, seeing Meggie's horrified expression. 'Silvertongue killed Basta, didn't he? Not that I saw it.' Farid glanced quickly down, as he always did in speaking of the hours when he had been dead.

Meggie stared at the castle gates. She thought she could hear Mo's voice talking about Sootbird. *And if he does . . . last time he saw me I was half dead. And another encounter will be the worse for him.*

The Bluejay. Stop thinking of him by that name, Meggie thought. Stop it!

'Come on!' Farid took her hand. 'Silvertongue said I was to take you to Roxane. Won't she just be glad to see me! But I expect she'll put on a friendly act if you're there too.'

'No.' Meggie freed her hand from his, good as it felt to be holding hands with him again at last. 'I'm staying here. I'm staying right here until Mo comes out again.'

Farid sighed and rolled his eyes, but he knew her well enough not to argue with her.

'Oh, wonderful!' he said, lowering his voice. 'If I know Silvertongue he's sure to spend forever looking at those wretched books. So at least let me kiss you, or the guards will soon be wondering why we're still standing around.'

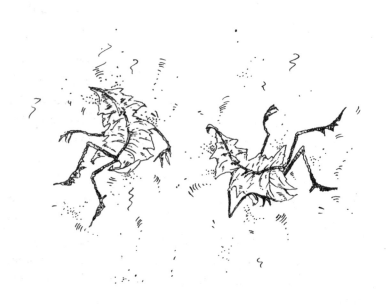

7

A Dangerous Visit

The question, given God's omniscient view,
Is: must what he foresees perforce come true?
Or is free choice of action granted me
To do a thing or else to let it be?
    Geoffrey Chaucer, *The Canterbury Tales (modernized)*

Humble. Humility and servility. He wasn't good at it. Did you ever notice that in the other world, Mortimer? he asked himself. Bow your head, don't stand too straight, let them look down on you even if you're taller than they are. Act as if you think it's perfectly natural for them to rule and everyone else to work.

It was so hard.

'Ah, you're the bookbinder Balbulus is expecting,' one of the guards had said, glancing at his black clothes. 'What was all that with the boy just now? Don't you like our pillory?'

Head lower, Mortimer! Go on. Pretend to be afraid. Forget your anger, forget the boy and his whimpering. 'It won't happen again.'

'Exactly! He . . . he comes from far away,' Fenoglio was quick to add. 'He has yet to get used to our new governor's rule. But if you'll allow us . . . Balbulus can be very impatient.' Then he had bowed and hastily drew Mo on with him.

Ombra Castle . . . it was difficult not to forget everything else when he stepped into the great courtyard. He remembered so many of the scenes from Fenoglio's book set here.

'Heavens above, that was a close thing!' whispered Fenoglio as they led the horse to the stables. 'I don't want to have to remind you again: you're here as a bookbinder! Play the Bluejay just once more and you're a dead man! Damn it, Mortimer, I ought never to have agreed to bring you here. Look at all those soldiers. It's like being in the Castle of Night!'

'Oh no, I assure you there's a difference,' Mo replied quietly, trying not to look up at the heads impaled on pikes that adorned the walls. Two belonged to a couple of the Black Prince's men, although he wouldn't have recognized them if the Strong Man hadn't told him about their fate. 'Although I didn't imagine the castle quite like this from your original description in *Inkheart*,' he whispered to Fenoglio.

'You're telling me?' Fenoglio murmured. 'First Cosimo had it all rebuilt, now the Milksop's leaving his mark on the place. He's had the gold-mockers' nests torn down, and look at all the shacks they've put up to hoard their loot! I wonder if the Adderhead's noticed yet how little of it ever reaches the Castle of Night. If he has, his brother-in-law will soon be in trouble.'

'Yes, the Milksop is pretty brazen about it.' Mo lowered his head as a couple of grooms came towards them. Even they were armed. His knife wouldn't be much use if anyone actually did recognize him. 'We stopped a few convoys intended for the Castle of Night,' he continued quietly when they had passed, 'and the contents of the chests always proved rather disappointing.'

Fenoglio stared at him. 'You're really doing it?'

'Doing what?'

The old man looked nervously around, but no one seemed to be taking any notice of them. 'Well, all the things they sing about!' he whispered. 'I mean . . . most of the songs are poor stuff, badly written, but the Bluejay is still my character, so . . . what does it feel like? What does it feel like, playing him?'

A maid carried two slaughtered geese past them. The birds' blood dripped on to the courtyard paving stones. Mo turned his head away. 'Playing? Is that what it still feels like to you – some kind of game?' His reply sounded touchier than he had intended.

Sometimes he'd really have given anything to read the thoughts in Fenoglio's head. And, who knew, maybe he would indeed read them some day in black and white, and find himself there on the page with words spun around him, like a fly caught in an old spider's web.

'I admit it's turned into a dangerous game, but I'm really glad you took the part! Because wasn't I right? This world *needs* the Blue—'

Mo interrupted Fenoglio – and put his fingers to his lips. A troop of soldiers passed them, and Fenoglio bit back the name he had first written down on a piece of parchment not so long ago. But the smile with which he watched the soldiers pass was the smile of a man who had planted an explosive device in his enemies' house, and was enjoying mingling with them knowing they had no idea he had laid that bomb.

Wicked old man.

Mo realized that the Inner Castle didn't look as Fenoglio had described it any more, either. He quietly repeated the words he had once read: *The Laughing Prince's wife had laid out the garden because she was tired of the grey stones all around her. She planted flowers from foreign lands, and when they came into bloom they made her dream of distant seas, strange cities and mountains where dragons lived. She allowed gold-breasted birds to breed, birds that perched in the trees like feathered fruits, and planted a seedling from the Wayless Wood, a tree with leaves that could talk to the moon.*

Fenoglio looked at him in surprise.

'Oh, I know your book by heart,' said Mo. 'Have you forgotten how often I read aloud from it after your words had swallowed up my wife?'

The gold-breasted birds had left the Inner Courtyard too. The Milksop's statue was reflected in a stone basin, and if the tree that talked to the moon ever existed then it had been felled. Dog-pens stood where there had once been a garden, and the new lord of Ombra's hounds pressed their noses to the silvered wire fencing. It's a long time since this was your story, old man, thought Mo as he and Fenoglio walked towards the Inner Castle. But, then, who was telling it now? Orpheus, maybe? Or had the Adderhead taken over as narrator, using blood and iron instead of pen and ink?

Tullio took them to Balbulus, Tullio the furry-faced servant said in Fenoglio's book to be the offspring of a brownie father and a moss-woman mother.

'How are you?' Fenoglio asked him as Tullio led them down the corridors. As if it had ever interested him how his creations were doing.

Tullio answered with a shrug of his shoulders. 'They hunt

me,' he said, his voice barely audible. 'Our new master's friends – and he has a lot of them. They chase me along the passages and shut me in with the hounds, but Violante protects me. She protects me even though her son is one of the worst of them.'

'Her son?' Mo asked.

'Yes, didn't Meggie tell you about him?' Fenoglio whispered back. 'Jacopo, a real little devil. His grandfather in miniature, although he's getting to look more like his father every day. Not that he ever shed a tear for Cosimo. Far from it. They say he daubed Cosimo's bust in the crypt with Balbulus's paints, and in the evenings he sits beside the Milksop or on Sootbird's lap instead of keeping his mother company. It's said he even spies on her for his grandfather the Adderhead.'

Mo had read nothing in Fenoglio's book about the door outside which Tullio finally stopped, rather breathless after climbing so many steep flights of stairs. He instinctively put out his hand to stroke the letters that covered it. 'They're so beautiful, Mo,' Meggie had murmured as the two of them sat high in their prison in the Castle of Night. 'Intertwined as if someone had written them on the wood in liquid silver.'

Tullio raised his small, furry fist and knocked. The voice calling them in could belong to no one but Balbulus. *Cold, self-satisfied, arrogant* . . . the words Meggie had used to describe the best illuminator in this world were not nice ones. Tullio stood on tiptoe, took hold of the door handle – and then let go of it again in alarm.

'Tullio!' The voice echoing up the staircase sounded very young, but it seemed used to giving orders. 'Where are you, Tullio? You must come and hold the torches for Sootbird.'

'Jacopo!' Tullio breathed the word as if it were the name of an infectious illness. He ducked and instinctively tried to shelter behind Mo's back.

A boy of perhaps six or seven came running upstairs. Mo had never seen Cosimo the Fair. The Milksop had had all his statues smashed, but Battista still had a few coins with his picture on them. A face almost too beautiful to be real, that was how everyone described him. His son had obviously inherited that beauty, although as yet it was only developing on his still round, childish face. But it was not an endearing face. The boy's eyes were watchful, and his mouth was as sullen as an old man's. His black tunic had an embroidered pattern showing his grandfather's emblematic adder with its flickering tongue, and even his belt was set with silver snakes, but around his neck dangled a silver nose – the Piper's trademark.

Fenoglio cast Mo a glance of alarm and stood in front of him, as if that would hide him from the boy.

You must come and hold the torches for Sootbird. Now what, Mo? He instinctively glanced down the stairs, but Jacopo had come alone, and this castle was large. His hand went to his belt all the same.

'Who's that?' Only the defiance in the clear voice sounded like a little boy's. Jacopo was breathing heavily from all that stair-climbing.

'He's . . . er . . . he's the new bookbinder, my Prince!' replied Fenoglio, bowing. 'I'm sure you remember how often Balbulus has complained of the clumsiness of our local bookbinders!'

'And this one's better?' Jacopo folded his little arms. 'He doesn't look like a bookbinder. Bookbinders are old, and all pale because they sit indoors the whole time.'

'Oh, we go out now and then too,' replied Mo. 'We go out to buy the best leather, new stamps, good knives, or to dry parchment in the sun if it's damp . . .'

He found it difficult to feel afraid of the boy, although he had heard so much that was bad about him. Cosimo's son reminded him of a boy he had known at school who was unlucky enough to be the headmaster's son. He used to stalk around the school yard like a copy of his father – and he was afraid of everything and everyone in the world. That's all very well, Mortimer, Mo told himself, but he was only a headmaster's son. This is the grandson of the Adderhead, so take care.

Jacopo frowned and looked disapprovingly at him. Obviously he didn't like the fact that Mo was so much taller than he was. 'You didn't bow! You have to bow to me.'

Mo felt Fenoglio's warning glance and bowed his head. 'My Prince.'

It was difficult. He would rather have chased Jacopo along the castle corridors in fun, the way he used to chase Meggie in Elinor's house, just to see if the child in him would emerge, carefully hidden as it was behind his grandfather's mannerisms.

Jacopo acknowledged his bow with a magnanimous nod, and Mo bowed his head again so that the boy wouldn't see his smile.

'My grandfather is having trouble with a book,' remarked Jacopo in his arrogant voice. 'A lot of trouble. Perhaps you can help him.'

Trouble with a book. Mo felt his heart miss a beat. In his mind's eye he saw the book before him again, felt the paper between his fingers. All those blank pages.

'My grandfather has had lots of bookbinders hanged

already because of that book.' Jacopo looked at Mo as if working out the size of the noose to fit his neck. 'He even had one flayed because the man had promised he could make the book better. Will you try all the same? But you'd have to ride to the Castle of Night with me so that my grandfather can see I was the one who found you, not the Milksop.'

Mo managed to get out of answering that as the door covered with letters opened and a man came out, an expression of annoyance on his face.

'What's all this?' he snapped at Tullio. 'First there's a knock but no one comes in, then so much talk that my brush slips. So, as you all clearly have not come to see me, I would be greatly obliged if you'd continue your conversation somewhere else. There are more than enough rooms in this castle where no real work is done.'

Balbulus . . . Meggie had described him very well. The slight lisp, the short nose and plump cheeks, the dark brown hair already receding from his forehead, although he was still quite a young man. An illuminator – and from what Mo had seen of his work, one of the best there had ever been, in either this world or his own. Mo forgot Jacopo and Fenoglio, he forgot the pillory and the boy in it, the soldiers down in the courtyard and even Sootbird. All he wanted was to go through that door. Even the glimpse of the workshop that he caught over Balbulus's shoulder made his heart beat as fast as a schoolboy's. He felt the same excitement as when he first held a book illustrated by Balbulus in his hand, when he was a prisoner threatened with death in the Castle of Night. This man's work had made him forget all that. Letters flowing as easily as if there were no more natural occupation for the human hand than writing, and then the pictures. Living, breathing parchment!

'I'll talk to people where and when I like! I'm the Adderhead's grandson!' Jacopo's voice was shrill. 'I'm going to tell my uncle how impertinent you've been again. I'm going to tell him this minute! I'll say he ought to take all your brushes away from you!' With one last glance at Balbulus he turned. 'Come on, Tullio. Or I'll shut you in with the hounds!'

The little servant went to Jacopo's side, head hunched between his shoulders, and the Adderhead's grandson inspected Mo again from head to foot before turning and hurrying down the stairs again – suddenly just a child after all, in a hurry to see a show.

'We ought to get out, Mortimer!' Fenoglio whispered to him. 'You should never have come to this place! Sootbird is here. It's not good, not good at all.'

But Balbulus was already impatiently beckoning the new bookbinder into his workshop. What did Mo care about Sootbird? He could think of nothing but what awaited him behind the door with the silver letters all over it.

He had spent so many hours of his life poring over the art of illumination, bending close to stained pages until his back ached, following every brush stroke with a magnifying glass, and wondering how such marvels could be captured on parchment. All the tiny faces, all the fantastic creatures, landscapes, flowers, miniature dragons, insects, so real that they seemed to be crawling off the pages. Letters as artfully entwined as if their lines had begun to grow only on that parchment.

Was all that waiting for him on the desks in there?

Maybe. But Balbulus stood in front of his work as if he were its guardian, and his eyes were so expressionless that Mo wondered how a man who bent so cold a gaze on the world could paint such pictures. Pictures so full of strength and fire . . .

'Inkweaver.' Balbulus nodded to Fenoglio with a look that seemed to sum him up: the unshaven chin, the bloodshot eyes, the weariness in the old man's heart. And what, Mo wondered, will he see in me?

'So you're the bookbinder?' Balbulus inspected him as thoroughly as if he planned to capture him on parchment. 'Fenoglio tells me truly wonderful things about your skill.'

'Oh, does he?' Mo couldn't help sounding distracted. He wanted to see those pictures at long last, but once again the illuminator barred his way as if by chance. What did this mean? Let me see your work, thought Mo. You ought to feel flattered that I've risked my neck to come here for its sake. Good heavens, those brushes really were incredibly fine. And then there were the paints . . .

Fenoglio dug a warning elbow into his ribs, and Mo reluctantly tore himself away from the sight of all these wonders and looked into Balbulus's expressionless eyes.

'I'm sorry. Yes, I'm a bookbinder, and I am sure you will want to see a sample of my work. I didn't have particularly good materials available, but . . .' He put his hand under the cloak that Battista had made (stealing so much black fabric couldn't have been easy), but Balbulus shook his head.

'You don't have to show me any evidence of what you can do,' he said, never taking his eyes off Mo. 'Taddeo, the librarian in the Castle of Night, has told me at length how impressively you proved your abilities there.'

Lost.

He was lost.

Mo sensed Fenoglio's appalled glance on him. Yes, look at me, he thought. Are the words 'reckless idiot' written as black as ink on my forehead?

However, Balbulus smiled. His smile was as hard to fathom as his eyes.

'Yes, Taddeo has told me about you at length.' Meggie had given a good imitation of the way his tongue touched his teeth as he spoke. 'Usually he is rather a reserved man, but he positively sung your praises to me in writing. After all, there aren't many of your trade who can bind death itself in a book, are there?'

Fenoglio gripped his arm so hard that Mo could feel the old man's fear. Did he think they could simply turn and walk out of the door? A guard would surely have been posted outside some time ago, and even if not, there were soldiers waiting at the bottom of the stairs. How quickly you got used to the way they could appear at any moment, armed with the power to take a man away, imprison him or kill him with impunity . . . how Balbulus's colours glowed! Vermilion, sienna, burnt umber . . . how beautiful they were. Beauty that had lured him into a trap. Most birds were trapped with bread and a few tasty seeds, but the Bluejay could be caught by words and pictures.

'I really don't know what you're talking about, highly esteemed Balbulus!' stammered Fenoglio. His fingers were still clutching Mo's arm. 'The . . . er . . . librarian at the Castle of Night? No. No, Mortimer's never worked on the other side of the forest. He comes from . . . from the north, yes, that's it.'

What a terrible liar the old man was. You'd have thought someone who made up stories could tell better lies.

However that might be, Mo himself was no good at lying

either, so he kept quiet, silently cursing his curiosity, his impatience, his recklessness, while Balbulus went on staring at him. What had made him think he could simply discard the part he was expected to play in this world by putting on a few black clothes? What had made him think he could go back to being Mortimer the bookbinder for a few hours here in Ombra Castle?

'Oh, be quiet, Inkweaver!' Balbulus snapped at Fenoglio. 'Just how much of a fool do you think I am? Of course I knew who he was the moment you mentioned him. "A true master of his art." Isn't that how you put it? Words can be very treacherous, as you really should know by now.'

Fenoglio did not reply. Mo felt for the knife that the Black Prince had given him when they set out from Mount Adder. 'From now on you must always have it with you,' the Prince had told him, 'even when you lie down to sleep.' Mo had followed his advice, but what use would a knife be to him here? He'd be dead before he reached the foot of the stairs. For all he knew, maybe Jacopo himself had immediately realized who was standing in front of him and had raised the alarm too. *Come quick, the Bluejay's flown into the cage of his own free will!*

I'm sorry, Meggie, thought Mo. Your father is an idiot. You rescued him from the Castle of Night only for him to get himself captured in another castle. Why hadn't he listened to her when she saw Sootbird in the marketplace?

Had Fenoglio ever written a song about the Bluejay's fear? The fear didn't come when he had to fight, not then. It came when he thought of fetters, chains and dungeons, and desperation behind barred doors. Like now. He tasted fear on his tongue, felt it in his guts and his knees. At least an illuminator's workshop is the right place for a bookbinder to die, he thought. But the Bluejay was back now, cursing the book-binder for being so reckless.

'Do you know what particularly impressed Taddeo?' Balbulus flicked a little powdered paint off his sleeve. Yellow as pollen, it clung to the dark blue velvet. 'Your hands. He thought it astonishing that hands which knew so much about killing could treat the pages of a book with such care. And you do have beautiful hands. Look at mine, now!' Balbulus spread his fingers and examined them with distaste. 'A peasant's hands. Large and coarse. Would you like to see what they can do all the same?'

And at last he stood aside and waved them over, like a con-juror raising the curtain on his show. Fenoglio tried to hold Mo back, but if he'd fallen into the trap, then he meant at least to taste the bait that would cost him his life.

There they were. Illuminated pages even better than those he had seen in the Castle of Night. Balbulus had adorned one of them with nothing but his own initial. The B spread right across the parchment, clad in gold and dark green and shel-tering a nest full of fire-elves. On the page beside it, flowers and leaves twined around a picture hardly the size of a play-ing card. Mo followed the tendrils with his eyes, discovered seed-heads, fire-elves, strange fruits, tiny creatures that he couldn't name. The picture so skilfully framed showed two men surrounded by fairies. They were standing outside a vil-lage, with a crowd of ragged men behind them. One of the two was black and had a bear by his side. The other wore a bird mask, and the knife in his hand was a bookbinder's knife.

'The Black Hand and the White Hand of Justice. The Prince and the Bluejay.' Balbulus looked at his work with barely concealed pride. 'I'll probably have to make some changes. You're even taller than I thought, and your bearing . . . but what am I talking about? I'm sure you're not anxious for this picture to resemble you too much – although of course it's meant only for Violante's eyes. Our new governor will never see it, because luckily there's no reason for him to toil up all the stairs to my workshop. To the Milksop's way of thinking, the value of a book is defined by the amount of wine it will buy. And if Violante doesn't hide it well, he'll soon have exchanged it – like all the other books my hands have made – for wine, or for a new silver-powdered wig. He can think himself truly lucky that I'm Balbulus the illuminator and not the Bluejay, or I'd be making parchment of his perfumed skin.'

The hatred in Balbulus's voice was black as the night painted in his pictures, and for a moment Mo saw in those expressionless eyes a flash of the fire that made the illuminator such a master of his art.

Footsteps resounded on the stairs, heavy and regular, footsteps of a kind that Mo had heard only too often in the Castle of Night. Soldiers' footsteps.

'What a pity. I really would have liked a longer chat!' Balbulus heaved a regretful sigh as the door was pushed open. 'But I'm afraid there are persons of much higher rank in this castle who want to talk to you.'

Three soldiers took Mo between them. Fenoglio watched in dismay as they tied his hands.

'You can go, Inkweaver!' said Balbulus.

'But this – this is all a terrible misunderstanding!' Fenoglio was trying really hard not to let his voice betray his fear, but even Mo wasn't deceived.

'Perhaps you shouldn't have described him in such detail

in your songs,' Balbulus observed wearily. 'To the best of my knowledge that's been his undoing once before. By way of contrast, look at my pictures. I always show him with his mask on!'

Mo heard Fenoglio still protesting as the soldiers pushed him down the stairs. Resa! No, this time he didn't have to fear for her. She was safe with Roxane at the moment, and the Strong Man was with her. But what about Meggie? Had Farid taken her to Roxane's farm yet? The Black Prince would look after both of them. He'd promised that often enough. And, who knew, perhaps they'd find their way back – back to Elinor in the old house crammed with books right up to the roof, back to the world where flesh and blood wasn't made of letters.

Mo tried not to think of where he would be by then. He knew just one thing: the Bluejay and the bookbinder would die the same death.

8

Roxane's Pain

'Hope,' said Sleet bitterly. 'I've learned to live without it.'
Paul Stewart, *Midnight Over Sanctaphrax*

Resa often rode over to see Roxane, although it was a long way and the roads around Ombra grew more perilous with every passing day. But the Strong Man was a good body-guard, and Mo let her go because he knew how many years she had lived in this world already, surviving even without him and the Strong Man.

Resa and Roxane had made friends tending the wounded together in the mine below Mount Adder, and their long journey through the Wayless Wood with a dead man had only deepened their friendship. Roxane never asked why Resa had wept almost as much as she did on the night when Dustfinger struck his bargain with the White Women. They had become friends not through talking, but by sharing experiences for which there were no words.

It was Resa who had gone to Roxane by night when she

heard her sobbing under the trees far from the rest of the company, Resa who had embraced and comforted her, although she knew there was no comfort for the other woman's sorrow. She did not tell Roxane about the day when Mortola shot Mo, leaving her alone with the fear that she had lost him for ever. Through all those many days and nights when she sat in a dark cave cooling his hot, feverish brow, she had only imagined how it would feel never to see him again, never to touch him again, never to hear his voice again. But the fear of pain was quite different from pain itself. Mo was alive. He talked to her, slept at her side, put his arms around her. Whereas Dustfinger would never put his arms around Roxane again. Not in this life. Roxane had nothing but memories left, and perhaps memories were sometimes worse than nothing.

And she knew that Roxane was feeling that pain for the second time. The first time, so the Black Prince had told Resa, the fire didn't even leave Roxane her dead husband's body. Perhaps that was why she guarded Dustfinger's body so jealously. No one knew the place where she had taken him, to visit him when longing wouldn't let her sleep.

It was when Mo's fever kept returning at night, and he was sleeping badly, that Resa first rode to Roxane's farm. She herself had often had to gather plants when she was in Mortola's service, but only plants that killed. Roxane had taught her to find their healing sisters. She told her which leaves were good for sleeplessness, which roots relieved the pain of an old wound, and that in this world it was wise to leave a dish of milk or an egg if you picked something from a tree, to please the wood-elves living in it. Many of the plants were strange to Resa, with unfamiliar odours that made her dizzy. Others she had often seen in Elinor's garden without guessing what power lay hidden in their inconspicuous stems and leaves. The Inkworld had taught her to see her own world more clearly and reminded her of something Mo had said long ago: 'I think we should sometimes read stories where everything's different from our world, don't you agree? There's nothing like it for teaching us to wonder why trees are green and not red, and why we have five fingers rather than six.'

Of course Roxane knew a remedy for Resa's sickness. She was just telling her what herbs would help the flow of her milk later on when Fenoglio, with Meggie and Farid, rode into the yard. Resa asked herself why the old man and her daughter wore such a guilty look on their faces. Of course she didn't guess the reason.

Roxane put her arms around Resa as Fenoglio, his voice faltering, told them what had happened. But Resa didn't know what to feel. Fear? Despair? Anger? Yes, anger. That was what she felt first of all. She was angry with Mo for being so reckless.

'How could you have let him go?' she snapped at Meggie, so sharply that the Strong Man jumped. The words were out before she could regret them. But her anger stayed with her: because Mo had gone to the castle even though he knew it was dangerous. And because he had done it behind her back. His daughter had been allowed to come with him, but to his wife he hadn't said a word.

Roxane stroked Resa's hair as she began to sob. Tears of rage, tears of fear. She was tired of feeling afraid.

Afraid of knowing Roxane's pain.

A Giveaway

'You're going to stop cruelty?' she asked. 'And greediness, and all those things? I don't think you could. You're very clever, but, oh no, you couldn't do anything like that.'

Mervyn Peake, *Titus Groan*

A dungeon awaited him, what else? And then? Mo remembered the death that the Adderhead had promised him only too clearly. *It could take days, many days and nights.* The fearlessness that had been his constant companion over the last few weeks, the cold calm that hatred and the White Women had implanted in him – they were gone as if he had never felt them. Since meeting the White Women he no longer feared death itself. It seemed to him familiar and at times even desirable. But dying was another matter, and so was imprisonment, which he feared almost more. He remembered, only too well, the despair waiting behind barred doors and the silence where even your own breath was painfully loud, every thought a torment, and where every hour tempted you simply to beat your head against the wall until you no longer heard and felt anything.

Mo had been unable to bear closed doors and windows since the days he had spent in the tower of the Castle of Night. Meggie seemed to have shed the fear of confinement like a dragonfly shedding its skin, but Resa felt as he did, and whenever fear woke one of them, they could find sleep again only in each other's arms.

Please, not a dungeon again.

That was what made fighting so easy – you could always choose death rather than captivity.

Perhaps he could seize a sword from one of the soldiers in one of the dark corridors, far from the other guards on duty. For guards stood everywhere with the Milksop's emblem on their chests. He had to clench his fists to keep his fingers from putting that idea into practice. Not yet, Mortimer, he told himself. Another flight of steps, burning torches on both sides. Of course, they were leading him down into the depths of the castle. Dungeons always lay high above or far below. Resa had told him about the cells in the Castle of Night, so deep in the mountainside that she had often thought she wouldn't be able to breathe in them. They weren't pushing and hitting him yet as the soldiers there had done. Would they be more civil when it came to torturing and quartering him too? Down and down they went, step by step. One in front of him, two behind him, breathing on the back of his neck. *Now, Mortimer! Try it now! There are only three of them!* Their faces were so young – children's faces, beardless, frightened under their assumed ferocity. Since when had children been allowed to play soldiers? Always, he answered himself. They make the best soldiers because they still think they're immortal.

Only three of them. But even if he killed them quickly they would shout, bringing more men down on him.

The stairs ended at a door. The soldier in front of him opened it. *Now! What are you waiting for?* Mo flexed his fingers, getting ready. His heart was beating a little faster, as if to set the pace for him.

'Bluejay.' The soldier turned to him, bowed, and left. There was a look of embarrassment on his face. In surprise, Mo scrutinized the other two. Admiration, fear, respect. The same mixture that he had met with so often, the result not of anything he had done himself, but of Fenoglio's songs. Hesitantly, he went through the open doorway – and only then did he realize where they had brought him.

The vault of the Princes of Ombra. Mo had read about that too. Fenoglio had found fine words for this place of the dead, words that sounded as if the old man dreamt of lying in such a vault himself some day. But in Fenoglio's book the most magnificent sarcophagus of all hadn't yet been there. Candles burnt at Cosimo's feet, tall, honey-coloured candles. Their perfume sweetened the air, and his stone image, lying on a bed of alabaster roses, was smiling as if in a happy dream.

Beside the sarcophagus, very erect as if to compensate for the lack of light, stood a young woman in black, her hair drawn severely back.

The soldiers bowed their heads to her and murmured her name.

Violante. The Adderhead's daughter. She was still known as Her Ugliness, although the birthmark that had earned her the name was only a faint shadow on her cheek now – it had begun to fade, people said, on the day when Cosimo came back from the dead. Only to return there soon.

Her Ugliness.

What a nickname. How did she live with it? But Violante's subjects used it with affection. Rumour had it that she secretly had leftovers from the princely kitchen taken to the starving villages by night, and fed those in need in Ombra by selling silverware and horses from the princely stables, even when the Milksop punished her for it by shutting her up in her rooms for days on end. She spoke up for those condemned to death and taken off to the gallows, and for those who vanished into dungeons – even though no one listened to her. Violante was powerless in her own castle, as the Black Prince had told Mo often enough. Even her son didn't do as she told him, but the Milksop was afraid of her all the same, for she was still his immortal brother-in-law's daughter.

Why had they brought him to her, here in the place where her dead husband lay at rest? Did she want to earn the price put on the Bluejay's head before the Milksop could claim it?

'Does he have the scar?' She didn't take her eyes off his face.

One of the soldiers took an awkward step towards Mo, but he pushed up his sleeve, just as the little girl had the night before. The scar left by the teeth of Basta's dogs long ago, in another life – Fenoglio had made a story out of it, and sometimes Mo felt as if the old man had drawn the scar on his skin with his own hands, in pale ink.

Violante came up to him. The heavy fabric of her dress trailed on the stone floor. She was really small, a good deal smaller than Meggie. When she put her hand to the embroidered pouch at her belt Mo expected to see the beryl that Meggie had told him about, but Violante took out a pair of glasses. Ground glass lenses, a silver frame – Orpheus's glasses must have been the model for this pair. It couldn't have been easy to find a master capable of grinding such lenses.

'Yes, indeed. The famous scar. A giveaway.' The glasses enlarged Violante's eyes. They were not like her father's. 'So Balbulus was right. Do you know that my father has raised the price on your head yet again?'

Mo hid the scar under his sleeve once more. 'Yes, I heard about that.'

'But you came here to see Balbulus's pictures all the same. I like that. Obviously what the songs say about you is true: you don't know what fear is, maybe you even love danger.'

She looked him up and down as thoroughly as if she were comparing him with the man in the pictures. But when he returned her glance she blushed – whether out of embarrassment or anger because he ventured to look her in the face, Mo couldn't have said. She turned abruptly, went over to her husband's tomb and ran her fingers over the stone roses as delicately as if she were trying to bring them to life.

'I would have done exactly the same in your place. I've always thought we were like each other. Ever since I heard the first song about you from the strolling players. This world breeds misfortune like a pond breeding midges, but it's possible to fight back. We both know that. I was already stealing gold from the taxes in the treasury before anyone sang those songs about you. For a new infirmary, a beggars' refuge, or somewhere for orphans to go . . . I just made sure that one of the administrators was suspected of stealing the gold. They all deserve to hang anyway.'

How defiantly she tilted her chin as she turned back to him. Almost the way Meggie sometimes did. She seemed very old and very young at the same time. What was she planning?

Would she hand him over to her father, to feed the poor with the price on his head, or so that she could buy enough parchment and paints for Balbulus at last? Everyone knew that she had even pawned her wedding ring to buy him brushes. Well, what could be more suitable? thought Mo. A bookbinder's skin, sold for new books.

One of the soldiers was still standing right behind him. The other two were guarding the door, obviously the only way out of the vault. Three. There were only three of them.

'I know all the songs about you. I had them written down.' The eyes behind the lenses in her glasses were grey and curiously light. As if you could see that they weren't very strong. They certainly didn't resemble the Adderhead's lizard-like eyes. She must have inherited them from her mother. The book in which death was held captive had been bound in the room where she and her ugly little daughter used to live after they fell into disfavour. Did Violante still remember that room? Surely she did.

'The new songs aren't very good,' she went on, 'but Balbulus makes up for that with his pictures. Now that my father's made the Milksop lord of this castle he usually works on them at night, and I keep the books with me so that they don't get sold like all the others. I read them when the Milksop is making merry in the great hall. I read them out loud so that the words will drown out all that noise: the drunken bawling, the silly laughter, Tullio crying when they've been chasing him again . . . and every word fills my heart with hope, the hope that you will stand there in the hall some day, with the Black Prince at your side, and kill them all. One by one. While I stand beside you with my feet in their blood.'

Violante's soldiers didn't move a muscle. They seemed to be used to hearing such words in their mistress's mouth.

She took a step towards him. 'I've had people searching for you ever since I heard from my father's men that you were in hiding on this side of the forest. I wanted to find you before they did, but you're good at staying out of sight. No doubt the fairies and brownies hide you, as the songs say, and the moss-women heal your wounds . . .'

Mo couldn't help it. He had to smile. For a moment Violante's face had reminded him so much of Meggie's when she was telling one of her favourite stories.

'Why do you smile?' Violante frowned, and for a moment he glimpsed the Adderhead in her light eyes. Careful, Mortimer.

'Oh, I know. You're thinking: she's only a woman, hardly more than a girl, she has no power, no husband, no soldiers. You're right, most of my soldiers lie dead in the forest because my husband was in too much of a hurry to go to war against my father. But I'm not so stupid! "Balbulus," I said, "spread word that you're looking for a new bookbinder. Perhaps we'll find the Bluejay that way. If what Taddeo said is true, he'll come just to see your pictures. And then, when he's in my castle, my prisoner, just as he was once a prisoner in the Castle of Night, I'll ask him to help me kill my immortal father."'

Violante's lips smiled in amusement as Mo looked sideways at her soldiers. 'Don't look so anxious! My soldiers are devoted to me. My father's men killed their brothers and fathers in the Wayless Wood!'

'Your father won't be immortal for very much longer.' The words came from Mo's lips unthinkingly; he hadn't meant to speak them aloud. Idiot, he told himself. Have you forgotten who this is facing you, just because something about her reminds you of your daughter?

But Violante smiled. 'Then what my father's librarian told me is indeed true,' she said, as softly as if the dead could overhear her. 'When my father began feeling unwell he thought at first that one of his maids had poisoned him.'

'Mortola.' Whenever Mo said her name he pictured her raising her gun.

'You know her?' Violante seemed as reluctant as he was to utter that name. 'My father had her tortured to make her say what poison she'd given him, and when she didn't confess she was thrown into a dungeon under the Castle of Night, but she disappeared one day. I hope she's dead. They say she poisoned my mother.' Violante stroked the black fabric of her dress as if she had been speaking of the quality of the silk and not her mother's death. 'Whether or not that's true, my father knows by now who's to blame for the way his flesh is rotting on his bones. Soon after your flight Taddeo noticed that the book was beginning to smell strange. And the pages were swelling. The clasps concealed it for a while, which presumably was your intention, but now they can hardly hold the wooden covers together. Poor Taddeo almost died of fear when he saw the state the book was in. Apart from my father himself, he was the only one who was permitted to touch it, and who knew where it was hidden . . . he even knows the three words that would have to be written in it! My father would have killed anyone else for possessing that knowledge. But he trusts the old man more than anyone else in the world, perhaps because Taddeo was his tutor for many years, and often protected him from my grandfather when he was a child. Who knows? Of course, Taddeo didn't tell my father what state the book was in. He'd have hung even his old tutor on the spot for bringing him such bad news. No, Taddeo secretly summoned every bookbinder between the Wayless Wood and the sea to the Castle of Night, and when none of them could help him, he took Balbulus's advice to bind a second book looking just like the first, which he showed my father when he asked for it. But meanwhile my father was feeling worse every day. Everyone knows about it by now. His breath stinks like stagnant pond water, and he's freezing, as if the White Women's breath is already wrapping him in their deadly cold. What a revenge, Bluejay! Endless life with endless suffering. That doesn't sound like the doing of an angel, more like the work of a very clever devil. Which of the two are you?'

Mo didn't answer. Don't trust her, a voice inside him said. But his heart, strangely enough, told him something else.

'As I said, it was a long time before my father suspected anyone but Mortola,' Violante went on. 'His suspicions even made him forget his search for you. But a day came when one of the bookbinders Taddeo had summoned to his aid told him what was wrong with the book, presumably hoping to be rewarded with silver for the news. My father had him killed – after all, no one must know about the threat to his immortality – but word soon spread. Now there's hardly a bookbinder left alive in Argenta. Every one of them who couldn't cure the book went to the gallows. And Taddeo has been thrown into the dungeons under the Castle of Night. "So that your flesh will rot away slowly like mine," my father's supposed to have said. I don't know if Taddeo is still alive. He's old, and the dungeons of the Castle of Night are enough to kill much younger men.'

Mo felt sick, just as he had in the Castle of Night when he

was binding the White Book to save Resa, Meggie and himself. Even then he had guessed that he was buying their lives at the cost of many others. Poor, timid Taddeo. Mo saw him in his mind's eye, crouching in one of those windowless dungeons. And he saw the bookbinders, he saw them very clearly, desolate figures swaying back and forth high in the air . . . He closed his eyes.

'Well, imagine that. Just as it says in the songs,' he heard Violante say. '*A heart more full of pity than any other beats in the Bluejay's breast.* You're really sorry that other people had to die for what you did. Don't be foolish. My father loves killing. If it hadn't been the bookbinders he'd have hung someone else! And in the end it wasn't a bookbinder, but an alchemist, who found a way to preserve the book. It's rumoured to be a very unappetizing way, and it couldn't reverse the harm you'd already done, but at least the book isn't rotting any more – and my father is looking for you harder than ever, because he still thinks only you can lift the curse you hid so skilfully between the empty pages. Don't wait for him to find you! Steal a march on him! Ally yourself with me. You and I, Bluejay – his daughter and the robber who has already tricked him once. We can be his downfall! Help me to kill him. Together we can do it easily!'

How she was looking at him – expectant as a child who has just told her dearest wish. Come with me, Bluejay, let's kill my father! What does a man have to do to his daughter, wondered Mo, to make her want something like that?

'Not all daughters love their fathers, Bluejay,' said Violante, as if she had read his thoughts, just as Meggie so often did. 'They say your daughter loves you dearly – and you love her. But my father will kill them, your daughter, your wife, everyone you love, and last of all he'll kill you too. He won't let you go on making him a laughing stock to his subjects. He'll find you even if you go on hiding as cleverly as a fox in its earth, because with every breath he draws, his own body reminds him of what you've done to him. Sunlight hurts his skin, his limbs are so bloated that he can't ride any more. He finds even walking difficult. Day and night he pictures what he wants to do to you and yours. He's made the Piper write songs about your death, such terrible songs that anyone who hears them can't sleep, or so they say, and soon he'll send the silver-nosed man to sing them here as well – and to hunt you down. The Piper has been waiting a long time for that order, and he'll find you. His bait will be your pity for the poor. He'll kill so many of them that their blood will lure you out of the forest at last. But if I help you—'

A voice interrupted Violante, a childish voice that was clearly used to getting a hearing from adults. It echoed down the endless stairway leading to the vault.

'He's bound to be with her, you just wait and see!' How excited Jacopo sounded! 'Balbulus is a very good liar, especially when he's lying for my mother. But when he does it he plucks at his sleeves and looks even more pleased with himself than usual. My grandfather's taught me to notice that kind of thing.'

The soldiers at the door looked enquiringly at their mistress, but Violante took no notice of them. She was listening to Jacopo outside the door, when another voice was heard and Mo saw, for the first time, a trace of fear in her fearless eyes. He knew the voice himself, and his hand went to the knife at his belt. Sootbird sounded as if the fire that he played with so clumsily had singed his vocal cords. 'His voice is like a warning,' Resa had once said of him, 'a warning to be on guard against his pretty face and the eternal smile on it.'

'What a clever lad you are, Jacopo!' Did the boy hear the sarcasm in his voice? 'But why don't we go to your mother's rooms?'

'Because she wouldn't be stupid enough to have him taken there. My mother is clever too, much cleverer than any of you!'

Violante went up to Mo and took his arm. 'Put the knife away!' she whispered. 'The Bluejay won't die in this castle. I refuse to hear that song. Come with me.'

She beckoned to the soldier standing behind Mo – a tall, broad-shouldered young man who held his sword as if he hadn't used it very often – and made her purposeful way past the stone coffins, as if this wasn't the first time she had had to hide someone from her son. More than a dozen tombs stood in the vault. Sleeping stone figures lay on top of most of them, with swords on their breasts, dogs at their feet, pillows of marble or granite under their heads. Violante hurried past them without a glance until she stopped by a coffin with a plain stone lid cracked right down the middle, as if the dead man inside had once pushed it open.

'If the Bluejay isn't here we'll go and scare Balbulus a bit, shall we?' There was jealousy in Jacopo's voice when he uttered Balbulus's name, as if he were talking about an older brother whom his mother preferred to him. 'We'll go back, and you can make fire lick around those books of his!'

The soldier's young face flushed red with effort as he heaved the lower part of the coffin lid aside. Mo kept his knife in his hand as he climbed into the sarcophagus. There was no dead body in it, but all the same Mo felt he could hardly breathe as he stretched out in the cold, cramped space. The coffin had clearly been made for a smaller man. Had Violante thrown his bones away so that she could hide her spies inside it? The darkness was almost total when the soldier pushed the cracked lid back into place. A little light and air came in through a few holes forming a flower pattern. Breathe steadily, Mo, breathe calmly, he told himself. He still had the knife in his hand; it was a pity none of the stone swords the dead were holding would be any use. 'Do you really think it's worth risking your own skin for a few painted goatskins?' Battista had enquired when he asked him to make the clothes and the belt. What a fool you are, Mortimer. Hasn't this world done enough to show you how dangerous it is? But Balbulus's painted goatskins had been very beautiful.

A knock. A bolt was pushed back. The voices came to his ears more distinctly now. Footsteps. Mo tried to peer through the holes, but he could see only another coffin, and the black hem of Violante's dress disappearing as she walked quickly away. His eyes weren't going to help him. He let his head sink back on to the cold stone and listened. How loud his breathing was. Could there be any sound more suspicious here among the dead?

Suppose it isn't just by chance that Sootbird has turned up now, something inside him whispered. Suppose Violante was only setting a trap for you? *Not all daughters love their fathers.* Suppose Her Ugliness was planning to give her father a very special present all the same? 'Look who I've caught for you. The Bluejay. He was disguised as a crow. I wonder who he thought he'd fool that way?'

'Your Highness!' Sootbird's voice echoed through the vault as if he were standing right beside the coffin where Mo lay.

'Forgive us for disturbing you in your grief, but your son wants me to meet a visitor you received today. He insists on it. He thinks the man is an old and very dangerous acquaintance of mine.'

'A visitor?' Violante's voice sounded as cool as the stone beneath Mo's head. 'The only visitor down here is death, and it's not much use warning anyone against death, is it?'

Sootbird laughed uneasily. 'No, certainly not, but Jacopo was talking about a flesh-and-blood visitor, a bookbinder, tall, dark hair . . .'

'Balbulus was interviewing a bookbinder today,' Violante replied. 'He's been looking for one for a long time now. Someone who knows his trade better than the bookbinders of Ombra.'

What was that noise? Of course. Jacopo hopping about on the flagstones. Obviously he sometimes acted like any other child after all. The hopping came closer. The temptation simply to stand up instead of lying there was very strong. It was difficult to keep your body as still as a corpse while you were still breathing. Mo closed his eyes so as not to see the stone around him. Keep your breath as shallow as you can, he told himself, breathe as quietly as the fairies.

The hopping stopped right beside him.

'You've hidden him!' Jacopo's voice reached Mo inside the sarcophagus as if he were speaking the words for Mo's ears alone. 'Shall we look in the coffins, Sootbird?'

The boy seemed to find the notion very enticing, but Sootbird laughed nervously. 'Oh, I'm sure that won't be necessary, if we tell your mother who she's dealing with. This bookbinder could be the very man your father is· looking for so desperately, Highness.'

'The Bluejay? The Bluejay, here in the castle?' Violante's voice sounded so incredulous that even Mo believed she was taken by surprise. 'Of course! I've told my father time and again: one day that robber's own daring will be his downfall. You're not to say a word of this to the Milksop. I want to catch the Bluejay myself, and then at last my father will realize who ought to be on the throne of Ombra! Have you reinforced the guards at the gates? Have you sent soldiers to Balbulus's workshop?'

'Er . . . no.' Sootbird was obviously confused. 'I mean . . . he isn't with Balbulus any more, he . . .'

'What? You fool!' Violante's voice was as sharp as her father's. 'Lower the portcullis over the gateway. At once! If my father hears that the Bluejay was in this castle, in my library, and simply rode away again . . .' How menacing she made those words sound in the chilly air! She was indeed clever; her son was right.

'Sandro!' That must be one of her soldiers. 'Tell the guards at the main gates to let the portcullis down. No one is to leave the castle. No one, do you hear? I only hope it's not too late already! Jacopo!'

'Yes?' There was fear and defiance in the high voice – and a trace of distrust.

'If he finds the gates closed, where could the Bluejay hide? You know every hiding place in this castle, don't you?'

'Of course!' Now Jacopo sounded flattered. 'I can show you all of them.'

'Good. Take three of the guards from outside the throne-room upstairs and post them at the most likely hiding places you know. I'll go and talk to Balbulus. The Bluejay! In my castle!'

Sootbird stammered something. Violante brusquely interrupted him, ordering him to go with her. Their footsteps and voices moved away, but Mo thought he could still hear them for some time on the endless stairs leading up and away from the dead, back to the world of the living, to the daylight where you could breathe easily . . .

Even when all was perfectly still again he lay there for a few more agonizing moments, listening until he felt as if he could hear the dead themselves breathing. Then he braced his hands against the stone lid – and hastily reached for his knife when he heard footsteps again.

'Bluejay!'

It was no more than a whisper. The cracked lid was pushed aside, and the soldier who had helped him into his hiding place reached out a hand to him.

'We must hurry!' he whispered. 'The Milksop has raised the alarm. There are guards everywhere, but Violante knows ways out of this castle that even Jacopo hasn't found yet. I hope,' he added.

As Mo clambered out of the sarcophagus, legs stiff from lying in its cramped space, he still had the knife in his hand.

The boy stared at it. 'How many have you killed?' His voice sounded almost awestruck. As if killing were a high art, like the painting of Balbulus. How old would the lad be? Fourteen? Fifteen? He looked younger than Farid.

How many? What was he to say to that? Only a few months ago the answer would have been so simple. Perhaps he'd even have laughed out loud at such a ridiculous question. Now he just said, 'Not as many as those who lie here,' although he wasn't sure that he was telling the truth.

The boy looked along the rows of the dead as if counting

them. 'Is it easy?'

Judging by the curiosity in his eyes, he really didn't seem to know the answer, despite the sword at his side and his shirt of chain mail.

Yes, thought Mo. Yes, it's easy . . . if you have a second heart beating in your breast, cold and sharp-edged as the sword you carry. A certain amount of hatred and anger, a few weeks of fear and helpless rage, and you'll have a heart like that. It beats time for you when you come to kill, a wild, fast rhythm. And only later do you feel your other heart again, soft and warm. It shudders in time with the other one at the thought of what you did. It trembles and feels pain . . . but that's only afterwards.

The boy was still looking at him.

'Killing is too easy,' said Mo. 'Dying is harder.'

Although Cosimo's stony smile claimed otherwise.

'Didn't you say we must hurry?'

The boy turned red under his shiny polished helmet. 'Yes . . . yes, of course.'

A stone lion kept watch in front of a niche behind the coffins, the emblem of Ombra on its breast – presumably the only example of the old coat of arms that the Milksop hadn't had smashed. The soldier put his sword between the lion's bared teeth, and the wall of the vault opened just far enough for a grown man to squeeze through it. Hadn't Fenoglio described this entrance? Words that Mo had read long ago came back to his mind, about one of Cosimo's ancestors who had escaped his enemies several times along the passage beyond. And words will save the Bluejay again, he thought. Well, why not? He's made of them. All the same, his fingers passed over the stone as if they needed to reassure themselves that the walls of the vault weren't just made of paper.

'The passage comes out above the castle,' the boy whispered to him. 'Violante couldn't get your horse from the stables. It would have attracted too much attention, but there'll be another waiting there. The forest will be swarming with soldiers, so be careful! And I'm to give you these.'

Mo put his hand into the saddlebags that the boy handed him.

Books.

'Violante says I'm to tell you they're a present for you, made in the hope that you will accept the alliance she offers you.'

The passage was endless, almost as oppressively narrow as the sarcophagus, and Mo was glad when at last he saw the light of day again. The way out was little more than a crack between a couple of rocks. The horse was waiting under the trees, and he saw Ombra Castle, the guards on the walls, the soldiers pouring out of the gates like a swarm of locusts. Yes, he would have to be very careful. All the same, he undid the saddlebags, hid among the rocks – and opened one of the books.

10

As If Nothing Had Happened

How cruel the earth, the willows shimmering,
the birches bending and sighing.
How cruel, how profoundly tender.

Louise Glück, *Lament*

Farid was holding Meggie's hand. He let her bury her face
in his shirt while he kept whispering that everything
would be all right. But the Black Prince still wasn't back, and
the crow sent out by Gecko brought the same news as Doria,
the Strong Man's younger brother, who had been spying for
the robbers ever since Snapper had saved him and his friend
from hanging. The alarm had been raised at the castle. The
portcullis was lowered, and the guards at the gate were boasting that the Bluejay's head would soon be looking down on
Ombra from the castle battlements.

The Strong Man had taken Meggie and Resa to the robbers' camp, although they would both have preferred to go
back to Ombra. 'That's what the Bluejay would want,' was all

111

he had said, and the Black Prince set off with Battista to the farm they'd called home for the last few weeks – such happy weeks, so deceptively peaceful in the turmoil of Fenoglio's world. 'We'll bring you your things,' was all the Prince had said, when Resa asked him what he was going there for. 'You can't go back.' Neither Resa nor Meggie asked why. They both knew the answer – because the Milksop would have the Bluejay questioned, and no one could be sure that a time wouldn't come when Mo might reveal where he had been hiding during those recent weeks.

The robbers themselves moved camp only a few hours after hearing of Mo's arrest. 'The Milksop has some very talented torturers,' Snapper remarked, and Resa sank down under the trees away from the others and buried her face in her arms.

Fenoglio had stayed in Ombra. 'Perhaps they'll let me see Violante. And Minerva's working in the castle kitchen tonight, maybe she'll find out something there. I'll do everything I can, Meggie!' he had promised as he said goodbye.

'Like getting into bed and drinking two jugs of wine!' was all Farid said to that, but he kept remorsefully silent when Meggie began to cry.

Why had she let Mo ride to Ombra? If only she'd at least gone to the castle with him, but she'd wanted to be with Farid so much. She saw the same accusation in her mother's eyes: you could have stopped him, Meggie, no one else but you could have done it.

When darkness began to fall Woodenfoot brought them something to eat. His stiff leg had earned him his name. Although not the fastest of the robbers, he was a good cook, but neither Meggie nor Resa could swallow a morsel. It was bitterly cold, and Farid tried to persuade Meggie to sit by the fire with him, but she just shook her head. She wanted to be alone with herself in the dark. The Strong Man brought her a blanket. His brother was with him, Doria. 'Not much good at poaching, but he's a first-class spy,' the Strong Man had whispered to her when he introduced them. The two brothers were not very much alike, although they had the same thick brown hair and Doria was already strong for his age (something that filled Farid with envy). He wasn't very tall. Doria only just came up to his elder brother's shoulder, and his eyes were as blue as the skin of Fenoglio's fairies, while the Strong Man's eyes were acorn-brown. 'We have different fathers,' the Strong Man had explained when Meggie expressed her surprise at the difference between them. 'Not that either of them's worth a lot.'

'You mustn't worry.' Doria's voice sounded very grown-up. Meggie raised her head.

He put the blanket around her shoulders, and stepped shyly back when she looked up at him, but he did not avoid her eyes. Doria looked everyone in the face, even Snapper – and most people looked away from Snapper.

'Your father will be all right, believe me. He'll outwit them all: the Milksop, the Adderhead, the Piper . . .'

'After they've hanged him?' asked Meggie. She sounded as bitter as she felt, but Doria just shrugged his shoulders.

'Nonsense. They were going to hang me too,' he said. 'He's the Bluejay! He and the Black Prince will save us all, you wait and see.' He made it sound as if it couldn't turn out any other way. As if he, Doria, were the only one who had read to the end of Fenoglio's story.

But Snapper, sitting under the trees with Gecko only a little way off, laughed hoarsely. 'Your brother's as big a fool as you!' he called over to the Strong Man. 'It's his bad luck he doesn't have your muscles, so I guess he won't live to be very old. The Bluejay is finished! And what does he leave behind as his legacy? The immortal Adderhead!'

The Strong Man clenched his fists and was about to go for Snapper, but Doria pulled him back when Gecko drew his knife and rose to his feet. The two of them often quarrelled, but suddenly they both raised their heads and listened. A jay was calling in the oak above them.

'He's back! Meggie, he's back!' Farid climbed down from his lookout post so fast that he almost lost his balance.

The fire had burnt low; only the stars shone down into the dark ravine where the robbers had pitched their new camp, and Meggie didn't see Mo until Woodenfoot limped over to him with a torch. Battista and the Black Prince were with him. They all seemed unharmed. Doria turned to her. *Well, Bluejay's daughter*, his smile seemed to be saying, *what did I tell you?*

Resa jumped up in such haste that she stumbled over her blanket. She made her way through the crowd of robbers standing around Mo and the Prince. As if in a dream, Meggie followed her. It was too good *not* to be a dream.

Mo was still wearing the black clothes that Battista had made him. He looked tired, but he did indeed seem to be uninjured.

'It's all right. Everything's all right,' Meggie heard him say as he kissed the tears from her mother's face, and when Meggie was there in front of him he smiled at her as if this were their old life, and he had only been on a short journey to cure a few sick books, not from a castle where people wanted to kill him.

'I've brought you something,' he whispered to her, and

only the way he hugged her so tight and for so long told her that he had been as frightened as she was.

'Leave him alone, will you?' the Black Prince told his men as they crowded around Mo, wanting to know how the Bluejay had escaped from Ombra Castle as well as the Castle of Night. 'You'll hear the story soon enough. And now, double the guard.'

They reluctantly obeyed, sat around the dying fire grumbling, or disappeared into the tents that had been patched together out of pieces of fabric and old clothes, offering only scant shelter from nights that were growing colder all the time. But Mo beckoned Meggie and Resa over to his horse and delved into the saddlebags. He brought out two books, handling them as carefully as if they were living creatures. He gave one to Resa and one to Meggie – and laughed when Meggie snatched hers so quickly that she almost dropped it.

'It's a long time since the two of us had a book in our hands, right?' he whispered to her with an almost conspiratorial smile. 'Open it. I promise you, you never saw a more beautiful book.'

Resa had taken her book too, but she didn't even look at it. 'Fenoglio said that illuminator was the bait for you,' she said in an expressionless voice. 'He told us they arrested you in his workshop.'

'It wasn't exactly what it seemed. As you can see, no harm came of it. Or I wouldn't be here, would I?'

Mo said no more, and Resa asked no further questions. She didn't say a word when Mo sat down on the short grass in front of the horses and drew Meggie down beside him.

'Farid?' he said, and Farid left Battista, whom he was obviously trying to question about events in Ombra, and went over to Mo with the same awe on his face that Meggie had seen on Doria's.

'Can you make some light for us?' Mo asked, and Farid knelt down between them and made fire dance on his hands, although Meggie could clearly see that he didn't understand how the Bluejay could sit there right after his narrow escape from the Milksop's soldiers, showing his daughter a book before he did anything else.

'Did you ever see anything so beautiful, Meggie?' Mo whispered as she caressed one of the gilded pictures with her finger. 'Apart from the fairies, of course,' he added with a smile as one of them, pale blue like the sky Balbulus painted, settled drowsily on the pages.

Mo shooed the fairy away as Dustfinger had always done, by blowing gently between her shimmering wings, and Meggie, beside him, bent her head over the pages and forgot her fears for him. She forgot Snapper, she even forgot Farid, who didn't so much as glance at what she couldn't tear her own eyes away from: lettering in sepia brown, as airy as if Balbulus had breathed it on to the parchment, dragons, birds stretching their long necks at the heads of the pages, initials heavy with gold leaf like shining buttons among the lines. The words danced with the pictures and the pictures sang for the words, singing their colourful song.

'Is that Her Ugliness?' Meggie laid a finger on the finely drawn figure of a woman. There she stood, slender beside the written lines, her face barely half the size of Meggie's little fingernail, yet you could see the pale birthmark on her cheek.

'Yes. And Balbulus made sure she'll still be recognized many hundreds of years from now.' Mo pointed to the name that the illuminator had written in dark-blue ink, clearly visible above the tiny head: *Violante*. The V had gold edging as fine as a hair. 'I met her today. I don't think she deserves her nickname,' Mo went on. 'She's rather too pale, and I think she could bear a grudge for a long time, but she fears nothing.'

A leaf landed on the open book. Mo flicked it away, but it clung to his finger with thin, spidery arms. 'Well, how about this!' he said, holding it up to his eyes. 'Is it one of Orpheus's leaf-men? His creations obviously spread fast.'

'And they're seldom very nice,' said Farid. 'Watch out. Those creatures spit.'

'Really?' Mo laughed softly and let the leaf-man fly away just as it was pursing its lips.

Resa watched the strange creature go, and abruptly straightened up. 'It's all lies,' she said. Her voice shook on every word. 'This beauty is only a lie. It's just meant to take our minds off the darkness, all the misfortune – and all the death.'

Mo put the book on Meggie's lap and got to his feet, but Resa stepped back.

'This isn't our story!' she said, in a voice loud enough for some of the robbers to turn and look at her. 'It's draining our hearts with all its magic. I want to go home. I want to forget all these horrors and not remember them until I'm back on Elinor's sofa!'

Gecko had turned too. He stared curiously at them while one of his crows tried to snatch a piece of meat from his hand. Snapper was listening as well.

'We can't go back, Resa,' said Mo, lowering his voice. 'Fenoglio isn't writing any more, remember? And we can't trust Orpheus.'

'Fenoglio will try to write us back if you ask. He owes it to you. Please, Mo! There can't be any happy ending here!'

Mo looked at Meggie, who was still kneeling beside Farid with Balbulus's book on her lap. What was he hoping for? Did he want her to contradict her mother?

Farid glared at Resa and let the fire between his fingers go out. 'Silvertongue?'

Mo looked at him. Yes, he had many names now. What had it been like when he was only Mo? Probably Meggie couldn't remember either.

'I must go back to Ombra. What am I to say to Orpheus?' Farid looked at him almost pleadingly. 'Will you tell him about the White Women?' There it was again, like fire burning on his face – his foolish hope.

'There's nothing to tell. I've said so before,' replied Mo, and Farid bowed his head and looked at his sooty hands as if Mo had snatched hope itself from his fingers.

He stood up. He still went barefoot, even though there was sometimes frost at night now. 'Good luck, Meggie,' he murmured, giving her a quick kiss. Then he turned without another word. Meggie was already missing him as he swung himself up on to his donkey.

Yes. Perhaps they really ought to go back . . .

She jumped when Mo put his hand on her shoulder.

'Keep the book wrapped in a cloth when you're not looking at it,' he said. 'The nights are damp.' Then he made his way past her mother and went over to the robbers, who were sitting around the embers of their dying fire as silently as if they were waiting for him.

But Resa stood there, staring at the book in her hands as if it were another book, the one that had swallowed her up entirely over ten years ago. Then she looked at Meggie.

'What about you?' she asked. 'Do you want to stay here, like your father? Don't you miss your friends, and Elinor and Darius? And your warm bed without any lice in it, the café down by the lake, the peaceful roads?'

Meggie wished so much she could give the answer that Resa wanted to hear, but she couldn't.

'I don't know,' she said quietly.

And that was the truth.

Sick with Longing

I lost a world the other day.
Has anybody found?
You'll know it by the row of stars
Around its forehead bound.

A rich man might not notice it;
Yet to my frugal eye
Of more esteem than ducats.
Oh, find it, sir, for me!

Emily Dickinson, _Collected Poems_

Elinor had read countless stories in which the main characters fell sick at some point because they were so unhappy. She had always thought that a very romantic idea, but she'd dismissed it as a pure invention of the world of books. All those wilting heroes and heroines who suddenly gave up the ghost just because of unrequited love, or longing for something they'd lost! Elinor had always enjoyed their sufferings – as a reader will. After all, that was what you wanted from books: great emotions you'd never felt yourself, pain you could leave behind by closing the book if it got too bad. Death and destruction felt deliciously real conjured up with the right words, and you could leave them behind between the pages as you pleased, at no cost or risk to yourself.

Elinor had wallowed in misery on the printed page, but she'd never thought that in real life, grey and uneventful as hers had been for many years, such pain could enter her own heart. You're paying the price now, Elinor, she often told herself these days. Paying the price for the happiness of those last months. Didn't books say that too: that there's always a price to pay for happiness? How could she ever have thought she would simply find it and be allowed to keep it? Stupid. Stupid Elinor.

When she didn't feel like getting up in the morning, when her heart faltered more and more frequently for no apparent reason, as if it were too tired to beat steadily, when she had no appetite even at breakfast time (although she had always preached that breakfast was the most important meal of the day), when Darius kept asking how she was with that anxious, owlish expression on his face, she began wondering whether becoming ill with longing was more than just a literary invention after all. Didn't she feel, deep down inside, that her longing was sapping her strength and her appetite, even her pleasure in her books? Longing.

Darius suggested going away to auctions of rare books, or famous book shops that she hadn't visited for a long time. He drew up lists of volumes not yet in her library, lists that would have filled Elinor with delighted excitement only a year ago. But now her eyes passed over the titles with as little interest as if she were reading a shopping list for cleaning products. What had become of her love for printed pages and precious bindings, words on parchment and paper? She missed the tug at her heart that she used to feel at the sight of her books, the need to stroke their spines tenderly, open them, lose herself in them. But it seemed as if all of a sudden her heart couldn't enjoy or feel anything, as if the pain had numbed it to everything but her longing for Meggie and her parents. Because by now Elinor had understood this too: a longing for books was nothing compared to what you could feel for human beings. The books told you about that feeling. The books spoke of love, and it was wonderful to listen to them, but they were no substitute for love itself. They couldn't kiss her like Meggie, they couldn't hug her like Resa, they couldn't laugh like Mortimer. Poor books, poor Elinor.

She began spending days on end in bed. She ate too little and then too much. Her stomach hurt, her head ached, her heart fluttered inside her. She was cross and absent-minded, and began crying like a crocodile over the most sentimental stories – because of course she went on reading. What else was there for her to do? She read and read and read, but she was stuffing herself with the letters on the page like an unhappy child stuffing itself with chocolates. They didn't taste bad, but she was still unhappy. And Orpheus's ugly dog lay beside her bed, slobbering on her carpet and staring at her with his sad eyes as if he were the only creature in the world who understood her sorrows.

Well, perhaps that wasn't quite fair. Presumably Darius, too, knew just how wretched she was feeling. 'Elinor, won't you go for a little walk?' he would ask when he had brought her breakfast in bed yet again, and she still hadn't appeared in the kitchen by twelve noon. 'Elinor, I found this wonderful edition of *Ivanhoe* in one of your catalogues. Why don't we go and take a look at it? The place isn't far away.' Or, as he had said only a few days ago, 'Please, Elinor, go and see the doctor! This can't go on!'

'The doctor?' she snapped at the poor man. 'And what do you expect me to say to him? "Well, doctor, it seems to be my heart. It feels this ridiculous yearning for three people who disappeared into a book. Do you have any pills for that kind of thing?"'

Of course Darius had had no answer. Without a word, he had just put down her tea – tea with honey and lemon, her favourite – beside the bed among the mountains of books piled on her bedside table, and gone downstairs again looking so sad that Elinor had a shockingly guilty conscience. All the same, she didn't get up.

She stayed in bed for three more days, and when she dragged herself into her library on the fourth day, still in her nightdress and dressing gown, to get something else to read, she found Darius holding the sheet of paper. The one that had taken Orpheus to the place where Elinor supposed Resa, Meggie and Mortimer still were.

'What on earth are you doing?' she asked, horrified. 'No one touches that piece of paper, understand? No one!'

Darius put the sheet back in its place and wiped a speck off the glass case with his sleeve. 'I was only looking at it,' he said in his gentle voice. 'Orpheus really doesn't write badly, does he? Although it sounds very much like Fenoglio.'

'Which is why it can hardly be described as Orpheus's writing,' said Elinor scornfully. 'He's a parasite. A louse preying on other writers – except that he feeds on their words, not their blood. Even his name is stolen from another poet! Orpheus!'

'Yes, I expect you're right,' said Darius as he carefully closed the glass case again. 'But perhaps you should call him a forger instead. He copies Fenoglio's style so perfectly that at first glance you can't tell the difference. It would be interesting to see how he writes when he has to work without a model. Can he paint pictures of his own? Pictures that don't look like someone else's?' Darius looked at the words under the glass lid as if they could answer his question.

'Why would I be interested in that? I hope he's dead and gone. Trodden underfoot.' Grim-faced, Elinor went up to the shelves and took out half a dozen books, supplies for another cheerless day in bed. 'Yes, trodden underfoot! By a giant. Or – no, wait! Even better – I hope his clever tongue is blue and sticking out of his mouth because they've hanged him!'

That brought a smile to Darius's owlish face.

'Elinor, Elinor!' he said. 'I think you could teach the Adderhead himself the meaning of fear.'

'Of course I could!' replied Elinor. 'Compared to me, the White Women are a bunch of sisters of mercy! But I'm stuck for the rest of my life in a story where there's no part for me but the role of a batty old woman!'

Darius didn't reply to that. However, when Elinor came downstairs again that evening to find another book, he was standing in front of the glass case once more, looking at the words Orpheus had written on the sheet of paper.

Back in the Service of Orpheus

Come close and consider the words.
With a plain face hiding thousands of other faces
and with no interest in your response,
whether weak or strong,
each word asks:
Did you bring the key?

Carlos Drummond de Andrade, *Looking for Poetry*

Of course, the city gates of Ombra were closed when Farid finally rode his stubborn donkey around the last bend in the road. A thin crescent moon shone down on the castle towers, and the guards were passing the time by throwing stones at the bones dangling from the gallows outside the city walls. The Milksop had left some skeletons hanging there, though, to spare his sensitive nose, the gallows were no longer in use. Presumably he thought that gallows left empty were too reassuring a sight for his subjects.

'Well, well, who comes here?' grunted one of the guards, a

tall thin fellow propping himself on his spear as if his legs alone wouldn't carry him. 'Take a look at this laddie!' he added, roughly seizing Farid's reins. 'Riding around all on his own in the middle of the night! Aren't you afraid the Bluejay will steal that donkey from under your skinny behind? After all, he had to leave his horse up at the castle today, so he could do with your donkey. And you he'll feed to the Black Prince's bear!'

'I've heard the bear eats nothing but men-at-arms because they crunch so nicely in his jaws.' As a precaution, Farid's hand went to his knife. He felt too tired to be humble – and perhaps it made him lightly reckless to know that the Bluejay had managed to get out of the Milksop's castle safe and sound. Yes, he too found himself calling Silvertongue by that name more and more often, although Meggie was always cross if she heard him.

'Ho, ho, hark at the lad, will you, Rizzo?' called the guard to the other man on duty. 'Maybe he stole the donkey himself to sell to the sausage-maker in Butchers' Alley before the poor beast drops dead under him!'

Rizzo came closer, smiling unpleasantly, and raised his lance until the ugly spearhead was pointing straight at Farid's chest. 'I know this fellow,' he said. He had two missing front teeth, which made him hiss like a snake. 'Saw him breathing fire once or twice in the marketplace. Aren't you the one they say learnt his trade from the Fire-Dancer?'

'Yes. What about it?' Farid's stomach muscles contracted. They always did when Dustfinger was mentioned.

'What about it?' Rizzo prodded him with the spearhead. 'Get off your decrepit donkey and give us a bit of a show. Maybe we'll let you into the city afterwards.'

They did finally open the gates – after he had turned night into day for almost an hour for their pleasure, making the fire grow flowers as he had learnt to do from Dustfinger. Farid still loved the flames, even though the crackling of their voices reminded him only too painfully of the man who had taught him all about them. But he no longer made them dance in public; he did it only for himself. The flames were all that was left to him of Dustfinger, and sometimes, when he missed him so much that his heart was numb with longing, he wrote his name in fire on a wall somewhere in Ombra and stared at the letters until they went out, leaving him alone, just as Dustfinger had left him alone.

Now that Ombra had lost its menfolk, it was usually as quiet as a city of the dead by night. Tonight, however, Farid ran into several troops of soldiers. The Bluejay had stirred them up like a wasps' nest and they were still buzzing around, as if that would bring the bold intruder back. Lowering his head, Farid dragged the donkey past them, and was glad when he finally reached Orpheus's house.

It was a magnificent building, one of the finest in Ombra, and the only one on this unrestful night with candlelight still shining through the windows. Torches burnt at the entrance – Orpheus lived in constant terror of thieves – and their flickering light brought the stone gargoyles above the gate to life. Farid always shuddered to see them stare down with their bulging eyes, their mouths wide open, their nostrils distended, looking as if they were about to snort in his face. He tried to put the torches to sleep with a whisper, as Dustfinger often did, but the fire wasn't listening to him. That happened more and more often now – as if to remind him that a pupil whose master was dead was a pupil for ever.

He was so tired. The dogs barked at him as he led the donkey across the yard to its stable. Back again. Back in the service of Orpheus. He would so much rather have rested his head in Meggie's lap, or sat by the fire with Silvertongue and the Black Prince. But for Dustfinger's sake he always came back here. Again and again.

Farid let Jink climb out of the rucksack on to his shoulder, and looked up at the stars as if he could find Dustfinger's scarred face there. Why didn't he appear to him in a dream and tell him how to bring him back? Didn't the dead sometimes do that for those they loved? Or did Dustfinger come only to Roxane, as he had promised, and to his daughter? No, if Brianna was visited by any dead man it was Cosimo. The other maids said she whispered his name in her sleep and sometimes put out her hand to him, as if he were lying beside her.

Perhaps he doesn't appear to me in my dreams because he knows I'm afraid of ghosts, thought Farid as he climbed the steps to the back door. The main entrance of the house, which led straight out into the square, was of course reserved for Orpheus himself and his fine customers. Servants, strolling players and delivery men had to plough through the muck in the yard and ring the bell at the modest little door hidden at the back of the house.

Farid rang three times, but nothing stirred. By all the demons of the desert, where was that Chunk? He had nothing to do but open a door now and then. Or was he snoring away like a dog outside Orpheus's bedroom door again?

However, when the bolt was finally pushed aside it wasn't Oss who let him in but Brianna. Dustfinger's daughter had been working for Orpheus for two weeks now, but presumably

Cheeseface had no idea whose daughter was doing his laundry and scrubbing his pots. Orpheus was so blind.

Without a word, Brianna held the door open, and Farid was equally silent as he passed her. There were no words between them except those that went unspoken: *My father died for you. He left us alone for you, only for you.* Brianna blamed him for every tear her mother shed. She had told him so in a low voice after their first day together in the service of Orpheus. 'For every single tear!' Yet again, he thought he felt her glance on the back of his neck like a curse when he turned his back to her.

'Where've you been all this time?' Oss seized him as he was stealing away to the place in the cellar where he slept. Jink hissed and ran off. Last time Oss kicked the marten he had almost broken Jink's ribs. 'He's been asking for you a hundred times over! Made me search every damn alleyway. I haven't had a wink of sleep all night because of you!'

'So? You sleep enough as it is!'

The Chunk hit him in the face. 'Less of your cheek! Go on, your master's waiting for you.'

One of the maids came towards them on the stairs. She blushed as she made her way past Farid. What was her name? Dana? A nice girl, she'd often slipped him a delicious piece of meat when Oss had stolen his food, and Farid had kissed her in the kitchen a few times for that. But she wasn't half as beautiful as Meggie. Or Brianna.

'I just hope he'll let me give you a good hiding!' Oss whispered before knocking on the door of Orpheus's study.

That was what Orpheus called the room, although he spent far less time studying in it than groping under one of the maids' skirts, or stuffing himself with the lavish dishes his cook had to prepare for him at any time of day or night. Tonight, however, he really was sitting at his desk, head bent over a sheet of paper, while his two glass men were arguing under their breath over whether it was better to stir ink to the left or the right. They were brothers called Jasper and Ironstone, and as different as day and night. Ironstone, the elder, loved lecturing his younger brother and ordering him about. Farid often wanted to wring his glass neck. He himself had two older brothers; they'd been one of the reasons why he had run away from home and joined a band of robbers.

'Shut up!' Orpheus snapped at the quarrelling glass men. 'What ridiculous creatures you are! Stir to the left, stir to the right – just make sure you don't spatter my whole desk with ink again while you're stirring.'

Ironstone looked accusingly at Jasper – of course! If anyone had spattered Orpheus's desk with ink, it had to be his little brother. But he preserved a grim silence as Orpheus put pen to paper again.

'Farid, you really must learn to read!' How often Meggie had told him that. And, with some difficulty, she had taught him a few letters of the alphabet. B for bear, R for robber ('look, Farid, there's a letter R in your name too'), M for Meggie, F for fire (wasn't it wonderful that his name began with the same letter?), and D . . . D for Dustfinger. He always got the rest mixed up. How were you supposed to remember those funny little things with their scrawled lines stretching all whichways? AOUIMTNP . . . it gave him a headache just to look at them. But yes, he must learn to read, he must. How else was he ever to find out whether Orpheus was really trying to write Dustfinger back?

'Snippets, nothing but snippets!' Orpheus pushed Jasper

aside with a curse as the glass man came up to sprinkle sand over the fresh ink. Grimly, he tore the sheet of paper he had been writing on into tiny scraps. Farid was used to that sight. Orpheus was seldom satisfied with what he put down on paper. He crumpled up what he had written, tore it in pieces, threw it on the fire with a curse, bullied the glass men and drank too much. But when he succeeded he was even more unbearable. He puffed himself up like a bullfrog, stalked proudly through Ombra like a newly-crowned king, kissed the maids with his moist, complacent lips, and let everyone know he had no equal. 'Let them call the old man Inkweaver!' he shouted, loudly enough to be heard all over the house. 'It suits him. He's nothing but a craftsman, while I . . . I am an enchanter! Ink-Enchanter, that's what they ought to call me. That's what they *will* call me someday!'

But tonight, yet again, the enchantment didn't seem to be working. 'Toad-twaddle! Goose-cackle! Leaden words!' he said angrily without raising his head. 'Just a mush of words, that's what you're smearing the paper with today, Orpheus: a watery, unseasoned, tasteless, slimy mush of words!'

The two glass men hastily scrambled down the legs of the desk and began picking up the shreds of paper.

'My lord, the boy is back.' No one could sound more servile than Oss. His voice bowed to Orpheus as readily as his massive body, but his fingers held the nape of Farid's neck in a steely grip.

Orpheus turned, his face like thunder, and stared at Farid as if he had finally pin-pointed the reason for his failure. 'Where the devil have you been? With Fenoglio all this time? Or helping your girlfriend's father to steal into the castle and out again? Oh yes, I've heard about his latest exploit.

Presumably they'll be singing the first bad songs about it tomorrow. That fool of a bookbinder really does play the ridiculous part the old man wrote him with touching enthusiasm.' Envy and contempt mingled in Orpheus's voice, as they so often did when he spoke of Silvertongue.

'He's not playing a part. He *is* the Bluejay.' Farid trod on Oss's foot hard enough to make him let go of his neck, and when the man tried to grab it again he pushed him away. With a grunt, the Chunk raised his big fist, but a glance from Orpheus halted him.

'Oh, really? Have you joined the ranks of his admirers too?' He put a clean sheet of paper on his desk and stared at it, as though that could fill it with the right words. 'Jasper, what are you doing down there?' he snapped at the glass man. 'How often do I have to tell you two that the maids can sweep up scraps of paper? Sharpen me another pen!'

Farid picked Jasper up, put him on the desk and earned a grateful smile. The younger glass man had to do all the unpleasant jobs – that was how his brother had fixed it – and sharpening pens was the most unpleasant of all, because the tiny blade they used slipped very easily. Only a few days ago it had cut deeply into Jasper's matchstick-thin arm, and Farid had discovered that glass men bleed like humans. Jasper's blood was transparent, of course. It had dripped on to Orpheus's paper like liquid glass, and Ironstone had slapped his little brother's face and called him a clumsy fool. For that, Farid had mixed some beer with the sand Ironstone ate. Since then Ironstone's limbs, usually clear as water (and he had been very proud of that), had been as yellow as horse's piss.

Orpheus went to the window. 'If you stay out and about so long again,' he said to Farid over his shoulder, 'I'll tell Oss to beat you like a dog.'

The Chunk smiled, and Farid cursed silently as he contemplated them both. But Orpheus was still looking up at the black night sky with a morose expression. 'Would you believe it?' he said. 'That old fool Fenoglio didn't even go to the trouble of naming the stars in this world. No wonder I keep running out of words! What's the moon called here? You'd think his senile old brain might at least have bothered about that, but no! He just called it "the moon", as if it were the same moon we saw from our windows in the other world.'

'Perhaps it really is the same moon. It was in my story too,' said Farid.

'Rubbish, of course it was different!' Orpheus turned to the window again, as if he had to explain to the entire world out there how badly made it was. '"Fenoglio," I ask him,' he went on in the self-satisfied voice that Ironstone always listened to devoutly, as if it were announcing truths never heard before, '"is Death a woman or a man in this world? Or is it perhaps just a door through which you pass into quite a different story, one that you yourself unfortunately omitted to write?" "How do I know?" he says. How does he know? Who else knows if he doesn't? He doesn't tell us in his book, anyway.'

In his book ... Ironstone, who had climbed up to join Orpheus on the windowsill, cast a reverent glance at the desk where the last copy of *Inkheart* lay beside the sheet of paper on which Orpheus was writing. Farid wasn't sure whether the glass man really understood that his entire world, himself included, had presumably slipped out of that same book. It usually lay there open, for when Orpheus was writing he kept leafing through it with restless fingers in search of the right words. He never used a single word that couldn't be found in

133

Inkheart, for he was firmly convinced that only words from Fenoglio's story could learn to breathe in this world. Others were just ink on paper.

'"Fenoglio," I ask, "are the White Women only servants?"' Orpheus went on, as Ironstone hung on every word from his soft – over-soft – lips. '"Do the dead stay with them, or do the White Women take them somewhere else?" "I expect so," the old fool replies. "I once told Minerva's children about a castle made of bones to comfort them for Cloud-Dancer's death, but I was only talking off the cuff." Off the cuff! Huh!'

'The old fool!' repeated Ironstone like an echo, but in his reedy, glass man's voice it was not a very impressive sound.

Orpheus turned and went back to his desk. 'With all your roaming around, I hope at least you didn't forget to tell Mortimer I want to talk to him? Or was he too busy playing the hero?'

'He says there's nothing to talk about. He says he doesn't know anything about the White Women except what everyone knows.'

'Oh, wonderful!' Orpheus reached for one of the pens that Jasper had sharpened so laboriously and snapped it in two. 'Did you at least ask whether he still sees them sometimes?'

'I'm sure he does.' Jasper's voice was as delicate as his limbs. 'Once the White Women have touched someone they never let him go. Or so the moss-women say.'

'I know that!' said Orpheus impatiently. 'I tried questioning a moss-woman about that rumour, but the nasty creature wouldn't talk about it. She just stared at me with her mousy eyes and said I eat too much rich food and drink too much wine!'

'They talk to the fairies,' Jasper said. 'And fairies talk to glass men. Although not all of them,' he added with a side-long glance at his brother. 'I've heard that the moss-women tell another tale of the White Women too. They say they can be summoned by anyone whose heart they've already touched with their cold fingers.'

'Oh, indeed?' Orpheus looked thoughtfully at the glass man. 'I hadn't heard that one before.'

'And it's not true! I've tried summoning them!' said Farid. 'Again and again!'

'You! How often do I have to explain that you died much too quickly?' Orpheus snapped contemptuously at him. 'You were in a great hurry to die, and just as great a hurry to come back. What's more, you're such a poor catch that I'd assume they don't even remember you! No, you're not the person to do it.' He went to the window again. 'Go and make me some tea!' he told Farid without turning. 'I have to think.'

'What kind of tea?'

Farid put Jasper on his shoulder. He took the little man with him whenever he could, to keep him safe from his big brother. Sometimes, when Orpheus didn't need either of them because he was taking his pleasure with one of the maids, or seeing his tailor for yet another fitting of some new clothes – which could last hours – Farid took Jasper with him to Seamstresses' Alley, where the glass women helped to thread the dressmakers' needles, tread seams smooth with their tiny feet, and tack lace to costly silk. For Farid had now also learnt that glass men don't just bleed, they fall in love too, and Jasper was head over heels in love with a girl who had pale yellow limbs. He was only too fond of watching her in secret through her mistress's workshop window.

'What kind of tea? How should I know? Something good

for stomach-ache,' replied Orpheus crossly. 'I've had a pain in my belly all day as if there were stag beetles in it. How am I supposed to get anything sensible down on paper in that state?'

Of course. Orpheus always complained of stomach-ache or a headache when his writing wasn't going well. I hope his belly torments him all night, thought Farid as he closed the study door behind him. I hope it plagues him until he writes something for Dustfinger at last.

13

A Knife through the Heart

So far as he was concerned, as yet, there might never have been such a thing as a single particle of sorrow on the gay, sweet surface of the dew-glittering world.

T.H. White, *The Once and Future King*

'At least he didn't tell you to go for the physician!' Jasper was doing his best to cheer Farid up as he carried him down the steep stairs to the kitchen. Yes indeed, the physician who lived beyond the city gate. Orpheus had sent Farid there only a few days ago. If you went to fetch him at night he threw logs of wood at you, or came to the door brandishing one of the pairs of pincers he used to draw teeth.

'Stomach-ache! Headache!' said Farid crossly. 'Cheeseface has been over-eating again, that's all!'

'Three roast gold-mockers filled with chocolate, fairy-nuts roasted in honey, and half a sucking pig stuffed with chestnuts,' said Jasper, counting it up. Then he ducked in alarm as he saw Jink by the kitchen door. The marten made Jasper nervous, even though Farid kept assuring him that while martens did like to chase glass men, they never, ever ate them.

There was only one maid still in the kitchen. Farid stopped in the doorway when he saw it was Brianna. That was all he needed. She was scrubbing the pots and pans from supper, her beautiful face grey with exhaustion. The working day began for Orpheus's maids before sunrise and often didn't end until the moon was high in the sky. Orpheus himself made a tour of inspection of the whole house every morning, looking for cobwebs and dust, a speck on one of the mirrors that hung everywhere, a tarnished silver spoon, or a shirt that still showed a dirty mark after laundering. If he found anything he would deduct a sum from all the maids' paltry wages on the spot. And he almost always did find something.

'What do you want?' Brianna turned, wiping her wet hands on her apron.

'Orpheus has stomach-ache,' muttered Farid, without looking at her. 'I'm to make him some tea.'

Brianna went to one of the kitchen dressers and took an earthenware jar off the top shelf. Farid didn't know which way to look as she poured hot water on the herbs. Her hair was the same colour as her father's, but wavy, and it shone in the candlelight like the red gold rings that the governor liked to wear on his thin fingers. The strolling players sang songs about Dustfinger's daughter and her broken heart.

'Why are you staring like that?' She took a sudden step towards him. Her voice was so cutting that Farid instinctively flinched back. 'Yes, I look like him, don't I?'

It was as if, all through the silence of the last few weeks, she had been sharpening her words until they were knives that she could thrust through his heart.

'*You* don't look in the least like him. I keep telling my mother so. You're only some good-for-nothing layabout who made out that he was my father's son, keeping the pretence up so long that in the end my father thought he had to die for you!'

Every word a knife, and Farid felt them piercing his heart.

Brianna's eyes were not like her father's. She had her mother's eyes, and they looked at Farid with the same hostility as Roxane's. He wanted to hit her to silence her beautiful mouth. But she resembled Dustfinger too much.

'You're a demon, an evil spirit bringing nothing but bad luck.' She handed him the ready-brewed tea. 'There, take Orpheus that. And tell him his stomach would feel better if he didn't eat so much.'

Farid's hands trembled as he took the mug.

'You don't know anything about it!' he said hoarsely. 'Nothing at all. I didn't want him to bring me back. Being dead felt much better.'

But Brianna only looked at him with her mother's eyes. And her father's face.

And Farid stumbled back up to Orpheus's room with the hot tea, while Jasper stroked his hair with his tiny glass hand, full of pity.

14

News from Ombra

And leafing through old books we sometimes find
A dark, oracular phrase is underlined.
You once were here, but in time out of mind.

Rainer Maria Rilke,
Improvisations from Capri in *Winter III*

Meggie liked it in the robbers' camp. Sometimes it almost seemed to Resa as if her daughter had always dreamt of living in shabby tents. She watched Battista making himself a new mask, asked the Strong Man to teach her how to speak to the larks, and accepted the wild flowers that his younger brother brought her with a smile. It was good to see Meggie smiling again more often, although Farid was still with Orpheus. But Resa missed the farm they had left behind. She missed the silence and seclusion, and the sense of being alone with Mo and Meggie after all the weeks when they had been apart. Weeks, months, years . . .

Sometimes, when she saw the two of them sitting by the fire with the robbers, she felt almost as if she were watching them at a game they had played all through the years when she hadn't been with them. *Come on, Mo, let's play robbers.*

The Black Prince had advised Mo not to go outside the camp for the time being, and for a few days he took that advice. But on the third night he disappeared into the forest once more, all alone, as if to go in search of himself. And on the fourth night he went out with the robbers again.

Battista had sung Resa the songs that were going around Ombra after Mo's venture into the city. The Bluejay had flown away, said the songs, escaping on the back of the Milksop's best horse. It was said that he had killed ten guards, imprisoned Sootbird in the vault and stolen Balbulus's finest books. 'How much of it is true?' she had asked Mo. He laughed. 'I'm afraid I can't be said to have flown!' he had whispered, caressing her belly in which their child was slowly growing. And then he had gone out with the Black Prince again. And she lay there night after night, listening to the songs Battista sang outside the tent, terrified for her husband.

The Black Prince had had two tents pitched for them right beside his own. They were patched together from old clothes that the robbers had dyed with oak bark so that they wouldn't show up too much among the surrounding trees: one tent for Meggie, one for the Bluejay and his wife. The mats of dried moss on which they slept were damp, and when Mo went out at night Resa shared the tent with her daughter for warmth. One day the grass was so white with hoarfrost in the morning that you could see the glass men's tracks in it. 'This will be a hard winter,' said the Strong Man, not for the first time.

One could still find giants' footsteps in the ravine where the camp lay. The rain of the last few weeks had turned them into ponds where gold-spotted frogs swam. The trees on the slopes of the ravine rose to the sky, almost as tall as the trees in the Wayless Wood. Their withering leaves covered the ground, which was cool now in autumn, with gold and flaming red, and fairies' nests hung among the branches like overripe fruit. If you looked south you could see a village in the distance, its walls showing pale as mushrooms between the trees, but it was such a poor village that even the Milksop's greedy tax-gatherers didn't bother to come this way. Wolves howled by night in the surrounding woods, pale grey owls like little ghosts flew over the shabby tents, and horned squirrels stole what food there was to steal among the camp fires.

There were a good fifty men living in the camp, sometimes more. The youngest were the two boys saved from hanging by Snapper, and now they both went spying for the Prince: Doria, the Strong Man's brother, who brought Meggie wild flowers, and his orphaned friend Luc. Luc helped Gecko to tame his crows. Six women cooked and mended for the robbers, but none of them went out at night with the men. Resa drew portraits of almost all of them, boys, men and women. Battista had found paper and chalk for her; where, he didn't say. She wondered, as she portrayed every face, if the lines on them had indeed been drawn by Fenoglio's words alone, or whether they weren't perhaps, after all, living their own lives in this world independently of the old man.

The women did not even join the men when they sat together talking. Resa always sensed the disapproving looks when she and Meggie sat down quite naturally with Mo and the Black Prince. Sometimes she returned those glances, staring Snapper in the face, and Gecko, and all the others who tolerated women in the camp only to cook food and mend clothes. She cursed the nausea that kept coming back and prevented her from at least going with Mo when he and the Prince walked in the surrounding hills, looking for a place offering better shelter for the winter.

They had been in the camp that Meggie called the Camp of Lost Giants for five days and five nights when Doria and Luc returned from Ombra about midday with news. It was obviously such bad news that Doria didn't even tell it to his brother, but went straight to the Black Prince's tent. A little later the Prince sent for Mo, and Battista assembled the men.

Doria glanced at his strong brother before stepping into the circle of robbers, as if drawing courage from him to tell his news. But his voice was clear and firm when he began to speak. He sounded so much older than he was.

'The Piper came out of the Wayless Wood yesterday,' he began. 'He took the road that approaches Ombra from the west, burning and looting as he went, letting it be known everywhere that the Milksop hasn't sent enough taxes to the Castle of Night, and he's here to collect more.'

'How many men-at-arms are there with him?' As usual, Snapper sounded brusque. Resa didn't like his voice. She didn't like anything about him.

Doria seemed to like the man who had saved his life no better than she did, judging by the look he gave him. 'A great many. More than us. Far more,' he added. 'I don't know the exact figure. The peasants whose houses they burnt didn't have time to count them.'

'Even if they *had* had time it wouldn't have been much use, would it?' replied Snapper. 'Everyone knows peasants can't count.'

Gecko laughed, and with him some of the robbers who

were always to be found near Snapper: Swindler, Grabber, the Charcoal-Burner, Elfbane, and several more.

Doria's lips tightened. He and the Strong Man were peasant-born, and Snapper knew it. His own father, apparently, had been a mercenary soldier.

'Tell them what else you heard, Doria.' The Black Prince's voice sounded weary as Resa had seldom heard it before.

The boy glanced at his brother once more. 'They're taking a head-count of the children,' he said. 'The Piper is drawing up lists of all of them over six years old and no more than five feet tall.'

A murmur rose among the robbers, and Resa saw Mo leaning over to the Prince to whisper something to him. How close to each other they seemed, and how naturally Mo sat there with the ragged robbers. As if he belonged to them as much as to her and Meggie.

The Black Prince straightened up. His hair wasn't long now, as it had been when Resa had first met him. Three days after Dustfinger's death he had shaved his head, the custom in this world after the death of a friend. For on the third day, it was said, the souls of the dead entered the realm from which there was no return.

'We knew the Piper would be coming sometime,' said the Black Prince. 'The Adder could hardly have failed to notice that his brother-in-law was keeping most of the taxes he collects for himself. But as you've heard, the taxes aren't the only reason why he's coming. We all know only too well what they use children for in Argenta.'

'What *do* they use them for?' Meggie's voice sounded so clear among the voices of all the men. You couldn't tell from the sound of it that it had already changed this world several times by reading a few sentences.

'What for? The tunnels in the silver mines are narrow, Bluejay's daughter,' replied Snapper. 'Be glad you're too large to be any use down there yourself.'

The mines. Resa's hand went instinctively to the place where her unborn child was growing, and Mo glanced at her as if the same thought had struck him too.

'Of course. The Adderhead has sent far too many children to the mines already. His peasants are beginning to resist. It seems the Piper has only just put down a revolt.' Battista's voice sounded as weary as the Prince's. There were too few of them to right all these wrongs. 'The children die quickly down there,' Battista went on. 'It's a marvel the Adder hasn't thought of taking ours before. Children with no fathers, only defenceless unarmed mothers.'

'Then we'll have to hide them!' Doria sounded as fearless as only a boy of fifteen can. 'The way you hid the harvest!'

Resa saw a smile appear on Meggie's lips.

'Hide them, oh yes, of course!' Snapper laughed with derision. 'A fabulous idea. Gecko, tell this greenhorn how many children there are in Ombra alone. He's a peasant's son, you know, can't count.'

The Strong Man was rising to his feet, but Doria cast him a warning glance, and his brother sat down again. 'I can pick my little brother up with one hand,' the Strong Man often said, 'but he's a hundred times cleverer than me.'

Gecko obviously had not the faintest notion how many children there were in Ombra, quite apart from the fact that he wasn't too good at counting himself. 'Well, there are a lot,' he faltered, while the crow on his shoulder pecked at his hair, presumably hoping to find a few lice. 'Flies and children –

that's the only two things still in plentiful supply in Ombra.'

No one laughed.

The Black Prince remained silent, and so did everyone else. If the Piper wanted those children, then he would take them.

A fire-elf settled on Resa's arm. She shook it off, and found herself longing for Elinor's house so much that her heart hurt as if the elf had burnt it. She longed for the kitchen, always full of the humming of the outsize fridge, for Mo's workshop in the garden, and the armchair in the library where you could sit and visit strange worlds without getting lost in them.

'Perhaps it's just bait!' said Battista, breaking the silence. 'You know how the Piper likes to leave bait lying around – and he knows very well that we can't simply let him take the children. Perhaps,' he added, glancing at Mo, 'perhaps he's hoping to catch the Bluejay that way at last!'

Resa saw Meggie instinctively moving closer to Mo. But his face remained unmoved, as if the Bluejay were someone else entirely.

'Violante's already told me the Piper would soon be coming here,' said Mo. 'But she said nothing about children.'

The Bluejay's voice . . . the voice that had fooled the Adderhead and beguiled the fairies. It did nothing of the kind to Snapper. It merely reminded him that he had once sat where the Bluejay was sitting now – at the Black Prince's side.

'You've been talking to Her Ugliness? Fancy that! So that's what took you to Ombra Castle. The Bluejay in conversation with the Adder's daughter.' Snapper twisted his coarse face into a grimace. 'Of course she didn't tell you anything about the children! Why would she? Quite apart from the fact that we can assume she doesn't even know about it! Her Ugliness has no more say than a kitchen maid about what goes on at the castle. That's how it always was, and that's how it always will be.'

'I've told you often enough, Snapper.' The Black Prince spoke more sharply than usual. 'Violante has more power than you think. And more men, too – even if they're all very young.' He nodded to Mo. 'Tell them what happened at the castle. It's time they knew.'

Resa looked at Mo. What did the Black Prince know that she didn't?

'Yes, come on, Bluejay, tell us how you got away unscathed this time!' Snapper's voice was so openly hostile now that some of the robbers exchanged uneasy glances. 'It really does sound like enchantment! First they let you out of the Castle of Night scot-free, now you're out of Ombra Castle as well. Don't say you made the Milksop immortal too in order to get away!'

Some of the robbers laughed, but their laughter sounded uncomfortable. Resa was sure that many of them really did take Mo for some kind of enchanter, one of those men whose names were best spoken only in whispers, because they were said to know dark arts and could bewitch ordinary mortals with no more than a glance. How else was it possible for a man who had arrived as if from nowhere to be able to handle a sword better than most of them? And he could read and write as well.

'Folk say the Adderhead's immortality doesn't bring him much joy!' objected the Strong Man.

Doria sat down beside him, his eyes fixed darkly on Snapper. No, the boy certainly didn't like his rescuer much. His friend Luc, on the other hand, followed Snapper and Gecko like a dog.

'So how does that help us? The Piper is looting and murdering worse than ever.' Snapper spat. 'The Adder is immortal. The Milksop, his brother-in-law, hangs at least one of us almost every day. And the Bluejay rides to Ombra and comes back unharmed.'

All was very, very quiet once more. Many of the robbers felt that the deal the Bluejay had done with the Adderhead in the Castle of Night was more than uncanny, even if ultimately Mo had tricked the Silver Prince. But the Adderhead was immortal all the same. Again and again he enjoyed giving a sword to some man the Piper had captured and making him thrust it through his body – only to follow that up by wounding the attacker with the same sword and giving him enough time to die to attract the White Women. That was the Adderhead's way of proclaiming that he no longer feared the daughters of Death, although it was also said that he still avoided getting too close to them. 'Death Serves the Adder' was the inscription he had had placed in silver lettering above the gates of the Castle of Night.

'No. I was not required to make the Milksop immortal.' Mo's voice sounded cold as he replied to Snapper, very cold. 'It was Violante who got me safely out of the castle. After asking me to help her kill her father.'

Resa placed her hand on her belly as if to keep the words away from her unborn child. But in her mind there was room for only one thought: he's told the Black Prince what happened in the castle, but he didn't tell me. *He didn't tell me . . .*

She remembered how hurt Meggie had sounded when Mo finally told them what he had done to the White Book before giving it to the Adderhead. 'You moistened every tenth page? But you can't have done! I was with you the whole time! Why didn't you say anything?' Although Mo had kept her mother's whereabouts a secret from her all those years, Meggie still believed that in the last resort he couldn't really have any secrets from her. Resa had never felt that. All the same, it hurt that he had told the Black Prince more than he told her. It hurt badly.

'Her Ugliness wants to kill her father?' Battista sounded incredulous.

'What's so surprising about that?' Snapper raised his voice as if to speak for them all. 'She's the Adder's spawn. What reply did you give her, Bluejay? Did you say you must wait until your damn book doesn't protect him from death any more?'

He hates Mo, thought Resa. He really hates him! But the look that Mo turned on Snapper was just as hostile, and Resa wondered, not for the first time, whether she simply used to overlook the anger in him, or whether it was as new as the scar on his chest.

'The Book will protect Violante's father for a long time yet.' Mo sounded bitter. 'The Adderhead has found a way to save it.'

Yet again there was murmuring among the robbers. Only the Black Prince didn't seem surprised. So Mo had told him that too. Had told him, and not her. He's turning into a different man, thought Resa. The words are changing him. This life is changing him. Even if it's only a game. If it's a game at all . . .

'But that's impossible. If you left the pages damp it will go mouldy, and you've always said yourself that mould kills books as certainly as fire.'

Meggie sounded so reproachful. Secrets . . . nothing eats

away at love faster.

Mo looked at his daughter. That was in another world, Meggie, said his eyes. But his mouth said something else. 'Well, the Adderhead has taught me better. The Book will go on protecting him from death – only if its pages stay blank.'

No, thought Resa. She knew what was coming next, and she felt like putting her hands over her ears, although she loved nothing in the world more than Mo's voice. She had almost forgotten his face in all those years in Mortola's service, but she had always remembered his voice. Now, however, it no longer sounded like her husband's. It was the voice of the Bluejay.

'It doesn't take long to write three words.' Mo did not speak loudly, but the whole Inkworld seemed full of his voice. It seemed to have belonged here for ever – among the tall, towering trees, the ragged men, the drowsy fairies in their nests. 'The Adderhead still believes that only I can save the Book. He'll give it to me if I go to him promising to cure it, and then . . . some ink, a pen, it doesn't take more than a few seconds to write three words. Suppose Violante can gain those few seconds for me?'

His voice painted the scene in the air, and the robbers listened as if they could see the whole thing before their eyes. Until Snapper broke the spell.

'You're out of your mind! Totally out of your mind!' he said hoarsely. 'I suppose by now you believe everything the songs say about you – how you're invulnerable! The invincible Bluejay! Her Ugliness will sell you, and her father will skin you alive if he gets his hands on you again. That won't take him much more than a few seconds! But your liking for playing the hero will cost all the rest of us our lives too!'

Resa saw Mo's fingers close around the hilt of his sword, but the Black Prince laid a hand on his arm. 'Maybe he'd have to play the hero less frequently if you and your friends did it more often, Snapper,' he said.

Snapper rose to his feet menacingly slowly, but before he could say anything the Strong Man spoke up, quick as a child trying to settle his parents' quarrel. 'Suppose the Bluejay is right? Perhaps Her Ugliness really does want to help. She's always been good to us strolling players! She even used to come and visit our camp. And she feeds the poor and sends for the Barn Owl to come to the castle when the Milksop's had some unfortunate fellow's hand or foot chopped off!'

'Yes, very generous of her, isn't it?' Gecko made a mocking face, as he so often did when the Strong Man said anything, and the crow on his shoulder uttered a croak of derision. 'What's so generous about giving away kitchen scraps and clothes no one wants any more? Does Her Ugliness go around in rags like my mother and my sisters? No! I expect Balbulus has run out of parchment, and she wants to buy more with the price on the Bluejay's head!'

Once again some of the robbers laughed. As for the Strong Man, he looked uncertainly at the Black Prince. His brother whispered something to him, and scowled at Gecko. Please, Prince! thought Resa. Tell Mo to forget what Violante said. He'll listen to you. And help him to forget the Book he bound for her father! Please!

The Black Prince glanced at her as if he had heard her silent pleading. But his dark face remained inscrutable. She often found Mo's face impossible to read these days.

'Doria!' the Prince said. 'Do you think you can get past the castle guards and ask around among Violante's soldiers? One of them may have heard more about what the Piper is here for.'

The Strong Man opened his mouth as if to protest. He loved his brother and did all he could to protect him, but Doria was at an age when a boy doesn't want protection any more.

'Of course. Easy,' he said with a smile that showed how happy he was to do as the Prince asked. 'I've known some of them ever since I could walk. Mostly they aren't much older than me.'

'Good.' The Black Prince stood up. His next words were for Mo, although he didn't look at him. 'As for Violante's offer, I agree with Gecko and Snapper. Violante may have a soft spot for strolling players and feel sorry for her subjects, but she's still her father's daughter, and we ought not to trust her.'

All eyes went to the Bluejay.

But Mo said nothing.

To Resa, that silence spoke louder than words. She knew it, just as Meggie did. Resa saw the fear on her daughter's face as she began talking earnestly to Mo. Yes, by now Meggie too probably felt what a hold this story had taken on her father. The letters were drawing him deeper and deeper down, like a whirlpool made of ink, and once again the terrible thought that had haunted Resa with increasing frequency these last few weeks came to her: that on the day when Mo had lain wounded in Capricorn's burnt-out fortress, close to death, perhaps the White Women really did take a part of him away with them to the place where Dustfinger had gone, and she would see that part of him again only there. In the place where all stories end.

15

Loud Words, Soft Words

When you go, space closes over like water behind you,
Do not look back: there is nothing outside you,
Space is only time visible in a different way,
Places we love we can never leave.

Ivan V. Lalic, *Places We Love*

'Please, Mo! Ask him!'

At first Meggie thought she had heard her mother's voice only in a dream, one of the dark dreams that sometimes came to her out of the past. Resa sounded so desperate. But when Meggie opened her eyes she could still hear her voice. And when she looked out of the tent she saw her parents standing among the trees only a short way off, little more than two shadows in the night. The oak against which Mo was leaning was huge, an oak such as Meggie had never seen outside the Inkworld, and Resa was clutching his arm as if to force him to listen to her.

'Isn't that what we've always done? When one of us didn't like a story any more, we closed the book! Mo, have you forgotten how many books there are? Let's find another to tell us its story, a book with words that will stay words and not make us a part of them!'

Meggie glanced at the robbers lying under the trees only a little way off. Many of them were sleeping in the open, although the nights were already very cold, but her mother's despairing voice didn't seem to have woken any of them.

'If I remember correctly, I was the one who wanted to close this book long ago.' Mo's voice sounded as cool as the air making its way in through the tent's ragged fabric. 'But you and Meggie wouldn't hear of another one.'

'How was I to know what this story would turn you into?' Resa's voice sounded as if she hardly knew how to hold back her tears.

Go back to sleep, Meggie told herself. Leave the two of them alone. But she stayed where she was, freezing in the cold night air.

'What are you talking about? What's it supposed to have made me into?'

Mo spoke softly, as if he didn't want to disturb the silence of the night, but Resa seemed to have forgotten where she was.

'What's it made you into?' Her voice was rising with every word. 'You wear a sword at your belt! You hardly sleep, you're out all night. Do you think I can't tell the cry of a real bluejay from a human imitation? I know how often Battista or the Strong Man came to fetch you when we were at the farm . . . and the worst of it is, I know how happy you are to go with them. You've found you have a taste for danger! You went to Ombra although the Prince warned you not to. And now you come back, after they almost caught you, and act as

154

if it were all a game!'

'What else is it?' Mo was still speaking so softly that Meggie could hardly hear him. 'Have you forgotten what this world is made of?'

'I couldn't care less what it's made of. You can die in it, Mo. You know that better than I do. Or have you forgotten the White Women? No, you even talk about them in your sleep. Sometimes I almost think you miss them.'

Mo did not reply, but Meggie knew Resa was right. Mo had talked to her about the White Women only once. 'They're made of nothing but longing, Meggie,' he had said. 'They fill your heart to the brim with longing, until you just want to go with them, wherever they take you.'

'Please, Mo!' Resa's voice was shaking. 'Ask Fenoglio to write us back again! He'll try to do it for you. He owes you that!'

One of the robbers coughed in his sleep, another moved closer to the fire . . . and Mo said nothing. When at last he did reply he sounded as if he were talking to a child. Even to Meggie he didn't speak like that. 'Fenoglio isn't writing at all these days, Resa. I'm not even sure whether he still can.'

'Then go to Orpheus! You've heard what Farid says. Orpheus has written rainbow-coloured fairies into this world, and unicorns and—'

'So? Maybe Orpheus can add something to Fenoglio's story here and there. But he'd have to write something of his own to take us back to Elinor. I doubt if he can do that. And even if he can – from all Farid says, he's not interested in anything but making himself the richest man in Ombra. Do you have the money to pay him for his words?'

This time it was Resa who remained silent – for so long

that she might have been mute again, as she was when she left her voice behind in the Inkworld.

It was Mo who finally broke the silence.

'Resa!' he said. 'If we go back now I'll be sitting in Elinor's house doing nothing but wondering how this story goes on, day in, day out. And no book in the world will be able to tell me that!'

'You don't just want to know how it goes on.' Now it was Resa's voice that sounded cool. 'You want to decide what happens. You want to be part of it! But who knows whether you'll ever find your way out of the letters on the page again, if you tangle yourself up in them even more?'

'Even more? What do you mean? I've seen Death here, Resa – and I have a new life.'

'If you won't do it for me,' – Meggie could hear how hard it was for her mother to go on – 'then go back for Meggie . . . and for our second child. I want my baby to have a father, I want the baby's father to be alive when it's born – and I want him to be the same man who brought its sister up.'

Once more Meggie had to wait a long time for Mo's answer. A tawny owl hooted. Gecko's crows cawed sleepily in the tree where they roosted at night. Fenoglio's world seemed so peaceful. And Mo stroked the bark of the tree against which he was leaning, as tenderly as he usually caressed the spine of a book.

'How do you know Meggie doesn't want to stay? She's almost grown up. And in love. Do you think she wants to go back while Farid stays here? Because stay he will.'

In love. Meggie's face was burning. She didn't want Mo to say what she herself had never put into words. In love – it sounded like a sickness without any cure, and wasn't that just how it sometimes felt? Yes, Farid would stay. She had so often told herself that, when she felt a wish to go back: Farid will stay even if Dustfinger doesn't return from the dead. He'll go on looking for him and longing for him, much more than he longs for you, Meggie. But how would it feel never to see him again? Would she leave her heart here and go around with an empty hole in her breast ever after? Would she stay alone – like Elinor – and only read about being in love in books?

'She'll get over it!' she heard Resa say. 'She'll fall in love with someone else.'

What was her mother talking about? She doesn't know me! thought Meggie. She never knew me. How could she? She was never there with us.

'What about your second child?' Resa went on. 'Do you want the baby born in this world?'

Mo looked round him, and once more Meggie felt something she had long known: by now her father loved this world as much as she and Resa had once done. Perhaps he even loved it more.

'Why not?' he retorted. 'Do you want it born in a world where what it longs for can be found only in books?'

Resa's voice shook when she replied, but now it was with anger. 'How can you say such a thing? Everything you find here was born in our world. Where else did Fenoglio get it all from?'

'How should I know? Do you really still think there's only one real world, and the others are just pale offshoots?'

Somewhere a wolf howled and two others responded. One of the guards came through the trees and put wood on the dying fire. His name was Wayfarer. None of the robbers went by the names they had been born with. He moved away again, after casting a curious glance at Mo and Resa.

'I don't want to go back, Resa. Not now!' Mo's voice sounded determined, but at the same time Meggie could tell he was trying to win her mother over, as if he still hoped to convince her that they were in the right place. 'It will be months yet before the baby's born, and maybe we'll all be back in Elinor's house by then. But right now, this is where I want to be.'

He kissed Resa on the forehead. Then he went away, over to the men standing on guard among the trees at the far end of the camp. And Resa dropped into the grass where she stood and buried her face in her hands. Meggie wanted to go to her and comfort her, but what could she say? *I want to stay with Farid, Resa. I don't want to find someone else.* No, that would hardly be much comfort to her mother. And Mo didn't come back either.

16

The Piper's Offer

The moment comes when a character does or says something you hadn't thought about. At that moment he's alive and you leave it to him.

Graham Greene, *Advice to Writers*

At last. Here they came. Trumpets rang out in a fanfare from the city gates, an arrogant metallic sound. Just like the man it announced, Fenoglio thought. The Milksop – the common people always found the most suitable names. He couldn't have thought of a better one himself, but then he hadn't invented this pallid upstart either! Not even the Adderhead had his arrival announced by long-stemmed trumpets, but his pigeon-chested brother-in-law had only to ride around the castle and they struck up.

Fenoglio drew Minerva's children closer to his side. Despina didn't mind at all, but her brother wriggled out of Fenoglio's grasp and climbed up, nimble as a squirrel, to a ledge on the wall where he would have a view down the street along which they'd soon be coming. The Milksop and his retinue, also known to the townsfolk as his pack of hounds. Had the Adder's brother-in-law already been told that almost all the women of Ombra were waiting for him at the castle gate? Yes, surely.

Why is the Piper counting our children? That was the question that had brought them here. They had already called it out to the guards, whose faces were unmoved and who had merely lowered their spears in the direction of the angry women. But the women hadn't gone home, all the same.

It was Friday, the day when the hunt rode out, and the crowd had been waiting hours for the return of their new master, who had set about killing all the game in the Wayless Wood from the moment of his arrival. Once again his servants would be carrying dozens of bloodstained partridges, wild boar, deer and hares through the streets of starving Ombra, past women who hardly knew where to find food for the next day. That was why Fenoglio hardly ever went out of doors, and even less on Fridays than on any other day of the week, but curiosity had brought him here today. Curiosity – a tiresome feeling!

'Fenoglio,' Minerva had said, 'can you look after Despina and Ivo? I have to go to the castle. We're all going. We want to make them tell us why the Piper is counting our children.'

You know why, Fenoglio wanted to say. But the desperation on Minerva's face silenced him. Let them hope their children weren't wanted for the silver mines, he told himself. Leave it to the Milksop and the Piper to take their hope away.

Oh, how tired he was of all this! He'd tried his hand at writing again yesterday, roused to anger by the arrogant smile with which the Piper rode into Ombra. He had picked up one of the sharpened pens that the glass man still placed encouragingly in front of him, sat down in front of a blank sheet of paper, and after an hour of waiting in vain told Rosenquartz off for buying paper that anyone could see was made of old trousers.

Ah, Fenoglio, he wondered, how many more stupid excuses will you think up for the way you've turned into an old man with no power over words any more?

Yes, he admitted it. He wanted to be master of this story, strongly as he had denied it after Cosimo's death. More and more often these days he set to work with pen and ink in search of the old magic – usually while the glass man was snoring in his fairy nest, because it was too embarrassing to have Rosenquartz as a witness of his failure. He tried it when Minerva had to give the children soup tasting little better than dishwater, when the horrible rainbow-coloured fairies jabbered away in their nest at the tops of their voices, keeping him awake, or when one of his creations – like the Piper yesterday – reminded him of the days when he had woven this world out of letters, intoxicated by his own skill with words.

But the paper stayed blank – as if all the words had stolen away to Orpheus, just because he took them and savoured them on his tongue. Had life ever tasted so bitter before?

In Fenoglio's gloomy mood he had even played with the idea of going back to that village in the other world, such a peaceful, well-fed place, so wonderfully free of fairies and stirring events, back to his grandchildren, who must be missing his stories. (And what fabulous stories he'd be able to tell them now!) But where could the words be found that would take him back? Certainly not in his empty old head, and he could hardly ask Orpheus to write them for him. He hadn't sunk as low as that yet.

Despina tugged at his sleeve. Cosimo had given him the tunic he was wearing, but it too was moth-eaten now, and as dusty as his brain that wouldn't think. What was he doing here outside this damn castle? The sight of it depressed him. Why wasn't he lying in bed?

'Fenoglio? Is it true that when people dig silver out of the ground they spit blood on it?' Despina's voice still reminded him of a little bird's. 'Ivo says I'm just the right size for the tunnels where they find most of the silver.'

Damn the boy! Why did he tell his little sister such stories?

'How often have I told you not to believe a word your brother says?' Fenoglio tucked Despina's thick black hair back behind her ears, and looked accusingly at Ivo. Poor fatherless little thing.

'Why shouldn't I tell her? She asked me!' Ivo was at the age when you despise even comforting lies. 'I don't expect they'll take you,' he said, leaning down to his sister. 'Girls die too quickly. But they'll take me and Beppo and Lino, and even Mungus, although he limps. The Piper will take us all. And then they'll bring us back dead just like our—'

Despina put her hand over his mouth quickly, as if her father might come back to life if only her brother didn't speak the bad word. Fenoglio could happily have seized and shaken the boy, but Despina would only have burst into tears on the spot. Did all little sisters adore their brothers?

'That's enough! Stop upsetting your sister!' he snapped at Ivo. 'The Piper's here to catch the Bluejay. Not for anything else. And to ask the Milksop why he isn't sending more silver to the Castle of Night.'

'Oh yes? Then why are they counting us?' The boy had grown up in the last few weeks. As if grief had wiped away the childishness on his face. At the tender age of ten, Ivo was now the man of the family – even if Fenoglio sometimes tried to lift the burden of that responsibility off his thin shoulders. The boy worked with the dyers, helped to pull wet fabric through the stinking vats day in, day out, and brought the smell home with him in the evening. But he earned more with that work than Fenoglio did as a scribe in the marketplace.

'They're going to kill us all!' he went on unmoved, his eyes fixed on the guards, who were still pointing their spears at the waiting women. 'And they'll tear the Bluejay to pieces, like they did last week with the strolling player who threw rotten vegetables at the governor. They fed the pieces to the hounds.'

'Ivo!' This was too much. Fenoglio tried to grab him by the ears, but the boy was too quick for him and ran away before he could get a hold. However, his sister stood there squeezing Fenoglio's hand as tightly as if there were nothing else for her to cling to in this shattered world.

'They won't catch him, will they?' Despina's little voice was so timid that Fenoglio had to bend down to hear what she was saying. 'The bear protects the Bluejay now as well as the Black Prince, doesn't he?'

'Of course!' Fenoglio stroked her jet-black hair again. The sound of hoof beats was coming up the street, echoing among the houses, with voices chatting as casually as if they scorned the silence of the women waiting there, while the sun sank behind the surrounding hills and turned the roofs of Ombra red. The noble lords were late coming back from the pleasures of the hunt today, their silver-embroidered garments spattered with blood, their bored hearts comfortably aroused by killing. Death could indeed be a great entertainer – when it was someone else's death.

The women crowded closer together. The guards drove them back from the gates, but they stayed outside the castle walls: old women, young women, mothers, daughters, grandmothers. Minerva was one of those in front. She had grown thin in the last few weeks. Fenoglio's story, that man-eating monster, was eating her alive. But Minerva had smiled when she heard that the Bluejay had gone to see some books in the castle and ridden away unscathed.

'He will save us!' she had whispered. In the evenings she sang, low-voiced, the songs going around Ombra, and very bad songs they were. About the White Hand and the Black Hand of Justice, the Jay and the Prince . . . a bookbinder and a knife-thrower against the Piper and his army of fire-raising men-at-arms. But why not? After all, didn't that sound like a good story?

Fenoglio picked Despina up as the soldiers escorting the hunting party rode by. Strolling players followed them down the street: pipers, drummers, jugglers, brownie-tamers, and of course Sootbird, who wasn't going to miss any fun, even if – so they said – he felt ill at the sight of people being blinded and quartered. Then came the hounds, dappled like the light in the Wayless Wood, with the kennel-boys who made sure the dogs were hungry on the day of the hunt, and finally the hunters, led by the Milksop, a skinny figure on a horse much too large for him. He was as ugly as his sister was said to be beautiful, with a pointed nose that seemed too short for his face and a wide, pinched mouth. No one knew why the Adderhead had made him, of all men, lord of Ombra. Perhaps it had been at the request of his sister who, after all, had given the Silver Prince his first son. But Fenoglio suspected it was more likely that the Adderhead had chosen his puny brother-in-law because he could be sure the Milksop would never rise against him.

What a feeble character, thought Fenoglio scornfully as the Milksop rode by with a supercilious expression on his face. Obviously this story was now filling even leading roles with cheap supporting actors.

As expected, the fine ladies and gentlemen had brought back plenty of game: partridges dangling from the poles to which the grooms had tied them like fruit that had just fallen, half a dozen of the deer he had thought up especially for this world, with reddish-brown coats that were still as dappled as a fawn's even in old age (not that these animals had been particularly old), hares, stags, wild boar . . .

The women of Ombra stared at the slaughtered game expressionlessly. Many put a telltale hand to their empty stomachs, or glanced at their ever-hungry children waiting in doorways for their mothers.

And then – then they carried the unicorn past.

Damn that Cheeseface!

There were no unicorns in Fenoglio's world, but Orpheus had written one here just so that the Milksop could kill it. Fenoglio quickly put his hand over Despina's eyes when they carried it by, its white coat pierced and bloodstained. Rosenquartz had told him not quite a week ago about the Milksop's commission. The fee for it had been high, and all Ombra had wondered what distant country Four-Eyes had brought that fairy-tale creature from.

A unicorn! What stories could have been told about it! But the Milksop wasn't paying for stories, quite apart from the fact that Orpheus couldn't have written them. He did it with my words, thought Fenoglio. With my words! He felt fury clenched like a stone in his belly. If he only had the money to hire a couple of thieves to steal the book which supplied that parasite with words! His own book! Or if, at least, he could have written a few treasures for himself! But he couldn't manage even that – he, Fenoglio, formerly court poet to Cosimo the Fair and creator of this once-magnificent world! Tears of self-pity came to his eyes, and he imagined them carrying Orpheus past, stabbed and bloodstained like the unicorn. Oh, yes!

'Why are you counting our children? We want you to stop it!'

Minerva's voice brought Fenoglio out of his vengeful daydreams. When she saw her mother step in front of the horses Despina wound her thin little arms so tightly around his neck that he could hardly breathe. Had Minerva lost her wits? Did she want her children to be not just fatherless but motherless too?

A woman riding just behind the Milksop pointed her gloved finger at Minerva with her bare feet and shabby dress. The guards moved towards her with their spears.

For heaven's sake, Minerva! Fenoglio's heart was in his mouth. Despina began crying, but it wasn't her sobs that made Minerva stumble back. Unnoticed, the Piper had appeared on the battlements above the gateway.

'You ask why we're counting your children?' he called down to the women.

As always, he was magnificently dressed. Even the Milksop looked like a mere valet by comparison. He stood on the battlements shimmering like a peacock with four crossbow-men beside him. Perhaps he had been up there for some time, watching to see how his master's brother-in-law would deal with the women waiting for him. His hoarse voice carried a long way in the silence that suddenly fell on Ombra.

'We count everything that's ours!' he cried. 'Sheep, cows, chickens, women, children, men – not that you have many of those left – fields, barns, stables, houses. We count every tree in your forest. After all, the Adderhead likes to know what he's ruling over.'

His silver nose still looked like a beak in the middle of his face. There were tales saying that the Adderhead had ordered a silver heart to be made for his herald too, but Fenoglio felt sure there was still a human heart beating in the Piper's breast. Nothing was more cruel than a heart made of flesh and blood, because it knew what gives pain.

'You don't want them for the mines?' The woman who spoke up this time did not step forward like Minerva, but hid among the others. The Piper did not answer at once. He examined his fingernails. The Piper was proud of his pink nails. They were as well manicured as a woman's, just as Fenoglio had described them. In spite of everything, it was still exciting to see his characters acting exactly as he had imagined.

You soak them in rosewater every evening, you villain, thought Fenoglio, as Despina stared at the Piper like a bird staring at the cat that wants to eat it. And you wear them as long as the nails of the ladies who keep the Milksop company.

'For the mines? What a delightful idea!'

It was so quiet now that the silver-nosed man didn't even have to raise his voice. In the setting sun his shadow fell over the women, long and black. Very effective, Fenoglio thought. And how stupid the Milksop looked. The Piper was keeping

167

him waiting outside his own gates like a servant. What a
scene. But this one wasn't his own invention . . .

'Ah, I understand! You think that's why the Adderhead
sent me here!' The Piper leant his hands on the wall and
looked down from the battlements, like a beast of prey wondering whether the Milksop or one of the women would taste
better. 'No, no. I'm here to catch a bird, and you all know the
colour of its feathers. Although, as I hear, he was black as a
raven during his last impudent exploit. As soon as that bird is
caught, I'll be riding back to the other side of the forest. Isn't
that so, Governor?'

The Milksop looked up at him and adjusted his sword, still
bloodstained from the hunt. 'If you say so!' he called in a voice
that he could control only with difficulty. He glanced angrily
at the women outside the gates, as if he'd never seen anything
like them before.

'I do say so.' The Piper smiled condescendingly down on
the Milksop. 'But on the other hand,' he said, and the pause
before he continued seemed endless, 'if this bird should escape
capture once more . . .' He paused again, for a long time, as if
he wanted to inspect each of the waiting women thoroughly.
'If any of those present here should go so far as to give him
shelter and a roof over his head, warn him of our patrols, sing
songs of how he pulls the wool over our eyes . . .' The sigh he
heaved came from the depths of his breast. 'Well, in that case,
no doubt I'd have to take your children with me in his place,
for after all, I can't go back to the Castle of Night empty-
handed, can I?'

Oh, the confounded silver-nosed bastard.

Why didn't you make him more stupid, Fenoglio? Because
stupid villains are so boring, he answered himself, and was

168

ashamed of it when he saw the despair on the women's faces.

'So you see, it's entirely up to you!' The strained voice still had something of the slushy sweetness for which Capricorn had loved it so much. 'Help me to catch the bird that the Adderhead longs to hear singing in his castle, and you can keep your children. Otherwise . . .' He wearily signed to the guards, and the Milksop, his face rigid with fury, rode towards the gates as they opened. 'Otherwise, I am afraid I'll have to remember that there is indeed always a need for small hands in our silver mines.'

The women were still staring at him with faces as empty of emotion as if there simply were no room in them for yet more despair.

'What are you still standing there for?' called the Piper as the servants carried the Milksop's dead game through the gateway below. 'Go away! Or I'll have boiling water poured over you. Not a bad idea at all, since I'm sure you could all do with a bath.'

As if numbed, the women moved back, looking up at the battlements as though the cauldrons were already heating up.

The last time Fenoglio's heart had raced like this was when the soldiers had appeared in Balbulus's workshop to take Mortimer away with them. He examined the faces of the women, the beggars crouching beside the pillory outside the castle walls, the frightened children, and fear spread through him. All the rewards set on Mortimer's head had not yet been able to buy the Silver Prince an informer in Ombra, but what now? What mother would not betray the Bluejay for her own child's sake?

A beggar pushed his way through the crowd of women, and as he limped past Fenoglio recognized him as one of the

169

Black Prince's spies. Good, he thought. Mortimer will soon know about the deal the Piper has offered the women of Ombra. But then what?

The Milksop's hunting party was moving on through the open castle gates, and the women set off for home, heads lowered, as if already ashamed of the act of betrayal the Piper had demanded of them.

'Fenoglio?' A woman stopped in front of him. He didn't know who she was until she pushed back the scarf that she had tied over her pinned-up hair like a peasant woman.

'Resa? What are you doing here?' Fenoglio instinctively looked round in alarm, but Mortimer's wife had obviously come without her husband.

'I've been looking for you everywhere!'

Despina clung around Fenoglio's neck and stared curiously at the strange woman. 'That lady looks like Meggie,' she whispered to him.

'Yes, because she's Meggie's mother.' Fenoglio put Despina down as Minerva came towards him. She was walking slowly, as if she felt dizzy, and Ivo ran to her and put his arm protectively around her.

'Fenoglio!' Resa took his arm. 'I have to speak to you!'

What about? It couldn't be anything good.

'Minerva, you go ahead,' he said. 'It will be all right, wait and see,' he added, but Minerva just looked at him as if he were one of her children. Then she took Despina's hand and followed her son, who was running on ahead. She walked as unsteadily as if the Piper's words were splinters of glass under her feet.

'Tell me your husband is hidden deep, deep in the forest and not planning any more idiocy like that visit to Balbulus!'

Fenoglio whispered to Resa as he led her away with him into Bakers' Alley. It still smelt of fresh bread and cake there, a tormenting aroma for most of the people of Ombra, who hadn't been able to afford such delicacies for a long time.

Resa covered her hair with the scarf again, and looked round as if she were afraid the Piper had come down from the battlements and was following her, but only a thin cat slunk past. Once there had been a great many pigs in the streets too, but they had been eaten long ago, most of them up at the castle.

'I need your help!' Good God, how desperate she sounded! 'You must write us home again. You owe us that! It's your songs that have put Mo in danger, and it's getting worse every day! You heard what the Piper said!'

'Stop, stop, stop!' He blamed himself often enough these days, but Fenoglio still didn't like to be blamed by others. And this accusation really was surely unjust. 'I never brought Mortimer here, Orpheus did. I really couldn't foresee that my inspiration for the Bluejay would suddenly be walking around here in flesh and blood!'

'But it happened!' One of the night watchmen who lit the lanterns was coming down the street. Darkness fell fast in Ombra. Another banquet would soon be beginning in the castle, and Sootbird's fire would stink to high heaven.

'If you won't do it for me,' said Resa, doing her best to sound composed, but Fenoglio could see the tears in her eyes, 'then do it for Meggie . . . and the brother or sister she's soon going to have.'

Another child? Fenoglio instinctively glanced at Resa's belly as if he could already see a new character in the story there. Was there no end to its complications?

171

'Fenoglio, please!'

What was he to say in reply? Should he tell her about the sheet of paper still lying blank on his table – or even admit that he liked the way her husband played the part he had written for him, that the Bluejay was his sole comfort in these dark days, the only one of his ideas that worked really well? No, better not.

'Did Mortimer send you?'

She avoided his eyes.

'Resa, does he want to leave too?' Leave this world of mine? he added in his thoughts. My world, still fabulous even if it's in a certain amount of turmoil at the moment? For, yes, Fenoglio knew only too well that he himself still loved it, despite its darkness. Perhaps *because* of its darkness. No. No, that wasn't why . . . or was it?

'He *must* leave! Can't you see that?' The last of the daylight was fading from the streets. The buildings stood very close together, and it was cold, and as still as if all Ombra were thinking of the Piper's threat. Shivering, Resa drew her cloak around her. 'Your words . . . they're changing him!'

'Oh, come on. Words don't change anyone!' Fenoglio's voice sounded louder than he had intended. 'Maybe my words have taught your husband things about himself he never knew before, but they were there all the time, and if he likes them now you can hardly call it my fault! Ride back, tell him what the Piper offered, say he'd better avoid anything like that visit to Balbulus in the near future, and for God's sake don't worry. He's playing his part very well! He plays it better than any of the other characters I made up, except maybe the Black Prince. Your husband is a hero in this world! What man wouldn't wish for that?'

The way she was looking at him, as if he were an old fool who didn't know what he was talking about! 'You know very well how heroes end up,' she said, carefully controlling her voice. 'They don't have wives or children, and they don't grow old. Find yourself another man to play the hero in your story, but leave my husband out of it! You must write us all back! Tonight!'

He hardly knew where to look. Her gaze was so clear – just like her daughter's. Meggie had always looked at him like that. A candle flared into life in the window above them. His world was sinking into darkness. Night was falling – close the curtains, tomorrow the story will go on . . .

'I'm sorry, but I can't help you. I'll never be able to write again. It brings nothing but misfortune, and there's enough of that here already.'

What a coward he was. Too cowardly for the truth. Why didn't he tell her that the words had abandoned him, that she was asking the wrong man? But Resa seemed to know it anyway. He saw so many emotions mingled on her face: anger, disappointment, fear – and defiance. Like her daughter, thought Fenoglio again. So uncompromising, so strong. Women were different, no doubt about it. Men broke so much more quickly. Grief didn't break women. Instead it wore them down, it hollowed them out, very slowly. That was what it was doing to Minerva . . .

'Very well.' Resa was in control of her voice, although it shook. 'Then I'll go to Orpheus. He can write unicorns into this world, he brought us all here. Why shouldn't he be able to send us home again too?'

If you can pay him, thought Fenoglio, but he didn't say it aloud. Orpheus would send her packing. He saved his words for the ladies and gentlemen in the castle who paid for his expensive clothes and his maids. No, she'd have to stay, and so would Mortimer and Meggie – and a good thing too, because who else was going to read his words, supposing they did obey him again some day. And who was to kill the Adderhead if not the Bluejay?

Yes, they had to stay. It was better that way.

'Off you go to Orpheus, then,' he said. 'And I wish you luck with him.' He turned his back to her, so that he wouldn't have to see the despair in her eyes any longer. Did he detect a trace of contempt there too? 'But you'd better not ride back in the dark,' he added. 'The roads are more dangerous every day.'

Then he left her. Minerva would be waiting with supper. He didn't turn back. He knew only too well how Resa would be gazing after him. Exactly like her daughter . . .

17

The Wrong Fear

You wish for something you don't really want, the dream says.
Bad dream. Punish him. Chase him from the house.
Tie him to the horses, let him run with them.
Hang him. He deserves it.
Feed him mushrooms. Poisonous ones.

Paavo Haavikko, *The Trees Breathe Gently*

Mo had spent two whole days and nights with Battista and the Black Prince looking for a place where a hundred or more children could be hidden. With the bear's help, they had finally found a cave. But it was a long way off. The mountainside where the cave lay concealed was steep and almost impassable, especially for children's feet, and a pack of wolves roamed the ravine next to it, but there was some hope that neither the Milksop's hounds nor the Piper would find them there. Not a great deal of hope, but for the first time in many days Mo's heart felt a little lighter.

Hope. Nothing is more intoxicating. And hardly any hope

was sweeter than the prospect of giving the Piper an unpleasant surprise and humiliating him in front of his immortal master.

They wouldn't have to hide all the children, of course, but many, very many of them must be hidden. If all went according to plan, Ombra would soon be not just without men but almost entirely without children, and the Piper would have to go from one remote farm to another if he wanted to steal any, hoping the Black Prince's men hadn't been there ahead of him helping the women to hide their little ones.

Yes, much would be gained if they succeeded in getting the children of Ombra to safety, and Mo was almost in high spirits as they returned to the camp. But when Meggie came to meet him with anxiety on her face, that mood was gone at once. Obviously there was more bad news.

Meggie's voice shook as she told him about the deal the Piper had offered the women of Ombra. *The Bluejay in exchange for your children.* The Black Prince didn't have to tell Mo what that meant. Instead of helping to hide the children, he himself would have to hide from every woman who had a child of the right age.

'You'd better take to living in the trees!' hiccupped Gecko. He was drunk, presumably on the wine they had stolen only last week from a couple of the Milksop's friends out hunting. 'After all, you can fly up there. Don't folk say that's how you escaped from Balbulus's workshop?'

Mo would happily have punched his drunken mouth, but Meggie reached for his hand, and the anger that sprang up in him so quickly these days ebbed away when he saw the fear on his daughter's face.

'What will you do now, Mo?' she whispered.

What indeed? He didn't know the answer. All he knew was that he would rather ride to the Castle of Night and surrender than hide. He quickly turned away so that Meggie wouldn't read his thoughts on his face, but she knew him so well. Too well.

'Perhaps Resa's right after all!' she whispered to him, while Gecko stared at them with bloodshot eyes, and even the Black Prince couldn't conceal his anxiety. 'Perhaps,' she added, almost inaudibly, 'we really ought to go back home to Elinor, Mo!'

She'd heard him and Resa quarrelling.

Involuntarily, he looked round for Resa, but he couldn't see her anywhere.

What will you do now, Mo?

Yes, what indeed? How was the last song about the Bluejay to go? *But they never caught the Jay, however hard they looked for him. He disappeared without trace, as if he had never been. However, he left the Book behind, the White Book that he had bound for the Adderhead, and with it the Adder's immortal tyranny.* No, that must not be the last song. No? What, then? *But one day a mother, fearing for her children, gave the Bluejay away. And he died the worst of all deaths ever suffered by any man in the Castle of Night.* Was that a better end to the story? Was there any better end at all?

'Come along!' Battista put an arm around his shoulders. 'I suggest we get drunk to drown this news. If the others have left any of the Milksop's wine, that is. Forget the Piper, forget the Adderhead, drown them all in good red wine.'

But Mo didn't feel like drinking, even if the wine silenced the voice he kept hearing inside himself since his quarrel with Resa. *I don't want to go back*, it said. *No, not yet . . .*

Gecko staggered back to the fire and pushed in between Snapper and Elfbane. They'd soon start fighting again; they always did when they were drunk.

'I'm going to get some sleep. That clears the head better than wine,' said the Black Prince. 'We'll talk tomorrow.'

The bear lay down outside his master's tent and looked at Mo.

Tomorrow.

What now, Mortimer?

It was getting colder every day. His breath was white vapour hanging in the air as he looked around for Resa again. Where was she? He'd picked her a flower with a shallow cup, pale blue, a species she hadn't yet drawn. Fairyglass, people called it, because it collected so much morning dew in its soft petals that the fairies used it as a mirror.

'Meggie, have you seen your mother?' he asked.

But Meggie didn't reply. Doria had brought her some of the wild boar that was roasting over the fire. It looked like a particularly good piece of meat. The boy whispered something to her. Was it his imagination, or had a rosy flush just risen to his daughter's face? In any case, she hadn't heard his question.

'Meggie, do you know where Resa is?' Mo repeated, taking great care not to smile when Doria cast him a quick and rather anxious glance. He was a good-looking lad, a little smaller than Farid, but stronger. Presumably he was wondering whether the songs about the Bluejay told the truth when they said he guarded his daughter like the apple of his eye. No, more like the finest of all books, thought Mo, and I sincerely hope you're not going to give her as much grief as Farid, because if you do the Bluejay will feed you to the Prince's bear without the slightest hesitation!

Luckily Meggie hadn't read his thoughts this time. 'Resa?'
She tasted the roast meat and thanked Doria with a smile. 'She
rode over to see Roxane.'

'Roxane? But Roxane is here.' Mo glanced at the tent used
as an infirmary for the sick. One of the robbers was in there,
curled up in pain – probably from eating poisonous fungi –
and Roxane stood outside the tent talking to two women who
were nursing him.

Meggie looked at her, bewildered. 'But Resa said she'd
arranged to meet Roxane.'

Mo pinned the flower that had been meant for her mother
to Meggie's dress. 'How long has she been gone?' He did his
best to sound casual, but Meggie was not to be deceived. Not
by him.

'She set out around midday! If she's not with Roxane, then
where is she?'

She was looking at him in bewilderment. No, she really had
no idea. He kept forgetting that she didn't know Resa nearly
as well as she knew him. A year was not a particularly long
time to get acquainted with your own mother.

Have you forgotten our quarrel? he wanted to reply. She's
gone to see Fenoglio. But he bit back the words. Fear made
his chest feel tight, and he'd only too gladly have believed it
was fear for Resa. But he was as bad at lying to himself as to
anyone else. He was not afraid for his wife, although he had
reason to be. He feared that, somewhere in Ombra, the words
were already being read aloud that would take him back to his
old world, like a fish caught in a river and flung back into the
pond it came from . . . Don't be stupid, Mortimer, he thought
angrily. Who is going to read the words, even if Fenoglio

really did write them for Resa? Well, a voice inside him whispered, who do you think?

Orpheus.

Meggie was still looking at him in concern, while Doria stood beside her hesitantly, unable to take his eyes off her face.

Mo turned. 'I'll be back soon,' he said.

'Where are you going? Mo!'

Meggie hurried after him when she saw him go over to the horses, but he did not turn again.

Why in such a hurry, Mortimer? the voice inside him mocked. Do you think you can ride faster than Orpheus can speak the words with his oily tongue? Darkness was falling from the sky like a scarf, a dark scarf smothering everything, the colours, the birdsong . . . Resa. Where was she? Still in Ombra, or on her way back already? And suddenly he felt the other fear – as bad as the fear of those words. The fear of footpads and nocturnal spirits, the memory of women they had found dead in the bushes. Had she at least taken the Strong Man with her? Mo uttered a quiet curse. No, of course not. He was sitting there with Battista and Wayfarer by the fire, and he had already drunk so much that he was beginning to sing.

He ought to have known. Resa had been very quiet since their quarrel. Had he forgotten what that meant? He knew that silence of hers. But he had gone off with the Black Prince instead of talking to her again about what made her so silent – almost as silent as in the days when she had lost her voice.

'Mo, what are you doing?' Meggie's voice sounded faint with fear. Doria had followed them. Meggie whispered something to him, and he set off towards the Prince's tent.

'Damn it, Meggie, what's the idea of that?' Mo tightened

the horse's girth. He wished his fingers weren't shaking so much.

'Where are you going to look for her? You can't leave this camp! Have you forgotten the Piper?'

She clung to him. Then Doria came back with the Prince. Mo cursed and put the horse's reins over its head.

'What are you doing?' The Black Prince stopped behind him, the bear at his side.

'I have to go to Ombra.'

'Ombra?' The Prince gently moved Meggie aside and reached for the reins.

What was he to say to him? Prince, my wife wants Fenoglio to write words that will make me disappear before your eyes, words that will turn the Bluejay back to what he once was – nothing but an old man's invention, vanishing as suddenly as he appeared?

'This is suicide. You're not immortal, whatever the songs say. This is real life. Don't forget that.'

Real life. What's that, Prince?

'Resa has ridden to Ombra. She set out hours ago. She's alone, and it's night. I must go after her.'

. . . and find out if the words have already been written. Written and read aloud.

'But the Piper's there. Are you going to make him a present of yourself? Let me send some men after her.'

'Which men? They're all drunk.'

Mo listened to the night air. He thought he could already hear the words that would send him back – words as powerful as those that had once protected him from the White Women. Above him the withering foliage rustled in the wind, and the drunken voices of the robbers by the fire came to him.

The air smelt of resin, autumn leaves and the fragrant moss that grew in Fenoglio's forest. Even in winter it was still covered with tiny white flowers that tasted like honey if you crushed them in your fingers. *I don't want to go back, Resa.*

A wolf howled in the mountains. Meggie turned her head in alarm. She was afraid of wolves, like her mother. I hope she stayed in Ombra, thought Mo. Even if that means I have to pass the guards. *Let's go back, Mo. Please!*

He swung himself up on the horse. Before he could stop her, Meggie was up there too, sitting behind him. As determined as her mother . . . she put her arms around him so firmly that he didn't even try to persuade her to stay behind.

'Do you see that, bear?' asked the Prince. 'Do you know what it means? It means there'll soon be a new song – about the Bluejay's sheer pig-headedness, and how the Black Prince sometimes has to protect him from himself.'

There were still two men sober enough to ride. Doria came too, getting up behind the Prince on his horse without a word. He wore a sword that was too large for him, but he could handle it well, and he was as fearless as Farid. They would be in Ombra before it was light, although the moon now stood high in the sky.

But words were so much faster than any horse.

18

A Dangerous Ally

All day long he was docile, intelligent, good
Though sometimes changing to a darker mood
He seemed hypocritical, could tell bitter lies,
In the dark he saw dots of colour behind closed eyes,
Clenched his fists, put his tongue out at his elder brother . . .
Arthur Rimbaud, *The Poet at Seven Years Old*

When Resa arrived Farid had just taken Orpheus his second bottle of wine. Cheeseface was celebrating. He was drinking to himself and his genius, as he called it. 'A unicorn! A perfect unicorn, snorting, pawing the ground with its hooves, ready to put its silly head in a virgin's lap any time! Why do you think there weren't any unicorns in this world, Oss? Because Fenoglio couldn't write them! Fluttering fairies, hairy brownies, glass men, yes, but no unicorns.'

Farid would happily have tipped the wine over Orpheus's white shirt to make it as red as the coat of the unicorn. The unicorn brought into this world by Orpheus only for the Milksop to kill it. Farid had seen it. He had been on the way to Orpheus's tailor to get yet another pair of trousers that had become too tight for Cheeseface altered. When they carried the unicorn by, he had felt so sick at the sight of those dull eyes that he had to sit down in a doorway. Murderer. Farid had been listening when Orpheus read the words that had brought it to life, such beautiful words that he had stood as if rooted to the spot outside the study door. *It came through the trees, white as wild jasmine flowers. And the fairies danced around it in dense swarms, as if they had been waiting, full of longing, for its arrival.*

Orpheus's voice had shown Farid the horn, the waving mane, had made him hear the unicorn snorting and scraping at the frozen grass with its hooves. For three whole days he had actually thought it might have been a good idea after all to bring Orpheus here. Three days, if he had counted them correctly – that was as long as the unicorn lived before the Milksop's hounds chased it onto the huntsmen's spears. Or was the tale Brianna told down in the kitchen the true version: that one of Sootbird's lovers had lured it to them with her smile?

Oss opened the door to Resa. When Farid looked past him, wondering who was knocking at such a late hour, he thought at first that the pale face emerging from the darkness was Meggie's. She looked so like her mother now.

'Is Orpheus at home?'

Resa spoke in a low voice, as if ashamed of every word she said, and when she saw Farid behind the Chunk she lowered her head like a child caught in the act of doing something forbidden.

What did she want with Cheeseface?

'Please tell him that Silvertongue's wife has to speak to him.'

When Oss showed her into the entrance hall Resa gave Farid a fleeting smile, but she avoided looking directly at him. Without a word, the Chunk indicated that she was to wait there, and stomped up the stairs. Resa's averted face told Farid that she wasn't going to tell him the reason for her visit, so he followed Oss, hoping to hear more in Orpheus's room.

Cheeseface was not alone when his bodyguard told him about his late-night visitor. There were three girls with Orpheus, none of them much older than Meggie, and they had been cooing at him for hours, telling him how clever, important and irresistible he was. The oldest was sitting on his plump knees, and Orpheus was kissing and fondling her so grossly that Farid would have liked to strike his fingers away. He was always being sent out to bring Orpheus the prettiest girls in Ombra. 'What are you making such a fuss about?' he had snapped, when Farid had at first refused to serve him in such a way. 'They inspire me. Haven't you ever heard of Muses? Off you go, or I'll never find the words you want so much!' So Farid obeyed him and took the girls who looked at him in the streets and the marketplace to Orpheus's house. And many of them did look at Farid; after all, nearly all the older boys in Ombra were either dead or served Violante. Most of them would go anywhere Farid took them for a few coins. They all had hungry brothers and sisters and mothers who needed the money. Some just wanted to be able to buy a new dress again.

'Silvertongue's wife?' You could tell from Orpheus's voice that he had already put away a whole bottle of heavy red wine, but his eyes still looked surprisingly clear through his thick glasses. One of the girls touched the glasses with her finger, as cautiously as if she were afraid that doing so might turn her into glass herself on the spot.

'Interesting. Bring her in. And you three, be off with you.'

Orpheus pushed the girl off his knees and smoothed his clothes down. Conceited bullfrog! Farid thought, pretending to have difficulty with the cork in the new wine bottle so that Orpheus wouldn't send him out of the room.

When Oss showed Resa in, the three girls hurried past her as if their mothers had caught them on Orpheus's lap.

'Well, what a surprise! Do sit down!' Orpheus waved to one of the chairs that had been specially made with his initials on them, and raised his eyebrows to express his surprise even further. He had rehearsed this little move, and that wasn't the only one. Farid had often found Orpheus practising facial expressions in front of his mirror.

Oss closed the door, and Resa sat down hesitantly, as if not sure whether she really wanted to stay.

'I hope you didn't come alone!' Orpheus sat down at his desk and observed his guest like a spider studying a fly. 'Ombra isn't the safest place by night, particularly not for a woman.'

'I have to speak to you.' Resa still kept her voice very low. 'Alone,' she added, with a sideways glance at Farid.

'Farid!' said Orpheus, without looking at him. 'Get out. And take Jasper with you. He's spattered himself with ink again. Wash him.'

Farid bit back the curse that was on the tip of his tongue, put the glass man on his shoulder and went to the door. Resa lowered her head as he passed her, and he saw that her fingers were shaking as she smoothed out her plain skirt. What was she doing here?

As usual, Oss tried to trip him up outside the door, but

Farid was used to such practical jokes now. He had even found a way to get his revenge for them. A smile from him, and the maids in the kitchen would see to it that the Chunk's next meal disagreed with him. Farid's smile was so much more attractive than Oss's.

All the same, he had to abandon any hope of listening at the door. Oss planted himself in front of it with a nasty smile. But Farid knew another place where the goings-on in Orpheus's study could be overheard. The maids said the wife of the previous owner of the house had liked to spy on her husband from this vantage point.

Jasper glanced at Farid in alarm when, instead of taking him down to the kitchen, he made for the stairs to the next floor. However, Oss suspected nothing, since Farid often had to fetch Orpheus a clean shirt or polish his boots. Orpheus's clothes had a room of their own, right beside his bedroom, and the spyhole was under the rails where his shirts hung. They smelt so strongly of roses and violets that Farid felt quite sick when he knelt down under them. One of the maids had shown him the hole in the floor when she had enticed him into the dressing room for a kiss. It was no bigger than a coin, but put your ear to it and you could hear every word spoken in the study downstairs, while if you looked through it with one eye you could see Orpheus's desk.

'Can I do it?' Orpheus was laughing as if he had never heard a more absurd question. 'There's no doubt about that! But my words have their price, and they don't come cheap.'

'I know.' Resa's voice still faltered as if she hated every word she spoke. 'I don't have silver like the Milksop, but I can work for you.'

'Work? Oh no, thank you very much, I'm not short of

maidservants.'

'Do you want my wedding ring? It must be worth something. Gold is rare in Ombra.'

'No, keep it. I'm not short of gold and silver either. But there's something else . . .' Orpheus gave a little laugh. Farid knew that laugh. It boded no good.

'It really is quite amazing how things sometimes turn out!' Orpheus went on. 'It certainly is. I might say you're the very person I need.'

'I don't understand.'

'Of course not. Forgive me. I'll put it more clearly. Your husband – I don't know just what name to give him, he has such a vast number of them, but however that may be,' laughed Orpheus again as if he had made a joke that only he could appreciate, 'your husband met the White Women not so long ago, and I confess I had something to do with that. It's said he has felt their fingers on his heart already, but unfortunately he won't talk to me about this remarkable experience.'

'What does that have to do with my request?'

It struck Farid for the first time how like Meggie's voice her mother's was. The same pride, the same vulnerability carefully hidden behind it.

'Well, I'm sure you remember that scarcely two months ago, on Mount Adder, I swore to bring a mutual friend of ours back from the dead.'

Farid's heart began to beat so violently that he was afraid Orpheus might hear it.

'I'm still determined to keep my promise, but unfortunately I've discovered that it's as difficult to find out what game Death is playing in this world as in ours. No one knows anything, no one's saying anything, and the White Women themselves – no doubt rightly called the daughters of Death – won't appear to me, wherever I look for them. Obviously they don't talk to any reasonably healthy mortal, even one with such extraordinary abilities as mine! I'm sure you've heard about the unicorn, haven't you?'

'Oh yes. In fact, I saw it.' Did Orpheus hear the abhorrence in Resa's voice? If so, even that probably made him feel flattered.

Farid felt Jasper nervously digging his glass fingers into his shoulder. He'd almost forgotten the glass man. Jasper was scared to death of Orpheus, even more scared than he was of his big brother. Farid put him down on the dusty floor and laid a warning finger on his lips.

'It was immaculate,' Orpheus went on in self-satisfied tones, 'absolutely immaculate . . . well, anyway, to return to the daughters of Death. It's said that they don't take it kindly when someone slips through their fingers. They follow such mortals into their dreams, wake them from sleep by whispering to them, even appear to them when they're awake. Has Mortimer been sleeping badly since he escaped the White Women?'

'What's the point of all these questions?' Resa sounded annoyed – and afraid.

'Is he sleeping badly?' Orpheus repeated.

'Yes.' Her reply was barely audible.

'Good! Very good! What am I saying? Excellent!' Orpheus's voice was so loud that Farid involuntarily took his ear away from the hole in the floor. He hastily pressed it in place again. 'In that case, then perhaps what I heard only recently about those pale ladies is true – and we come to the matter of my fee!'

Orpheus sounded very excited, but this time it didn't seem to have anything to do with the prospect of silver.

'There's a rumour – and rumours, as I am sure you know, often contain a kernel of truth in both this and any other world,' said Orpheus, speaking in a velvety voice, as if to make it easy for Resa to swallow every word, 'there's a rumour that those whose hearts the White Women have touched,' – here he inserted a little pause for effect – 'can summon them at any time. No fire is needed, such as Dustfinger used, no fear of death, only a voice that's familiar to them, a heartbeat known to their fingers . . . and they'll appear! I expect by now you can guess what payment I want? In return for the words I write you, I want your husband to call the White Women for me. So that I can ask them about Dustfinger.'

Farid held his breath. It was as if he had heard the Devil in person bargaining. He didn't know what to think or feel. Indignation, hope, fear, joy . . . he felt them all at once. But in the end one idea blotted out all the others: Orpheus wants to bring him back! He really is trying to bring Dustfinger back!

Down in the study there was such deathly silence that finally Farid put his eye, rather than his ear, to the spyhole. But all he could see was the careful parting in Orpheus's pale fair hair. Jasper knelt beside him, looking anxious.

'The best place for him to try it is probably a graveyard.' Orpheus sounded as confident as if Resa had already agreed to the deal. 'If the White Women really do show themselves, they'll attract less attention there – and the strolling players could make up a very moving song about this latest Bluejay adventure.'

'You're abominable, just as abominable as Mo says!' Resa's

voice was trembling.

'Ah, does he indeed? Well, I take that as a compliment. And do you know what? I think he'll be glad to summon them! As I was saying, a fine heroic song could be written about it all. A song praising his courage to the skies, celebrating the magic of his voice.'

'Call them yourself if you want to talk to them.'

'Sad to say, that's what I can't do. I thought I'd made that clear enough, so . . .'

Farid heard the door slam. Resa was going! He picked up Jasper, made his way out through Orpheus's clothes, and ran downstairs. Oss was so surprised when he shot past that he even forgot to put out a leg to trip him. Resa was already in the hall. Brianna was just giving her her cloak.

'Please!' Farid barred Resa's way to the door, ignoring both Brianna's hostile glance and Jasper's cry of alarm as he almost slipped off the boy's shoulder. 'Please! Perhaps Silvertongue really can summon them. Just get him to call them up, and then Orpheus can ask them how to get Dustfinger back! You want him to come back too, don't you? He protected you from Capricorn. He stole into the dungeons of the Castle of Night for you. His fire saved you all when Basta was lying in wait for you on Mount Adder!'

Basta . . . on Mount Adder . . . for a moment the recollection silenced Farid as if Death had laid hands on him again. But then he went on, faltering, although Resa's face remained as cold as ice. 'Please! I mean, it's not like when Silvertongue was wounded . . . and even then they couldn't do him any harm! He is the Bluejay!'

Brianna was staring at Farid as if he had lost his mind. Like everyone else, she thought Dustfinger was gone for ever.

Farid could have hit them all for thinking so!

'It was wrong of me to come here.' Resa tried to push him aside, but Farid thrust her hands away.

'He only has to call them up!' he shouted at her. 'Ask him!'

But Resa pushed him out of her way again, so roughly this time that he stumbled against the wall and the glass man clung to his shirt. 'If you tell Mo I was here,' she said, 'I'll swear you were lying!'

She was already in the doorway when Orpheus's voice halted her. No doubt he had been standing at the top of the stairs for some time, waiting to see what would come of the quarrel. Oss stood behind him with the stolid expression that he always wore when he didn't understand what was going on.

'Let her go. She very obviously doesn't want to let anyone help her.' Every word Orpheus spoke dripped contempt. 'Your husband will die in this story. You know that, or you wouldn't have come here. Maybe Fenoglio even wrote the right song about it himself before he ran out of words. "The Bluejay's Death", touching and very dramatic, heroic as befits such a character, but it certainly won't end with *and they lived happily ever after*. Be that as it may – the Piper struck up the first verse of the real song today. And, clever as he is, he wove a noose out of maternal love to put around your high-minded robber's neck. Is there any deadlier rope? Your husband will certainly walk straight into the trap in the most heroic way imaginable; he's playing the part Fenoglio created for him so enthusiastically, and his death will be the subject of another very impressive song. But I hope that when his head's on a spike above the castle gates you'll remember I could have kept him alive.'

The voice in which Orpheus said this conjured up the picture he described so clearly that Farid thought he could see Silvertongue's blood trickling down the castle walls while Resa stood in the doorway with her head bent, as if Orpheus's words had broken her own neck.

For a moment Fenoglio's whole story seemed to hold its breath again.

Then Resa raised her head and looked at Orpheus.

'Curse you!' she said. 'I wish I could call up the White Women myself and get them to take you away, here and now.'

She went down the steps outside the door unsteadily, as if her knees were trembling, but she did not turn back again.

'Close the door, it's cold!' ordered Orpheus, and Brianna obeyed. But Orpheus himself remained standing there at the top of the stairs, staring at the closed door.

Farid looked uncertainly up at him. 'Do you really believe Silvertongue can summon the White Women?'

'Ah, so you were eavesdropping. Good.'

Good? What did that mean?

Orpheus stroked back his pale hair. 'I'm sure you know where Mortimer is hiding at the moment, don't you?'

'Of course not! No one—'

'Spare me the lies!' snapped Orpheus. 'Go to him. Tell him why his wife came to see me, and ask if he's prepared to pay the price I demand for my words. And if you want to see Dustfinger again, the answer you bring me back had better be yes. Understand?'

'The Fire-Dancer's dead!' Nothing in Brianna's voice showed that she was speaking of her father.

Orpheus gave a little laugh. 'Well, so was Farid, my beauty, but the White Women were ready to do a deal. Why wouldn't they do the same thing again? It just has to be made attractive to them, and I think I now know how. It's like fishing. You only need the right bait.'

What kind of bait did he mean? What was more desirable to the White Women than the Fire-Dancer? Farid didn't want to know the answer. All he wanted was to think that all might yet end well. That bringing Orpheus here had been right after all . . .

'What are you standing around for?' Orpheus shouted down at him. 'Get moving! And you,' he added to Brianna, 'bring me something to eat. I think it's time for a new Bluejay song. And this time I, Orpheus, will write it!'

Farid heard him humming to himself as he returned to his study.

19

Soldiers' Hands

Does the walker choose the path or the path the walker?
Garth Nix, *Sabriel*

Ombra seemed more than ever like a city of the dead as Resa went back to the stable where she had left her horse. In the silence among the buildings she kept hearing Orpheus saying the same words over and over again, as clearly as if he were walking behind her: *But I hope that when his head's on a spike above the castle gates you'll remember I could have kept him alive.* Her tears almost blinded her as she stumbled through the night. What was she to do? Oh, what was she to do? Go back? No. Never.

She stopped.

Where was she? Ombra was a labyrinth of stone, and the years when she had known her way around its narrow streets were long gone.

Her own footsteps echoed in her ears as she walked on. She was still wearing the boots she had on when Orpheus read Mo and her here. He had almost killed Mo once already. Had she forgotten that?

A hiss overhead made her jump. It was followed by a dull crackling, and above the castle the night turned as scarlet as if the sky had caught fire. Sootbird was entertaining the Milksop and his guests by feeding the flames with alchemical poisons and menace until they writhed, instead of dancing as they used to dance for Dustfinger.

Dustfinger. Yes, she wanted him to come back too, and her heart froze when she imagined him lying among the dead. But it froze even more when she thought of the White Women reaching their hands out to Mo for a second time. Yet wouldn't they come for him anyway, if he stayed in this world? *Your husband will die in this story . . .*

What was she to do?

The sky above her turned sulphurous green; Sootbird's fire had many colours. The street down which she was walking, faster all the time, ended in a square she had never seen before. Dilapidated houses stood here. A dead cat lay in one doorway. At a loss, she went over to the well in the middle of the square – and spun around when she heard footsteps behind her. Three men moved out of the shadows among the buildings. Soldiers wearing the Adderhead's colours.

Now what, she wondered? She had a knife with her, but what use was that against three swords? One of the men had a crossbow too. She had seen only too often what bolts from such a weapon could do. You should have worn men's clothes, she told herself. Hasn't Roxane told you often enough that no woman in Ombra goes out after dark, for fear of the Milksop's men?

'Well? I suppose your man's as dead as all the rest, right?'

The soldier facing her was not much taller than she was, but the other two towered more than a head above her.

Resa looked up at the houses, but who was going to come to her aid? Fenoglio lived on the other side of Ombra, and Orpheus – well, even if he could hear her from here, would he and his gigantic servant help her after she'd refused to do a deal with him? Try it, Resa. Scream! Perhaps Farid at least will come and help you. But her voice failed her, as it had when she'd lost it in this world for the first time . . .

Only one window showed a light in the surrounding houses. An old woman put her head out, and hastily retreated when she saw the soldiers. Resa seemed to hear Mo saying, 'Have you forgotten what this world is made of?' So if it really consisted only of words, what would those words say about her? *But there was a woman there who was lost twice in the Inkworld, and the second time she never found her way back again.*

Two of the soldiers were now right behind her. One of them put his hands on her hips. Resa felt as if she had read about what was now happening already somewhere, sometime . . . stop trembling, she told herself. Hit him, claw at his eyes! Hadn't Meggie told her how to defend herself if something like this ever happened?

The smallest of the three men came close to her, a dirty, expectant smile on his narrow lips. What did it feel like to get pleasure out of other people's fear?

'Leave me alone!' At least her voice was obeying her again. But no doubt such voices were often heard in Ombra by night.

'Why would we want to do that?' The soldier behind her smelt of Sootbird's fire. His hands reached out for her. The others laughed. Their laughter was almost the worst thing of all. Through the sound of it, however, Resa thought she heard something else. Footsteps – light, quick footsteps. Farid?

'Take your hands off me!' This time she shouted it as loud as she could, but it wasn't her voice that made the men spin round.

'Let her go. At once.'

Meggie's voice sounded so grown-up that at first Resa didn't realize it was her daughter's. She walked out from among the houses holding herself very upright, just as she had walked into the arena that was the scene of Capricorn's festivities.

The soldier holding Resa dropped his hands like a boy caught doing something wrong, but when he saw no one but a girl step out of the darkness he made a grab for his victim again.

'Another one?' The smaller man turned and sized Meggie up. 'All the better. See that, you two? What did I tell you about Ombra? It's a place full of women, so it is!'

Stupid words, and they were his last. The knife thrown by the Black Prince hit him in the back. Like shadows coming to life, the Prince and Mo emerged from the night. The soldier holding Resa pushed her away and drew his sword. He shouted a warning to the other man, but Mo killed them both so quickly that Resa felt she hadn't even had time to draw breath. Her knees gave way, and she had to lean against the nearest wall. Meggie ran to her, asking anxiously if she was injured. But Mo just looked at her.

'Well? Is Fenoglio writing again?' That was all he said.

He knew why she had ridden here. Of course.

'No!' she whispered. 'No, and he won't write anything either. Nor will Orpheus.'

The way he was looking at her! As if he didn't know

whether he could believe what she said. He'd never looked at her like that before. Then he turned without a word, and helped the Prince to haul the dead men away into a side street.

'We're going back through the dyers' stream!' Meggie whispered to her. 'Mo and the Prince have killed the guards there.'

So many men dead, Resa. Just because you want to go home. There was blood all over the paving stones, and when Mo dragged away the soldier who had been holding her, the man's eyes still seemed to stare at her. Was she sorry for him? No. But it sent a shiver down her spine to hear her daughter, too, speak so casually of killing. And what did Mo feel about it? Did he feel anything any more? She saw him wiping the blood off his sword with one of the dead men's cloaks, and looking her way. Why couldn't she read his thoughts in his eyes now, as she used to?

Because it was the Bluejay she saw there. And this time she had summoned him herself.

The walk to the dye works seemed endless. Sootbird's fire was still lighting up the sky, and they twice had to hide from a troop of drunken soldiers, but finally the acrid smell of the dyers' vats rose to their nostrils. Resa covered her mouth and nose with her sleeve when they came to the stream that carried the effluent away to the river through a grating in the city wall, and as she followed Mo into the stinking liquid she felt so sick that she could hardly take a deep enough breath to plunge down under the grating herself.

As the Black Prince helped her to the bank she saw one of the dead guards lying among the bushes. The blood on his chest looked like ink in the starless night, and Resa began crying. She couldn't stop, not even when they finally reached the river and washed the stinking water out of their hair and clothes as best they could.

Two robbers were waiting with horses further along the bank, at the place where the river-nymphs swam and the women of Ombra dried their washing on the flat rocks by the waterside. Doria was there too, without his brother the Strong Man. He put his shabby cloak around Meggie's shoulders when he saw how wet she was. Mo helped Resa into the saddle, but still said not a word. His silence made her shiver more than her wet clothes, and it was the Black Prince and not Mo who brought her a blanket. Had Mo told the Prince what she had gone to do in Ombra? No, surely not. How could he have explained without telling him what power words had in this world?

Meggie knew why she had ridden to Ombra too. Resa saw it in her eyes. They were watchful – as if her daughter were wondering uneasily what she would do next. Suppose Meggie learnt that she'd even asked Orpheus for help? Would she understand that the only reason had been Resa's fears for her father?

It was beginning to rain as they set off. The wind drove the icy raindrops into their faces, and above the castle the sky glowed dark red, as if Sootbird were sending a warning after them. Doria fell behind on the Prince's orders, to obliterate their tracks, and Mo rode ahead in silence. When he looked round once his glance was for Meggie, not her, and Resa was thankful for the rain on her face that kept anyone from seeing her tears.

20

A Sleepless Night

When despair for the world grows in me
and I wake in the night at the least sound
in fear of what my life and my children's lives may be,
I go and lie down where the wood drake
rests in his beauty on the water, and the great heron feeds.
I come into the peace of wild things
who do not tax their lives with forethought
of grief. I come into the presence of still water.
And I feel above me the day-blind stars
waiting with their light. For a time
I rest in the grace of the world, and am free.

Wendell Berry, *The Peace of Wild Things*

'I'm sorry.' Resa meant it.

I'm sorry. Two words. She whispered them again and again, but Mo sensed what she was really thinking behind her words: she was a captive again. Capricorn's fortress, his village in the mountains, the dungeons, the Castle of Night . . . so many prisons. Now a book was keeping her prisoner, the same book that had imprisoned her once before. And when she'd tried to escape, he had brought her back.

'I'm sorry too,' he said. He said it as often as she did – and knew that she was waiting to hear very different words. *Very well, let's go back, Resa. We'll find a way somehow!* But he didn't say it, and the unspoken words gave rise to a silence they had never known, even when Resa was mute.

At last they lay down to sleep, although the sky was growing lighter outside, exhausted by the fear they had both felt and by what they *didn't* say to each other. Resa fell asleep quickly, and as he looked at her sleeping face he remembered all the years when he had longed to see her asleep beside him. But even that idea brought him no peace – and at last he left Resa alone with her dreams.

He stepped out into the waning night, passed the guards, who ribbed him about the stench of the dye works that still clung to his clothes, and walked through the narrow ravine where they had set up camp, as though, if he only strained his ears hard enough, the Inkworld would whisper to him and tell him what to do.

He knew, only too well, what he *wanted* to do . . .

Finally he sat down by one of the ponds that had once been a giant's footprint, and watched the dragonflies whirring above the cloudy water. In this world they really did look like tiny winged dragons, and Mo loved sitting there, following their strange shapes with his eyes and imagining how huge the giant who had left such a footprint must have been. Only a few days ago he and Meggie had waded into one of the ponds to find out how deep the footprints were. The memory made him smile, although he was not in any smiling mood. He could still feel the shuddering sensation that killing left behind it. Did the Black Prince feel it too, even after all these years?

Morning came hesitantly, like ink mingling with milk, and Mo couldn't say how long he had been sitting there, waiting for Fenoglio's world to tell him what ought to be done next, when a familiar voice quietly spoke his name.

'You shouldn't be here on your own,' said Meggie, sitting down beside him on the grass. It was white with frost. 'It's dangerous to be so far away from the guards.'

'What about you? I ought to be a stricter father, and forbid you to take a step outside the camp without me.'

She gave him an understanding smile and wrapped her arms around her knees. 'Nonsense. I always have a knife with me. Farid taught me how to use it.' She looked so grown-up. He was a fool, still wanting to protect her.

'Have you made it up with Resa?'

Her anxious expression made him feel awkward. Sometimes it had been so much easier to be alone with her.

'Yes, of course.' He put out a finger, and one of the dragonflies settled on it. It looked as if it were made of blue-green glass.

'And?' Meggie looked inquiringly at him. 'She asked them both, didn't she? Fenoglio and Orpheus.'

'Yes. But she says she didn't come to an agreement with either of them.' The dragonfly arched its slender body. It was covered with tiny scales.

'Of course not. What did she expect? Fenoglio isn't writing any more, and Orpheus is expensive.' Meggie frowned.

He stroked it with a smile. 'Watch out, or those lines will stay, and it's rather too early for that, don't you think?' How he loved her face. He loved it so much. And he wanted it to look happy. There was nothing in the world he wanted more.

'Tell me one thing, Meggie. Be honest with me – perfectly honest.' She was a far better liar than he was. 'Do you want to go back too?'

She bent her head and tucked her smooth hair back behind her ears.

'Meggie?'

She still didn't look at him.

'I don't know,' she said at last, quietly. 'Maybe. It's a strain, feeling afraid so often. Afraid for you and Resa, afraid for Farid, for the Black Prince and Battista, for the Strong Man . . .' She raised her head and looked at him. 'You know Fenoglio likes sad stories. Maybe that's where all the unhappiness comes from. It's just that sort of story . . .'

That sort of story, yes. But who was telling it? Not Fenoglio. Mo looked at the frost on his fingers. Cold and white. Like the White Women . . . sometimes he woke from sleep with a start because he thought he heard them whispering. Sometimes he still felt their cold fingers on his heart, and sometimes – yes – sometimes he almost wanted to see them again.

He looked up at the trees, away from all the whiteness below. The sun was breaking through the morning mist, and the last few leaves shone pale gold on branches that were now almost bare. 'What about Farid? Isn't he a reason to stay?'

Meggie lowered her head again. She was taking great care to sound casual. 'Farid doesn't mind whether I'm here or not. He thinks only of Dustfinger. It's been even worse since he died.'

Poor Meggie. She'd fallen in love with the wrong boy. But when did love ever bother about that?

She tried very hard to hide her sadness when she looked at

him again. 'What do you think, Mo? Is Elinor missing us?'

'You and your mother certainly. I'm not so sure about me.' He imitated Elinor's voice. *'Mortimer! You've put that Dickens back in the wrong place. And why do I have to tell a bookbinder not to eat jam sandwiches in a library?'*

Meggie laughed. Well, that was something. It was getting harder every day to make her laugh. But next moment her face was grave again. 'I do miss Elinor very much. I miss her house, and the library, and the café by the lake where she always took me for an ice cream. I miss your workshop, and you driving me to school in the morning and imitating Elinor and Darius quarrelling, and my friends always wanting to come and visit us because you make them laugh. I'd love to tell them everything that's happened to us, not that they'd believe a word of it. Although – perhaps I could take a glass man back with me as proof.'

For a moment she seemed to be far, far away, taken back to her old world, not by the words of Fenoglio or Orpheus, but by her own. But they were still sitting beside a pond in the hills around Ombra, and a fairy fluttered into Meggie's hair and pulled so hard that she shrieked, and Mo was quick to shoo the little creature away. It was one of the rainbow-coloured fairies, Orpheus's creations, and Mo thought he detected something of her maker's malice in the tiny face. Giggling happily, she carried her pale blonde plunder up to her nest, which shimmered in as many colours as the fairy herself. Unlike the blue fairies, those made by Orpheus didn't seem to grow drowsy as winter came on. The Strong Man even claimed that they stole from the blue fairies too as they slept in their nests.

A tear hung on Meggie's lashes. Perhaps the fairy had

caused it, or perhaps not. Mo gently wiped it away.

'I see. So you do want to go back.'

'No! I tell you, I don't know!' She was looking at him so unhappily. 'What will become of Fenoglio if we simply disappear? And what would the Black Prince think, and the Strong Man, and Battista? What will become of them? And Minerva and her children, and Roxane . . . and Farid?'

'Yes, what?' said Mo. 'How would the story go on without the Bluejay? The Piper will take the children, because even the desperate mothers won't be able to find the Bluejay for him. Of course the Black Prince will try to save them – he'll be the true hero of this story, and he'll play the part well. But he's already played the hero too long, he's tired – and he doesn't have enough men. So the men-at-arms will kill him and all his followers one by one: the Prince, Battista, the Strong Man and Doria, Gecko and Snapper – well, perhaps those two will be no great loss. Then the Piper will probably chase the Milksop out and rule Ombra himself for a while. Orpheus will read unicorns here for him, or a few war machines . . . yes, I'm sure the Piper would rather like those. Fenoglio will drown his sorrows in wine and drink himself to death. And the Adderhead will be immortal. Some day he'll reign over a nation of the dead. I think the end of the story would go something like that, don't you?'

Meggie looked at him. In the light of the new morning her hair looked like spun gold. Resa's hair had been just the same colour when he had first seen her, in Elinor's house.

'Yes. Perhaps,' said Meggie quietly. 'But would the story really end so very differently if the Bluejay stayed? How could he give it a happy ending all by himself?'

'Bluejay?' A couple of toads jumped into the water in alarm

as the Strong Man ploughed his way through the under-growth.

Mo straightened up. 'Maybe you'd better not call that name quite so loud in the forest,' he said, lowering his own voice.

The Strong Man looked as horrified as if men-at-arms were already standing among the trees. 'Sorry,' he muttered. 'My head doesn't work well so early in the morning, and all that wine last night . . . it's the boy. You know, the one who works for Orpheus, the one that Meggie—' He stopped short at the sight of Meggie's expression. 'Oh, whatever I say sounds stupid!' he groaned, pressing his hand to his round face. 'Plain stupid! But that's how the words come out of my mouth. I can't help it!'

'Farid. His name is Farid. Where is he?' Meggie's face lit up, although she was making a great effort to look indifferent.

'Farid, of course. Funny sort of name. Like something out of a song, eh? He's in the camp. But he wants to speak to your father.'

Meggie's smile was extinguished as quickly as it had come to her lips. Mo put his arm around her shoulder, but a father's hug was no use to a lovesick girl. Damn the boy.

'He's all worked up. He must have ridden here so fast his donkey can hardly stand. He woke the whole camp, asking: "Where's the Bluejay? I have to speak to him!" No one could get anything else out of him!'

'The Bluejay!' Mo had never heard Meggie sound so bitter before. 'I've told him a thousand times already not to call you that. How can he be so stupid?'

The wrong boy. But what did the heart care about that?

21

Sharp Words

Oh, please! he felt his heart say to him. Oh, please, let me *leave!*

John Irving, *The Cider House Rules*

'Darius!' Elinor couldn't bear the sound of her own voice any more. It was horrible – grouchy, irritable, impatient. She hadn't sounded like that in the old days, had she?

Darius almost dropped the books he was bringing in, and the dog raised his head from the rug she had bought to keep him from ruining her wonderful wooden floor with his slimy slobber. Quite apart from the fact that you were always slipping on it.

'Where's the Dickens we bought last week? For goodness' sake, how long does it take you to put a book back in its proper place? Am I paying you to sit in my armchair reading? That's what you do when I'm not here, admit it!'

Oh, Elinor. How she hated the words coming out of her mouth, and yet there was no keeping them back: bitter and venomous, spat out by her unhappy heart.

Darius bowed his head, as he always did when he was trying not to show her how hurt he was. 'It's where it belongs,
Elinor,' he said in his gentle voice, which only infuriated her
more than ever. She'd been able to have magnificent quarrels
with Mortimer, and Meggie had been a real little fighter. But
Darius! Even Resa, mute as she was, used to stand up to
Elinor better.

Owl-faced coward. Why didn't he call her names? Why
didn't he throw the books at her feet instead of clutching them
so lovingly to his scrawny chest, as if he had to protect them
from her?

'Where it belongs?' she repeated. 'Do you think I can't
even read these days?'

How anxiously the stupid dog was looking at her. Then he
let his massive head sink to the rug again with a grunt.

Darius put the stack of books he was carrying down on the
nearest glass case, went up to the shelf where Dickens made
himself at home, taking up a lot of space in between Defoe
and Dumas (the man had written just too many books, that
was his trouble), went straight to the volume she wanted and
took it out. Without a word, he gave it to Elinor. Then he set
about sorting the books he had brought into the library.

She felt so stupid, and Elinor hated to feel stupid. It was
almost worse than feeling sad.

'It's dirty!'

Stop it, Elinor, she told herself. But she couldn't. The
words simply came out of her mouth. 'When did you last dust
the books? Do I have to do that for myself too?'

Darius kept his thin back turned to her. He took the words
without flinching, like an undeserved beating.

'What's the matter? Has your stuttering tongue finally given up? Sometimes I wonder whether you have a tongue at all! Mortola ought to have taken you with her instead of Resa – even when she was mute, Resa was more talkative than you.'

Darius put the last book on the shelf, straightened another, and marched towards the door, holding himself very straight.

'Darius! Come back!'

He didn't even turn.

Damn. Elinor hurried after him, holding the Dickens which, she had to admit, really wasn't so very dusty. To be perfectly honest, it wasn't dusty in the least. Of course it's not, Elinor! she told herself. As if you didn't know how devotedly Darius removes the tiniest speck of dust from the books every Tuesday and Friday. Her cleaning lady always laughed at the fine brush he used for the purpose.

'Darius! For heaven's sake, don't make such a big deal of it!'

No reply.

The dog overtook her on the stairs, and looked down at her from the top step with his tongue hanging out.

'Darius!'

By that stupid dog's slobber – where was he?

His room was right next to the one Mortimer had used as an office. The door was open, and so was his suitcase, lying on the bed. It was the case she had bought him for their first trip together. Buying books with Darius had always been a pleasure (and she had to admit that he'd kept her from making many silly mistakes).

'What . . .?' How heavy her sharp tongue suddenly felt. 'What the devil are you doing?'

Well, what did she think? Very obviously, he was packing the few clothes he possessed.

'Darius!'

He put the drawing of Meggie that Resa had given him on to the bed, with the notebook Mortimer had bound for him, and the bookmark that Meggie had made him from a bluejay's feathers.

'The dressing gown,' he said hesitantly, as he put the photograph of his parents in the case, the one that always stood by his bed. 'Do you mind if I take it with me?'

'Don't ask such silly questions! Of course not! It was a present, for heaven's sake. But where are you going?'

Cerberus trotted into the room and went to the bedside cupboard. Darius always kept a few biscuits in the drawer.

'I don't know yet . . .'

He folded the dressing gown just as carefully as his other clothes (it was much too large for him, but how would she have known his size?), put the drawing, the notebook and the bookmark in the case and closed it. Of course, he couldn't manage to close the catches. He was so clumsy sometimes!

'Unpack that again! At once! This is silly.'

But Darius shook his head.

'Heavens above, you can't go as well and leave me all alone!' Elinor herself was frightened by the despair in her voice.

'You're alone even when I'm here, Elinor,' said Darius, in a strained voice. 'You're so unhappy! I can't stand it any more!'

The stupid dog gave up snuffling around the bedside table and stood in front of her, looking sad. He's right, said his watering doggy eyes.

As if she didn't know! She couldn't stand herself any more either. Had she been like this long ago? Before Meggie, Mortimer and Resa came to live with her? Maybe. But then there'd only been the books around, and they weren't complaining. Although, to be honest, she'd never been as hard on the books as she was on Darius.

'All right, you go, then!' Her voice began shaking in the most ridiculous way. 'Leave me alone. You're right. Why would you want to watch me getting more insufferable every day, always waiting for some miracle to bring them back? Perhaps I ought to shoot myself or drown myself in the lake, instead of perishing slowly in this miserable way. Writers sometimes do that, and it sounds good in stories.'

Oh, the way he was looking at her with his long-sighted eyes! (She really ought to have bought him new glasses long ago. His present pair looked just too silly.) Then he opened the case again and stared at his possessions. He took out Meggie's bookmark and stroked the boldly-patterned blue feathers. Bluejay feathers. Meggie had glued them to a strip of pale yellow card. It looked very pretty.

Darius cleared his throat. He cleared it three times.

'Oh, very well!' he said at last, in a voice that he carefully kept level. 'You win, Elinor. I'll try it. Fetch me that sheet of paper. Or you probably *will* go and shoot yourself someday.'

What? What was he saying? Elinor's heart began to race, as if hurrying on ahead of her into the Inkworld to see the fairies, the glass men, and the people she loved so much more than she loved any book.

'You mean . . .?'

Darius nodded, resigned, like a warrior who has fought too many battles. 'Yes,' he said. 'Yes, Elinor.'

212

'I'll get it!' Elinor turned on her heel. Everything that had made her heart so heavy these last few weeks, turning her limbs to an old woman's – it was all gone! Vanished without trace.

But Darius called her back. 'Elinor! We ought to take some of Meggie's notebooks too – and some practical things, like . . . like a lighter, for instance.'

'And a knife!' Elinor added. After all, Basta was where they were going, and she had sworn that when next she met him she'd have a knife in her own hand.

She almost fell down the stairs, she was in such a hurry to get back to the library. Cerberus bounded after her, panting with excitement. Did he guess, in some corner of his doggy heart, that they were following his old master to the place where he'd gone when he had disappeared?

He's going to try it! He's going to try it! Elinor couldn't think of anything else. She didn't think of Resa's lost voice, Cockerell's stiff leg or Flatnose's mutilated face. Everything's going to be all right, that was all she thought as, with trembling fingers, she took the words that Orpheus had written out of the glass case. This time there won't be any Capricorn to frighten Darius. This time he'll read beautifully. Oh, dear God, Elinor, you're going to see them again!

213

22

Taking the Bait

If Jim had been able to read he might now have noticed a remarkable circumstance ... but the fact was that Jim couldn't read.

Michael Ende, *Jim Knopf and the Wild 13*

A dwarf about twice the size of a glass man. Definitely not furry like Tullio – no, the dwarf was to have skin as white as alabaster, a head too big for it, and bandy legs. At least the Milksop always knew just what he wanted, even if his orders had come noticeably less often since the Piper arrived in the city. Orpheus was just wondering whether to give the dwarf red hair or the white hair of an albino when Oss knocked, and at his master's grunt of 'Enter' put his head around the door. Oss had revolting table manners, and was not much given to washing himself, but he never forgot to knock.

'There's another letter for you, my lord!'

Ah, how good it made him feel being called that! *My lord ...*

Oss came in, bowed his bald head (he sometimes overdid

the servility) and handed Orpheus a sealed piece of paper. Paper? That was strange. The fine gentlemen usually sent their orders written on parchment, and the seal didn't look familiar either. Well, never mind that. This would be the third order today; business was good. The Piper's arrival had made no difference to that. This world could have been made for him! Hadn't he always known it, ever since he first opened Fenoglio's book with his sweaty schoolboy fingers? His accomplished lies didn't get him jailed as a forger or con man here; they valued his talents at their true worth in this world – and all Ombra bowed to him when he crossed the marketplace in his fine clothes. Fabulous.

'Who's the letter from?'

Oss shrugged his ridiculously broad shoulders. 'Dunno, my lord. Farid gave it to me.'

'Farid?' Orpheus sat up straight. 'Why didn't you say so at once?' He quickly snatched the letter from Oss's clumsy fingers.

Orpheus – of course he didn't begin 'Dear Orpheus'. Even in the salutation of a letter the Bluejay told no lies! – *Farid has told me what you want in return for the words my wife has asked you for. I agree.*

Orpheus read the words three times, four, five times, and yes, there it was in black and white.

I agree.

The bookbinder had taken the bait! Could it really be that easy?

Yes, why not? Heroes are fools. Hadn't he always said so? The Bluejay had fallen into the trap, and all he had to do was snap it shut. With a pen, some ink . . . and his tongue.

'Go away! I want to be alone!' he snarled at Oss, who was

standing there looking bored and throwing nuts at the two glass men. 'And take Jasper with you!' Orpheus liked talking to himself out loud when he was writing his ideas down, so the glass man had better be out of the room. Jasper sat on Farid's shoulder far too often, and on no account must the boy learn what Orpheus was planning to write now. It was true that the stupid boy wanted Dustfinger back even more fervently than he did, but Orpheus wasn't so sure that he would sacrifice his girlfriend's father in return. No, by now Farid worshipped the Bluejay as much as everyone else here did.

Ironstone gave his brother a gleefully malicious glance as Oss picked Jasper up from the desk with fleshy fingers.

'Parchment!' Orpheus ordered, as soon as the door had closed behind the two of them, and Ironstone busily spread the best sheet they had on the desk.

Orpheus, however, went to the window and looked out at the hills from which, presumably, the Bluejay's letter had come. Silvertongue, Bluejay . . . fine names they'd given him, and yes, Mortimer was certainly very much braver and more noble than Orpheus himself was, but such a paragon couldn't compete with him in cunning. The good are stupid.

You have his wife to thank for this, Orpheus, he told himself as he began pacing up and down (nothing helped him to think better). If his wife wasn't so afraid of losing him, you might never have found the bait you need!

Oh, it would be fantastic! His greatest triumph! Unicorns, dwarves, rainbow-coloured fairies . . . not bad at all, but as nothing compared to what he'd do now! He would bring the Fire-Dancer back from the dead. Orpheus. Had the name he had taken ever suited him better? But he would be wilier than the singer whose name he had stolen. He would indeed. He would send another man into the realm of Death in the Fire-Dancer's place – and he'd make sure that he didn't come back.

'Do you hear me, Dustfinger, in the cold land where you are now?' whispered Orpheus, while Ironstone busily stirred the ink. 'I've caught the bait to buy your freedom, the most wonderful bait of all, decked out with the finest pale-blue feathers!'

He began humming, as he always did when he was pleased with himself, and picked up Mortimer's letter again. What else had the Bluejay written?

It will be as you require. By the Devil's cloven hoof, he was writing in the style of public proclamations, like the robbers of the old days. *I will try to call up the White Women, and in return you will write words to take my wife and daughter back to Elinor's house. But all you are to say about me is that I will follow them later.*

Well, well. What was this?

Surprised, Orpheus lowered the sheet of paper. Mortimer wanted to stay? Why? Because his noble and heroic heart wouldn't let him steal away now that the Piper had made his threat? Or did he just like playing the part of a robber too much?

'Well, never mind which, noble Bluejay,' said Orpheus softly (oh, how he liked the sound of his own voice!). 'It won't turn out the way you think it will. Because I have plans of my own for you!'

High-minded idiot! Hadn't Mortimer ever read any tale of robbers right through? No happy ending for Robin Hood, for Angelo Duca, for Dick Turpin and all the rest of them. Why would there be a happy ending for the Bluejay? No, he was going to play just *one* part: the bait on the hook, a tasty bait – and one condemned to certain death.

And I will write the last song about him! thought Orpheus as he strode up and down with a spring in his step, as if he already felt the right words inside him all the way down to his toes. *Good people, hear the amazing tale of the Bluejay who brought the Fire-Dancer back from the dead but then, sad to say, lost his own life.* Heart-rending. Like Robin Hood's death at the hands of the treacherous nun, or Angelo Duca's end on the gallows beside his dead friend, with the hangman riding him to death on his shoulders. Yes, every hero needs a death like that. Even Fenoglio wouldn't write it in any other way.

Ah, but he hadn't finished reading the letter yet! What else did that most noble of robbers have to say? *Hang a piece of blue cloth in the window when you have written the words.* (How romantic! A real robber's idea. He really did seem to be turning more and more into the character made by Fenoglio in his image!) *I will meet you at the graveyard of the strolling players on the following night. Farid knows where it is. Come alone, bringing one servant at the most. I know you are on friendly terms with the new governor, and I will not show myself until I am certain that none of his men is with you. Mortimer.* (Well, well, so he actually still signed his old name. Who did he think he was fooling?)

Come alone? Oh yes, I'll come alone, thought Orpheus. And you won't be able to see the words I've sent on ahead of you!

He rolled up the letter and slid it under his desk.

'Everything ready, Ironstone? A dozen sharpened pens, ink stirred slowly while you take sixty-five breaths, a sheet of the best parchment?'

'A dozen pens. Sixty-five breaths. The very best parchment.'

'What about this list of words?' Orpheus looked at his bitten fingernails. He had recently taken to bathing them in rosewater every morning, but unfortunately that just made them tastier. 'Your useless brother left his footprints all over the words beginning with B.'

The list. The list of all the words used by Fenoglio in *Inkheart*, arranged in alphabetical order. He had only recently told Jasper to prepare it – his brother had terrible handwriting. But unfortunately the glass man had only just reached the letter D, so Orpheus still had to look everything up in Fenoglio's book if he wanted to be sure that any words he used were in *Inkheart* too. It was a nuisance, but it had to be done, and so far his method had proved its merits.

'All ready!' Ironstone nodded eagerly.

Good! The words were already coming. Orpheus sensed them like a tingling of his scalp. As soon as he picked up the pen he could hardly dip it in the ink fast enough. Dustfinger . . . the tears still came to his eyes when he remembered seeing him lying dead in the mine. Certainly one of the worst moments of his life.

And how the promise he'd given Roxane had come to haunt him, even if she had never believed a word of it! He had given it with the dead man at his feet, *'I'll find words as precious and intoxicating as the scent of a lily, words to beguile Death and open the cold fingers he has closed around Dustfinger's warm heart!'* He had been looking for those words ever since he arrived in this world – even if Farid and Fenoglio thought he did nothing but write unicorns and rainbow-coloured fairies into it. But after his first failed attempts he had accepted the bitter fact that beauty of sound alone was not enough in this case. Words like lilies would never bring Dustfinger back.

Death demanded a more substantial price – a price paid in flesh and blood.

Incredible that he hadn't hit upon the idea of Mortimer before – the man who had made Death a laughing stock to the living when he had bound an empty book to make the Adderhead immortal!

So away with him! This world needed only one silver tongue, and it was his. Once he had fed Mortimer to Death, and Fenoglio's brain was wrecked by the drink, only he would go on telling this story, on and on – with a suitable part in it for Dustfinger and a not inconsiderable part for himself.

'Yes, call up the White Women for me, Mortimer!' whispered Orpheus as he filled the parchment with word after word in his elegant script. 'You'll never know what I've whispered into their pale ears first! *"Look what I've brought you! The Bluejay. Take him to your cold lord with greetings from Orpheus, and give me the fire-eater in exchange."* Ah, Orpheus, Orpheus, they can say many things about you, but they can never call you stupid.'

He dipped his pen in the ink with a soft laugh – and spun round when the door opened behind him. Farid came in. Damn it, where was Oss? 'What do you want?' he snapped at the boy. 'How often do I have to tell you to knock before coming in? Next time I'll throw the inkwell at your stupid head. Bring me wine! The best we have.'

How the lad looked at him as he closed the door. He hates me, thought Orpheus.

He liked that idea. In his experience only the powerful were hated, and that was what he meant to be in this world.

Powerful.

23

The Graveyard of the Strolling Players

He sits down on a hill and sings. They are songs of magic, strong enough to wake the dead to life. Softly, cautiously, his song rises, then it grows louder and more insistent, until the turf opens up and the cold earth cracks.

Tor Age Bringsværd, *The Wild Gods*

The strolling players' graveyard lay above a deserted village. Carandrella. It had kept its name, although the inhabitants had left long ago. Why and where they went no one knew now – an epidemic, some said, while others spoke of famine, and others again of two warring clans who had slaughtered one another and driven any survivors out. Whichever story was true, it wasn't in Fenoglio's book, and nor was this graveyard where the peasants had buried their dead among the Motley Folk, so that now they slept side by side for ever.

A narrow, stony path wound its way from the abandoned cottages up the furze-grown slope, and ended on a rocky headland. Standing there you could look far south over the tree-tops of the Wayless Wood towards Argenta, where the sea lay somewhere beyond the hills. The dead of Carandrella, they said in Lombrica, have the best view in the country.

A crumbling wall surrounded the graves. The gravestones were of the pale stone that was also used to build houses here. Stones for the living, stones for the dead. Names were incised on some of them, scratched clumsily as if whoever wrote them had learned the letters only to preserve the sound of a beloved name, rescuing it from the silence of death.

Meggie felt as if the stones were whispering those names to her as she walked past the graves – Farina, Rosa, Lucio, Renzo. Those stones that bore no names seemed like closed mouths, sad mouths that had forgotten how to speak. But perhaps the dead didn't mind what their names had once been?

Mo was still talking to Orpheus. The Strong Man was sizing up his bodyguard Oss as if wondering which of them had the broader chest.

Mo. Don't do it! *Please.*

Meggie looked at her mother, and abruptly turned her face away when Resa returned her glance. She was so angry with her. It was all because of Resa's tears, and because she had ridden off to see Orpheus, that Mo was here now.

The Black Prince had come with them as well as the Strong Man – and Doria, although his brother had told him to stay behind. Like Meggie, he was standing among the graves, looking around him at the things lying in front of the gravestones: faded flowers, a wooden toy, a shoe, a whistle. A fresh flower lay on one grave. Doria picked it up. The flower was white, like the beings they were waiting for. When he saw Meggie looking at him he came over to her. He really wasn't at all like his brother. The Strong Man wore his brown hair short, but Doria's was wavy and shoulder-length. Sometimes Meggie felt as if he had come out of one of the old fairy-tale books that Mo gave her when she had just learnt to read. The pictures in the books had been yellow with age, but Meggie used to look at them for hours, firmly convinced that the fairies who featured in some of the tales had painted them with their tiny hands.

'Can you read the letters on the stones?' Doria was still holding the white flower as he stopped in front of her. Two fingers of his left hand were stiff. His father had broken them long ago in a drunken rage when Doria tried to protect his sister from him. At least, that was how the Strong Man told the story.

'Yes, of course.' Meggie looked her father's way again. Fenoglio had sent him a message, delivered by Battista. *You can't trust Orpheus, Mortimer!* All useless.

Don't do it, Mo. *Please!*

'I'm looking for a name.' Doria sounded shyer than usual. 'But I can't . . . I can't read. It's my sister's name.'

'What was she called?'

If the Strong Man was right, Doria had been fifteen on the very day when the Milksop was going to hang him. Meggie thought he looked older. 'Ah, well,' the Strong Man had said. 'Could be he's older. My mother's not that good at counting. She can't even remember my birthday.'

'Her name was Susa.' Doria looked at the graves as if the name alone could conjure up his sister. 'My brother says she's supposed to be buried here, only he can't remember just where.'

They found the gravestone. It was overgrown with ivy, but the name was still clearly legible. Doria bent down and moved the ivy leaves aside. 'She had hair as bright as yours,' he said. 'Lazaro says my mother turned her out because she wanted to go and live with the strolling players. He never forgave her for that.'

'Lazaro?'

'My brother. You call him the Strong Man.' Doria traced the letters with his finger. They looked as if someone had scratched them into the stone with a knife. The first S was overgrown with moss.

Mo was still talking to Orpheus. Orpheus handed him a sheet of paper: the words he had written at Resa's request. Was Mo going to read them this very night, if the White Women really did appear? Would they all be back in Elinor's house before it was day? Meggie didn't know whether the idea made her feel sad or relieved. She didn't want to think about it, either. All she wanted was for Mo to get on his horse and ride away again, and for her mother's tears never to have brought him here.

Farid was standing a little way off with Jink on his shoulder. At the sight of him, Meggie's heart felt the same chill as when she looked at Resa. Farid had taken Orpheus's demand to Mo knowing what danger it could mean for her father, knowing too that if the deal went through they might never see each other again. But all that meant nothing to Farid. He cared for only one person, and that was Dustfinger.

'They say you come from far away, you and the Bluejay.' Doria had drawn the knife from his belt and was scratching the moss away from his sister's name. 'Is it different there?'

What could she say to that? 'Yes,' she murmured at last. 'Very different.'

'Really? Farid says there are coaches that can drive without horses, and music that comes out of a tiny black box.'

Meggie couldn't help smiling. 'Yes, that's right,' she said quietly.

Doria placed the white flower on his sister's grave and stood up. 'Is it true that there are flying machines in that country too?' How curious he was! 'I once tried making myself wings. I even flew a little way with them, but not very far.'

'Yes, there are flying machines there as well,' replied Meggie distractedly. 'Resa can draw them for you.'

Mo folded the sheet of paper that Orpheus had given him. Her mother went over to him and began talking to him urgently. Why bother? He wouldn't listen to her. 'There's no other way, Meggie,' was all he had said, when she herself had begged him not to agree to the offer made by Orpheus. 'Your mother is right. It's time to go back. This is getting more dangerous every day.' And what could she say to that? The robbers had moved camp three times over the last few days because of the Piper's patrols, and they had heard that women were going to Ombra Castle all the time, claiming to have seen the Bluejay, in the hope of saving their children.

Oh, Mo.

'He'll come to no harm,' said Doria behind her. 'You wait and see, even the White Women love his voice.'

Nonsense. Nothing but poetic nonsense!

When Meggie went over to Mo her boots left traces in the hoarfrost as if a ghost had been walking over the graveyard. Mo's face was so serious. Was he afraid? Well, what do you think, Meggie? she asked herself. He wants to call the White Women. *They're made of nothing but longing, Meggie.*

Farid looked awkwardly away as she passed him.

'Please! You don't have to do it!' Resa's voice sounded far

too loud among all the dead, and Mo gently laid his hand on her lips.

'I want to,' he said. 'And you mustn't be afraid. I know the White Women better than you think.' He tucked the folded sheet of paper into her belt. 'There. Take good care of it. If for any reason I'm unable to read it, then Meggie will do it.'

If for any reason I'm unable to read it . . . if they kill me with their cold white hands, the way they killed Dustfinger. Meggie opened her mouth – and shut it again when Mo looked at her. She knew that look. *No arguing. Forget it, Meggie.*

'Good. Very well, then. I've done my part of the bargain. I . . . er, I don't think we should wait any longer!' Orpheus was visibly impatient. He was stepping from foot to foot, with an unctuous smile on his lips. 'They're said to like it when the moon is shining, before it disappears behind the clouds . . .'

Mo just nodded and signalled to the Strong Man, who gently led Resa and Meggie away from the graves to an oak growing at the side of the graveyard. At a gesture from his brother, Doria joined them under the tree.

Orpheus too took a couple of steps back, as if it were too dangerous to stand beside Mo now.

Mo exchanged a glance with the Black Prince. What had he told him? That he was going to try calling the White Women only for Dustfinger's sake? Or did the Prince know about the words that act would buy the Bluejay? No, surely not.

Side by side, the two of them walked among the graves. The bear trotted after them. As for Orpheus, he and his bodyguard hurried over to the oak where Meggie and Resa were standing. Only Farid stayed put as if rooted to the spot, on his face both fear of the beings whom Mo was about to summon, and longing for the man they had taken away with them.

A light wind blew over the graveyard, cool as the breath of those they were waiting for, and Resa instinctively took a step forward, but the Strong Man drew her back.

'No,' he said quietly, and Resa stood still in the shade of the branches and stared, like Meggie, at the two men who had now stopped in the middle of the graveyard.

'Show yourselves, daughters of Death!'

Mo's voice sounded as calm as if he had called on them many times before. 'You remember me, don't you? You remember Capricorn's fortress, you remember following me into the cave, and how faintly my heart beat against your white fingers. The Bluejay wants to ask you about a friend. Where are you?'

Resa put a hand to her heart. It must be beating as fast as Meggie's.

The first White Woman appeared right beside the gravestone where Mo was standing. She had only to reach out her arm to touch him, and she did touch him, as gently as if she were greeting a friend.

The bear moaned and lowered his head. Then he retreated step by step, and did something he had never done before. He left his master's side. But the Black Prince stood his ground next to Mo, although his dark face showed fear such as Meggie had never seen on it before.

Mo's face, however, gave nothing away when the pale fingers caressed his arm. The second White Woman appeared to his right. She put her hand to his breast, to the place where his heart was beating. Resa cried out and took another step forward, but the Strong Man held her back again.

'They won't harm him. Watch!' he whispered to her.

Another White Woman appeared, then a fourth, and a

fifth. They surrounded Mo and the Black Prince until Meggie saw the two men only as shadows among those misty figures. They were so beautiful – and so terrible – and for a moment Meggie wished Fenoglio could see them too. She knew how proud he would have been of the sight, proud of the flightless angels he had created.

More and more kept coming. They seemed to form from the white vapour that Mo and the Prince exhaled into the air. Why were there so many? Meggie saw the same enchantment that she felt on Resa's face too, even on Farid's, although he was so frightened of ghosts.

But then the whispering began, in voices that seemed as ethereal as the pale women themselves. It grew louder and louder, and enchantment turned to fear. Mo's outline blurred, as if he were dissolving in all the whiteness. Doria looked at his brother in alarm. Resa called Mo's name. The Strong Man tried to hold her back once more, but she tore herself away and began to run. Meggie ran after her, plunging into the mist of translucent bodies. Faces turned to her, as pale as the stones over which she stumbled. Where was her father?

She tried to push the white figures aside, but she only reached into a void again and again, until suddenly she touched the Black Prince. There he stood, his face ashen, his sword in his trembling hand, looking around him as if he had forgotten where he was. But the White Women were no longer whispering. They dissolved like smoke blowing in the wind. The night seemed darker when they were gone. So dark. And so terribly cold.

Resa called Mo's name again and again, and the Prince looked round desperately, his useless sword in his hand.

But Mo was not there.

24

To Blame

Time, let me vanish. Then what we separate by our very own presence can come together.
Audrey Niffenegger, *The Time Traveller's Wife*

Resa waited among the graves until day began to dawn, but Mo did not come back.

She felt Roxane's pain now, except that she didn't even have a dead man to mourn. Mo was gone as if he had never existed. The story had swallowed him up, and she was to blame.

Meggie was crying. The Strong Man held her in his arms while tears ran down his own broad face.

'It's your fault!' Meggie had kept shouting, pushing Resa and Farid away, not even letting the Prince comfort her. 'You two persuaded him! Why did I save him after Mortola shot him, if they were going to take him now?'

'I'm so sorry. I really am so very sorry.'

Orpheus's voice still clung to Resa's skin like something venomously sweet. When the White Women disappeared, he had stood there as if waiting for something, making an effort to hide the smile that kept returning to his lips. But Resa had seen it. Indeed she had . . . and so had Farid.

'What have you done?' He had seized Orpheus by his fine clothes and hammered at the man's chest with his fists. Orpheus's bodyguard tried to grab Farid, but the Strong Man held him off.

'You filthy liar!' Farid had cried, sobbing. 'You double-tongued snake! Why didn't you ask them anything? You were never going to ask them anything, were you? You just want-ed them to take Silvertongue! Ask him! Ask him what else he wrote! He didn't just write the words he promised Silvertongue – there was a second sheet too! He thinks I don't know what he gets up to because I can't read – but I can count. There were *two* sheets – and his glass man says he was reading out loud last night.'

He's right, a voice whispered inside Resa. Oh God, Farid is right!

Orpheus, however, had taken great pains to look genuine-ly indignant. 'What's all this stupid talk?' he had cried. 'Do you think I'm not disappointed myself? How can I help it if they took him away with them? I've fulfilled my part of the bargain! I wrote exactly what Mortimer asked for! But did I get a chance to ask them about Dustfinger? No! All the same, I won't ask for my words back. I hope it's clear to all of you here,' and he looked at the Black Prince, who still had his sword in his hand, 'that *I'm* the one who gets nothing out of this deal!'

The words he had written were still tucked into Resa's belt. She had been going to throw them after him when he rode away, but then she had kept them after all. The words that were to take them back . . . she hadn't even looked to see what they said. They had been bought at too high a price. Mo was gone, and Meggie would never forgive her. She had lost them both, again, for the sake of those words.

Resa leant her forehead against the gravestone beside her. It was a child's grave; a tiny shirt lay on it. *I'm so sorry.* Once again she remembered Orpheus's deep, soft voice mingled with her daughter's sobbing. Farid was right. Orpheus was a liar. He had written what was to happen, and his voice made it come true. He had got rid of Mo because he was jealous of him, as Meggie had always said – and she had helped him to do it.

With trembling fingers she unfolded the paper that Mo had tucked into her belt. It was damp with dew, and Orpheus's coat of arms stood above the words, lavish as a prince's. Farid had told them how he had commissioned it from a designer of crests in Ombra – a crown for the lie that he came from a royal family, a pair of palm trees for the foreign land he claimed to come from, and a unicorn, its winding horn black with ink.

Mo's own bookbinder's mark was a unicorn too. Resa felt tears coming again. The words blurred before her eyes as she began to read them. The description of Elinor's house was a little stilted. But Orpheus had found the right words for her homesickness and her fear that this story could make her husband into someone else . . . how did he know so well what went on in her heart? From you yourself, Resa, she thought bitterly. You took all your despair to him. She read on – and stopped short.

And mother and daughter went away, back to the house full of books, but the Bluejay stayed – promising to follow them when the time came and he had played his part . . .

I wrote exactly what Mortimer asked for! she heard Orpheus saying, his voice full of injured innocence.

No. It couldn't be true! Mo had wanted to go with her and Meggie . . . hadn't he?

You'll never know the answer, she told herself, bent double over the little grave from the pain in her heart. She thought she heard the child inside her weeping too.

'Let's go, Resa!' The Black Prince was there beside her, offering her his hand. His face showed no reproach, although it was sad, very sad. Nor did he ask about the words that Orpheus had written. Perhaps he believed the Bluejay had really been an enchanter after all. The Black Prince and the Bluejay, the two hands of justice – one black, the other white. Now there was only the Prince again.

Resa took his hand and rose to her feet with difficulty. Go? Go where? she felt like asking. Back to the camp, where an empty tent is waiting and your men will look at me with more hostility than ever?

Doria brought her horse. The Strong Man was still standing with Meggie, his big face as tearstained as her daughter's. He avoided her eyes. So he too blamed her for what had happened.

Go where? Back?

Resa was still holding the sheet of paper with Orpheus's words on it. Elinor's house. How would it feel to go back there without Mo? If Meggie would agree to read the words at all. *Elinor, I've lost Mo. I wanted to protect him, but* . . . no, she didn't want to have to tell that story. There was no going back. There was nothing any more.

'Come along, Meggie.' The Black Prince beckoned Meggie

over. He was about to put her up with Resa on her horse, but Meggie recoiled.

'No. I'll ride with Doria,' she said.

Doria brought his horse to her side. Farid gave the other boy a scowl when he lifted Meggie up behind him.

'And why are you still here?' Meggie snapped at him. 'Still hoping to see Dustfinger suddenly materialize in front of you? He won't come back, any more than my father will – but I'm sure Orpheus will take you in again, after all you've done for him!'

Farid flinched like a beaten dog at every word. Then he turned in silence and went to his donkey. He called for the marten, but Jink didn't come, and Farid rode away without him.

Meggie didn't watch him go.

She turned to Resa. 'You needn't think I'm going back with you!' she said sharply. 'If you need a reader for your precious words, go to Orpheus, like you did before!'

Again, the Black Prince didn't ask what Meggie was talking about, although Resa saw the question on his weary face. He stayed at Resa's side as they rode the long way back. The sun claimed hill after hill for its own, but Resa knew that night would not end for her. It would live in her heart from now on. The same night, for ever and ever. Black and white at the same time, like the women who had taken Mo away with them.

The End and the Beginning

HERE IS A SMALL FACT. You are going to die.

Markus Zusak, *The Book Thief*

They brought it all back: the memory of pain and fear, of the burning fever and their cold hands on his heart. But this time everything was different. The White Women touched Mo and he did not fear them. They whispered the name that they thought was his, and it sounded like a welcome. Yes, they were welcoming him in their soft voices, heavy with longing, the voices he heard so often in his dreams – as if he were a friend who had been away for a long time, but had come back to them at last.

There were many of them, so many. Their pale faces surrounded him like mist, and everything else disappeared beyond it: Orpheus, Resa, Meggie, the Black Prince, who had been standing beside him only a moment ago. Even the stars vanished, and so did the ground beneath his feet. Suddenly he

was standing on rotting leaves. Their fragrance hung sweet
and heavy in the cold air. Bones lay among the leaves, pale
and polished. Skulls. Arm bones and leg bones. Where was
he?

They've taken you away with them, Mortimer, he thought.
Just as they took Dustfinger.

Why didn't the idea make him afraid?

He heard birds above him, many birds, and when the
White Women withdrew he saw air-roots overhead, hanging
from a dark height like cobwebs. He was inside a tree as hollow as an organ pipe and as tall as the castle towers of Ombra.
Fungi grew from its wooden sides, casting a pale green light
on the nests of birds and fairies. Mo put out his hand to the
roots to see if his fingers still had any feeling in them. Yes,
they did. He ran them over his face, felt his own skin, the
same as ever, warm. What did that mean? Wasn't this death,
after all?

If not, what was it? A dream?

He turned, still as if he were asleep, and saw beds of
moss. Moss-women slept on them, their wrinkled faces as
ageless in death as in life. But on the last mossy bed lay a
familiar figure, his face as still as when Mo had last seen it.
Dustfinger.

Roxane had kept the promise she made in the old mine.
*And he will look as if he were only sleeping long after my hair is
white, for I know from Nettle how you go about preserving the
body even when the soul is long gone.*

Hesitantly, Mo approached the motionless figure. Without
a word, the White Women made way for him.

Where are you, Mortimer, he wondered? Is this still the
world of the living, even though the dead sleep here?

235

Dustfinger did indeed look as if he were sleeping. A peaceful, dreamless sleep. Was this where Roxane visited him? Presumably it was. But how did he himself come to be here?

'Because this is the friend you wanted to ask about, isn't he?' The voice came from above, and when Mo looked up into the darkness he saw a bird sitting among the web of roots, a bird with gold plumage and a red mark on its breast. It was staring down at him from a bird's round eyes, but the voice that came from its beak was the voice of a woman.

'Your friend is a welcome guest here. He has brought us fire, the only element that does not obey me. And my daughters would gladly bring you here too, because they love your voice, but they know that voice needs the breath of living flesh. And when I ordered them to bring you here all the same, as your penalty for binding the White Book, they persuaded me to spare you, telling me you have a plan which will appease me.'

'And what might that be?' It was strange to hear his own voice in this place.

'Don't you know? Even though you're ready to part with everything you love for it? You are going to bring me the man you took from me. Bring me the Adderhead, Bluejay.'

'Who are you?' Mo looked at the White Women. Then he looked at Dustfinger's still face.

'Guess.' The bird ruffled up its golden feathers, and Mo saw that the mark on its breast was blood.

'You are Death.' Mo felt the word heavy on his tongue. Could any word be heavier?

'Yes, so they call me, although I might be called by so many other names!' The bird shook itself, and golden feathers covered the leaves at Mo's feet. They fell on his hair and shoulders, and when he looked up again there was only the skeleton of a bird sitting among the roots. 'I am the end and the beginning.' Fur sprouted from the bones. Pointed ears grew on the bare skull. A squirrel was looking down at Mo, clutching the roots with tiny paws, and the voice with which the bird had spoken now came from its little mouth.

'The Great Shape-Changer, that's the name I like!' The squirrel shook itself in its own turn, lost its fur, tail and ears and became a butterfly, a caterpillar at his feet, a big cat with a coat as dappled as the light in the Wayless Wood – and finally a marten that jumped on to the bed of moss where Dustfinger lay, and curled up at the dead man's feet.

'I am the beginning of all stories, and their end,' it said in the voice of the bird, in the voice of the squirrel. 'I am transience and renewal. Without me nothing is born, because without me nothing dies. But you have interfered with my work, Bluejay, by binding the Book that ties my hands. I was very angry with you for that, terribly angry.'

The marten bared its teeth, and Mo felt the White Women coming close to him again. Was he about to die now? His chest felt tight, he was breathing with difficulty, as he had when he felt them near him before.

'Yes, I was angry,' whispered the marten, and its voice was the voice of a woman, but it suddenly sounded old. 'However, my daughters calmed my rage. They love your heart as much as your voice. They say it is a great heart, very great, and it would be a pity to break it now.'

The marten fell silent, and suddenly the whispering that Mo had never forgotten came again. It surrounded him; it was everywhere. 'Be on your guard! Be on your guard, Bluejay!'

Be on his guard against what? The pale faces were looking at him. They were beautiful, but they blurred as soon as he tried to see them more distinctly.

'Orpheus!' whispered the pale lips.

And suddenly Mo heard Orpheus's voice. Its melodious sound filled the hollow tree like a cloyingly sweet fragrance. *'Hear me, Master of the Cold,'* said the poet. *'Hear me, Master of Silence. I offer you a bargain. I send you the Bluejay, who has made mock of you. He will believe that he has only to call on your pale daughters, but I am offering him to you as the price for the Fire-Dancer. Take him, and in return send Dustfinger back to the land of the living, for his tale is not yet told to its end. But the Bluejay's story lacks only one chapter, and your White Women shall write it.'* So the poet wrote and so he read, and as always his words came true. The Bluejay, presumptuous as he was, summoned the White Women, and Death did not let him go again. But the Fire-Dancer came back, and his story had a new beginning.

Be on your guard . . .

It was a few moments before Mo really understood. Then he cursed his stupidity in trusting the man who had nearly killed him once already. He desperately tried to remember the words Orpheus had written for Resa. Suppose he was trying to make an end of Meggie and Resa as well? Remember, Mo! What else did he write?

'Yes, you were indeed stupid,' Death's voice mocked him. 'But he was even more stupid than you. He thinks I can be bound with words, I who rule the land where there are no words, although all words come from it. Nothing can bind me, only the White Book, because you have filled its pages with white silence. Almost daily, the man it protects sends me a poor wretch he has killed as a messenger of his mockery. I would happily melt the flesh from your bones for that! But my daughters read your heart like a book, and they assure me that you will not rest until the man whom the Book protects is mine again. Is that true, Bluejay?'

The marten lay down on Dustfinger's unmoving breast.

'Yes!' whispered Mo.

'Good. Then go back and rid the world of that Book. Fill it with words before spring comes, or winter will never end for you. And I will take not only your life for the Adderhead's, but your daughter's too, because she helped you to bind the Book. Do you understand, Bluejay?'

'Why two?' asked Mo hoarsely. 'How can you ask for two lives in return for one? Take mine, that's enough.'

But the marten only stared at him. 'I fix the price,' it said. 'All you have to do is pay it.'

Meggie. No. No. Go back, Resa, Mo thought. Get Meggie to read what Orpheus wrote and go back! Anything is better than this. Go back! Quickly!

But the marten laughed. And once again it sounded like an old woman's laughter.

'All stories end with me, Bluejay,' Death said. 'You will find me everywhere.' And as if to prove it, the marten turned into the one-eared cat that liked to steal into Elinor's garden to hunt her birds. The cat jumped nimbly off Dustfinger's breast and rubbed around Mo's legs. 'Well, what do you say, Bluejay? Do you accept my conditions?'

And I will take not only your life for the Adderhead's but your daughter's too.

Mo glanced at Dustfinger. His face looked so much more peaceful in death than it had in life. Had he met his younger daughter on the other side, and Cosimo, and Roxane's first husband? Were all the dead in the same place?

The cat sat down in front of him and stared at him.

'I accept,' said Mo, so hoarsely that he could hardly make out his own words. 'But I make a condition too: give me the Fire-Dancer to go with me. My voice stole ten years of his life. Let me give them back to him. And there's another thing . . . don't the songs say that the Adderhead's death will come out of the fire?'

The cat crouched down. Fur fell red on the rotting leaves. Bones covered themselves with flesh and feathers again, and the gold-mocker with its bloodstained breast fluttered up to settle on Mo's shoulder.

'You like to make what the songs say come true, do you?' the bird whispered to him. 'Very well, I will give him to you. Let the Fire-Dancer live again. But if spring comes and the Adderhead is still immortal, his heart will stop beating at the same time as yours – and your daughter's.'

Mo felt dizzy. He wanted to seize the bird and wring its golden neck to silence that voice, so old and pitiless, with irony in every word. Meggie. He almost stumbled as he went to Dustfinger's side once more.

This time the White Women were reluctant to make way for him.

'As you see, my daughters don't like to let him go,' said the old woman's voice. 'Even though they know he will come back.'

Mo looked at the motionless body. The face was indeed so much more tranquil than it had been in life, and all of a sudden he wasn't sure whether he was really doing Dustfinger a favour by calling him back.

The bird was still on his shoulder, so light in weight, so sharp of claw.

'What are you waiting for?' asked Death. 'Call him!'

And Mo obeyed.

26

A Familiar Voice

What remains to him? Tall Time wonders. What thoughts
and smells, what names? Or are there only sensations and a
clutter of incompatible words?

Barbara Gowdy, *The White Bone*

They had gone. Had left him alone with all the blue that
clashed with the red of the fire. Blue as the evening sky,
blue as cranesbill flowers, blue as the lips of drowned men and
the heart of a blaze burning with too hot a flame. Yes, sometimes it was hot in this world too. Hot and cold, light and
dark, terrible and beautiful, it was everything all at once. It
wasn't true that you felt nothing in the land of Death. You felt
and heard and smelt and saw, but your heart remained
strangely calm, as if it were resting before the dance began
again.

Peace. Was that the word?

Did the guardians of this world feel it too, or did they long
for something else? The pain they didn't know, the flesh they
didn't dwell in. Perhaps. Or perhaps not. He couldn't tell

from their faces. He saw both there: peace and longing, joy and pain. As if they knew about everything in this world and the other, just as they themselves were made of every colour at once, all the colours of the rainbow merging into white light. They told him that the land of Death had other places too, darker than the one where they had brought him and where no one stayed for long – except for him. Because he called up fire for them.

The White Women both feared and loved fire. They warmed their pale hands at it, laughing like children when he made it dance for them. They *were* children, young and old at the same time, so old. They made him form trees and flowers of fire, a fiery sun and moon, but for himself he made the fire paint faces, the faces he saw when the White Women took him with them to the river where they washed the hearts of the dead. Look into it, they whispered to him. Look into it, then those who love you will see you in their dreams. And he leant over the clear blue water and looked at the boy and the woman and the girl whose names he had forgotten, and saw them smiling in their sleep.

Why don't I know their names any more? he asked.

Because we've washed your heart, they said. Because we've washed it in the blue water that parts this world from the other one. It makes you forget.

Yes. He supposed it did. For whenever he tried to remember he saw nothing but the blue, cool and caressing. It was only when he called up fire and its red glow spread that the pictures came again, the same pictures that he saw in the water. But his longing for them fell asleep before it had woken fully.

What was my name? he sometimes asked, and then they

laughed. Fire-Dancer, they whispered, that was your name and always will be, because you'll stay with us for all eternity and never go away like all the others, away to another life . . .

Sometimes they brought him a girl, a little girl. She stroked his face and smiled like the woman he saw in the water and the flames. Who's that? he asked. She's been here and went away again, they said she was your daughter.

Daughter . . . the word sounded like pain, but his heart merely remembered and did not feel it. It felt only love, nothing but love. There was nothing else any more.

Where were they? They had never before left him alone, not once since he had come here . . . wherever here was.

He had grown so used to the pale faces, to their beauty and their soft voices.

But suddenly he heard another voice, very different from theirs. He knew it. And he knew the name it was calling.

Dustfinger.

He hated that voice . . . or did he love it? He didn't know. He knew only one thing: it brought back everything he had forgotten – like a violent pain suddenly jolting his still heart into beating again. Hadn't that voice caused him pain once before, so much pain that it almost broke his heart? Yes, he remembered! He pressed his hands to his ears, but in the world of the dead you don't hear with your ears alone, and the voice made its way right inside him like fresh blood flowing into veins that had frozen long ago.

'Wake up, Dustfinger!' it said. 'Come back. The story isn't over yet.'

The story . . . he felt the blue pushing him away, he felt firm flesh surrounding him again, and a heart beating in a chest far too small for it.

Silvertongue, he thought. It's Silvertongue's voice. And suddenly all the names came back to him: Roxane, Brianna, Farid . . . and the pain was back again, and time, and longing too.

Lost and Back Again

For it so happens that I have never been able to convince
myself that the dead are utterly dead.

Saul Bellow, *Henderson the Rain King*

It was dark when Gwin woke Roxane. She still didn't like
the marten, but she couldn't bring herself to chase him
away. She had seen him sitting on Dustfinger's shoulder too
often. Sometimes she thought she still felt the warmth of his
hands on Gwin's brown coat. Since his master's death the
marten had allowed Roxane to stroke him. He never used to
let her do that before. But he also used to kill her chickens
before, and now he spared them, as if that were part of their
unspoken agreement – his thanks for her letting him, and no
other living creature, follow her when she went to his master.
Only Gwin shared her secret and kept her company when she
sat beside the dead man for an hour, sometimes two, losing
herself in the sight of his still face.

He's back! said Gwin's bristling coat as he jumped up on
her breast, but Roxane didn't understand. She pushed the

marten away when she saw how dark it still was outside, but he persisted, hissing at her and scratching at the door. Of course she thought at once of the patrols that the Milksop was only too likely to send to isolated farms at night. Heart thudding, she reached for the knife that lay under her pillow and threw on her dress, while the marten pawed more and more impatiently at the door. Luckily he hadn't yet woken Jehan. Her son was fast asleep. Her goose wasn't giving the alarm either . . . which was strange.

Barefoot, she went to the door, knife in hand, and listened, but there was nothing to be heard outside, and when she cautiously went out into the open air she felt as if she heard the night itself breathing deeply and regularly, like someone asleep. The stars shone down on her like flowers made of light, and their beauty hurt her weary heart.

'Roxane . . . '

The marten shot past her.

It couldn't be true. The dead did not come back, even when they had promised they would. But the figure emerging from the shadows near the stable was so very familiar.

Gwin hissed when he saw the other marten sitting on his master's shoulder.

'Roxane.' He spoke her name as if he wanted to savour it on his tongue, like something he hadn't tasted for a long time.

It was a dream, one of the dreams she had almost every night. Dreams in which she saw his face so clearly that she touched it in her sleep, and next day her fingers still remembered his skin. Even when he put his arms around her, carefully, as if he wasn't sure whether he had forgotten how to hold her, she didn't move – because her hands did not believe they would really feel him, her arms did not believe they could hold him again. But her eyes could see him. Her ears heard him breathing. Her skin felt his, as warm as if the fire were inside him, after he had been so terribly cold.

He had kept his promise. And even if he was coming to her only in a dream it was better than nothing . . . so much better.

'Roxane! Look at me. Look at me.' He took her face between his hands, caressed her cheek, wiped away the tears she so often felt on her skin when she woke. And only then did she draw him close to her, let her hands tell her that she wasn't just embracing a ghost. It couldn't be true. She wept as she pressed her face to his. She wanted to hit him for having left her for the boy's sake, for all the pain she had already felt on his account, so much pain, but her heart gave her away, as it had the first time he came back. It always gave her away.

'What is it?' He kissed her once more.

The scars. They were gone, as if the White Women had washed them away before sending him back to life.

She took his hands and laid them against his cheeks.

'Well, who'd have thought it!' he said, stroking his own skin with his fingers as if it were a stranger's. 'They've really gone! Basta wouldn't like that at all.'

Why had they let him go? Who had paid the price for him, as he had paid it for the boy?

Why did she ask? He was back. That was all that mattered, back from the place from which there was no return. Where all the others were. Her daughter, the father of her son, Cosimo . . . so many dead. But he had come back. Even if she saw in his eyes that, this time, he had been so far away that something of him was still left there.

'How long will you stay this time?' she whispered.

He did not answer at once. Gwin rubbed his head against his neck and looked at him, as if he too wanted to know the answer.

'As long as Death allows,' he replied at last, and placed her hand on his beating heart.

'What does that mean?' she whispered.

But he closed her mouth with a kiss.

28

A New Song

Bright hope arises from the dark
And makes the mighty tremble.
Princes can't fail to see his mark,
Nor can they now dissemble.
With hair like moleskin smooth and black,
And mask of bluejay feathers,
He vows wrongdoers to attack,
Strikes princes in all weathers.

Fenoglio, *The Bluejay Songs*

'The Bluejay's come back from the dead!' It was Doria who brought the Black Prince the news. The boy stumbled into his tent just before dawn, so breathless that he could hardly get the words out. 'A moss-woman saw him. By the Hollow Trees where the healers bury their dead. She says he's brought the Fire-Dancer back too. Please! May I tell Meggie?'

Incredible words. Far too wonderful to be true. All the same, the Black Prince set off at once for the place where the Hollow Trees grew – after making Doria promise not to tell anyone else what he had told him: neither Meggie nor her mother, neither Snapper nor any of the other robbers, not even his own brother, who was lying outside by the fire, fast asleep.

'But they say the Piper's heard about it too!' the boy faltered.

'That's unfortunate,' replied the Prince. 'Let's hope I find him before the Piper does.'

He rode fast, so fast that the bear was soon snorting with disapproval as he trotted along beside him. Why such haste? For a foolish hope? Why did his heart always insist on believing that there was a light in all the darkness? Where did he keep getting new hope from, after he had been disappointed countless times? *You have the heart of a child, Prince.* Hadn't Dustfinger always told him so? *And he's brought the Fire-Dancer back too.* It couldn't be true. Such things happened only in songs, and in the stories that mothers told their children in the evening to drive away night-time fears.

Hope can make you careless, he should have known that too. The Black Prince didn't see the soldiers until they emerged ahead of him through the trees. A good number of them. He counted ten. They had a moss-woman with them, her thin neck already rubbed sore by the rope on which they were pulling her along. Presumably they had caught her to make her lead them to the Hollow Trees, for hardly anyone knew the place where the healers buried their dead. They themselves, so rumour said, made sure that all the paths to it were hidden by undergrowth. But after helping Roxane to take Dustfinger there, the Black Prince knew the way.

It was a sacred place, but in her fear the moss-woman had indeed led the men-at-arms the right way. The crowns of the dead trees could already be seen in the distance. They rose, as grey as if morning had stripped them bare, among the oaks, which were still autumnal gold, and the Prince prayed the Bluejay wasn't there. Better to be with the White Women than in the Piper's hands.

Three men-at-arms came up on him from behind, swords in their hands. The moss-woman sank to her knees as her captors drew their own swords and turned to their new quarry. The bear reared up on his hind legs and bared his teeth. The horses shied, and two of the soldiers retreated, but there were still a great many of them – too many for a knife and a pair of claws.

'Well, guess what! Obviously the Piper's not the only one stupid enough to believe moss-women's gossip!' Their leader was almost as pale as the White Women, and his face was sprinkled with freckles. 'The Black Prince, none other! There was I cursing my luck, sent riding into this damn forest to catch a ghost, and who should stumble into my path but his black brother! The price on your head isn't as high as the price for the Bluejay, but it'll make us all rich men!'

'You're wrong there. Touch him and you'll be dead men instead.'

And his voice wakens the dead from sleep and makes the wolf lie down with the lamb . . . The Bluejay stepped out from behind a beech tree as naturally as if he had been waiting for the soldiers there. *Don't call me Bluejay – it's only a name from the songs!* He had said that to the Prince so often, but what else was he to call him?

Bluejay. They were whispering his name, their voices hoarse with terror. Who was he? The Prince had often wondered. Did he really come from the land where Dustfinger had spent so many years? And what kind of country was it? A land where songs came true?

Bluejay.

The bear roared him a welcome that made the horses rear, and the Jay drew his sword very slowly, as he always did, the sword that had once belonged to Firefox and had killed so many of the Black Prince's men. The face beneath the dark hair seemed paler than usual, but the Prince could see no fear in it. Presumably you forgot what fear was once you visited Death.

'Yes, as you see, I'm really back from the dead. Even if I still feel Death's claws in me.' He spoke dreamily, as if a part of him were still with the White Women. 'I'm willing to show you the way if you want. It's entirely up to you. But if you do prefer to live a little longer,' he added, flourishing his sword in the air as if he were writing their names, 'then let him go. Him and the bear.'

They just stared at him, and their hands, resting on their swords, trembled as if they were reaching out for their own deaths. Nothing is more terrifying than fearlessness, and the Black Prince went to the Bluejay's side and felt that the words were like a shield for them, the words sung quietly up and down the country . . . all about the White Hand and the Black Hand of Justice.

There'll be a new song now, thought the Prince as he drew his sword, and his heart felt so foolishly young that he could have fought a thousand men. As for the Piper's soldiers, they wrenched their horses' heads round and fled – from just two men. And the words.

When they had gone the Bluejay went over to the moss-woman, who was still kneeling in the grass with her hands pressed to her bark-brown face, and undid the rope from her neck.

'A few months ago one of you tended a bad wound I had,' he said. 'It wasn't you, was it?'

The moss-woman let him help her up, but she looked at him suspiciously. 'What do you mean by that? That we all look the same to human eyes?' she snapped. 'Well, we feel the same about you. So how am I supposed to know if I ever set eyes on you before?'

And she limped away without another look at her rescuer, who stood there watching her go as if he had forgotten where he was.

'How long have I been away?' he asked when the Black Prince joined him.

'Over three days.'

'As long as that?' Yes, he had been far away, very far away. 'Of course. Time runs differently when you meet Death, isn't that what they say?'

'You know more about it than I do now,' replied the Prince.

The Bluejay made no comment on that.

'Have you heard who I brought with me?' he asked at last.

'It's difficult for me to believe such good news,' said the Black Prince huskily, but the Bluejay smiled and ran a hand over the Prince's short hair.

'You can let it grow again,' he said. 'The man you shaved it for is breathing again. He's left his scars with the dead, that's all.'

It couldn't be true.

'Where is he?' His heart still ached from the night when he had kept watch with Roxane at Dustfinger's side.

'No doubt with Roxane. I didn't ask him where he was going. We were neither of us particularly talkative. The White Women leave silence behind them, Prince, not words.'

'Silence?' the Black Prince laughed, and embraced him. 'What are you talking about? They've left joy behind, pure joy! And hope, hope again at last! I feel younger than I've felt for years! As if I could tear up trees by the roots – well, maybe not that beech, but many others. By this evening, everyone will be singing that the Bluejay fears Death so little that he seeks it out, and the Piper will tear the silver nose off his face in a rage . . .'

The Bluejay smiled again, but his look was still grave – very grave for a man who has just come back from the dead unscathed. And the Black Prince realized that there was bad news behind the good news, a shadow behind all the light. But they didn't speak of that. Not yet.

'What about my wife and my daughter?' asked the Bluejay. 'Have they . . . have they already gone?'

'Gone?' The Black Prince looked at him in surprise. 'No. Where would they go?'

Relief and worry were mingled equally in the other man's face.

'Sometime I'll explain all that to you too,' he said. 'Sometime. But it's a long story.'

A Visitor to Orpheus's Cellar

So many lives,
So many things to remember!
I was a stone in Tibet

A tongue of bark
At the heart of Africa
Growing darker and darker. . .

Derek Mahon, *Lives*

When Oss, gripping Farid firmly by the back of his neck,
told him that Orpheus wanted to see him in his study at
once, he took two bottles of wine with him. Cheeseface had been
drinking like a fish ever since their return from the graveyard of
the strolling players, but the wine didn't make Orpheus talkative like Fenoglio, just extremely malicious and unpredictable.

As so often, he was by the window when Farid entered the
study. He was swaying slightly, and staring at the sheet of
paper that he'd studied over and over again these last few days,

cursing, crumpling it up and then smoothing it out again.

'There it is in black and white, every letter perfect as a pic-ture, and it sounds good too, it sounds damn good!' he said thickly as his finger kept tapping the words. 'So why, by all the infernal spirits, did the bookbinder come back again too?'

What was Cheeseface talking about? Farid put the wine bottles on the table and stood there waiting. 'Oss says you want to speak to me?' he asked.

Jasper was sitting beside the jug of pens, making frantic signals, but Farid couldn't work out what they meant.

'Ah yes, Dustfinger's angel of death.' Orpheus put the paper down on his desk and turned to him with a nasty smile.

Why on earth did you come back to him? Farid asked him-self, but he had only to think of the hatred on Meggie's face in the graveyard to answer his own question. Because you didn't know where else to go.

'Yes, I sent for you.' Orpheus looked at the door. Oss had followed Farid into the room, more silently than you would have thought possible for a man of his size, and before Farid had time to realize why Jasper was waving to him so franti-cally, Oss's meaty hands had seized him.

'So you haven't heard the news yet!' said Orpheus. 'Of course not. If you had I'm sure you'd have gone chasing straight off to him.'

Off to who? Farid tried to wriggle free, but Oss pulled his hair so hard that tears of pain came to his eyes.

'He really doesn't know. How touching.' Orpheus came so close to him that the smell of the wine on his breath made Farid feel sick.

'Dustfinger,' said Orpheus in his velvety voice. 'Dustfinger is back.'

Farid immediately forgot all about Oss's rough fingers and Orpheus's unpleasant smile. There was nothing in him but joy, like a violent pain, too much for his heart to bear.

'Yes, he's back,' Orpheus went on. 'Thanks to my words – but the rabble out there are saying the Bluejay brought him back!' he added, with a dismissive gesture to the window. 'Curse them. May the Piper make maggot-flesh of them all!'

Farid wasn't listening. His own blood was roaring in his ears. Dustfinger was back! Back!

'Let go of me, Chunk!' Farid drove his elbows into Oss's stomach and tugged at his hands. 'Dustfinger will turn his fire on you!' he shouted. 'That's what he'll do, the moment he hears you two didn't let me go to him at once!'

'Really?' Orpheus blew wine-laden breath into his face again. 'I'm more inclined to think he'll be grateful to me – or do you suppose he'd like you to bring him to his death again, you ill-omened brat? I warned him about you once before. He wouldn't listen to me then, but he'll have learnt better now, believe you me. If I had the book you came from here, I'd have read you back into your own story long ago, but sad to say it's out of print in this world.'

Orpheus laughed. He liked to laugh at his own jokes. 'Lock him in the cellar,' he told the Chunk, 'and as soon as it's dark you can take him out to the hill where the gallows stand, and wring his neck. No one will notice a few bones more or less up there.'

Jasper put his hands over his eyes when Oss picked Farid up and threw him over his shoulder. Farid shouted and kicked, but the Chunk hit him in the face so hard that he almost lost consciousness.

'The Bluejay! The Bluejay! *I* sent him to the White Women! I did it!' he heard Orpheus's voice ringing down the stairs after them. 'So why, by the devil's tail, didn't Death keep him? Didn't I make that high-minded idiot sound tempting enough with the finest words I could write?'

At the bottom of the stairs Farid made another attempt to free himself, but Oss hit him in the face again so hard that blood ran from his nose, and then shifted him to his other shoulder. A maid, alarmed, stuck her face out of the kitchen doorway as he carried Farid past – it was the little brown-haired girl who was always making up to him, but she didn't help him. How could she?

'Get out!' was all Oss growled at her before dragging Farid down to the cellar. He tied him to one of the pillars supporting Orpheus's house, stuffed a dirty rag into his mouth, and left him alone, but not without giving him another vigorous kick first.

'See you later, when it's dark!' he grunted before trudging back upstairs, and Farid was left behind with the cold stone at his back and the taste of his own tears in his mouth.

It hurt so much to know that Dustfinger was back, and all the same he would never see him again. But that's how it will be, Farid, he told himself. And, who knows, maybe Cheeseface is right. Perhaps you'd only bring him to his death again!

His tears burnt his face, so sore from Oss's blows. If only he could have called up fire to consume Orpheus, complete with his house and the Chunk, even if it meant that he too would burn! But he couldn't move his hands, and his tongue could not conjure up a word of fire, so he just crouched there sobbing, as he had sobbed on the night of Dustfinger's death, waiting for evening to come and Oss to fetch him and wring his neck, under the same gallows where he had dug up silver for Orpheus.

Luckily the marten had gone. Oss would certainly have killed him too. But presumably Jink had found his way to Dustfinger long ago. The marten would have sensed that he was back. Why didn't you sense it yourself, Farid? he wondered. Never mind, at least Jink was safe. But what would become of Jasper if he couldn't protect him any more? Orpheus had often shut the glass man up in a drawer without any light or sand, just for cutting paper clumsily or splashing ink on his master's sleeve!

'Dustfinger!' It did him good to at least try to whisper the name and know he was alive. How often Farid had imagined what it would be like to see him again. Longing made him tremble as if he were shaken by a fever. Which of the martens had jumped on Dustfinger's shoulder first to lick his scarred face, he wondered, Gwin or Jink?

The hours went by, and after a while Farid managed to spit out the gag. He tried gnawing through the rope that Oss had used to tie him up, but even a mouse could have done better. Would they look for him when he was lying dead and buried on the gallows hill? Dustfinger, Silvertongue, Meggie . . . oh, Meggie. He would never kiss her again. Not that he'd done that so very often recently. All the same . . . that bastard Cheeseface! Farid called down every curse he could remember on him – curses from this world, his own world, and the one where he had met Dustfinger. He shouted them all out loud, because that was the only way they worked – and fell silent in alarm when he heard the cellar door above him opening.

Was it evening already? Probably. How could anyone tell in this damp, mouldy hole? Would Oss break his neck like a rabbit's or simply press his fat hands down over his mouth until he couldn't breathe any more? Don't think about it, Farid, you'll find out soon enough. He pressed his back against the pillar. Perhaps he could at least kick Oss's nose in. A well-aimed kick at that stupid face when he was taking off Farid's bonds, and it would break like a dry twig. He desperately braced himself against the rough rope, but unfortunately Oss was good at tying people up. *Meggie! Can't you send a few words to save me as you did for your father?* Fear was making his arms and legs weak. He listened to the footsteps coming down the stairs. They were surprisingly quiet for the Chunk. And suddenly two martens scurried towards him.

'By all the fairies, that moon-faced fellow really has been making money,' a voice whispered in the darkness. 'What a grand house!' A flame began dancing, then a second, a third, a fourth, a fifth . . . five flames, just bright enough to light up Dustfinger's face – and Jasper sitting on his shoulder with a shy smile.

Dustfinger.

Farid's heart felt so light that he wouldn't have been surprised if it had simply floated out of him. But what had happened to Dustfinger's face? It looked different. As if all the years had been washed away, all the sad, lonely years, and—

'Your scars – they're gone!'

Farid could only whisper. Happiness muted his words like cotton wool. Jink jumped up to him and licked his bound hands.

'Yes, and would you believe it – I think Roxane misses

them.' Dustfinger reached the bottom step of the stairs and knelt down beside him. From above, agitated voices came down to them.

Drawing a knife from his belt, Dustfinger cut through Farid's bonds. 'Hear that? I'm afraid Orpheus is about to find out he has a visitor.'

Farid rubbed his numb wrists. He couldn't take his eyes off Dustfinger. Suppose he was only a ghost after all – or even worse, nothing but a dream? But then would Farid have felt his warmth, and the beating of his heart when he leant over him? No more of the dreadful silence that had surrounded Dustfinger in the mine. And he smelt of fire.

The Bluejay had brought him back. Yes, it must have been him. Whatever Orpheus said. Oh, he'd write his name in fire on the city walls of Ombra – Silvertongue, Bluejay, whichever name he liked! Farid put out his hand and timidly touched Dustfinger's face, so familiar and yet so strange.

Dustfinger laughed quietly and raised him to his feet. 'What is it? Do you want to make sure I'm not a ghost? I expect you're still afraid of them, aren't you? Suppose I *was* a ghost?'

By way of answer Farid flung his arms around him so impetuously that Jasper, with a sharp little scream, slid off Dustfinger's shoulder. Luckily he caught the glass man before Gwin did.

'Careful, careful!' whispered Dustfinger, putting Jasper on to Farid's shoulder. 'You're still as clumsy as a young calf. You have your glass friend to thank for my being here. He told Brianna what Orpheus was planning to do to you, and she rode to Roxane.'

'Brianna?' The glass man blushed when Farid put him on

his arm. 'Thank you, Jasper!'

Then he spun round. Orpheus's voice came ringing down the cellar stairs. 'A stranger? What are you talking about? How did he get past you?'

'It's the maid's fault!' Farid heard Oss protesting. 'The red-haired maid let him in through the back door!'

Dustfinger listened to the sounds above, smiling the old mocking smile that Farid had missed so much. Sparks were dancing on his shoulders and his hair. They seemed to be shining even under his skin, and Farid's own skin was hot, as if the fire had been licking it since he touched Dustfinger.

'The fire . . .' he whispered. 'Is it in you?'

'Maybe,' Dustfinger whispered back. 'I'm probably not entirely what I was, but I can do a few interesting new things.'

'New things?'

Farid looked at him, eyes wide, but the voice of Orpheus came down again from above. 'Smells of fire, does he? Let me past, you human rhinoceros! Is his face scarred?'

'No. Why?' Oss sounded offended.

And footsteps came down the stairs again, heavy and uncertain footsteps this time. Orpheus hated climbing either up or down stairs, and Farid heard him cursing.

'Meggie read Orpheus here!' he whispered as he pressed close to Dustfinger's side. 'I asked her to do it because I thought he could bring you back!'

'Orpheus?' Dustfinger laughed again. 'No, it was only Silvertongue's voice I heard.'

'His voice perhaps, but it was my words that brought you back!' Orpheus stumbled down the last few steps, his face red from the wine. 'Dustfinger. It really is you!' There was genuine delight in his voice.

Oss appeared behind Orpheus, fear and rage on his coarse face. 'Look at him, my lord!' he managed to get out. 'He's not human. He's a demon, or a spirit of the night. See those sparks on his hair? When I tried to hold on to him I almost burnt my fingers – as if the executioner had put red-hot coals in my hands!'

'Yes, yes,' was all Orpheus said. 'He comes from far away, very far away. Such a journey can change a man.' He was staring at Dustfinger as if afraid he might dissolve into thin air at any moment – or, more likely, into a few lifeless words on a sheet of paper.

'I'm so glad you're back!' he stammered, his voice awkward with longing. 'And your scars have gone! How amazing. I didn't write that. Well, anyway . . . you're back! This world is worth only half as much without you, but now it will all be as wonderful as it was when I first read about you in *Inkheart*. It was always the best of all stories, but now you'll be its hero – you alone, thanks to my art that took you home and now has even brought you back from the realm of Death!'

'Your art? More likely Silvertongue's courage.' Dustfinger made a flame dance on his hand. It took on the shape of a White Woman so distinctly that Oss cowered against the cellar wall in terror.

'Nonsense!' For a moment Orpheus sounded like a boy with hurt feelings, but he soon had himself in hand again. 'Nonsense!' he repeated, with more self-control this time, although his tongue was still rather thick from the wine. 'Whatever he told you, it isn't true. I did it all.'

'He didn't tell me anything. He didn't have to. He was there, he and his voice.'

'But I had the idea – and I wrote the words! He was only

my tool.' Orpheus spluttered the last word as furiously as if he were spitting it into Silvertongue's face.

'Ah yes . . . your words! Very cunning words, according to all I've heard from him.' The image of the White Woman was still burning on Dustfinger's hand. 'Maybe I ought to take those words to Silvertongue so that he can read them once more and find out what kind of part you intended him to play in all this.'

Orpheus stood up very straight. 'I wrote them like that for you, only for you!' he cried in an injured voice. 'That was all I cared about – for you to come back. Why would that book-binder interest me? After all, I had to offer Death something!'

Dustfinger blew gently into the flame burning on his hand. 'Oh, I understand you very well!' he said quietly, while the fire formed the shape of a bird, a golden bird with a red breast. 'I understand a good deal now that I've been on the other side, and I know two things for sure: Death obeys no words, and Silvertongue – not you – went to the White Women.'

'He was the only one who could call them. What was I supposed to do?' cried Orpheus. 'And he did it for his wife! Not for you!'

'Well now, I'd call that a good reason.' The fiery bird fell apart in Dustfinger's hand. 'And as for the words . . . to be honest, I like his voice so much better than yours, even if the sound of it didn't always make me happy. Silvertongue's voice is full of love. Yours speaks only of yourself. Quite apart from the fact that you're much too fond of reading words no one knows about, or forgetting a few you promised to read. Isn't that so, Farid?'

Farid just stared at Orpheus, his face rigid with hate.

'Be that as it may,' Dustfinger went on as the flame in his hand licked out of the ashes again, forming the shape of a tiny skull, 'I'll take the words with me. And the book.'

'The book?' Orpheus stepped back as if the fire on Dustfinger's hand had turned into a snake.

'Yes, *Inkheart*, you stole it from Farid, remember? That hardly makes it yours . . . even if you seem to be busily making use of it, from all I hear. Rainbow-coloured fairies, spotted brownies, unicorns . . . they say there are even dwarves in the castle now. What's the idea of all that? Weren't the blue fairies beautiful enough for you? The Milksop kicks the dwarves, and you bring unicorns here only to die.'

'No, no!' Orpheus raised his hands defensively. 'You don't understand! I have great plans for this story. I'm still working on them, but believe me, it will be wonderful! Fenoglio left so much unsaid, there was so much he didn't describe – I'm going to change it all, I'm going to improve it . . .'

Dustfinger turned his hand over and dropped the ashes on the floor of Orpheus's cellar. 'You sound like Fenoglio himself – but I'd guess you're much worse than he is. This world is spinning its own threads. The two of you only confuse them – take them apart and put them together again in ways that don't really fit, instead of leaving it to the people who live in the place to improve it.'

'Like who, for instance?' Orpheus's voice turned vicious. 'The Bluejay? Since when has he belonged here?'

Dustfinger shrugged his shoulders. 'Who knows? Perhaps all of us belong in more than one story. Now, bring me the book. Or shall I ask Farid to go and get it?'

Orpheus was staring at him as bitterly as a rejected lover.

'No!' he got out at last. 'I need it. The book stays here.

You can't take it away from me. I'm warning you. Fenoglio's
not the only one who can write words to harm you! I can—'

'I'm not afraid of words any more,' Dustfinger interrupted
impatiently. 'Neither yours nor Fenoglio's. And neither of you
was able to dictate how I'd die. Have you forgotten that?' He
reached into the air, and a burning torch grew from his hand.
'Bring me the book,' he said, giving it to Farid. 'Bring everything he's written. Every word.'

Farid nodded. He was back. Dustfinger was back!

'You must take the list too!' Jasper's voice was as slight as
his limbs. 'The list he made me draw up. Of all the words
Fenoglio used! I'm as far as the letter F.'

'Ah, not a bad idea! A list. Thank you, glass man.'
Dustfinger smiled. No, his smile hadn't changed. Farid was so
glad he hadn't left that behind with the White Women.

He put Jasper on his shoulder and went to the stairs. Jink
ran after him. Orpheus tried to bar his way, but he flinched
back when the torch left his glasses clouded and its flame
singed his silk shirt. Oss was braver than his master, but in
response to a whisper from Dustfinger the torch reached out
to him with fiery hands, and before Oss had recovered from
his fright Farid was past him. Agile as a gazelle, he leapt up
the stairs, his heart full of happiness, and the taste of sweet
revenge on his tongue.

'Jasper!' Orpheus called after him. 'I'm going to smash you
into such tiny splinters that no one will even be able to see
what colour you were!'

The glass man dug his fingers into Farid's shoulder, but he
didn't turn round.

'As for you, you lying little camel-driver –' Orpheus's voice
broke – 'I'll make you disappear into a story full of horrible

things specially written for you!'

The threat halted Farid for a moment, but then he heard Dustfinger's voice.

'Take care with your threats, Orpheus. If anything ever happens to the boy, or if he suddenly disappears – the fate you clearly intended for him this time – then I'll come to visit you again. And as you know, I never go anywhere without fire.'

'It was for you!' Farid heard Orpheus shouting. 'I did it all for you! Is this the thanks I get?'

Ironstone hurled furious abuse at Farid and his younger brother as soon as he realized what they were looking for in his master's study. But Jasper, unmoved, helped Farid to find first the book and then every scrap of paper that Orpheus had ever written on. Ironstone threw sand and sharp pens at them, he wished every imaginable disease that can afflict a glass man on Jasper, and finally flung himself heroically on the last sheet of paper that Jasper was rolling up on Orpheus's desk, but Farid merely pushed him roughly aside.

'Traitor!' shrieked Ironstone at his brother as Farid closed the door of the study behind him. 'I hope you're smashed into a thousand pieces!' But Jasper did not turn back, any more than he had at the threats made by Orpheus.

Dustfinger was already waiting at the front door of the house.

'Where are they?' asked Farid anxiously as he hurried towards him. There was no sign of Orpheus or Oss, but he could hear their angry voices.

'In the cellar,' said Dustfinger. 'I lost a little fire on the stairs. We'll be well into the forest before it goes out.'

Farid nodded, and turned as one of the maids appeared at the top of the stairs, but it wasn't Brianna.

'My daughter left,' said Dustfinger, as if he had read his thoughts. 'And I doubt if she'll be coming back to this house.'

'She hates me!' Farid stammered. 'Why did she help me?'

Dustfinger opened the door, and the martens scurried out. 'Perhaps she likes Orpheus even less than you,' he said.

30

Sootbird's Fire

Life's but a walking shadow, a poor player
That struts and frets his hour upon the stage
And then is heard no more. It is a tale
Told by an idiot, full of sound and fury
Signifying nothing.

William Shakespeare, *Macbeth*

Fenoglio was happy. He was happy even though Ivo and Despina had taken it into their heads to drag him off to the marketplace, where Sootbird was giving yet another show. The criers had been announcing it for days, and naturally Minerva wasn't letting the children go alone. The Milksop had had a platform specially made so that everyone could watch his court fire-eater's incompetent performance. Did they hope such things would make the people forget that the Fire-Dancer was back? Never mind, not even Sootbird could cast a shadow over Fenoglio's cheerful mood. His heart hadn't been so light since he had set off with Cosimo for the Castle of Night. And he wasn't going to think of what had happened after that; no, that chapter was closed. His story had struck up a new song, and whose doing was that? His own! Who else had brought the Bluejay into the story, the man who had run rings around the Piper and the Milksop and brought the Fire-Dancer back from the dead? What a character! Orpheus's creations were grotesque by comparison: garishly coloured fairies, dead unicorns, dwarves with a blue tinge to their hair. Yes, that calf's-head could bring such creatures into being, but only he, Fenoglio, could think up men like the Black Prince and the Bluejay. Well – he had to admit that only Mortimer had made the Bluejay flesh and blood. But the words had come first, all the same, and it was he who had written them, every single one!

'Ivo! Despina!' Where were they, dammit? It was easier to catch Orpheus's rainbow-coloured fairies than those children! Hadn't he told them not to run too far ahead? Children were swarming all over the street, coming out of all the houses to forget, at least for an hour or so, the burdens the world had laid on their frail shoulders. It was no fun being a child in these dark times. The boys had become men too young, and the girls found their mothers' sadness hard to bear.

At first Minerva hadn't wanted to let Ivo and Despina go. There were too many soldiers in town, and too much work waiting at home, but Fenoglio had won her over, although he didn't like the thought of the stink that Sootbird would be spreading again. On a day when he was so happy, however, he wanted the children to be happy too, and while Sootbird put on his pathetic show he would simply dream of Dustfinger breathing fire in Ombra's marketplace in the near future. Or he would imagine the Bluejay riding into Ombra and chasing the Milksop out of the gates like a mangy dog, knocking the silver nose off the Piper's face, and then, together with the Black Prince, founding a realm of justice, ruled by the people! Or, perhaps not entirely. This world hadn't reached that point yet, but never mind. It would be wonderful, it would move all hearts, and he, Fenoglio, had set the story on the course that would save it when he had written the first song about the Bluejay. In the end he'd done everything right! Well, perhaps Cosimo had been a mistake, but where would the excitement be in a story if it wasn't dark from time to time?

'Inkweaver! Where are you?' Ivo was waving to him impatiently. Did the boy think an old man could wriggle through this tide of children's bodies like an eel? Despina turned and smiled in relief when Fenoglio waved to her. But then her little head disappeared among all the others again.

'Ivo!' called Fenoglio. 'Ivo, keep an eye on your sister, can't you?'

Good heavens, he'd never known how many children there were in Ombra! Many of them were dragging their smaller brothers and sisters along after them as they flocked to the marketplace. Fenoglio was the only grown man to be seen, and few of the mothers had come. No doubt most of the children had stolen away on the sly – from workshops and stores, from housework or the stables. They had even come from the surrounding farms in their poor shabby clothes. Their clear voices were like the twittering of a flock of birds among the buildings. It was unlikely that Sootbird had ever had such an excited audience before.

He was already standing on the platform in the black and red costume worn by fire-eaters, but his clothes weren't patched together from rags like those of his brothers in the trade. They were made of the finest velvet, as befitted a prince's favourite. His ever-smiling face gleamed with the grease he used to protect it from the flames, but by now the fire had licked it so often that it looked like the masks Battista made from leather.

Sootbird was smiling again now as he looked down on the sea of little faces, crowding around the platform as eagerly as if he could release them from all their troubles, from hunger, from their mothers' sadness and from missing their dead fathers. Fenoglio saw Ivo at the very front, but where was Despina? Ah, over there, right beside her big brother. She waved excitedly to him, and he waved back as he joined the mothers waiting outside the houses. He heard them whispering about the Bluejay, and how he'd protect their children now that he had brought the Fire-Dancer back from the dead. Yes, the sun was shining on Ombra again. Hope was back, and he, Fenoglio, had given it a name. The Bluejay . . .

Sootbird took off his cloak, which was so heavy and expensive that the price of it could surely have fed all the children crowded there in the marketplace for months. A brownie climbed up to him on the platform, hung about with bags full of the alchemists' powders that the inept fire-eater fed to the flames to make them obey him. Sootbird still feared the fire. You could see that clearly. Perhaps he feared it now more than ever, and Fenoglio felt uncomfortable, watching him begin his show. Flames sprayed and hissed, breathing out poison-green smoke that made the children cough. The fire formed shapes: menacing fists, claws, snapping mouths. Sootbird had been learning. He no longer waved a couple of torches about and breathed flames so poorly that everyone whispered Dustfinger's name. The fire he was playing with, though, seemed to be quite different. It was fire's dark brother, a nightmare made of flames, but the children watched the bright, evil spectacle, both fascinated and frightened. They jumped when the fire reached red claws out to them, and groaned in relief when it turned to nothing but smoke – although the smoke still hung in the air, acrid and making their eyes water. Was what people whispered true? Was it a fact that this smoke befuddled your senses so that you saw more than was really there? Well, if so, it doesn't work for me, thought Fenoglio as he rubbed his smarting eyes. A set of wretched conjuring tricks, that's all I see!

Tears were running down his nose, and when he turned to wipe the soot and smoke out of his eyes he saw a boy come stumbling down the road from the castle. The lad was older than the children in the square, old enough to be one of Violante's beardless soldiers, but he wore no uniform. His face seemed strangely familiar to Fenoglio. Where had he seen him before?

'Luc!' the boy shouted. 'Luc! Run! All of you run!' He stumbled, fell, and crawled into a doorway just in time before the man pursuing him on horseback could ride him down. It was the Piper. He reined in his horse, while behind him a dozen men-at-arms surged along the road down from the castle. More of them came from every direction, Smiths' Street, Butchers' Street. They were coming out of every street and alley that led to the marketplace, riding in almost leisurely fashion on their great horses, armoured like their masters.

But the children kept staring up at Sootbird, suspecting nothing. They hadn't heard the boy's cries of warning. They didn't see the soldiers. They just stared at the fire while their mothers called their names. By the time the first of them turned it was too late. The men-at-arms drove back the weeping women, while more and more soldiers surged out of every street, enclosing the children in a ring of iron.

Horrified, the little ones spun around. Amazement suddenly turned to pure fear. And the way they cried! How was Fenoglio ever to forget that crying? He stood there helplessly, his back to a wall, while five men-at-arms kept their lances pointed at him and the women. No more were needed. Five lances to keep the little group in check. One of the women ran for it all the same, but a soldier rode her down. Then they formed a circle of swords as Sootbird, at a nod from the Piper, extinguished his flames and bowed to the weeping children with a smile.

They drove them up to the castle like a flock of lambs. Some of the little ones were so frightened that they ran here and there among the horses, and were left lying on the paving of the road like broken toys. Fenoglio called the names of Ivo and Despina, but his voice merged with all the others, with all the screaming and sobbing. When the men-at-arms let the mothers go, he too stumbled over to the children who had been left behind, bleeding. He stared at the pale faces, terrified of recognizing Despina or Ivo. They weren't there, but Fenoglio felt as though he knew the faces all the same. Such small faces. Too young to die, too young for pain and terror. Two White Women appeared, his angels of death. And the mothers bent over the children and closed their ears to that white whispering. Three were dead, two boys and a girl. They no longer needed the White Women to make the crossing to the other side.

The lad who had stumbled along the street shouting his warning in vain was kneeling beside one of the dead boys. He stared up at the platform, his young face old with hatred. But

Sootbird was gone, as if he had dissolved into the venomous smoke that hung in dense swathes over the marketplace. Only the brownie still stood there looking down, dazed, at the women bending over the children. Then, as slowly as if he had fallen out of ordinary time, he began collecting the empty bags left behind by Sootbird. A few of the women had run after the soldiers and the children they were taking away. The rest knelt there, wiped blood from the foreheads of the injured and felt their small limbs.

Fenoglio couldn't bear it any more. He turned and walked back, unsteadily, to the street where Minerva's house stood. Women came the other way, brought out of their houses by the screaming. They ran past him. It was too much! Too much! Minerva herself came running towards him. He stammered a few broken words, pointed to the castle. She ran after the other women.

It was such a fine day. The sun was as warm as if winter were still a long way off.

How was he ever going to forget that weeping? Fenoglio was amazed that his legs could still carry his tear-drenched heart up the stairs.

'Rosenquartz!' He supported himself on his table, looked for parchment, paper, anything he could write on. 'Rosenquartz! Damn it all, where are you?'

The glass man peered out of the nest where Orpheus's rainbow-coloured fairies lived. What the devil was he doing up there? Wringing their silly necks?

'If you were thinking of sending me off to spy on Orpheus again, forget it!' Rosenquartz called down to him. 'That Ironstone has gone and pushed the glass man Orpheus got to replace his brother out of the window! He's so badly smashed he looks like the remains of a wine bottle!'

'I don't need you to go spying!' snapped Fenoglio, in a voice muffled by tears. 'Sharpen me some pens! Get stirring that ink, and jump to it!'

Ah, this weeping.

He sank down on his chair and buried his face in his hands. Tears ran through his fingers and dripped on to the table. Fenoglio couldn't remember ever having cried so much. Even Cosimo's death had left him dry-eyed. Ivo! Despina!

He heard the glass man landing on his bed. Hadn't he told him not to jump out of the fairy nests? Never mind. Let him break his glass neck if he liked. So much misfortune! There must be an end to it, or his old heart really would break!

He heard Rosenquartz hastily clambering up the table leg. 'Here you are,' said the glass man in a muted voice, offering him a freshly sharpened quill.

Fenoglio wiped the tears away from his face with his sleeve. His fingers were shaking as he took the pen. The glass man pushed a piece of paper over to him and quickly set about stirring the ink.

'Where are the children?' he asked. 'Weren't you going to the marketplace with them?'

Another tear. It fell on the blank sheet, and the paper greedily soaked it up. Just like this wretched story, thought Fenoglio. Feeding on tears! Suppose Orpheus had written what happened in the marketplace? Folk said he had hardly left his house since the day of Dustfinger's visit to him, and he kept throwing bottles out of the window. In his rage, could he have written words to kill a few children?

Stop it, Fenoglio, don't go thinking about Orpheus! Write something yourself! He wished the paper wasn't so blank.

'Come on!' he whispered. 'Come here, words, will you? They're children! Children! Save them!'

'Fenoglio?' Rosenquartz was looking at him with concern. 'Where are Ivo and Despina? What's happened?'

But all Fenoglio could do was bury his face in his hands again. Where were the words to open those accursed castle gates, break the lances, roast Sootbird in his own fire?

It was Minerva who told Rosenquartz what had happened – when she came back from the castle without her children. The Piper had made another speech.

'He says he's tired of waiting,' Minerva told him in a toneless voice. 'He's giving us a week to bring him the Bluejay. Or he'll take our children away to the mines!'

Then she went down to her empty kitchen, where no doubt the bowls from which Ivo and Despina had eaten that morning still stood. And Fenoglio sat there in front of the blank sheet of paper which showed nothing but the traces of his tears. Hour after hour, until late into the night.

31

The Bluejay's Answer

'I *want* to be of use,' Homer began, but Dr. Larch wouldn't listen.

'Then you are not permitted to hide,' said Larch. 'You are not permitted to look away.'

John Irving, *The Cider House Rules*

Resa, her face pale, was writing in her best script. Just as she had long ago when she used to sit in men's clothes in Ombra marketplace, earning her living as a scribe. Orpheus's former glass man was stirring the ink for her. Dustfinger had brought Jasper back to the robbers' cave with him. And Farid too.

This is the Bluejay's answer, wrote Resa, with Mo standing beside her. *In three days' time he will give himself up to Violante, widow of Cosimo and mother of the rightful heir of Ombra. In exchange the Piper will set free the children of Ombra whom he tricked into his power. This agreement shall be sealed with his master's seal, so that they may be safe for all time.*

Only when this condition is met will the Bluejay be prepared

279

to cure the White Book that he bound for the Adderhead in the Castle of Night.

Meggie saw her mother's hand falter again and again as she wrote. The robbers stood around, watching her. A woman who could write . . . apart from Battista, none of them had that skill, not even the Black Prince. They had all tried to keep Mo from giving himself up – even Doria, who had done his best to warn the children of Ombra, and then had to watch as the Piper caught them, and his best friend Luc was killed.

In vain. Only one person hadn't even attempted to make Mo change his mind: Dustfinger.

It seemed almost as if he'd never been away, even though his face now had no scars. The same smile, enigmatic as ever, the same swift movements. He was here one moment, gone the next. Like a ghost. Meggie found herself thinking so again and again – yet at the same time she sensed that Dustfinger was more alive than ever before, more alive than anyone.

Mo looked her way, but Meggie wasn't sure that he really saw her. Ever since he had come back from the White Women, he seemed to be more the Bluejay than ever.

How could he give himself up as a prisoner? The Piper would kill him!

Resa had finished writing the letter. She looked at Mo as if hoping, just for a moment, that he would throw the parchment on the fire. But he only took the pen from her hand and added his sign under the deadly words – a pen and a sword forming a cross, in the way peasants made their mark instead of signing their names, because they didn't understand letters.

No.

No!

Resa bowed her head. Why didn't she say anything? Why

couldn't she shed some tears to make him change his mind this time? Had she used them all up on that endless night among the graves when they stood waiting in vain for him to come back? Did Resa know what Mo had promised the White Women in return for letting him and Dustfinger go again? 'I may soon have to go away,' was all he had told Meggie. And when she had asked, full of fear, 'Go away? Where to?' all he had said was, 'Don't look at me so anxiously! Wherever I go, I've visited Death and come back safe and sound. It can hardly be more dangerous than that, can it?'

She ought to have asked more questions, but Meggie had felt too glad, indescribably glad, that she hadn't lost him for ever . . .

'You're out of your mind! I've said so before and I'll say it again!'

Snapper was drunk. He stood there red in the face, his brusque voice breaking the oppressive silence so suddenly that the glass man dropped the pen Mo had handed him.

'Giving yourself up to the Adder's spawn in the hope that she can protect you from the Piper! He'll soon teach you better. And even if Silvernose leaves you alive – do you still think his master's daughter will help you to write in that damn book? You must have left your reason behind with Death! Her Ugliness will sell you for the throne of Ombra. And the Piper will send the children to the mines all the same!'

Many of the robbers murmured agreement, but they fell silent when the Black Prince went to Mo's side.

'How are *you* going to get the children out of the castle, then, Snapper?' he asked evenly. 'I don't like to think of the Bluejay riding through the castle gates of Ombra either, but if he doesn't give himself up, then what? I couldn't answer him when he asked that question, and believe me, I've been thinking of nothing else since Sootbird's performance! Are we to attack the castle with the few men we have? Will you lie in ambush when they take the children through the Wayless Wood? How many men-at-arms will be guarding them? Fifty? A hundred? How many dead children do you expect to see if you try freeing them that way?'

The Black Prince scrutinized the ragged men standing around him. Many of them lowered their heads, but Snapper defiantly thrust out his chin. The scar on his neck was as red as a fresh cut.

'I'll ask you once again, Snapper,' said the Black Prince quietly. 'How many children would die if we tried rescuing them like that? Would we manage to save even one?'

Snapper didn't reply. He just stared at Mo. Then he spat, turned, and marched away, followed by Gecko and a dozen others. But Resa took the written sheet of parchment without a word and folded it so that Jasper could seal it. Her face was as expressionless as if it were made of stone, like the face of Cosimo the Fair in the vault in Ombra Castle, but her hands were trembling so much that finally Battista went over and folded the parchment for her.

Three days once again. Mo had been gone with the White Women for that long as well – three endless days that had made Meggie believe her father was dead beyond recall this time, and it was her mother's fault. And Farid's too. She hadn't exchanged a single word with either of them during those three days, and when Resa approached her she had pushed her away.

'Meggie, why are you looking at your mother like that?' Mo had asked her on the first day after his return. Why? The

White Women took you away because of her, she wanted to say, and then didn't. She knew she was being unfair, but the coolness between her and Resa was still there. She couldn't forgive Farid either.

He was standing beside Dustfinger, and was the only one who didn't look depressed. Of course. Why would Farid care that her father was about to hand himself over to the Piper? Dustfinger was back. Nothing else counted. He had tried to make up their quarrel. 'Come on, Meggie. No harm came to your father – and he brought Dustfinger back!' Yes, that was all that interested him. And all that ever would.

Jasper had let sealing wax drop on to the parchment, and Mo pressed his stamp on it, the one he'd carved for the book of Resa's drawings. A unicorn's head. The bookbinder's seal for the robber's promise. Mo gave Dustfinger the letter, exchanged a few words with Resa and the Black Prince, and came over to Meggie.

When she was still so small that she stood no higher than his elbow, she would often push her head under his arm when something scared her. But that was long ago. 'What does Death look like, Mo?' she had asked. 'Did you really see Death himself?' The memory didn't seem to frighten him, but his eyes had immediately wandered far, far away. 'Death has many shapes, but the voice of a woman.' 'A woman?' Meggie had asked in surprise. 'But Fenoglio would never give a woman such a big part in his story!'

And Mo had laughed and replied, 'I don't think it was Fenoglio who wrote Death's part, Meggie.'

She wouldn't look up at him when he stopped in front of her. 'Meggie?' He put his hand under her chin so that she had to meet his eyes. 'Don't look so sad. Please!'

Behind him, the Black Prince took Battista and Doria aside. She could imagine what instructions he had for them. He was sending them to Ombra, to spread the news among the desperate mothers there that the Bluejay would not let their stolen children down. But what about his own daughter? Meggie thought, and was sure that Mo saw the accusation in her eyes.

Without a word, he took her hand and drew her away from the tents, away from the robbers, and away from Resa, who was still standing by the fire. She was wiping the ink from her fingers, wiping and wiping, while Jasper watched sympathetically. It was as if she were trying to wipe away the words she had written.

Mo stopped under one of the oak trees. Their branches stretched above the camp like a sky made of wood and yellowing leaves. He held Meggie's hand and ran his forefinger over it as if he were surprised to find how large it was now – yet her hands were still so much slimmer than his. A girl's hands . . .

'The Piper will kill you.'

'No, he won't. But if he tries I'll be happy to show him how sharp a bookbinder's knife is. Battista is going to sew me a place to hide a knife again, and believe me, I'll be very happy if that child-murderer gives me an opportunity to try it out on him.' Hatred fell over his face like a shadow. The Bluejay.

'The knife won't be any help. He'll kill you just the same.' She sounded stupid. Like a defiant child. But she was so afraid for him.

'Three children are dead, Meggie. Go to Doria and ask him to tell you again how they herded them together. They'll kill them all if the Bluejay doesn't give himself up!'

The Bluejay. He sounded as if he meant someone else. How dim did he think she was?

'It's not your story, Mo! Let the Black Prince save the children.'

'How? The Piper will kill them all if he tries.' There was so much fury in his eyes. And for the first time Meggie realized that Mo wasn't riding to the castle only to save the living children, but also to avenge the dead. That idea frightened her even more.

'Yes, I see. Perhaps you're right. Perhaps there really isn't any other way,' she said. 'But at least let me come with you! So that I can help you. Like in the Castle of Night!' It seemed only yesterday that Firefox had pushed her into Mo's cell. Had he forgotten how glad he'd been to have her with him? Had he forgotten that it was she, with some help from Fenoglio, who had saved him?

No, she was sure he hadn't. But Meggie had only to look at him to know that in spite of everything he would go alone this time. All alone.

'Do you remember the robber stories I used to tell you?' he asked.

'Of course. They all end badly.'

'And why? It's always the same. Because the robber wants to protect someone he loves, and they kill him for that. Right?'

Oh, he was so clever. Had he said the same thing to her mother? But I know him better than Resa, thought Meggie, and I know far more stories than she does. 'What about the highwayman poem?' she asked. Elinor had read it to her countless times. She could still hear her sighing, 'Oh, Meggie, why don't you read it aloud for a change? We don't have to mention it to your father, but I'd just love to see that highwayman galloping through my house!'

Mo smoothed the hair back from her forehead. 'What about it?'

'The girl he loves warns him about the soldiers, and he escapes! Daughters can do that kind of thing too.'

'Yes, indeed! Daughters are very good at rescuing their fathers. No one knows that better than me.' He had to smile. She loved his smile. Suppose she never saw it again? 'But don't you remember how the poem ends for the girl too?' he added.

Of course Meggie remembered. *Her musket shattered the moonlight, shattered her breast in the moonlight.* And in the end the soldiers killed the highwayman after all. *And he lay in his blood on the highway, with the bunch of lace at his throat.*

'Meggie . . .'

She turned her back to him. She didn't want to look at him any more. She didn't want to feel afraid for him any more. She simply wanted to be angry with him, that was all. Just as she was angry with Farid, angry with Resa. Loving someone merely meant pain. Nothing but pain.

'Meggie!' Mo took her shoulders and turned her round. 'Suppose I don't ride to Ombra – how would you like the song they'd sing then? *And one morning the Bluejay disappeared and was never seen again. But the children of Ombra died on the other side of the forest, like their fathers, and the Adderhead reigned for all eternity because of the White Book that the Bluejay had bound for him.*'

Yes, he was right. That was a terrible song, yet Meggie knew one that would be even worse: *But the Bluejay rode to the castle to save the children of Ombra, and died there. And although the Fire-Dancer wrote his name in the sky with fiery letters so that the stars whisper it every night, his daughter never saw him again.*

That was how it would turn out, yes. But Mo was listening to a different song.

'Fenoglio's not going to write us a happy ending this time, Meggie!' he said. 'I'll have to write it myself, but with actions instead of words. Only the Bluejay can save the children. Only he can write the three words in the White Book.'

She still didn't look at him. She didn't want to hear what he was saying. But Mo went on in the voice she loved so much, the voice that had sung her to sleep, comforted her when she was sick, and told her stories about the mother who had disappeared.

'I just want you to promise me something,' he said. 'You and your mother must look after each other while I'm gone. The two of you can't go back. There's no trusting Orpheus's words! But the Prince will protect you, and so will the Strong Man. He's promised me on his brother's life, and he's certainly a much better protector than I am. Do you hear, Meggie? Whatever happens, stay with the robbers. Don't go to Ombra, and don't follow me to the Castle of Night if they take me there! I wouldn't be able to think straight if I found out that you two were in danger. Promise me!'

Meggie bowed her head so that he wouldn't read her answer in her eyes. No. No, she wasn't going to make him any promises. And she was sure Resa hadn't either. Or had she? Meggie glanced over at her mother. She looked terribly sad. The Strong Man was beside her. Unlike Meggie, he had forgiven Resa once Mo had come back safe and sound.

'Meggie, please listen to me!' Usually Mo began making jokes when he thought the mood was getting too serious, but obviously that had changed too. His voice sounded as serious and down-to-earth as if he were discussing a school trip with her. 'If I don't come back,' he said, 'you must get Fenoglio to write words to take you and your mother home to Elinor in our old world. He can't have forgotten how to do it entirely, after all. Then you can read his words and take the three of you back, you and Resa – and your brother.'

'Brother? I want a sister.'

'Ah, do you?' Now he was smiling after all. 'Good. I want another daughter too. My first has grown too big to be picked up in my arms.'

They looked at each other, and there were so many words that Meggie wanted to say, but not one that really expressed what she was feeling.

'Who's going to take the letter to the castle?' she asked quietly.

'We don't know yet,' replied Mo. 'It won't be easy to find someone who'll be allowed access to Violante.'

Three days to go from the time Her Ugliness would get the letter and the Piper would accept the terms. Meggie hugged him as hard as she used to when she was a small child. 'Please, Mo!' she said softly. 'Don't go! Please! Let's all go back. Resa was right!'

'Go back? Meggie! Go back now, just when it's getting exciting?' he whispered to her. So he hadn't changed so very much after all. He still cracked jokes when he thought things were getting too serious. She loved him so much.

Mo took her face between his hands. He looked at her as if he were going to say something to her, and for a moment Meggie thought she read in his eyes that he was as frightened for her sake as she was for his.

'Believe me, Meggie!' he said. 'I'm also riding to that castle

288

to protect you. Someday you'll understand that. Didn't the two of us already know in the Castle of Night that I was binding the White Book for the Adderhead only to write those three words in it some time in the future?'

Meggie shook her head so hard that Mo hugged her again. 'Yes, Meggie!' he said quietly. 'Yes, we did.'

At Last

There, in the night, where none can spy
all in my hunter's camp I lie,
and play at books that I have read
till it is time to go to bed.
These are the hills, these are the woods,
these are my starry solitudes,
and there the river by whose brink
the roaring lions come to drink.

R.L. Stevenson, *The Land of Story Books*

Darius read wonderfully, although in his mouth the words
sounded very different from the way Mortimer would
have read them (and of course very different again from the
voice of Orpheus, that defiler of books). Perhaps Darius's art
was most like Meggie's. He read with the innocence of a child,
and it seemed to Elinor as if, for the first time, she saw the
boy he had once been – a thin, bespectacled boy who loved
books as passionately as she did, but with the difference that
for him the pages came to life.

Darius's voice was not as full and beautiful as Mortimer's, nor did it have the enthusiasm that lent Orpheus's voice its power. No, Darius took the words on his tongue as carefully as if they might break apart there, might lose their meaning if they were spoken in too loud and firm a tone. All the sadness of the world lay in Darius's voice: the magic of the weak, the quiet and cautious, and their knowledge of the pitiless minds of the strong . . .

The music of Orpheus's words amazed Elinor as much as on the day she first heard him read them. Those words didn't sound at all like the work of the vain fool who had thrown her books at the library walls. Well, that's because he stole them from someone else, thought Elinor, and then she thought of nothing more at all.

Darius's tongue didn't stumble once – perhaps because this time not fear but love made him read. He opened the door between the letters on the page so gently that Elinor felt as if they were stealing into Fenoglio's world like two children slipping into a forbidden room.

When she suddenly found a wall behind her she dared not believe what her fingers were feeling. *At first you think it's a dream.* Wasn't that how Resa had described it? Well, if this is a dream, thought Elinor, then I never intend to wake up! Her eyes greedily drank in the images suddenly flooding in on her: a square, a well, houses leaning against each other as if they were too old to stand up straight, women in long dresses (most of them very shabby), a flock of sparrows, pigeons, two thin cats, a cart and an old man shovelling garbage into it . . . heavens above, the stench was almost unbearable, but all the same Elinor breathed it in deeply.

Ombra! She was in Ombra! What else could her

surroundings be? A woman drawing water at the well turned and looked suspiciously at the heavy dark-red velvet dress Elinor was wearing. Oh, drat it! She had hired the dress from a theatrical costume agency, along with the tunic Darius was wearing. She'd asked for 'something medieval', and now here she stood looking as conspicuous as a peacock among a flock of crows!

Never mind. You're here, Elinor! When something pulled her hair rather roughly, tears of joy came to her eyes. With a practised move, she caught the fairy who was about to make off with a grey strand of it. How she'd missed those tiny, fluttering creatures! But hadn't they been blue? This one shimmered in all the iridescent colours of a soap bubble. Captivated, Elinor closed her hands around her catch and examined the fairy through her fingers. The little creature looked rather sleepy. This was wonderful! When the tiny teeth dug into her thumb and the fairy escaped Elinor laughed out loud, making two women put their heads out of the nearby windows.

Elinor!

She clapped her hand to her mouth, but she could still feel laughter like sherbet powder fizzing on her tongue. Oh, she was so happy, so idiotically happy. She hadn't felt like this since she was six years old and stole into her father's library to get at the books he wouldn't let her read. Perhaps you ought to drop dead here and now, Elinor, she told herself. At this very moment. How can things get any better?

Two men in colourful garments were crossing the square. Strolling players! They didn't look quite as romantic as Elinor had imagined the Motley Folk, but never mind . . . they were minstrels, and a brownie was carrying their instruments. His hairy face looked so bemused when he saw her that Elinor instinctively felt her nose. Had something happened to her face? No, surely her nose had always been that size, hadn't it?

'Elinor?'

She turned. Darius! For heaven's sake, she'd completely forgotten him. What was he doing under the rubbish cart?

Looking bewildered, he crawled out from between the wooden wheels and plucked a few not-very-clean blades of straw off his tunic. Oh, Darius! Of all places in the Inkworld, he had to land under a load of garbage! Just like him! He was a walking disaster area. And the way he was looking around him – as if he'd fallen among thieves. Poor Darius. Wonderful Darius. He was still holding the sheet of paper with Orpheus's words on it, but where was the bag with all the things they'd meant to bring?

Just a moment, Elinor, *you* were going to bring it. She looked around – and instead of the bag saw Cerberus beside her, snuffling at the strange paving stones with great interest.

'H-h-he'd have starved to death if we'd left him behind,' stuttered Darius, still brushing straw off his tunic. 'A-a-anyway I suppose he can lead us to his master, and maybe he'll know where we can find the others.'

Not a bad idea, Elinor told herself. I'd never have thought of that. But what was making him stammer again?

'Darius! You did it!' she whispered, hugging him so hard that his glasses slipped. 'Thank you! Thank you so, so much!'

'Hey, you there, where'd that dog come from?'

Cerberus pressed close to Elinor's legs, growling. Two soldiers were facing them. *The soldiers are worse than the highwaymen.* Hadn't Resa told her that too? *Most of them will kill for fun some time or other.*

Involuntarily, Elinor took a step back, but she just came up against the wall of the house behind her.

'Well, cat got your tongues?' One of the men punched Darius in the belly with his gloved fist, so hard that he doubled up.

'What do you think you're doing? Leave him alone!' Elinor's voice didn't sound half as fearless as she had hoped. 'That's my dog.'

'Yours?' The soldier approaching her had only one eye. Fascinated, Elinor stared at the place where the other eye had once been. 'Only princesses may keep dogs. Trying to tell me you're a princess?'

He drew his sword and ran the blade over Elinor's dress. 'And what sort of clothes are those? You think they make you look a fine lady? What seamstress made that dress? She ought to be put in the pillory, so she ought!'

The other soldier laughed. 'The strolling players wear such garments!' he said. 'She's a minstrel woman rather past her prime.'

'A minstrel woman? Nah, too ugly for that.' The one-eyed man scrutinized Elinor as if he were about to strip her dress off.

She longed to tell him what she thought of his own appearance, but Darius cast her a pleading glance, and the point of the sword pressed menacingly against her stomach as if the one-eyed soldier was thinking of boring a second navel in it. Look down, Elinor! Remember what Resa said. Women keep their eyes lowered in this world.

'Please!' With difficulty, Darius scrambled to his feet. 'We . . . we're strangers here. W-w-we come from far away . . .'

'And you come to Ombra?' The soldiers laughed. 'By the

Adderhead's silver, who'd come here of his own free will?'

The one-eyed man was staring at Darius. 'Take a look at this!' he said, lifting off his glasses. 'He's got the same kind of frame thing as Four-Eyes, the fellow that got the unicorn and the dwarf for the Milksop.'

Making a big performance of it, he perched the glasses on his own nose.

'Hey, take that off!' The other man uneasily retreated.

The one-eyed soldier blinked at him through one thick lens and grinned. 'I can see all your lies. All your black lies!'

Laughing, he threw the glasses at Darius's feet.

'Wherever you come from,' he said, reaching out for Cerberus's collar, 'you're going back without any dog. Dogs belong to princes. This one's an ugly brute, but the Milksop will like it all the same.'

Cerberus bit the gloved hand so hard that the soldier screamed and fell to his knees. The other man drew his sword, but Orpheus's dog wasn't half as stupid as he was ugly. With the soldier's glove still in his jaws, he turned and ran for his life.

'Quick, Elinor!' Darius swiftly snatched up his twisted glasses and dragged her away with him, while the soldiers, cursing, stumbled off in pursuit of the hell-hound. Elinor couldn't remember when she had last run so fast – and even if her heart still felt like a young girl's, her legs were the legs of a rather too stout old woman.

Elinor, this was not the way you imagined your first hours in Ombra, she told herself as she followed Darius down an alley so narrow that she was afraid of getting stuck between the houses. But even if her feet hurt, and she could still feel the tip of that one-eyed oaf's sword in her stomach – never mind! She was in Ombra! At last she was behind the letters on the page! That was all that mattered. And it was hardly to be expected that life would be as tranquil here as in her house at home – leaving aside the fact that it hadn't been so tranquil there either recently. Well, never mind that . . . she was here! She was here at last! In the only story with an ending that she really wanted to know, because all the people she loved were in it.

But it's a pity the dog has gone, she thought, as Darius stopped at the end of the alley, unsure which way to go. Cerberus's ugly nose would have come in very useful in this maze of alleyways, and she was probably going to miss him too. Resa, Meggie, Mortimer – she felt like shouting their names through the streets. Where are you? I'm here, I'm here at last!

But perhaps *they're* not here any more, Elinor, a voice inside her whispered, while the strange sky above them grew dark. Perhaps the three of them died long ago. Hush, she thought. Hush, Elinor. That thought wasn't allowed. It simply was not allowed.

33

Herbs for Her Ugliness

The soul is silent.
If it speaks at all
it speaks in dreams.

Louise Glück, *Child Crying Out*

Violante went down to the dungeons where the Milksop
had imprisoned the children several times a day, with two
maids who were still loyal to her, and one of the boys who
served her as soldiers. Child soldiers, the Piper called them,
but her father had made sure that these boys weren't children
any more when he had their fathers and brothers slaughtered
in the Wayless Wood. And the children in the dungeons soon
wouldn't be children either. Fear was making them grow up
fast.

The mothers stood outside the castle, begging the guards
at least to let them go in to see their youngest children. They
brought clothes, dolls, food, in the hope that at least some of
it might end up in the hands of their sons and daughters. But
the guards threw most of these things away, although Violante

297

kept sending her maids to them to collect what the mothers had brought.

Fortunately the Piper did at least allow her to do that. Fooling the Milksop was easy. He was even more stupid than his doll-like sister, and had never realized how Violante was spinning her web behind his back. But the Piper was clever, and only two things made it possible to manipulate him: his fear of the Adderhead and his vanity. Violante had flattered the Piper from the day he first rode into Ombra. She made out that she was glad he had come, saying she was tired of the Milksop's feeble stupidity. She told the Piper how he squandered money, and commissioned Balbulus to write out the Piper's dark songs on his best parchment and illuminate them (even though the commission made Balbulus so furious that he broke three of his most valuable brushes before her eyes).

After Sootbird had lured the children into the trap on the Piper's orders, Violante had praised the silver-nosed man for his wiliness – and was sick in her bedchamber later. Nor did she let him see that these days she couldn't sleep because she thought she heard the children crying in the dungeons by night. She wasn't letting him know that.

She had been just four herself when her father had her and her mother shut up in the Old Chamber in the Castle of Night, but her mother had taught her to hold her head high all the same. 'You've a man's heart, Violante,' her father-in-law had once told her. Sad, stupid old man. To this day she didn't know if he had been paying her a compliment or expressing disapproval. She knew only that all the things she most wanted belonged to men: freedom, knowledge, strength, cleverness. Power . . .

Was the thirst for revenge masculine too, or a wish to rule, or impatience with others? She'd inherited all those from her father.

Her Ugliness . . .

Her disfiguring birthmark had faded, but the name stuck. It was part of her, like her very pale face and ridiculously slight body. 'Her Craftiness, that's what they ought to call you,' Balbulus sometimes said. No one knew her better than Balbulus. No one saw through her more clearly, and Violante knew that whenever Balbulus hid a fox in one of his pictures he meant her. Her Craftiness. She was certainly crafty. The sight of the Piper made her physically ill, but she smiled at him as she had learnt to do from watching her father: with condescension mingled with a touch of cruelty. She wore shoes that made her look taller (Violante had always hated being so short) but she did nothing to make her face prettier, since it was her opinion that beautiful women might be desired but were never respected, certainly not feared. Anyway, she would have felt ridiculous with her lips painted red or her brows plucked to a narrow arch.

Some of the child prisoners were injured. The Piper had allowed Violante to send the Barn Owl to tend them, but there was no persuading him to let them go. 'Not until we've caught our bird,' he had replied to her request. 'They're here as bait for him!'

And Violante had seen it in her mind's eye – she saw them dragging the Bluejay to the castle once the mothers weeping down there outside the gates had given him away. He was bleeding like the unicorn that the Milksop had killed in the forest. That image remained with her, even clearer than the pictures that Balbulus painted, but in her dreams she saw another. In that one the Bluejay killed her father and set a crown on her head, on her mouse-brown hair . . .

'The Bluejay will soon be a dead man,' Balbulus had said to her only yesterday. 'I hope he'll at least ensure that his death makes a good picture.'

Violante could have struck him in the face, but her anger had never yet impressed him. 'Take care, Your Ugliness,' he had murmured to her. 'You're always giving your love to the wrong men. But at least the last one had blue blood.'

She should have had his tongue cut out for such impertinence – her father would have done it on the spot – but then who would tell her the truth, much as it might hurt? Brianna used to. But Brianna had gone.

Outside, the second night was falling on the children in the dungeons, and Violante had just asked one of her maids to bring her hot wine, hoping that for a few hours it would at least make her forget those little faces, the small hands clutching her skirt, when Vito entered her room.

'Your Highness!' The boy was just fifteen, and the oldest of her soldiers, the son of a smith. A dead smith, of course. 'Your former maidservant is at the gate. Brianna, that woman healer's daughter.'

Tullio cast Violante a doubtful glance. He had wept when she had turned Brianna out. For that she wouldn't allow him to come to her room for more than two days.

Brianna. Had Violante's own thoughts summoned her? The name still sounded so comforting. She'd probably spoken it more often than her son's. Why was her silly heart beating faster? Had it already forgotten how much pain the girl had caused it? Her father was right: the heart was a weak, changeable thing, bent on nothing but love, and there could be no more fatal mistake than to make it your master. Reason must be in charge. It comforted you for the heart's foolishness, it sang mocking songs about love, derided it as a whim of nature, transient as flowers. So why did she still keep following her heart?

It was her heart that leapt up at the sound of Brianna's name, while her reason asked: what does she want here? Does she miss her comfortable life? Is she tired of being a maid scrubbing floors for Four-Eyes, who bows so low to the Milksop that his chin almost collides with his plump knees? Or is she going to beg me to let her go down into the vault to kiss my dead husband's mouth?

'Brianna says she's bringing herbs from her mother for the children in the dungeon. But she'll give them only to you in person.'

Tullio looked pleadingly at her. He had no pride, but a loyal heart. Too loyal. Yesterday a few of the Milksop's friends had shut him in the dog-pens with the hounds again. Her own son had been with them.

'Good. Go and bring her in, Tullio!' Your voice can give you away, but Violante knew how to make hers sound indifferent. Only once had she shown what she really felt, when Cosimo had come back – and then she felt all the more ashamed to find that he preferred her maidservant to her.

Brianna.

Tullio shot eagerly off, and Violante patted her hair, which was severely pinned back, and looked dubiously at her dress and the jewels she was wearing. Brianna had that effect on people. She was so beautiful that everyone felt clumsy and colourless in her presence. Violante had once liked that. She had hidden behind Brianna's beauty, relishing the fact that her maid made others feel as she herself always did – ugly. It had pleased her that so much beauty served her, admired her, perhaps even loved her.

Tullio was smiling foolishly all over his furry face as he came back with Brianna. She hesitated as she entered the room where she had spent so many hours. It was said that she wore a coin with Cosimo's picture around her neck, and kissed it so often that by now the face could hardly be made out. But grief had only made her more beautiful. How could that be? How could there be any justice in the world if even beauty wasn't fairly shared out?

Brianna sank down in a low curtsey – no one could do it more charmingly – and handed Violante a basket full of herbs. 'My mother has heard from the Barn Owl that some of the children are hurt, and many won't eat. These herbs may help. She has written to tell you how they work and how they must be given.' Brianna took a sealed letter out from under the leaves, handing it to Violante with another curtsey.

A seal, for a healer's instructions?

Violante sent away the maid who was busy turning back her bed – she didn't trust the girl – and picked up her new reading glasses. The same glazier who had made a new frame for the glasses worn by Four-Eyes – a gold frame, of course – had made hers. She had paid him with her last ring. The glasses did not reveal lies to her, as it was said those that Four-Eyes wore did. Balbulus's lettering was not much clearer than when seen through the beryl she normally used, but at least the world wasn't red any more, and she could see better with both eyes at once, even though she couldn't wear the glasses for too long without straining her eyes. 'You read too much!' Balbulus was always saying, but what was she to do? Without words she would die, she'd simply die, even faster than her mother had done.

The seal of the letter was a unicorn's head. Whose seal was that?

Violante broke it – and instinctively glanced at the door when she realized who had written to her. Brianna followed her glance. She had lived in this castle long enough to know that the walls and doors had ears, but fortunately written words made no sound. Nonetheless, Violante felt as if she could hear the Bluejay's voice as she read – and she understood exactly what he was telling her, even if he had hidden his real words behind the written ones with great skill.

The written words spoke of the children and how the Bluejay was giving himself up in exchange for their freedom. They promised her father that the White Book would be cured if the Piper let the children go. But the hidden words said something else, something that only she could read between the lines. They said that at last the Bluejay was ready to strike the bargain she had offered him beside Cosimo's coffin.

He would help her to kill her father.

We can do it easily together.

Could they really? She lowered the letter. What had she been thinking when she made that promise?

She sensed Brianna's eyes on her, and abruptly turned her back to the girl. *Think, Violante!* She pictured what would happen, step by step, image by image, as if leafing through one of Balbulus's books.

Her father would come to Ombra as soon as the Bluejay had given himself up. That much was certain. After all, he still hoped that the man who had bound the White Book for him could cure its ills. And as he trusted no one else with the

Book, he would have to bring it to the Bluejay himself. Of course, her father would come with the intention of killing the Jay. He was desperate, half crazed with what the rotting pages were doing to him, and even on the journey he would be thinking how to put his enemy to death in the most painful possible way. But first he must hand the book over to that enemy. And as soon as the Bluejay had the White Book in his hands it would all depend on her. How much time does it take to write three words? She must gain him that time. Just three words, a few seconds when he was unobserved, a pen and some ink, and then not the Bluejay but her father would die – and Ombra would be hers.

Violante felt her breath coming fast, her own blood roaring in her ears. Yes, it could work. But it was a dangerous plan, and far more dangerous for the Bluejay than for her. Nonsense, it *will* work, said her reason, her cool reason, but her heart was beating so fast that she felt dizzy. Once he's in the castle, her reason kept asking, how are you going to protect him? What about the Piper and the Milksop?

'Your Highness?'

Brianna's voice sounded different. As if something in her had broken. Good! I hope she sleeps badly, thought Violante. I hope her beauty fades while she's on her knees scrubbing floors. But when she turned and looked at Brianna, all she wanted was to hold her close and laugh with her again, the way they used to laugh.

'There's something else I'm to tell you.' Brianna didn't lower her eyes when she looked at Violante. She was still as proud as ever. 'These herbs will taste very bitter. They will help only if you use them properly. In the worst case, they can even be deadly. It's all up to you.'

As if she had to have that explained to her! But Brianna was still looking at her. Protect him, said her eyes. If you don't, then all is lost!

Violante stood up straight as a ramrod.

'I understand you very well!' she said brusquely. 'I am sure that the children will be very much better in three days' time. Their troubles will be over, and I'll use the herbs with all the necessary care. Take that message back. And now go. Tullio will escort you back to the gates.'

Brianna sank into another curtsey. 'Thank you. I know they'll be in the best of hands with you.' She rose, hesitantly. 'I know you have plenty of maids,' she added quietly, 'but if you ever want my company again, please send for me! I miss you.' She uttered the last words so softly that Violante could hardly hear them.

I miss you too. The words were on the tip of Violante's tongue, but she didn't let them pass her lips. Be quiet, heart, you stupid forgetful thing.

'Thank you,' she said. 'But I don't feel like hearing songs at present.'

'No. Of course not.' Brianna turned as pale as when Violante had hit her, after she had been with Cosimo and then lied to Violante about it. 'But who's reading to you? Who's playing with Jacopo?'

'I'm reading to myself.' Violante was proud of the cold rejection in her voice, although her heart felt so differently. 'As for Jacopo, I don't see much of him. He goes around wearing a tin nose that he had the smith make him, he sits on the Piper's knee and tells everyone he'd never have been stupid enough to let Sootbird entice *him* into the marketplace.'

Brianna put her hand to her throat. She really did wear a

coin there. 'Do you sometimes see him too?'

'See who?'

'Cosimo. I see him every night in my dreams. And in the day I sometimes feel as if he were standing behind me.'

Stupid creature. In love with a dead man. What did she still love about him? His beauty was food for worms now, and what else was there in Cosimo for anyone to love? No, Violante had buried her love with him. It had gone away like the silly happiness you feel after a jug of wine.

'Would you like to go down to the vault?' Violante couldn't believe that her mouth had uttered those words.

Brianna was looking at her incredulously.

'Tullio will take you down. But don't expect too much – you'll find no one but the dead there. Tell me, Brianna,' she added (ugly Violante, cruel Violante), 'were you disappointed when the Bluejay brought your father and not Cosimo back from the dead?'

Brianna bent her head. Violante had never been able to find out whether she loved her father or not. 'I would very much like to go down to the vault,' she said quietly. 'If you'll allow me.'

Violante nodded to Tullio, and he took Brianna's hand.

'Three more days and everything will be all right,' said Violante, when Brianna was at the door. 'Injustice is not immortal. It can't be!'

Brianna nodded, as abstractedly as if she hadn't been listening. 'Send for me,' she said again.

Then she was gone, and Violante was already missing her as the door closed. So? she thought. Is there any feeling you understand better? Losing people and missing them – that's what your life consists of.

She folded up the Bluejay's letter and went over to the tapestry that had hung in her bedchamber since she first slept there at the age of seven. It showed a unicorn hunt, woven in a time when unicorns had been creatures of fantasy and were not carried dead through Ombra after a hunt. But even the unicorns of fantasy had had to die. Innocence doesn't live long in any world. Ever since Violante had met the Bluejay the unicorn had reminded her of him. She had seen the same innocence in his face.

How are you going to protect him, Violante? How?

Wasn't it the same in all stories? Women didn't protect the unicorns. They brought them to their death.

The guards at her door looked tired, but they hastily straightened their backs when she came out. Child soldiers. They both had small siblings down in the dungeon.

'Wake the Piper!' she told them. 'Tell him I have important news for my father.'

Her father. The word never failed to take effect, but none tasted more unpleasant to her. Just six letters, and she felt small and weak and so ugly that people avoided looking at her. She remembered her seventh birthday only too well. It was the only day when her father had obviously been happy to have such an unattractive child. 'A good revenge!' he had told her mother. 'Giving my ugliest daughter to my enemy's handsome son for his wife.'

Father.

When would there be no one she had to call father any more?

She pressed the Bluejay's letter to her heart.

Soon.

34

Burnt Words

Time seemed to have just gone, in big clumps, or all the day was happening at once, or something, I was wondering so hard about what was to come, I was watching so hard the differences from our normal days. I wished I had more time to think, before she went right down, all the way down; my mind was going breathless, trying to get all its thinking done.

Margo Lanagan, *Black Juice*

They were setting off at sunrise. The Piper had accepted Mo's conditions: the children of Ombra would be set free as soon as the Bluejay kept his promise and handed himself over to the Adderhead's daughter. Some of the robbers were going to disguise themselves as women and wait outside the castle with the mothers, and Dustfinger would accompany Mo to Ombra as a fiery warning to the Piper. But the Bluejay would ride into the castle alone.

Don't call him that, Meggie, she told herself.

There were only a few hours now until dawn. The Black

Prince was sitting by the fire, wide awake, with Battista and Dustfinger, who didn't appear to need any sleep at all now that he was back from the dead. Farid was sitting beside him, of course, and Roxane. But Dustfinger's daughter had moved into Ombra Castle. Violante had taken Brianna back on the morning when the Piper had announced his agreement with the Bluejay.

Mo wasn't sitting by the fire with them. He had gone to lie down and get some sleep, and Resa was with him. How could he sleep tonight? The Strong Man was sitting outside the tent as if he must at least keep watch over the Bluejay.

'You should sleep too, Meggie,' Mo had told her when he saw her sitting a little way from the others under the trees, but Meggie had only shaken her head. It was rainy, and her clothes were as damp and chilly as her hair, but it wasn't much better inside the tents, and she didn't want to lie there with the rain telling her how the Piper would greet her father.

'Meggie?' Doria sat down in the wet grass beside her. His hair was wavy from the rain. 'Are you riding to Ombra too?'

She nodded. Farid glanced at them.

'I'll steal into the castle as soon as your father has ridden through the door, I promise you,' said Doria. 'And Dustfinger will stay near the castle too. We'll protect him.'

'What are you saying?' Meggie's voice sounded sharper than she had intended. 'You can't protect him, not just the two of you! The Piper will kill him. Are you thinking, she's only a girl, tell her lies to comfort her? I was with my father in the Castle of Night. I've faced the Adderhead. They'll kill him!'

Doria did not reply. He stayed silent for a long time, and she felt sorry she'd snapped at him like that. She wanted to say so, but she too remained silent, her head bent so that he wouldn't see the tears she'd been holding back for hours. What he'd said had started them flowing. And now he'd be thinking, she's a girl, she cries.

She felt Doria's hand on her hair. He was stroking it as gently as if to wipe away the rain. 'He won't kill him,' he whispered to her. 'The Piper is far too frightened of the Adderhead for that!'

'But he hates my father! Hate is sometimes stronger than fear! And if the Piper doesn't kill him, then the Milksop will do it, or the Adderhead himself. He'll never get out of that castle alive, never!'

How her hands were shaking – as if all her fear was in her fingers. But Doria clasped them so firmly in his own hands that they couldn't shake any more. He had strong hands, although his fingers weren't much longer than her own. Farid's hands were slender by comparison.

'Farid says you saved your father once with words when he was wounded. He says you did it just with words.'

Yes, but she had no words this time.

Words . . .

'What is it?' Doria let go of her hands and looked at her with a question in his eyes. Farid was still watching them, but Meggie ignored him. She planted a kiss on Doria's cheek. 'Thank you!' she said, quickly getting to her feet.

Of course he didn't understand what she was thanking him for. Words. The words that Orpheus had written! How could she have forgotten them?

She ran through the wet grass to the tent where her parents were sleeping. Mo will be terribly angry, she thought, but he'll live! Hadn't she read what would happen next into this story more than once already? It was time to do it again, even if that meant it wouldn't end as Mo wanted. The Black Prince would just have to tell the rest of it. He'd find a way to make it turn out well, even without the Bluejay's aid. For the Bluejay must leave – before her father died with him.

The Strong Man had nodded off. His head had sunk on to his chest, and he was snoring slightly as Meggie crept past him.

Her mother was awake. She had been crying.

'I need to talk to you!' Meggie whispered to her. 'Please!'

Mo was fast asleep. Resa cast a glance at his sleeping face and then followed Meggie outside. They still weren't speaking to each other very much. Meggie found it impossible to forget that night among the graves. Yet now she was about to do exactly what her mother had intended when she rode to Ombra in secret.

'If it's about tomorrow,' said Resa, taking her hand, 'don't tell anyone, but I'm going to Ombra with them, even though your father doesn't want me to. I want at least to be near him when he rides into the castle . . .'

'He's not going to ride into the castle.'

Rain was still falling through the fading leaves as if the trees were shedding tears, and Meggie longed for Elinor's garden. The rain sounded so peaceful there. Here it whispered of nothing but death and danger. 'I'm going to read the words.'

Dustfinger turned, and for a moment Meggie was afraid he could see what she planned to do in her face and tell Mo, but he turned away again and kissed Roxane's black hair.

'What words?' Resa looked at her blankly.

'The words Orpheus wrote for you!' The words for which Mo almost died, she wanted to add. Now they would save his life.

Resa looked back at the tent where Mo was sleeping. 'I

311

don't have them any more,' she said. 'I burnt them when your father didn't come back.'

No.

'They couldn't have protected him anyway!'

A glass man appeared among dripping wet nettles, pale green, like many of the glass men who still lived in the forest. He sneezed and scurried away in alarm at the sight of Meggie and Resa.

Her mother placed her hands on Meggie's shoulders. 'He didn't want to come with us, Meggie! He told Orpheus to write something just for us. Your father wants to stay, even now, and neither you nor I can force him to go back. He'd never forgive us.'

Resa tried to stroke her daughter's wet hair back from her forehead, but Meggie pushed her hand away. It couldn't be true. She was lying. Mo would never stay here without his wife and daughter . . . would he?

'And perhaps he's right. Perhaps everything will turn out well,' said her mother quietly. 'And one day we'll be telling Elinor how your father saved the children of Ombra.' Resa's voice didn't sound half as hopeful as her words. 'Bluejay,' she whispered as she glanced at the men sitting by the fire. 'The first present your father ever gave me was a bookmark made of bluejay feathers. Isn't that strange?'

Meggie didn't answer. And Resa caressed her wet face once more and went back to the tent.

Burnt.

It was still dark, but a few freezing fairies were already beginning to dance. Mo would soon be setting out, and there was nothing that could stop him. Nothing.

Battista was sitting alone between the roots of the great oak which the guards climbed at night. You could see almost as far as Ombra from its highest branches. He was making a new mask. Meggie saw the blue feathers in his lap and knew who would soon be wearing it.

'Battista?' Meggie knelt down beside him. The ground was cold and damp, but the moss among the roots was as soft as the cushions in Elinor's house.

He looked at her, his eyes full of sympathy. His glance was even more comforting than Doria's hands. 'Ah, the Bluejay's daughter,' he said in the voice that the Strong Man called Battista's marketplace voice. 'What a beautiful sight at such a dark hour. I've sewn your father a good place to hide a sharp knife. Can a poor strolling player ease your heart in some other way?'

Meggie tried to smile. She was so tired of tears. 'Can you sing me a song? One of the songs the Inkweaver wrote about the Bluejay? It has to be one of those! The best you know. A song full of power and . . .'

'Hope?' Battista smiled. 'Of course. I could fancy such a song too. Even if,' he added, lowering his voice to a conspiratorial tone, 'even if your father doesn't like having them sung when he's around. But I'll sing it so quietly that my voice won't wake him. Let's see, which is the right song for this dark night?' He thoughtfully stroked the mask on his lap. It was nearly finished. 'Yes,' he whispered at last. 'I know!' And he began singing in a soft voice:

Piper, beware, your end is near,
The Adder's power dwindles.
He writhes, he goes in mortal fear,
Nothing his strength rekindles.

Though you seek the Jay in country and town,
No sword can wound him, no hound run him down,
And when you think you'll succeed in your quest,
You find that the bird has flown the nest.

Yes, those were the right words. Meggie got Battista to sing them to her until she could remember every line. Then she sat down a little way from everyone else, under the trees, where the firelight still kept the darkness of night away, and wrote the song down in the notebook that Mo had bound for her long ago, in that other life, after a quarrel that now seemed so strange. *Meggie, you'll lose yourself in the Inkworld.* Didn't he say something like that to her at the time? And now he himself didn't want to leave this world; he wanted to stay here alone, without her.

Words written down in black and white. It was a long, long time since she'd read anything aloud. When did she last do it? When she brought Orpheus here? Don't think about that, Meggie. Think of the other times, the Castle of Night, the words that helped when Mo was wounded . . .

Piper, beware, your end is near.

Yes, she could still do it. Meggie felt the words gathering weight on her tongue as she wove them into her surroundings . . .

The Adder's power dwindles.
He writhes, he goes in mortal fear,
Nothing his strength rekindles . . .

She sent the words to find Mo in his sleep, made him armour out of them, armour that even the Piper and his dark master couldn't pierce . . .

> *Though you seek the Jay in country and town,*
> *No sword can wound him, no hound run him down,*
> *And when you think you'll succeed in your quest,*
> *You find that the bird has flown the nest.*

Meggie read Fenoglio's song over and over again. Until the sun rose.

35

The Next Verse

Through this toilsome world, alas!
Once and only once I pass;
If a kindness I may show;
If a good deed I may do
To a suffering fellow man,
Let me do it while I can.
No delay, for it is plain
I shall not pass this way again.

Anonymous, *I Shall Not Pass This Way Again*

It was a cold day, misty and colourless, and Ombra looked as if it were wearing a grey dress. The women had gone to the castle at daybreak, silent as the day itself, and now they were standing there and waiting without a word.

There was not a cheerful sound to be heard, no laughter, no weeping. It was simply quiet. Resa stood with the mothers as if she too were waiting for a child to come back, instead of expecting to lose her husband. Did the baby she was carrying under her aching heart sense its mother's despair this morning?

Suppose it never saw its father? Had that thought ever made Mo hesitate? She hadn't asked him.

Meggie stood beside her, her face under such rigid control that it frightened Resa more than if she had been crying. Doria was with her, dressed as a maidservant with a headscarf over his brown hair, because boys of his age were conspicuous in Ombra now. His brother hadn't come with them. All Battista's skill with disguises couldn't have made the Strong Man look like a woman, but more than a dozen robbers had been able to steal past the guards at the gate with their faces shaved, wearing stolen dresses and with scarves over their heads. Even Resa didn't notice them among all the women. The Black Prince had told his men to go to the mothers as soon as their children were free and persuade them to bring their sons and daughters to the forest the next day, so that the robbers could hide them in case the Piper broke his word and came to take them away to the mines after all. For who was going to ransom them a second time, once the Bluejay was caught?

The Black Prince himself hadn't come to Ombra with them. His dark face would have attracted far too much attention. Snapper, who had opposed Mo's plan to the last, had also stayed in the camp, like Roxane and Farid. Of course Farid had wanted to go with the others, but Dustfinger had forbidden it, and after what had happened on Mount Adder Farid did not go against such orders.

Resa glanced at Meggie again. She knew that if she could find any comfort today it would be only in her daughter. Meggie was grown-up now, Resa realized that this morning. I don't need anyone, said her face. It said so to Doria, who was still standing beside her, to her mother, and perhaps above all to her father.

A whisper ran through the waiting crowd. Reinforcements joined the guards on the castle walls, and Violante appeared behind the battlements above the gates, so pale that it looked as if the rumours about her were true: the Adderhead's daughter, they said, almost never left her dead husband's castle. Resa had never seen Her Ugliness before. But of course she had heard of the mark that had disfigured her face like a brand since birth, and then faded on Cosimo's return. It was hardly visible now, but Resa noticed that Violante's hand instinctively went to her cheek when she saw all the women staring up at her. Her Ugliness. Had they shouted that name up to her in the past, whenever she appeared on the battlements? Some of the women were whispering it even now, but Violante was neither ugly nor beautiful. She held herself very erect, as if to make up for her lack of height, but between the two men who stationed themselves beside her she looked so young and vulnerable that Resa felt fear close like a claw around her heart. The Piper and the Milksop. Violante looked like a child between the two of them. How was this girl to protect Mo?

A boy pushed his way in beside the silver-nosed minstrel. He wore a metal nose too, but there was a real flesh-and-blood nose under it. This must be Jacopo, Violante's son. Mo had mentioned him. He obviously thought more of the Piper's company than his mother's, judging by the admiring looks he gave his grandfather's herald.

Resa felt dizzy when she saw the man with the silver nose standing up there so proudly. No, Violante couldn't protect Mo from him. He commanded Ombra now, not she, and not the Milksop who stood looking down at his subjects as haughtily as if the mere sight of them turned his stomach. The Piper, in contrast, seemed as pleased with himself as if the day belonged to him alone. Didn't I tell you so? his glance mocked them. I'll catch the Bluejay, and then I'll take your children all the same.

Why had she come? Why was she doing this to herself? Because she wanted to convince herself that it was all really happening, that she wasn't just reading about it?

The woman next to her reached for her arm. 'He's coming!' she whispered to Resa. There were whispers everywhere. 'He's coming! He's really coming!' Resa saw the sentries on the watchtowers by the gate giving the Piper a signal. Of course he was coming. What had they expected? Did they think he wouldn't keep his word?

The Milksop adjusted his wig and smiled at the Piper as triumphantly as if he personally, single-handed, had driven into his path the quarry he'd been hunting so long, but the Piper ignored him. He was staring at the street leading up from the city gate, his eyes as grey as the sky above him and just as cold. Resa remembered those eyes only too well. She also remembered the smile that now stole over his thin lips. He had smiled in just the same way in Capricorn's fortress whenever there was going to be an execution.

And then she saw Mo.

There he was all of a sudden, where the street ended, mounted on the black horse that the Prince had given him after he had to leave his own behind at Ombra Castle. The mask that Battista had made him was dangling around his neck. He didn't need the mask any more to be the Bluejay. The bookbinder and the robber had the same face now.

Dustfinger was behind him. He was riding the horse that had carried Roxane to the Castle of Night, bringing Fenoglio's words to save them. But there were no words for what was going to happen now. Or were there? Was the terrible silence weighing down on them all made of words?

No, Resa, she thought. This story has no author any more. What happens now is written by the Bluejay in his own flesh and blood – and for a moment, as he rode out of the alley, even she could call Mo by no other name. The Bluejay. How hesitantly the women made way for him, as if they themselves suddenly thought the price he was going to pay for their children too high. But at last they formed a lane just wide enough for the two riders, and every hoof beat made Resa clutch the folds of her dress more tightly.

What's the matter? Didn't you always love to read such stories? she thought bitterly, her heart in her mouth. Wouldn't you have liked this story too? The robber setting the children free by giving himself up to his enemies . . . admit it, you'd have loved every word! Except that the heroes of such stories don't usually have wives. Or daughters.

Meggie was still standing there as if none of this was anything to do with her, but her eyes were fixed on her father as if her gaze could protect him. Mo rode past, so close that Resa could have touched his horse. Her knees felt weak. She reached for the arm of the nearest woman, feeling so faint and ill that she could hardly keep on her feet. Look at him, Resa, she told herself. That's what you're here for, to see him once again, aren't you?

Did he feel fear? The fear that had made him wake abruptly from sleep on so many nights, his fear of bars and fetters? *Resa, leave the door open.*

Dustfinger is with him, she thought, trying to comfort herself. Dustfinger is right behind him, and he left all his own fears behind with Death. But Dustfinger will stay with him only as far as the castle gates, whispered her heart, and the Piper is waiting beyond them. She felt her knees giving way again until suddenly Meggie's arm was under hers, holding it as firmly as if her daughter were the older of the two of them. Resa turned her face into Meggie's shoulder, while the women around her looked longingly at the castle gates, which were still firmly closed.

Mo reined in his horse. Dustfinger was still just behind him, his face as expressionless as only he could make it. She wasn't yet used to the sight of him without his scars. He looked so much younger. Many eyes rested on him, the Fire-Dancer whom the Bluejay had brought back from the dead.

'The Piper won't be able to touch him!' whispered the woman beside her, murmuring it like a magic spell. 'No, how can he hold the Bluejay captive if even Death couldn't do it?'

Perhaps the Piper is more murderous than Death, Resa felt like replying, but she said nothing. She held her peace and looked up at the man with the silver nose.

'So here you really are! The Bluejay, in person!' His hoarse voice carried a long way in the silence that had settled over Ombra again. 'Or do you still claim to be someone else, as you did back at the Castle of Night? How shabby you look. A dirty vagabond. I really thought you'd send someone in your place, hoping we wouldn't find him out behind the mask too soon.'

'Oh, I don't think you as stupid as that, Piper!' Mo's face was full of contempt as he looked up at the silver-nosed man. 'Although shouldn't we change your name and call you after your new trade in future? Butcher of Children, how do you like that?'

Resa had never heard such hatred in Mo's voice before.

The voice that could call the dead back to life. How intently everyone was listening. And in spite of all the hate and anger in it, it still sounded so soft and warm by comparison with the Piper's.

'Call me what you like, bookbinder!' The Piper put his gloved hands on the battlements. 'I hear you know something about butchery yourself. But why did you bring the fire-eater with you? I don't remember inviting him! Where are his scars? Did he leave them with the dead?'

The battlements caught fire just where the Piper was leaning, and the flames whispered words that only Dustfinger understood. The silver-nosed tyrant flinched back, cursing, and struck at the sparks that were settling on his fine clothes, while Jacopo ducked into safety behind his back and stared, fascinated, at the whispering fire.

'I left certain things with the dead, Piper. And I brought certain others back.' Dustfinger didn't raise his voice, but the flames went out as if they were creeping away into the stone, to wait there for more words of fire. 'I'm here to warn you not to treat your guest badly. Fire is as much his friend as mine now, and I don't have to tell you what a powerful friend it can be.'

His face pale with anger, the Piper rubbed the soot from his gloves, but before he could reply the Milksop leant over the battlements.

'Guest?' he cried. 'Do you call that the right word for a robber who already has an appointment to meet the hangman in the Castle of Night?' His voice reminded Resa of the cackling of Roxane's goose.

Violante pushed him aside as if he were one of her servants. How small she was.

'The Bluejay is giving himself up as my prisoner, Governor! That was the agreement. And he is under my protection until my father comes.' Her voice was sharp and clear, astonishingly strong for such a slight body, and for a moment Resa took heart. Perhaps she really can protect him after all, she thought, and saw the same hope on Meggie's face.

Mo and the Piper were still staring at each other. Their hatred seemed to spin threads between the two of them, and Resa couldn't help thinking of the knife that Battista had sewn so carefully into Mo's clothes. She didn't know whether it frightened or reassured her to know that he had it with him.

'Very well! Let's call him our guest!' the Piper called down. 'Which means that we ought to show him our own special brand of hospitality! After all, we've been waiting for him long enough.'

He raised his hand, still sooty from Dustfinger's fire, and the guards at the gate levelled their spears at Mo. Some of the women screamed. Resa thought she heard Meggie's voice too, but she herself was mute with fear. The sentries on the towers bent their crossbows.

Violante put her son aside and took a step towards the Piper. But Dustfinger simply made the fire lick around his fingers as if he were playing with an animal, and Mo drew his sword. The Piper knew very well whose weapon it had once been.

'What's the idea? Send the children out, Piper!' Mo cried, and this time his voice was so cold that Resa hardly recognized it as his. 'Send them out, or you can tell your master that the flesh will go on rotting on his bones because you couldn't bring him the Bluejay alive, only dead!'

One of the women began sobbing. Another pressed her

hand to her mouth. Just behind the two of them Resa saw Minerva, Fenoglio's landlady. Of course, her children were among the captives. But Resa didn't want to think of Minerva's children, or the children of the other women. She saw nothing but the spears pointing at Mo's unarmed breast and the crossbows aimed at him from the walls.

'I'm warning you, Piper!' Once more Violante's voice allowed Resa to breathe again. 'Let the children go.'

The Milksop cast a longing glance at the crossbows. For a moment Resa was afraid he would give the order to shoot, so that he himself could lay the Bluejay at the Adderhead's feet, his own personal hunting trophy. But instead the Piper leant forward and gave the guards a signal.

'Open the gates!' he said, in a deliberately weary tone. 'Let the children out and the Bluejay in!'

Resa buried her head in her daughter's shoulder again. Meggie was still as self-controlled as her father, but she went on looking as if she feared to lose him the moment she took her eyes off him.

The gates slowly opened. They groaned and stuck until the guards pushed at them.

And then they came out. Children. So many children. They surged out as if they had been waiting behind the heavy gates for days. The little ones were in such a hurry to get outside the walls that they stumbled, but the bigger children helped them to their feet again. Fear was written on all their faces, a fear much greater than themselves. The youngest began running as soon as they saw their mothers, threw themselves into their waiting arms and burrowed their way in among the women as if into a safe hiding place. But the older children walked back to freedom slowly, almost hesitantly.

They looked distrustfully at the guards they had to pass, and stopped when they saw the two men waiting on their horses outside the gate.

'Bluejay!' It was only a whisper, but it came from many mouths, louder and louder until the name seemed to be written on the air. 'Bluejay, Bluejay.' The children nudged each other, pointed to Mo – and stared in awe at the sparks surrounding Dustfinger like a swarm of tiny fairies. 'Fire-Dancer.'

More and more children stopped in front of the two horses, surrounded their riders, touched them as if to see if the men they knew only from the songs sung secretly by their mothers at their bedsides were really flesh and blood. Mo leant down from his horse. He waved the children aside, quietly saying something to them. Then he gave Dustfinger one last glance, and turned his horse towards the open gateway.

They would not let him go.

Three children barred his way, two boys and a girl. They reached for his reins and wouldn't let him pass into the place they had just left, to be lost behind its walls like them. More and more of them crowded around him, held him, shielding him from the spears of the guards while their mothers called for them.

'Bluejay!'

The Piper's voice made the children turn. 'Through those gates with you now, or we'll take them all back, and hang a dozen in cages over the gateway where the ravens can eat them!'

The children didn't move. They just stared at the silver-nosed man, and the boy beside him who was younger than they were. But Mo picked up his reins again and made his way through them as carefully as if each child were his own, and the children stood there while their mothers called them, watching him ride through the huge gateway. All alone.

Mo looked over his shoulder once more before he rode past the guards, as if he knew that Resa and Meggie had followed him after all, and Resa saw the fear on his face. She was sure that Meggie had seen it too. As he rode on again the gates were already beginning to close.

'Disarm him!' Resa heard the Milksop shout, and the last thing she saw was soldiers, dozens of soldiers, dragging Mo off his horse.

36

A Surprising Visitor

God took a deep breath. Another complaint! When would Man come to him without a complaint? But he shot up his eyebrows, smiled with delight, and cried: 'Man! How are the carrots coming on?'

Ted Hughes,
The Secret of Man's Wife, from *The Dreamfighter*

Oh, how good it was to see Despina's little face again! Even if she looked tired and sad, scared as a bird that had fallen out of its nest. And Ivo – had he been so tall before that wretched Sootbird took to stealing children? How thin he was . . . and was that blood on his tunic? 'The rats bit us,' he said, acting grown-up and fearless as he had so often since his father's death, but Fenoglio saw the fear in his childish eyes. Rats!

He just couldn't stop hugging and kissing them, he was so relieved. And so he should be. He forgave himself much, he forgave himself easily, but if his story had killed Minerva's children – he wasn't sure how he would have come to terms

327

with that. But they were alive, and he himself had called the man who saved them into being.

'What will they do to him now?' Despina freed herself from his arms, her big eyes dark with worry. Damn it, that was the trouble with children – they were always asking the very questions you so carefully avoided yourself. And then they gave the very answers you didn't want to hear!

'They'll kill him,' said Ivo, and his little sister's eyes filled with tears.

How could she be crying for a stranger? She'd seen Mortimer for the first time today. It's because your songs have taught her to love him, Fenoglio, that's how. They all love him, and today will write that love in their hearts for ever. Whatever the Piper did to him, from now on the Bluejay was as immortal as the Adderhead. Indeed, he was far more reliably immortal, since the Adderhead could always be killed by three words. But words would keep Mortimer alive even if he died behind the castle walls – all the words now being whispered and sung down there in the streets would keep him alive.

Despina wiped the tears from her eyes and looked at Fenoglio in the hope that he would contradict her brother, and of course he did, for her sake and his own. 'Ivo!' he said sternly. 'What nonsense are you talking? Do you think the Bluejay didn't have a plan when he gave himself up? Do you think he's just going to the Piper like a rabbit falling into a trap?'

A smile of relief came to Despina's lips, and the shadow of a doubt appeared on Ivo's face.

'No, of course he isn't!' said Minerva, who still hadn't spoken a word since she had brought the children up to his room.

'He's a cunning fox, not a rabbit! He'll outwit them all!' And Fenoglio heard the seed that his songs had sown begin to grow in her voice too. Hope – the Bluejay still stood for hope in the midst of all the darkness.

Minerva took the children away with her. Of course. She would be going to feed them up with everything she could still find in the house, and Fenoglio was left alone with Rosenquartz, who had been stirring the ink without a word while Fenoglio lavished kisses on Despina and Ivo.

'Outwit them all, will he?' he said in his reedy little voice as soon as Minerva closed the door behind her. 'How? Do you know what I think? I think it's all up with your fabulous robber! And he'll have a particularly nasty execution, that's what! I can only hope it will be in the Castle of Night. No one ever stops to think what all those screams of agony do to a glass man's poor head.'

Heartless glassy little fellow! Fenoglio threw a cork at him, but Rosenquartz was used to such missiles and dodged it. Why had he taken on such a pessimistic glass man? Rosenquartz had his left arm in a sling. After Sootbird's performance Fenoglio had persuaded him to go and spy on Orpheus one more time, and Orpheus's horrible glass man really had pushed the poor creature out of the window. Luckily Rosenquartz had landed in the gutter, but Fenoglio still didn't know if the child-catching scene had been Orpheus's idea. No! He couldn't possibly have written it! Orpheus could write nothing without the book, and it seemed – for Rosenquartz had discovered this much – that Dustfinger had actually stolen it from him. Anyway, the scene was much too good for that calf's-head to have written, wasn't it?

He'll outwit them all . . .

Fenoglio went to the window, while the glass man adjusted his sling with a reproachful sigh. Did Mortimer really have a plan? Damn it, how was he to know? Mortimer wasn't really one of his characters, even if he was playing the part of one. Which is extremely annoying, Fenoglio thought. Because if he *had* been one of them, presumably I'd know what's really going on behind those thrice-damned walls.

He stared darkly over the roof tops to the castle. Poor Meggie. And no doubt she'd blame him for everything again. Her mother certainly did. Fenoglio remembered Resa's pleading look only too well. *You must write us back again. You owe us that!* Yes, perhaps he really should have tried. Suppose they killed Mortimer? Wouldn't it be better for them all to go back to their world then? What would he want to do here once the Bluejay was dead? Watch the immortal Adder and the Piper tell his story?

'Of course he's here! Didn't you hear what she said? Up the stairs. Do you see any other stairs around here? For heaven's sake, Darius!'

Rosenquartz forgot his broken arm and looked at the door.

What woman's voice was that?

There was a knock, but before Fenoglio could call, 'Come in,' the door opened and a rather powerful female form entered his room so impetuously that he instinctively took a step back, knocking his head against the sloping roof. The dress she wore looked as if it had come straight from some cheap theatrical production.

'There we are! This is him, the author!' she announced, looking him up and down with such contempt that Fenoglio was aware of every hole in his tunic. I've seen this woman before, he thought.

'And what's going on here, may I ask?' She jabbed her finger into his chest as hard as if to stab him straight to his old heart. And he'd seen the thin fellow behind her as well. Of course . . . wait . . .

'Why is the Adderhead's flag hoisted in Ombra? Who is that frightful fellow with the silver nose? Why were they threatening Mortimer with spears, and since when, for goodness' sake, has he gone about wearing a sword?'

The bookworm. Of course! That's who she was. Elinor Loredan. Meggie had told him about her often enough. Fenoglio had last seen her through bars, stuck in one of the dog-pens in the arena where Capricorn's festivities were held. And the timid man with the owlish look was Capricorn's stammering reader! Though, with the best will in the world, Fenoglio couldn't remember his name. What were these two doing here? Were tourist visas for his story being handed out these days?

'I admit I was relieved to see Mortimer alive,' his uninvited guest went on. (Did she ever stop to get her breath back?) 'And thank goodness he seems to be sound and healthy, although I didn't like to see him riding into that castle alone at all. But where are Resa and Meggie? And what about Mortola, Basta, and that puffed-up mooncalf Orpheus?'

Good lord, the woman was just as awful as he'd imagined her! Her companion – Darius, yes, that was his name – was staring at Rosenquartz with such a captivated expression that the glass man, flattered, passed a hand over his pale pink hair.

'Quiet!' thundered Fenoglio. 'Shut up, for heaven's sake!'

It had no effect. Not the slightest. 'Something's happened to them! Admit it! Why was Mortimer alone?' Once again she jabbed him in the chest. 'I just know something's happened to

Meggie and Resa, something terrible . . . a giant has trodden on them, they've been impaled on spikes, they—'

'Nothing of the kind!' Fenoglio interrupted. 'They're with the Black Prince!'

'The Black Prince?' Her eyes became almost as large as her bespectacled companion's. 'Oh!'

'Yes, and if something terrible happens to anyone here it's going to be Mortimer. Which is why . . .' said Fenoglio, grabbing her arm, not very gently, and dragging her to the door, '. . . I want to be left in peace, for heaven's sake, so that I can think!'

That really did shut her up. But not for long.

'Something terrible?' she asked.

Rosenquartz took his hands away from his ears.

'What do you mean? Who writes what happens here? You do, isn't that so?'

Oh, wonderful! Now her fat fingers were prodding at his sorest point!

'No, definitely not!' he told her sharply. 'This story is now telling itself, and today Mortimer prevented it from taking a very unpleasant turn! But unfortunately that looks as if it will cost him his neck, in which case I can only advise you to take his wife and daughter and go back with them to where you came from, as fast as possible! Because you've obviously found a way, haven't you?'

With these words he opened the door, but Signora Loredan simply closed it again.

'Cost him his neck? What do you mean?' With a jerk, she freed her arm from his grasp. (Heavens above, the woman was as strong as a hippopotamus.)

'I mean that, very regrettably, he's likely to be hung or

332

beheaded or quartered, or whatever else strikes the Adderhead as the right kind of execution for the man who's his worst enemy!'

'His worst enemy? Mortimer?' She was frowning incredulously – as if Fenoglio were an old fool who didn't know what he was talking about!

'It was him. *He* made him into a robber.'

That was Rosenquartz. The miserable traitor! He was pointing a glass finger at his master so mercilessly that Fenoglio felt like picking him up from his desk and breaking him in two at the waist.

'It's the songs,' murmured Rosenquartz to their two visitors, as if he'd known them for a lifetime. 'Obsessed by them, that's what he is, and Meggie's poor father has been caught up in his fine words like a fly in a spider's web!'

This was too much. Fenoglio marched towards Rosenquartz, but the bookworm woman barred his way.

'Don't you dare do anything to that poor defenceless glass man!' She was glowering at him like a bulldog. Good God, what a fearsome female! 'Mortimer, a robber? He's the most peace-loving person I know.'

'Oh, really?' Fenoglio's voice rose to such a pitch that Rosenquartz put his hands over his ridiculously tiny ears again. 'Well, perhaps even the most peace-loving person gets to feel less so when he's been shot and nearly killed, parted from his wife, and locked in a dungeon for weeks on end. And none of that was my work, whatever this lying glass man may say! Far from it. But for the words I wrote, I imagine Mortimer would be dead by now.'

'Shot and nearly killed? Dungeon?' Signora Loredan cast a helpless glance at her bespectacled companion.

'This sounds like a long story, Elinor,' he said in his quiet voice. 'Maybe you should listen to it.'

But before Fenoglio could say anything in response to that, Minerva put her head round the door. 'Fenoglio,' she said, glancing briefly at his visitors. 'Despina won't give me a moment's peace. She's worried about the Bluejay, she wants you to tell her how he's going to save himself.'

This was too much. Fenoglio sighed deeply and tried to ignore Rosenquartz's snort of derision. He ought to take the glass man into the Wayless Wood and leave him there, that's what he ought to do.

'Send her to me,' he said, although he hadn't the faintest idea what to tell the little girl. What had become of the days when his head was brimming over with ideas? They were suffocated by all this misfortune, that was what had become of them!

'The Bluejay? Didn't the man with the silver nose call Mortimer that?'

Oh, good heavens, he'd forgotten his visitors entirely for a moment.

'Get out of here!' he snarled. 'Out of my room, out of my story! There are far too many visitors here already. Go away.'

But the brazen woman sat down on the chair at his desk, folded her arms, and planted her feet on his floor as if planning to let them take root there. 'No, I won't. I want to hear the story,' she said. 'The whole story.'

This was going from bad to worse. What an unlucky day – and it wasn't over yet.

'Inkweaver?' Despina was standing in the doorway, her face tear-stained. When she saw the two strangers she instinctively stepped back, but Fenoglio went over and took her little hand.

'Minerva says you want me to tell you about the Bluejay?'

Despina nodded shyly, without taking her eyes off his visitors.

'Well, that comes in handy.' Fenoglio sat down on his bed and took her on his lap. 'My two visitors here want to hear something about the Bluejay too. Suppose you and I tell them the whole story?'

Despina nodded. 'How he outwitted the Adderhead and brought the Fire-Dancer back from the dead?' she whispered.

'Exactly,' said Fenoglio, 'and then the two of us will discover how it goes on. We'll just weave the rest of the song. After all, I'm the Inkweaver, right?'

Despina nodded, looking at him so hopefully that his old heart felt heavy in his breast. A weaver who's run out of threads, he thought. Or, no – the threads were there, they were all there – he just couldn't weave them together any more.

Signora Loredan was suddenly sitting perfectly still, looking at him as expectantly as Despina. The owl-faced man was staring at him too, as if he couldn't wait to hear the words come from his lips. Only Rosenquartz turned his back on Fenoglio and went on stirring the ink again, as if to remind him how long it was since he had last used it.

'Fenoglio!' Despina's hand caressed his wrinkled face. 'Go on, tell me!'

'Yes, go on!' said the bookworm woman. Elinor Loredan. He still hadn't asked how she came to be here. As if there weren't enough questions in this story already. And the stammerer wasn't going to be a particularly valuable addition to it either!

Despina tugged at his sleeve. Where did all the hope in her

reddened eyes come from? How had that hope survived Sootbird's guile, and all the fear in the dark dungeon? Children, thought Fenoglio as he took Despina's small hand firmly in his. If anyone could ever bring back the words, he supposed it would be the children.

37

Only a Magpie

What was she, then, in the lean time,
In the year's meagre quarter?
She was bird and enchanter, was mistress
Of fire and water.

Franz Werfel, *Invocations 1918–1921*

The house where Fenoglio was lodging reminded Orpheus of places where he himself had lived not so long ago: a shabby building, crooked, leaning sideways, with mouldy walls and windows offering a view only of other dilapidated houses. The rain fell inside it too, because in this world windowpanes were only for the rich! Pitiful. How he hated hiding in the darkest corner of the back yard, where spiders crawled into his velvet sleeves and chicken droppings ruined his expensive boots. But what else could he do? Ever since Basta had killed a strolling player before her very eyes, Fenoglio's landlady went for anyone loitering in her yard with a pitchfork. And Orpheus had to know. He had to know if Fenoglio was writing again. He just hoped that useless glass man would

337

come back before he was up to his knees in mud!

A thin chicken strutted by, and beside him Cerberus growled. Orpheus hastily held his muzzle shut. He'd been glad when Cerberus suddenly came scratching at his door, of course, but one question had immediately spoiled his pleasure – how did the dog come to be here? Was Fenoglio writing again after all? Had Dustfinger taken the book to the old man? None of it made any sense, but he had to know. Who but Fenoglio could have dreamt up the touching scene performed by the Bluejay outside the castle? How much everyone loved the bookbinder for it! Even though by now the Piper must have beaten him half to death, he had become godlike when he rode through the gates of that damn castle. The Bluejay as a noble sacrificial lamb. If that didn't sound like Fenoglio he'd eat his hat!

Naturally Orpheus had sent Oss with the glass man at first, but his bodyguard had let Fenoglio's landlady catch him. There was no dark corner where that great hulk could lurk unseen, and Ironstone hadn't even reached the stairs leading to Fenoglio's room. A chicken had chased him through the mud and a cat had almost bitten his head off – you certainly couldn't say that glass men made ideal spies, but their small size came in so handy! The same was true of fairies, of course, but they forgot the least little errand before they'd even flown out of the window – and after all, Fenoglio himself used his glass man as a spy, although he was lamentably unfit for the job.

No, Ironstone was much better at it. However, unlike Fenoglio's glass man he suffered from vertigo, which made it impossible for him to cross roof tops, and even on the ground he was so bad at finding his way that Orpheus found it better

to put him down at the foot of Fenoglio's stairs, if he wanted
to be sure he wouldn't get hopelessly lost.

But where the devil was he now? Admittedly climbing
those stairs was like scaling a mountain for a glass man, but
all the same . . . There was a goat bleating noisily in the shed
behind which Orpheus was standing – it had probably caught
the dog's scent – and some kind of liquid was seeping through
the leather of his boots. Its smell was suspiciously appealing
to Cerberus, who was snuffling around in the mud so greedily
that Orpheus had to keep tugging him away from it.

Ah, here came Ironstone at last! He jumped from step to
step, nimble as a mouse. Fabulous. For a glass man, he was a
tough little fellow. It was to be hoped that what he'd found
out was worth the ruin of those expensive boots.

Orpheus bent down to Cerberus's collar and took off the
chain, which for want of a dog leash he had ordered in Smiths'
Alley. Cerberus trotted over to the stairs and plucked the
protesting glass man off the bottom step. Ironstone claimed
that the dog's slobber brought his glass skin out in a rash, but
how else was he going to get through the mud with those thin
legs of his? An old woman looked out of her window as the
dog trotted back to Orpheus, but luckily it wasn't Fenoglio's
landlady.

'Well?' Cerberus dropped the glass man into his outstretched hands. Ugh! Dog slobber really was disgusting.

'He's not writing. Not a line!' Ironstone passed his sleeve
over his moist face. 'I told you so, master! He's drunk himself
silly. His fingers shake if he so much as sees a pen!'

Orpheus looked up at Fenoglio's room. Light showed
underneath the door. Ironstone, who was slippery as an eel,
always crawled through the broad crack underneath it.

'Are you sure?' He fastened the chain to Cerberus's collar again.

'Absolutely sure! And he doesn't have the book either. He has visitors, though.'

The old woman tipped a bucket of water out of her window. Always supposing it was water. Once again Cerberus was snuffling around with far too much interest.

'Visitors? I don't want to know about them. But whatever it looks like, I'm sure he's writing again!'

Orpheus looked up at the dilapidated houses. A candle burnt in every window. They were burning all over Ombra. For the Bluejay. Curse him! Curse them all: Fenoglio and Mortimer, his stupid daughter – and Dustfinger. He cursed the Fire-Dancer most of all. Dustfinger had betrayed him – stolen from him, Orpheus, whose heart had been given to him for so many years, who had read him home to his own story and snatched him away from Death! What was it they called him now? The Bluejay's fiery shadow. A shadow! It served him right. He, Orpheus, would have made him more than a shadow in this story, but that was over and done with. He had declared war on them all. He was going to write them a story that was to his own liking – just as soon as he had the book back!

A child came out of the house and ran barefoot over the muddy yard to disappear into one of the outbuildings. Time to get out of here. Orpheus mopped the dog slobber off Ironstone with a cloth, put him on his shoulder, and stole away before the child came out again. Away from this filth – not that it was much better in the streets.

'Blank sheets, nothing but blank sheets, master!' Ironstone whispered to him as they hurried back through the night to Orpheus's house. 'No more than a few sentences, and those were crossed out . . . that's all, I swear! His glass man almost spotted me today, but I managed to hide in one of his master's boots just in time. You can't imagine how it stank in there!'

Oh yes, he could. 'I'll have one of the maids soap you all over.'

'No, no, better not. Last time the soapsuds left me belching for more than an hour, and my feet went white as milk!'

'So? You think I'm letting a glass man who stinks of sweaty feet march all over my parchment?'

A night watchman came towards them, swaying as he walked. Why were those fellows always drunk? Orpheus pressed a few copper coins into the man's wrinkled hand, in case he was thinking of calling a patrol. Now that the Bluejay was a prisoner in the castle, troops of soldiers were out and about in Ombra night and day.

'How about the book? Did you really search for it thoroughly?'

Two boards in Butchers' Alley sang the praises of fresh unicorn meat. Ridiculous. Where was anyone supposed to get that? Orpheus turned into Glaziers' Alley, although Ironstone hated going that way.

'Well, it wasn't easy.' Ironstone looked nervously at the notices advertising artificial limbs for broken glass men. 'Like I told you, he has visitors, and with all those eyes to notice things, getting around his room was tricky! I even searched his clothes, all the same, and he nearly shut me up in his chest! But no luck. He doesn't have the book, master, I swear he doesn't!'

'Death and the devil!' Orpheus felt an almost irresistible urge to throw or break something. Ironstone knew these moods of his by now, and clung to his sleeve to be on the safe side.

Who but the old man could have the book? Even if Dustfinger had given it to Mortimer, he certainly hadn't taken it to his dungeon with him! No, Dustfinger himself must have kept it. Orpheus felt a burning sensation in his stomach, as bad as if one of Dustfinger's martens were sitting there gnawing his guts. He was familiar with this pain, which always attacked him when something wasn't going as he wanted. A stomach ulcer, that was it. For sure. So? he asked himself. Mind you don't make it even worse, or do you want to have to go to one of the local quacks and have your blood let?

Ironstone was crouching on his shoulder, silent and depressed, probably thinking about the soapy water ahead of him. However, Cerberus was sniffing every wall he padded past. No wonder dogs liked this world – it stank to high heaven. I'd change that too, thought Orpheus. And I'd write myself a better spy, one as tiny as a spider and definitely not made of glass. But you won't be writing anything here any more, Orpheus, a voice whispered inside him, because you've lost the book!

Cursing, he quickened his pace, hauling Cerberus impatiently along with him – only to tread in cat dirt. Mud, chicken droppings, cat dirt . . . his boots were ruined, and where was he going to get the silver for a new pair? His last attempt to write himself a chest of treasure on the gallows hill had been a dismal failure, producing coins as thin as silver foil.

At last. There it was in all its glory. His house. The finest house in Ombra. His heartbeat always quickened when he saw the front steps shining in the darkness, white as alabaster, and the coat of arms over the entrance that made even Orpheus himself believe he was of royal descent. No, up to now things really hadn't gone badly for him here. He had to keep reminding himself of that when he felt like smashing glass men, or wishing a plague of boils on the neck of a certain skinny Arab boy. Not to mention ungrateful fire-eaters!

Orpheus stopped suddenly. A bird was perching on the steps. It sat as if it intended to build a nest right there on the spot. It didn't fly away even when Orpheus came closer, but just stared at him with its black button-eyes. Birds – he hated them. They left their droppings everywhere. And all that fluttering, those sharp beaks, those feathers full of mites and worm eggs . . .

Orpheus undid the chain from Cerberus's collar. 'Go on, catch it!'

Cerberus loved to chase birds, and now and then he even caught one. But this time he put his tail between his back legs and retreated as if a snake were wriggling there on the steps of Orpheus's house. What the devil . . .?

The bird jerked its head and hopped one step lower.

Cerberus ducked, and the glass man clung uneasily to Orpheus's collar. 'It's a magpie, master!' he whispered in his ear. 'They . . .' His voice almost failed him. 'They smash glass men and collect the coloured splinters for their nests! Please, master, chase it away!'

The magpie jerked its head again and stared at him. This was a strange bird, decidedly strange.

Orpheus bent and threw a stone at it. The magpie spread its wings and uttered a hoarse cry.

'Oh, master, master, it's going to smash me to pieces!' wailed Ironstone, clinging to his ear. 'Grey glass men are very rare!'

This time the magpie's cry sounded like laughter.

'You still look as stupid as ever, Orpheus.'

He knew the voice at once.

The magpie stretched its neck. It coughed as if it were choking on grain pecked up too greedily. Then it spat out some seeds on the alabaster-white steps – one, two, three seeds – and began to grow.

Cerberus cowered behind his legs, and Ironstone was trembling so pitifully that his limbs clattered like china in a picnic basket.

But the magpie went on growing. Feathers became black clothes, grey hair pinned severely back, fingers hastily counting the seeds that the bird's beak had spat out on to the steps. Mortola looked older than Orpheus remembered her, much older. Her shoulders were hunched, even when she stood up. Her fingers curled over like the claws of a bird, her face was gaunt under the high cheekbones, and her skin was the colour of yellowed parchment. But her eyes were still piercing, and made Orpheus bow his head like a boy being scolded.

'How – how do you do that?' he stammered. 'Fenoglio's book says nothing about shape-shifters! Only about Night-Mares and—'

'Fenoglio! What does he know?' Mortola plucked a feather off her black dress. 'Everything changes shape in this world, only most have to die first. But there are ways and means –' and as she spoke she carefully dropped the seeds she had picked up into a leather bag – 'for people to free themselves from their own shapes without any need for the White Women.'

'Really?' Orpheus immediately began wondering what kind of possibilities that opened up for this story, but Mortola didn't give him any time to think it over.

'You've settled into this world in fine style, haven't you?' she murmured, looking up at his house. 'Four-Eyes, the milky-bearded merchant from across the sea, who trades in unicorns and dwarves and can read every wish of the new lord of Ombra in his eyes – well, I thought to myself, bless me if that isn't my dear friend Orpheus! He's obviously managed to read himself here. And you've even brought that nasty dog along with you.'

Cerberus bared his teeth, but Ironstone was still trembling. Glass men really were absurd creatures. And to think Fenoglio was proud of them!

'What do you want?' Orpheus did his best to sound cool and superior, not like the frightened little boy he became only too easily in Mortola's presence. She still terrified him, he had to admit it.

Footsteps echoed through the night, presumably from one of the patrols sent out by the Piper to comb Ombra in case the Black Prince found some way of freeing his noble fellow-fighter after all.

'Do you always welcome your guests outside the door?' hissed Mortola. 'Come on, time we went in!'

Orpheus had to bring the bronze knocker down on the wood three times before Oss opened the door. He blinked sleepily down at Mortola.

'Is this that wardrobe-man from the other world or a new one?' asked Mortola, pushing her way past Oss with her skirts rustling.

'A new one,' muttered Orpheus, whose mind was still trying to work out whether it was a good thing she was back or not. Wasn't she supposed to be dead? But it was becoming clearer all the time that you couldn't rely on Death in this world. Which was both reassuring and alarming.

He took Mortola, not to his study, but into the reception room. The old woman looked around as if everything in it was hers. No, very likely it wasn't a good thing she was back. And what did she want of him? He could imagine: Mortimer. For sure she still wanted to kill him. Mortola didn't abandon such plans easily – particularly not where her son's murderer was concerned. In this case, however, other people looked like they were ahead of her in line.

'So now the bookbinder really is the Bluejay!' she remarked, as if Orpheus had spoken his thoughts out loud. 'How many more ridiculous songs are they going to sing about him? Hailing him as their saviour . . . as if *we* hadn't brought him to this world in the first place! And the Adderhead, instead of hunting him down after he killed his best men on Mount Adder, blames Mortola for his escape, and for the way the flesh is rotting on his own bones. I knew at once it must be the White Book. Silvertongue is wily, but his innocent look deceives them all, and the Adder handed me, not him, over to the torturers, to get the name of the poison. I still feel the pain of it today, but I outwitted them – I made them bring me seeds and herbs, saying I'd brew them an antidote for their master. Instead I made myself wings to fly away. I listened to the wind and to the gossip in marketplaces to find the book-binder, and I discovered he really was playing the robber, and the Black Prince had found him a hiding place. It was a good hiding place, too, but I found it all the same.' Mortola pursed her lips while she spoke, as if she felt she still had a beak. 'How I had to control myself not to peck his eyes out when I saw him again! There's no hurry, Mortola, I thought. Being in a hurry has spoilt your fine revenge once already. Sprinkle a few poisonous berries in his food, leaving him to writhe like a worm and die slowly enough for you to enjoy your revenge. But some stupid crow pecked the berries out of his dish, and the next time I tried it the bear snapped at me with his stinking muzzle and pulled out two of my tail feathers. I tried again in the camp where the Black Prince took them – him and his daughter and that deceitful maid – but the wrong man ate from that dish. Poisonous fungi, they said, he's eaten poisonous fungi!'

Mortola laughed, and Orpheus shuddered when he saw her fingers curving as if they were still clinging to a branch. 'It's like a jinx! Nothing can kill him, neither poison nor a bullet. It's as if everything in this world were bent on protecting him – every stone, every animal, even the shadows among the trees! The Bluejay! Death itself let him go, and did a deal with him for the Fire-Dancer. Oh, very impressive! But at what price? He hasn't told even his wife the price, only Mortola knows it! No one pays any attention to the magpie in the tree, but she hears everything – what the trees whisper at night, what spiders write in damp branches with their silver threads: they say that Death will take the Bluejay and his daughter if he doesn't deliver the Adderhead's life before winter ends. And they say the Adder's own daughter plans to help the Jay to write the three words in the White Book.'

'What?' Orpheus had been only half listening. He knew Mortola's hate-filled tirades, endless and self-glorifying, but he pricked up his ears at that last remark. Violante in league with the Bluejay? Yes, it made sense. Of course! That was why Mortimer had handed himself over expressly to her! He might have known it. That paragon of virtue hadn't let

347

himself be made prisoner only out of nobility of mind. The noble robber was intent on murder.

Orpheus began pacing up and down, while Mortola went on uttering curses in so hoarse a voice that the words sounded hardly human.

Violante – Orpheus had offered her his services as soon as he had settled in Ombra, but she had rejected them, saying that she already had a poet . . . not very nice of her.

'Oh yes, he plans to kill the Adder! Stole into the castle like a marten into a poultry yard! Even the fairies sing about it as they do their silly dances, but only the magpie listens!' Mortola bent double. Even her coughing sounded like a croak. She was crazy! How she looked at him, with her pupils so black and fixed that they looked more like the eyes of a bird than of a human being. Orpheus shuddered.

'Yes, yes, I know his plans!' she whispered. 'And I tell myself: Mortola, let him live, hard as that is for you. Kill his wife, or even better the daughter he dotes on, and flutter up on to his shoulder when he hears the news, so that you can hear his heart breaking. But let him live until the Adderhead gives him the White Book, because the Adder too must die for all the pain he gave me. And should the Silver Prince really be stupid enough to let his worst enemy lay hands on the Book that can kill him, all the better! The magpie will be there, and not the Bluejay but Mortola will write those three words. Yes, I know what they are. And Death will take both the Bluejay and the Adderhead, and in return for such rich pickings will finally give back what that accursed bookbinder took from me with his silver tongue – my son!'

What the devil? Orpheus nearly choked on the wine he had just raised to his lips. The old witch was still dreaming of

Capricorn's return! Well, why not, since first Cosimo and then Dustfinger had come back from the dead? But he could think of more interesting turns for this story to take than the return of Mortola's fire-raising son.

'You really believe the Adderhead will bring the White Book here?' Ah, he felt there were great things in the offing, developments full of promise. Maybe all was not lost, even if Dustfinger had stolen Fenoglio's book from him. There were other ways to play a significant part in this story. The Adderhead in Ombra! What possibilities that opened up . . .

'Of course he'll come! The Adder is more of a fool than most people think.' Mortola sat down on one of the chairs that stood ready for Orpheus's distinguished clients. The wind blew through the unglazed windows and made the candles flicker. Shadows danced like black birds on the whitewashed walls.

'So will the Silver Prince let the bookbinder outwit him for the second time?' Orpheus himself was surprised by the hatred in his voice. To his astonishment, he realized that he now wished for Mortimer's death almost as passionately as Mortola. 'Even Dustfinger runs after him these days!' he uttered. 'Obviously Death has made him forget what that hero once did to him!' He took his glasses off and rubbed his eyes, as if he could wipe away the memory of Dustfinger's cold face. Yes, that was the only reason why Dustfinger had turned against him! Because Mortimer had bewitched him with his accursed voice. He bewitched them all. It was to be hoped that the Piper would cut his tongue out before they quartered him. He wanted to watch as the Milksop's hounds tore him to pieces, as the Piper sliced up his skin and his noble heart. Oh, if only he could have written *that* song about the Bluejay!

Mortola's coughing brought Orpheus back from his blood-thirsty dreams.

'It's only too easy to swallow these seeds!' she gasped, bent double in the chair, her hands clutching the arms like claws. 'You have to put them under your tongue, but they're slippery little things, and if too many of them go astray and down to your stomach, the bird sometimes comes back when you haven't summoned it.' She jerked her head like the magpie, opened her mouth as if it were a beak and pressed her fingers to her pale lips.

'Listen!' she managed to say as the fit shook her again. 'I want you to go to the castle as soon as the Adderhead reaches Ombra, and warn him against his daughter! Tell him to ask Balbulus the illuminator how many books about the Bluejay Violante has ordered from him. Convince him that his daughter is obsessed with his worst enemy and will do all in her power to save him. Tell him in the finest words you can think up. Use your voice, the way Silvertongue will try to use his. You're very keen on boasting that your voice is more impressive than Mortimer's! Prove it!'

Mortola retched – and spat another seed out into the palm of her hand.

She was clever, even if she was totally crazy, and it was surely best to let her believe she could go on acting as if she were his mistress, although all that retching made him feel so unwell he could almost have spat out his own wine. Orpheus brushed a little dust off his elaborately embroidered sleeves. His clothes, his house, all the maids . . . how could the old woman be blind enough to think he'd ever serve her again? As if he'd come into this world to carry out other people's plans! No, here he served only himself. So he had sworn.

'It doesn't sound a bad idea.' Orpheus was taking great pains to keep his tone of voice as deferential as usual. 'But what about all the Bluejay's noble friends? He won't be hoping for support from Violante alone. What about the Black Prince?' And Dustfinger, he added silently, but he did not speak the name. He was going to take his own revenge on Dustfinger.

'The Black Prince, yes. Another high-minded idiot. My son had trouble with him from time to time himself.' Mortola put the seed she had spat out away with the others. 'I'll take care of him. Him and Silvertongue's daughter. That girl's almost as dangerous as her father.'

'Nonsense!' Orpheus poured himself more wine. Wine made him braver.

Mortola inspected him scornfully. Yes, she obviously still thought him a subservient fool. All the better. She rubbed her thin arms, shuddering as if the feathers were trying to pierce through her skin again.

'What about the old man? The one who, they say, wrote Silvertongue's daughter the words I took from her in the Castle of Night? Is he still writing foolhardy recklessness into the Bluejay's heart?'

'No, Fenoglio isn't writing any more. All the same, I'd have no objection if you killed him. Far from it – he's a terrible know-all.'

Mortola nodded, but she didn't really seem to be listening any more. 'I must go,' she said, rising unsteadily from her chair. 'Your house is as musty as a dungeon.'

Oss was lying outside the door when Mortola opened it. 'So this is your bodyguard?' she asked. 'You don't seem to have many enemies.'

Orpheus slept poorly that night. He dreamt of birds, hundreds of birds, but when dawn came and Ombra emerged from the shadows of night like a pale fruit, he went to the window of his bedroom full of new confidence.

'Good morning to you, Bluejay!' he said under his breath, eyes turned to the towers of the castle. 'I hope you passed a sleepless night! I dare say you still think the roles in this story have been cast by now, but you've played its hero long enough. Curtain up, Act Two: enter Orpheus. In what part? The part of the villain, of course. Isn't that always the best role in a play?'

38

A Greeting to the Piper

There was a smell of Time in the air tonight. [. . .] What
did Time smell like? Like dust and clocks and people. And
if you wondered what Time sounded like, it sounded like
water running in a dark cave and voices crying and dirt
dropping down upon hollow box-lids, and rain.

Ray Bradbury, *The Martian Chronicles*

Farid wasn't with the party when the Bluejay rode to
Ombra Castle. 'You're staying in the camp.' Dustfinger
didn't have to say any more to make Farid worry about caus-
ing his death again, and the fear was like a hand clutching his
throat. The Strong Man waited among the empty tents with
him, because the Black Prince refused to believe that he could
pass for a woman. They sat there for many hours, but when
Meggie and the others at last came back Dustfinger wasn't
with them, any more than the Bluejay was.

'Where is he?' The Black Prince was the only person Farid
dared to ask, although his face was so grave that even the bear
didn't venture near him.

'Where the Bluejay is,' replied the Prince, and when he saw Farid's look of dismay he added, 'No, not in the dungeon. I mean near him, that's all. Death has bound those two together, and nothing but death is going to part them again.'

Near him.

Farid looked at the tent where Meggie slept. He thought he could hear her crying, but he dared not go to her. She hadn't yet forgiven him for persuading her father to do that deal with Orpheus, and Doria was sitting outside her tent. He was to be found near Meggie a good deal too often for Farid's liking, but luckily he appeared to understand as little about girls as his strong brother.

The men back from Ombra were sitting around the fire, heads bent. Some of them didn't even take off the women's clothes they had been wearing, but the Black Prince gave them no time to drown their fears for the future in wine. He sent them out hunting. They would need good stocks of provisions if they were to hide the children of Ombra from the Piper: dried meat, warm furs.

But that didn't interest Farid. He no more belonged to the robbers than he had to Orpheus. He didn't even belong to Meggie. He belonged with only one person, and he had to keep away from him, for fear of bringing him to his death.

Darkness was just falling, and the robbers were still smoking meat and stretching skins between the trees, when Gwin came scurrying out of the forest. Farid thought the marten was Jink until he saw the greying muzzle. Yes, it was Gwin all right. Since Dustfinger's death he had looked at Farid like an enemy, but tonight he nibbled his calves the way he used to when he wanted to play, and chattered until Farid followed him.

The marten was quick, too quick even for Farid, who could

outrun most people, but Gwin kept stopping to wait for him with his tail twitching impatiently, leaving Farid to follow as fast as the darkness allowed, because he knew who had sent the marten.

They found Dustfinger where the castle walls became the city boundary of Ombra, and the mountainside on which the city stood rose so steeply that no more houses could stand there. Nothing but thorny bushes covered the slope, and the castle wall towered up without any windows, forbidding as a clenched fist, broken by only a few barred slits that let just enough air into the dungeons for the prisoners not to stifle to death before they were executed. No one stayed long in the castle dungeons of Ombra. Sentence was quickly passed and executions quickly carried out. Why feed someone for long if you were going to hang him anyway? It was only the Bluejay's judge who was coming from the far side of the forest specially for him. Five days, so the whisper went, it would take the Adderhead five days to reach Ombra in his black-draped coach – and no one knew whether the Bluejay would live as long as a single day after his arrival.

Dustfinger stood with his shoulders back against the wall and his head bent, as if he were listening. The deep shadows cast by the castle made him invisible to the guards pacing back and forth on the battlements.

Dustfinger turned only when Gwin bounded towards him. Farid looked anxiously up at the guards before running to him, but they weren't looking for a boy, or a man on his own. One man wouldn't be able to set the Bluejay free. No, the Milksop's soldiers were watching for the arrival of many men, men coming out of the nearby forest or using ropes to help them down the steep slope above the castle – although the

Piper must know that even the Black Prince wouldn't venture to storm Ombra Castle.

The sky above the towers shone with the dark green of Sootbird's fire. The Milksop was celebrating. The Piper had ordered all the minstrels among the strolling players to compose songs about his own cunning and the defeat of the Bluejay, but very few had obeyed. Most of them kept silent, and their silence sang another song – a song of the sadness in Ombra and the tears of the women who had their children back, but had lost their hope.

'Well, what do you think of Sootbird's fire?' Dustfinger whispered as Farid came to lean against the castle wall beside him. 'Our friend has learnt a few things, wouldn't you say?'

'He's still useless!' Farid whispered back, and Dustfinger smiled, but his face grew grave again as he looked up at the windowless walls.

'It's nearly midnight,' he said quietly. 'At this time the Piper likes to show prisoners his hospitality with fists, clubs and boots.' He laid his hands on the wall and passed them over it, as if the stones could tell him what was going on in the cells behind them. 'He's not with him yet,' he whispered. 'But it won't be long now.'

'How do you know?' Sometimes it seemed to Farid as if someone else had come back from the dead, not the man he had known.

'Well, Silvertongue, Bluejay, whatever you like to call him . . .' Dustfinger whispered, 'since his voice brought me back I've known what he feels as if Death had transplanted his heart into my breast. Now, catch me a fairy, or the Piper will half kill him before sunrise. Bring me one of the rainbow-coloured kind. Orpheus has given them his own vanity, which comes in handy. You can get them to do anything for a few compliments.'

The fairy was soon found. Orpheus's fairies were all over the place, and although winter didn't make them as drowsy as Fenoglio's blue fairies, it was child's play to pluck one from her nest at this hour of the night. She bit Farid, but he blew in her face as Dustfinger had taught him, until she was gasping for air and forgot all about biting. Dustfinger whispered something to her, and next moment the tiny thing was fluttering up to the barred slits in the wall and disappeared through one of them.

'What did you tell her?' Above them, Sootbird's venomous fire went on devouring the night. It swallowed up the sky, the stars and the moon, and the smoke hanging in the air was so acrid that Farid's eyes were streaming.

'Oh, just that I promised the Bluejay I'd send the most beautiful fairy of all to visit him in his dark dungeon. And by way of thanks she'll whisper him the news that the Adderhead will reach Ombra in five days' time, even if the moss-women pave his way here with curses, and that meanwhile we'll try to keep the Piper's mind occupied, so that he can't spend too much time beating up his prisoners.' Dustfinger clenched his left hand into a fist. 'You haven't yet asked me why I sent for you,' he said, blowing gently into the fist he had made. 'I thought you might like to see this.'

He laid his fist against the castle wall, and fiery spiders scuttled out from between his fingers. They hurried up the stones, more and more of them, as many as if they had been born there in Dustfinger's hand.

'The Piper's afraid of spiders,' he whispered. 'He fears them more than swords and knives, and if these creep into his fine clothes he may forget, just for a while, how much he enjoys beating his prisoners at night.'

Farid clenched his own fist. 'How do you make them?'

'I don't know – which, I'm afraid, means I can't teach you. Any more than I can teach you this.' Dustfinger placed his hands together. Farid heard him whispering, but he couldn't make out the words. When a fiery bluejay flew out of Dustfinger's hands and soared into the night sky on wings of blue and white fire, he felt a pang of envy like a wasp-sting.

'Oh, show me!' he whispered. 'Please! Let me try, at least!'

Dustfinger looked at him thoughtfully. One of the guards above them was raising the alarm. The fiery spiders had reached the castle battlements. 'Death taught me the trick of it, Farid,' he said softly.

'Well? So I was dead too, like you, although not for so long!'

Dustfinger laughed. He laughed so loudly that a sentry looked down, and he quickly drew Farid back with him into the blackest shadows.

'You're right. I'd quite forgotten!' he whispered, as the guards on the wall shouted in confusion and shot arrows at the fiery jay. The arrows smouldered and went out among its feathers. 'Very well, copy me! Try this.'

Farid quickly curved his fingers, feeling the excitement he always felt when he was going to learn something new about fire. It wasn't easy to repeat the strange words that Dustfinger whispered, and Farid's heart leapt when he really did feel a fiery tingling between his fingers. Next moment spiders were swarming all over the wall from his hand too, their burning bodies hurrying up the stones like an army of sparks. He smiled proudly at Dustfinger. But when he tried the bluejay, only a few pale moths fluttered out from between his fingers.

'Don't look so disappointed!' whispered Dustfinger as he sent two more bluejays flying into the night. 'There's plenty more to learn. But we'd better hide from our silver-nosed friend now.'

Ombra Castle wore a burning coat as they made their way through the trees, and Sootbird's fire had gone out. The sky belonged to the fire conjured up by Dustfinger. The Piper sent patrols out, but Dustfinger made the flames give birth to wolves and big cats, snakes slithering out of the branches, fiery moths that flew in the faces of the men-at-arms. The forest at the foot of the castle seemed to be all aflame, but the fire did not take hold, and Farid and his master were shadows among all the red, untouched by the fear they were spreading.

Finally the Piper had water poured from the battlements. It froze to ice in the branches of the trees, but Dustfinger's fire burnt on, shaping new creatures all the time, and died down only in the morning, like a spectre of the night. The fiery bluejays, however, went on circling in the air above Ombra, and when the Milksop sent his hounds into the for-est where the flames were now extinguished, fiery hares threw them off any track they found. But Farid sat with Dustfinger in a thicket of thorn apple and brownie-thorn, feeling happi-ness warm his heart. It was so good to be near Dustfinger again, as he had been in the old days, during all the nights when he had watched over him or kept him from bad dreams. Now, however, there didn't seem to be anything he had to protect him from. Except yourself, Farid, he thought, and his happiness was gone like the fiery creatures that Dustfinger had conjured up to protect the Bluejay.

'What's the matter?' Dustfinger looked at him as if it

wasn't only Silvertongue's thoughts he could read.

Then he took Farid's hand and blew gently into it, until a woman made of white fire rose from his fingers. 'They're not as bad as you think,' Dustfinger whispered to him, 'and if they come for me again it won't be because of you. Understand?'

'What do you mean?' Farid's heart missed a beat. 'Are they going to come for you again? Why? Soon?' The White Woman on his hand changed into a moth, fluttered away, and dissolved in the grey light of dawn.

'That depends on the Bluejay.'

'What does?'

Dustfinger placed a warning hand over his mouth and pushed the thorny tendrils aside. Soldiers had taken up positions under the window slits of the dungeons. They were staring at the forest, eyes wide with fear. Sootbird was with them. He was examining the castle wall as if he could read in the stones how Dustfinger had set the night on fire. 'Look at him!' Dustfinger whispered. 'He hates the fire, and the fire hates him.'

But Farid didn't want to talk about Sootbird. He reached for Dustfinger's arm. 'They mustn't come to take you away again! Please!'

Dustfinger looked at him. His eyes were so different since he had come back. There was no fear in them now, only the old watchfulness. 'I'll say it again. It all depends on the Bluejay. So help me to protect him, because he's going to need protection. Five days and nights in the Piper's power – that's a long time. I think we'll all be glad when the Adderhead finally arrives.'

Farid wanted to ask more questions, but he saw in Dustfinger's face that he would get no further answers. 'How about Her Ugliness? Don't you believe she can protect him?'

'Do you?' Dustfinger asked back.

A fairy was struggling through the thorny undergrowth. She almost tore her wings on the branches, but finally, exhausted, she perched on Dustfinger's knee. It was the fairy he had sent out to look for the Bluejay. She had found him, and was bringing back his thanks. Nor did she forget to mention that he had assured her that she was indeed the most beautiful fairy he had ever set eyes on.

39

Stolen Children

when I was a child
i was a squirrel a bluejay a fox
and spoke with them in their tongues
climbed their trees dug their dens
and knew the taste
of every grass and stone
the meaning of the sun
the message of the night

        Norman H. Russell, *The Message of the Rain*

It was snowing, tiny icy flakes, and Meggie wondered whether her father could see the snowflakes falling from wherever he was held captive. No, she told herself, the dungeons of Ombra lie too deep under the castle, and the idea that Mo was missing his first sight of snow in the Inkworld made her almost as sad as knowing that he was a prisoner.

Dustfinger was protecting him, as the Black Prince had so often assured her. Battista and Roxane kept saying so as well. But Meggie could think of nothing but the Piper, and how frail and young Violante had looked beside him.

The Adderhead was only two days' journey away now, so Nettle had said yesterday. Two days, and everything would be decided.

Two days.

The Strong Man drew Meggie to his side and pointed through the trees. Two women were looking for a way through the snow-covered thickets. They had a couple of boys and a girl with them. The children of Ombra had been disappearing one by one ever since the Bluejay gave himself up. Their mothers took them out into the fields, down to the river to do their laundry, into the forest to look for firewood – and came back alone. There were four places where the Prince's men waited for the children. News of their whereabouts was passed on from mouth to mouth, and there was a woman as well as a robber waiting at each of those places, so that it wouldn't be too hard for the children to let go of their mothers' hands.

Resa, Battista and Gecko were receiving them at the infirmary run by the Barn Owl. Roxane and Elfbane waited at the place where the healers gathered the bark of oak trees. Two more women met children by the river, and Meggie, with Doria and the Strong Man, waited for them in a charcoalburner's abandoned hut not far from the road to Ombra.

The three children hesitated when they saw the Strong Man, but their mothers led them on, and when Doria caught a couple of snowflakes on his outstretched tongue the youngest, a girl of about five, began giggling.

'Suppose we just make the Piper angry again by hiding them with you?' asked the child's mother. 'Suppose he's given up any idea of taking the children away now the Bluejay is his prisoner? It was all about the Bluejay, wasn't it?'

Meggie could have hit her for the coldness in her voice.

'Yes, and this is his daughter!' said the Strong Man, putting a protective arm around Meggie's shoulders. 'So don't talk as if you didn't care what became of him! You'd never have got your child back but for her father, have you forgotten that already? But the Adderhead will still need children for his mines, and yours would be easy prey.'

'That's his daughter? The witch?' The other woman drew her children close to her, but the girl looked curiously at Meggie.

'You sound like the Adder's men!' The Strong Man held Meggie more firmly, as if to ward off the words. 'What's the matter with you? Do you want to know your children are safe or don't you? You can always take them back to Ombra and hope the Piper doesn't come knocking at your door!'

'But where are you taking them?' The younger woman had tears in her eyes.

'If I told you, you'd be able to give it away.' The Strong Man put the smaller boy up on his shoulders as if he weighed no more than a fairy.

'Can we come too?'

'No, we can't feed so many. It will be difficult enough to fill the children's bellies.'

'And how long do you mean to hide them for?' How desperate every word sounded.

'Until the Bluejay has killed the Adderhead.'

The women looked at Meggie.

'How can he possibly do that?'

'He'll kill him, you wait and see,' replied the Strong Man, and his voice sounded so confident that for a precious moment even Meggie forgot all her fears for Mo. But the moment passed, and once again she felt the snow on her skin, as cold as the end of all things.

Doria put the little girl on his back and smiled at Meggie. He was tireless in his efforts to cheer her up. He brought her berries hard with frost, flowers covered with rime – the last flowers of the year – and made her forget her troubles by asking her about the world she came from. She was beginning to miss him when he wasn't near her.

The little girl cried when the women left, but Meggie stroked her hair and told her what Battista had said about the snow: many of the snowflakes, he had told her, were tiny elves who kissed your face with icy lips before melting on your warm skin. The child stared up at the whirling snow, and Meggie went on talking, letting the words comfort her too while the world around turned white, letting herself go back to the days when Mo used to tell her stories – before he was part of a story himself. It was a long time since Meggie had been able to say whether it was her story as well.

The snow did not fall for long, and left only a fine, light dusting on the cold ground. Twelve more women brought their children to the abandoned charcoal-burner's hut, their faces full of anxiety and concern, and full of doubt too. Were they doing the right thing? Some of the children didn't even look back at their mothers as the women left, others ran after them, and two cried so hard that their mothers took them away again, back to Ombra where the Piper was waiting for them like a silver spider in its web. By the time darkness fell, nineteen children stood under the trees with their powdering of snow, huddled together like a flock of goslings. The Strong Man looked like a giant beside them as he signalled to them to go with him. Doria conjured acorns out of their little noses and plucked coins from their hair when one of them started crying. The Strong Man showed them how he listened to the birds, and let three children ride on his shoulders all at once.

As for Meggie, she told them stories as darkness fell over them, stories Mo had told her so often that she thought she heard his voice with every word she spoke. They were all exhausted by the time they reached the robbers' camp. The place was teeming with children. Meggie tried to count them, but soon gave up. How were the robbers to fill so many mouths, when the Black Prince could hardly feed his own men?

What Snapper and Gecko thought of all this showed only too clearly in their faces. Nursemaids, that was the whisper going around the camp. Is this what we went into the forest for? Snapper, Gecko, Elfbane, Woodenfoot, Wayfarer, Blackbeard . . . many of them were saying so. But who was the slightly-built man with the gentle face standing beside Snapper, looking around as if he had never seen his surroundings before? He looked like . . . no. No, it couldn't be true. Meggie rubbed her eyes. She was obviously so tired that she was seeing ghosts. But suddenly two strong arms went around her, hugging her so hard that she gasped for air.

'Why, just look at you! You're almost as tall as me now, you shameless girl!'

Meggie turned.

Elinor.

What was happening? Had she lost her mind? Had it all been nothing but a dream, and now she was waking up? Would the trees dissolve next, would everything disappear – the robbers, the children – and she'd see Mo standing beside her bed asking if she intended to sleep right through breakfast?

Meggie pressed her face into Elinor's dress. It was velvet,

and looked like a theatrical costume. Yes, she was dreaming. Definitely. But then what was still real? Wake up, Meggie! she told herself. Come on, wake up!

The slightly-built stranger standing next to Snapper smiled shyly at her as he held his twisted spectacle frame up to his eyes, and yes, it really was Darius!

Elinor hugged her again, and Meggie began to cry. She wept into Elinor's peculiar dress, shedding all the tears she had been holding back since Mo rode to Ombra Castle.

'Yes, yes, I know! It's just terrible,' said Elinor as she awkwardly stroked Meggie's hair. 'You poor thing. I've already given that scribbler fellow a piece of my mind. Conceited old fool! But you wait, your father will show that silver-nosed Fiddler a thing or two!'

'He's the Piper.' Meggie had to laugh although the tears went on running down her face. 'The Piper, Elinor!'

'Well, whatever! How's anyone supposed to remember all these strange names?' Elinor looked around her. 'That Fenoglio deserves to be hung, drawn and quartered for all this, but of course he doesn't see it that way. I'm glad we'll be able to keep an eye on him now. He refused to let Minerva come here on her own, I suppose just because he couldn't stand the thought of not having her to cook and mend for him!'

'You mean Fenoglio's here too?' Meggie wiped her tears away.

'Yes. But where's your mother? I can't find her anywhere.'

Meggie's face seemed to show that she still wasn't on good terms with Resa, but Battista came between them before Elinor could ask her about that.

'Bluejay's daughter, will you introduce me to your splendidly-dressed friend?' He bowed to Elinor. 'To what guild of the strolling players do you belong, gracious lady? Let me guess. You're an actress. Your voice would surely fill any marketplace!'

Elinor stared at him in such horror that Meggie quickly came to her aid. 'This is Elinor, Battista – my mother's aunt . . .'

'Ah, one of the Bluejay's family!' Battista bowed even lower. 'Presumably that information will keep Snapper there from wringing your neck. He's trying to convince the Black Prince that you and this stranger –' he indicated Darius, who joined them with a shy smile – 'are spies of the Piper's.'

Elinor spun round so abruptly that she drove her elbow into Darius's stomach. 'The Black Prince?' She blushed like a girl as she saw him and his bear standing with Snapper. 'Oh, he's magnificent!' she breathed. 'And so is his bear – the bear looks just the way I imagined him! Ah, this is all so wonderful, so incredibly wonderful!'

Meggie felt her tears drying up. She was so glad Elinor was here, so very glad indeed.

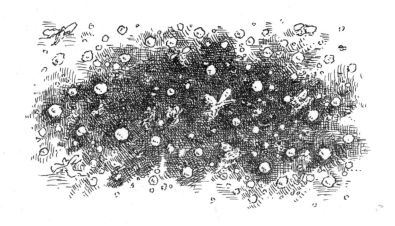

40

A New Cage

Westley closed his eyes. There was pain coming and he had
to be ready for it. He had to prepare his brain, he had to
get his mind controlled and safe from their efforts, so that
they could not break him.

William Goldman, *The Princess Bride*

This time they came earlier than on the nights before.
Night was only just falling outside. Not that it was ever
light in Mo's cell, but night brought a different kind of darkness, and with it came the Piper. Mo sat up as straight as he
could in chains, and prepared to be kicked and struck. If only
he hadn't felt so stupid, so infinitely stupid. The fool who of
his own free will had stumbled into his enemies' net. Not a
robber any more, not a bookbinder, only a fool.

The cells in the dungeons of Ombra were no more comfortable than the cells in the tower of the Castle of Night. In
these dark holes, hardly high enough for a man to stand up,
the same fear lurked as in all dungeons. Yes, the fear was
back. It had been waiting for him at the gates, it had almost

choked him when the Milksop's men had bound his hands.

Captured. Helpless . . .

Think about the children, Mortimer! Only the memory of their faces soothed him when he cursed himself for what he had done and endured the blows and kicks that the night brought with it. Dustfinger's fire at least made the Piper leave him in peace from time to time, but it also infuriated Silvernose more and more. In his mind Mo still heard the voice of the fairy who had fluttered up on to his shoulder that first night. He still saw the fiery spiders scuttering into the Piper's velvet garments. Mo had laughed at him for the panic in his face – but he had paid for that, several times.

Two more days, Mortimer, two days and two nights. Then the Adderhead will arrive. And then what? Yes, he was a fool to hope he might yet be able to give Death and her pale daughters what they demanded.

Would Resa realize that he had also ridden to the castle for Meggie's sake when the White Women came for their daughter? Would she understand that he hadn't told her anything about it so that fear for Meggie wouldn't eat away at her own heart?

The two soldiers who entered his cell had soot on their hands and faces. They always came in pairs, but where was their silver-snouted master? Without a word, they hauled Mo to his feet. The chains were heavy and cut into his skin.

'The Piper's going to be visiting you in another cell today!' they muttered to him. 'One that your friend's fire can't find.'

They went further down, down and down, past holes from which the smell of rotting flesh rose. Once Mo thought he saw a fiery snake creeping through the darkness, but one of his guards hit him when he turned to look at it.

The cell into which they pushed him was much larger than the one he had been kept in before. There was dried blood on the walls, and the air was both cold and musty.

The Piper kept him waiting, and when he finally arrived, followed by two more soldiers, he too had soot on his face. The men who had dragged Mo here made way respectfully for their master, but Mo saw how anxiously they looked around – as if they were waiting for Dustfinger's fiery spiders to crawl out of the walls any minute now. Mo could sense Dustfinger searching for him. It was as if his thoughts were putting out feelers for Mo, but the dungeons in Ombra lay almost as deep as those in the Castle of Night.

Perhaps tonight he would use the knife that Battista had sewn into the hem of his shirt – although his hands hurt so much that he probably wouldn't even be able to hold it, let alone stab with it. But it felt good to have it with him when the fear became unbearable. The fear and the hatred.

'Your fire-eating friend is getting bolder all the time, but that won't help you tonight, Bluejay. I'm tired of it!' The Piper's face was white under the soot that blackened even his silver nose. One of the soldiers hit Mo in the face. Two more days . . .

The Piper looked at his soot-smeared gloves with distaste. 'All Ombra is laughing at me. "Look at the Piper," they whisper. "The Fire-Dancer is running rings around his men, and the Black Prince is hiding the children from him! The Bluejay will save us after all." Well, enough of that! When I've finished with you tonight they won't think so any more.'

He came so close to Mo that his nose was almost prodding his enemy's face. 'What about it? Don't you want to use your wonderful voice to call for help? Call all your ragged friends, the Prince and his bear, the Fire-Dancer – or how about Violante? Her hairy servant is always on my heels, snooping, and hardly an hour goes by without her telling me that you're no use to her father unless you're alive. But her father is nothing like as terrifying these days as he used to be. You've made sure of that yourself.'

Violante. Mo had seen her only once, when they were dragging him off his horse in the castle courtyard. How could he have been stupid enough to believe she'd be able to protect him? He was lost. And Meggie with him. Despair rose in him, such black despair that he felt sick, and the Piper smiled.

'Ah, you're afraid. I like that. I ought to write a song about it. But from now on the only songs sung will be about me – dark songs, the kind I enjoy. Very dark.'

With a foolish grin, one of the soldiers went up to Mo holding a stick studded with iron.

'"The Bluejay will run away from them again!" That's what they say!' The Piper took a step back. 'But you're never going to run away from anything any more. From now on you're going to crawl, Bluejay. Crawl to me.'

The two men who had brought him here seized Mo. They forced him up against the bloodstained wall, while the third man raised the iron-studded stick. The Piper stroked his silver nose.

'You'll need your hands for the Book, Bluejay. But why would the Adder mind if I break your legs? And even if he did . . . as I was saying, the Adderhead's not what he used to be.'

Lost.

Oh God. Meggie, he thought. Had he ever told her such a terrible story as this? 'No, Mo, no fairy tales!' she always used to say when she was little. 'They're much too sad.' Not as sad as this one.

'What a pity my father was unable to hear your little speech for himself, Piper.' Violante did not raise her voice much, but the Piper whipped round as if she had shouted at him. The soldier with the silly grin lowered the stick, and the others retreated, making way for the Adderhead's daughter. Violante was almost invisible in the black dress she wore. How could they call her ugly? At this moment Mo felt he had never seen a more beautiful face. He hoped the Piper didn't notice how his legs were trembling. He begrudged the silver-nosed man that satisfaction.

A small, furry face appeared beside Violante. Tullio. Had he fetched her? Her Ugliness had half a dozen of her beardless soldiers with her too. They looked so young and vulnerable compared to the Piper's men, but their young hands held crossbows, weapons to be respected even by seasoned men-at-arms.

But the Piper quickly recovered.

'What do you want here?' he snarled at Violante. 'I'm only making sure your precious prisoner doesn't fly the coop again. It's bad enough for his fiery friend to make us all a laughing stock. Your father's not going to like that one bit.'

'And you are not going to like what I'm about to do.' There was no emotion at all in Violante's voice. 'Tie them up!' she ordered her soldiers. 'Take the chains off the Bluejay and tie him up too, but so that he can still ride.'

The Piper reached for his sword, but three of Violante's young men overpowered him and dragged him down. Mo could physically feel their hatred for the man. They'd happily have killed the Piper, he saw it on their young faces, and obviously the Piper's men saw it too, for they let themselves be tied up without resisting.

'You ugly little snake!' The Piper's noseless voice sounded even stranger when he raised it. 'So the Milksop was right! You're hand in glove with that pack of robbers. What do you want? The throne of Ombra, and perhaps your father's too?'

Violante's face was as still as if Balbulus had painted it. 'I want just one thing,' she replied. 'I want to deliver the Bluejay to my father intact, so that he can still be useful to him. And in return for that service I will indeed demand the throne of Ombra. Why not? I have ten times more right to it than the Milksop.'

The soldier who removed Mo's chains was the boy who had opened the sarcophagus for him in Cosimo's vault. 'I'm sorry!' he murmured as he tied him up. He didn't pull the rope very tight around Mo's arms, which were chafed and sore, but it still hurt, and all the time Mo never took his eyes off Violante. He could hear Snapper's hoarse voice in his ears only too clearly. *She'll sell you for the throne of Ombra.*

'Where are you taking him?' The Piper spat in the face of the soldier tying him up. 'Even if you hide him with the giants, I'll find you!'

'Oh, I've no intention of hiding him,' replied Violante with composure. 'I shall take him to my mother's castle. My father knows the way. And if he is to agree to my conditions, he must go there. I'm sure you'll tell him that.'

She'll sell you.

Violante's glance moved over Mo as indifferently as if they had never met before. The Piper kicked Mo with his bound legs as Violante's soldiers led him out of the cell, but what was a kick compared to the iron-studded stick he had been about to use?

'You're a dead man, Bluejay!' he shouted after him before one of Violante's soldiers gagged him. 'Dead!'

Not yet, Mo wanted to reply. Not yet.

A maid was waiting outside the barred door. Only when Mo passed her did he see that it was Brianna. So Violante really had taken her back. She nodded to him before following her mistress. Three guards lay unconscious in the passage. Violante stepped over them and followed the corridor down which Mo had been brought, to a narrow tunnel branching off to the left. Tullio hurried ahead, and her soldiers followed in silence, with Mo between them.

Her mother's castle . . .

Whatever Violante's intentions, he was very thankful to her that he still had the use of his legs.

The tunnel seemed endless. How did the Adderhead's daughter know so much about the secret ways around this castle?

'I read about this tunnel.' Violante turned to him as if she had heard his thoughts. Or perhaps he was thinking out loud, after all those hours alone in the dark?

'Fortunately for us, I am the only person who uses the castle library,' Violante went on. How she was looking at him – as if to determine whether he still trusted her! Oh yes, she was like her father. She loved the game of fear and power, just as the Adderhead did, the constant measuring of her strength against others, even to the point of death. So why did he still trust her all the same, in spite of his helplessness?

Two more tunnels branched off into the darkness, just as narrow as the first. When Tullio looked enquiringly at her, Violante pointed without hesitation to the one on the left. She was a strange woman, so much older than her years. Such coldness, such self-control. *Never forget whose daughter she is.* The Black Prince had so often urged Mo to remember that, and he was beginning to understand the warning better now. Violante was surrounded by the same aura of cruelty that he had felt in the company of her father, the same impatience with others, the same belief that she was cleverer than most people, better . . . more important.

'Your Highness?' It was the soldier behind Mo. They all treated their mistress with great respect. 'What about your son?'

Violante did not turn as she replied. 'Jacopo stays here. He'd only give us away.' Her voice was cold. Did you have to learn from your own parents how to love your child? If so, he supposed it was no wonder the Adderhead's daughter didn't know much about it.

Mo felt wind on his face. Air that smelt of more than just earth. The tunnel was getting wider. He heard rushing water, and as they came out into the open he saw Ombra high above him. Snow was falling from the black sky, and the river glinted beyond almost leafless bushes. Horses were waiting by the bank, guarded by a soldier, but a boy was holding a knife to the soldier's neck. Farid. Dustfinger stood beside him, sparks in his snow-dusted hair, the two martens at his feet.

When Violante's soldiers aimed their crossbows at him, he only smiled. 'Where are you taking your prisoner, Adder's daughter?' he asked. 'I'm the shadow he brought back from the dead with him, and his shadow follows him wherever he goes.'

Tullio hid behind Violante's black skirts as if he were afraid Dustfinger would send him up in flames at any moment. But Violante signalled to her soldiers to lower their crossbows. Brianna just looked at her father.

'He's not my prisoner,' said Violante. 'But I don't want my father hearing that from one of his countless spies. Hence the bonds. Shall I remove them all the same, Bluejay?'

She brought out a knife from under her cloak. Mo exchanged a glance with Dustfinger. He was glad to see him, although his heart still had to accustom itself to that feeling. The sight of Dustfinger had filled him with very different emotions for too many years. But since Death had touched them both they seemed to be made of the same flesh. And the same story. Perhaps there was only a single story anyway?

Don't trust her! said Dustfinger's glance. And Mo knew that he would read his own unspoken answer in his face. *I must.*

'I'll keep the bonds on,' he said, and Violante hid the knife among the folds of her dress again. Snowflakes clung to its black fabric like tiny feathers.

'I am taking the Bluejay to the castle where my mother grew up,' she said. 'I can protect him there. Here I can't.'

'The Castle in the Lake?' Dustfinger took a bag from his belt and gave it to Farid. 'That's a long way. A good four days' ride on horseback.'

'You've heard of the castle?'

'Who hasn't? But it was abandoned many years ago. Have you ever been there?'

Violante's chin jutted so defiantly that she reminded Mo of Meggie again. 'No, I never have, but I remember all my mother told me about it, and I've read everything that's ever been written about the castle. I know it better than if I *had* been there.'

Dustfinger merely looked at her. Then he shrugged his

shoulders. 'If you say so. The Piper isn't there – that's one good thing, and it's said to be easy to defend.' He scrutinized Violante's young soldiers as if counting their years of life. 'Yes, very likely the Bluejay will be safer there.'

The snowflakes settling on Mo's bound hands cooled his sore skin. He would hardly be able to use them unless he could move them more freely, at least at night. 'And you're sure your father will follow us to the castle?' His voice sounded as if the despair of the dungeon still clung to it.

Violante smiled. 'Oh yes, indeed he will. He'll follow you anywhere. And he will bring the White Book with him.'

The White Book. The snow fell as if to paint the whole world as white as its empty pages. Winter had come. Your heartbeats are numbered, Mortimer, he told himself. And Meggie's. Meggie's . . . how could he still love this world in spite of everything? How was it that his eyes couldn't see enough of the distant trees, so much taller than the trees he had climbed as a boy, and his gaze sought fairies and glass men as if they'd always been a part of his world? *Remember, Mortimer, there was once a very different world*, a voice whispered inside him. But whatever it whispered, it was wasting its time. Even his own name sounded strange and unreal, and he knew that if there had been a hand trying to close Fenoglio's book for ever, he would have stopped it.

'We have no horse for you, Fire-Dancer.' Violante's voice was hostile. She didn't like Dustfinger. Well, he had felt just the same himself for a long time, hadn't he?

Dustfinger gave such a mocking laugh that Violante just stared at him even more coldly. 'Ride on. I'll find you,' he said.

He was gone even before Violante's men brought Mo a

horse, and so was Farid. There were only a few sparks still left glowing in the snow where they had been standing. Mo saw the awe on the faces of Violante's soldiers – as if they had seen a ghost. And perhaps that wasn't too far off, as a name for a man who had come back from the dead.

Still nothing was moving in the castle. No sentry raised the alarm as the first of the young soldiers rode his horse into the river. No one shouted from the battlements that the Bluejay was escaping again. Ombra was asleep, and the snow covered it with a white blanket, while Dustfinger's fiery bluejays still circled above the roof tops.

Pictures from the Ashes

Dumbledore shook his head. 'Curiosity is not a sin,' he said. 'But we should exercise caution with our curiosity . . . yes, indeed . . .'

J.K. Rowling, *Harry Potter and the Goblet of Fire*

The cave that Mo and the Black Prince had found, long before Sootbird staged his show, was two hours' journey north of Ombra on foot. That was a long way for children to walk, and winter had come to the Inkworld, with rain that turned to snow more and more often. White moths were suddenly hanging from the bare branches like leaves made of ice, and grey-feathered owls had begun hunting the fairies.

'My own fairies sleep at this time of year,' Fenoglio had said in self-defence, when Despina began crying because an owl had torn two of the tiny creatures to pieces before her eyes. 'But the silly creatures Orpheus has made flutter around as if they'd never heard of winter!'

The Black Prince led them uphill and downhill, through

thickets and stony debris, along such overgrown paths that they usually had to carry the smaller children. Meggie's back was soon aching, but Elinor strode on as if she couldn't wait to see as much as possible of this strange world – although she went to a great deal of trouble to conceal her delight from the creator of the whole thing. Fenoglio was walking right behind them most of the time, with Resa and Darius. The little girl Resa was carrying looked so like Meggie that, whenever Meggie herself turned round to her mother, it was like looking back to a time that had never been. Mo used to carry her when she was little, always Mo. But when she saw Resa pressing her face into the little girl's hair Meggie wished it had been different. Perhaps then Mo's absence wouldn't have hurt her quite so much.

When Resa felt sick halfway to the cave, Roxane told her not to carry any of the children any more. 'Be careful!' Meggie heard her say. 'You don't want to be telling your husband you've lost his child when he comes back, do you?'

It was obvious now that Resa was pregnant, and sometimes Meggie wanted to put her hand on the place where the child was growing, but she didn't. Tears had sprung to Darius's eyes when he heard about the pregnancy, and Elinor had cried, 'Well, everything *has* to turn out all right now,' hugging Resa so hard that she must almost have squashed the unborn child. But Meggie kept catching herself thinking: I don't need any sister. Or any brother either. I just want my father back! However, when one of the little boys she had been carrying on her back thanked her with a smacking kiss on her cheek, she felt – for the first time, and quite unexpectedly – that she was looking forward to the new baby, and she began imagining what it would be like to have a brother or sister putting small fingers into her own hand.

They were all glad that Roxane had come with them. Her son had not been among the children taken captive by the Piper and Sootbird, but she had brought Jehan along all the same. Roxane was wearing her long black hair loose again, as the minstrel women did. She smiled more often these days too, and when some of the children started crying because it was such a long way, Meggie heard her sing for the first time. She sang very quietly, but it was enough for Meggie to understand what Battista had once said: *When Roxane sings she takes all the sadness from your heart and makes music out of it.* How could she be so happy when Dustfinger wasn't with her? 'Because now she knows that he will always come back to her,' Battista said. Did Resa know the same of Mo?

Meggie didn't see the entrance to the cave until she was very close to it. Tall fir trees hid it, thorn-apple, and bushes with white down hanging from their branches, long and soft as human hair. Meggie's skin was still itching hours after she had followed Doria through the dense thickets.

The crack in the rock leading to the cavern inside was so narrow that the Strong Man had to duck his head and squeeze through it sideways, but the cave itself was tall as a church inside, and the children's voices echoing back from the rock walls were so loud that it seemed to Meggie as if they could be heard all the way to Ombra.

The Black Prince posted six guards outside. They climbed high into the tops of the surrounding trees. He sent four more men back to obliterate their tracks. Doria went as well, and sitting on his shoulder was Jasper who had attached himself to Doria now that Farid had gone. It was an almost hopeless task to hide the prints of so many small feet, and Meggie could see from the Prince's face how much he would have liked to take the children even further away, far from the Piper and the Milksop's hounds.

The Black Prince had let half a dozen women come with their children, for he knew his men well enough to realize that they weren't much use as foster mothers. Roxane, Resa and Minerva helped the women to make the cave more comfortable, laying blankets and lengths of cloth between the rocky walls, bringing in more dry leaves so that everyone could sleep more easily, spreading furs over the leaves and piling up stones to make separate niches where the smallest children could bed down. They made a hearth to cook on, took stock of the provisions the robbers had brought – and kept straining their ears for noises outside, terrified of suddenly hearing the barking of dogs, or soldiers' voices.

'See how greedily they're stuffing their little mouths!' grunted Snapper, when the Black Prince first had food served out to the children. 'Our provisions are hardly going to last a week at this rate. And then what?'

'By then the Adderhead will be long dead,' replied the Strong Man, his tone defiant, but Snapper just laughed scornfully.

'Oh yes? And the Bluejay will kill the Piper at the same time, will he? He'll need more than three words for that. And what about the Milksop and his men-at-arms?'

Yes, what about them? No one knew the answer to that. 'Violante will throw them all out once her father's dead!' said Minerva. But Meggie still found it hard to trust Her Ugliness.

'He'll be all right, Meggie!' Elinor kept saying. 'Don't look so sad. If I get the hang of this whole story – which isn't so easy, since our good friend the author there likes making things complicated,' she added with a reproachful glance at Fenoglio, '– then they won't touch a hair of your father's head, because he has to cure that Book for the Adderhead. Which presumably he can't do, but that's another problem. Anyway, you wait and see. Everything will end well!'

If only Meggie could have believed her, as she used to believe Mo. 'It will be all right, Meggie!' That was all he had to say, and she would lay her head against his shoulder in the certain knowledge that he would fix everything. How long ago that was. So very long ago.

The Black Prince had sent Gecko's tame crows to Ombra – to the Barn Owl and his informers in the castle – and Resa stood outside the cave for hours on end, searching the sky for black feathers. But the only bird Gecko brought into the cave on the second day was a bedraggled magpie, and in the end it was Farid, not one of the crows, who brought them news of the Bluejay.

He was shaking with cold when one of the guards took him to the Black Prince, and his face had the forlorn expression it wore every time Dustfinger had sent him away. Meggie took Elinor's hand as he stammered out his news: Violante was taking Mo to her mother's castle as her prisoner. Dustfinger would follow them. The Piper had hit and threatened Mo . . . Violante had been afraid he would kill him. Resa buried her face in her hands, and Roxane put an arm around her.

'Her mother's castle? But Violante's mother is dead!' By now Elinor knew her way around Fenoglio's story better than its author himself. She moved among the robbers as if she had always been one of them, got Battista to sing her minstrel songs, asked the Strong Man to show her how to talk to the birds, and made Jasper explain how many different kinds of glass men there were. She kept tripping on the hem of her peculiar dress, she had smudges on her forehead and spiders in her hair, but Elinor looked happier than she had ever been before.

'It's the castle where her mother grew up. Dustfinger knows it.' Farid took a bag from his belt and wiped some soot off the leather. Then he looked at Meggie. 'We made spiders and wolves out of fire to protect your father!' There was no mistaking the pride in his voice.

'But all the same Violante thought he wasn't safe in the castle.' Resa's voice sounded accusing: you can't protect him, in fact, none of you can protect him. He's on his own.

'The Castle in the Lake.' The Black Prince spoke its name as if he did not particularly like Violante's idea either. 'There are many songs about that castle.'

'Dark songs,' added Gecko. The magpie had flown to him and was perching on his shoulder. It was a skinny bird, and it stared at Meggie as if it would like to peck her eyes out.

'What kind of songs?' Resa's voice was husky with fear.

'Oh, ghost stories, that's all. Fanciful nonsense!' Fenoglio pushed past Resa. Despina was clinging to his hand. 'The Castle in the Lake was abandoned long ago, so people fill it with stories, but that's all they are.'

'How reassuring!' The glance that Elinor cast Fenoglio made his face turn red.

He was in a gloomy mood. Since their arrival at the cave he had been complaining non-stop about the cold, the crying children, or the stench of the bear. Most of the time he sat behind a wall of stones he had built in the darkest corner of the cave, quarrelling with Rosenquartz. Only Ivo and Despina could get a smile out of him – and Darius, who had joined the old man as soon as they had arrived at the cave and, as he helped Fenoglio to build his wall, started timidly asking him about the world he had created. 'Where do the giants live?' 'Do water-nymphs live longer than human beings?' 'What kind of country lies beyond the mountains?' Darius obviously asked the right questions, for Fenoglio didn't lose patience with him as he had with Orpheus.

The Castle in the Lake.

Fenoglio shook his head when Meggie went to him to find out more about the place to which Her Ugliness was taking her father. 'It wasn't among the main scenes of the story,' was all he would say, grumpily. 'One of many settings. Just scenery! Read my book if you want to know more about it – if Dustfinger ever lets it out of his hands again, that is! If you ask me, he ought really have given it to me, although we still don't seem to be on speaking terms. After all, I wrote it, but there we are. At least Orpheus doesn't have it any more.'

The book.

In fact Dustfinger had passed *Inkheart* on long ago, but Meggie kept that knowledge to herself, for Farid had asked her to.

He had handed it over to her mother as swiftly as if Basta might emerge behind him to steal it, just as he had back in the other world. 'Dustfinger says it will be safest with you, because you know how powerful the words in it are,' he had murmured. 'The Black Prince doesn't understand that. But keep it hidden and let nobody know you have it! Orpheus mustn't get it back. Dustfinger is fairly sure, though, that he won't look for it in your hands.'

Resa had taken the book only with some reluctance, and finally she hid it in the place where she slept. Meggie's heart beat faster as she took it out from under the blanket. She hadn't held Fenoglio's book in her hands since Mortola had given it to her in Capricorn's arena to read the Shadow into being. It was a strange feeling to open it now that she was in the world it described, and for a moment Meggie feared the pages might suck in everything around her. The rocky ground where she was sitting, the blanket under which her mother slept, the white ice-moth that had lost its way in the cave, the children laughing as they ran after it . . . had all that really come into existence between these covers? The book seemed so meaningless compared to the marvels it described, just a few hundred printed pages and a dozen pictures not half as good as those that Balbulus painted, all in a silvery-green linen binding. Yet it wouldn't have surprised Meggie to find her own name on the pages, or the names of her mother, Farid, or Mo – although, no, her father bore another name in this world.

Meggie had never had the chance to read Fenoglio's whole story. Where was she to begin now? Was there a picture of the Castle in the Lake? She was quickly leafing through the pages when she suddenly heard Farid's voice behind her.

'Meggie?'

She closed the book guiltily, as if every word in it was a secret. How stupid of her. This book didn't know anything about all her fears, it knew nothing of the Bluejay, nor even of Farid . . .

She didn't think of him now as often as she used to. It was almost as if, with Dustfinger's return, the chapter about Farid and herself had ended, and the story was beginning again, extinguishing part of the tale it had told before with every new word.

'Dustfinger gave me something else to bring back here.'

Farid glanced at the book on her lap as if it were a snake. But then he knelt down beside her and took from his belt the soot-blackened bag that his fingers had been caressing while he delivered his news to the Prince.

'He gave it to me for Roxane,' said Farid quietly, as he sprinkled a fine circle of ashes on the rocky ground. 'But you looked really upset, so . . .'

He didn't finish his sentence. Instead he whispered words that only he and Dustfinger understood – and the fire suddenly licked up from the ashes as if it had been sleeping there. Farid lured it out, praised and enticed it, until it burnt with such heat that the heart of the flames became white as paper, and a picture appeared, difficult to make out at first, then more and more distinct.

Hills, densely wooded . . . soldiers on a narrow path, many soldiers . . . two women riding among them. Meggie recognized Brianna at once by her hair. The woman in front of her must be Her Ugliness, and there – with Dustfinger beside him – rode Mo. Meggie instinctively put her hand out to him, but Farid held her fingers fast.

'He has blood on his face,' she whispered.

'The Piper.' Farid spoke to the flames again, and the picture spread out, showing the path turning towards mountains that Meggie had never seen before, much higher than the hills around Ombra. Snow lay on the way ahead, as it did on the slopes in the distance, and Meggie saw Mo breathing into his cold hands. He looked so strange in the fur-trimmed cloak he wore – like a character in a fairy tale. He *is* a character in a fairy tale, Meggie, a voice inside her whispered. The Bluejay . . . was he still her father too? Had Mo ever looked so serious? Her Ugliness turned to him; of course it was Her

Ugliness, who else? They were talking, but the fire showed only silent images.

'You see? He's all right. Thanks to Dustfinger.' Farid stared into the fire with longing, as if that could take him back to Dustfinger's side. Then he heaved a sigh and blew gently on the flames until they turned dark red as if blushing at the pet names he soothed them with.

'Will you follow him?'

Farid shook his head. 'Dustfinger wants me to look after Roxane.' Meggie could sense his bitterness for herself. 'What will *you* do?' He looked at her with the question in his eyes.

'What am I supposed to do?'

Whisper words, that's all I can do, she added in her mind. All the words the minstrels sing about the Bluejay: how he calms the waves with his voice, how he is invulnerable and fast as the wind, how the fairies protect him, and the White Women watch over his sleep. Words. They were the only means she had of protecting Mo, and she whispered them day and night, in every private moment, sending them after him like the crows that the Black Prince had sent to Ombra.

The flames had gone out, and Farid was heaping up the warm ashes with his hands when a shadow fell on him. Doria stood behind them, holding hands with two children. 'Meggie, the woman with the loud voice is looking for you.'

The robbers had many names for Elinor. Meggie couldn't help smiling, but Farid cast a none-too-friendly glance at Doria. He carefully put the ashes back in his bag, and rose to his feet. 'I'll be with Roxane,' he said, kissing Meggie on the mouth. He hadn't done that for weeks. Then he pushed past Doria and strode away without looking back once.

'He kissed her!' one of the children whispered to Doria,

just loud enough for Meggie to hear. The child was a girl, and she blushed when Meggie returned her gaze, and hastily hid her face in Doria's side.

'So he did,' Doria whispered back. 'But did she kiss him back?'

'No!' said the boy on his right, sizing up Meggie as if wondering whether kissing her would be fun.

'That's a good thing, then,' said Doria. 'A very good thing.'

An Audience with the Adderhead

You cannot fully read a book without being alone. But through this very solitude you become intimately involved with people whom you might never have met otherwise, either because they have been dead for centuries or because they spoke languages you cannot understand. And nonetheless, they have become your closest friends, your wisest advisors, the wizards that hypnotize you, the lovers you have always dreamed of.

Antonio Munoz Molina, *The Power of the Pen*

Just after midnight the Adderhead's retinue reached Ombra. Orpheus had made Oss wait under the gallows by the city gate for three nights on end, so that he would be sure to hear of the Silver Prince's arrival as soon as the Milksop did.

All was ready. The Piper had had every door and window in the castle draped with black cloth so that it would be night there for his master even during the day, and the felled trees that the Milksop intended to burn on the castle hearths lay

391

ready in the courtyard, although everyone knew that no fire could drive away the cold that had made its way into the Adderhead's flesh and bones. The one man who could perhaps have done it had escaped from the castle dungeons, and all Ombra wondered how the Silver Prince would take that news.

Orpheus sent Oss to the castle that very night. After all, it was common knowledge that the Adderhead hardly slept at all.

'Say I have information of the utmost importance for him. Say it's about the bookbinder and his daughter.' Having little confidence in his bodyguard's intellectual capacities, he repeated the words half a dozen times, but Oss did his errand well. After just over three hours, hours spent by Orpheus pacing restlessly up and down his study, he came back with the message that the audience was granted, but only on condition Orpheus went to the castle at once, since the Adderhead must rest before he set out again.

Set out again? Aha. So he's playing his daughter's game! Orpheus thought as he hurried up the path to the castle. Very well. Then it's up to you to show him he can't win the game without your help! Involuntarily he licked his lips to keep them smooth for this great task. Never before had he spun his web around such magnificent prey. Curtain up, he whispered to himself again and again. Curtain up!

The servant who led him through the black-draped corridors to the throne-room said not a single word. It was hot and dark in the castle. Like hell, thought Orpheus. And wasn't that suitable? Didn't people often compare the Adderhead with the devil himself? You had to hand it to Fenoglio, this was a villain of real stature. Beside the Adderhead, Capricorn had been just a cheap play-actor, an amateur – although no doubt Mortola saw it differently. But who cared what Mortola thought now?

A shudder of delight ran down Orpheus's plump shoulders. The Adderhead! Sprung from a clan that had cultivated the art of evil for generations. There was no cruel act that at least one of his ancestors hadn't committed. Cunning, the lust for power, total lack of any conscience: those were the family's outstanding characteristics. What a combination! Orpheus was excited. His hands were damp and sweating like a boy's on his first date. Again and again he ran his tongue over his teeth as if to sharpen them that way, prepare them for the right words. 'Believe me,' he heard himself saying, 'I can lay this world at your feet, I can make it into anything you like, but for that you must find me a certain book. It is even more powerful than the Book that made you immortal, far more powerful!'

Inkheart . . . no, he wasn't going to think of the night he had lost it, not now, and he certainly wasn't going to think of Dustfinger!

It was no lighter in the throne-room than in the corridors. A few lost-looking candles burnt among the columns and around the throne. On Orpheus's last visit (as far as he could remember, that was when he had delivered the dwarf to the Milksop), the way to the throne had been lined by stuffed animals, bears, wolves, spotted great cats, and of course the unicorn he had written here, but they were all gone now. Even the Milksop was bright enough to realize that in view of the sparse taxes he had sent to his brother-in-law, these hunting trophies were unlikely to impress the Adderhead. Nothing but darkness filled the great hall now, making the black-clad guards between the columns almost invisible. Only their weapons glinted in the flickering light of the fire that burnt behind the throne. Orpheus went to great pains to stride past them looking unimpressed, but unfortunately he stumbled over the hem of his coat twice, and when he finally stood in front of the throne itself, the Milksop was sitting there, and not his brother-in-law.

Orpheus felt a stab of disappointment, sharp as a knife. He quickly bowed his head to hide it, and tried to find the right things to say, flattering but not too servile. Talking to the powerful called for special skills, but he'd had practice. There had always been people more powerful than he was in his life. His father had been the first, never satisfied with his awkward son who liked books better than working in his parents' shop: those endless hours among the dusty shelves, an ever-friendly smile when he had to serve the tourists who flocked in instead of leafing through a book with hasty fingers, avidly looking for the place where he had last had to leave the world of print. Orpheus couldn't count the slaps he'd earned over his forbidden passion for reading. One every tenth page was probably about it, but the price had never seemed too high. What was a slap for ten pages of escapism, ten pages far from everything that made him unhappy, ten pages of real life instead of the monotony that other people called the real world?

'Your Grace!' Orpheus bent his head even lower. What a ridiculous sight the Milksop was under his silver-powdered wig, his scrawny neck emerging so pathetically from his heavy velvet collar. His pale face was as expressionless as ever – as if his creator had forgotten to give it eyebrows, just sketching in the eyes and lips lightly.

'You want to speak to the Adderhead?' Even the Milksop's voice was not impressive. Malicious tongues mocked it, saying he wouldn't have to change it very much to use it as a decoy call to the ducks he liked shooting out of the sky.

How that feeble fool is sweating, thought Orpheus as he smiled deferentially. Well, I expect I'd be sweating in his place. The Adderhead had come to Ombra to kill his worst enemy, only to discover instead that his herald and his brother-in-law had let their valuable prisoner get away. Really, it was amazing that they were both still alive.

'Yes, Your Honour. Whenever it is convenient to the Silver Prince!' Orpheus was delighted to realize that in this empty hall his voice sounded even more effective than usual. 'I have information for him that could be of the greatest significance.'

'About his daughter and the Bluejay?' The Milksop plucked at his sleeves with a deliberately bored expression. Perfumed bonehead.

'Indeed.' Orpheus cleared his throat. 'As you know, I have important clients, influential friends. News comes to my ears that doesn't even reach castles. This time it is alarming news, and I want to make sure that your brother-in-law hears of it.'

'And what might this news be?'

Careful, Orpheus!

'As to that, Your Grace . . .' he really was taking great pains to sound regretful, 'I would rather tell it only to the Adderhead himself. After all, it concerns his daughter.'

'Whom he will hardly feel like discussing at present!' The Milksop adjusted his wig. 'Sly, ugly creature!' he uttered. 'Abducts my prisoner to steal the throne of Ombra from me! Threatens to kill him if her own father doesn't follow her into the mountains like a dog! As if it hadn't been difficult enough to catch that puffed-up Bluejay! But why do I bother to tell you all this? I suppose because you brought me the unicorn. The best hunt of my life.' In melancholy mood, he stared at

Orpheus with eyes almost as pale as his face. 'The more beautiful the game the greater the pleasure of killing it, don't you agree?'

'Words of wisdom, Your Highness, words of wisdom!' Orpheus bowed again. The Milksop loved people to bow to him.

Glancing nervously at the guards, he now leant down to Orpheus. 'I would so much like another unicorn!' he whispered. 'It was a huge success with all my friends. Do you think you can get me another? Maybe a little larger than the last one?'

Orpheus gave the Milksop a confident smile. What a talkative, empty-headed fool he was, but then – every story needed such characters. They usually died quite early on. It was to be hoped that this general rule held good for the Adderhead's brother-in-law.

'Naturally, Your Highness! That ought not to be any problem,' murmured Orpheus, choosing every word with care, even though this princely fool wasn't worth the trouble. 'But first I must speak to the Silver Prince. Rest assured that my information really is of the utmost importance. And you,' he added, giving the Milksop a crafty smile, 'will receive the throne of Ombra. Get me an audience with your immortal brother-in-law and the Bluejay will meet his well-deserved end at last. Violante will be punished for her deceitfulness, and for your triumphal celebrations I'll get you a Pegasus, which will surely impress your friends even more than the unicorn. You could hunt it with both crossbows and hawks!'

The Milksop's pale eyes widened with delight. 'A Pegasus!' he breathed as he impatiently waved one of the guards over. 'Fabulous indeed! I'll get you your audience, but let me advise you,' and here he lowered his voice to a whisper, 'not to go too close to my brother-in-law. The stink coming off him has already killed two of my dogs!'

The Adderhead kept Orpheus waiting another hour. It passed as painfully slowly as few hours had before in his whole life. The Milksop asked him about other creatures that might be hunted, and Orpheus promised basilisks and six-legged lions while his mind put the right words together for the Silver Prince. Every one of them must ring true. After all, the Lord of the Castle of Night was as famous for his clever mind as for his cruelty. Orpheus had done a great deal of thinking since Mortola visited him, and he always came to the same conclusion: he could make his dreams of wealth and influence come true only at the Adderhead's side. Even in a state of physical decay, the Silver Prince still played the leading part here. With his help, Orpheus might perhaps get back the book that had made this world such a wonderful toy before Dustfinger stole it. Not to mention the other book, the one enabling its owner to play with that toy for all eternity . . .

How modest you are, Orpheus, he had whispered to himself when the idea first took shape in his mind. Two books, that's all you ask! Just two books – and one of them full of blank pages and in rather poor condition!

Ah, what a life he could lead. Orpheus the all-powerful, Orpheus the immortal, hero of the world he had loved even as a child!

'He's coming! Bow low!' The Milksop jumped up so hastily that his wig slipped down over his receding forehead, and Orpheus came out of his delightful daydreams with a start.

A reader doesn't really see the characters in a story; he feels them. Orpheus had discovered that for the first time when, aged nearly eleven, he had tried describing or drawing characters from his favourite books. As the Adderhead came towards him out of the darkness, it was exactly like the day when he first encountered him in Fenoglio's book: he felt fear and admiration, he sensed the evil that surrounded the Silver Prince like black light, and an abundance of power that made it difficult to breathe. But Orpheus had imagined the Silver Prince very much taller. And of course Fenoglio's description had said nothing about that devastated face, the pale and puffy flesh, the swollen hands. Every step the Adderhead took seemed to hurt him. His eyes were bloodshot under their heavy lids. They watered even in the sparse candlelight, and the stench given off by his bloated body made Orpheus want desperately to cover his own mouth and nose.

The Adderhead didn't deign to look at him as he walked past, breathing heavily. Only when he was sitting on the throne did those reddened eyes turn to his visitor. A lizard's eyes, so Fenoglio had described them. Now they were inflamed slits under swollen lids, and the red jewels that the Adderhead wore in both nostrils were sunk deep, like nails driven into the white flesh.

'You want to tell me something about my daughter and the Bluejay?' He struggled for breath after every other word, but that made his voice no less menacing. 'What is it? That Violante loves power as much as I do, so she's stolen it from me? Is that what you want to tell me? If so, then say goodbye to your tongue, because I'll have it torn out. I greatly dislike having my time wasted – however much of it I now have at my disposal.'

His tongue torn out . . . Orpheus gulped. Not a nice idea at all – but he still had it at the moment. Even if the stench wafting down from the throne made speaking almost impossible.

'My tongue could come in very useful to you, Your Grace,' he replied, with difficulty suppressing an urge to retch. 'But of course you're free to tear it out at any time.'

The Adderhead's mouth twisted into an unpleasant smile. Pain carved fine lines around his lips. 'What a delightful offer. I see you take me seriously. Very well, what do you have to say?'

Curtain up, Orpheus, he thought again. On you go, this is your big scene!

'Your daughter Violante,' Orpheus let the name die away for effect before he went on, 'wants more than just the throne of Ombra. She wants yours too. Which is why she is planning to kill you.'

The Milksop clutched his chest, as if giving the lie to those who claimed that he had a dead partridge there instead of a heart. However, the Adderhead merely stared at Orpheus with his inflamed eyes.

'Your tongue is in great danger,' he said. 'Violante can't kill me, have you forgotten that? No one can.'

Orpheus felt the sweat running down his nose. The fire behind the Adderhead crackled as if it were calling Dustfinger. Oh, devil take it, he was so frightened. But then wasn't he always frightened? Look him straight in the eye, Orpheus, and trust your voice!

Those eyes were terrible. They stripped the skin from his face. And the swollen fingers lay on the arms of the throne like dead flesh.

'Oh yes, she can. If the Bluejay has told her the three words.' His voice really did sound astonishingly composed.

Good, Orpheus, very good.

'Ah, those three words . . . so you've heard about them too. Well, you are right. She could get them out of him under torture. Although I would expect him to say nothing for a very long time . . . and he could always give her the wrong words.'

'Your daughter doesn't have to torture the Bluejay. She's in league with him.'

Yes!

Orpheus saw, from the disfigured face, that such an idea really hadn't occurred to the Silver Prince yet. Ah, this game was fun. This was just the part he wanted to play. They'd soon all be sticking to his cunning tongue like flies on flypaper.

The Adderhead remained silent for an agonizingly long time.

'Interesting,' he said at last. 'Violante's mother had a weakness for strolling players. I'm sure a robber would have taken her fancy just as much. But Violante is not like her mother. She's like me, although she doesn't care to hear people say so.'

'Oh, I have no doubt of that, Your Highness!' Orpheus injected just enough deference into his voice. 'But why has the illuminator who works in this castle had to do nothing but illustrate songs about the Bluejay for over a year? Your daughter has sold her jewels to pay for paints. She's obsessed by that robber, he dominates her mind. Ask Balbulus! Ask him how often she sits in the library staring at the pictures he's painted of the man! And ask yourself, how is it possible for the Bluejay to have escaped from this castle twice in the last few weeks?'

'I can't ask Balbulus anything.' The Adderhead's voice seemed made for this black-draped hall. 'The Piper is having him hunted out of town at this very moment. He cut his right hand off first.'

That really did silence Orpheus for a moment. His right hand. Instinctively, he touched his own writing hand. 'Why . . . er . . . if I may ask, Your Highness, why did he do that?' he managed in a thread of a voice.

'Why? Because my daughter thought highly of his art, and I hope the stump of his wrist will make it clear to her how very angry I am. For Balbulus will of course take refuge with her. Where else would he go?'

'Indeed. How clever of you.' Orpheus involuntarily moved his fingers as if to reassure himself that they were still there. He had run out of words; his brain was a blank sheet of paper and his tongue a dried-up pen.

'Shall I let you into a secret?' The Adderhead licked his cracked lips. 'I like what my daughter has done! I can't allow it, but it pleases me. She doesn't care for being ordered around. Neither the Piper nor my pheasant-murdering brother-in-law – ' here he cast a look of disgust at the Milksop – 'has realized that. As for the Bluejay, it may well be that Violante is only pretending to him that she will protect him. She's wily. She knows as well as I do that it's easy to trick heroes. You just have to make a hero believe you're on the side of what's right and just, and he'll go trotting after you like a lamb to the slaughter. But in the end Violante will sell me her noble robber. For the crown of Ombra. And who knows . . . perhaps I really will let her have it.'

The Milksop was looking straight ahead as fixedly as if he hadn't heard those last words spoken by his overlord and brother-in-law. However, the Adderhead leant back and patted his bloated thighs. 'I think your tongue is mine,

Four-Eyes,' he said. 'Any last words before you're left as mute as a fish?'

The Milksop smiled unpleasantly, and Orpheus's lips began to tremble as if they already felt the pincers. No. No, this couldn't be happening. He hadn't found his way into this story just to end up a mute beggar in the streets of Ombra.

He gave the Adderhead what he hoped was an enigmatic smile and clasped his hands behind his back. Orpheus knew that this posture made him look rather imposing; he had rehearsed it often enough in front of the mirror. But now he needed words. Words that would cast ripples in this story, circling outwards like stones thrown into still water.

He lowered his voice as he began to speak again. A word weighs more heavily if it is softly uttered.

'Very well, then these are my last words, Your Highness, but rest assured that they will also be the last words you remember when the White Women come for you. I swear to you by my tongue that your daughter plans to kill you. She hates you, and you underestimate her romantic weakness for the Bluejay. She wants the throne for him, and for herself. That's the only reason why she freed him. Robbers and princes' daughters have always been a dangerous mixture.'

The words grew in the dark hall as if they had a shadow. And the Adderhead's hooded gaze rested on Orpheus as if to poison him with its own evil.

'But that's ridiculous!' The Milksop's voice made him sound like an injured child. 'Violante is little more than a girl, and an ugly one at that. She'd never dare turn against you!'

'Of course she would!' For the first time the Adderhead's voice rose, and the Milksop compressed his narrow lips in alarm. 'Violante is fearless, unlike my other daughters. Ugly, but fearless. And very cunning . . . like this man.' Once again his eyes, clouded with pain, turned to Orpheus.

'You're a viper like me, am I right? Poison runs in our veins, not blood. It consumes us too, but it is deadly only to others. It also runs in Violante's veins, so she will betray the Bluejay, whatever else she may intend at the moment.' The Adderhead laughed, but it turned into a cough. He struggled for breath, gasping as if water were filling his lungs, but when the Milksop bent over him in concern he pushed him roughly away. 'What do you want?' he spat at his brother-in-law. 'I'm immortal, remember?' And he laughed again, a wheezing, gasping laugh. Then the lizard eyes moved back to Orpheus.

'I like you, milk-faced viper. You seem much more like a member of my family than that fellow.' With an impatient gesture, he thrust the Milksop aside. 'But he has a beautiful sister, so one has to take the brother on with her. Do you have a sister as well? Or can you be of use to me in some other way?'

This is going well, thought Orpheus. Very well indeed! Now I'll soon be weaving my own thread through the fabric of this story – and what colour will I choose? Gold? Black? Maybe blood red?

'Oh,' he said, casting a weary glance at his fingernails – another effective trick, as the mirror had shown him. 'I can be useful to you in many ways. Ask your brother-in-law. I make dreams come true. I tailor things to your own wishes.'

Careful, Orpheus, you don't have the book back yet. What are you promising?

'Oh, a magician, are you?' The contempt in the Adderhead's voice was a warning.

'No, I wouldn't call it that,' Orpheus was quick to reply.

'Let's just say my art is black. As black as ink.'

Ink! Of course, Orpheus! he told himself.

Why hadn't he thought of that before? Dustfinger had stolen his favourite book from him, it was true, but Fenoglio had written others. Why wouldn't the old man's words still work even if they didn't come from *Inkheart*? Where were the Bluejay songs that Violante was said to have collected so carefully? Didn't people say she'd ordered Balbulus to fill several books with them?

'Black? A colour I like.' The Adderhead, groaning, heaved himself out of his throne. 'Brother-in-law, give the little viper a horse. I'll take him with me. It's a long way to the Castle in the Lake, and perhaps he'll help me to pass the time.'

Orpheus bowed so deeply that he almost toppled over. 'What an honour!' he stammered – you always had to give powerful people the feeling that you could hardly speak in their presence. 'But in that case, might I most humbly ask Your Highness a favour?'

The Milksop cast him a distrustful glance. What if that fool had bartered Balbulus's books of Fenoglio's songs for a few casks of wine? He'd read him an attack of the plague!

'I am a great lover of the art of book illumination,' Orpheus went on, without taking his eyes off the Milksop, 'and I've heard wonderful things about the library in this castle. I'd very much like to see the books, and perhaps take one or two on the journey. Who knows, I may even be able to entertain you with their contents on the way!'

Indifferently, the Adderhead shrugged his shoulders. 'Why not? If you'll work out, while you're at it, how much silver those that my brother-in-law hasn't yet exchanged for wine are worth.'

The Milksop bent his head, but Orpheus had seen the vicious dislike in his eyes.

'Of course.' Orpheus bowed as low as he could.

The Adderhead came down the steps of the throne and stopped in front of him, breathing heavily. 'When making your estimate, you should take into account the fact that books illuminated by Balbulus have risen in value!' he remarked. 'After all, he won't be producing any new works without his hand, and that certainly makes those already in existence more valuable, don't you agree?'

Once again Orpheus found it hard not to retch as the Adderhead's foul breath met his face, but all the same he managed to produce an admiring smile.

'How extremely clever of you, Your Highness!' he replied. 'The perfect penalty! May I ask what punishment you intend for the Bluejay? Perhaps it would be appropriate to separate him from his tongue first, since everyone goes into such raptures about his voice?'

But the Adderhead shook his head. 'No, no. I have better plans for the Bluejay. I'm going to flay him alive and make his skin into parchment, and we want him to be able to scream as it's done to him, don't we?'

'Of course!' breathed Orpheus. 'What a truly fitting punishment for a bookbinder! May I suggest that you write a warning to your enemies on this very special parchment and have it hung up in marketplaces? I will happily provide you with suitable words. In my trade one must be able to use words with skill.'

'Well, well, you're obviously a man of many talents.' The Adderhead was examining him with something like amusement.

Now, Orpheus! he told himself. Even if you do find Fenoglio's songs in the library, there's no substitute for that one book. Tell him about *Inkheart*!

'I assure you, all my talents are at your disposal, Highness,' he faltered. 'But to practise my arts to perfection I need something that was stolen from me.'

'Indeed? And what might that be?'

'A book, Your Grace! The Fire-Dancer has stolen it, but I believe he did it at the request of the Bluejay, who is certain to know where it is now. So if you were to ask him about it as soon as he is in your power . . .'

'A book? Did the Bluejay bind you a book too, I wonder?'

'Oh no. No!' Orpheus waved the mere notion away. 'He has nothing to do with *this* book. No bookbinder captured its power inside the covers. It's the words in it that make it powerful. With those words, Your Grace, this world can be re-created, and every living thing in it made subject to your own purposes.'

'Indeed? For instance, trees would bear silver fruit? It could be night for ever if I wanted?'

How he was staring at him – like a snake staring at a mouse! Not a word out of place now, Orpheus!

'Oh, yes.' Orpheus nodded eagerly. 'I brought your brother-in-law a unicorn with the aid of that book. And a dwarf.'

The Adderhead cast the Milksop a derisive glance. 'Yes, that sounds like the kind of thing my good brother-in-law would want. My wishes would be rather different.'

He scrutinized Orpheus with satisfaction. Obviously the Adderhead had realized that the same kind of heart beat in both their breasts – black with vanity and the desire for vengeance, in love with its own cunning, full of contempt for those whose hearts were ruled by other feelings. Orpheus knew what state his own heart was in, and he feared only that those inflamed eyes might also uncover what he hid even from himself: his envy of the innocence of others, his longing for an unblemished heart.

'What about my rotting flesh?' The Adderhead passed his swollen fingers over his face. 'Can you cure that too with this book, or do I still need the Bluejay to do it?'

Orpheus hesitated.

'Ah. I see . . . you're not sure.' The Adderhead's mouth twisted, his dark lizard eyes almost lost in his flesh. 'And you're clever enough not to promise what you can't perform. Well, I'll return to your other promises and give you a chance to ask the Bluejay about the book that was stolen from you.'

Orpheus bowed his head. 'Thank you, Your Grace!' Oh, this was going well. Very well indeed.

'Highness!' The Milksop was hurrying down the steps of the throne. His voice really was like a duck quacking, and Orpheus imagined not a wild boar or his fabulous unicorn being carried through the streets of Ombra as a trophy of the hunt, but the Milksop himself, his silver-powdered wig full of blood and dust. However, he'd be a poor sight in comparison with the unicorn.

Orpheus exchanged a quick glance with the Adderhead, and for a moment it seemed to him as if they were seeing the same picture.

'You ought to rest now, my prince,' said the Milksop, with obviously exaggerated concern. 'It was a long journey, and another lies ahead of you.'

'Rest? How am I supposed to rest when you and the Piper have let the man who turned me into a piece of rotting meat escape? My skin is burning. My bones are icy. My eyes feel as if every ray of light pierced them with a pin. I can't rest until that accursed Book has stopped poisoning me and the man who bound it is dead. I picture it to myself every night, brother-in-law – just ask your sister – every night I pace up and down, unable to sleep, imagining him wailing and screaming and begging me for a quick death, but I'll have as many torments ready for him as that murderous Book has pages. He'll curse it even more often than I do – and he'll very soon find out that my daughter's skirts are no protection from the Adderhead!'

Once again a racking cough shook him, and for a moment his swollen hands clutched Orpheus by the arm. Their flesh was pale as a dead fish. It smells like a dead fish too, thought Orpheus. Yet he's still the lord of this story.

'Grandfather!' The boy emerged from the darkness as suddenly as if he had been standing in the shadows all this time. He had a pile of books in his small arms.

'Jacopo!' The Adderhead swung round so abruptly that his grandson stood rooted to the ground. 'How often do I have to tell you that even a prince doesn't walk into the throne-room unannounced?'

'I was here before the rest of you!' Jacopo raised his chin and pressed the books to his chest, as if they could shield him from his grandfather's anger. 'I often come in here to read – over there, behind my great-great-great-grandfather's statue.' He pointed to the statue of a very fat man standing among the columns.

'In the dark?'

'You can see the pictures the words paint in your head better in the dark. Anyway, Sootbird gave me these.' He put out his hand, showing his grandfather a couple of candles.

The Adderhead frowned, and bent down to his grandson. 'You will not read in the throne-room as long as I'm here. You won't even put your head around the door. You will stay in your own room, or I'll have you shut in with the hounds like Tullio, understand? By the emblem of my house, you look more and more like your father. Can't you at least cut your hair?'

Jacopo held the gaze of those reddened eyes for an astonishingly long time, but finally he bowed his head, turned without a word and stalked away, the books still held in front of him like a shield.

'He really is coming to look more like Cosimo all the time!' remarked the Milksop. 'But he gets his arrogance from his mother.'

'No, he gets it from me,' the Adderhead told him. 'A very useful quality for him when he sits on the throne.'

The Milksop cast an anxious glance after Jacopo. But the Adderhead struck his brother-in-law's chest with his swollen fist. 'Summon your men!' he ordered him. 'I have work for you to do.'

'Work?' Looking ill at ease, the Milksop raised his brows. He had dusted them with silver, like his wig.

'Yes, for a change you won't be hunting unicorns, you'll be hunting children. Or do you want to let the Black Prince get away with hiding those brats in the forest, while you and the Piper are busy letting my daughter lead you by the nose like dancing bears?'

The Milksop twisted his pale mouth, looking injured. 'We had to prepare for your arrival, dear brother-in-law, and try to catch the Bluejay again—'

'In which attempt you weren't particularly successful!' the Adderhead brusquely interrupted him. 'Luckily my daughter has told us where we can find him, and while I recapture the bird you two so generously allowed to go free, you can bring the children here for me – along with that knife-thrower who calls himself a prince, so that he can watch me skin the Jay. I fear his own skin is too black to make parchment, so I'll have to think of something else for him. Fortunately I am very inventive in such matters. But, to be sure, they say the same of you, don't they?'

The Milksop flushed, obviously flattered, although it was clear that the prospect of hunting children through the forest didn't excite him half as much as a unicorn hunt, perhaps because they were prey that couldn't be eaten.

'Good.' The Adderhead turned and walked on unsteady legs towards the door of the hall. 'Send me Sootbird and the Piper!' he called over his shoulder. 'He should be through with chopping off hands by now. And tell the maids that Jacopo will go with me to the Castle in the Lake. No one spies on his mother better than that child, even though she doesn't especially like him.'

The Milksop stared at him expressionlessly. 'As you please,' he murmured in a thin voice.

But the Adderhead turned once more as the servants scurried to open the heavy door for him.

'As for you, milkface.' Orpheus couldn't help instinctively giving a start. 'I set off at sunset. My brother-in-law will tell you where you must be then. You'll have to bring your own servant, and a tent. And make sure you don't bore me. Parchment could always be made of your skin too.'

'Your Highness!' Orpheus bowed again, although he was

feeling weak at the knees. Had he ever played a more dangerous game? But everything will be all right, he told himself.
You wait and see, Orpheus. This story is yours. It was written for you alone. No one loves it better, no one understands
it better, certainly not the old fool who wrote it in the first
place!

The Adderhead had been gone for some time, but Orpheus
still stood there as if beguiled by the promise of the future.

'So you're a magician. Fancy that.' The Milksop was
inspecting him as if he were a caterpillar that had turned into
a black moth before his eyes. 'Is that why the unicorn was so
easy to hunt? Because it wasn't real?'

'Oh, it was real enough,' replied Orpheus with a patroniz-
ing smile. It was made of the same stuff as you, he added in
his mind. This Milksop creature really was a pathetic character. As soon as he could make the words come to life again
he'd write a totally ridiculous kind of death for him. Suppose
he had him torn to pieces by his own hounds? No. He'd make
him choke to death on a chicken bone at one of his banquets,
and then have him falling on his silver-dusted face into a large
dish of black pudding. That was it. Orpheus couldn't help
smiling.

'That smile will soon be wiped off your face!' the Milksop
hissed at him. 'The Adderhead doesn't like having his expectations disappointed.'

'Oh, I'm sure you know that better than anyone,' replied
Orpheus. 'Now kindly show me the library.'

Four Berries

On my wall hangs a Japanese mask
of gilded wood, the mask of an evil demon.
With sympathy, I see
the veins at his temples swelling,
showing what a strain it is to be bad.

Bertolt Brecht, *The Mask of Evil*

The marten was worse than the bear. He was watching her, he was chattering her name into the boy's ear (fortunately the boy didn't understand him) and chasing her away. But a time came when the marten followed the boy outside, and the bear just raised his heavy head when she hopped up to the bowl of soup that one of the women had put in front of his master.

Nothing was easier to poison than soup. The Black Prince was arguing with Snapper once again, and his back was turned as she dropped the dark red berries into the dish. Five tiny berries, that was all it would take to send the prince of the robbers to another kingdom, one where his bear wouldn't be able to follow him. But just as she was about to let the fifth berry fall from her beak the wretched marten shot towards her, as if even outside he had scented what she was planning. The berry rolled away, and Mortola prayed to all the devils in hell that four would be enough to kill.

The Black Prince. Another high-minded fool. Presumably his heart felt a pang every time he saw a cripple. He'd never help her to get hold of the book that would let her bargain with Death, not he. But fortunately men like that were less common than white ravens, and most of them died young. Such men didn't want what made other hearts beat faster: riches, power, fame. No, the Black Prince wasn't interested in any of that. Justice made his heart beat faster. Pity. Love. As if life hadn't treated him just as badly as the others. Kicks and blows, pain and hunger. He'd known more than enough of all that. So where did the pity that motivated him come from? And the warmth of his silly heart, the laughter in his face? He simply didn't see the world as it really was, that was the explanation – neither the world nor the people he felt so sorry for. Because if you did see them for what they were, what on earth would make you want to fight and even die for them?

No, if anyone could help her to get her hands on the White Book before the Bluejay wrote in it and ransomed himself from Death, it was Snapper. He was a man after Mortola's own heart. Snapper saw people as they really were: greedy and cowardly, full of self-interest, cunning. Only one kind of injustice had made *him* a robber, injustice to himself. Mortola knew all about him. One of the Laughing Prince's stewards had seized his farm, the way the powerful classes so often simply took what they wanted. That, and nothing else, had driven him into the forest. Yes, she could deal with Snapper.

Mortola knew exactly how to harness him for her own purposes once the Black Prince was out of the way. 'What are you all still doing here, Snapper?' she would whisper to him. 'There are more important things in life than looking after a few snotty-nosed children! The Bluejay knows why he's really landed you with them. He's planning to sell you all! You must kill him before he throws in his lot with the Adderhead's daughter. How did he try fooling you – by saying he only wanted to write in the White Book to kill the Adderhead? Nonsense! He wants to make himself immortal! And there's something else I'm sure he hasn't told you. The White Book doesn't just keep Death at bay – it makes its owner rich beyond the dreams of avarice!'

Oh yes, Mortola knew how Snapper's eyes would light up at those words. He didn't understand what made the Bluejay tick. Nor would he understand that she herself wanted the Book only to buy her son back from Death. But he would certainly set off at once with the prospect of gold and silver before his eyes. As soon as the Black Prince couldn't stop him any more . . . and luckily the berries worked fast.

Gecko called to her. He had filled his hand with breadcrumbs and was holding it up as if there were nothing tastier in the world. What a fool. Thought he knew something about birds. Well, perhaps he really did. After all, she was no ordinary bird. Mortola uttered a hoarse laugh. It sounded strange, coming from that pointed beak, and the Strong Man raised his head and looked up at the rocky ledge where she was perching. Yes, *he* knew about birds and what they said. She'd have to watch him carefully. 'Oh, never mind, kek-kek-kek, kraaa!' said the magpie in her, the magpie that thought only of worms and shiny things and the gleam of its black feathers. 'They're all fools, fools, such fools. But I am clever. Come along, old woman, let's fly after the Bluejay and peck his eyes out. What fun!'

Every day it was getting more difficult to keep her wings still when the magpie wanted to spread them, and Mortola had to shake her bird's head harder and harder to make it think human thoughts. Sometimes she couldn't even remember for sure what human thoughts were like.

Now the feathers would shoot out through her skin even without the seeds. She had already swallowed too many, and the poison was wandering through her body and sowing the bird in her blood. Never mind. You'll find a way to drive it out, Mortola, she thought. But first the bookbinder must be dead and her son alive again! His face . . . what did it look like? She could hardly remember.

The Black Prince was still arguing with Snapper, as he did so often these days. Eat it! Start eating, you fool! Two other robbers came along – the pock-marked actor who was always at the Prince's side, and Gecko, who saw the world as Snapper did. One of the women came over to them, brought the actor a bowl of soup too and pointed to the one she had put in front of the Prince.

That's right, listen to her! Sit down! Eat! Mortola thrust her head forward. She felt how her human body wanted to shake off the feathers, how it longed to spread and stretch. Yesterday a couple of children had almost caught her shape-shifting. Silly, noisy nuisances. She'd never liked children – except her own son, and she had never let even him see that she loved him. Love ruined you. It made you soft, gullible . . .

There. He was eating. At last. Yes, enjoy it, Prince! The bear trotted up to his master and snuffled at the bowl. Get out, you clumsy great brute. Let him eat it. Four berries. Five would have been better, but with a little luck four would do the trick. It was useful that the trees they grew on were far from rare. Two of them stood only a little way below the cave. Resa was always warning the children not to try their berries.

The Black Prince put the bowl to his mouth and drank the dregs. Good. He'd soon feel Death twisting his guts. Mortola uttered a triumphant croak and spread her wings. Gecko raised his hand with the breadcrumbs again as she flew away over his head. Idiot. They were all stupid, very, very stupid. But that was just as well.

The women began ladling soup out for the children, and Silvertongue's daughter stood far away at the back of the long line. There'd be enough time to pick a few berries for her too. More than enough time.

44

The Hand of Death

Death is great.
Laugh as we may,
we are its own.
In life's bright day
It weeps its way
Into our hearts.

Rainer Maria Rilke, *Closing Piece*

Minerva made good soup. Meggie had often eaten it when she was staying with Fenoglio, and the aroma rising from the steaming bowls was so delicious that for a moment the huge, chilly cave really seemed like home. 'Please, Meggie, do eat something!' Resa had said. 'I don't have an appetite any more than you do, but it's not going to help your father if we starve to death because we're so worried about him.'

No, she supposed not. When she'd asked Farid to call up the fiery pictures for her again, the flames had shown nothing. 'You can't force them!' Farid had muttered in annoyance as he put the ashes back into his bag. 'The flames like to play, so you have to pretend you don't really want anything from them. But how am I supposed to do that when you're staring at them as if it were a matter of life and death?'

Well, what else was it? Even the Black Prince was anxious about Mo. He had decided to follow Violante to the Castle in the Lake with a few men. He was going to set off tomorrow, but he wouldn't take Resa and Meggie with him. 'Of course not,' Meggie's mother had whispered bitterly. 'This world belongs to men.'

Meggie picked up the wooden spoon that Doria had carved for her (it was a very good spoon) and listlessly stirred the soup. Jasper peered at it longingly. Of course. Glass men loved human food, although it wasn't good for them. Jasper was spending more and more time with Doria, even though Farid was back. Meggie wasn't surprised. Farid had been far from talkative since Dustfinger sent him away again. Most of the time he walked restlessly in the surrounding hills or tried to call up pictures in the fire. So far Roxane had looked into the flames only once. 'Thank you,' she had said to Farid afterwards, her voice cool. 'But I'd rather go on listening to my heart. It usually tells me whether he's all right.'

'There, isn't that just what I told Dustfinger?' Farid had said, annoyed. 'So why did he send me to her? She doesn't need me. She'd bewitch me away if she could.'

Doria offered Jasper his spoon.

'Don't give him any!' said Meggie. 'He can't digest it! Ask him.' She was very fond of Jasper. He was so much friendlier than Rosenquartz, who liked nothing better than losing his temper and quarrelling with Fenoglio.

'She's right,' muttered Jasper gloomily, but his sharp little nose sniffed, as if at least to fill his glass body with the forbidden aroma. The children sitting around Meggie giggled. They all liked the glass man, and Doria often had to rescue him from their small hands. They liked the marten too, but Jink snapped and spat when the fuss the children made of him got to be too much. The glass man, however, had little defence against human fingers.

The soup really did smell good. Meggie dipped her spoon into her bowl – and jumped when the magpie that had flown to Gecko fluttered over to her own shoulder. By now the bird seemed to belong in the cave, like Jink and the bear, but Resa disliked it.

'Get away!' she said, shooing the magpie off Meggie's shoulder. The bird croaked angrily and jabbed at Resa with its beak. Meggie was so startled that she spilt the hot soup over her hands.

'Sorry.' Resa mopped the liquid off Meggie's fingers with the hem of her dress. 'I can't stand that bird. I expect it's because it reminds me of Mortola.'

The Magpie – of course. It was a long time since Meggie had thought about Capricorn's mother, but then she hadn't been there when Mortola had shot Mo. Resa had.

'It's only a bird,' said Meggie, her thoughts already far away again, following her father. She had found very little about the Castle in the Lake in Fenoglio's book. *Deep in the mountains, in the middle of a lake . . . an endless bridge over black water.* Was Mo riding over that bridge now? Suppose she and Resa simply followed the Black Prince? *Do you hear, Meggie? Whatever happens, stay with the robbers! Promise me!*

Resa pointed to the bowl in her lap. 'Do please eat it, Meggie!'

But Meggie turned to Roxane, who was quickly making her

way past the children as they sat there eating. Her beautiful face was paler than Meggie had seen it since Dustfinger's return. Resa stood up, looking anxious.

'What's happened?' She took Roxane's arm. 'Is there any news? Has anything been heard of Mo? You must tell me!'

But Roxane shook her head. 'The Prince . . .' The anxiety in her voice was plainly audible. 'He's not well, and I don't know what it is. He has terrible stomach cramps. I have a few roots here that may help him.'

She moved on, but Resa held her back again. 'Stomach cramps? Where is he?'

Meggie heard the bear's howl from far away. The Strong Man was looking like a desperate child as they made their way towards him. Battista was there too, with Woodenfoot and Elfbane. The Black Prince lay on the ground. Minerva was kneeling beside him, trying to get some liquid into his mouth, but he writhed in pain, pressed his hands to his body and struggled for breath. Sweat stood out on his forehead.

'Quiet, bear!' he gasped. He could hardly get the words past his lips; he had bitten them in his pain until they bled. But the bear went on howling and snorting as if his own life was at stake.

'Let me by.' Resa pushed them all aside, even Minerva, and took the Prince's face between her hands.

'Look at me!' she said. 'Please, look at me!'

She wiped the sweat from his brow and looked into his eyes.

Roxane came back with a few roots in her hand, and the magpie flapped its way over to Gecko's shoulder.

Resa stared at it.

'Strong Man!' she said, so quietly that no one but Meggie

heard her. 'Catch that bird.'

The magpie jerked its head as the Black Prince writhed in Minerva's arms.

The Strong Man looked at Resa, his face streaming with tears, and nodded. But when he took a step towards Gecko, the magpie flew away and perched on a ledge high up below the roof of the cave.

Roxane knelt beside Resa.

'He's lost consciousness,' said Minerva. 'And see how shallow his breathing is!'

'I've seen cramps like these before.' Resa's voice was trembling. 'The berries that cause them are dark red, not much bigger than a pinhead. Mortola liked to use them because they're easily mixed with food, and they bring a very painful death. There are two of the trees they grow on just below this cave! I've warned the children not to eat the berries.' She looked up at the magpie again.

'Is there an antidote?' Roxane straightened her back. The Black Prince lay there as if dead, and the bear pushed his muzzle into his master's side and moaned like a human being.

'Yes. A flower with tiny white blooms that smell of carrion.' Resa was still looking up at the bird. 'The root alleviates the effect of the berries.'

'What's wrong with him?' Fenoglio made his way past the women, a look of concern on his face. Elinor was with him. The pair of them had spent all morning in Fenoglio's corner of the cave, arguing about what was good in his story and what wasn't. Whenever someone came near them they lowered their voices like conspirators, as if any of the children or the robbers could have understood what they were talking about.

Elinor put her hand to her mouth with alarm when she saw

the Black Prince lying there motionless. She looked incredulous, as if she had found a wrongly printed page in a book.

'Poisoned.' The Strong Man stood up, clenching his fists. His face was the dark red colour that it usually turned only when he was drunk. He took Gecko by his scrawny neck and shook him like a rag doll. 'Did you do this?' he cried. 'Or was it Snapper? Come on, tell us or I'll beat it out of you! I'll break all your bones until you're writhing in agony too!'

'Let him go!' Roxane snapped. 'That's not going to help the Prince now!'

The Strong Man let go of Gecko and started sobbing. Minerva put her arms round him. But Resa looked up at the magpie again.

'The plant you describe sounds like deathbud,' Roxane told her, while Gecko, coughing, rubbed his neck and cursed the Strong Man roundly. 'It's very rare. And even if it grew here it would have died down in the cold long ago. Isn't there anything else?'

The Black Prince came to his senses and tried to sit up, but he fell back with a groan. Battista knelt down beside him and looked at Roxane in search of help. The Strong Man too turned his tearful eyes on her like a pleading dog.

'Don't stare at me like that!' she cried, and Meggie heard the desperation in her voice. 'I can't help him. Try giving him retchwort,' she told Minerva. 'And I'll go and look for deathbud roots, though I'm afraid there's not much point.'

'Retchwort will only make it worse,' said Resa in a toneless voice. 'Believe me, I've seen this often enough.'

The Black Prince gasped in agony and buried his face against Battista's side. Then his body suddenly went limp, as if it had lost its battle against the pain. Roxane quickly knelt down beside him, putting her ear to his chest and her fingers on his mouth. Meggie tasted her own tears on her lips, and the Strong Man began sobbing like a child.

'Still alive,' said Roxane. 'But only just.'

Gecko slipped away, probably to tell Snapper what was going on. But Elinor whispered something to Fenoglio. He turned away angrily, but Elinor held him back and went on talking insistently to him. 'Don't make such a fuss!' Meggie heard her whisper. 'Of course you can do it! Are you going to leave him to die?'

Meggie was not the only one to have heard those last words. The Strong Man, bewildered, mopped the tears off his face. The bear groaned again and nuzzled his master's side. But Fenoglio still stood there, staring at the unconscious Prince. Then he took a hesitant step in Roxane's direction.

'This . . . er . . . this flower, Roxane . . .'

Elinor stayed right behind him, as if she had to make sure he said the right thing. Fenoglio looked at her in annoyance.

'What?' Roxane looked at him.

'Tell me more about it. Where does it grow? How tall is it?'

'It likes moist, shady places, but why ask? I told you, it'll have died down in the frost long ago.'

'White flowers, tiny. Shady, moist surroundings.' Fenoglio passed his hand over his tired face. Then he turned abruptly and took Meggie's arm.

'Come with me,' he told her in a low voice. 'We must hurry.'

'Moist and shady,' he murmured as he led Meggie off with him. 'Right, so if they grew at the entrance of a brownie's burrow, protected by the warm air coming out of the burrow where a few brownies are hibernating ... yes, that makes sense. Yes!'

The cave was almost empty. The women had taken the children out so that they wouldn't hear the Prince's cries of pain. A few small groups of robbers still sat there in silence, staring at one another as if wondering which of them had tried to kill their leader. Snapper was near the entrance with Gecko, and he returned Meggie's glance with such a black expression that she quickly looked the other way.

Fenoglio, however, did not avoid his eyes. 'I wonder if it was Snapper,' he whispered to Meggie.' Yes, I really do wonder.'

'If anyone ought to know it's you!' muttered Elinor, who had followed them. 'Who else made up that horrible fellow?'

Fenoglio spun round as if something had stung him. 'Now you listen to me, Loredan! I've been patient with you so far because you're Meggie's aunt—'

'Great-aunt,' Elinor corrected him, unmoved.

'Whatever. I never invited you into this story, so you will kindly spare me any remarks about my characters in future!'

'Oh, will I?' Elinor's voice rose. It was loud enough to echo right through the huge cave. 'And suppose I'd spared you my comment just now? Your befuddled brain would never have thought of getting the flower here by—'

Fenoglio pressed his hand roughly over her mouth. 'How many more times do I have to tell you?' he hissed. 'Not a word about writing, understand? I haven't the faintest desire to be drawn and quartered as a wizard because of a stupid woman.'

'Fenoglio!' Meggie pulled him forcibly away from Elinor. 'The Black Prince! He's dying!'

Fenoglio stared at her for a fraction of a second, as if he thought her interruption was in the worst possible taste, but then, without a word, he retreated to the corner where he slept. Stony-faced, he cleared a wineskin aside and found a bundle of papers under a few clothes. To Meggie's surprise, most of the sheets already had writing on them.

'Curse it all, where's Rosenquartz?' he muttered as he took a blank sheet. 'Out and about with Jasper again, no doubt. The moment two of them get together they forget their work and go looking for wild glass women. As if the glass women would give one of those pink good-for-nothings so much as a glance!'

Paying no attention to the written pages, he put them aside. So many words. How long ago had he begun writing again? Meggie tried reading the first of the sheets. 'Only a few ideas,' muttered Fenoglio when their eyes met. 'Trying to see how all this could yet end well. What part your father will play in the story . . .'

Meggie's heart turned over, but Elinor got in ahead of her.

'Aha! So it was you who wrote all that about Mortimer after all: letting himself be taken prisoner, then riding to that castle, while my niece cries her eyes out at night!'

'No, it wasn't me!' Fenoglio snapped at her angrily, as he quickly hid the written sheets under his clothes again. 'I didn't have him talking to Death either – though I must say I really like that part of the story. I tell you, these are just some ideas! Useless scribbling that leads nowhere! And it'll probably be the same with what I'm trying to do now. But I'll have a shot at it all the same. So kindly be quiet! Or do you want to talk the Black Prince into his grave?'

As Fenoglio dipped his pen in the ink, Meggie heard a

slight sound behind her. With a clearly embarrassed expression, Rosenquartz emerged from behind the rock on which Fenoglio's writing things stood. The pale green face of a wild glass woman appeared behind him. Without a word, she scurried away past Fenoglio and Meggie.

'I don't believe it!' thundered the old man, in such a loud voice that Rosenquartz put his hands over his ears. 'The Black Prince is at death's door, and you're gadding about with a wild glass woman!'

'The Prince?' Rosenquartz looked at Fenoglio in such dismay that he calmed down at once. 'But, but—'

'Stop all that gabbling and stir the ink!' Fenoglio snapped. 'And if you were going to say something clever like, "But the Prince is such a good man!" that never kept anyone alive yet in any world, did it?' He dipped his pen in the ink so vigorously that it splashed Rosenquartz's pink face, but Meggie saw that the old man's fingers were shaking. 'Come on, then, Fenoglio!' he whispered to himself. 'It's only a flower. You can do it!'

Rosenquartz was watching him with concern, but Fenoglio just stared at the blank sheet before him. He stared at it like a torero facing a bull.

'The entrance to the brownie burrow where the plant grows lies where Elfbane sets his snares!' he murmured. 'And the flowers smell so horrible that the fairies give them a wide berth. But moths love them, grey moths with wings patterned as if a glass man had painted tiny death's-heads on them. Can you see them, Fenoglio? Yes . . .'

He put pen to paper, hesitated – and began to write.

New words. Fresh words. Meggie thought she could hear the story taking a deep breath. Nourishment at last, after all the time when Orpheus had merely fed it with Fenoglio's old words.

'There we are! He only has to be brought up to the mark, you see. He's a lazy old man,' Elinor whispered to her. 'Of course he can still do it, even if he won't believe it himself. You don't forget that kind of thing. I mean, could you forget how to read?'

I don't know, Meggie was going to reply, but she said nothing. Her tongue was waiting for Fenoglio's words. Healing words. Like the words she had once read for Mo.

'Why is the bear howling like that?' Meggie felt Farid's hands on her shoulders. She supposed he had been off in some place where the children couldn't find him, to try conjuring up fire again, but judging by his glum face the flames had refused to show anything.

'Oh no! Him too!' cried the exasperated Fenoglio. 'Why did Darius and I pile up all these rocks? So that anyone and everyone can march into my bedroom? I need peace! This is a matter of life and death!'

'Life and death?' Farid looked at Meggie in alarm.

'The Black Prince . . . he . . . he . . .' Elinor was trying to sound composed, but her voice was shaking.

'Not another word!' said Fenoglio, without looking up. 'Rosenquartz! Sand!'

'Sand? Where am I supposed to find sand?' Rosenquartz's voice rose shrilly.

'Oh, you really are useless! Why do you think I dragged you off to this wilderness with me? For a nice holiday so that you can chase green glass women?' Fenoglio blew on the wet ink and handed Meggie the sheet he had just written. He looked unsure of himself.

'Make them grow, Meggie!' he said. 'A few last healing leaves, warmed by the breath of sleeping brownies, picked before the winter freezes them.'

Meggie stared at the paper. There it was again, the story she had last heard when she had brought Orpheus here.

Yes. The words obeyed Fenoglio once again. And she would teach them how to live.

Written and Unwritten

The characters have their own lives and their own logic,
and you have to act accordingly.

Isaac Bashevis Singer, *Advice to Writers*

Roxane found the plants exactly where Fenoglio had
described: in the entrance of a brownie burrow where
Elfbane set his snares. And Meggie, holding Despina's hand,
watched again as the words that she had only just read became
reality.

*The leaves and flowers defied the cold wind, as if the fairies
had planted them so that they could dream of summer when they
saw them. But the smell rising from the flowers was the odour of
decomposition and decay, and it had given the plant its name:
deathbud. The flowers were put on graves to placate the White
Women.*

*Roxane brushed the moths off the leaves, dug up two plants
and left two others, for fear of angering the wood-elves. Then she
hurried back to the cave, where the White Women were already
standing at the Black Prince's side, grated the roots, brewed them*

*using the method Resa had described to her, and spooned the hot
liquid into the Prince's mouth. He was already very weak, yet
what they had hardly dared to hope for happened: the brew less-
ened the effect of the poison, lulled it to sleep, and brought back
the strength of life.*

*And the White Women disappeared, as if Death had called
them to another place.*

Those last sentences had been easy to read, but many anxious hours passed before they too became reality. The poison
was not giving in without a struggle, and the White Women
came and went. Roxane strewed herbs to keep them away, as
she had learnt to do from Nettle, but the pale faces kept
appearing again, barely visible against the grey walls of the
cave, and a time came when Meggie felt they were looking not
just at the Prince, but at her too.

Don't we know you? their eyes seemed to ask. *Didn't your
voice protect the man who has been ours twice?* Meggie returned
their glance for little longer than it takes to draw a breath, yet
she immediately felt the longing that Mo had spoken of: longing for a place that lay far beyond all words. She took a step
towards the White Women to feel their cool hands on her
beating heart, to let them wipe away all her fear and pain, but
other hands held her back, warm, firm hands.

'Meggie, for heaven's sake don't look at them!' Elinor murmured. 'Come on, let's get you out into the fresh air. Why,
you're as pale as those creatures themselves!'

And she wouldn't take no for an answer, but led Meggie
outside to where the robbers were consulting together and the
children played under the trees, as if they had forgotten what
was going on in the cave. The grass was white with hoarfrost,
white as the figures waiting for the Black Prince, but the spell

of the White Women was broken as soon as Meggie heard the children's laughter. They were throwing fir cones for the marten and shouting as he chased them. Life seemed so much stronger than death, death so much stronger than life. Like the ebb and flow of the tide.

Resa was standing outside the cave too, wrapping her arms around herself for warmth, although the Strong Man had put a rabbit-skin cloak over her shoulders. 'Have you seen Snapper?' she asked Elinor. 'Or Gecko and his magpie?'

Battista joined them. He looked exhausted. This was the first time he had left the Prince's side. 'They've gone,' he said. 'Snapper, Gecko and ten others. They went after the Bluejay as soon as it was clear that the Prince wasn't likely to be able to follow him.'

'But Snapper hates Mo!' Resa's voice was so loud that several robbers turned to look at her, and even the children paused their game. 'Why would he want to help him?'

'I'm afraid he has no intention of helping him,' Battista replied quietly. 'He's been telling the others he's going because the Bluejay plans to betray us and make his own bargain with Violante. And he said your husband hasn't told us the whole truth about the White Book.'

'What kind of truth?' Resa's voice was failing her.

'Snapper says,' Battista replied quietly, 'that the Book doesn't just make its owner immortal, it makes him immensely rich. That sounds a lot more tempting to most of our men than immortality. They'd betray their own mothers for a book like that. So why, they ask themselves, wouldn't the Bluejay plan on doing the same to us?'

'But that's all lies! The Book makes its owner immortal, nothing more.' Meggie didn't care that her voice was rising.

Let them all hear her, all of them putting their heads together, whispering about her father!

Elfbane turned to her, an unpleasant smile on his thin face. 'Oh yes? And how would you know that, little witch? Didn't your father keep it a secret from you that the Book was making the Adderhead's flesh rot on his bones?'

'What if he did?' Elinor asked Elfbane angrily, putting a protective arm around Meggie. 'She still knows one thing: she can certainly trust her father more than a poisoner. Because who else poisoned the Prince if not your beloved Snapper?'

There was a rather unfriendly murmuring among the robbers, and Battista drew Elinor over to his side.

'Mind what you say!' he whispered to her. 'Not all Snapper's friends went with him. And if you ask me, poison doesn't sound much like Snapper. A knife, yes, but poison . . .'

'Oh no? Then who else would it be?' Elinor retorted.

Resa looked up at the sky as if the answer might be found there. 'Did Gecko take his magpie with him?' she asked.

Battista nodded. 'Yes, luckily. The children are scared of it.'

'With good reason.' Resa looked up at the sky again, and then at Battista. 'What exactly does Snapper mean to do?' she asked. 'Tell me.'

Battista just shrugged wearily. 'I don't know. Maybe he's going to try to steal the Book from the Adderhead before he reaches the Castle in the Lake. Or maybe he's going straight there to get it for himself after the Bluejay has written the three words in it. Whatever his plan is, there's nothing we can do. The children need us, and until the Prince gets better he needs us too. Remember, Dustfinger is with the Bluejay. Snapper won't have an easy time of it with the pair of them!'

Now forgive me, but I must go back to the Prince.'

Snapper won't have an easy time of it with the pair of them! Yes, but what if he really did steal the White Book from the Adderhead on the way, and the Adderhead arrived at the Castle in the Lake knowing that even the Bluejay couldn't help him now? Wouldn't he kill Mo then and there? And even if Mo did get a chance to write those three words on the blank pages . . . what if Snapper poisoned him afterwards, as ruthlessly as he'd presumably poisoned the Prince, just to get his hands on the Book?

What if, what if . . . those questions kept Meggie awake even when all had long been sleeping around her, and finally she got up to go and see how the Black Prince was.

He was sleeping. The White Women had gone, but his dark face was still as grey as if their hands had bleached his skin. Minerva and Roxane were taking turns to sit at his side, and Fenoglio was with them, as if he must watch over his own words if they were to remain effective.

Fenoglio . . . Fenoglio could write again.

What did the sheets of paper he had hidden under his clothes say?

'Why did you make up the Bluejay for your robber songs, why didn't you just write about the Black Prince?' Meggie had asked him long ago.

'Because the Prince was tired,' Fenoglio had replied. 'The Black Prince needed the Bluejay as much as the poor people who whispered his name at night. The Prince had been part of this world for too long to believe it could really be changed. And his men never doubted that he was flesh and blood like them. They're not nearly so sure about your father. Do you understand now?'

Meggie understood only too well. But Mo *was* flesh and blood, and she was sure that Snapper didn't doubt it. When she returned to the sleepers, Darius had taken two of the children on to his lap and was quietly telling them a story. The little ones often woke him in the middle of the night because he knew how to drive away their bad dreams with stories, and Darius patiently resigned himself to his task. He liked Fenoglio's world, although it probably frightened him more than Elinor – but would he change it with his voice if Fenoglio asked him to? Would he read aloud what Meggie herself might not want to?

What was on the sheets of paper that Fenoglio had hidden so hastily from her and Elinor?

What did they say?

Go and look, Meggie, she told herself. You won't be able to sleep anyway.

As she went round behind the wall marking off the place where Fenoglio slept, she heard Rosenquartz's quiet snoring. His master was sitting with the Black Prince, but the glass man lay on the clothes under which Fenoglio had hidden the written pages. Meggie carefully picked him up, surprised as usual to feel how cold his transparent limbs were, and laid him on the cushion that Fenoglio had brought with him from Ombra. Yes, the pages were still exactly where he had hidden them from Elinor and her. There were more than a dozen, covered with words written in haste – scraps of sentences, questions, snippets of ideas that presumably made no sense to anyone but their author: *the pen or the sword? Who does Violante love? Careful, the Piper . . . Who writes the three words?* Meggie couldn't decipher all of it, but on the very first page, in capital letters, were the words that made her heart beat faster: *The Song of the Bluejay.*

'Just ideas, Meggie, as I told you. Only questions and ideas.'

Fenoglio's voice made her spin round in such alarm that she almost dropped the pages on the sleeping Rosenquartz.

'The Prince is rather better,' said Fenoglio, as if she had come to him to hear that. 'It really does look as if my words have kept someone alive for once, instead of killing them. But then again, perhaps he's only alive because this story thinks he can still be useful to it. How would I know?' He sat down beside Meggie with a sigh and gently took what he had written from her hand.

'Your words saved Mo too, before all this,' she said.

'Yes, maybe.' Fenoglio brushed his hand over the dry ink as if that would dust the words free of anything harmful. 'All the same, you don't trust them now any more than I do, do you?'

He was right. She had learnt both to love and to fear the words.

'Why *The Song of the Bluejay?*' she asked softly. 'You can't write any more about him! He's my father now! Make up a new hero. I'm sure you can invent one. But let Mo be Mo again, just Mo and no one else.'

Fenoglio looked at her thoughtfully. 'Are you sure that's what your father himself wants? Or don't you mind about that?'

'Of course I do!' Meggie's voice was so sharp that Rosenquartz woke with a start. He looked around him with a bewildered expression – and fell asleep again. 'But Mo certainly wouldn't want you catching him in your words like a fly in a spider's web. You're changing him!'

'Nonsense! Your father himself decided to be the Bluejay! I just wrote a few songs, and you've never read a single one of them aloud! So how would they change anything?'

Meggie bowed her head.

'Oh no!' Fenoglio looked at her, horrified. 'You *did* read them?'

'After Mo rode to the castle. To protect him, to make him strong and invulnerable. I read them aloud every day.'

'Well, who'd have thought it! Then let's hope the words in the songs work as well as those I've written for the Black Prince.' Fenoglio put an arm around her shoulders, as he had often done when they were both Capricorn's prisoners – in another world, in another story. Or was it the same story after all?

'Meggie,' he said quietly. 'Even if you go on reading my songs aloud, even if you read them a dozen times a day – we both know they haven't made your father the Bluejay. If I'd chosen him as the model for the Piper, do you think he'd have become a murderer? Of course not! Your father is like the Black Prince! He feels for the weak. *I* didn't write that into his heart – it was always there! Your father didn't ride to Ombra Castle because of my words but for the children asleep out there. Perhaps you're right. Perhaps this story is changing him, but he's changing the story too! He's telling the next part of it through what he does, Meggie, not because of what I write. Even if the right words might be able to help him . . .'

'Protect him, Fenoglio!' Meggie whispered. 'Snapper's after him, and he hates Mo.'

Fenoglio looked at her in surprise. 'What do you mean? You actually want me to write something about him? Heavens, it was confusing enough when I had only my own characters to worry about!'

And you let them die without giving it a thought, Meggie told herself, but she didn't say so aloud. After all, Fenoglio had saved the Black Prince today – and he had really feared for him. What would Dustfinger have said about this sudden fit of sympathy?

Rosenquartz started snoring again.

'Hear that?' asked Fenoglio. 'Can you tell me how such a ridiculously small creature can snore at such volume? Sometimes I feel like stuffing him in the inkwell overnight just to get some peace and quiet!'

'You're a terrible old man!' Meggie reached for the written pages again and ran her finger along the words jotted down there. 'What does all this mean? *The pen or the sword? Who writes the three words? Who does Violante love?*'

'Well, those are only some of the questions to be answered as this story goes on. All good stories hide behind a tangle of questions, and it isn't easy to find out their dodges. And this story certainly has a mind of its own, but,' and here Fenoglio lowered his voice as if the story itself could be eavesdropping, 'if you ask the right questions it will whisper all its secrets to you. A story like this is a very talkative thing.'

Fenoglio read aloud what he had written. '*The pen or the sword?* A very important question. But I don't know the answer yet. Perhaps it will be both. Well, however that may be . . . *Who will write the three words?* Your father let himself be taken prisoner to do that, but who knows . . . will the Adderhead really allow his daughter to trick him? Is Violante as clever as she thinks, and *who does Her Ugliness love?* I am afraid she's fallen in love with your father. I think she fell in love with him a long time ago, before she ever met him.'

'What?' Meggie looked at him in astonishment. 'What are

you talking about? Violante isn't much older than me and Brianna!'

'Nonsense! Not in years, perhaps, but with all the experience she's had, she's at least three times your age. And like so many princes' daughters she has a very romantic notion of robbers. Why do you think she made Balbulus illuminate all my Bluejay songs? And now he's riding along beside her in flesh and blood. Not unromantic, is it?'

'You're dreadful!' Meggie's indignant voice woke Rosenquartz again.

'Why? I'm only explaining what would have to be taken into account if I were really to try bringing this story to a good end, although it may have had different ideas itself for some time. Suppose I'm right? Suppose Violante loves the Bluejay and your father rejects her? Will she protect him from the Adderhead all the same? What role will Dustfinger take? Will the Piper see what game Violante is playing? Questions, nothing but questions! Believe you me, this story is a labyrinth! It looks as if there were several ways to go, but only one is right, and there's a nasty surprise ready to punish you for every false step. This time, though, I'll be prepared. This time I'll see the traps it's setting me, Meggie – and I'll find the right way out. But for that I have to ask questions. For instance: where's Mortola? I can't get that question out of my mind. And what, by all inky devils, is Orpheus up to? Questions, more and more questions . . . but Fenoglio is back in the game again! And he's saved the Black Prince!'

Every wrinkle in his old face expressed self-satisfaction.

Oh, he really was a terrible old man!

46

The Castle in the Lake

There is something about it that opens no door to words.
John Steinbeck, *Travels with Charlie*

They rode north, further and further north. On the morning of the second day, Violante had Mo's hands, bound until now for fear of her father's spies, loosened after one of her soldiers told her that otherwise the Bluejay would soon lose the use of them. More than fifty soldiers had been waiting for them barely a mile out of Ombra. Hardly any of them were older than Farid, and they all looked as determined as if they would follow Violante to the end of the world.

With every mile they put behind them the woods were darker and the valleys deeper. The hills became mountains. Snow already lay on some of the passes, so that they had to dismount and lead their horses, and on the second night rain fell, covering the white snow with treacherous ice. The mountain range through which they were riding seemed almost uninhabited. Only very occasionally did Mo see a village in the distance, an isolated farmhouse or a charcoal-burner's hut.

It was almost as if Fenoglio had forgotten to populate this part of his world.

Dustfinger joined them when they first stopped to rest. He did it as naturally as if nothing were simpler than to pick up the trail that Violante's soldiers were so carefully obliterating. The soldiers looked at him in the same respectful but wary way as they looked at Mo. Bluejay . . . Fire-Dancer . . . of course they knew the songs, and their eyes asked: are these men made of the same flesh as us?

For himself, Mo knew the answer – although he sometimes wondered whether by now ink, rather than blood, flowed through his veins. He wasn't so sure about Dustfinger. The horses shied when they saw him, although he could calm them with a whisper. He hardly slept or ate, and he plunged his hands into fire as if it were water. But when he talked about Roxane or Farid, there was human love in his words, and when he looked round for his daughter surreptitiously, as if he were ashamed of it, it was with the eyes of a mortal father.

It was good to ride, just to ride on while the Inkworld unfurled before them like elaborately folded paper. And with every mile Mo doubted more and more that all this had really been made by Fenoglio's words. Wasn't it more likely that the old man had simply been a reporter describing a tiny part of this world, a fraction of it that they had long ago left behind? Strange mountains rimmed the horizon, and Ombra was far away. The Wayless Wood seemed as distant as Elinor's garden, the Castle of Night nothing but a dark dream.

'Have you ever been in these mountains before?' he once asked Dustfinger, who rode beside him in silence most of the time. Sometimes Mo thought he could hear the other man's thoughts. *Roxane*, they whispered. And Dustfinger's eyes kept wandering to his daughter, who was riding at Violante's side and didn't deign to give her father a glance.

'No, I don't think so,' replied Dustfinger, and it was the same as every time Mo spoke to him: it seemed as if he were calling him back from that place for which there were no words. Dustfinger didn't talk about it, and Mo asked no questions. He knew what the other man was thinking. The White Women had touched them both, sowing in their hearts a longing for that place, a constant, wordless, bittersweet longing.

Dustfinger looked over his shoulder as if in search of a familiar view. 'I never rode north in the old days. The mountains frightened me,' he said, and smiled as if he were smiling at his old self, who had known so little of the world that a few mountains could scare him. 'I was always drawn to the sea. The sea and the south.'

Then he fell silent again. Dustfinger had never been very talkative, and his journey to the land of Death hadn't changed that. So Mo left him to his silence and wondered, once more, whether the Black Prince had heard yet from Farid that the Bluejay was no longer in Ombra, and how Meggie and Resa had taken the news. It was so hard to leave them further behind with every step his horse took, even if he did it knowing that the further away he was, the safer they were. Don't think about them, he told himself. Don't wonder when or whether you'll see them again. Tell yourself the Bluejay never had a wife or a daughter. Just for a while.

Violante turned in the saddle as if to make sure she hadn't lost him. Brianna whispered something to her, and Violante smiled. Her Ugliness had a beautiful smile, although you seldom saw it. It showed how young she still was.

They were riding up a densely wooded hill. Sunlight fell

through the branches of the almost leafless trees, and in spite
of the snow covering the moss and roots further up the slopes
there was still a smell of autumn here, of rotting leaves and
the last fading flowers. Fairies, drowsy with the onset of winter, flitted through the grass, which was yellow now and stiff
with frost. Brownie tracks crossed their path, and Mo thought
he heard wild glass men scurrying about under the bushes that
grew on the slope above them. One of Violante's soldiers
began to sing quietly, and the sound of his young voice made
Mo feel as if everything he had left behind were fading: his
concern for Resa and Meggie, the Black Prince, the children
of Ombra and the threat of the Piper, even his bargain with
Death. There was only the path, the endless path winding up
into the strange mountains, and the desire in his heart that he
couldn't tame, a wish to ride further and further on into this
bewildering world. What did the castle to which Violante was
leading them look like? Were there really giants in the mountains? Where did the path end? Did it ever end at all? Not for
the Bluejay, a voice inside him whispered, and for a moment
his heart beat like the heart of a ten-year-old boy, as fearless
and as fresh.

He sensed Dustfinger's eyes resting on him. 'You like this
world of mine.'

'Yes. Yes, I do.' Mo himself could hear the guilt in his
voice.

Dustfinger laughed louder than Mo had ever heard him
laugh before. He looked so different without the scars – as if
the White Women had healed his heart as well as his face.
'And you're ashamed of it!' he said. 'Why? Because you still
think everything here is just made of words? It is indeed a
strange thing: look at you! Anyone might think you belonged

here as much as me. Are you sure someone didn't just read you over into that other world of yours?'

Mo didn't know whether or not he liked that idea. 'Fairly sure,' he answered.

The wind blew a leaf against his chest. Tiny limbs hung from it, a frightened face, pale brown like the leaf itself. Orpheus's leaf-men had obviously spread quickly. The strange creature bit Mo's finger when he reached for it, and the next gust of wind blew it away.

'Did you see them last night too?' Dustfinger turned in the saddle. The soldier riding behind them avoided his eyes. There is no land more foreign than the realm of Death.

'See who?'

Dustfinger responded with a mocking smile.

There had been two of them. Two White Women. They had been standing among the trees just before daybreak.

'Why do you think they're following us? To remind us that we still belong to them?'

Dustfinger merely shrugged his shoulders, as if the answer wasn't important and the question was the wrong one. 'I see them every time I close my eyes. *Dustfinger!* they whisper. *We miss you. Does your heart hurt again? Do you feel the burden of time? Shall we lift it from you? Shall we make you forget once more?* I tell them no. Let me feel all of it a little longer. Who knows, perhaps you'll be taking me back soon anyway. Me,' he added, looking at Mo, 'and the Bluejay.'

Dark clouds were gathering above them, as if they had been waiting beyond the mountains, and the horses grew restless, but Dustfinger calmed them with a few quiet words.

'What do they whisper to you?' he asked Mo, looking at him as if he knew the answer already.

'Ah.' It was difficult to talk about the White Women. As difficult as if they held his tongue down as soon as he tried. 'Usually they simply stand there as if they were waiting for me. And if they do speak to me they always say the same thing: *only Death will make you immortal, Bluejay.*'

He hadn't told anyone that before, not the Black Prince or Resa or Meggie. What would be the point? The words would only have frightened them.

But Dustfinger knew the White Women – and the one they served. 'Immortal,' he repeated. 'Yes, they like to say such things, and no doubt they're right. But what about you? Are you in a hurry for immortality?'

Mo could find no answer for that.

Ahead, Violante turned her horse around. The path had brought them to the crest of a mountain, and far below lay a lake with a castle reflected in its waters, drifting on the ripples like a stone fruit floating a long way from the bank. Its walls were as dark as the spruce trees that grew on the slopes of the surrounding mountains, and an almost endless bridge, narrow as a ribbon of stone and supported on countless piers, led over the water to land, where two ruined watchtowers stood among a few abandoned huts.

'The Impregnable Bridge!' whispered one of the soldiers, and all the stories he had heard about this place were echoed in that whisper.

It began to snow again, tiny, wet flakes that disappeared in the dark lake as if it were devouring them. Violante's young soldiers stared at their destination in dismal silence. It was not a very inviting sight. But their mistress's face lit up like a young girl's.

'What do you say, Bluejay?' she asked Mo, putting her

gold-framed glasses on her nose. 'Look at it. My mother described this castle to me so often that I feel as if I'd grown up here myself. I only wish these glasses were stronger,' she added impatiently, 'but even from here I can see that it's beautiful!'

Beautiful? Mo would have called the castle sinister. But perhaps, to the Adderhead's daughter, that was one and the same thing.

'Now do you see why I've brought you here?' Violante asked. 'No one can take this castle. Even the giants couldn't harm it when they still came to this valley. The lake is too deep, and the bridge is just wide enough for a single horseman.'

The path leading down to the banks of the lake was so steep that they had to lead their horses. It was as dark under the dense spruce trees as if their needles ate up the daylight, and Mo felt his heart grow heavy again. But Violante walked on impatiently, and the rest of them could hardly keep up with her as they passed through the trees that grew so close together.

'Night-Mares!' whispered Dustfinger, when the silence among the trees grew as dark as the needles that covered the ground. 'Black Bogles, Red-Caps . . . everything that would terrify Farid lives here. Let's hope this castle really is uninhabited.'

When they were standing on the banks of the lake at last, mist hung above the water, and the bridge and the castle rose from the white vapour as if they had just been born out of it. Stony growths from the depths of the water. The huts on the bank looked much more real now, although it was obvious that they had been standing empty for a very long time. Mo led his horse to one of the watchtowers. The door was charred, the interior black with soot.

Violante came to his side. 'A nephew of my grandfather's was the last who tried to capture this castle. He never got across the lake. My grandfather bred predatory fish in it. They're said to be larger than horses, and they crave human flesh. The lake guards this castle better than any army could. There were never many soldiers here, but my grandfather always made sure there were enough provisions to withstand a siege. Cattle were kept in the castle, and he had vegetables grown and fruit trees planted in several of the inner court-yards. All the same, so my mother told me, she had to eat fish more often than she liked.'

Violante laughed, but Mo looked out over the dark water uneasily. It was as if, through the drifting swathes of mist, he saw all the dead soldiers who had tried to cross the Impregnable Bridge. The lake was like a copy of the Inkworld itself, both beautiful and terrible. Its surface was smooth as glass, but the edge of the bank was marshy, and swarms of buzzing insects, obviously unaffected by the wintry weather, hovered among reeds now white with rime.

'Why did your grandfather live in such a remote place?'

'Because he was tired of human beings. Is that surprising?' Violante was still looking as captivated as if she couldn't believe that at last her short-sighted eyes were seeing what she had only known through words before. So often it is words or pictures that first tell us what we long for.

'My mother's chambers were in the tower on the left. My grandfather had the tower built when giants still came here.' Violante's voice sounded as if she were talking in her sleep. 'At that time this lake was the only place outside the cities where you could be safe from them, because they couldn't cross it. But they loved to look at their reflection in its waters, and that's why it was also called the Giants' Mirror. My mother was afraid of them. She used to hide under the bed when she heard their footsteps, but all the same she wondered how big they would be if they were standing right in front of her, not on the distant bank. Once, when she was about five years old and a giant and his child appeared on the bank, she wanted to run over to them. But one of her nursemaids caught up with her where the bridge begins, and my grandfather had her shut up in the tower there for three days and nights, as a punishment.' Violante pointed to a tower that rose like a needle among the others. 'That tower was the only place in the castle that my mother didn't like to talk about. It had pictures of Night-Mares and lake monsters on its walls, of wolves and snakes and robbers attacking travellers. My grandfather had the pictures painted to show his daughters how dangerous the world beyond the lake was. The giants often used to take human beings – especially children – away as toys. Have you heard that?'

'I've read about it,' replied Mo.

The happiness in her voice moved him, and he wondered, not for the first time, how it was that the book which had told him so much about fire-elves and giants said so little about the Adderhead's daughter. To Fenoglio, Violante had been only a minor character, an ugly, unhappy little girl, no more. Perhaps you could learn from her how small parts can be made into major roles if you play them in your own way.

Violante seemed to have forgotten that he was standing beside her. Indeed, she seemed to have forgotten everything, even that she had come here to kill her father. She was looking at the castle as if she hoped to see her mother appear on the battlements at any moment. But at last she turned abruptly.

'Four of you stay by the watchtowers!' she ordered her soldiers. 'The rest come with me. But ride slowly if you don't want the sound of your horses' hooves to entice the fishes. My mother used to tell me how they'd pulled dozens of men down from the bridge.'

An uneasy murmur rose among her soldiers. They really were little more than children.

But Violante took no notice. She picked up her skirts, black like everything Mo had ever seen her wear, and let Brianna help her up on to her horse. 'You'll see,' she said. 'I know this castle better than if I'd lived here. I've studied all the books there are about it. I know its ground plan and all its secrets.'

'Has your father ever been here?' Dustfinger asked the question just as it had formed in Mo's mind too.

Violante picked up her reins. 'Only once,' she said, without looking at Dustfinger. 'When he was courting my mother. But that's a long time ago. All the same, he's sure to remember that no one can take this castle.'

She turned her horse. 'Come, Brianna,' she said, and rode towards the bridge. But her horse shied back when it saw the stone path across the water. Without a word, Dustfinger brought his mount to Violante's side, took the reins from her hand and led her horse on to the bridge behind his. The sound of their hooves echoed over the water as Violante's men followed him.

Mo was the last to ride on to the bridge. Suddenly the whole world seemed to be made of water. Mist drifted into his face, and the castle swam on the lake before him like a dark dream: towers, battlements, bridges, oriels, windowless walls with the wind and the water eating at them. The bridge seemed to go on for ever, and the gate to which it led looked out of reach, but at last it began to grow larger with every step that his horse took. The towers and walls filled the sky like a menacing song, and Mo saw dark shadows glide through the water, like watchdogs picking up the scent of their coming.

What did the castle look like, Mo? he heard Meggie asking. *Describe it!*

What would he say? He looked up at the towers, as many of them as if a new one grew every year, at the maze of oriels and bridges and the stone griffin above the gateway. 'It didn't look like a happy ending, Meggie,' he heard himself reply. 'It looked like a place from which no one ever comes back.'

The Role of Women

Why would I need a book?
The wind leafs through the trees
Speaking softly at its ease
Words that I sometimes repeat.
And Death, breaking eyes like a flower
Does not have mine in its power . . .

Rainer Maria Rilke, *Book of Pictures*

Men's clothes. Resa had stolen them from the sleeping Elfbane: a pair of trousers and a long, warm shirt. Very likely they were his pride and joy. Few of the robbers owned more than what they wore on their backs, but over the next few days she was going to need those clothes more than Elfbane.

It was long ago that the Inkworld had forced Resa to wear men's clothing, yet as soon as she put on the rough trousers the memory came back as if it were only yesterday. She remembered how often the knife had scratched her scalp as she cut her hair short, and how her throat had hurt from the constant attempt to make her voice sound deeper. This time she'd just pin up her hair, and presumably she wouldn't have to pretend to be a man, but trousers were so much more practical than a dress on overgrown paths, and she would have to take such paths if she wanted to follow Mo.

'Promise me!' He had never asked her more fervently for anything. 'Promise me you'll both stay in hiding, never mind what happens, never mind what you hear. And if it all goes wrong –' (what a clever way of getting around saying *if I die*) – 'then Meggie must try to read the two of you back.'

Back where? To Elinor's house, where every nook and cranny reminded her of him, and his workshop stood in the garden? Quite apart from the fact that Elinor herself was on this side of the letters now. But Mo didn't know that, any more than he knew she had burnt the words that Orpheus had written.

No. There was no going back home without him. If Mo died in the Inkworld, then so would she . . . hoping that the White Women would take her to wherever he was.

Dark thoughts, Resa, she told herself, placing her hand on her belly. It was so long since Meggie had been growing in there, but her fingers still remembered – all the days when she had felt her body in vain, and then the moment when she suddenly sensed the baby moving under her skin. There was no moment like it, and she could hardly wait to feel the tiny feet kicking below her ribs, the child inside her turning and stretching. It couldn't be long now. If only she didn't have to feel so anxious about the child's father.

'Come along, let's go looking for him, to warn him about the Magpie and Snapper!' she whispered to her unborn child. 'We've been standing back and watching for too long. From now on we'll play our part, even if Fenoglio hasn't written us one.'

Only Roxane knew what she was planning, no one else. Not Elinor, not Meggie. They'd both have wanted to come too. But she must go alone, although that would make Meggie angry with her once again. She still hadn't entirely forgiven Resa for riding to Orpheus, or for that night in the graveyard. Meggie didn't forgive easily when her father's wellbeing was at stake. He was the only one she always forgave.

Resa took Fenoglio's book out from under the blanket beneath which she slept. She had asked Battista to make a leather bag for it, of course without telling him that he himself, more than likely, had been born between its pages. 'That's a strange book,' he had remarked. 'What scribe writes such ugly letters? And what kind of binding is that? Had the bookbinder run out of leather?'

She wasn't sure what Dustfinger would have said about her plan. It still touched her that he had entrusted the book to her. But now she must do as she thought right.

She looked across the cave at her daughter. Meggie was sleeping beside Farid, but Doria slept only a little further off, his face turned towards her. Orpheus's former glass man lay beside him, the boy's hand over him like a blanket. How young Meggie still looked in her sleep! Resa almost bent down to push the hair back from her daughter's forehead. It still hurt to think of all the years she had spent away from her; it hurt so much. Hurry up, Resa, she told herself. Day is already beginning to dawn outside. Soon they'd all be awake, and then they wouldn't let her leave.

Elinor murmured something in her sleep as Resa slipped

past her, and the guard at the cave entrance glanced her way when she went round behind the wall that Fenoglio had built, as if to ward off the world he himself had made. He and his glass man were snoring in competition, like a bear and a grasshopper. Rosenquartz's tiny fingers were black with ink, and the sheet of paper beside him was covered with freshly-written words, but nearly all of them had been crossed out.

Resa put the bag containing the book down beside the wineskin for which Fenoglio was still inclined to reach, even though Elinor lost no opportunity to lecture him on his drinking. She put the letter she had written him between the pages, so that it stuck out of the bag like a white hand. He couldn't miss it.

Fenoglio, she had written – it had taken her a long time to look for the right words, and she still wasn't sure she had found them – *I am giving* Inkheart *back to the man who wrote it. Perhaps your own book can tell you how this story is going to end, and will whisper you words to protect Meggie's father. Meanwhile I will try to make sure, in my own way, that the song of the Bluejay doesn't end sadly. Resa.*

The sky was turning red as she stepped out of the cave, and it was bitterly cold. Woodenfoot was standing guard under the trees. He watched suspiciously as she turned north. Perhaps he didn't even recognize her in men's clothing. Some bread and a waterskin, a knife, the compass that Elinor had brought from their old world – that was all she was taking. It wouldn't be the first time she'd had to manage on her own in this world. But she hadn't gone far before she heard heavy footsteps behind her.

'Resa!' The Strong Man sounded injured, like a child

catching his sister in the act of running away. 'Where are you going?'

As if he didn't know.

'You can't follow him! I promised him I'd look after you – you and your daughter.' He held her firmly, and anyone held firmly by the Strong Man wasn't going to get away.

'Let me go!' she snapped at him. 'He doesn't know about Snapper. I have to follow him! You can look after Meggie.'

'Doria will do that. I've never seen him look at a girl the way he looks at her. And Battista's there too.' He was still holding her. 'It's a long way to the Castle in the Lake. Very long and very dangerous.'

'Roxane has told me how to get there.'

'Oh yes? And did she tell you about the Night-Mares? And the Red-Caps, and the Black Elves?'

'They haunted Capricorn's fortress too, and every one of his men was worse. So go back. I can look after myself.'

'I'm sure. And you can take on Snapper and the Piper too.' Without another word he took the waterskin from her. 'The Bluejay will kill me when he sees you!'

The Bluejay. Suppose she met only him, and not her husband, at the castle? Mo might understand why she had followed him, but not the Bluejay.

'Let's go.' The Strong Man marched off. He was as obstinate as he was strong. Not even the Black Prince could make him change his mind once he'd made it up, and Resa didn't even try. It would be good to have his company, very good. She hadn't often been alone in the forests of the Inkworld, and she didn't like to remember the times when she was.

'Strong Man?' she asked when they had left the cave where her daughter was sleeping far behind. 'What did you think of the magpie that flew to Gecko?'

'That was no magpie,' he said. 'It had a woman's voice. But I didn't say anything. The others would only have said I was crazy again.'

Waiting

We shall not cease from exploration
And the end of all our exploring
Will be to arrive where we started
And know the place for the first time.

T.S. Eliot, *Little Gidding*

The Castle in the Lake was an oyster that had closed itself off from the world. Not a single window had a view of the mountains around. Not a single window looked out on the lake lapping at its dark walls. Once you had left the gate behind you there was only the castle: its dark and narrow courtyards, covered bridges linking its towers, walls painted with worlds like nothing that existed in the world outside these windowless fortifications. They showed gardens and gently rolling hills populated by unicorns, dragons and peacocks, and above them an eternally blue sky with white clouds drifting over it. The pictures were everywhere, in the rooms, along the corridors, on the courtyard walls. You saw them through every window (and there were many windows inside the castle).

Painted views of a world that didn't exist. But the moist breath of the lake made paint flake off the stones, so that it seemed in many places as if someone had tried to wipe the painted lies off the walls.

Only from the towers, where the view was not interrupted by walls, oriels and roofs, could you see the world that really surrounded the castle, the great lake and the mountains that lay around it. Mo was immediately drawn to the battlements, where he could feel the sky above him and look at the world which fascinated him so much that he kept making his way deeper and deeper into it, even though it might not be any more real than the pictures on the walls. But Violante just wanted to see the rooms with windows looking out on painted worlds, rooms where her mother had played in the past.

She moved through the Castle as if she had come home, tenderly caressing the furniture, which was grey with dust, scrutinizing every piece of earthenware that she found under the cobwebs, and examining the pictures on the walls as closely as if they told her tales of her mother. 'This was the room where she and her sisters did their lessons. Look, those were their desks! They had a horrible tutor!' 'This was where my grandmother slept!' 'This was where they kept the hounds, this was the dovecote for the pigeons who carried their messages.'

The longer Mo followed her, the more it seemed to him that this painted world was exactly what Violante's short-sighted eyes wanted to see. Perhaps she felt safer in a world resembling the scenes in Balbulus's books – invented, easily controlled, timeless and unchanging, every corner of it familiar.

Would Meggie have liked to see painted unicorns from her

window, he wondered, eternally green hills, clouds that were always the same? No, he answered himself, Meggie would have climbed up to the towers like him.

'Did your mother ever tell you if she was really happy here?' Mo couldn't keep the doubt out of his voice, and Violante heard it. The girlish softness that changed her face so much disappeared at once, and the Adderhead's daughter was back.

'Of course! Very happy. Until my father made my grandfather give him her hand in marriage and took her away to the Castle of Night!' She looked at him defiantly, as if her mere gaze could force him to believe her – and to love this castle.

There was one room that didn't let you forget the outside world. Mo first found it when he was exploring on his own, searching for some place where he wouldn't feel that he was a prisoner again, if in a beautifully painted dungeon this time. Daylight dazzled him as he suddenly stepped into a hall in the west wing of the castle. It had so many windows that they turned the walls into lace. Light, reflected from the water of the lake, danced on the ceiling, and the mountains seemed to line up outside as if they wanted nothing more than to be seen through all those windows. The beauty of the view took Mo's breath away, although it was a dark beauty, and his eyes instinctively went to the sombre mountain slopes in search of any trace of human beings. He filled his lungs with the cold air carried in on the wind, and did not see that he was not alone until he turned and looked south, to where Ombra lay somewhere beyond the mountains. Dustfinger was sitting in one of the windows, the wind in his hair, his face turned towards the cold sun.

'The strolling players call it the Hall of a Thousand

Windows,' he said, without turning, and Mo wondered how long he had been sitting there. 'They say that Violante's mother and sisters had poor eyesight because their father would never let them look into the distance, for fear of what awaited them there. Daylight began to hurt their eyes. They couldn't even make out the pictures on the walls of their rooms clearly any more, and a physician who came here with a couple of the Motley Folk told Violante's grandfather that his daughters would go blind unless he let them see the real world now and then. So the Prince of Salt – that was what people called him, because he'd made a fortune in the salt trade – had these windows made in the walls and ordered his daughters to look out of them for an hour every day. But while they did so a minstrel had to tell them about the terrors of the outside world – the heartlessness and cruelty of human beings, disease running rife and hungry wolves – so that they'd never want to go out into it and leave their father.'

'What a strange story,' said Mo. As he went over to Dustfinger's side he could feel his longing for Roxane as strongly as if it were his own.

'It's only a story now,' said Dustfinger. 'But it all really happened, here in this place.' He blew a gentle breath into the cool air, and close beside them three girls were formed out of fire. They stood close together, staring into the distance, where the mountains were as blue as yearning.

'It's said they tried to run away with the strolling players several times. Their father tolerated the Motley Folk only because they brought him news from other princely courts. But neither the girls nor the strolling players ever got any further than the first trees. Their father had them caught and brought his daughters back to the castle. As for the strolling

players, he had them tied up there –' Dustfinger pointed to a
rock on the banks of the lake – 'and the girls had to stand at
the window –' (the figures did exactly what Dustfinger
described) – 'freezing cold and trembling with fear, until
giants came and dragged the strolling players away.'

Mo couldn't take his eyes off the fiery girls. The flames
depicted their fear and loneliness as expressively as Balbulus
could have done with his brush. No, Violante's mother had
not been happy in this castle, whatever her daughter said.

'What's he doing?'

Suddenly Violante was standing behind them. Brianna and
Tullio were with her.

Dustfinger snapped his fingers, and the flames lost their
human form and twined around the window like a fiery plant.
'Don't worry. There'll just be a little soot left on the stones,
and for the moment,' he added, glancing at Brianna, who was
staring into the flames as if enchanted, 'it looks beautiful,
don't you think?'

It did. The fire surrounded the window with red leaves and
flowers of gold. Tullio instinctively took a step towards it, but
Violante roughly pulled him back to her side. 'Put it out, Fire-
Dancer!' she ordered Dustfinger. 'This minute.'

Shrugging his shoulders, Dustfinger obeyed. A whisper,
and the fire went out. Violante's anger did not impress him,
and that alarmed the Adderhead's daughter. Mo could see it
in her eyes.

'It did look beautiful, don't you agree?' he asked, passing
his finger over the sooty sill. It was as if he could still see the
three girls standing at the window.

'Fire is never beautiful,' said Violante with scorn. 'Have
you ever seen anyone die by fire? They burn for a long time.'

She obviously knew what she was talking about. How old had she been when she first saw someone die at the stake, how old when she first saw a hanging? How much darkness could children bear before darkness became a part of them for ever?

'Come with me, Bluejay!' Violante turned abruptly. 'There's something I want to show you. Only you! Brianna, get some water and wash that soot off.'

Brianna hurried away without a word, but not without casting a quick glance at her father, who held Mo back as he was about to follow Her Ugliness.

'Beware of her!' he whispered. 'Princes' daughters have a weakness for mountebanks and robbers.'

'Bluejay!' Violante's voice was sharp with impatience. 'Where are you?'

Dustfinger painted a fiery heart on the floor.

Violante was waiting on the staircase in the tower as if afraid of the windows. Perhaps she liked shadows because she still felt the mark on her cheek from which her cruel nickname came. Meggie had been called very different pet names when she was little: 'my pretty', 'sweetheart', 'honey' . . . Meggie had grown up in the certainty that the mere sight of her filled him with love. Presumably Violante's mother had shown her daughter that kind of love, but everyone else had looked at her and shuddered, or felt pity at the most. Where had Violante hidden, as a child, from all those glances of dislike and all that pain? Had she taught her heart to despise everyone who could show the world a pretty face? Poor Adder's daughter, thought Mo as he saw her standing on the dark staircase, so lonely in her dark heart . . . no, Dustfinger was wrong. Violante loved nothing and no one, not even herself.

She hurried down the steps as if running away from her

own shadow. She always walked fast and impatiently, picking up her long skirts as if cursing the clothes women had to wear in this world at every step she took.

'Come with me. I want to show you something. My mother always told me the library of this castle was in the north wing, with the unicorn pictures. I don't know when it was moved, or why, but see for yourself . . . the tower guardroom, the scribe's room, the women's room,' she whispered as she walked. 'The bridge to the north tower, the bridge to the south tower, the aviary courtyard, the hounds' courtyard . . .' She really did move around the castle as if she had lived in it for years.

How often had she studied the books describing this place? Mo could hear the lake as she led him through a courtyard containing empty cages, gigantic cages made of metalwork as elaborate as if the bars were meant to be substitute trees for the birds inside. He heard water breaking on the stones, but the walls surrounding this courtyard were painted with beech and oak trees, and flocks of birds sitting in their branches: sparrows, larks, wild doves, nightingales and falcons, crossbills and robin redbreasts, woodpeckers and hummingbirds dipping their beaks into red flowers. A bluejay sat beside a swallow.

'My mother and her sisters loved birds. So my grandfather didn't just have them painted on the walls, he had live birds brought here from the most distant lands, and filled these cages with them. He had the cages covered in winter, but my mother crept in under the covers. Sometimes she would sit for hours in one of the cages, until the nursemaids found her and plucked the birds' feathers from her hair.'

She hurried on. A covered passage under a gateway, another courtyard. Kennels, hunting scenes on the walls, and above it all the sound of the water of the lake, so far away and yet so close. Of course Violante's mother loved birds, thought Mo. She wished she had wings too. No doubt she and her sisters dreamt of flying away when they climbed into the cages and waited for their fine dresses to be covered with feathers.

It saddened him to think of the three lonely girls, but all the same he would have loved to show Meggie the cages and the painted birds, the unicorns and dragons, the Hall of a Thousand Windows, even the Impregnable Bridge that seemed to be hovering over the lake when you looked down on it from above. You'll tell Meggie about all this one day, he said to himself, as if just imagining it could make the words true.

Another staircase, another covered bridge like a tunnel suspended between the towers. The door at which Violante stopped was stained black, like all the doors in the castle. The wood had swelled, and she had to brace her shoulder against it to open it.

'It's terrible!' she said, and she was right. Mo couldn't make out much in the long room. Two narrow windows let in only a little light and air, but even if he hadn't been able to see anything he would have smelt it. The books were stacked like firewood by the damp walls, and the cold air smelt so strongly of mould that he put his hand over his mouth and nose.

'Look at them!' Violante picked up the nearest book and held it out to him, tears in her eyes. 'They're all like that!'

Mo took the book from her hand and tried to open it, but the pages had stuck together in a single blackened, musty-smelling lump. Mould covered the cut edges of the pages like foam. The covers were eaten away. What he was holding wasn't a book any more – it was the corpse of a book, and for a moment Mo felt nausea as he thought that he had condemned the Book he had bound for the Adderhead to the same fate. Did it look as bad as this one by now? Hardly, or it would have killed the Adderhead long ago, and the White Women wouldn't be reaching out their hands to Meggie.

'I've looked at so many of them. Hardly any of them are in a better state! How can it have happened?'

Mo put the ruined book back with the others.

'Well, wherever the library originally was, I'm afraid there's no safe place for books in this castle. Even if your grandfather tried to forget the lake outside, it's still there. The air is so damp that the books started rotting, and since no one knew how to save them I suppose they were put in this room, in the hope that they'd dry out more quickly here than in the library. A bad mistake. They must have been worth a fortune.'

Violante pressed her lips together and passed her hand over the crumbling covers, as if stroking a dead pet's coat for the last time. 'My mother described them to me even more vividly than the rest of this castle! Luckily she took some to the Castle of Night with her, and then I took most of those to Ombra. As soon as I arrived I asked my father-in-law to send for the other books too. After all, this castle had been empty for years. But who listens to an eight-year-old girl? "Forget the books, and the castle where they stand," that's what he said whenever I asked him. "I'm not sending my men to a place like the Castle in the Lake, not for the finest books in the world. Haven't you heard of the fish your grandfather bred in the lake, and the eternal mists? Not to mention the giants." As if giants hadn't disappeared from these mountains years ago! He was such a fool! A greedy, gluttonous fool!' Anger took the sadness from her voice.

Mo looked around. The idea of the treasures that had once been hidden between all these wrecked covers nauseated him more than the stench of mould.

'You can't do anything for the books now, can you?'

He shook his head. 'No. There's no remedy for mould. Although you say that the Adderhead has found one. I don't suppose you know what it is?'

'Oh yes. But you won't like it.' Violante picked up one of the spoilt books. This one would still open, but the pages fell apart in her fingers. 'He's had the White Book dipped in fairy blood. They say that if that hadn't worked he'd have tried human blood.'

Mo felt as if he could see the blank pages he had cut in the Castle of Night soaking up the blood. 'That's appalling!' he said.

It obviously amused Violante that such a ridiculous piece of cruelty could shake him. 'Apparently my father mixed the fairy blood with the blood of fire-elves so that it would dry more quickly,' she went on, unmoved. 'Their blood is very hot, did you know that? Hot as liquid fire.'

'Indeed?' Mo's voice was hoarse with disgust. 'I hope you aren't planning to try the same remedy with these books. Believe me, it wouldn't help them now.'

'If you say so.'

Was he just imagining the disappointment in her voice?

He turned round. He didn't want to see the dead books any more. Nor did he want to think of those pages drenched in blood.

As he came through the doorway, Dustfinger moved away from the painted wall of the corridor. It was almost as if he were stepping out of a book again. 'We have a visitor,

Silvertongue,' he said. 'Although not the one we were expecting.'

'Silvertongue?' Violante appeared in the open doorway. 'Why do you call him that?'

'Oh, it's a long story.' Dustfinger gave her a smile which she did not return. 'I assure you the name fits him at least as well as the one you give him. And he's had it very much longer.'

'Has he?' Violante looked at Dustfinger with barely concealed dislike. 'Is that what they call him among the dead too?'

Dustfinger turned and ran his finger over the gold-mocker sitting among the painted branches of a rose bush. 'No. No one goes by any name among the dead. We're all alike there. Mountebanks and princes. You'll find that out yourself some day.'

Violante's face froze, and once again it looked like her father's. 'My husband once came back from the dead too. But he didn't tell me mountebanks were so highly honoured there.'

'Did he tell you anything about it at all?' Dustfinger replied, looking so directly at Violante that she turned pale. 'I could tell you a long tale about your husband. I could tell you I've seen him twice among the dead. But I think you should greet your visitor now. He's not in a very good way.'

'Who is this visitor?'

Dustfinger plucked a fiery brush out of the air.

'Balbulus?' Violante looked at him in disbelief.

'Yes,' said Dustfinger. 'And the Piper has left the mark of your father's anger on him.'

49

Masters New and Old

'No problem!' cried Butt the Hoopoe. 'Any story worth its salt can handle a little shaking up.'

Salman Rushdie, *Hassan and the Sea of Stories*

How his behind hurt! As if he'd never be able to sit on it again. Damn all this riding about the place. It was one thing to go through the streets of Ombra on horseback, his head held high, attracting envious glances. But it was no fun following the Adderhead's coach for hours in the dark, along rough paths where you were liable to break your neck the whole time.

For Orpheus's new master travelled only by night. As soon as dawn came he had his black tent pitched to hide there from the light of day, and only when the sun set did he heave his rotting body back into the coach standing ready for him. It was drawn by two horses as black as the velvet that lined the coach. Orpheus had cast a surreptitious glance inside it the first time they stopped to rest. The Adder's crest was embroidered on the cushions in silver thread, and they looked much softer than the saddle he'd been sitting in for days. He wouldn't have minded a coach like that himself, but he had to ride behind it with Jacopo, Violante's horrible brat, who kept demanding something to eat or drink, and showed such dog-like devotion to the Piper that he wore a tin nose over his own. It still surprised Orpheus that the Piper wasn't travelling with them. Well, of course – he'd let the Bluejay escape. Presumably the Adderhead had sent him back to the Castle of Night to punish him. But why, for heaven's sake, didn't his master have more than four dozen men-at-arms to escort them? Orpheus had counted them twice, but that was all. Did the Adderhead think this handful of men was enough against Violante's child soldiers, or did he still trust his daughter? If so, then the Silver Prince was either considerably more stupid than he was reputed to be, or the rot had attacked his brain, which might well mean that Mortimer would be playing the hero again and he, Orpheus, had backed the wrong side. A terrible idea, so he was very careful not to think of it too often.

They made such painfully slow progress in the heavy coach that Oss could keep up with the horses on foot. Cerberus had been left behind in Ombra. The Adderhead, too, thought keeping dogs was a privilege of the nobility . . . it really was high time the rules of this world were rewritten.

'Slow as snails!' grumbled one of the men-at-arms behind him. Those fellows stank to high heaven, as if competing with their master's odour. 'You wait and see, by the time we reach that damn castle the Bluejay will have flown again.' Idiots in armour. They still hadn't realized that the Bluejay had ridden to Ombra Castle with a plan in mind, and that plan had not yet been put into practice.

Ah, they were stopping at last. What a relief to his poor

bones! The sky was still black as pitch, but presumably Thumbling had spotted a fairy dancing at the approach of dawn in spite of the cold.

Thumbling . . .

The Adderhead's new bodyguard could teach anyone the meaning of fear. He was as thin as if Death had taken him once already, and the scaly snake from his master's crest was tattooed across his larynx, so that when he spoke it writhed on his skin as if it were alive. A very unsettling sight, but luckily Thumbling didn't talk much. He did not owe his name to his stature. Indeed, Thumbling was rather taller than Orpheus, not that it was likely anyone in this world knew the fairy tale of the same name and its tiny central character. No, this Thumbling apparently got his name from the cruel things he could do with his thumbs.

Orpheus hadn't found anything about him in Fenoglio's book, so presumably he was one of those characters who – if Fenoglio himself was to be believed – had been hatched out by the story itself, like midge larvae in a marshy pond. Thumbling dressed like a peasant, but his sword was better than the Piper's, and it was said that, like Silvernose, he had no sense of smell, which was why the two of them could be near the Adderhead without being overcome by nausea, unlike everyone else.

Lucky for them, thought Orpheus as he slid off his horse, groaning with relief.

'Rub it down!' he ordered Oss testily. 'And then pitch my tent, and jump to it.' Orpheus thought his bodyguard extremely foolish since he had set eyes on Thumbling.

Orpheus's tent was not particularly large. He could hardly stand up in it, and it was so cramped that he almost knocked it down when he turned around, but he hadn't been able to read himself a better one in a hurry, even though he had searched all his books for a rather grander version. His books . . . well, they were his now, anyway. Formerly the property of the library of Ombra Castle, but no one had stopped Orpheus when he'd helped himself to them.

Books.

How excited he had been, standing in the Laughing Prince's library. He had been so sure that he'd find at least one book there containing words by Fenoglio. And he had, indeed, come upon a book of Bluejay songs on the very first lectern. His fingers had been shaking as he freed the book from its chain (the locks were easily picked; he knew how to do these things). Got you now, Mortimer, he had thought. I'll knead you into shape like dough. You won't know who and where you are once I get my tongue around your robber's name! He had been all the more painfully disappointed when he read the first words. Oh, those leaden sounds, those badly-rhymed lines! Fenoglio couldn't have written any of the songs in that book. Where were the old man's songs? Violante took them with her, you fool, he told himself. Why didn't you think of that before?

The disappointment still hurt. But who said only Fenoglio's words could come alive in this world? Weren't all books ultimately related? After all, the same letters filled them, just arranged in a different order. Which meant that, in a certain way, every book was contained in every other!

However that might be, what Orpheus had read so far during those endless hours in the saddle was not, unfortunately, very promising. It seemed that there wasn't a single storyteller in this world who understood his art, or at least not in the

Laughing Prince's library. What a pitiful collection of beautifully handwritten tedium, what wooden babbling! And the
characters! Not even *his* voice would bring them to life.

Originally Orpheus had intended to impress the
Adderhead with a sample of his skill the next time they
stopped to rest, but he still hadn't found anything that tasted
better on his tongue than dry paper. Damn it all!

Of course the Adderhead's tent was already pitched.
Thumbling always sent a few servants on ahead so that his
master could stumble out of the coach and straight into it. It
was a fabric palace, the dark lengths of cloth embroidered with
silver snakes shimmering in the moonlight as if thousands of
slugs had been crawling over the material.

Suppose he summons you now, Orpheus said to himself.
Didn't you promise him entertainment? He still heard the
Milksop's malicious words only too clearly: *My brother-in-law
doesn't like to have his expectations disappointed.*

Orpheus shivered. He sat down under a tree, feeling
wretched, lit a candle and fished another book out of the saddlebags, while Oss went on struggling with the tent.

Children's stories! Oh, for heaven's sake! Damn it, damn
it, damn it . . . or not? Wait a minute! This sounded familiar!
Orpheus's heartbeat quickened. Yes, these were Fenoglio's
words, no doubt about it.

'That's my book!' Small fingers snatched the book from
Orpheus's hands. There stood Jacopo, lips pouting, brows
drawn together above his eyes – probably in imitation of his
grandfather. He wasn't wearing the tin nose. Maybe it had
become rather a nuisance after a while.

With difficulty, Orpheus resisted the temptation to tug the
book out of those slender hands. Not a clever move. Be nice

to the little devil, Orpheus!

'Jacopo!' He gave him a broad and slightly deferential smile, the kind a prince's son would like, even if the prince in question was dead. 'This is your book? Then I'm sure you know who wrote it, don't you?'

Jacopo stared darkly at him. 'Tortoise-Face.'

Tortoise-Face. What a fabulous name for Fenoglio.

'Do you like his stories?'

Jacopo shrugged. 'I like the songs about the Bluejay better, but my mother won't let me have them.'

'That's not very nice of her, is it?' Orpheus stared at the book that Jacopo was clutching so possessively to his chest. He felt his hands sweating with desire for it. Fenoglio's words . . . suppose the words in that book worked as well as the words in *Inkheart* itself?

'How would it be, Jacopo . . .' (oh, how happily he could have wrung his stupid princely neck!), 'how would it be if I told you a few robber stories, and you lent me that book in return?'

'Can you tell stories? I thought you sold unicorns and dwarves.'

'I can do that too!' And I'll have you impaled on a unicorn's horn if you don't give me the book this minute, thought Orpheus, hiding his savage reflections behind an even broader smile.

'What do you want the book for? It's for children. Only for children.'

Horrible little know-all. 'I want to look at the pictures.'

Jacopo opened the book and leafed through the parchment pages. 'They're boring. Just animals and fairies and brownies. I can't stand brownies. They stink, and they look like Tullio.'

He looked at Orpheus. 'What will you give me if I lend it to you? Do you have any silver?'

Silver. It ran in the family – although Jacopo resembled his dead father far more than his grandfather.

'Of course.' Orpheus put his hand into the bag at his belt. Just you wait, princeling, he thought. If this book can do what I suspect it can, I'll think up a few nasty surprises for you.

Jacopo put out his hand, and Orpheus dropped a coin bearing his grandfather's head into it.

The little hand stayed open, demanding more. 'I want three.'

Orpheus snarled with annoyance, and Jacopo clutched the book a little more firmly.

Greedy little bastard. Orpheus dropped two more coins into the child's hand, and Jacopo was quick to close his fingers over them. 'That's for one day.'

'One day?'

Oss trudged towards them. His toes were sticking out of his boots; he was always needing new boots for his elephantine feet. Too bad. Let him go barefoot for a while.

'Your tent is ready, my lord.'

Jacopo stuffed the coins into the bag at his own belt, and held the book out to Orpheus with a gracious expression.

'Three silver coins, three days!' said Orpheus, taking the book. 'And now get out before I change my mind.'

Jacopo ducked, but the next moment he remembered whose grandson he was.

'That's no way to talk to me, Four-Eyes!' he cried shrilly, treading on Orpheus's foot so hard that he screamed. The soldiers who were sitting under the trees, freezing in the cold, laughed, and Jacopo stalked away like a shrunken copy of the Adderhead.

Orpheus felt the blood shoot to his face. 'What kind of bodyguard are you?' he snapped at Oss. 'Can't you even protect me from a six-year-old?'

With that, he limped towards his tent.

Oss had lit an oil lamp and spread a bearskin on the cold forest floor, but Orpheus missed his own house the moment he stepped inside. 'All because of Mortimer and his stupid robber games!' he grumbled as he sat down on the bearskin in a bad temper. 'I'll send him to hell, and Dustfinger with him. From all I hear, those two seem to be inseparable these days. And if there isn't any hell in this world, well, I'll write one especially for them. Even Dustfinger won't like that kind of fire!'

Write . . . he avidly opened the book he had bargained for with that avaricious little devil. Bears, brownies, fairies . . . the child was right, these were children's stories. It wouldn't be easy to read something out of them to tempt the Adderhead, who was sure to summon him soon, for who else was going to help him pass the sleepless night?

More brownies. The old man seemed to have a soft spot for them. A very sentimental story about a glass woman in love . . . another featuring a nymph madly in love with a prince . . . for heaven's sake, even Jacopo could hardly be expected to take much interest in that. Was a robber at least mentioned somewhere? Or, if not that, a bluejay calling? Yes, that would do it: he could step into the Adderhead's tent and, with just a few words, read the enemy he'd been hunting so long into his presence. But instead he found woodpeckers, nightingales, even a talking sparrow – no bluejay. Curse it, curse it, curse it! He hoped his three silver coins had been a good investment. *Nose-Nipper* . . . hmm, that at least sounded like a creature he could use to get his own back on the boy. But wait a moment! *There, where the forest was at its darkest . . .* Orpheus's lips formed the words soundlessly *. . . and where not even the brownies ventured out to search for mushrooms . . .*

'This camp is a very uncomfortable place to stay, master!' Ironstone was suddenly there beside him, looking gloomy. 'How long do you think we'll be travelling?'

The glass man was getting greyer every day. Perhaps he missed quarrelling with that treacherous brother of his. Or maybe it was because he kept catching woodlice and maggots and eating them with obvious relish.

'Don't disturb me!' Orpheus snapped at him. 'Can't you see I'm reading? And what's that leg clinging to your jacket? Haven't I told you not to eat insects? Do you want me to chase you away into the forest to join the wild glass men?'

'No. No, I really don't! I won't let another word pass my lips, Your Grace – and no insects either!' Ironstone bowed three times. (How Orpheus loved his servility!) 'Just one more question. Is that the book that was stolen from you?'

'No, unfortunately – only its little brother,' replied Orpheus without looking up. 'And now for heaven's sake shut up!'

. . . and where not even the brownies ventured out to search for mushrooms, he read on, *lived the blackest of all shadows, the worst of all nameless terrors. Night-Mare it was now called, but once it had borne a human name, for Night-Mares are human souls so evil that the White Women cannot wash the wickedness from their hearts, and send them back again . . .*

Orpheus raised his head. 'Well, well, what a dark story!' he murmured. 'What was the old man thinking of? Had that ghastly imp annoyed him so much that he set out to sing him a very special lullaby? This sounds rather as if Jacopo's grandfather might like it too. Yes.' Once again he bent over the pages on which Balbulus had painted a shadow with black fingers reaching through the letters on the page. 'Oh yes, fabulous!' he whispered. 'Ironstone, bring me pen and paper – and quick, or I'll feed you to one of the horses.'

The glass man obeyed eagerly, and Orpheus set to work. Half a sentence stolen here, a few words there, a snippet plucked from the next page to link them. Fenoglio's words. Written with a rather lighter touch than in *Inkheart* – you almost thought you could hear the old man chuckling – but the music was the same. So why shouldn't the words from this story act like those from the other book – the one so shamefully stolen from him?

'Yes. Yes, that sounds just like the old man's work!' whispered Orpheus as the paper soaked up the ink. 'But it needs a little more colour . . .' He was leafing through the illuminated pages, looking for the right words, when the glass man suddenly gave a shrill scream and scurried into hiding behind his hand.

There was a magpie in the opening of the tent.

Alarmed, Ironstone clutched Orpheus's sleeve (he was brave only when dealing with smaller specimens of his own kind), and Orpheus's hope that this might be just an ordinary magpie was dashed as soon as the bird opened her beak.

'Get out!' she spat at the glass man, and Ironstone scurried outside on his thin, spidery legs, although the Adderhead's men threw acorns and fairy-nuts at him.

Mortola. Of course Orpheus had known she'd turn up again sooner or later, but why couldn't it have been later? A magpie, he thought as she hopped towards him. If I could turn myself into an animal or a bird I'd make sure to choose something more impressive. How bedraggled she looked. Presumably a marten had been after her, or a fox. A pity it hadn't eaten her.

'What are you doing here?' she snapped. 'Did I say anything about offering your services to the Adderhead?'

She sounded completely crazy, apart from the fact that her harsh voice lost all its terrors when it came out of a yellow beak. Your story's finished, Mortola, thought Orpheus. Over. Whereas mine is only just beginning . . .

'Why are you sitting staring at me like that? Did he believe what you told him about his daughter and the Bluejay? Well, come on, out with it!' She pecked angrily at a beetle that had wandered into the tent, crunching it up so noisily that Orpheus felt sick.

'Oh, yes, yes,' he said, irritated. 'Of course he believed me. I was very convincing.'

'Good.' The magpie fluttered up on to the books that Orpheus had stolen from the library and peered down on what he had been writing. 'What's all this? Has the Adderhead ordered a unicorn from you too?'

'No, no. That's nothing. Just a . . . er . . . a story I'm supposed to be writing for his pest of a grandson.' Orpheus placed his hand over the words, as if by chance.

'What about the White Book?' Mortola preened her ruffled feathers. 'Have you found out where the Adderhead is hiding it? He must have it with him!'

'Death and the devil, of course not! Do you think the Adderhead carries it about with him publicly?' This time Orpheus didn't even try to keep the contempt out of his voice, and Mortola pecked his hand so hard that he screeched.

'I don't like your tone, Moonface! He must have it somewhere, so look for it, seeing that you're here. I can't take care
of everything.'

'When did you ever take care of anything?' Oh, why don't
I wring her skinny neck, he said to himself, wiping the blood
from the back of his hand. The way my father used to kill
chickens and pigeons.

'Is that any way to speak to me?' The magpie pecked at his
hand again, but this time Orpheus snatched it away in time.
'Do you think I've just been perching on a branch doing nothing? I've rid the world of the Black Prince and made sure that
his men will help me in future, not the Bluejay.'

'Really? The Prince is dead?' Orpheus took a great deal of
trouble to sound unimpressed. That would hurt Fenoglio. The
old man was ridiculously proud of his character. 'What about
the children he stole? Where are they?'

'In a cave northeast of Ombra. The moss-women call it the
Giants' Chamber. There are still a few robbers with them, and
some women. It's a stupid hiding place, but since the
Adderhead thought it was a good idea to send his brother-in-
law to look for them, the children are probably safe there for
a good while yet. Folk say even a rabbit can outwit that man.'

Interesting! And wasn't that a piece of news that could convince the Adderhead of his own usefulness?

'What about the Bluejay's wife and daughter? Are they
there too?'

'Certainly.' Mortola hissed as if something were stuck in
her throat. 'I was going to poison the little witch as well and
send her after the Prince, but her mother chased me away. She
knows too much about me, far too much!'

This was getting better and better.

But Mortola could read his thoughts on his face. 'Don't look so stupidly pleased with yourself! You're not to tell the Adderhead a word about any of this. They're both mine. I'm not leaving them to the Silver Prince this time, just for him to let them go again, understand?'

'Of course! My lips are sealed!' Orpheus immediately assumed his most innocent expression. 'What about the others – the robbers who are going to help you?'

'They're following you. They'll lie in ambush for the Adder tomorrow night. They think it's their own idea, but I planted it in their silly heads! Where can the Book fall into their hands more easily than in the middle of the forest? Snapper's staged hundreds of such attacks in the past, and he won't have to deal with the Piper. The stupid Adder has left his best watchdog behind – I suppose to punish him for letting the Bluejay escape. But he's only cutting into his own rotting flesh, and perhaps the Magpie will redeem her own son from Death with his corpse as early as tomorrow. It's a pity that if I do I won't see the White Women take the bookbinder away, but that can't be helped. Take him away they will, and this time they won't let him go again. Who knows? Perhaps Death will be so pleased to have both the Adderhead and the Bluejay that the White Book will be forgotten. Then I can write my son's name in it and never fear for him again!'

She was talking feverishly, faster and faster with every sentence, cackling as if she would choke on the words if she didn't get them out fast enough.

'Hide in the bushes when they attack!' she added. 'I don't want Snapper killing you too by mistake. I may need you yet if the fool happens to fail!'

She really does still trust you, Orpheus, he thought. He

could almost have laughed out loud. What had happened to Mortola's mind? Did she think of nothing but worms and beetles now? A poor prospect for her, thought Orpheus, and a very good one for me.

'Good. Excellent,' he said, while his brain thought swiftly of the best way to use all this information. Only one thing was perfectly clear: if the White Book fell into Mortola's hands, he himself would have lost the game. Death would take the Adderhead, Mortola would write her son's name in the White Book, and he himself wouldn't even get back the book that Dustfinger had stolen from him, to say nothing of immortal life! He would be left with nothing but the stories Fenoglio had written for a spoilt child. No, there was no alternative, he must go on backing the Adderhead.

'Why are you standing there gaping like a mooncalf?' Mortola's voice sounded more like a bird's hoarse cry with every word.

'My lord!' Oss put his head into the tent, looking alarmed. 'The Adderhead wants to see you. They say he's in a terrible temper.'

'I'm coming.' Orpheus almost trod on the magpie's tail feathers as he stumbled out of the tent. She hopped aside with an angry cackle.

'Horrible creature!' grunted Oss, kicking out at her. 'You want to shoo it away, my lord. My mother says magpies are thieves reborn.'

'I don't like it either,' whispered Orpheus. 'I tell you what, why not wring its neck while I'm gone?'

Oss's mouth twisted in an unpleasant smile. He liked such tasks. Perhaps he wasn't such a bad bodyguard after all. No, he wasn't.

Orpheus passed his hand once more over his hair (old man's hair, they called it here; no one else in Ombra was such a pale blond) and made for the Adderhead's tent. He wouldn't be able to read the Bluejay here for him, and whatever was hidden in Jacopo's book must wait until his audience with the Silver Prince was over, but thanks to Mortola he had something else to offer now.

The Adderhead's tent was as black beneath the trees as if night had left a piece of itself behind there. And suppose it had? Night was always kinder to you than day, Orpheus, he told himself as Thumbling pushed back the dark cloth of the tent flap, his face expressionless. Didn't darkness and silence make it so much easier to dream the world to your own taste? Yes, perhaps he ought to make it always night in this world, once he had *Inkheart* back again . . .

'Your Highness!' Orpheus bowed low as the Adderhead's face emerged from the darkness like a distorted moon. 'I bring news I've just learnt from listening to the wind. I think you'll like it . . .'

50

Lazy Old Man

One day God felt he ought to give his workshop a spring-clean . . . It was amazing what ragged bits and pieces came out from under his workbench, as he swept. Beginnings of creatures, bits that looked useful but had seemed wrong, ideas that he'd mislaid and forgotten . . . There was even a tiny lump of sun. He scratched his head. What could be done with all this rubbish?

Ted Hughes, *Leftovers*, from *The Dreamfighter*

Here she came again! Elinor Loredan! The name sounded almost as if he'd thought her up himself. Cursing, Fenoglio pulled the blanket over his face. Wasn't it bad enough that she was a know-all, a bluestocking, and stubborn as a mule? Did she have to be an early riser too? He supposed day was just beginning to dawn outside.

'Hm, that doesn't look particularly inspired!' Her eyes had gone straight to the blank sheet of paper lying beside him. How horribly bright and cheerful she sounded. 'Don't they say the Muses' kisses are sweetest early in the morning? I think I read that somewhere.'

Huh. As if she knew anything about kissing – and hadn't he earned his sleep, when there wasn't a decent drop of wine to be had in this wretched cave? Hadn't he just saved the Black Prince's life? Very well, the Prince's legs were still rather weak, and he wasn't eating much, as Minerva kept saying with concern. But then, all those children had to be fed, not an easy task at this time of year, and the little ones were hungry the whole time – when they weren't asking him or Darius for a story, Farid for some tricks with fire, or Meggie for a few songs about the Bluejay. She sang them better than Battista by now.

Perhaps that's something I ought to do, thought Fenoglio, ostentatiously turning his back on Signora Loredan. Write some more game here for us to hunt – something easily brought down, with plenty of meat on it and a good flavour.

'Fenoglio!' She'd actually pulled the blanket off him! This was incredible!

Rosenquartz put his head out of the pocket where he had taken to sleeping, and rubbed his eyes.

'Good morning, Rosenquartz. Get some paper out and sharpen the pens.'

That tone of voice! Just like a hospital nurse! Fenoglio sat up with a groan. He really was too old to be sleeping on the floor of a damp cave! 'That's *my* glass man, and he does what *I* tell him to do!' he grunted, but before he knew it Rosenquartz was scurrying past him with a syrupy-sweet smile on his pale pink lips.

What by all the ink-devils was he playing at? The glass-headed traitor! How eagerly he did as she told him, whereas if he, Fenoglio, asked Rosenquartz for something it didn't arrive half so quickly.

'Wonderful!' whispered Signora Loredan. 'Thank you, Rosenquartz.'

Elinor. It's not the name I'd have given her, thought Fenoglio as he forced his feet into his boots, shivering. Something more warlike would fit her much better . . . Penthesilea or Boadicea or some such Amazon . . . heavens, it was cold in this cave too! Can't you change the weather somehow, Fenoglio? Could he?

As he blew on his cold hands his uninvited visitor held out a steaming mug to him. 'Here you are. Doesn't taste particularly good, but it's hot. Coffee made from tree bark – you know, Rosenquartz really is a delightful glass man!' she whispered to him in a confidential tone. 'Jasper is very nice too, but so shy. And then there's that pink hair!'

Flattered, Rosenquartz ran his fingers over it. Glass men's ears were certainly as keen as any owl's, which was why – even with their fragile limbs – they made such good spies. Fenoglio could cheerfully have stuffed the vain little creature into his empty wineskin.

He took a sip of the hot brew – it really did taste nasty – got to his feet, and dipped his face in the basin of water that Minerva always left ready for him in the evening. Did he just imagine it, or was there a thin layer of ice on the surface?

'You really don't understand the first thing about writing, Loredan!' he growled. That was it, Loredan! That's what he'd call her in future. It suited her much better than the flowery 'Elinor'. 'For one thing, early in the morning is the worst possible time. The brain is like a wet sponge at that hour. And for another, real writing is a question of staring into space and waiting for the right ideas.'

'Well, you certainly are very good at staring into space!'

Oh, what a sharp tongue she had. 'Next you'll be telling me that tipping brandy and mead down your throat encourages the flow of ideas too.'

Had Rosenquartz just nodded in agreement? He'd chase him out into the forest, where his wild cousins would teach him to eat snails and beetles.

'Well then, Loredan, I'm sure you've known all along how this story ought to turn out! Let me guess: I suppose a frozen sparrow told you the ending yesterday when you were sitting outside the cave, gazing at my forest and my fairies, totally beguiled by them!' Damn it, another tear in his trousers. And Battista had hardly any thread left for mending clothes.

'Inkweaver?' Despina came round the wall that allowed him, for a few precious moments, to forget where he was. 'Do you want any breakfast?'

Dear, kind Minerva. She still looked after him as if they were back in her house in Ombra. Fenoglio sighed. The good old days . . .

'No thank you, Despina,' he replied, looking sideways at his other visitor. 'Tell your mother that unfortunately someone ruined my appetite first thing today.'

Despina and Elinor exchanged a glance that could only be called conspiratorial. Good heavens, were even Minerva's children on Loredan's side now?

'Resa has been gone for two days, not to mention Snapper, but what was the good of leaving you the book if you're just going to sleep the day away or drink bad wine with Battista?'

Dear God, how delightful this world had been when he hadn't had that voice ringing in his ears the whole time!

'You owe it to Mortimer to give him a few words to help him. Who else is going to do it? The Black Prince is too weak, and Mortimer's poor daughter is just waiting for you to give her something to read aloud at long last. But oh, no, no. *It's too cold, the wine is bad, the children make too much noise, how's anyone supposed to write?* You don't run out of words when it comes to complaining!'

There! Rosenquartz was nodding again! I'll mix soup in his sand, thought Fenoglio, so much soup that he writhes with stomach cramps like the Black Prince – and I won't write a single word to cure him!

'Fenoglio, are you listening to me?' She was looking at him as reproachfully as a teacher asking where his homework was!

The book, yes. Resa had left it here for him. So what use was that supposed to be? It just reminded him how easy he had once found storytelling, before he put every word down on paper knowing that it could become reality.

'It can't be all that difficult! Mortimer has done almost all the work for you in advance! He's going to pretend to the Adderhead that he can heal the Book, then Violante will distract her father's attention, and Mortimer will write the three words in it. Maybe afterwards there'll be a duel with the Piper – that kind of thing always reads well – I suppose the Fire-Dancer will put on a show too, although personally I still don't like him – and yes, you could have Resa playing a part as well. She could keep that horrible Snapper occupied, I don't know just how, but I'm sure you'll think of something . . .'

'Be quiet!' thundered Fenoglio in such a loud voice that Rosenquartz, terrified, took refuge behind the inkwell. 'What outrageous nonsense! That's just typical. Readers and their ideas! Yes, Mortimer's plan sounds really good. Plain and simple, but good. He overcomes the Adderhead with Violante's help, writes the three words, Adderhead dead, Bluejay saved,

Violante ruler of Ombra – oh yes, it *sounds wonderful*. I tried writing it like that last night. It doesn't work! Dead words! This story doesn't like taking an easy path. It has other ideas, I can smell that in the air. But what are they? I brought the Piper into it, I gave Dustfinger his fair share of the action, but then – something or other was missing. *Someone* or other was missing! Someone who's going to thwart Mortimer's fine plan with a vengeance. Snapper? No, he's too stupid. But who? Sootbird?'

She was looking at him so anxiously. Well, well. At last she understood. But the next moment she was as defiant as ever. It was a wonder she didn't stamp her foot like a child. She *was* a child, disguised as a rather stout middle-aged woman.

'But that's all nonsense! You're the author. You, and no one else.'

'Oh yes? So why is Cosimo dead, then? Did I write about Mortimer binding the book in a way that would leave the Adderhead rotting alive? No. Was it my idea to make Snapper jealous of him, and Her Ugliness suddenly want to kill her father? Definitely not. I just planted this story, but it's growing the way it wants to, and everyone expects me to know in advance what kind of flowers it will have!'

Good God, that incredulous look. As if he'd been talking about Santa Claus. But finally she thrust her chin out (it was quite an imposing chin), and that never boded well.

'Excuses! Nothing but excuses! You can't think of anything, and Resa's on the way to that castle. Suppose the Adderhead gets there long before she does? Suppose he doesn't trust his daughter, and Mortimer is dead before—'

'And suppose Mortola is back, as Resa says?' Fenoglio brusquely interrupted her. 'Suppose Snapper kills Mortimer because he's jealous of the Bluejay? Suppose Violante hands Mortimer over to her father after all, because she can't bear to be rejected by yet another man? What about the Piper, what about Violante's spoilt son, what about all that?' His voice grew so loud that Rosenquartz hid under his blanket.

'Stop shouting!' Suddenly Signora Loredan sounded unusually subdued. 'Poor Rosenquartz's head will be splitting.'

'No, it won't, because his head is as empty as a sucked-out snail's shell. Mine, on the other hand, has to think about difficult problems, matters of life and death – but it's my glass man that gets your sympathy, and you drag me out of bed after I've been lying awake half the night straining my ears trying to get this story to tell me where it wants to go!'

She fell silent. She actually fell silent. She bit her surprisingly feminine lower lip and plucked a few burrs off the dress that Minerva had given her, lost in thought. That dress was always picking up dead leaves, burrs and rabbit droppings – and no wonder, the way she kept wandering around the forest. Elinor Loredan certainly loved his world, though of course she would never admit it – and she understood it almost as well as he did.

'How . . . how would it be if you could at least gain us a little time?' She still sounded far less sure of herself than usual. 'Time to think, time to write! Time that might really give Resa a chance to warn Mortimer of Snapper and that magpie. Perhaps a wheel could come off the Adderhead's coach. He travels by coach, doesn't he?'

Well, yes. Not such a stupid idea. Why hadn't he thought of it himself?

'I can try,' he growled.

'Oh, wonderful.' She smiled with relief – and was

immediately more self-confident again. 'I'll ask Minerva to make you some nicer tea,' she added, looking back over her shoulder. 'Tea is better for thinking than wine, I'm sure. And don't be cross with Rosenquartz.'

The glass man smiled at her in a nauseating way, and Fenoglio gave him a slight nudge with his foot that sent him over on his back.

'Stir the ink, you slimy-tongued traitor!' he said, as Rosenquartz scrambled to his feet, looking offended.

Minerva really did bring him some tea. It even had a little lemon in it, and outside the cave the children were laughing as if everything in the world was all right. Well, *make* it all right, Fenoglio, he told himself. Loredan has a point. You're still the author of this story. The Adderhead is on his way to the Castle in the Lake, where Mortimer is waiting. The Bluejay is preparing for his finest song. Write it for him! Write Mortimer's part to its end. He's playing it with as much conviction as if he'd been born with the name you gave him. The words are obeying you again. You have the book. Orpheus is forgotten. This is still your story, so give it a good ending!

Yes. He'd do it. And Signora Loredan would finally be left speechless and show him the respect she owed him. But first he had to delay the Adderhead (and forget that had been Elinor's idea in the first place).

Outside the children were shouting noisily. Rosenquartz was whispering to Jasper, who was sitting among the freshly-sharpened pens and watching him, wide-eyed. Minerva brought some soup, and Elinor peeped over the wall as if he couldn't see her there. But soon Fenoglio was beyond noticing any of that. The words were carrying him away as they had in the past, letting him ride on their inky backs, leaving him blind and deaf to his surroundings, until he heard only the crunch of coach wheels on frozen ground and the sound of black-painted wood splitting. Soon both glass men were dipping pens in the ink for him, the words came so fast. Splendid words. Words worthy of Fenoglio. He'd quite forgotten how the letters on the page could intoxicate you. No wine could compete with them . . .

'Inkweaver!'

Fenoglio raised his head, irritated. He was already deep in the mountains, on his way to the Castle in the Lake, aware of the Adderhead's bloated flesh as if it were his own.

Battista stood there, concern in his face, and the mountains vanished. Fenoglio was back in the cave, surrounded by robbers and hungry children. What was the matter? The Black Prince hadn't taken a turn for the worse again, had he?

'Doria is back from one of his scouting expeditions. The boy's dead on his feet; he must have been running half the night. He says the Milksop is on his way here, and he knows about the cave. No one has any idea who told him.' Battista rubbed his pockmarked cheeks. 'They have hounds with them. Doria says they'll be here this evening. That means we must leave.'

'Leave? And go where?'

Where could they take all the children, many of them half crazed with homesickness by now? Fenoglio saw from Battista's face that the robber had no answer to that question either.

Well, so now what would clever Signora Loredan say? How was anyone supposed to write in these circumstances? 'Tell the Prince I'll be with him right away.'

Battista nodded. As he turned, Despina pushed past him. Her little face was anxious. Children know at once when something's wrong. They are used to having to guess what grown-ups don't tell them.

'Come here!' Fenoglio beckoned her over, while Rosenquartz fanned the words he had just written with a maple leaf. Fenoglio sat Despina on his lap and stroked her fair hair. Children . . . he forgave his villains so much, but since the Piper had started hunting children down, there was only one ending he wanted to write to the man's story, and it was a bloody one. If only he'd already written it! But it would have to wait now, like the song of the Bluejay. Where could they take the children? Think, Fenoglio, think!

He desperately rubbed his lined brow. Heavens, no wonder thinking dug such deep furrows in your face.

'Rosenquartz!' he told the glass man sharply. 'Find Meggie. Tell her she must read what I've written, even though it isn't quite finished. It'll have to do.'

The glass man scurried off so fast that he knocked over the wine Battista had brought, and the covers of Fenoglio's bed were stained as if soaked in blood. The book! He snatched it out from under the damp fabric in concern. *Inkheart*. He still liked that title. What would happen if *these* pages were moistened? Would his whole world begin to rot? But the paper was dry, only one corner of the binding was slightly damp. Fenoglio rubbed it with his sleeve.

'What's that?' Despina took the book from him. Of course – where would she ever have seen a book before? She hadn't grown up in a castle or a rich merchant's house.

'This is a thing that has stories in it,' said Fenoglio.

He heard Elfbane calling the children together, the alarmed

491

voices of the women, the first sounds of weeping. Despina listened anxiously too, but then she stared at the book again.

'Stories?' She leafed through the pages as if expecting the words to fall out. 'What stories? Have you told them to us already?'

'Not this one.' Fenoglio gently took the book from her hand and stared at the page where she had opened it. His own words looked back at him, written so long ago that they sounded like someone else's work . . .

'What kind of a story is it? Will you tell it to me?'

He stared at his old words, written by a different Fenoglio, a Fenoglio whose heart had been so much younger, so much lighter – and not so vain, no doubt Signora Loredan would add.

Great marvels lay north of Ombra. Hardly any of its inhabitants had ever set eyes on those wonders, but the songs of the strolling players told tales about them and when the peasants wanted to escape their toil in the fields for a few precious moments they would imagine themselves standing on the banks of the lake which, so it was said, the giants used as their mirror. They would picture the nymphs thought to live in it rising from the water and taking them away to castles made of pearls and mother-of-pearl. As the sweat ran down their faces they would sing softly, songs that told of snow-white mountains and of the nests human beings had built in a mighty tree when the giants had begun stealing their children.

Nests . . . a mighty tree . . . stealing their children. Good heavens, that was it!

Fenoglio picked Jasper up and put him on Despina's shoulder. 'Jasper will take you back to your mother,' he said, and strode away past her. 'I must go to the Prince.'

Signora Loredan is right, he thought as he made his way swiftly through the crowd of excited children, weeping mothers and robbers standing around helplessly. You're a foolish old man. Your befuddled brain doesn't even remember your own stories any more! Orpheus may well know more about your own world than you do by now.

But his vain self, lurking somewhere between his forehead and his breastbone, answered back at once. *How are you supposed to remember them all, Fenoglio? There are just too many of them. Your imagination is inexhaustible.*

Yes. Yes, he was indeed a vain old man. He admitted it. But he had very good reasons for his vanity.

51

The Wrong Helpers

We never know we go – when we are going
We jest and shut the door;
Fate following behind us blots it,
And we accost no more.

Emily Dickinson, Collected Poems

Mortola was perching in a poison yew, surrounded by needles nearly as black as her plumage. Her left wing hurt. Orpheus's servant had almost broken it with his meaty fingers, and only her beak had saved her. She'd pecked his ugly nose until it bled, but she hardly knew how she had managed to flutter out of the tent. She had been able to fly only short distances since then, but even worse, she couldn't change back from her bird shape, although it was a long time since she had swallowed any of the seeds. How long since she had taken human form? Two days, three days? The magpie didn't count days, the magpie thought of nothing but beetles and worms (ah, plump, pale worms!), winter and wind and the fleas in her feathers.

The last person she had seen when she was in human shape was Snapper. And yes, he would follow the good advice she had given him in a whisper, and attack the Adderhead in the forest, but all the thanks he'd given her was to call her a damn witch, and try to seize her so that his men could kill her. She had bitten his hand, hissed at the others until they retreated, and there in the bushes she had swallowed the seeds again so that she could fly to Orpheus – only to have his servant almost break her wings! *Peck his eyes out! Peck all their eyes out! Dig your claws into their stupid faces!*

Mortola uttered a pitiful cry, and the robbers looked up at her as if she were announcing their death. They didn't realize that the magpie was the old woman they'd wanted to kill. They didn't realize anything. What were they going to do with the Book without her help, if they ever really did get their grubby hands on it? They were as stupid as the pale worms she pecked out of the earth. Did they think they just had to shake the Book, or tap its rotting pages, for the gold she'd promised them to come raining down? No, most likely they thought nothing at all as they sat down there among the trees, waiting for darkness to fall. Only a few hours before they planned to ambush the Adderhead's black coach, what were they doing? Drinking home-distilled spirits stolen from some charcoal-burner, dreaming of the wealth to come, bragging that they'd kill first the Adder and then the Bluejay. What about the three words? That's what the magpie wanted to call down to them. Which of you fools can write them in the White Book? However, Snapper at least had obviously thought of that point.

'And once we have the Book,' he was babbling, 'we'll catch the Bluejay and force him to write the three words in it, and then as soon as the Adder is dead and we're wallowing in gold we'll kill him too, because I'm sick and tired of hearing all those stupid songs about him.'

'Yes, let folk sing about us in future!' mumbled Gecko, putting a piece of bread soaked in brandy into the beak of the crow on his shoulder. The crow, alone among them, kept staring up at Mortola. 'We'll be more famous than anyone! More famous than the Bluejay, more famous than the Black Prince, more famous than Firefox and his fire-raisers. More famous than . . . what was his old master's name?'

'Capricorn.'

The name pierced Mortola's heart like a red-hot needle, and she cowered on the branch where she was perching, shaken by yearning for her son. Ah, to see his face once more, bring him food once more, cut his pale hair . . .

She uttered another shrill cry, and her pain and hatred echoed through the dark valley where the robbers were planning to attack the lord of the Castle of Night.

Her son. Her son. Her wonderful, cruel son. Mortola plucked feathers from her own breast as if that could drive the pain out of her heart.

Dead. Lost. And his murderer was playing the noble robber, his praises sung by the stupid rabble who used to tremble before her son! The murderer's shirt had been dyed red, the life had almost flowed out of him, but that little witch of a daughter had saved him. Was she whispering somewhere even now? I'll peck both their faces to pieces, I'll do such a good job of it that the treacherous maid won't recognize them . . . Resa . . . she saw you back at the cave, Mortola, she saw you, but what's she going to do about it? The bookbinder went alone, and she's playing the game that all women play in this world, the waiting game . . . *ah, caterpillar!*

She pecked furiously at the hairy body. *Caterpillar, caterpillar*, cried the voice inside her. Damn this bird-brain. What had she been thinking of just now? Killing. Yes. Revenge. The bird knew that feeling too. She felt her feathers ruffling up, her beak striking at the wood of the branch where she sat, as if it were the Bluejay's body.

A cold wind blew through the tree, shaking its evergreen branches. Rain fell on Mortola's plumage. Time to fly down under the dark yews that would hide her from the robbers, and try, yet again, to shake off the bird-shape, be human flesh once more.

But the bird thought: no! Time to tuck her beak into her feathers, time to let the rustling branches sing her to sleep. Nonsense! She ruffled herself up, shook her silly little head, called her own name back to mind. Mortola. Mortola. Capricorn's mother . . .

What was that? The crow on Gecko's shoulder jerked its head and spread its wings. Snapper unsteadily got to his feet, drew his sword, and shouted to the others to do the same. But there stood the Adder's men already, among the trees. Their leader was a lean, hawk-faced man, his eyes as expressionless as the eyes of a corpse. Almost casually, he thrust his sword into the first robber's chest. Three soldiers attacked Snapper. He slit them open, although his hand must still be hurting from Mortola's teeth, but his men were dying like flies around him. Folk would sing songs about them, yes, but they'd be songs mocking the fools who had thought they could ambush the Adderhead as easily as any rich merchant.

Mortola gave another pitiful cry, while swords were plunged into the bodies below her. These helpers had been no use at all. Now she had no one left but Orpheus, with his ink-magic and his velvety voice.

The hawk-faced man wiped his sword on a dead robber's cloak and looked around. Mortola instinctively ducked, but her magpie form stared greedily down at the glittering weapons, at the rings and belt buckles. How pretty they'd look in her nest, shining bright enough to bring down the stars from the sky by night!

None of the robbers was left standing. Even Snapper was on his knees by now. The hawk-faced man made a sign to his soldiers, and they dragged Snapper over to him. Die now, fool, thought Mortola bitterly. And the old woman you planned to strike down will watch you die!

The hawk-faced man asked Snapper something, hit him in the face, asked again. Mortola put her head on one side so as to hear them better and fluttered a few branches farther down, staying under cover of the needles.

'He was dying when we set out.' Snapper's voice still sounded defiant, but it was also hoarse with fear. The Black Prince. They were talking about him. I did it, Mortola wanted to cackle. I, Mortola, poisoned him! Ask the Adderhead if he remembers me!

She flew lower still. Was the lean killer talking about children? He knew about the cave, did he? How? If only her stupid head could think straight!

One of the soldiers drew his sword, but the hawk-faced leader told him brusquely to sheathe it again. He stepped back, signalling to his men to do so too. Snapper, still on his knees among his dead companions, raised his head in surprise. But the magpie, who had been about to fly down to pull rings off dead fingers and peck at silver buttons, froze on her branch and shook with fear, because something in her stupid bird-brain was crying out: *death, death, death!* And there it came, mildewed black among the trees, panting like a huge dog, shapeless yet somehow human – a Night-Mare. Snapper fell to pleading instead of cursing, and the hawk-faced man watched him with his dead eyes as his followers retreated far into the trees. But the Night-Mare made for Snapper as if night itself were opening a mouth full of a thousand teeth, bringing him the worst of all deaths.

Well, so what? Away with him, thought Mortola as her feathered body shook like an aspen tree. Away with the fool! He was no use to me. Orpheus must help me now. Orpheus . . .

Orpheus. It was as if the name took shape the moment it came into her mind.

No, it couldn't be so. It couldn't be Orpheus suddenly standing there under the trees, with the Night-Mare cowering like a dog at his foolish smile.

Who told the Adderhead about the robbers, Mortola? Who told him?

Orpheus examined the trees with his glassy eyes. Then he raised his pale, plump hand and pointed to the magpie, who ducked when his finger swung her way.

Fly, Mortola, she thought. *Fly!*

The arrow hit her in mid-air, and pain drove the bird away. She no longer had wings as she fell, falling and falling through the cold air. Human bones broke when she hit the ground. And the last thing she saw was Orpheus's smile.

52

The Dead Men in the Forest

It was evening all afternoon.
It was snowing
And it was going to snow.
The blackbird sat
In the cedar-limbs.
   Wallace Stevens, *Thirteen Ways of Looking at a Blackbird*

On, further and further on. Resa was feeling sick again, but she didn't say so. Whenever the Strong Man turned to look anxiously at her she smiled, so that he wouldn't slow down because of her. Snapper had more than half a day's start on them, and she was trying not to think about the magpie at all.

Go on, she told herself, go on. It's only a little sickness. Chew the leaves Roxane gave you and keep going. The forest through which they had been walking for days was darker than the Wayless Wood. She had never been in this part of the Inkworld before. It was like opening a new chapter, one she'd never yet read. 'The strolling players call it the forest where night sleeps,' the Strong Man had told her as they were passing through a ravine so dark, even by day, that she could hardly see her hand before her eyes. 'But the moss-women have given it the name of the Bearded Forest, because of all the healing lichens growing on the trees.' Resa liked that name better. With the frost lying on them, many trees did indeed look like ancient, bearded giants.

The Strong Man was good at reading tracks, but even Resa could have followed the trail left by Snapper and his men. Their footprints had frozen in many places, as if time had stopped. In other places they were obliterated by the rain, as if it had washed away the men themselves at the same time. The robbers hadn't taken any trouble to conceal their tracks. Why should they? They were the pursuers.

It rained a lot. At night the rain often turned to hail, but luckily there were enough evergreen trees under whose branches they could keep reasonably dry. At sunset it turned bitterly cold, and Resa was very glad of the fur-lined coat that the Strong Man had given her. Thanks to that coat and the coverings of moss that he cut from the trees for them both, she could sleep at night in spite of the cold.

Go on, Resa, she thought, keep going. The magpie flies fast, and Snapper is quick with his knife. A bird uttered a hoarse cry in the trees above her, and she looked up in alarm, but it was only a crow and not a magpie gazing down at her.

'Caw!' The Strong Man replied to the black bird with a croak of his own (even the owls talked to him), and then suddenly stopped. 'What the devil's that?' he murmured, scratching his shorn head.

Resa too stopped, alarmed. 'What's the matter? Have you lost the way?'

'Me? Not in a thousand years, not in any forest in the world! Certainly not this one.' The Strong Man bent down and investigated the tracks on the fallen leaves, now frozen stiff. 'My cousin taught me to poach here. He showed me how to talk to the birds and make blankets from the bearded lichen on the trees. And he showed me the Castle in the Lake. No, Snapper's lost his way, not me. He's bearing much too far west!'

'Your cousin?' Resa looked at him curiously. 'Is he among the robbers too?'

The Strong Man shook his head. 'He joined the fire-raisers,' he said, without looking at Resa. 'Disappeared when Capricorn did and never came back. He was a tall, ugly fellow, but I was always stronger, even when we were both little boys. I often wonder what's become of him. He may have been one of those damn fire-raisers, but he was still my cousin, see what I mean?'

Tall and ugly . . . Resa thought back to Capricorn's men. Flatnose? Oh, Strong Man, Mo's voice brought him to his death, she thought. Would you still go on protecting Mo if you knew? Yes, he probably would.

'Let's follow Snapper's tracks,' she said. 'I want to know why he strayed from his path!'

They found him and his men very soon, in a clearing brown with withered leaves. The dead men lay there as if the trees had shed them along with their foliage. Ravens were already pecking at their flesh. Resa shooed the birds away – and stepped back in horror when she saw Snapper's body.

'What did that?'

'A Night-Mare!' The Strong Man's reply was barely audible.

'A Night-Mare? But they kill through fear, nothing else. I've seen it!'

'Yes, but only if they're prevented from eating their victims. They eat them too if they're allowed.'

Mo had once given her a dragonfly's cast-off case. Every limb could still be traced under the empty skin it had shed. There wasn't much more than that left of Snapper. Resa threw up there and then beside the dead men.

'I don't like this.' The Strong Man examined the blood-soaked leaves. 'Looks almost as if the men who killed them watched the Night-Mare eat him . . . as if they'd brought it with them, like the Prince brings his bear!' He looked around, but nothing stirred. Only the ravens perched in the trees, waiting.

The Strong Man drew Gecko's cloak over his dead face. 'I'm going to follow the trails and find out where the killers came from.'

'You don't need to.' Resa bent over one of the dead robbers and raised his left hand. The thumb was missing. 'Your little brother told me the Adderhead has a new bodyguard, a man known as Thumbling. They say he used to be one of the torturers in the Castle of Night until his master promoted him. Doria says he's notorious for cutting a thumb off every man he kills. He makes little pipes out of the thumb-bones to mock the Piper with them . . . and it seems he has a very large collection.' Resa began trembling, even though she no longer had to fear Snapper. 'She'll never be able to protect him,' she whispered. 'Violante can't protect Mo. They'll kill him!'

The Strong Man helped her to her feet and awkwardly put his arms around her.

'What do we do now?' he asked. 'Go back?'

But Resa shook her head. The killers had a Night-Mare with them. A Night-Mare. She looked round.

'The magpie,' she said. 'Where's the magpie? Call her!'

'I told you, she doesn't sound like a real bird,' said the Strong Man, but all the same he imitated a magpie's cry. There was no reply, but just as the Strong Man was about to try again Resa saw the dead woman.

Mortola was lying a little way from the others, with an arrow in her breast. Resa had often imagined what it would feel like to see the woman she had served for so long lying dead at last. She had so often wanted to kill Mortola herself, but now she felt nothing at all. A few black feathers lay beside the corpse in the snow, and the fingernails of Mortola's left hand were still like a bird's claws. Resa bent down and took the bag from Mortola's belt. There were some tiny black seeds in it, the same as the seeds still sticking to Mortola's pale lips.

'Who's that?' The Strong Man stared at the old woman in disbelief.

'The woman who used to mix poisons for Capricorn. You must have heard of her. She was his mother.'

The Strong Man nodded, and involuntarily took a step back.

Resa tied Mortola's bag to her own belt. 'When I was one of her maids . . .' (she couldn't help smiling at the surprise in the Strong Man's eyes) '. . . when I was still one of her maids, it was said that Mortola had discovered a plant with seeds that could change your shape. *Little Death*, the other maids called it, and they whispered that it sent you crazy if you used it too often. They showed me the plant – it can be used as a deadly poison too, but I always thought its other quality was just a fairy tale. Obviously I was wrong.' Resa picked up one of the magpie feathers and laid it on Mortola's pierced breast. 'And they also said that Mortola had given up using Little Death after a fox nearly killed her in her bird-shape. But as soon as I saw the magpie in the cave I felt sure it was her.'

She rose to her feet.

The Strong Man pointed to the bag at her belt. 'Sounds to me like you'd better leave those seeds here.'

'Should I?' replied Resa. 'Yes, maybe you're right. Come on, let's go. It will soon be dark.'

53

Human Nests

Take note:
words hide in the night
in caves of music and image.
Still humid and pregnant with sleep
they turn in a winding river and by neglect are transformed.
Carlos Drummond de Andrade, *Looking for Poetry*

Meggie's feet were so cold that she could hardly feel her toes, in spite of her boots. They were still the pair she had brought from the other world. Only on their endless march over the last few days had they all realized what good shelter the cave had offered from the coming winter – and how flimsy their clothes were. The rain was even worse than the cold. It dripped off the trees and turned the ground to mud that froze when evening came. One little girl had already sprained her ankle, and Elinor was carrying her. Everyone who could was carrying one of the smaller children, though there weren't enough of them to go round. Snapper had taken his men with him, and Resa and the Strong Man had gone too.

The Black Prince carried three children at once, two in his arms and one on his back, although he was still hardly eating anything, and Roxane kept making him stop to rest. Meggie pressed her face into the hair of the little boy who was clinging round her neck. Beppe. He reminded her of Fenoglio's grandson. Beppe didn't weigh much – the children hadn't had enough to eat for days – but after all the hours that Meggie had spent trudging through the mud with the little boy in her arms he seemed as heavy as an adult. 'Meggie, sing me one of those songs!' he kept saying, and she sang in a soft voice that was reedy with weariness. Songs about the Bluejay, of course. By now she sometimes forgot that she was also singing about her father. When she closed her eyes now and then in sheer exhaustion she saw the castle Farid had shown her in the fire, a growth of dark stone reflected on a misty lake. She'd tried desperately to catch a sight of Mo somewhere among the walls, but she couldn't see him.

She was alone. She was even more alone now that Resa had gone. In spite of Elinor, in spite of Fenoglio, in spite of all the children, and definitely in spite of Farid. But out of this feeling of being abandoned, which only Doria could sometimes dispel, something else had grown: a sense that she must protect those who, like herself, were on their own, without father or mother, seeking shelter in a world that was as strange to them as to Meggie, although these children had never known any other.

Fenoglio himself, who was leading them, had only written about this world without knowing it, yet now they had nothing but his words to guide them.

He was walking at the front with the Black Prince. Despina clung to his back, though she was older than some of the children who had to walk. Her brother was up ahead with the older boys. They were running about among the trees as though they didn't feel tired at all. The Black Prince kept calling them back, telling them to do as the older girls did and carry the little ones. Farid and Doria were so far in advance of the rest of the party that Meggie hadn't seen them for nearly an hour. They were looking for the tree that Fenoglio had described to the Black Prince, so persuasively that the Prince had decided they should set off at once. And indeed, what other hope did they have?

'How much further?' Meggie heard Despina ask, not for the first time.

'Not very far now, not very far,' replied Fenoglio, but did he really know?

Meggie had heard him telling the Black Prince about the human nests. *They look like huge fairies' nests, but people lived in them, Prince! Many people. They built the nests when giants started coming for their children, and they chose such a tall tree that even the largest giants couldn't reach up to it.*

'Which goes to show,' he had whispered to Meggie, 'that it's sensible not to make your giants too big when you're writing a story about them!'

'Human nests?' she had whispered back. 'Have you only just thought that up?'

'Don't be ridiculous! What makes you think that?' Fenoglio sounded offended. 'Have I asked you to read them into existence? No. This world is so well equipped that you can manage very well without stopping to make up something new every five minutes – although that fool Orpheus thinks otherwise. I hope by now he's begging in the streets of Ombra – that'd serve him right for making my fairies rainbow-coloured!'

'Beppe, walk for a little, will you?' Meggie put the boy down, although he resisted, and instead picked up a little girl who was so tired that she could hardly keep on her feet.

'How much further?' A question that she had asked Mo so often herself, on those endless drives when they were going to cure another few sick books. 'Not far now, Meggie!' She could almost hear her father's voice, and for a moment her weariness made her imagine he was putting his jacket around her cold shoulders, but it was only a branch brushing against her back, and when she slipped on the wet leaves that covered the ground like a carpet, only Roxane's hand kept her from falling.

'Careful, Meggie,' she said, and for a moment her face seemed as familiar as Resa's.

'We've found the tree!' Doria appeared in front of them so suddenly that some of the smaller children hid, alarmed, behind the grown-ups. He was drenched with rain and trembling with cold, but he looked happy – happier than he had been for many days.

'Farid stayed there. He's going to climb the tree and see if the nests are still fit to live in!' Doria spread his arms wide. 'They're huge! We'll have to construct something to help us haul the little ones up, but I have an idea.'

Meggie had never heard him talk so fast or so much before. One of the little girls ran towards him, and Doria picked her up and whirled her round in a circle with him, laughing. 'The Milksop will never find us up there!' he cried. 'Now we only have to learn to fly and we can live as free as the birds!'

The children all began talking excitedly, until the Black Prince raised his hand. 'Where is the tree?' he asked Doria. His voice was heavy with fatigue. Sometimes Meggie feared that the poison had broken something in him, casting a shadow over the light that had always been a part of him before.

'Right ahead, there!' Doria pointed through the trees that dripped with rain.

Suddenly even the weariest feet could walk again. 'Quiet!' the Prince warned the children as they shouted louder and louder, but they were too excited to obey, and the forest echoed to the sound of their clear voices.

'There, told you so, didn't I?' Suddenly Fenoglio was walking beside Meggie, his eyes full of his old pride in the world he had written. It was easily aroused.

'Yes, you did.' Elinor got in before Meggie with the answer. She was obviously feeling cross in her damp clothes. 'But I haven't seen these fabulous nests of yours yet, and I must say the prospect of perching up at the top of a tree in this weather doesn't exactly sound enticing.'

Fenoglio glared at Elinor with contempt. 'Meggie,' he asked in a low voice, 'what's that lad there called? You know, the Strong Man's brother.'

'You mean Doria?'

Doria glanced around as she spoke his name, and Meggie smiled at him. She liked the way he looked at her. His glance warmed her heart in a way quite unlike Farid's. In a very different way.

'Doria,' murmured Fenoglio. 'Doria. Sounds somehow familiar to me.'

'Hardly surprising,' said Elinor sarcastically. 'The Dorias were a very famous aristocratic Italian family.'

Fenoglio gave her a look that was far from friendly, but he never got a chance to reply.

'There they are!'

Ivo's voice was so loud in the gathering dusk that Minerva

instinctively put her hand over his mouth.

And there they really were.

Human nests.

They looked just as Fenoglio had described them in his book. He had read the passage aloud to Meggie. *Gigantic nests in the crown of a mighty tree, with evergreen branches reaching so high into the sky that its top seemed lost in the clouds.* The nests were round, like fairies' nests, but Meggie thought she saw bridges between them, ladders and nets made of twining tendrils. The children gathered around the Black Prince and stared up, enchanted, as if he had led them to a castle in the clouds. But Fenoglio looked happiest of all.

'Aren't they fabulous?' he cried.

'They're a very long way up, that's for sure!' Elinor sounded far from enthusiastic.

'Well, that's the whole point!' replied Fenoglio brusquely, but Minerva and the other women were also looking at the nests in dismay.

'What happened to the people who used to live up there?' asked Despina. 'Did they fall out of the nests?'

'Of course not!' said Fenoglio impatiently, but Meggie could see he hadn't the faintest idea what had happened to the original nest-dwellers.

'Oh no, I suppose they just wanted to get back to the ground!' said Jasper in his clear little voice.

The two glass men were sitting in the deep pockets of Darius's coat. He was the only one who had anything like proper winter clothing, but he was always ready to share his coat generously with a few of the children. He let them slip in under the warm fabric like chicks under a mother hen's wings.

The Black Prince looked up at the strange dwellings, scrutinized the tree that they would have to climb – and said nothing.

'We can pull the children up in nets,' said Doria. 'The creepers will make ropes. Farid and I have tried them. They'll hold.'

'This is the best possible hiding place!'

It was Farid's voice calling to them. Nimble as a squirrel, he came climbing down the trunk as if he had lived in trees in his old life, not the desert. 'Even if the Milksop's hounds find us we can defend ourselves from up here!'

'With luck they won't find us at all,' said the Black Prince. 'I hope we'll be able to hold out up there until . . .'

They all looked at him expectantly. Until – yes, until when?

'Until the Bluejay's killed the Adderhead!' said one of the children so confidently that the Prince had to smile.

'Yes, exactly. Until the Bluejay's killed the Adderhead.'

'And the Piper!' added one of the boys.

'Of course, the Piper too.' Hope and anxiety were equally balanced in the glance that Battista exchanged with the Black Prince.

'That's right, he'll kill them both, and then he'll marry Her Ugliness and they'll reign over Ombra and live happily ever after!' Despina's smile was as delighted as if she could already see the wedding before her eyes.

'No, no!' Fenoglio looked at her, as horrified as if her words might come true the next moment. 'The Bluejay already has a wife, Despina, doesn't he? Have you forgotten Meggie's mother?'

Despina glanced at Meggie in alarm and put her hand over her mouth, but Meggie just stroked her smooth hair. 'Sounds like a good story all the same,' she whispered to the child.

'Start getting ropes up into the tree,' the Black Prince told Battista, 'and ask Doria just how he plans to haul the nets up. The rest of you, climb to the top of the tree and see which nests are still sound.'

Meggie looked up at the dense thicket of branches. She had never set eyes on a tree like it before. The bark was reddish brown, but as rough as the bark of an oak, and the trunk did not branch until high up in the tree, although it had so many bulges that you could find footholds and handholds everywhere. In some places huge tree fungi formed platforms. Hollows gaped in the towering trunk, and crevices full of feathers showed that human beings were not the only creatures to have nested in this tree. Perhaps I should ask Doria if he can really build me wings, Meggie said to herself, and suddenly she thought of the magpie that had frightened her mother so much.

Why hadn't Resa taken her along? Because she thinks I'm still a small child, she told herself.

'Meggie?' One of the children slipped her cold fingers into Meggie's hand. Elinor had nicknamed the little girl Fire-Elf because of her hair, which was as red as if Dustfinger had sprinkled it with sparks. How old was she? Four? Five? Many of the children didn't know their own ages.

'Beppe says there are birds that eat children up there.'

'Nonsense. Anyway, how would he know? You think Beppe's been up there already?'

Fire-Elf smiled in relief and looked sternly at Beppe. But her face grew grave again as, her fingers still clutching Meggie's hand firmly, she listened with the others to Farid reporting to the Black Prince.

'The nests are so large that I should think five or even six of us can sleep in each of them!' He sounded so excited. 'Many of the bridges are crumbling, but there are enough creepers and timber up there to repair them.'

'We have hardly any tools,' Doria pointed out. 'We must make do with our knives and swords.'

The robbers looked in some alarm at their swordbelts.

'The crown of the tree is dense enough to give us good shelter from the wind, but there are gaps in it in some places,' Farid went on. 'I guess they were lookout points for the guards. We'll have to pad and line the nests, as the fairies do.'

'Maybe some of us had better stay down here,' Elfbane put in. 'We have to go hunting and—'

'Oh, you can hunt up there!' Farid interrupted. 'There are flocks of birds, and I've seen large squirrels, and creatures like rabbits with fingers that cling to the branches. Though there are wild cats up there as well . . .'

The women looked at each other, frightened.

'. . . and bats, and long-tailed brownies,' Farid went on. 'There's a whole world up there! It has caves in it, and a lot of the branches are so wide you can easily walk along them. Flowers and mushrooms grow there! It's fabulous. Wonderful!'

Fenoglio was smiling all over his wrinkled face, like a king hearing praise of his domain, and even Elinor looked wistfully up the rough trunk for the first time. Some of the children wanted to climb the tree at once, but the women stopped them. 'Go and collect leaves,' they told them, 'and moss and birds' feathers – anything you can find to make soft linings.'

The sun was already low as the robbers began stretching ropes, weaving nets, and building wooden platforms to be hauled up the tall trunk. Battista went back with some of the men to wipe out their tracks, and Meggie saw the Black Prince looking at his bear, at a loss. How was he going to get the bear up the tree? What would happen to the packhorses? So many questions, and he still wasn't at all sure that they had outrun the Milksop.

Meggie was just helping Minerva to tie creepers together to make a net for provisions when Fenoglio drew her aside, a conspiratorial expression on his face.

'You won't believe this!' he murmured to her when they were standing among the mighty roots of the tree. 'And don't you dare tell Loredan about it. She'd only accuse me of having delusions of grandeur again!'

'What don't you want me to tell her?' Meggie looked at him blankly.

'Well, that boy, you know who I mean – the one who keeps looking at you and brings you flowers and turns Farid green with jealousy. Doria . . .'

Above them the crown of the tree was bathed with red in the light of the setting sun, and the nests hung among its branches like black fruits.

Feeling embarrassed, Meggie turned her face away. 'What about him?'

Fenoglio looked round as if afraid that Elinor might appear behind him next moment. 'Meggie,' he said, lowering his voice, 'I think I made him up too, just like Dustfinger and the Black Prince!'

'Oh, nonsense, what are you talking about?' Meggie whispered back. 'Doria probably wasn't even born when you were writing your book!'

'Yes, yes, I know! That's the confusing part of it! All these children,' said Fenoglio, with a sweeping gesture towards the children searching busily for moss and feathers under the trees, 'my story lays them like eggs, entirely without my aid. It's a very fertile story! But that boy . . .' Fenoglio lowered his voice as if Doria could hear him, although he was far away with Battista, kneeling on the forest floor and turning knives into machetes and saws. 'Meggie, this is where it gets so crazy: I wrote a story about him, but the character with his name was grown-up! And even stranger – the story was never published! Presumably it's still lying in a drawer in my old desk, or my grandchildren have made it into balls of paper to throw for the cats!'

'But that's impossible. He can't be the same person.' Meggie unobtrusively glanced at Doria. She liked the sight of him; she liked it very much. 'What's this story about?' she asked. 'What does this grown-up Doria do?'

'He builds castles and city walls. He even invents a flying machine, a clock to measure time, and – ' here Fenoglio looked at Meggie – 'and a printing machine for a famous bookbinder.'

'Really?' Meggie suddenly felt warm, the way she used to when Mo had told her a particularly good story. For a famous bookbinder. Just for a moment she forgot all about Doria and thought only of her father. Perhaps Fenoglio had already written the words that would keep Mo alive, perhaps he'd written them long ago. Oh, please, she begged Fenoglio's story, let the bookbinder be Mo!

'Doria the Enchanter, I called him,' Fenoglio whispered. 'But it's with his hands that he works enchantment, like your father. And now, listen to this: it gets even better! This Doria has a wife who is said to come from a distant land, and she often gives him his ideas in the first place. Isn't that strange?'

'What's so strange about it?' Meggie felt herself blushing, and just at that moment Farid looked at her. 'Did you give her a name?' she asked Fenoglio.

Awkwardly, the old man cleared his throat. 'Well, you know I sometimes neglect my women characters a bit, and I couldn't find the right name, so I just called her his wife.'

Meggie had to smile. Yes, that was very like Fenoglio. 'Doria has two stiff fingers on his left hand,' she pointed out. 'So how could he do all the things you say?'

'But I wrote him those stiff fingers!' cried Fenoglio out loud, forgetting to be quiet. Doria raised his head and glanced at them, but luckily the Black Prince went up to him just at that moment.

'His father broke them,' Fenoglio went on more quietly. 'When he was drunk. He was going to hit Doria's sister, and Doria tried to protect her.'

Meggie leant back again the tree trunk. She felt as if she could hear its heart beating behind her, a gigantic heart in the wood. It was all a dream, just a dream. 'What was this sister's name?' she asked. 'Susa?'

'How should I know?' retorted Fenoglio. 'I can't remember everything. Maybe she didn't have a name any more than his wife did. Anyway, it will just make him all the more famous later when people find out he can build such marvels in spite of his stiff fingers!'

'I see,' murmured Meggie – and caught herself wondering what Doria would look like when he grew up. 'That's a love-ly story,' she said.

'I know,' agreed Fenoglio, leaning back with a self-satisfied sigh against the tree he had described in his book so many years ago. 'But not a word to the boy about all this, of course.'

'Of course not. Did you leave any more stories like that in your desk drawers? Do you know what will happen to Minerva's children, and to Beppe and Fire-Elf?'

Fenoglio never got around to answering that question.

'Well, isn't that wonderful!' Elinor was standing in front of them with her arms full of moss. 'Tell me, Meggie, isn't the fellow beside you the laziest man in this world – and any other? Everyone else is working while he stands here staring into space!'

'Oh yes, and what about Meggie?' Fenoglio retorted indignantly. 'Anyway, you'd none of you have *anything* to do if the laziest man in all the worlds hadn't thought up this tree, and the nests in its branches!'

Elinor was not in the least impressed. 'We're probably all going to break our necks in those wretched nests,' was all she said. 'And I'm not sure if this is any better than the mines.'

'Calm down, Loredan. In any case, the Piper wouldn't want *you* for the mines,' replied Fenoglio. 'You'd get stuck in the first tunnel.'

Meggie left them to their quarrel. Lights were beginning to dance among the trees. At first Meggie thought they were glow-worms, but when some of them settled on her arms she saw that they were tiny moths, shining as if moonlight clung to them.

A new chapter, she thought, looking up at the nests. A new place. And Fenoglio can tell me about Doria's future, but he doesn't know what his story is going to say about my father. Why didn't Resa take me with her?

Because your mother is a clever woman, Fenoglio would have told her. Who but you is going to read my words if I find the right ones? Darius? No, Meggie, you're the best teller of this tale. If you really want to help your father, your place is here beside me. And Mortimer would certainly see it just the same way!

Yes, she supposed he would.

One of the moths settled on her hand, shining on her finger like a ring. *This Doria has a wife who is said to come from a distant land, and she often gives him his ideas in the first place.* Yes. That really was strange.

54

The White Whispering

Had I the heavens' embroidered cloths,
Enwrought with golden and silver light,
The blue and the dim and the dark cloths
Of night and light and the half light,
I would spread the cloths under your feet:
But I, being poor, have only my dreams;
I have spread my dreams under your feet;
Tread softly because you tread on my dreams.

William Butler Yeats,
Aedh Wishes for the Cloths of Heaven

From the tower battlements, Dustfinger looked down on a lake as black as night, where the reflection of the castle swam in a sea of stars. The wind passing over his unscarred face was cold from the snow of the surrounding mountains, and Dustfinger relished life as if he were tasting it for the first time. The longing it brought, and the desire. All the bitterness, all the sweetness, even if it was only for a while, never for more than a while, everything gained and lost, lost and found again.

Even the blackness of the trees intoxicated him with joy. The night blackened them as if to prove once and for all that this world was nothing but ink. And didn't the snow on the mountain peaks look like paper?

Even so . . .

Above his head the moon burnt a silver hole in the night, and the stars surrounded it like fire-elves. Dustfinger tried to remember whether he had seen the moon in the realm of the dead too. Perhaps. Why did death make life taste so much sweeter? Why could the heart love only what it could also lose? Why? Why . . .

The White Women knew some of the answers, but they hadn't told him all of them. Later, they had whispered when they let him go. Another time. You will often come to us. And often go again.

Gwin sat on the battlements with him, listening uneasily to the lapping of the water. The marten didn't like the castle. Behind him, Silvertongue stirred in his sleep. Without a word, the two of them had decided to sleep up here on the tower behind the battlements, even though it was cold. Dustfinger didn't like sleeping in closed rooms, and Silvertongue seemed to feel the same. Although perhaps he slept up here only because Violante roamed the painted rooms even at night – as restlessly as if she were looking for her dead mother, or as if her sleeplessness would hasten the Adder's arrival. Did any daughter ever wait so impatiently to kill her father?

Violante was not the only one who couldn't sleep. Her illuminator was sitting in the room full of dead books, trying to teach his left hand the art that his right had once mastered so superbly. He sat there hour after hour, at a desk that Brianna had dusted for him, forcing his unpractised fingers to trace leaves and tendrils, birds and tiny faces, while the useless stump of his right wrist held down the parchment he had, with forethought, brought with him.

'Shall I find you a glass man in the forest?' Dustfinger had asked him, but Balbulus had only shaken his head.

'I don't work with glass men,' he replied morosely. 'They're too liable to leave their footprints all over my pictures!'

Silvertongue slept uneasily. Sleep brought him no peace, and it seemed worse tonight than the nights before. Presumably they were with him again. When the White Women slipped into your dreams you didn't see them. They came to Silvertongue more often than to Dustfinger himself, as if to make sure that the Bluejay didn't forget the bargain he had struck with their mistress, the Great Shape-Changer who made all things wither and blossom, grow and decay.

They were with him now, their cool fingers stroking his heart. Dustfinger could feel it as if it were his own. Let him sleep, he thought. Let him rest from the fear that day brings him: fear for himself, fear for his daughter, fear that he's done the wrong thing. Leave him alone.

He went over to him and placed his hand on his breast. Silvertongue woke with a start, pale-faced. Yes, they had been with him, and Dustfinger made fire dance on his fingers. He knew the chill that those visitors left behind. It was fresh and clear, pure as snow, but it both froze and burnt the heart.

'What were they whispering this time? *Bluejay, immortality is very close?*'

Silvertongue pushed aside the fur under which he was sleeping. His hands shook as if he had been holding them too long in cold water.

Dustfinger let the fire grow, and then gently pressed his hand to the other man's heart again. 'Better?'

Silvertongue nodded. He did not push the hand away, even though it was still hotter than human skin. 'Did they pour fire into your veins to bring you back to life?' Farid had asked Dustfinger. 'Perhaps,' he had replied. The idea pleased him.

'Heavens, they must really love you,' he said when Silvertongue got to his feet, still drowsy. 'Unfortunately they sometimes forget that their love always leads to death.'

'Yes. Yes, they forget that. Thank you for waking me.' Silvertongue went over to the battlements and looked out into the night. '*He's coming, Bluejay.* That's what they were whispering this time. *He's coming.* But,' he turned and looked at Dustfinger, 'they said the Piper was preparing the way for him. What do you think they mean by that?'

'Whatever it means,' said Dustfinger, stepping to his side, 'the Piper will have to cross the bridge, like his master, so we'll see him coming in good time.' It still struck Dustfinger as strange that he could speak the Piper's name without feeling fear. But it seemed as if he had left his fears behind with the dead for ever.

The wind ruffled the surface of the lake. Violante's soldiers marched up and down on the bridge, and Dustfinger thought he could hear their mistress's restless footsteps up here on the battlements. Violante's footsteps – and the scratching of Balbulus's pen.

Silvertongue looked at him. 'Show me Resa. The way you conjured up Violante's mother and her sisters out of the fire.'

Dustfinger hesitated.

'Come on,' said Silvertongue. 'I know you're almost as

familiar with her face as I am.'

I've told Mo everything. That was what Resa had whispered to him in the dungeons of the Castle of Night. Obviously she had not been lying. Of course not, Dustfinger told himself. She can't tell a lie any more than the man she loves can.

He traced a figure in the night and made the flames paint it.

Silvertongue instinctively put out his hand, but snatched his fingers away when the fire stung them.

'What about Meggie?' Love was written all over his face. No, he hadn't changed, whatever anyone said. He was like an open book, with his burning heart and a voice that could conjure up whatever he wanted – just as Dustfinger could conjure up images with fire.

The flames painted Meggie in the night, filling her with warm life. It looked so real that her father turned away abruptly, because his hands wanted to reach into the fire again.

'Your turn now.' Dustfinger left the fiery figures standing behind the battlements.

'Mine?'

'Yes, tell me about Roxane. Live up to your name, Silvertongue.'

The Bluejay smiled and leant back against the stones. 'Roxane? That's easy,' he said softly. 'Fenoglio has written wonderful things about her.'

When he began to speak, his voice took hold of Dustfinger like a hand touching his heart. He felt the words on his skin as if they were Roxane's hands. *Dustfinger had never seen a more beautiful woman before. Her hair was as black as the night that he loved. Her eyes were the darkness under the trees, ravens' feathers and the sooty breath of the fire. Her skin reminded him of moonlight on the wings of the fairies . . .*

Dustfinger closed his eyes and could hear Roxane breathing beside him. He wanted Silvertongue to go on and on until the words became flesh and blood, but Fenoglio's words soon came to an end, and Roxane was gone.

'And Brianna?' Silvertongue spoke her name, and Dustfinger could already see his daughter standing there in the night, turning her face away as she usually did when he came close to her. 'Your daughter is here, but you hardly dare look at her. Shall I show you Brianna too?'

'Yes,' said Dustfinger softly, 'show me Brianna.'

Silvertongue cleared his throat, as if to make sure that his voice was at its full strength. 'There's nothing written about your daughter in Fenoglio's book, except for her name and a few words about the small child that she isn't any more. So I can only say what everyone can see about her.'

Dustfinger's heart contracted, as if afraid of the words that were coming. His daughter, his daughter who was a stranger to him.

'Brianna has inherited her mother's beauty, but everyone who sets eyes on her thinks of you too.' Silvertongue spoke the words carefully, as if plucking every one of them out of the night, assembling Brianna's face out of the stars. 'There's fire in her hair and in her heart, and when she looks in the mirror she thinks of her father . . .'

And bears him a grudge for coming back from the dead without bringing Cosimo too, thought Dustfinger. Hush, he wanted to tell Silvertongue, forget my daughter. Tell me more about Roxane instead. But he kept silent, and Silvertongue went on.

'Brianna is so much more grown-up than Meggie, but

sometimes she looks like a lost child whose own beauty seems uncanny to her. She has her mother's grace and her beautiful voice – even the Prince's bear listens when Brianna sings – but all her songs are sad, saying that those we love will be lost someday.'

Dustfinger felt tears on his face. He had forgotten how they felt, so cool on his skin. He wiped them away with his hot fingers.

But Silvertongue went on, his voice as gentle as if he were speaking of his own daughter. 'She looks at you when she thinks you won't notice. She follows you with her eyes as if looking for herself in your face. And no doubt she wishes both of us would tell her what it's like among the dead, and whether we saw Cosimo there.'

'I saw two of him,' said Dustfinger softly. 'I expect she'd gladly exchange me for either of them.'

He turned and looked down at the lake.

'What is it?' asked Silvertongue.

Without a word, Dustfinger pointed down. A fiery serpent was crawling through the night. Torches. The waiting was over. The guards on the bridge began to move. One of them ran back to the castle to take the news to Violante.

The Adderhead was coming.

55

The Wrong Time

'Is he your latest?' asked Man.
'Hard to say,' God replied, peering into the Newt's eyes.
'He might have been here a while. Some things take an awful lot of work. But others – they just seem to turn up, somehow. All ready-made. Very odd!'

Ted Hughes,
The Playmate, from *The Dreamcatcher and Other Stories*

*D*ustfinger saw the torches down in the forest. Of course. The Adderhead feared daylight. Damn it all, the ink was too thick again.

'Rosenquartz!' Fenoglio wiped the pen on his sleeve and looked around in search of the glass man. Walls made of branches elaborately woven together, the writing-board Doria had made him, his bed of leaves and moss, the candle that Farid kept relighting for him when the wind blew it out – but no Rosenquartz.

Very likely he and Jasper hadn't yet given up hope of finding glass women, even up here. After all, Farid had been fool enough to tell them he'd seen at least two – 'as pretty as fairies,' the idiot had added! Ever since then the two glass men had been clambering around in the branches so eagerly that it was only a question of time when they would break their silly necks. Stupid creatures.

Well, never mind. Fenoglio dipped his pen back into the thick ink. He must just make do with things as they were. He loved his new perch for writing, so high that his world was truly at his feet, even if the glass man kept playing truant and it was terribly cold at night. Nowhere before had he felt so strongly that the words were coming to him as if of their own accord.

Yes, he'd write the Bluejay his very best song up here in the crown of a tree. What place could be more suitable? The last picture the flames showed Farid had been reassuring: Dustfinger behind the castle battlements, Mortimer asleep . . . it could only mean that the Adderhead hadn't reached the castle yet. Well, how could he, Fenoglio? he thought with satisfaction. You broke his coach wheel in the middle of the darkest part of the forest. That should hold the Silver Prince up for at least two days, if not more. Plenty of time for writing, now that the words loved him again.

'Rosenquartz!' If I have to call him once more, thought Fenoglio, I personally am going to throw him out of this tree.

'I'm not hard of hearing, thank you very much. Far from it. I hear better than you.' The glass man emerged from the darkness so suddenly that Fenoglio left a large blot of ink on the paper right beside the Adderhead's name. Well, he hoped that was a good omen. Rosenquartz dipped a thin twig in the ink and started stirring without a word of apology, without a word to explain where he had been. Concentrate, Fenoglio.

Forget the glass man. Write.

And the words came. They came easily. The Adderhead was on his way back to the castle where he had once paid court to Violante's mother, and his immortality was a burden to him. In his swollen hands he held the White Book that tormented him worse than his own torturers could have done. But soon there would be an end to it, because his daughter was going to hand over the man who had done all this to him. How sweet revenge would taste when the Bluejay had cured the book and his own rotting flesh! Dream of your revenge, Silver Prince, thought Fenoglio as he wrote down the Adderhead's dark thoughts. Think of nothing but your revenge – and forget that you've never trusted your daughter!

'Well, fancy that, he's writing!' The words were only a whisper, but the Adderhead's face, so clear a moment ago that Fenoglio could have touched it, blurred and changed into the face of Signora Loredan. Meggie was with her. Why wasn't the child asleep? It didn't surprise Fenoglio in the least that her deranged aunt clambered around the branches by night, very likely in pursuit of every shining moth, but Meggie – she was tired to death after insisting on climbing the trunk with Doria, instead of being pulled up like the children.

'Yes, he's writing,' he growled. 'And he'd probably have finished long ago if people didn't keep interrupting him the whole time.'

'What do you mean, the whole time?' replied Loredan. She sounded aggressive again, and she looked so silly in the three dresses she was wearing, one on top of the other. It was amazing she could find so many in her considerable size. Luckily Battista had been able to make jackets for the children out of the monstrous garment she'd been wearing when she had stumbled into Fenoglio's world.

'Elinor—' Meggie tried to interrupt her, but no one could ever stop that busy tongue, as Fenoglio had discovered by now.

'The whole time, he says!' Now she was letting wax from her candle drop on to the paper too! 'Is he hard at work day and night making sure the children don't fall out of these damn nests, is he climbing up and down this wretched tree to bring up something to eat? Is he repairing the walls so that the wind doesn't kill us all, is he keeping watch? No, but people are interrupting him *the whole time*.'

Splash. Another drop of candle wax. And what a nerve she had, leaning over to look at the words he'd just written. 'This really doesn't sound bad,' she informed Meggie, as if Fenoglio had dissolved into the cold forest air before their eyes. 'No, not at all bad.'

It was beyond belief.

Now Rosenquartz too was bending over his lines, wrinkling up his glassy forehead so much that it looked as if water were tracing folds there.

'Oh, and do you, by any chance, want to deliver your opinion as well before I go on writing?' Fenoglio asked him sharply. 'Anything in particular you fancy? You want me to put a heroic glass man into the story, or a fat woman who always knows best and will drive the Adderhead to such distraction that he'll hand himself over to the White Women of his own free will? That would be one solution, I suppose.'

Meggie came up to him and put her hand on his shoulder. 'You don't know how much longer you'll need, do you?' Her voice sounded so desolate. Not at all like a voice that had already changed this world several times.

'It won't be long now.' Fenoglio took great care to sound confident. 'The words are coming. They—'

He fell silent.

From outside came the hoarse, long-drawn-out cry of a falcon. Again and again. The guards' alarm signal. Oh no.

The nest into which Fenoglio had settled hung over a branch broader than any street in Ombra, but once again he felt dizzy when he climbed down the ladder Doria had made him so that he wouldn't have to let himself down on a rope. On the Black Prince's orders, ropes woven by the robbers from bark and climbing plants had been stretched everywhere. In addition, the tree itself had so many air-roots and branches hanging down that there was always something to hold on to. Yet none of that could make you forget the deep void yawning under the slippery boughs. The fact is, Fenoglio, you're no squirrel, he told himself as he clung to a few woody shoots and peered down. But for an old man you're not doing too badly up here.

'They're hauling in the ropes!' Signora Loredan, unlike him, was surprisingly agile as she moved through the air along the wooden paths.

'I can see that for myself!' growled Fenoglio. They were hauling up all the ropes that went down to the foot of the tree. That boded no good.

Farid came climbing down to them. He often joined the guards posted by the Black Prince in the top branches of the tree. Heavens, how could any human being climb like that? The boy was almost as good at it as his marten.

'Torches! They're coming closer!' he said breathlessly. 'And do you hear the dog barking?' He looked accusingly at Fenoglio. 'Didn't you say no one knew about this tree? Didn't you claim it had been forgotten, and the nests with it?'

Blaming him. Of course. Something goes wrong, and it's all Fenoglio's fault!

'Well? Dogs find forgotten places too!' he snapped at the boy. 'Why not ask who wiped our tracks out? Where's the Black Prince?'

'Down on the ground with his bear. Trying to hide him. The stupid creature just refuses to be hauled up!'

Fenoglio listened. Sure enough, he heard dogs. Damn it, damn it, damn it!

'So what about it?' Of course Signora Loredan was acting as if none of it bothered her at all. 'They can't get us down, can they? A tree like this must be easy to defend!'

'They can starve us out, though.'

Farid understood more about situations like this, and Elinor Loredan suddenly looked rather anxious after all. And who was she staring at?

'Ah, so now I'm your last hope again, is that right?' Fenoglio imitated her voice. 'Write something, Fenoglio, go on! It can't be all that difficult!'

The children clambered out of the nests where they slept. They ran along the branches as if they were meadow foot-paths, peering down in alarm. They looked like pretty beetles in the gigantic tree. Poor little things.

Despina ran to Fenoglio. 'They can't get up the tree, can they?'

Her brother just looked at him.

'Of course not,' said Fenoglio, although Ivo's eyes accused him of lying. Ivo was spending more and more time with Roxane's son Jehan these days. The two boys got on well. They both knew too much about the world for lads of their age.

Farid took Meggie's arm. 'Battista says we ought to get the children into the top nests. Will you help me?'

Of course she nodded – she still liked him far too much – but Fenoglio held her back. 'Meggie stays here. I might need her.'

Naturally, Farid immediately knew what he was talking about. In his black eyes Fenoglio saw the reborn Cosimo riding through the streets of Ombra, and the dead men lying among the trees in the Wayless Wood.

'We don't need your words!' said the boy. 'I'll send fire raining down on them if they try to climb up!'

Fire? An alarming word in a forest.

'Well, perhaps I can think of something better,' said Fenoglio, and sensed Meggie's desperate eyes on him. What about my father? they asked. Yes, what about him? Which set of words was more urgent now? Damn it, damn it, damn it!

A few of the children began crying, and below him Fenoglio saw the torches that Farid had mentioned. They shone in the night like fire-elves, but with far more menace.

Farid led Despina and Ivo away with him. The other children followed. Darius went to them, his thin hair untidy from sleep, and took the small hands that reached out in search of his. He glanced in concern at Elinor, but she just stood there staring darkly at the depths below, her hands clenched into fists.

'Let them come!' she said fiercely, her voice shaking. 'I hope the bear will 'eat them all! I hope those men who hunt children will all be hacked to pieces!'

A lunatic of a woman, but she took the words right out of Fenoglio's mouth. Meggie's eyes were still fixed on him.

'Why are you looking at me like that? What am I supposed

to do, Meggie?' he asked. 'This story is telling itself in two places again. Which of them needs the words more urgently? Am I supposed to grow a second head, or—?'

He stopped abruptly.

Signora Loredan was still firing off a salvo of curses at the ground below. 'Child-murderers! Vermin! Cockroaches in armour! You ought to be crushed underfoot!'

'What was that you just said?' Fenoglio sounded more brusque than he had intended.

Elinor looked at him blankly.

Crushed underfoot . . .! Fenoglio stared at the torches down below. 'Yes!' he whispered. 'Yes. It could be rather dangerous. But how am I to . . .?'

He turned and swiftly climbed the ladder to his nest again. The nest where the words were hatched out. That was the place for him now.

But of course Loredan followed him.

'You have an idea?'

He did, and he certainly wasn't going to let her know that, once again, she had given it to him. 'I have an idea, that's right. Meggie, be ready, please.'

Rosenquartz handed him a pen. He was afraid, Fenoglio saw it in his glass face. It was a deeper pink than usual. Or had he been sneaking wine again? For the two glass men were now eating grated bark like their wild cousins, and the result was a little green mingling with Rosenquartz's pale pink. Not a very good colour combination.

Fenoglio put a blank sheet of paper on the board that Doria had so cleverly cut to size for him. For heaven's sake, he'd never yet managed to write two stories at once!

'What about my father, Fenoglio?' Meggie knelt down

beside him. She looked so desperate!

'He still has time.' Fenoglio dipped his pen in the ink. 'Get Farid to look into the fire if you're worried, but I can assure you it's not easy to repair a coach wheel in a hurry. The Adderhead won't be at the castle for a day or so at the most. And I promise, as soon as I've dealt with what's going on here I'll get back to writing the words for the Bluejay. Don't look so sad! How are you going to help him if the Milksop shoots us all out of this tree? Now, give me the book. You know the one I mean.'

He knew where to look. He had described them at the very beginning, in the third or fourth chapter.

'Come on, tell us!' Loredan's voice was quivering with impatience. 'What are you going to do?' She came closer to get a look at the book, but Fenoglio slammed it shut in front of her nose.

'Be quiet!' he thundered, not that that made any difference to the noise coming in from outside. Was the Milksop here already?

Write, Fenoglio.

He closed his eyes. He could see him already. Very clearly. How exciting – given a task like this, writing was twice as much fun!

'What I mean is—'

'Elinor, do keep quiet!' he heard Meggie say.

And then the words came. Yes, this nest was a good place to write in.

56

Fire and Darkness

What was Right, what was Wrong? What distinguished Doing from Not Doing? If I were to have my time again, the old King thought, I would bury myself in a monastery, for fear of a Doing which might lead to woe.

                    T.H. White, *The Once and Future King*

'How many did you count?'

'Nearly fifty.' They were trying hard to sound casual, but Violante's child-soldiers were frightened, and Mo wondered – not for the first time – whether they had ever really fought before, or if they knew about war only from the deaths of their brothers and fathers.

'Only fifty? Then he really does trust me!' There was no mistaking the triumph in Violante's voice. The Adderhead's daughter thought nothing of fear. It was an emotion that she was very good at suppressing – one among many – and Mo read contempt in her eyes when she saw the fear on her young soldiers' faces. But it could be seen on Brianna's face too, and even on Tullio's furry features.

'Is the Milksop with him?'

The boys, as Mo still couldn't help calling them, shook their heads.

'What about the Piper? Surely he's brought the Piper too, hasn't he?'

More head-shaking. Mo exchanged a glance of surprise with Dustfinger.

'To your posts!' Violante ordered. 'We've discussed it often enough. You don't even let my father on to the bridge. He can send a single envoy, no more. We'll keep him waiting for two or maybe three days. That's what he himself does with his enemies.'

'He won't like that.'

'He's not meant to like it. Now, off you all go. I want to speak to the Bluejay alone.' Violante cast Dustfinger an imperious glance. '*Entirely* alone.'

Dustfinger did not move. Only when Mo nodded to him did he turn and leave, as silently as if he were the other man's shadow.

Violante went over to the window. They were in the room that had once been her mother's. On the walls, unicorns grazed peacefully among the spotted cats that Mo had often seen in the forest, and the window had a view of the aviary courtyard, with the empty cages and painted nightingales, now faded by daylight. The Adderhead seemed far, far away, in another world.

'So he hasn't brought the Piper,' said Violante. 'All the better. I suppose he sent him back to the Castle of Night, to punish him for letting you escape.'

'Do you really think so?' Mo examined the peacefully grazing unicorns on the walls. They reminded him of other pictures, hunting scenes in which their white coats were pierced by lances. 'Last night the White Women told me a different tale.'

He could still hear them whispering: *The Piper is preparing the way for him.*

'Really? Well, be that as it may . . . if he's coming after all, then we must kill him too. We can let the others go, but not the Piper.'

Was she really so sure of herself?

Violante still had her back turned to him. 'I'll have to have you bound again. Otherwise my father isn't likely to believe you're really my prisoner.'

'I know. Get Dustfinger to do it. He knows how to tie people up so that they can easily free themselves.' He learnt it from a boy my daughter's in love with, added Mo in his mind. Where was Meggie now? With her mother, he hoped. And with the Black Prince. In safety.

'When my father is dead – ' Violante spoke the word cautiously, so perhaps she wasn't so sure of succeeding as she made out – 'the Milksop isn't going to give up the throne of Ombra to me without a fight. He'll probably get support from his sister in the Castle of Night. I hope you and I will still be allies?' For the first time she looked at him.

What was he to say? *No, once your father is dead I'm going away.* Was he?

Violante turned her back to him again before asking her next question. 'Do you really have a wife?'

'Yes.'

Princes' daughters have a soft spot for robbers and mountebanks.

'Send her away. I'll make you Prince of Ombra.'

Mo thought he heard Dustfinger laughing. 'I'm no prince, Your Highness,' he replied. 'I'm a robber – and a bookbinder. Two parts are more than enough for one man to play.'

She turned again, and scrutinized him as if she couldn't believe he meant it seriously. If only he could read her face better. But the mask Violante wore was even more inscrutable than those Battista made for performing his farces.

'You don't even want to think my offer over?'

'As I said: two parts are enough,' repeated Mo, and for a moment Violante's face was so like her father's that his heart missed a beat.

'Very well. As you say,' she said. 'But I will ask you again when all this is over.'

She looked out of the window once more. 'I've told my soldiers to shut you up in the tower called the Needle. I won't consign you to one of the holes my grandfather used as dungeons. They're built so that the lake can fill them with just enough water to keep prisoners from actually drowning.' She looked at him, as if to see whether the idea frightened him. Yes, it does, thought Mo. So?

'I will receive my father in the Hall of a Thousand Windows,' Violante went on. 'That's where he came to court my mother. I'll have you brought once I'm sure he has the White Book with him.'

The way she put her hands together – it was like a schoolgirl reciting in class. He still felt affection for her; she moved him. He wanted to protect her from all the pain of the past and the darkness in her own heart, although he knew no one could do that. Violante's heart was a locked room, with dark pictures on the walls.

'You will pretend that you can heal the White Book, just

as we planned. I'll have everything made ready – Balbulus has told me what you'd need – and when you seem to be starting work I'll distract my father's attention so that you can write the three words. I'll make him angry. That's usually the best way to distract him. He has a savage temper. If we're lucky he won't even notice you're putting pen to paper. They say he has a new bodyguard, so that could be a problem. But I'm sure my men can deal with him.'

My men. They're children, thought Mo, but fortunately Dustfinger was here too. No sooner had the name come into his mind than Dustfinger himself stepped through the doorway.

'What do you want?' Violante snapped.

Dustfinger ignored her. 'It's very quiet out there,' he told Mo in a low voice. 'The Adderhead is taking the news that he's to be kept waiting surprisingly well. I don't like it.' He went back to the door and looked down the passage. 'Where are the guards?' he asked Violante.

'Where would they be? I sent them down to the bridge. But two of my men are stationed in the courtyard. Now it's time for you to play the part of my prisoner, Bluejay. Yet another part. You see? Sometimes there are more than two.' She went to the window and called to the guards, but only silence answered her.

Mo felt it at the same moment. He felt the story taking a new turn. Time suddenly seemed to weigh more heavily, and a strange uneasiness took hold of him. As if he were on stage and had missed his cue.

'Where are they?' Violante turned, and for a moment she looked almost as young and frightened as her soldiers. She went to the door and called for them again, but no one replied.

Only the silence.

'Keep close to me!' Dustfinger whispered to Mo. 'Whatever happens. Fire is sometimes a better defence than the sword.'

Violante was still listening intently. The sound of footsteps was coming closer – stumbling, unsteady footsteps. Violante stepped back from the door as if afraid of what was coming. The soldier who collapsed at her feet was covered with blood – his own blood. It was the boy who had let Mo out of the sarcophagus. Did he know more about killing now?

He stammered something that Mo didn't understand until he bent over him. 'The Piper . . . they're everywhere.' The boy whispered more, but Mo couldn't make it out. He died with the faltering words still on his lips, mingling with his blood.

'Is there another entrance? One you haven't told us about?' Dustfinger seized Violante's arm roughly.

'No!' she stammered. 'No!' And she tore herself away from him as if it were he who had killed the boy at her feet.

Mo reached for her hand and led her out into the corridor, away from the voices suddenly echoing through the silent castle on all sides. But their flight ended at the next set of steps. Dustfinger sent his marten scurrying off as soldiers barred their way, bloodstained men who hadn't been boys for a long time. Aiming crossbows at them, they drove them to the hall where Violante's mother and her sisters had learnt to dance in front of a dozen silver mirrors. Now the Piper was reflected in them.

'Well, well, isn't the prisoner in chains? How careless, Your Ugliness.' As always, the silver-nosed man held himself erect, proud as a peacock. But Mo was less surprised by the

sight of him than by seeing the man at his side. Orpheus. He
had never expected Orpheus to come here. He had forgotten
him as soon as Dustfinger told him how he had taken the
book, and all the words in it, away from him. *You're a fool,
Mortimer.* As so often, his face showed what he was thinking,
and Orpheus gloated over his surprise.

'How did you get into the castle?' Violante pushed away
the men holding her, and went up to the Piper, who might
have been no more than an uninvited guest. His soldiers
retreated before her as if they had forgotten who their master
was. The Adderhead's daughter – it was a mighty title, even
if she was the ugly daughter.

However, it did not impress the Piper. 'Your father knew
a more comfortable way in than that draughty bridge,' he
replied in a world-weary tone. 'He thought you didn't know
it, so it wouldn't be guarded. Obviously it was your grandfather's best-kept secret, but in fact it was your mother who
showed it to your father when she stole away from this castle
with him. A romantic story, don't you think?'

'You're lying!' Violante looked around like a hunted animal, but all she saw was her own reflection next to the Piper's.

'Really? Your men know better. I haven't had them all
killed. Boys like them make excellent soldiers, because they
still think themselves immortal.' He took a step towards Mo.

'I could hardly wait to see you again, Bluejay. "Send me on
ahead," I asked the Adderhead. "So that I can catch you the
bird who flew away from me. I'll stalk him like a cat, along
secret ways, and seize him while he's still looking out just for
you."'

Mo wasn't listening. He read Dustfinger's thoughts as if
they were his own. *Now, Bluejay!* they whispered, and as a

fiery snake crawled up the legs of the soldier on his right he drove his elbow into the chest of the man behind him. Fire licked up from the floor, baring teeth of flame and setting light to the clothes of the men guarding them. Screaming, they staggered back, while the fire formed a protective ring around their two prisoners. Two soldiers raised their crossbows, but the Piper struck down their arms. He knew his master would not forgive him once more if he brought him the Bluejay dead. His face was pale with rage. But Orpheus smiled.

'Very impressive! It really is!' He went up to the fire and inspected the flames intently as if to find out how Dustfinger summoned them up. But then his gaze went to Dustfinger himself.

'No doubt you really could rescue the bookbinder all by yourself,' he said gently. 'But unluckily for him, you've made an enemy of me. What a mistake. I didn't come with the Piper. I serve his master now. He's waiting for night to fall before paying a call on the Bluejay, and he sent me ahead to prepare everything for his arrival. Including, among other things, the sad task of dispatching the Fire-Dancer to the realm of Death for the last time.'

The regret in his voice sounded almost genuine, and Mo remembered the day in Elinor's library when Orpheus had bargained with Mortola for Dustfinger's life.

'That's enough talking. Get rid of him, Four-Eyes!' cried the Piper impatiently, as his men tore off their burning clothes. 'I want to get my hands on the Bluejay at last!'

'Yes, yes, you'll have him in a minute!' replied Orpheus. He sounded irritated. 'But first I want my share!'

He came so close to the fire that its light reddened his pale face.

'Who did you give Fenoglio's book to?' he asked Dustfinger through the flames. 'Him?' He nodded in Mo's direction.

'Maybe,' replied Dustfinger, and smiled.

Orpheus bit his lip like a child who has to hold back tears. 'Very well, smile away!' he said huskily. 'Mock me! But you'll soon be sorry for what you did to me.'

'Will I?' replied Dustfinger, unmoved, as if the soldiers still aiming crossbows at them were not there at all. 'How are you going to frighten a man who's died once already?'

This time it was Orpheus who smiled, and Mo wished he had a sword, even though he knew that it wouldn't help him.

'Piper, what is this man doing here? Since when has he served my fa . . .' Violante's voice died away as Orpheus's shadow moved, like an animal waking from sleep.

A shape grew out of it, panting like a large dog. No face could be made out in that blurred, pulsating blackness, only eyes, cloudy and angry. Mo felt Dustfinger's fear, and the fire died down as if the dark figure had taken its breath away.

'I don't suppose I have to explain what a Night-Mare is, do I?' said Orpheus in a velvety voice. 'The strolling players say they are the dead sent back by the White Women because even they couldn't wash the dark stains from their souls. So they condemn them to wander without human bodies, driven by their own darkness, in a world that is no longer theirs . . . until they are finally extinguished, eaten away by the air they can't breathe, burnt by the sun from which no body protects them. But until that happens they are like hungry dogs – very hungry.'

He took a step back. 'Take him!' he told the shadowy form. 'Get him, good dog! Take the Fire-Eater for your own, because he broke my heart.'

Mo moved closer to Dustfinger's side, but Dustfinger pushed him back. 'Get away, Bluejay!' he said sharply. 'This thing is worse than death!' The flames around them went out, and the Night-Mare, breathing heavily, stepped into the soot-ringed circle. Dustfinger did not shrink from it. He simply stood there as the shapeless hands reached for him, and then the life just went out of him, extinguished like a flame.

Mo felt as if his own heart stopped when the other man fell. But the Night-Mare bent over Dustfinger's motionless body, snuffling like a disappointed dog, and Mo remembered something that Battista had once told him: Night-Mares were interested only in living flesh and avoided the dead, fearing to be taken back by them to the realm they had escaped for a short time.

'Oh, what happened?' cried Orpheus. He sounded like a disappointed child. 'Why was it so quick? I wanted to watch him dying for longer!'

'Seize the Bluejay!' Mo heard the Piper calling. 'Go on, do it!' But his soldiers just stared at the Night-Mare. It had turned, and its dull gaze was now bent on Mo.

'Orpheus! Call it off!' The Piper's voice almost cracked. 'We still need the Bluejay!'

The Night-Mare moaned as if its mouth were trying to find words – if it had a mouth at all. For a second Mo thought he could make out a face in the blackness. Evil seeped through his skin, covering his heart like mildew. His legs gave way, and he struggled desperately for breath. Dustfinger had been right; the creature was worse than death.

'Back, dog!' Orpheus's voice made the Night-Mare freeze. 'You don't get him until later.'

Mo fell to his knees beside Dustfinger's motionless body. He wanted to lie down beside him, to stop breathing too, stop feeling, but the soldiers hauled him up and bound his hands. He hardly felt it. He could still barely breathe.

When the Piper came up to him, Mo saw him as if through a veil. 'Somewhere in this castle they say there's a courtyard, an aviary with bird cages in it. Put him in one of those.' He drove his elbow into Mo's stomach, but all Mo felt was that he could breathe again as the Night-Mare withdrew, merging with Orpheus's shadow.

'Stop! The Bluejay is still my prisoner!' Violante barred the soldiers' way as they were dragging Mo along with them.

But the Piper pushed her roughly aside. 'He was never your prisoner,' he said. 'Just how stupid do you think your father is? Take her to her room!' he ordered one of the soldiers. 'And throw the Fire-Dancer into the courtyard, outside the cage where you lock up the Bluejay. After all, we shouldn't part a shadow from its master, should we?'

Another of Violante's soldiers was lying outside the door, his young face showing his terror as he saw death coming. They lay everywhere. The Castle in the Lake – and the Bluejay with it – belonged to the Adderhead. So that was how the song ended.

'What a terrible ending!' Mo could almost hear Meggie saying. 'I don't want to listen to this book, Mo. Don't you have another story?'

57

Too Late

'Rat,' said the Mole, 'I simply can't go and turn in, and go to sleep, and *do* nothing, even though there doesn't seem to be anything to be done.'

Kenneth Grahame, *The Wind in the Willows*

The lake. Resa wanted to run when she saw the water shining through the trees at the foot of the slope, but the Strong Man held her back, pointing without a word to the tents lining the bank. The black tent could belong to only one man, and Resa leant against one of the trees growing on the steep hillside and felt all her strength failing her. They were too late. The Adderhead had reached this place before them. Now what?

She looked at the castle lying there in the middle of the lake, like a black fruit that the Silver Prince was about to pluck. Its dark walls looked menacing – and inaccessible. Was Mo really there? Even if he was, so was the Adderhead. And the bridge leading across the lake to it was guarded by a dozen soldiers. Now what, Resa?

'We can't go over the bridge, that's for sure,' the Strong Man whispered to her. 'I'll have a look around. You wait here. Maybe there's a boat somewhere.'

But Resa hadn't come all this way to wait. It was difficult finding a way over the steep slopes by the banks, and there were soldiers stationed everywhere among the trees, but their eyes were on the castle. The Strong Man led her away from the tents to the eastern bank of the lake, where trees grew all the way down to the water. Perhaps they could try to swim across the lake under cover of darkness? But it would be cold, very cold, and there were grim stories about the water of this lake and the creatures living in it. Resa's hand went to the child in her belly as she followed the Strong Man. She felt as if it had gone into hiding deep inside her.

Suddenly the Strong Man took her arm and pointed to some rocks projecting into the lake. Two soldiers emerged among them, as suddenly as if they had come up out of the water. As they climbed to the bank, Resa saw horses waiting under the spruce trees only a few paces from the rocks.

'What does that mean?' whispered the Strong Man as even more soldiers appeared on the rocks. 'Can there be another way into the castle? I'll go and look. But you're not coming with me this time. Please! I promised the Bluejay. He'd punch my nose in anyway if he knew you were here.'

'No, he wouldn't,' Resa whispered back, but she stayed where she was, and the Strong Man slipped away as she stood under the trees, freezing, and watching him go. The water of the lake was lapping on the bank almost to the toes of her boots, and she thought she could see faces under the mirror-like surface, faces pressed flat like patterns on the back of a ray. Shuddering, she retreated – and heard footsteps behind her.

'Hey, you there.'

She spun round. A soldier was standing among the trees, sword in hand. Run, Resa!

She was faster than he was, with his weapons and heavy shirt of mail, but he called another man up, and this one had a crossbow. Faster, Resa! From tree to tree, hiding and then running, as children do. As she would have played with Meggie if she'd been there when her daughter was still small. All those years missed . . .

An arrow drove into the tree beside her. Another buried itself in the ground just in front of her feet. *Don't follow me, Resa. I have to know you'll be there when I come back.* Oh, Mo. It's so much harder to wait, just to keep on waiting.

She ducked behind a tree and drew her knife. They were coming closer, weren't they? Run on, Resa. But her legs were weak with fear. Breathing heavily, she staggered to the shelter of the next tree – and felt a large hand over her mouth.

'Call and tell them you're surrendering!' the Strong Man whispered. 'But don't go towards them. Make them come to you.'

Resa nodded and put the knife away. The two soldiers called something to each other. She felt sick with fear as she put out her arm from behind the tree and asked them not to shoot, her voice trembling. She waited until the Strong Man had crawled away – with astonishing agility for a man of his size – before she emerged from the shelter of the tree with her hands in the air. The eyes under the soldiers' helmets widened in surprise as they saw she was a woman. Their smiles boded no good, even though they lowered their weapons, but before one of them could grab her, the Strong Man was behind them, and winding an arm around the neck of each. Resa turned away as he killed them. She threw up in the damp grass, hand pressed to her belly, afraid the child had sensed her terror.

'They're all over the place!' The Strong Man pulled her to her feet. His shoulder was bleeding so freely that it dyed his shirt red. 'One of them had a knife. "Watch out for knives, Lazaro," that's what Doria always says. That little fellow's far cleverer than me.' He was swaying so much that Resa had to support him. They staggered on together, further into the trees.

'The Piper is here too,' the Strong Man whispered. 'Those were his men we saw on the rocks. Seems there's a tunnel under the lake there, all the way to the castle. And I'm afraid there's more bad news.'

He looked round. Voices came over from the banks of the lake. Suppose the men's bodies were found? The Strong Man led her to a burrow in the ground that smelt of brownies.

Resa heard the sobbing as soon as she made her way into it. The Strong Man was groaning as he crawled in after her. Something furry crouched there in the darkness. At first Resa thought it really was a brownie. Then she remembered the description Meggie had given her of Violante's servant. What was his name? Yes, Tullio.

She reached for the furry hand. Violante's servant stared at her, eyes wide with fear.

'What's happened? I'm the Bluejay's wife! Please, is he still alive?'

He went on staring at her with his dark eyes, which were round like an animal's. 'They're all dead,' he whispered. Resa's heart began to falter as if it had forgotten how to beat. 'There's blood everywhere. They've locked Violante in her room, and as for the Bluejay . . .'

What had they done to him? No, she didn't want to hear. Resa closed her eyes as if that would take her back to Elinor's house, the peaceful garden, where she could go over to Mo's workshop . . .

'The Piper has shut him up in a cage.'

'Does that mean he's still alive?'

The quick nod allowed her heart to beat more regularly again.

'They still need him!'

Of course. How could she have forgotten?

'But the Night-Mare has eaten the Fire-Dancer.'

Oh no. It couldn't be true. Resa buried her face in her hands.

'Is the Adderhead already in the castle?' the Strong Man asked.

Tullio shook his head and began sobbing again.

The Strong Man looked at Resa. 'Then he'll be riding over tonight. And the Bluejay will kill him.' It sounded as if he were reciting a magic spell.

'How?' Resa cut a strip of fabric from his tunic with her knife and bandaged his wound, which was still bleeding hard. 'How is he going to write the words if Violante can't help him any more and Dustfinger is . . .' She did not utter the word 'dead', as if she could make it untrue by leaving it unspoken.

Footsteps could be heard outside, but they moved away again. Resa undid Mortola's bag from her belt.

'No, Lazaro,' she said softly – it was the first time she had used the Strong Man's name. 'The Bluejay will not kill the Adderhead. They will kill *him*, once the Adderhead finds out that Mo can't cure the White Book. And that will be very soon.'

She sprinkled a few of the tiny seeds into her hand. Seeds that taught the soul what only Death could usually teach: how to take on another form.

'What are you doing?' The Strong Man tried to take the bag away from her, but Resa clutched it in both hands.

'You have to place them under your tongue,' she whispered, 'and take care not to swallow them. For if you do that too often the animal will grow too strong, and you forget what you were before. Capricorn had a dog that was said to have been one of his men once, until Mortola tried out these seeds on him. A day came when the dog attacked her, and they killed it. At the time I thought it was just a story to scare the maids.'

She shook all but four of the seeds back into the bag. Four tiny seeds, almost round like poppy seeds, but lighter in colour. 'Take Tullio and go back to the cave!' she told the Strong Man. 'Tell the Black Prince what we saw. Tell him about Snapper too. And take care of Meggie!'

He was looking at her unhappily.

'You can't help me here, Lazaro!' she whispered. 'You can't help either me or the Bluejay. Go back and protect our daughter. And comfort Roxane. Or – no, perhaps you'd better not tell her anything yet. I'll do it myself.'

She licked the seeds up from her hand. 'You never know what kind of creature you'll turn into,' she whispered. 'But I hope it will have wings.'

58

Help from Mountains Far Away

He thinks of the old days, when everything was created. It was so long ago! He and his brothers killed the monstrous giant Ymer then and made the whole world from his corpse. His blood became the sea, his flesh the land, mountains and cliffs arose from his bones, trees and grass grew out of his hair.

Tor Age Bringsværd, *The Wild Gods*

Meggie waited . . . while her ears were filled with screams. While Farid put out Sootbird's black fire with white flames. While Darius soothed the children by telling them stories, his soft voice louder than usual to drown out the noise of fighting, and Elinor helped the other women to cut the ropes that the Milksop's men had shot up into the tree on arrows.

Meggie waited, quietly singing the songs Battista had taught her – all the songs full of hope and light, defiance and courage – while down at the foot of the tree the robbers were fighting for the children's lives and their own. Every scream reminded Meggie of the battle in the forest in which Farid had died. But this time she feared for two boys, not one.

Her eyes didn't know who to look for first, Farid or Doria, black hair or brown. Sometimes she couldn't see either of them, they moved so fast in the branches, both of them following the fire that Sootbird sent up into the huge tree like burning tar. Doria beat it out with cloths and mats, while Farid mocked Sootbird from above and sent his own flames to nest on the murderous fire like doves until their fiery plumage smothered it. He had learnt a great deal from Dustfinger. Farid was no novice now, and Meggie saw jealousy distort Sootbird's leathery face, while the Milksop sat on his horse among the trees, observing the fighting men with as little expression on his face as if he were watching his hounds bring down a stag.

The robbers were still defending the tree, even though they were hopelessly outnumbered. But how much longer could they fight?

Where was he? Where was the creature she and Fenoglio had called to their aid? It had all been so quick with Cosimo!

No one knew what Meggie had read aloud a few hours ago except Fenoglio and the two glass men, who had listened to her open-mouthed. They hadn't even had a chance to tell Elinor about it, since the Milksop's attack had been so sudden.

'You have to give him time!' Fenoglio had told Meggie when she put down the sheet of paper bearing his words. 'He has to come from far away, or it couldn't be done.'

Just so long as he didn't arrive only after they were all dead . . .

The Black Prince was bleeding from his shoulder. Almost all the robbers were wounded by now. It would be too late. Too late.

Meggie saw Doria just avoiding an arrow, Roxane comforting the crying children, and Elinor and Minerva desperately trying to cut another rope before the Milksop's men could climb it. Oh, when would he come? When?

And, suddenly, she felt the sensation, exactly as Fenoglio had described it: a trembling that shook the tree to its topmost branches. Everyone felt it. The men fighting stopped and looked at each other in alarm. *The ground quivered beneath his footsteps.* That was what Fenoglio had written.

'Are you really sure he'll be peaceful?' Meggie had asked anxiously.

'Of course I am!' Fenoglio had replied in some annoyance. But Meggie couldn't help thinking of Cosimo, who hadn't turned out as Fenoglio imagined him. Or had he? Who could say what exactly went on in the old man's head? Perhaps Elinor was more likely to guess than the rest of them.

The quivering grew stronger. Branches broke, shoots, saplings. Flocks of birds flew up from the undergrowth, and the battle cries under the tree turned to screams of terror as the giant pushed his way out of the thickets.

No, he wasn't as tall as the tree.

'Of course not!' Fenoglio had said. 'Of course they're not as tall as *that*! It would be silly! Anyway, didn't I tell you these nests were built on purpose to keep the people who lived in them safe from the giants? Well, there you are! He won't be able to reach up to any of them, but the Milksop will run for it as soon as he sees the giant, that's for sure. He'll run as fast as his spindly legs can carry him!'

And that was what the Milksop did, although he left it to his horse to do the running. He was the first to turn and flee. Sootbird was so terrified that he burnt himself on his own flames, and the robbers themselves stood firm only because the Black Prince made them. It was Elinor who let the first rope down to the men and snapped at the other women as they stood there, petrified, staring at the giant. 'Throw down ropes!' Meggie heard her shouting. 'And get on with it, or do you want him to crush them underfoot?'

Brave Elinor.

The robbers began climbing, while the screams of the soldiers rang through the forest, retreating further into the distance all the time. However, now it was the giant's turn to stop and stare up at the children, who in turn were staring down at him with both delight and terror on their little faces.

'They like human children. That's the problem,' Fenoglio had murmured to Meggie before she began to read. 'After a time they begin catching them, like butterflies or hamsters. But I've tried to write one here who's too lethargic to do that. Although it presumably means he won't be a very clever specimen.'

Did the giant look clever? Meggie couldn't say. She had imagined him as quite different. His mighty limbs were not grossly massive, and he moved only a little more ponderously than the Strong Man. For a moment, as he stood there among the trees, it seemed to Meggie that he, not the robbers, was the right size for this forest. His eyes were strange. They were rounder than human eyes, and rather like a chameleon's. The same could be said of his skin. The giant was naked, like the fairies and elves, and his skin changed colour with every movement he made. When he first appeared it had been pale brown, like the bark of a tree, but now it was patterned with red like the last of the berries hanging in an almost leafless hawthorn bush that came up to his knees. Even his hair changed colour – sometimes green, then suddenly pale like the sky. All this made him almost invisible among the trees. As if the air were moving. As if the wind, or the spirit of this forest, had taken visible shape in him.

'Aha! Here he is at last! Fabulous!' Fenoglio appeared behind Meggie so suddenly that she almost stumbled off the branch where she was standing. 'Yes, we know our craft, you and I! I wouldn't say a word against your father, but in my view you're the true mistress of this art. You're still child enough to see the pictures behind the words as clearly as only children can. Which is probably why this giant doesn't look at all the way I imagined him.'

'But I didn't imagine him like this either,' Meggie said in a whisper, as if any loud word might attract the giant's attention.

'Really? Hm.' Fenoglio took a cautious step forward. 'Well, never mind that. I can't wait to hear what Signora Loredan thinks of him, I really can't.'

Meggie could see what Doria, for one, thought of the giant. He was perched in the crown of the tree and couldn't take his eyes off the apparition. And Farid was looking as captivated as he usually did only when Dustfinger was showing him a new trick, while Jink, sitting on his lap, bared his teeth in alarm.

Meggie felt pleased. She had done it again! She had used Fenoglio's words and her voice to go on telling the story. And, as on those other occasions, she felt exhausted and proud at the same time – and a little afraid of what she had summoned up.

'So now do you have the words for my father ready?'

'The words for your father? No, but I'm working on them.'

Fenoglio rubbed his lined forehead as if he had to wake up a few thoughts slumbering there. 'I'm afraid a giant wouldn't be much help to your father, but trust me. I'll get that done tonight too. When the Adderhead reaches the castle Violante will receive him with my words, and the two of us will bring this story to a good ending once and for all. Oh, he really is magnificent!' Fenoglio leant forward to get a better look at his creation. 'Although I wonder where he gets those chameleon eyes. I never wrote a word about them! Never mind, it makes him look . . . well, interesting. Perhaps I ought to write a few more giants like him here. It's a shame they hide away in the mountains now.'

The robbers did not appear to agree with him. They were still climbing the ropes as hastily as if the Milksop's men were after them. By now only the Black Prince and his bear stood at the foot of the tree.

'What's the Prince doing still down there?' Fenoglio leant so far forward that Meggie instinctively grabbed his tunic. 'For heaven's sake, why doesn't he leave the damn bear alone? These giants don't have particularly good eyesight. He'll be trodden underfoot if the giant stumbles just once!'

Meggie tried to haul the old man back. 'The Black Prince would never leave the bear alone, you know he wouldn't!'

'But he must!' She had seldom seen Fenoglio so concerned. Obviously he really was fonder of the Prince than most of his characters.

'Come on up!' he called down to him. 'Come on, Prince!'

But the Black Prince went on talking to his bear as if the animal were a sulky child, while the giant stood there staring up at the children. Several women shrieked when he reached out his hand. They pulled the children away, but however far the giant stretched, his mighty fingers couldn't reach the nests, just as Fenoglio had said.

'Made to measure!' the old man whispered. 'See that, Meggie?' Yes, this time he obviously had thought of everything.

The giant looked disappointed. He reached up once more, and then took a step to one side. His heel missed the Black Prince by no more than a twig's breadth. The bear roared and stood up on his hind legs – and the giant, in surprise, looked down at what was there between his feet.

'Oh, no!' faltered Fenoglio. 'No, no, no!' he shouted down to his creation. 'Not him! Leave the Prince alone. That's not what you're here for! Go after the Milksop. Take some of his men, if you want anyone! Go on, go away!'

The giant raised his head, looking to see who was shouting like that, but then he bent and picked up the Prince and the bear with as little ceremony as Elinor picking caterpillars off her roses.

'No!' stammered Fenoglio. 'What's going on now? What went wrong this time? He'll break every bone in the Prince's body!'

The robbers hung from their ropes, frozen rigid. One of them threw his knife down at the giant's hand. The giant pulled it out with his lips like a thorn and dropped the Black Prince as he might have dropped a toy. Meggie flinched as he struck the ground and lay there without moving. She heard Elinor scream, while the giant hit out at the men on the ropes as if they were wasps trying to sting him.

Everyone was shouting in confusion. Battista ran to one of the ropes to go to the Prince's aid. Farid and Doria followed him, and even Elinor ran after him, while Roxane stood there, horrified, with her arms around two crying children. As for Fenoglio, he was shaking at the ropes hanging from the tree in helpless fury.

'No!' he shouted down once more. 'No, you just can't do that!'

And suddenly one of the ropes tore away and he fell into the void below. Meggie tried to grab him, but she arrived too late. Fenoglio was falling, with an expression of surprise on his wrinkled face, and the giant caught him in mid-air like a ripe fruit dropping from the tree.

The children had stopped screaming. The women and the robbers were silent too as the giant sat down at the foot of the tree and examined his catch. He put the bear carelessly on the ground, but as he did so his glance fell on the unconscious Prince, and he picked him up again. Roaring, the bear went to his master's aid, but the giant just flicked him away with his hand. Then he rose to his feet, looked up at the children one last time, and strode away with Fenoglio in his right hand and the Black Prince in his left.

59

The Bluejay's Angels

I ask you:
What would you do if you were me? Tell me. Please tell me!
But you're far from this. Your fingers turn the strangeness of these pages that somehow connect my life to yours. Your eyes are safe. The story is just another few hundred pages of your mind. For me, it's here. It's now.

Markus Zusak, *I Am the Messenger*

Orpheus had seen Violante for the first time at one of the Milksop's banquets, and even then he had wondered what it would be like to rule Ombra at her side. All his maids were more beautiful than the Adderhead's daughter, but Violante had something that they did not possess: arrogance, ambition, the lust for power. All of that appealed to Orpheus, and when the Piper led her into the Hall of a Thousand Windows his heart beat faster as he saw how high she still held her head, even though she had staked everything on a single card and lost.

Her gaze passed over them all as if they were the losers – her father, Thumbling, the Piper. She had only a fleeting glance for Orpheus, but never mind. How was she to know what a prominent part he would play in the future? The Adderhead would still be stuck in the mud with a broken wheel if he hadn't read him four new coach wheels on the spot. How everyone had stared! Even Thumbling had learnt to respect him.

The Hall of a Thousand Windows had no windows any more. Thumbling had had them draped with black cloth, and only half a dozen torches gave light in the darkness, just enough of it to show the Adderhead the face of his worst enemy.

When they pushed Mortimer in, Violante's haughty mask cracked, but she quickly pulled herself together. Orpheus saw, with satisfaction, that they had not treated the Bluejay particularly gently, but he could still stand, and the Piper had certainly made sure his hands were unharmed. They could have cut out his tongue, though, thought Orpheus, thus putting an end to all the fulsome praise of his voice once and for all. But then it occurred to him that Mortimer still had to tell him where Fenoglio's book was, since Dustfinger hadn't given its whereabouts away.

The torchlight fell only on Mortimer. The Adderhead sat in darkness. He clearly didn't want to give his prisoner the satisfaction of seeing his bloated body. Anyone could smell it, though.

'Well, Bluejay? Did my daughter describe this meeting of ours rather differently to you? Very likely.' The Adderhead's breath rattled in his throat like an old man's. 'I was very glad when Violante suggested this castle as our meeting place, although the journey here wasn't easy. The castle gave me happiness once before, if not for very long. And I was sure that her mother hadn't told her about the secret passage. She told her daughter a great deal about this castle, but little of it had anything to do with reality.'

Violante's face remained expressionless. 'I don't know what you're talking about, Father,' she said. What an effort she was making not to look at Mortimer. Touching.

'No, you don't know anything, that's the point.' The Adderhead laughed. 'I often had people posted to overhear what your mother told you in the Old Chamber. All the stories about her happy childhood days, the sweet lies told to make her ugly little daughter dream of a place so different from the castle where she really grew up. Reality isn't usually much like what we say about it, but you always confused the words with the truth. Just the same as your mother – you could never distinguish between what you want and the way things really are, could you?'

Violante did not reply. She simply stood there, as upright as ever, staring into the darkness where her father was concealed.

'When I met your mother for the first time in this hall,' the Adderhead went on in his hoarse voice, 'she wanted nothing but to get away from here. She'd have tried to run away if her father had given her any chance. Did she tell you that one of her sisters fell to her death climbing out of one of these windows? Or that she herself was almost drowned by the water-nymphs when she tried swimming across the lake? Presumably not. Instead, she made out that I forced her father to give me her hand in marriage, and took her away from here against her will. Who knows, perhaps she even believed that story herself in the end?'

'You're lying.' Violante was trying very hard to sound composed. 'I don't want to hear any more.'

'But hear it you will,' said the Adderhead, unmoved. 'It's time you stopped hiding behind pretty stories and heard the facts. Your grandfather was only too inclined to make sure that any suitors of his daughters disappeared. So your mother showed me the tunnel – the one that enabled the Piper to get into the castle entirely unnoticed. She was madly in love with me at the time, whatever she may have said to you.'

'Why are you telling me these lies?' Violante still held her head high, but her voice was trembling. 'It wasn't my mother who showed you the tunnel. It must have been one of your spies. And she never loved you, either.'

'Believe what you like. I assume you don't know very much about love.' The Adderhead coughed, and rose from the chair where he was sitting with a groan. Violante retreated as he stepped into the torchlight.

'Yes, see what your noble robber has done to me,' said the Adderhead as he slowly approached Mortimer. It was getting more and more painful for him to walk, Orpheus had seen that often enough on the endless journey to this bleak castle, but the Silver Prince still stood as straight as his daughter.

'But let's not discuss the past any more,' he said, when he was so close to Mortimer that his prisoner had the full bene-fit of the odour he gave off, 'or about the way my daughter may have envisaged this bargain. Convince me that it really doesn't make sense for me to flay you alive at once – and do the same to your wife and daughter. Yes, you left them with the Black Prince, but I know about the cave where they're hid-ing. I assume that my useless brother-in-law has captured them by now and will be taking them to Ombra.'

Ah, that really got through to Mortimer. Guess who told the Adderhead about the cave, noble robber, thought Orpheus, smiling broadly when Mortimer looked at him.

'So now . . .' The Adderhead drove his gloved fist into his prisoner's chest just where Mortola had wounded him. 'What are the prospects? Can you reverse your own trick? Can you cure the Book you so craftily used to deceive me?'

Mortimer hesitated for only a moment. 'Of course,' he replied. 'If you give it to me.'

Very well. Orpheus had to admit that Mortimer's voice still sounded impressive, even in these dire straits (although his own sounded far, far better). But the Adderhead wasn't to be beguiled this time. He struck Mortimer in the face so hard that he fell to his knees.

'Do you seriously expect to fool me again?' he snarled. 'How stupid do you think I am? No one can cure this book! Dozens of your fellow craftsmen have died to give me that information. No, it's past saving, which means that my flesh will rot for all eternity, and every day I'll be tempted to write the three words in it myself and put an end to all this. But I have thought of a better solution, and I'll require your services for it once more after all, which is why I am truly grateful to my daughter for taking such good care of you. After all,' he added, glancing at the Piper, 'I know what a hot temper my silver-nosed herald has.'

The Piper was going to say something, but the Adderhead merely raised his hand impatiently and turned back to Mortimer.

'What kind of solution?' The famous voice sounded hoarse. Was the Bluejay afraid now after all? Orpheus felt like a boy enjoying a particularly exciting passage in a book. I hope he's afraid, he thought. And I hope this is one of the last chapters he appears in.

Mortimer's face twisted when the Piper pressed his knife against his ribs. Oh yes, he's obviously made the wrong enemies in this story, thought Orpheus. And the wrong friends. But that was high-minded heroes for you. Stupid.

'What kind of solution?' The Adderhead scratched his itching flesh. 'You'll bind me another book, what else? But this time you won't go unobserved for a single second. And once this new book with its spotlessly white pages protects me from Death again, we'll write your name in the other one – so that you can know for a while how it feels to be rotting alive. After that I'll tear it to pieces, page by page, and watch as you feel your flesh tearing and you beg the White Women to come for you. Doesn't that sound like a solution satisfactory to all parties?'

Ah. A new White Book. Not a bad idea, thought Orpheus. But my name would suit its brand-new pages so much better! Stop dreaming, Orpheus, he told himself.

The Piper had his knife to Mortimer's throat. 'Well, what's your answer, Bluejay? Want me to carve it into you with my knife?'

Mortimer said nothing.

'Answer!' the Piper snarled at him. 'Or shall I do it for you? There's only one answer, anyway.'

Mortimer still said nothing, but Violante appointed herself to speak for him. 'Why should he help you if you're going to kill him in any case?' she asked her father.

The Adderhead shrugged his heavy shoulders. 'I could let him die in a rather less painful way, or just send his wife and daughter to the mines instead of killing them. After all, we've bargained for those two once before.'

'But this time they're not in your hands.' Mortimer's voice sounded as if he were very far away. He's going to say no, thought Orpheus in astonishment. What a fool.

'Not yet, but they soon will be.' The Piper let his knife slide down Mortimer's chest, and its point traced a heart over the place where the real one beat. 'Orpheus has given us a very detailed description of the place where they're hiding. You heard. The Milksop is presumably taking them to Ombra at this very moment.'

For the second time Mortimer looked at Orpheus, and the hatred in his eyes was sweeter than the little cakes that Oss was sent to buy for him in Ombra market every Friday. Well, there'd be no more Oss now. Unfortunately the Night-Mare had eaten him when it slipped out of Fenoglio's words – it had taken Orpheus some time to get it under control. But he could always find a new bodyguard.

'You can get down to work at once. Your noble patroness, very usefully, has made sure everything you'll need is here!' spat the Piper, and this time blood flowed when he pressed his knife against Mortimer's throat. 'Obviously she wanted to provide every last detail to make us think you were really still alive only to cure the Book. What a farce. Ah, well, she always had a weakness for strolling players.'

Mortimer ignored the Piper as if he were invisible. He looked only at the Adderhead. 'No,' he said. The word hung heavily in the dark hall. 'I will not bind you another book. Death would not forgive me a second time for that.'

Violante instinctively took a step towards Mortimer, but he took no notice of her.

'Don't listen to him!' she told her father. 'He'll do it! Just give him a little time.' Oh, so she really was fond of the Bluejay. Orpheus frowned. One more reason to wish him to the devil.

The Adderhead looked thoughtfully at his daughter. 'Why would you want him to do it?'

'Well, you . . .' For the first time Violante's voice betrayed uncertainty. 'He'll make you well again.'

'So?' The Silver Prince was breathing heavily. 'You want to see me dead. Don't deny it. I like that! It shows that my blood flows in your veins. Sometimes I think I really should put you on the throne of Ombra. You'd certainly fill the position better than my silver-powdered brother-in-law.'

'Of course I would! I'd send six times as much silver to the Castle of Night, because I wouldn't be squandering it on banquets and hunting parties. But for that you must leave me the Bluejay – once he's done what you want.'

Impressive. She was actually still making conditions. Oh yes, I like her, thought Orpheus. I like her very much. She just has to have her weakness for lawless bookbinders driven out of her. But then . . . what possibilities!

Obviously the Adderhead was appreciating his daughter more and more as well. He laughed louder than Orpheus had ever heard him laugh before. 'Look at her!' he cried. 'Bargaining with me even though she stands there empty-handed! Take her to her room,' he ordered one of his soldiers. 'But watch her carefully. And send Jacopo to her. A son should be with his mother. You, however,' he said, turning to Mortimer, 'will finally agree to my demand, or I'll have my bodyguard torture a 'yes' out of you.'

The Piper, aggrieved, lowered his knife when Thumbling stepped out of the darkness. Violante cast him an uneasy glance, and resisted when the soldier dragged her away with him – but Mortimer still remained silent.

'Your Grace!' Orpheus took a respectful step forward (at least, he hoped it looked respectful). 'Let *me* get him to consent!'

A whispered name (for you just have to call the creatures by their right names, like dogs), and the Night-Mare emerged from Orpheus's shadow.

'Not the Night-Mare!' the Piper said forcefully. 'You want to see the Bluejay dead on the spot, like the Fire-Dancer? No.' He had Mortimer hauled to his feet again.

'Didn't you hear? I'm dealing with this, Piper.' Thumbling took off his black gloves.

Orpheus tasted disappointment like bitter almonds on his tongue. What a chance to show the Adderhead how useful he was! If he'd only had Fenoglio's book so that he could use it to write the Piper right out of this world. And that Thumbling fellow too.

'My lord! Please, listen to me!' He stepped in front of the Adderhead. 'May I ask for the answer to an additional question to be extracted from the prisoner in the course of what, I'm sure, he will find a rather uncomfortable process? You'll remember the book I told you about, the book that can change this world in any way you like! Please get him to say where it is!'

But the Adderhead just turned his back. 'Later,' he said, and dropped back, with another groan, into the chair where the shadows hid him. 'We're talking about only one book now, a book with white pages. You can start, Thumbling,' said his gasping voice in the darkness. 'But take care of his hands.'

When Orpheus felt the sudden chill on his face, he thought at first that the night wind was blowing through the black-draped windows. But there they were, standing beside the Bluejay, as white and terrible as they had been in the grave-yard of the strolling players. They surrounded Mortimer like flightless angels, their limbs made of mist, their faces white as bleached bone. The Piper stumbled back so hastily that he fell and cut himself on his own knife. Even Thumbling's face lost its look of indifference. And the soldiers who had been guarding Mortimer flinched back like frightened children.

It couldn't be true! Why were they protecting him? As thanks to him for tricking them more than once? For stealing Dustfinger away from them? Orpheus felt the Night-Mare cower like a beaten dog. So even the Night-Mare feared them? No. No, for heaven's sake! This world really must be rewritten. And he was the man to do it. Yes, indeed. He'd find a way.

What were they whispering?

The pale light spread by the daughters of Death drove away the shadows where the Adderhead was concealed, and Orpheus saw the Silver Prince fighting for breath in his dark corner, putting his shaking hands over his eyes. So he was still afraid of the White Women, even though he had killed so many men in the Castle of Night to prove that he wasn't. All lies. The Adderhead, in his immortal body, was breathless with fear.

But Mortimer stood among Fenoglio's angels of death as if they were a part of him – and smiled.

60

Mother and Son

The scent of moist dirt and fresh growth washes in over me, watery, slippery, with an acid taste to it like the bark of a tree. It smells like youth; it smells like heartbreak.

Margaret Atwood, *The Blind Assassin*

Of course the Adderhead had Violante locked in her mother's former chamber. He knew very well that she would just hear the many lies his late wife had told her all the more clearly there. It couldn't be true. Her mother had never lied to her. Mother and father had always meant good and bad, truth and lies, love and hate. It had been so simple! But now her father had taken that from her too. Violante searched inside herself for her pride and the strength she had always preserved, but all she found was an ugly little girl sitting in the dust of her hopes, at the heart of her mother's shattered image.

She leant her forehead against the barred door and listened for the Bluejay's screams, but she heard only the guards talking outside her door. Oh, why hadn't he said yes? Because he thought she'd still be able to shield him? Thumbling would soon teach him better. She couldn't help thinking of the minstrel whom her father had had quartered because he had sung for her mother, and the servant who had brought her books and was starved to death in a cage outside her window. She had given him parchment to eat. How could she have promised the Bluejay protection when those who were on her side had always gone to their deaths?

'Thumbling will slice strips off his skin!' Jacopo's voice hardly reached her. 'They say he does it so skilfully that his victims don't die. He's said to have practised on dead bodies!'

'Be quiet!' She felt like slapping his pale face. He was growing more and more like Cosimo every day, although he would so much rather have been like his grandfather.

'You can't hear anything from here. They'll take him down to the cellar near the dungeons. I've been there. All the instruments are still in place – rusty, but they're still fit for use: chains, knives, screws, iron spikes . . .'

Violante looked at him, and he fell silent. She went to the window, but the cage where they had first imprisoned the Bluejay was empty. Only the Fire-Dancer lay dead outside it. Strange that the ravens hadn't touched him. As if they were afraid to.

Jacopo took the plate of food that one of the maids had brought him and sulkily picked at it. How old was he now? She couldn't remember. At least he'd stopped wearing that tin nose since the Piper had made fun of him for it.

'You like him.'

'Who?'

'The Bluejay.'

'He's better than any of them.' Once again she listened at

the door. Why hadn't he said yes? Then perhaps she might yet have been able to save him.

'If the Bluejay makes another book, will Grandfather still go on smelling so bad? I think he will. I think he'll just fall down dead some day. He looks dead already, really.' How indifferent he sounded. A few months ago Jacopo had still adored her father. Were all children like that? How would she know? She had just one child. Children . . . Violante still saw them running out of the castle gate in Ombra and into their mothers' arms. If the Bluejay died for them, were they really worth it?

'I don't like looking at Grandfather any more!' Jacopo shuddered and put his hands over his eyes. 'If he dies I'll be king, won't I?' The chill in his clear voice both impressed and alarmed Violante.

'No, you won't. Not after your father attacked him. His own son will be king. King in the Castle of Night *and* in Ombra.'

'But he's only a baby.'

'So his mother will reign for him. And the Milksop.' What's more, Violante added in her thoughts, your grandfather is still immortal, and no one seems able to do anything about it. Not for all eternity.

Jacopo pushed his plate aside and strolled over to Brianna. She was embroidering a picture of a horseman who looked suspiciously like Cosimo, although Brianna said he was the hero of an old fairy tale. It did Violante good to have Brianna with her again, although the girl had been even more silent than usual since the Night-Mare had killed her father. Perhaps she had loved him after all. Most daughters loved their fathers.

'Brianna!' Jacopo thrust a hand into her beautiful hair.

'Read to me. Go on. I'm bored.'

'You can read for yourself. In fact you can read very well.' Brianna removed his fingers from her hair and went on with her embroidery.

'I'll fetch the Night-Mare!' Jacopo's voice rose shrilly, as it always did when he didn't get his own way. 'I'll fetch it to eat you like your father. Oh no, I forgot, it didn't eat him. He's lying dead out in the courtyard, with ravens pecking around him.'

Brianna didn't even raise her head, but Violante saw her hands trembling so violently that she pricked her finger.

'Jacopo!'

Her son turned to her, and for a moment Violante thought his eyes were begging her to say more. Shake me! Hit me! Punish me! said those eyes. Or take me in your arms. I'm scared. I hate this castle. I want to go away.

She hadn't wanted children. She didn't know how to deal with them. But Cosimo's father had begged for a grandson. How was she supposed to deal with a child? She could hardly manage to keep her own painful heart together. If only it had at least been a girl. The Bluejay had a daughter. Everyone said he loved her very much. Perhaps he'd give in after all for the daughter's sake, and bind her father a second book. If the Milksop really did catch the girl. And then? She didn't want to think about his wife. Perhaps she was dying anyway. The Milksop liked treating those he hunted cruelly.

'Read! Read to me!' Jacopo was still standing in front of Brianna. He snatched the embroidery from her lap, so roughly that she pricked her hand again.

'That looks like my father.'

'No, it doesn't!' Brianna cast a quick glance at Violante.

'Yes, it does. Why don't you ask the Bluejay to bring him back from the dead? The way he brought *your* father back?'

Once Brianna would have slapped him, but Cosimo's death had broken something in her. She was soft now, like the inside of a shellfish, soft and full of pain. All the same, her company was better than none, and Violante slept much more easily when Brianna sang for her in the evenings.

Outside, someone pushed back the bolt.

What did that mean? Were they coming to tell her that the Piper had killed the Bluejay after all? That Thumbling had broken him like so many men before? And if so, she asked herself, what difference does it make? Your heart is broken into pieces anyway.

But it was Four-Eyes who came in. Orpheus, or Moonface, as the Piper derisively called him. Violante still couldn't understand how he had insinuated himself into her father's good graces so swiftly. Perhaps it was his voice. It was almost as beautiful as the Bluejay's, but something in it made Violante shudder.

'Your Highness!' Her visitor bowed so low that the bow verged on mockery.

'Has the Bluejay given my father the right answer after all?'

'No, I'm afraid not. But he is still alive, if that's what you wanted to know.' His eyes looked so innocent through those round glasses – glasses that she had copied from him, except that unlike Four-Eyes Violante didn't always wear hers. Sometimes she preferred to see the world through a blur.

'Where is he?'

'Ah, so you've seen the empty cage. Well, I suggested to the Adderhead different accommodation for the Bluejay. You presumably know about the dungeons where your grandfather used to throw his prisoners. Once in there, I'm sure our noble robber will very soon give up the idea of resisting your father's wishes. But let's come to the reason for my visit.'

His smile was sweet as syrup. What did he want from her?

'Your Highness.' His voice stroked Violante's skin like the hare's foot that Balbulus used to smooth parchment. 'Like you, I am a great lover of books. Sad to say, I hear that the library of this castle is in a terrible condition, but it has also come to my ears that you still have a few books with you. Would it be possible for me to borrow one, or maybe even two? Of course I would show my appreciation of the loan in every possible way.'

'What about *my* book?' Jacopo pushed in front of Violante, his arms folded in the pose his grandfather used to adopt before his swollen arms had made even that gesture painful. 'You haven't given it back to me yet. You owe me –' he counted on his short fingers – 'you owe me twelve silver coins.'

The look Orpheus gave Jacopo was neither warm nor sweet, but his voice was still both. 'Why, of course! What a good thing you've reminded me of it, Prince. Come to my room and I'll give you the coins and your book back. But now let me speak to your mother, will you?' With an apologetic smile, he turned back to Violante.

'Well, what do you say?' he asked, lowering his voice to a confidential tone. 'Would you lend me one, Your Highness? I've heard wonderful things about your books, and believe me, I will treat them with the utmost care.'

'She only has two with her.' Jacopo pointed to the chest beside the bed. 'And they're both about the Blue—'

Violante clapped her hand over his mouth, but Orpheus

was already making for the chest.

'I'm sorry,' she said, barring his way. 'I am too much attached to these books to let them out of my hands. And as I'm sure you have heard, my father has seen to it that Balbulus can't illuminate any more books for me.'

Orpheus hardly seemed to be listening. He was staring spellbound at the chest. 'May I at least take a look at them?'

'Don't let him have them!'

Clearly Orpheus hadn't even noticed Brianna. His face froze when he heard her voice behind him, and his plump fingers clenched into fists.

Brianna stood up and returned his hostile glance with composure. 'He does strange things with books,' she said. 'Books and the words in them. And he hates the Bluejay. My father said he tried selling him to Death.'

'Poor confused creature!' stammered Orpheus, but he was visibly nervous as he adjusted his glasses. 'She was my maid, as presumably you know, and I caught her stealing. No doubt that's why she says such things about me.'

Brianna went as red as if he had thrown hot water in her face, but Violante moved to her side to defend her. 'Brianna would never steal,' she said. 'Now go away, please. I can't give you the books.'

'Oh, so she'd never steal?' Orpheus was clearly having some difficulty in giving his voice its old velvety sound. 'As far as I know she stole your husband from you, didn't she?'

'Here you are!'

Before Violante could react Jacopo was standing in front of Orpheus, holding her books. 'Which one do you want? She likes reading the thicker book most. But this time you must pay me more than you paid for my own book!'

Violante tried to snatch the books from his hands, but Jacopo was surprisingly strong, and Orpheus hastily opened the door.

'Quick. Take these books to safe keeping!' he ordered the soldier on guard outside.

The man had no difficulty in getting the books away from Jacopo. Orpheus opened them, read a few lines first from one, then from the other – and gave Violante a triumphant smile.

'Yes, exactly the reading matter I need,' he said. 'You'll get them back as soon as they've served their purpose. But these books,' he added to Jacopo, pinching his cheek roughly, 'I'm borrowing for free, you greedy son of a dead prince! And we can forget about any payment for your other book too, or do you want to meet my Night-Mare? I'm sure you've heard of it.'

Jacopo just stared at him with a mixture of fear and hatred on his thin face.

Orpheus, however, bowed and went out through the door-way. 'I really can't thank you enough, Your Highness,' he said by way of farewell. 'You have no idea how happy these books make me. Now the Bluejay is certain to give your father the right answer soon.'

Jacopo was chewing his lip hard as the guard outside shot the bolt again. He always did that when something hadn't gone the way he wanted. Violante slapped his face so hard that he stumbled against her bed and fell. He began crying with-out a sound, his eyes fixed on her like a dog that has been punished.

Brianna helped him up and wiped his tears away with her dress.

'What is Four-Eyes going to do with the books?' Violante was shivering. She was shivering all over. She had a new enemy.

'I don't know,' Brianna replied. 'All I do know is that my father took one away from him because he had done great harm with it.'

Great harm.

Now the Bluejay is certain to give your father the right answer soon.

61

Clothed and Unclothed

Archimedes finished his sparrow, wiped his beak politely on the bough, and turned his eyes full on the Wart. These great, round eyes had, as a famous writer has expressed it, a bloom of light upon them like the purple bloom of powder on a grape.

'Now that you have learned to fly,' he said, 'Merlyn wants you to try the Wild Geese.'

T.H. White, *The Once and Future King*

It was easy to fly, so easy. The skill of it came with the body, with every feather and every delicate bone. For the seeds had turned Resa into a bird. The transformation caused painful spasms which had terrified Lazaro the Strong Man, but she hadn't turned into a magpie like Mortola. 'A swift!' the Strong Man had whispered when she flew to his hand, dizzy to find everything suddenly so much larger.

'Swifts are nice birds, very nice. It suits you.' He had very gently stroked her wings with his forefinger, and it seemed so strange that she couldn't smile at him with her beak. But she could speak in her human voice, which alarmed poor Tullio even more.

Her feathers warmed her, and the guards on the banks of the lake didn't even look up as she flew over their heads. Obviously they hadn't yet found the soldiers the Strong Man had killed. The crests on their grey cloaks reminded Resa of the dungeons of the Castle of Night. Forget them, she thought, as she spread her wings on the wind. That's in the past. But perhaps you can still change what's yet to come. Or was life after all only a tangle of threads spun by fate, and there was no escaping it? Don't think, Resa, she told herself, fly!

Where was he? Where was Mo?

The Piper has locked him up in a cage. Tullio hadn't been able to say just where that cage stood. In a courtyard, he had stammered, a courtyard full of painted birds. Resa had heard about the painted walls of the castle. From the outside, however, its walls were almost black, built of the dark stone also found on the banks of the lake. She was glad she didn't have to cross the bridge, which was swarming with soldiers. It was raining, and the raindrops made endless circles on the water below her. But her body weighed very little, and flying was a wonderful sensation. She saw her reflection underneath her. It shot across the waves like an arrow, and at last the towers rose to meet her, the fortified walls, the slate-grey roofs, and among them courtyards – gaping dark holes in the pattern of the stone. She spotted trees with bare branches, dog-runs, a frozen garden, and soldiers everywhere. But cages . . .?

When she finally found them at first she saw only Dustfinger, lying where he had been thrown on the grey paving stones like a bundle of old clothes. Oh, God. She would never have wanted to see him like that again. There was a child standing beside him, staring at the still body as if waiting for it to move – just as it had done once before, if the songs of the strolling players told the truth. And they do tell the truth, Resa wanted to call down. I've felt his warm hands. I've seen him smile again and kiss his wife. But when she saw him lying there it was as if he had never moved since he died in the mine.

She didn't see the cages until she dived below the slate roof tops. They were all empty. No trace of Mo. Empty cages and an empty body. She wanted to let herself drop like a stone, hit the paving and lie there as motionless as Dustfinger.

The child turned. He was the boy she had last seen standing on the battlements in Ombra. Violante's son. Even Meggie, who would usually take any child on her lap with such tenderness, spoke of him only with dislike. Jacopo. For a moment he stared up at Resa as if he could see the woman under the feathers, but then he bent over the dead man again, touched the rigid face – and straightened up when someone called his name. There was no mistaking that strained nasal voice.

The Piper.

Resa flew up to the ridge of a roof.

'Come along, your grandfather wants to see you!' The Piper took the boy by the scruff of his neck and pushed him roughly towards the nearest flight of steps.

'What for?' Jacopo's voice sounded like a ridiculous echo of his grandfather's, but it was also the voice of a little boy lost among all the grown-ups, fatherless – and motherless, judging by all Roxane had said about Violante's lack of love for him.

'What do you think he wants you for? He's certainly not pining away for your peevish company.' The Piper thumped Jacopo on the back with his fist. 'He wants to know what your mother says when you're alone in her room with her.'

'She doesn't talk to me.'

'Oh, I don't like to hear that. What are we to do with you if you're no use as a spy? Maybe we ought to feed you to the Night-Mare! It's a long time since the creature had anything to eat, and if your grandfather gets his way it won't get to taste the Bluejay in a hurry either.'

Night-Mare.

So Tullio had told the truth. As soon as the voices died away Resa fluttered down to Dustfinger. But the swift couldn't weep any more than she could smile. Fly after the Piper, Resa, she told herself as she perched on the stones, wet with rain. Look for Mo. There's no more you can do for the Fire-Dancer now, any more than you could before. She was only thankful that the Night-Mare hadn't feasted on him as it had on Snapper. His cheek was so cold when she pressed her feathered head against it.

'How did you come by that pretty dress of feathers, Resa?'

The whisper came from nowhere – out of the rain, the moist air, the painted stone – but surely not from the cold lips. Yet it was Dustfinger's voice, husky and soft at the same time, ever familiar. Resa swiftly turned her bird's head – and heard his quiet laughter.

'Didn't you look round like that for me before, back in the dungeons of the Castle of Night? I was invisible then too, as far as I remember, but it's far more entertaining to be without a body. Although you can't enjoy the entertainment too long. I'm afraid if I let my body lie here much longer it won't fit me any more, and then I suppose not even your husband's voice could bring me back. Apart from the fact that without the help of the flesh you soon forget who you are. I admit I'd almost forgotten already – until I saw you.'

It was like seeing a sleeper wake when the dead man moved. Dustfinger pushed back the damp hair from his face and looked down at himself, as if to make sure that his body did still fit him. It was just as Resa had dreamt it the night after his first death, when he did not wake again. Not until Mo brought him back to life.

Mo. She fluttered up on to Dustfinger's arm, but he put a warning finger to his lips as she opened her beak. He called Gwin with a soft whistle, then looked up at the steps which the Piper had climbed with Jacopo, to the windows on their left and on again to the oriel tower casting its shadow down on them. 'The fairies tell tales of a plant that turns human beings into animals and animals into humans,' he whispered. 'But they also say it's dangerous to use it. How long have you been wearing your feathered clothing?'

'About two hours.'

'Then it's time to take it off again. Luckily this castle has many forgotten chambers, and I explored them all before the Piper arrived.' He put out his hand, and Resa perched on his skin, now warm again. He was alive! Wasn't he?

'I brought back a few very useful abilities from the realm of Death!' whispered Dustfinger as he carried her down a passage painted with fish and water-nymphs so true to life that Resa felt as if the lake had swallowed them up. 'I can take off this body like a garment, I can give fire a soul, and I can read your husband's heart better than the letters you took such trouble to teach me.'

He pushed a door open. No window let any light into the room beyond, but Dustfinger whispered, and the walls were covered with sparks as if they were growing a fiery coat.

When Resa spat out the seeds she had been holding under her tongue, two were missing, and for a terrible moment she was afraid she would be a bird for ever, but her body still remembered itself. When she had human limbs again she instinctively stroked her belly and wondered whether the child inside it was changed by the seeds too. The idea frightened her so much that she was almost sick.

Dustfinger picked up a swift's feather lying at her feet and looked at it thoughtfully.

'Roxane is well,' said Resa.

He smiled. 'I know.'

He seemed to know everything. So she told him nothing about either Snapper or Mortola, or how the Black Prince had nearly died. And Dustfinger did not ask why she had followed Mo.

'What about the Night-Mare?' Even speaking the word frightened her.

'I slipped through its black paws just in time.' He rubbed a hand over his face as if to wipe a shadow away. 'Luckily creatures of its kind aren't interested in dead men.'

'Where did it come from?'

'Orpheus brought it here with him. It follows him like a dog.'

'Orpheus?' But that was impossible! Orpheus was in Ombra, drowning his sorrows in drink and wallowing in self-pity, as he had been doing ever since Dustfinger stole the book from him.

'That's right, Orpheus. I don't know how he fixed it, but

he serves the Adder now. And he's just had your husband thrown into one of the dungeons under the castle.'

Footsteps could be heard above them, but they soon died away.

'Take me to him!'

'You can't go there. The cells are deep down and well guarded. I may be able to do it alone, but two of us would attract far too much attention. This castle will be teeming with soldiers once they discover that the Fire-Dancer is back from the dead again.'

You can't go there . . . wait here, Resa . . . it's too dangerous. She was tired of hearing this kind of thing. 'How is he?' she asked. 'You said you can read his heart.'

She saw the answer in Dustfinger's eyes.

'A bird will attract less attention than you would,' she said, and put the seeds in her mouth before he could stop her.

62

Black

You are the bird whose soft wings came
When I cried out at night, waking from sleep.
Cried only with my arms, because your name
Is like a chasm, a thousand long nights deep.
Rainer Maria Rilke, *The Guardian Angel*

The cell they threw Mo into was worse than the tower in the Castle of Night or the dungeon in Ombra. They had let him down on a chain, his hands bound, deeper and deeper down until the dark settled on his eyes like blindness. And the Piper had stood there above him, describing in his nasal whine how he was going to bring Meggie and Resa here and kill them before his eyes. As if the Piper's words made any difference. Meggie was lost already. Death would take her as well as him. But perhaps the Great Shape-Changer would at least spare Resa and their unborn child if Mo refused to bind the Adderhead another book. Ink, Mortimer, black ink surrounds you, he thought. It was difficult to breathe in this damp void. But it made him feel strangely calm to think it was no longer up to him to go on with this story, on and on all the time. He was so tired of it . . .

He dropped to his knees. The damp stone felt like the bottom of a well. As a child he had always been afraid of falling into a well and starving to death, helpless and alone. He shuddered, longing for Dustfinger's fire, for its light and warmth. But Dustfinger was dead. Extinguished by Orpheus's Night-Mare. Mo thought he could hear it breathing beside him, so distinctly that he looked for its red eyes in all that blackness. But there was nothing. Or was there?

He heard footsteps, and looked up.

'Well, how do you like it down there?'

Orpheus was standing on the edge of the shaft. The light of his torch didn't reach the bottom of it; the cell lay too deep for that, and Mo instinctively stepped back so that the darkness would hide him. Like a caged animal, he thought.

'Oh, so you're not talking to me any more? Very understandable.' Orpheus smiled with self-satisfaction, and Mo's hand went to where his knife had been hidden, the knife so carefully concealed by Battista. Thumbling had found it all the same. Mo imagined thrusting it into Orpheus's flabby body. Again and again. The pictures that his helpless hatred conjured up were so full of blood that they sickened him.

'I'm here to tell you how this story goes on. Just in case you still think you play a leading part in it.'

Mo closed his eyes and leant back against the damp wall. Let him talk, he told himself. Think of Resa, think of Meggie. Or perhaps he'd better not. How had Orpheus heard about the cave?

All is lost, a voice inside him whispered. Everything. The composure that he had felt since the appearance of the White

Women was gone. Come back, he wanted to whisper. Please! Protect me! But they didn't come. Instead, words ate into his heart like pale maggots. Where did they come from? All is lost. Stop it, he told himself. But the words ate their way on, and he writhed as if in physical pain.

'You're so quiet! Ah, do you feel it already?' Orpheus laughed, happy as a child. 'I knew it would work. I knew it when I read the first song. Oh yes, I have a book again, Mortimer. In fact I have three of them, full to the brim with Fenoglio's words, and two of them are all about the Bluejay. Violante brought them to this castle. Wasn't that kind of her? I had to make some changes, of course – move a few words here, a few more there. Fenoglio is very kind to the Bluejay, but I was able to put that right.'

Fenoglio's Bluejay songs. All neatly written down by Balbulus. Mo closed his eyes.

'And, by the way, the water isn't my doing!' Orpheus called down to him. 'The Adderhead has had the sluices to the lake opened. You won't drown, it doesn't rise high enough for that, but it won't be pleasant.'

At the same moment Mo felt the water rising up his legs as if the darkness had turned liquid, so cold and black that he fought for breath.

'No, the water isn't my idea,' Orpheus went on, sounding bored. 'I know you too well by now to think that fear of that kind would change your mind. Presumably you're hoping your obstinacy may yet mollify Death, now that you haven't kept your part of the bargain. Oh yes, I know about the deal you did with Death, I know everything . . . but however that may be, I'll drive the obstinacy out of you. I'll make you forget your high-minded virtues. I'll make you forget everything

589

except the fear, because the White Women can't protect you from my words.'

Mo wanted to strike the man dead. With his bare hands. But they were bound, he reminded himself

'At first I was going to write something about your wife and daughter, but then I said to myself: no, Orpheus, that way he won't feel the words himself!' How the moon-faced creature was enjoying every syllable he spoke. As if he had dreamt of this moment. There he is up above, thought Mo, and here I am down in a black cell, helpless as a rat that he could kill at any moment.

'No,' Orpheus went on. 'No, I said to myself. Let him feel the power of your words for himself. Show him that from now on you can play with the Bluejay like a cat playing with a mouse. Except that your claws are made of letters!'

And Mo felt the claws. It was as if the water were seeping through his skin and straight into his heart. So black. Then came the pain. As violent as if Mortola had shot him a second time, and so real that he pressed his hands to his chest, thinking he would feel his own blood between his fingers. Although the darkness blinded him, he saw it stain his shirt and his hands, and felt his strength fading away as it had before. He could hardly stand upright; he had to brace his back against the wall to keep from slipping into the water that was already up to his waist. Resa. Oh God. Resa, help me.

Despair shook him like a child. Despair and helpless rage.

'I wasn't sure at first what would work best.' Orpheus's voice cut through the pain like a blunt knife. 'Should I send a few unpleasant water-monsters to visit you? I have the book here that Fenoglio wrote for Jacopo. It has some rather nasty creatures in it. But I decided on another, far more interesting way! I decided to drive you mad with beings out of your own head, come to haunt you with old fears, old anger and old pain all dammed up in your heroic heart, locked away but not forgotten. Bring it all back to him, Orpheus! I told myself. With some added images that he's always been afraid of: a dead wife. A dead child. Send them all down to him in the darkness, let him drown in his own anger. Who feels like a hero when he's trembling with fright and knows it comes from nowhere but himself? How does the Bluejay feel when he dreams of bloody slaughter? How does it feel to doubt your own sanity? Yes, I told myself, if you want to break him, that's the way. Let him lose himself, let the Bluejay howl like a mad dog, let him trap himself in his own fear. Let loose the Furies who can kill him so cleverly from the inside.'

Mo felt what Orpheus was describing even as the other man spoke, and he realized that Orpheus had already read the words aloud some time ago, with a tongue as powerful as his own. Yes, it was a new Bluejay song. Telling how he lost his mind in a damp, black cell, how he nearly drowned himself in his despair, and how at last he begged for mercy and bound the Adderhead another White Book, his hands still shaking from hours in the dark.

The water had stopped rising, but Mo felt something brush past his legs. Breathe slowly, Mortimer, breathe very steadily. Shut out the words, don't let them in. You can do it. But how, when a gunshot had just entered his breast again, when his blood was mingling with the water and everything in him cried out for revenge? He felt feverish again, feverish and yet so cold. He bit his lip to keep Orpheus from hearing him groan, pressed his hand to his heart. Feel it; there isn't really any blood there. Meggie isn't dead, even if you see that image as clearly as Orpheus could write the scene. No, no, no! But the words whispered: yes! And he felt as if he were breaking into a thousand tiny shards.

'Throw your torch down, guard! I want to see him.'

The torch fell. It dazzled Mo, and drifted on the dark water for a moment before going out.

'Well, well, so you do feel them! You feel every single word, don't you?' Orpheus looked down at him like a child looks at a worm he has put on a hook, fascinated to see it writhe. Mo wanted to put his head under the water until he couldn't breathe any more. Stop it, Mortimer, he told himself, what is he doing to you? Defend yourself. But how? He felt like sinking into the water just to escape the words, but he knew that even there they would be waiting for him.

'I'll be back in an hour's time!' Orpheus called down. 'Of course, I couldn't resist reading at least a few nasty creatures into the water for you, but don't worry, they won't kill you. Who knows, perhaps you'll even find them a welcome diversion from what your mind shows you? Bluejay . . . yes, you really ought to be careful when you choose what part to play. Get them to call me as soon as you realize that your high-minded approach is out of place here. Then I'll write you a few words to save you. Along the lines of: *but morning came, and the Bluejay's madness left him . . .*'

Orpheus laughed, and went away. Leaving him alone with the water and the darkness and the words.

Bind the Book for the Adderhead. The sentence formed in Mo's mind as if written in perfect calligraphy. *Bind him another White Book and all will be well.*

Again pain shot through him so violently that he cried out. He saw Thumbling taking his fingers in a pair of pincers, saw the Milksop dragging Meggie out of a cave by her hair, saw the dogs snapping at Resa. He was shivering with fever, or was it from the cold? It's only in your mind, Mortimer! He struck his forehead against the stone. If only he could have seen something, anything but Orpheus's images. If only he could have felt something other than the words. Press your hands on the stone, go on, dip your face in the water, strike yourself with your fists, that's all that's real, nothing else. Oh yes?

Mo sobbed, and pressed his bound hands to his forehead. He heard a fluttering above him. Sparks sprang up in the blackness. The dark retreated as if someone were removing a blindfold from his eyes. Dustfinger? No, Dustfinger was dead. Even if his heart refused to believe it.

The Bluejay is dying, the voice inside him whispered, the Bluejay is losing his mind. And he heard fluttering again. Of course. Death was coming to visit him, and she wasn't sending the White Women to protect him again. This time she was coming herself to take him away, because he had failed. Death would take first him, then Meggie . . . but perhaps even that was better than the words Orpheus had written.

It was all black, so black, in spite of the sparks. He could still see them. Where did they come from? He heard the fluttering again, and suddenly he felt someone beside him. A hand was laid on his forehead, caressed his face. Such a familiar hand.

'What is it? Mo!'

Resa. This was impossible. Was Orpheus conjuring up her face, only to drown her the next moment before his eyes? He had never known that Orpheus could write so well. And how warm her hands were!

'What's the matter with him?'

Dustfinger's voice. Mo looked up and saw him, exactly where Orpheus had been standing. Madness. He was caught in a dream until Orpheus released him.

'Mo!' Resa took his face between her hands. Only a dream. But what did that matter? It was so good to see her. He sobbed with relief, and she held him tight. 'You must get away from here!'

She couldn't be real.

'Listen to me, Mo! You must get away.'

'You can't be here.' How heavy his tongue was.

'Yes, I can.'

'Dustfinger is dead.' Resa . . . she looked so different with her hair pinned up.

Something swam between them. Spikes stuck up from the water, and Resa flinched in alarm. Mo drew her close and hit out at the swimming thing. Still as if in a dream. Dustfinger threw a rope down. It didn't come low enough, but at a whisper from above it began growing longer, lengthened by fibres made of flames.

Mo reached for it, and let it go again.

'I can't leave this place.' The sparks made the water filling the cell seem as red as blood. 'I can't.'

'What are you talking about?' Resa pressed the fiery rope into his damp hands.

'Death. Meggie.' He had lost the words, too, in all the darkness. 'I have to find the Book, Resa.'

She put the rope back into his hands once more. They would have to climb fast to keep it from burning their skin. Mo began climbing, but it seemed as though the darkness clung to him like a black scarf. Dustfinger helped him up over the rim of the shaft. Two guards lay there, dead or unconscious.

Dustfinger looked at him, looked into his heart, saw everything in it.

'Those are terrible pictures,' he said.

'Black as ink.' Mo's voice was hoarse. 'A greeting from Orpheus.'

The words were still there. Pain. Despair. Hatred. Rage. His heart seemed to fill with them at every breath he took. As if the dark dungeon were inside him now.

He took a sword from one of the guards and drew Resa close. He felt her trembling under the men's clothes she wore. Perhaps she really was here. But how? And why wasn't the Fire-Dancer lying dead outside the cages any more? Suppose these are only pictures conjured up by Orpheus, he thought as he followed Dustfinger. Suppose he's showing them to me only to fling me even deeper into the darkness? Orpheus. Strike him dead, Mortimer, him and his words. His own hatred frightened him almost more than the darkness; it was so full of blood, so intemperate.

Dustfinger went ahead as fast as if he were leading them along paths he knew. Flights of steps, gateways, endless passages, with never any hesitation, as if the stones themselves told him the way. Wherever he went, sparks sprang from the walls, spreading out and painting the black with gold. They met soldiers three times. Mo killed them with as much relish as if he were killing Orpheus. Dustfinger had to make him go on, and Mo saw the fear on Resa's face. He reached for her hand, like a drowning man – and felt the darkness still inside him.

63

Ah, Fenoglio

And so the poet's testament ends here,
And as he leaves this world upon his bier,
Take you your leave of him, saying thank God
We're rid of him, let's have the next man now,
To make a fair round dozen beneath the sod
Just as the good old custom used to vow.
In life and death alike, let's not pretend
Anyone mourns for such a vagrant's end.

Adapted from François Villon,
A Ballade with which Villon Concludes his Testament

In the hand of a giant. His own giant! Not bad, eh? No reason to be sad about it. If only the Black Prince had looked rather livelier! If, if, if, Fenoglio, he told himself. If only you'd finished writing the words for Mortimer! If only you had some idea how this story is to go on now . . .

The huge fingers held him both firmly and carefully, as if they were used to carrying small humans around. Not necessarily a reassuring idea. Fenoglio really didn't want to become some giant child's toy. He had little doubt that it would be one of the nastiest ways of meeting one's end. But would anyone ask his opinion? No.

Which brings us back to the one crucial question, thought Fenoglio as his stomach, bumped about as it was, slowly but surely began to feel as if he'd eaten too many of Minerva's stuffed pigs' trotters. The one great crucial question.

Was there another man writing this story?

Was there a scribbler sitting somewhere in the hills that he himself had described so vividly, another writer who had sent him falling into this giant's hand? Or was the wretch sitting in the other world, the real world that hadn't been written, the way he used to sit there himself, putting *Inkheart* down on paper?

Oh, come on! What would that make you, Fenoglio? he asked himself, both annoyed and badly shaken, as he always was when that question occurred to him. No, he wasn't dangling from strings like the stupid puppet that Battista sometimes showed in marketplaces (although it did look a little like him). No, no, no. No strings for Fenoglio, no strings controlling either his words or his fate. He liked to keep his life in his own hands and didn't want any interference – although he admitted that he himself was very fond of pulling strings. But there it was: his story had simply swerved off course. No one was writing it. It was writing itself! And now it had come up with this stupid idea of the giant carrying him off!

Although his stomach rebelled, Fenoglio cast another glance at the depths below him. It was definitely a long way down, but why should that bother him after he'd fallen from the tree like a ripe fruit? The sight of the Black Prince gave considerably more cause for concern. He really did look alarmingly lifeless lying in the giant's other hand. What a shame. All the trouble he'd gone to to keep the man alive – all the words, the herbs in the snow, Roxane's nursing, all for nothing! Damn it! Fenoglio swore so loudly that the giant raised him to his eyes to look at him. This was too much!

Would it help to smile? Was it any use talking to him? Well, if you don't know the answer, Fenoglio, you old fool, he told himself, then who does?

The giant stopped. He was still staring at him. He had opened his fingers out slightly, and Fenoglio took the opportunity of stretching his old limbs.

Words, words were wanted again – and of course, as always, they had to be exactly right. Perhaps it was a blessing to be mute and unable to rely on words at all!

'Er . . .' What a wretched start, Fenoglio! 'Er. What's your name?' Oh, for heaven's sake!

The giant puffed air into his face and said something. The sounds that passed his lips were certainly words, but Fenoglio didn't understand them. How could that be possible?

Good heavens, how the giant was looking at him! Fenoglio's eldest grandson had looked like that when he found a big black beetle in his kitchen. The boy was both fascinated and troubled by it. And then the beetle began wriggling, and Pippo had dropped it in alarm and trodden on it. So keep still, Fenoglio! No wriggling, not the least little wriggle, however much your old bones ache. Good God, those fingers. Each of them as long as one of his own arms!

But clearly the giant had lost interest in him for the moment. He was examining his other catch with obvious concern. Finally he shook the Black Prince as if he were a watch that had run down, and sighed when he still didn't move.

With another deep sigh he sank to his knees – astonishingly gently, given his size – looked sadly at the black face, and then carefully laid the Prince on the thick moss under the trees. It was just what Fenoglio's grandchildren had done with the dead birds they took away from their cat. They'd had exactly the same look on their faces as they laid the small bodies to rest among his roses. Pippo used to make a cross out of twigs for every dead animal, but the giant didn't do that for the Black Prince. He didn't bury him either. He just covered him with dry leaves, very carefully, as if he didn't want to disturb his sleep. Then he rose to his feet again, looked at Fenoglio – perhaps to make sure that he, at least, was still breathing – and went on, every stride as long as a dozen human footsteps, perhaps more. Going where? Away from everything, Fenoglio, far away!

He felt those mighty fingers closing more tightly around him again, and then – he couldn't believe his ears! – the giant began humming the same tune that Roxane sang to the children in the evening. Did giants sing human songs? Whether they did or not, this one was obviously happy with himself and the world, even if the toy with the black face was broken. Perhaps he was thinking about giving the other strange creature that had fallen into his hand so suddenly to his son. Oh no! Fenoglio shuddered. Suppose the giant child pulled him apart the way children sometimes dismember insects?

You fool, he thought, you arrogant old fool! Loredan was right. Delusions of grandeur, that's your trouble! How could you think there are words to control a giant?

Another stride, and then another . . . goodbye for ever, Ombra. Presumably he'd never find out now what became of the children. And Mortimer.

Fenoglio closed his eyes. And suddenly he thought he heard his grandchildren's high, insistent voices: *Grandfather, play dead for us.* Of course! Nothing easier. How often he'd lain there on his sofa without moving, even when they prodded his stomach and his wrinkled cheeks with their little fingers. *Play dead.*

Fenoglio uttered a loud groan, made his limbs go limp and fixed his eyes.

There. The giant stopped and looked at him in dismay. Keep your breathing shallow, Fenoglio told himself. It would be better not to breathe at all, but then your stupid old head would probably burst.

When the giant puffed into his face once again he almost sneezed. But Fenoglio's grandchildren had puffed in his face too, although with considerably smaller mouths, and breath that didn't smell quite so strong. Keep still, Fenoglio.

Still.

The mighty face became a mask of disappointment. Another sigh rose from that broad chest. A cautious prod with his forefinger, a few incomprehensible words, and the giant knelt down. The downward plunge made Fenoglio feel dizzy, but he went on playing dead. The giant looked around for help, as if someone might come fluttering down from the trees to revive his toy. A few snowflakes fell from the grey sky – it was getting colder again – and settled on the giant's huge arms. They were as green as the moss all around, as grey as the bark of the trees, and then finally white, as the snow began to fall more thickly.

The giant sighed and murmured to himself. Obviously he really was severely disappointed. Then he put Fenoglio down on the ground as carefully as he had set down the Black

Prince, gave him one last experimental prod with his finger –
don't move, Fenoglio told himself! – and sprinkled a handful
of dry oak leaves on his face. They had woodlice in them, and
other creatures of the forest floor, most of which had a great
many legs, and all of them immediately looked for new hiding
places in Fenoglio's clothes. Keep playing dead, he thought;
didn't Pippo once put a caterpillar on your face? And much to
his disappointment, you still didn't move!

And he did not move, not even when something very hairy
crawled over his nose. He waited for the footsteps to go away
and the ground beneath him to stop vibrating like a drum.
Away went the helper he had called. Away he went, leaving
Fenoglio alone again with all his other creations. Now what?

All was still. There was only the faintest vibration left in
the distance, and Fenoglio pushed the dead leaves off his face
and chest and sat up, groaning. His legs felt as if someone had
been sitting on them, but they would still carry him. But
which way should he go? Follow the giant's footsteps back-
wards, of course, he thought. After all, they ought to take you
straight back to the tree with the nests. You'll be able to read
the tracks easily enough for yourself.

There. There was the last footprint. How his ribs hurt! He
wondered if one of them was broken. If so, he too would have
a claim on Roxane's attentions at last. Not an unpleasant
prospect. Although something else awaited him on his return:
Signora Loredan's sharp tongue. She'd certainly have something to say about his experiment with the giant. And then
there was the Milksop . . .

Involuntarily, Fenoglio quickened his pace in spite of his
aching ribs. Suppose the Milksop had come back and brought
them all down from the tree by now, Loredan and the

children, Meggie and Minerva. Roxane and all the others? Oh, why hadn't he simply written that the Milksop and his men were struck down by the plague? That was the trouble with writing: there were such an infinite number of turns the story could take. How were you to know which one was right? Go on, admit it, Fenoglio, he thought, a giant just sounded more magnificent. Quite apart from the fact that the plague would hardly have stayed down at the foot of the tree.

For a moment he stood listening, afraid the monster might come back. Monster, Fenoglio? What did that giant do that was so monstrous? Did he bite off your head or tear a leg off? There you are, then.

Even what happened to the Black Prince had been an accident. Where was the place where the Prince had been left? Everything looked the same under the trees, and the giant's strides were so long that you could lose your way between his footprints.

Fenoglio looked up at the sky. Snowflakes settled on his forehead. Darkness was falling too. That was all he needed! He immediately remembered every creature with which he had populated the night in this world. He wouldn't want to meet a single one of them. There! What was that? Footsteps! He stumbled back against the nearest tree.

'Inkweaver!'

A man was coming towards him. Battista? Fenoglio was so glad to see his pockmarked face! He felt there wasn't a more beautiful face in the whole world.

'You're alive!' cried Battista as he came up. 'We thought the giant had eaten you!'

'The Black Prince . . .' Fenoglio was truly surprised to feel such pain in his heart for the Prince.

Battista led him away. 'I know. The bear found him.'

'Is he . . .?'

Battista smiled. 'No, he's as alive as you. Although I'm not sure whether all his bones are still unbroken. Seems like Death just doesn't fancy the taste of him! First poison, now a giant – or maybe the White Women simply don't like his face! But we'd better make sure we get back to the nests as soon as we can. I'm afraid the Milksop will come back. He's certainly as terrified of his brother-in-law as he was of the giant!'

The Black Prince was sitting among the roots of the tree where the giant had laid him to rest, his back against the trunk, while the bear tenderly licked his face. The leaves that the giant had so considerately placed over him still clung to his clothes and his hair. He was alive! To his own annoyance, Fenoglio felt a tear running down his nose. He could have thrown his arms around the Prince's neck.

'Inkweaver! How did you get away?' His voice showed that he was in pain, and Battista gently pushed him back when he tried to sit up straighter.

'Oh, you showed me how, Prince!' said Fenoglio hoarsely. 'The giant was obviously only interested in live toys.'

'Just as well for us,' replied the Prince, closing his eyes. He deserves better, thought Fenoglio. Better than so much pain and all that fighting.

Something rustled in the undergrowth. Fenoglio spun round in alarm, but it was only two more robbers and Farid, with a stretcher made of branches. The boy nodded to him, but he clearly wasn't half as glad as the others to see him safe. How those black eyes were looking at him! The fact was, Farid knew too much about Fenoglio and the part he played in this world. Don't look at me so accusingly, he wanted to protest.

What else were we to do? Meggie thought it was a good idea too – well, to be honest, she had expressed a few doubts.

'I don't understand where that giant came from so suddenly!' said Battista. 'Even when I was a child the giants were little more than a fairy tale. I don't know any of the strolling players who ever set eyes on one, except for Dustfinger, and he would always venture further into the mountains than the rest of us.'

Without a word, Farid turned his back on Fenoglio and cut a few more twigs for the stretcher. Presumably the bear would happily have carried his master on his furry back, and Battista had some difficulty in persuading him to get out of the way when they lifted the Black Prince and put him on the stretcher. Only when his master spoke gently to him did the bear calm down, and he lumbered along beside the Prince looking dejected.

Well, come on, Fenoglio, the old man told himself, what are you waiting for? Go after them, he muttered as he followed Battista, his legs aching. No one's going to carry you. And you'd better pray to whatever you believe in that the Milksop isn't back!'

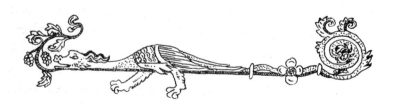

64

Light

All these, however, were mere terrors of the night, phantoms of the mind that walk in darkness.

Washington Irving, *The Legend of Sleepy Hollow*

The fire was everywhere. It ate its way along the walls and licked down from the ceiling, crept out of the stone, and gave as much light as if the sun itself had risen in the darkened castle to scorch his bloated flesh.

The Adderhead shouted at the Piper until he was hoarse. He struck him in his bony chest with his fists, longing to ram the man's silver nose into his face, deep into the sound flesh that he envied him so much.

The Fire-Dancer was back from the dead for the second time, and the Bluejay had escaped from one of the cells which, so his father-in-law had always claimed, no prisoner ever left alive. 'Flown away!' whispered his soldiers. 'The bird has flown, and now he's roaming the castle like a hungry wolf. He'll kill us all!'

The Adderhead had handed over the two guards of the cell

605

to Thumbling for punishment, but the Bluejay had already killed six more, and the rumours grew louder with every dead man they found. His soldiers were running away, over the bridge or along the tunnel under the lake, anywhere to get away from the bewitched castle that now belonged to the Bluejay and the Fire-Dancer. Some of them had even jumped into the lake, never to climb out again. The rest were shaking in their shoes like a crowd of terrified children, while the painted walls burnt and the light scorched the Adder's brain and his skin.

'Bring me Four-Eyes!' he shouted, and Thumbling dragged Orpheus into his room. Jacopo crept in at the door too, like a worm that had dug its way out of damp earth.

'Put out the fire!' How his throat hurt! As if the sparks were in there too. 'Put it out at once and bring me back the Bluejay, or I'll cut your slimy tongue out! Is this why you persuaded me to throw him into that cell? So that he could fly away?'

The pale-blue eyes blurred behind the man's glasses – and the flattering tongue sounded as if it had been bathed in precious oil. But it was impossible to mistake the fear in it.

'I told the Piper he ought to post more than two guards outside the cell,' said the sly little snake. So much cleverer than Silvernose, so much mock innocence, even the Adderhead couldn't quite see through it. 'Only a few more hours and the Jay would have been pleading with you to let him bind the book. Ask the guards. They heard him down there writhing like a worm on the hook, groaning and sighing—'

'The guards are dead. I handed them over to Thumbling and told him to make sure their screams could be heard all over the castle.'

Thumbling adjusted his black gloves. 'Four-Eyes is telling the truth. The guards kept bleating over and over that the Bluejay was in a very bad state down in that cell. They heard him screaming and groaning, and they checked a couple of times to make sure he was still alive. I'd like to know how you did it,' he said, his hawk-like gaze resting on Orpheus for a moment. 'But anyway, they said the Jay kept whispering one name again and again . . .'

The Adderhead put his hands over his burning eyes. 'What name? My daughter's name, by any chance?'

'No, the name of some other woman,' replied Thumbling.

'Resa. His wife, Your Highness.' Orpheus smiled. The Adderhead was not sure whether his smile expressed deference or self-satisfaction.

The Piper cast a vicious glance at Orpheus. 'My men will soon have caught his wife. And his daughter too!'

'And what use is that to me now?' The Adderhead pressed his fists into his eyes, but he could still see the fire all the same. Pain was cutting him into slices, stinking slices, and now the man to whom he owed it all had fooled him for the second time. He needed the Book! A new Book to heal his flesh. It was hanging off his bones like mud – heavy, damp, stinking mud.

Bluejay.

'Take two of those who tried to run away up on to the bridge where everyone can see them,' he said grimly. 'And you, fetch that dog of yours!' he snapped at Orpheus. 'It must be hungry.'

The men screamed like animals as the black shadow devoured them, and the Adderhead imagined that the cries echoing all the way to his room were the Bluejay's. The man owed him many screams.

Orpheus listened with a smile, and the Night-Mare returned to him like a faithful dog after its meal. Panting, it merged with Orpheus's shadow, and its darkness made even the Adderhead shudder. Orpheus, however, adjusted his glasses with a satisfied expression. Their round lenses reflected the sparks burning on the walls. Four-Eyes.

'I'll bring you back the Bluejay,' he said, and even against his will the Adderhead felt the confidence in that velvety voice soothing him once again. 'He hasn't escaped you, however it may seem. I have bound him in invisible chains. I forged them myself with my black art, and wherever he's hiding those chains will pull at him and bring back old pain. He knows I am the one sending him the pain, and he knows it will never end as long as I live. So he'll try to kill me. Set Thumbling to guard my room, and the Bluejay will stumble into his arms. He's not our problem any more. But the Fire-Dancer is.'

The hatred in his pale face surprised the Adderhead. Usually such hatred comes only after love.

'So, he's back from the dead again!' Loathing clung to every word that Orpheus spoke, slowing his smooth tongue. 'He's acting as if he were lord of this castle, but take my advice and his fire will soon be extinguished!'

'And what advice might that be?'

Orpheus smiled.

'Send Thumbling to your daughter. Have her thrown into one of the cells, and spread word that she helped the Bluejay to escape. That'll stop all the nonsense talked that makes your soldiers tremble with fear. As for her beautiful maidservant, lock her up in the cage where the Bluejay himself was held. And tell Thumbling he needn't treat the girl too gently.'

The fire was still reflected in Orpheus's glasses. They made his eyes almost invisible, and for a moment the Adderhead felt something he had never felt before – fear of another man. It was an interesting sensation. Like a tingling on the back of the neck, a slight pressure in the stomach . . .

'Exactly what I planned to do,' he said – and read in Orpheus's face that he knew he was lying. I'll have to kill him, thought the Adderhead. As soon as the new Book is bound.

No man should be cleverer than his master. Particularly not when he controlled so dangerous a dog.

65

Made Visible

But writing broke away from the gods and in that rupture
much of its power was lost.

Salman Rushdie, *The Power of the Pen*

'You must go! You're not safe anywhere in this castle!'
Dustfinger kept saying it, again and again, and Mo kept
shaking his head.

'I have to find the White Book.'

'Let me look for it. I'll write the three words. Even I can
write well enough for that!'

'No, that wasn't the bargain. Suppose Death comes for
Meggie all the same? I bound the Book, I must rid the world
of it. And the Adder wants to see you dead as much as me.'

'I'll simply slip out of my skin again.'

'You only just found your way back into it last time.'

How familiar the two of them sounded with each other.
Like two sides of a coin, like two faces of the same man.

'What bargain are you talking about?'

610

They looked at Resa as if they both wished her far, far away. Mo was pale, but his eyes were dark with anger, and his hand kept going to his old wound. What had they done to him down in that terrible cell?

Dust lay like snow in the room where they were hiding. The plaster on the ceiling was so damp that it had crumbled away in places. The Castle in the Lake was sick. Perhaps it was already dying, but on its walls lambs still slept beside wolves, dreaming of a world that never was. The room had two narrow windows. A dead tree stood in the courtyard below.

Walls, parapets, oriel towers, bridges . . . a stony trap, and Resa wanted her wings back. How her skin was itching. As if the feathered quills were just waiting to pierce through again.

'Mo, what kind of bargain?' She came between the two men.

When he told her she began crying. Now at last she understood. He was promised to Death whether he stayed or fled. Caught in a trap made of stone and ink. And so was their daughter.

He took her in his arms, but he wasn't really with her. He was still down in the cell, drowning in hate and fear. His heart was beating so violently that she was afraid it might break in his breast.

'I'll kill him,' she heard him say as she wept into his shoulder. 'I ought to have done it long ago. And after that I'll look for the Book.'

She knew only too well who he meant. Orpheus. He pushed her gently away from him and picked up his sword. It was covered with blood, but he wiped the blade clean on his sleeve. He still wore the black clothes of a bookbinder, although it was a long time since that had been his trade. He made for the door with determination, but Dustfinger barred his way.

'What's your idea?!' he said. 'Very well, so Orpheus read the words, but you are making them come true!' He raised his hands, and fire wrote the words in the air, terrible words, all speaking of only one thing. The Bluejay's Last Song.

Mo stretched out his hand as if to extinguish them, but they scorched his fingers and burnt his heart.

'Orpheus is just waiting for you to come to him!' said Dustfinger. 'He's going to serve you up to the Adderhead on a platter made of ink. Resist it! It's not a pleasant feeling to read the words that guide your actions. No one knows that better than I do, but they didn't come true for me either. They have only as much power as you give them. You won't go to Orpheus, I will. I don't know much about killing. Even dying didn't teach me that, but I can steal the books from which he takes the words. And once you can think straight again, we'll look for the White Book together.'

'Suppose the Adder's soldiers find Mo here first?' Resa was still staring at the burning words. She read them again and again.

Dustfinger passed his hand over the picture fading on the walls of the room, and the painted wolf began to move. 'I'll leave you a watchdog, though not quite such a fierce one as Orpheus's, but it will howl when the soldiers come, and I hope it can hold them off long enough to give you time to find another hiding place. Fire will teach the Adder's men to fear every shadow.'

The wolf with its burning coat leapt off the wall and followed Dustfinger out. However, the words that had been written in the air were still there, and Resa read them again:

But when the Bluejay would not bow to the Adderhead only one man knew what to do, a stranger who had come from far away to be the Adder's adviser. He understood that the Bluejay could be broken by only one man, and that was himself. So he summoned up all that the Bluejay didn't dare to acknowledge: the fear that made him fearless, the anger that made him invincible. He had him thrown into darkness to fight himself there – to fight the pain still inside him, never forgotten, never healed, all the fear that fetters and chains had given him, the anger that had sown the seeds of fear. He painted dreadful pictures in his heart, pictures of . . .

Resa read no more. The words were too terrible. But the fire had burnt the last sentences into her memory.

. . . and the Bluejay, broken by his own darkness, pleaded with the Adderhead to be allowed to bind him a second Book, even more beautiful than the first. But as soon as the Silver Prince had the Book in his hands he condemned him to die the slowest of all deaths, and the minstrels sang the Last Song of the Bluejay.

Mo had turned his back on the words. He stood there with the dust of countless years around him like grey snow, looking at his hands as if he wasn't sure whether they still did as he told them or obeyed the words burning behind him.

'Mo?' Resa kissed him. She knew that he wouldn't like what she was about to do.

He looked at her absently, his eyes full of darkness.

'I will look for the White Book. I'll find it and write the three words in it for you.' *So that the Adderhead dies before Orpheus's words come true,* she added in her mind, *and before the name Fenoglio gave you kills you.*

By the time Mo understood what she had said, she was

613

already lifting the seeds to her mouth. He tried to knock them out of her hand, but she already had them under her tongue.

'No, Resa!'

She flew through the fiery letters. Their heat singed her breast.

'Resa!'

No, this time he was the one who must wait. Stay where you are, she thought. Please, Mo.

66

Love Disguised as Hate

Where did this love come from? I don't know; it came to
me like a thief in the night [. . .]. All I could hope was that
my crimes were so monstrous that the love was no bigger
than a mustard-seed in the shadow of them, and I wished
I'd committed even greater ones to hide it more deeply still
. . . But the mustard-seed had taken root and was growing,
and the little green shoot was splitting my heart wide open
[. . .].

Philip Pullman, *The Amber Spyglass*

The Adderhead wanted fairy blood, a whole tub full, to
bathe his itching skin. Orpheus was writing fairies' nests
into the bare branches of the cherry trees growing under his
window when he heard soft footsteps behind him. He dropped
his pen so abruptly that it spattered Ironstone's grey feet with
ink. The Bluejay!

Orpheus thought he could already feel the sword between
his shoulder blades: after all, he himself had stoked the
Bluejay's blood-lust, drowning him in anger and helpless rage.

How had he managed to get past the guards? There were three outside his door, and Thumbling was waiting in the next room.

However, when Orpheus turned he found not Mortimer but Dustfinger standing behind him.

What was he doing here? Why wasn't he outside the cage where his sobbing daughter sat, letting the Night-Mare eat him?

Dustfinger.

Less than a year ago the mere thought of seeing him would have made Orpheus drunk with happiness – in the bleak room where he was living at the time, surrounded by books that spoke of the longing in his heart but never satisfied it. Longing for a world that bowed to his will, longing to escape his grey failure of a life at last, to become the Orpheus that slumbered inside him, the man whom those who mocked him never saw. Perhaps longing was the wrong word. It sounded too tame, too gentle and resigned. It was a raging desire that drove him, desire for everything he didn't have.

Oh yes, the sight of Dustfinger would have made him very happy back then. But now his heart beat faster for other reasons. The hate he felt still tasted like love, but that didn't tame it. And suddenly Orpheus saw the opportunity for such perfect revenge that he spontaneously smiled.

'Well, if it isn't my old childhood friend. My faithless friend.' Orpheus pushed Violante's Bluejay book under the parchment on which he was writing.

Ironstone ducked behind the inkwell in fear. Fear. Not necessarily a bad feeling. Sometimes it could be very stimulating.

'I suppose you're here to steal a few more books from me?' he went on. 'That won't do the Bluejay any good. The words have been read, and they'll pursue him. That's the price you pay for making a story your own. But how about you? Have you seen your daughter recently?'

Dustfinger's expression gave nothing away. He really didn't know yet! Ah, love. What a perfect tool of revenge. Even the fearless heart that Dustfinger had brought back from the dead was powerless against it.

'You really should go to her. She's sobbing in the most heart-rending way, tearing her beautiful hair.'

The look in his eyes! Got you, thought Orpheus. Got you both on the hook now, you and the Bluejay.

'My black dog is guarding your daughter,' he went on, and every word tasted as good as spiced wine. 'I expect she's terribly afraid. But I've ordered my dog not to feast on her sweet flesh and soul . . . just yet.'

There – so fear *could* sting Dustfinger after all. His unscarred face turned pale. He stared at Orpheus's shadow, but the Night-Mare did not emerge from it. The Night-Mare was outside the cage where Brianna sat weeping and calling for her father.

'I'll kill you if it so much as touches her. I don't know much about killing, but for you I'd learn!' Dustfinger's face seemed so much more vulnerable without the scars. His clothes and hair were covered with fiery sparks.

Orpheus had to admit it – the Fire-Dancer was still his favourite character. Whatever Dustfinger did to him, however often he betrayed him, it didn't change that. His heart loved him like a dog. All the more reason to remove him from this story once and for all – although it was still a shame. Orpheus could hardly believe he had come here only to protect the Bluejay. Such high-minded nobility didn't suit him at all. No, it was time the Fire-Dancer returned to playing a part that was more like himself.

'You can ransom your daughter!' Orpheus let every word melt on his tongue.

Oh, sweet revenge. The marten on Dustfinger's shoulder bared its teeth. Nasty brute.

Dustfinger stroked its brown coat. 'How?'

Orpheus rose to his feet. 'Well . . . first by putting out the lights you've so skilfully brought to this castle. At once.'

The sparks on the walls flared up as if reaching out to burn him, but then they died down. Only those on Dustfinger's hair and clothes still shone. Yes. What a terrible weapon love could be. Was any knife sharper? Time to thrust it even deeper into his faithless heart.

'Your daughter is crying her eyes out in the same cage that held the Bluejay,' Orpheus went on. 'Of course she looks much more beautiful in there, with that fiery hair. Like a precious bird . . .'

The sparks swirled around Dustfinger like a red mist.

'Bring us the bird who really belongs in that cage. Bring us the Bluejay and your lovely daughter is free. But if you don't bring him, I'll feed my black dog on her flesh and her soul. Don't look at me like that! As far as I'm aware you've played the part of traitor once already. I wanted to write you a better part, but you wouldn't hear of it!'

Dustfinger said nothing, just looked at him.

'You stole the book from me!' Orpheus's voice almost failed him, the words still tasted so bitter. 'You ranged yourself on the bookbinder's side, although he snatched you out of your own story, instead of backing me, the man who brought you home! That was cruel, very cruel.' Tears rose to his eyes.

'What did you think – that I'd just accept such treachery? No, my plan was to send you back to the dead without a soul, hollow as an insect sucked dry, but I like this revenge even better. I'll make you a traitor again. How that will pierce the bookbinder's noble heart!'

The flames were leaping from the walls again. They licked up from the floor scorching Orpheus's boots. Ironstone moaned with fear and buried his head in his glass arms. Dustfinger's anger showed in the flames, burning on his face, raining down from the ceiling in sparks.

'Keep your fire away from me!' Orpheus cried. 'I'm the only one who can command the Night-Mare, and your daughter will be the first it eats when it next feels hungry. Which will be soon. I want a trail of fire laid to wherever the Bluejay is hiding, and I'll be the man who shows it to the Adderhead, understand?'

The flames on the walls went out for the second time. Even the candles on the desk burnt out, and all was dark in Orpheus's room. Only Dustfinger himself was still enveloped in sparks, as if the fire were in him.

Why did the look in his eyes make Orpheus feel such shame? Why did his heart still feel love? He closed his eyes, and when he opened them again Dustfinger was gone.

As Orpheus stepped out of the door the guards who were supposed to be keeping watch outside his room came stumbling along the corridor, their faces twisted with fear. 'The Bluejay was here!' they stammered. 'He was all made of fire, and then he suddenly dissolved into smoke. Thumbling has gone to tell the Adderhead.'

Idiots. He'd feed them all to the Night-Mare.

Don't lose your temper, he told himself. You'll soon bring

the Adderhead the real Bluejay. And your Night-Mare will eat the Fire-Dancer too.

'Tell the Silver Prince to send some men to the courtyard under my window,' he snarled at the guards. 'They'll find enough fairies' nests there to fill a tub with their blood for him.'

Then he went back to his room and read the nests into the trees. But he saw Dustfinger's face through the letters, as if he were living behind them. As if all the words spoke only of him.

67

The Other Name

I write your name. Two syllables. Two vowels. Your name inflates you, is bigger than you. You repose in a corner, sleeping; your name awakes you. I write it. You could not be named otherwise. Your name is your juice, your taste, your savor. Called by another name, you vanish. I write it. Your name.

Susan Sontag, *The Letter Scene*

The Castle in the Lake had been built to protect a few unhappy children from the world, but the longer Mo walked in its corridors the more he felt as if it had been waiting for another task to fulfil one day: to drown the Bluejay in his own darkness between its painted walls. Dustfinger's fiery wolf ran ahead as if it knew the way, and while Mo followed he killed four more soldiers. The castle belonged to the Fire-Dancer and the Bluejay, he read it in their faces, and the anger that Orpheus aroused in him made him strike so often that their blood drenched his black clothes. Black. Orpheus's words had turned his heart black too.

You ought to have asked them which way to go instead of killing them, he thought bitterly as he bent to pass through an arched gateway. A flock of doves fluttered up. No swifts. Not one. Where was Resa? Well, where did he suppose? In the Adderhead's bedchamber, searching for the Book he had once bound to save her. A swift could fly fast, very fast, and his own steps were heavy as lead from the words Orpheus had written.

There. Was that the tower into which the Adderhead had retreated? It was as Dustfinger had described it. Two more soldiers . . . they staggered back in horror when they saw him. Kill them quickly, Mo, before they scream. Blood. Blood as red as fire. Hadn't red once been his favourite colour? Now the sight of it made him feel ill. He clambered over the dead men, took the silver-grey cloak from one of them, put on the other man's helmet. Maybe the disguise would spare him the killing if he met any more of them.

The next corridor looked familiar, but there were no guards in sight. The wolf loped on, but Mo stopped outside a door and pushed it open.

The dead books. The Lost Library.

He lowered his sword and went in. Dustfinger's sparks glowed in here too, burning the smell of mould and decay out of the air.

Books. He leant the bloodstained sword against the wall, stroked their stained spines, and felt the burden of the words lifting from his shoulders. He was not the Bluejay, not Silvertongue, just Mortimer. Orpheus had written nothing about the bookbinder.

Mo picked up a book. Poor thing, it was a wreck. He took up another and then another – and heard a rustling sound. His hand immediately went to his sword, and Orpheus's words reached for his heart again.

A few piles of books fell over. An arm pushed its way past all the printed corpses, followed by a second arm, without a hand. Balbulus.

'Ah, it's you they're looking for!' He straightened up, ink on the fingers of his left hand. 'Since I hid in here from the Piper, not a soldier's come through this door until today. I expect the mouldy smell keeps them away. But today there've been two here already. They've certainly kept a better watch on you than on me! So, how did you escape them?'

'With the help of fire and feathers,' said Mo, leaning his sword against the wall again. He didn't want to remember. He wanted to forget the Bluejay, just for a few moments, and find happiness instead of misery among parchment and leather-bound covers.

Balbulus followed his glance. No doubt he saw the longing in it. 'I've found a few books that are still good for something. Do you want to see them?'

Mo listened for sounds outside. The wolf was silent, but he thought he heard voices. No. They died away again.

Just for a few moments, then.

Balbulus gave him a book not much bigger than his hand. It had a few holes nibbled in it, but it had obviously escaped mildew. The binding was very well made. His fingers had missed leafing through written pages so much. His eyes were so hungry for words that carried him away, instead of capturing and controlling him. How very much his hand wanted to hold a knife that cut not flesh but paper.

'What's that?' whispered Balbulus.

It had turned dark. The fire on the walls had gone out, and

Mo couldn't see the book in his hands any more.

'Silvertongue?'

He turned.

Dustfinger stood in the doorway, a shadow rimmed with fire.

'I've been talking to Orpheus.' His voice sounded different. The composure that Death had left in him was gone. His old desperation, almost forgotten by both of them, was back.

'What's happened?'

Dustfinger lured fire back out of the darkness and made it build a cage among the books, a cage with a girl in tears inside it.

Brianna. Mo saw on Dustfinger's face the same fear he had so often felt himself. Flesh of his flesh. Child. Such a powerful word. The most powerful of all.

Dustfinger had only to look at him, and Mo read it all in his eyes: the Night-Mare watching his daughter, the price he would have to pay to ransom her.

'So?' Mo listened for sounds outside. 'Are the soldiers already out there?'

'I haven't laid the trail yet.'

Mo sensed Dustfinger's fear sharply, as if Meggie were the girl in the cage, as if it were her weeping that came out of the fire.

'What are you waiting for? Lead them here!' he said. 'It's time my hands bound a book again – even if the job must never be finished. Let them capture the bookbinder, not the Bluejay. They won't notice the difference. And I'll banish the Bluejay forever, bury him deep in the dungeon cell below, with the words that Orpheus wrote.'

Dustfinger breathed into the darkness, and instead of the

cage the fire formed the sign that Mo had imprinted on the spines of so many books: a unicorn's head. 'If that's what you want,' he said quietly. 'But if you're playing the bookbinder again, then what part is mine?'

'Your daughter's rescuer,' said Mo. 'My wife's protector. Resa has gone to look for the White Book. Help her to find it, and bring it to me.'

So that I can write the end in it, he thought. Three words, that's all it takes. And suddenly a thought occurred to him and made him smile in all the darkness. Orpheus had not written anything at all about Resa, not a single binding word. Who else had he forgotten?

68

Back

Sometimes a thousand twangling instruments
Will hum about mine ears; and sometimes voices,
That, if I then had wak'd after long sleep,
Will make me sleep again: and then, in dreaming,
The clouds methought would open and show riches
Ready to drop upon me; that, when I wak'd
I cried to dream again.
> William Shakespeare, *The Tempest, Act 3 Scene 2*

Roxane was singing again. For the children who couldn't sleep for fear of the Milksop. And everything Meggie had ever heard about her voice was true. Even the tree seemed to be listening to her, the birds in its topmost branches, the animals living among its roots, the stars in the dark sky. There was so much comfort in Roxane's voice, although what she sang was often sad, and Meggie heard her longing for Dustfinger in every word. It was a comfort to hear about longing, even if it filled her heart to the brim. Longing for sleep free of fear, and carefree days, for firm ground underfoot, a full stomach, the streets of Ombra, mothers . . . and fathers.

Meggie was sitting high up in the tree, outside the nest where Fenoglio had sat writing. She didn't know who to worry about first: Fenoglio and the Black Prince; Farid, who had followed the giant with Battista; or Doria, who had climbed down again to find out if the Milksop had really left. She tried not even to think of her parents, but suddenly Roxane began the song about the Bluejay that Meggie loved most, because it described his captivity in the Castle of Night with his daughter. Some of the songs were more heroic, but only this one also spoke of her father, and it was her father she missed. 'Mo?' she would so much have liked to ask, putting her head on his shoulder. 'Do you think the giant is taking Fenoglio to his children as a toy? Do you think he'll tread on Farid and Battista and crush them if they try to rescue the Prince? Do you think anyone can love two boys with just one heart? Have you seen Resa? And how are you, Mo, how are you?'

'Has the Bluejay killed the Adderhead yet?' one of the children had asked Elinor only yesterday. 'Will he come back soon to save us from the Milksop?'

'Of course he will!' Elinor had replied, glancing at Meggie. Of course . . .

'The boy's not back yet,' she heard Elfbane say to Woodenfoot down below her. 'Shall I go and look for him?'

'Why do that?' replied Woodenfoot, lowering his voice. 'He'll come back if he can. And if he doesn't, then they've caught him. I'm sure the soldiers are down there somewhere. I just hope Battista will be careful when he comes back himself.'

'How can he be careful?' asked Elfbane, with a grim laugh. 'The giant behind him, the Milksop in front of him, and the Prince probably dead. We'll soon be striking up our own last song, and it won't sound half as good as the songs Roxane sings.'

Meggie buried her face in her arms. Don't think about it, Meggie, she told herself, just don't think about it. Listen to Roxane. Dream that everything will be all right. That they'll all come back safe and sound: Mo, Resa, Fenoglio, the Black Prince, Farid – and Doria. What does the Milksop do to prisoners? No, don't think about it, don't ask such questions.

Voices drifted up from down below. Leaning forward, she tried to make something out in the darkness. Was that Battista's voice? She saw fire, just a small flame, but it gave a bright light. There was Fenoglio! And the Black Prince on a stretcher beside him.

'Farid?' she called down.

'Hush!' hissed Elfbane, and Meggie pressed her hand to her mouth. The robbers were letting down ropes, and a net to take the Prince.

'Quick, Battista!' Roxane's voice sounded so different when she wasn't singing. 'They're coming!'

She didn't need to say any more. Horses snorted among the trees, twigs broke under the tread of many boots. The robbers threw down more ropes, and some let themselves down the trunk. Arrows came out of the darkness. Men swarmed out from the surrounding trees like silver beetles. 'Wait and see – they'll bide their time until Battista comes back. With the Prince!' Hadn't Doria said so? That was why he had gone down himself. And he hadn't come back.

Farid made the fire flare up. He and Battista placed themselves in front of the Black Prince to protect him. The bear was with them too.

'What is it? What's going on?' Elinor was kneeling beside

Meggie, her hair in wild confusion as if bristling with fear. 'I'd actually dropped off to sleep, would you believe it?'

Meggie did not reply. What could she do? Oh, what could she do? She made her way over to the forked branch where Roxane and the other women were kneeling. Only two of the robbers were with them. All the others were letting themselves down the trunk to help the Prince, but it was a long way to the ground, a terribly long way, and a rain of arrows came from below. Two men fell, screaming, and the women covered the children's eyes and ears.

'Where is he?' Elinor leant so far forward that Roxane pulled her back by force. 'Where is he?' she cried again. 'Someone tell me, is that old fool still alive?'

Fenoglio looked up at them as if he had heard her voice, his lined face full of fear, the fighting all around him. One man fell dead at his feet, and Fenoglio picked up his sword.

'Look at that, will you?' cried Elinor. 'What's he doing? Does he think he can play the hero in his own damn story?'

I must go down, thought Meggie. I must help Farid and look for Doria! Where was he? Lying dead somewhere among the trees? No, he can't be. Fenoglio wrote about him! Wonderful things. He can't be dead. All the same . . .

She ran to the ropes, but Elfbane stopped her. 'Climb up the tree!' he said urgently. 'All the women and children must get as far up the tree as they can!'

'Oh yes, and what are we going to do when we reach the top?' snapped Elinor. 'Wait for them to pick us off?'

There was no answer to that question.

'They have the Prince!' Minerva's voice sounded so desperate that everyone looked round. Some of the women began sobbing. Sure enough, they had the Black Prince. They were dragging him off the stretcher where he lay. The bear lay motionless beside him with an arrow in his coat. Battista had been captured too. Where was Farid?

Where the fire was.

Farid made it bite and burn, but Sootbird was there too, his leathery face pale above his red and black costume. Fire ate fire, the flames licked up the trunk. Meggie thought she could hear the tree groaning. Several smaller trees had already caught fire. The children were crying hard enough to melt anyone's heart.

Oh, Fenoglio, thought Meggie, we don't have much luck with the people we call to our aid. First Cosimo, now the giant.

The giant.

His face appeared among the trees as suddenly as if the mere word had summoned him. His skin had turned dark as the night, and he wore the reflection of the stars on his brow. One foot trod out the fire that was eating at the roots of their tree. The other foot missed Farid and Sootbird so narrowly that Meggie's own scream echoed in her ears.

'Yes! Yes, he's back!' she heard Fenoglio shout. He staggered towards the mighty feet and climbed on to one of its toes as if it were a lifeboat.

But the giant looked up at the crying children enquiringly, as if he had come for something that he couldn't find.

The Milksop's men abandoned their prisoners and ran for their lives again, with their lord in front on his snow-white horse. Only Sootbird stood his ground with a small troop, sending his fire to lick at the giant. The giant stared at the flames, bewildered, and stumbled back when they caught his toes.

'No, please!' Meggie called down. 'Please don't go away again. Help us!'

And suddenly Farid was standing on the giant's shoulder, making flakes of fire rain down from the night. They settled on the clothes of Sootbird and his men like burning burrs, until they flung themselves down on the forest floor and rolled over and over on the dry leaves. As for the giant, he looked at Farid in astonishment, plucked him off his shoulder as easily as a moth, and placed him on his raised palm. How large his fingers were. Terribly large. And how small Farid looked standing there beside them.

Sootbird and his men were still beating at their burning clothes. The giant stared down at them, irritated. He rubbed his ear as if their screams hurt him, closed his hand around Farid as if he were a precious find, and with the other hand flicked the screaming men away into the forest like a child brushing a spider off its clothes. Then he put his hand to his ear again and looked up at the tree, still searching for something – as if he had suddenly remembered what he had come for.

'Roxane!'

It was Darius's voice that Meggie heard echoing through the tree, hesitant and firm at the same time. 'Roxane! I think he came back because of you. Sing!'

631

69

In the Adderhead's Bedchamber

Resa flew after one of the servants who were carrying buckets of blood and water to the Adderhead's bedchamber. He sat there in a silver tub, red up to his neck, gasping and cursing, such a terrible sight that Resa feared for Mo more than ever. What revenge would make up for such suffering?

Thumbling looked around when she flew to the wardrobe by the door, but she ducked in good time. It could be useful to be small. Dustfinger's sparks were burning on the walls. Three soldiers were flicking at them with damp cloths, while the Adderhead put his bloodstained hand over his smarting eyes. His grandson stood beside the tub, arms folded, as if that would protect him from his grandfather's bad temper. What a small, thin child he was, as handsome as his father and

632

delicately built like his mother. But unlike Violante, Jacopo didn't resemble his grandfather at all, although he imitated the Adderhead's every gesture.

'She didn't.' He thrust out his chin. He had copied that from his mother, although presumably he didn't know it.

'Oh no? Then who else helped the Bluejay if not your mother?'

A servant poured the contents of his bucket over the Adderhead's back. Resa felt sick when she saw the blood running over the pale nape of his neck. Jacopo too looked at his grandfather with both fear and disgust – and quickly glanced away when the Adderhead caught him at it.

'Yes, you just look at me!' he snarled at his grandson. 'Your mother helped the man who did this to me.'

'She didn't. The Bluejay has flown away! Everyone says he can fly, and they say he's invulnerable too.'

The Adderhead laughed. His breath whistled. 'Invulnerable? I'll show you just how invulnerable he is once I've caught him again. I'll give you a knife and you can find out for yourself.'

'But you won't catch him.'

The Adderhead smacked his hand down in the bath of blood, splashing Jacopo's pale tunic with red. 'Watch out. You're getting more and more like your mother.'

Jacopo seemed to be wondering whether this was a good thing or not.

Where was the White Book? Resa looked around her. Chests, clothes thrown over a chair, the bed untidy. The Adderhead slept poorly. Where did he hide it? His life depended on the Book, his immortal life. Resa looked for a casket, perhaps a precious cloth in which it was wrapped, even though it stank and was rotting . . . but suddenly the room went completely dark, so dark that only sounds remained: the splashing of the bloody water, the soldiers breathing hard, Jacopo's cry of alarm.

'What's that?'

Dustfinger's sparks had suddenly died down. Resa felt the bird's heart in her breast beating even faster than usual. What had happened? Something must have happened, and it couldn't be anything good.

One of the soldiers lit a torch, putting his hand around the flame to keep it from dazzling his master.

'At last!' The Adderhead's voice sounded both relieved and surprised. He waved to the servants, and they went on pouring the contents of their buckets over his itching skin. Where had they caught all the fairies? Fairies slept at this time of year.

The door opened as if the story itself were answering her, and Orpheus came in. 'Well?' he asked with a deep bow. 'Were there enough fairies, Your Highness? Or shall I get you some more?'

'This will do for the time being.' The Adderhead filled his hands with the red water and dipped his face into it. 'Do you have anything to do with the fire going out?'

'Do I have anything to do with it?' Orpheus smiled with such self-satisfaction that Resa longed to fly down and peck his pale face to pieces with her beak. 'I do indeed,' he went on. 'I've persuaded the Fire-Dancer to change sides.'

No. It couldn't be true. He was lying.

The bird in her pecked at a fly, and Jacopo looked up. Keep your head down, Resa, she told herself, even though it's dark. She wished the feathers on her breast and throat weren't so white.

'Good. But I hope you didn't promise him any reward for it!' The Adderhead plunged deep into the bloody water. 'He's made me a laughing-stock to my men. I want to see him dead, and dead beyond recall this time. But that can wait. What about the Bluejay?'

'The Fire-Dancer will lead us to him. For no reward at all.' The words were terrible enough, but the beauty of Orpheus's voice made them even worse. 'He'll lay a trail of flames, and your soldiers will only have to follow it.'

No. No. Resa began trembling. Dustfinger surely hadn't betrayed Mo again. No.

A suppressed cry came from her bird-breast, and Jacopo looked up at her again. But even if he did see her, there was nothing there but a trembling swift lost in the dark human world.

'Is everything ready for the Bluejay to set to work at once?' asked Orpheus. 'The sooner he's finished, the sooner you can kill him.'

Oh, Meggie, what kind of being did you read here? Resa thought desperately. With his shining glasses and flatteringly beautiful voice, Orpheus seemed to her like a demon.

The Adderhead heaved himself out of his bath, groaning. He stood there as bloodstained as a newborn child. Jacopo instinctively flinched back, but his grandfather beckoned him closer.

'My lord, you need to stay in the bath longer for the blood to take effect!' said one of the servants.

'Later!' replied the Adderhead impatiently. 'You think I want to be sitting in the tub when they bring me my worst enemy? Give me those towels!' he told Jacopo sharply. 'And

635

quick, or do you want me to put you in the dark cell with your mother? Did I say you were getting more like her? No, it's your father you look like – more and more like him all the time.'

With a black look, Jacopo handed him the towels lying ready beside the tub.

'Clothes!'

The servants hurried over to the chests, and Resa hid in the dark again, but the voice of Orpheus followed her like a deadly scent.

'Your Grace, I . . . er . . .' He cleared his throat. 'I've kept my promise. The Bluejay will soon be your prisoner again, and he'll bind you a new book. I think I've earned a reward.'

'Oh, do you?' The servants were putting black garments on the Adderhead's blood-red skin. 'And what were you thinking of?'

'Well. Do you remember the book I mentioned to you? I would still very much like to have it back, and I'm sure you can find it for me. But if that can't be done at once –' oh, the vanity of the gesture as he smoothed his pale fair hair! '– I would also accept your daughter's hand in marriage as my reward for the delivery of the Bluejay.'

Orpheus.

Resa thought of the day when she had first set eyes on him, in Elinor's house, accompanied by Mortola and Basta. At the time she had only noticed that he didn't resemble the men with whom Mortola usually liked to surround herself. He looked strangely harmless, almost innocent, with that childlike face. How stupid she had been. He was worse than any of them, much, much worse.

'Your Highness.' That was the Piper's voice. Resa hadn't

heard him come in. 'We've caught the Bluejay. Him and the book illuminator. Shall we bring the Jay straight to you?'

'Aren't you going to tell us how you caught him?' purred Orpheus. 'Did you pick up his scent with that silver nose of yours?'

The Piper replied in as reluctant a voice as if every word bit his tongue. 'The Fire-Dancer gave him away. With a trail of flames.'

Resa wanted to spit out the seeds so that she could shed human tears.

But Orpheus laughed out loud, happy as a child. 'And who told you about that trail? Come on, out with it!'

It took the Piper a long time to answer. 'You, who else?' he said hoarsely at last. 'And some day I'll find out what devilry you used to do it.'

'Well, he's done it, anyway!' said the Adderhead. 'After you let the Jay escape twice. Take the prisoner to the Hall of a Thousand Windows. Chain him to the table where he's to bind the book, and have every move he makes watched. If this new Book makes me sick too, I'll cut your heart out with my own hands, Piper, and believe me, a heart's not as easily replaced as a nose.'

Bird-thoughts were obscuring Resa's mind. It frightened her, but how was she to reach Mo without wings? And even if you do fly to him, she asked herself, what then? Are you going to peck out the Piper's eyes so that he can't see the Bluejay escape? Fly away, Resa, it's all over, she thought. Save your unborn child even if you can't save its father. Go back to Meggie. Birdlike fears filled her, birdlike fears and human pain – or was it the other way around? Was she going crazy? Crazy like Mortola?

She perched there, trembling, waiting for the bedchamber to empty and for the Adderhead to go and see his prisoner. Why did Dustfinger give him away, she wondered. Why? What did Orpheus promise him? What can be worth more than the life Mo gave him back?

The Adderhead, Orpheus, the Piper, the soldiers, two servants with the cushions to support their master's aching flesh – Resa saw them all go, but just as she thought she was alone and was putting her head over the edge of the wardrobe, there stood Jacopo staring straight up at her.

One of the servants came back to fetch the Adderhead his coat.

'See that bird up there?' Jacopo asked. 'Catch it for me!'

But the servant dragged him unceremoniously to the door. 'You don't give the orders around here! Go and see your mother. I'm sure she'll be glad of company where she is now!'

Jacopo resisted, but the servant pushed him roughly through the doorway. Then he closed the door – and came over to the wardrobe. Resa retreated. She heard him pushing something in front of the wardrobe. Fly into his face, she told herself. But then where? The door was closed, the windows draped. The servant threw a black coat at her. She fluttered against the door, against the walls, heard the man cursing. Where could she go? She flew up to the chandelier hanging from the ceiling, but something hit her wing. It hurt, it hurt badly, and she fell.

'You just wait, I'll wring your neck! Who knows, maybe you won't taste bad. Sure to be better than what our fine master gives us to eat.' Hands reached for her. She tried to fly away, but her wing hurt, and the man's fingers held on tightly. In desperation, she pecked them with her beak.

'Let it go!'

Bewildered, the servant turned, and Dustfinger struck him to the ground. There was fire behind him. A traitor's fire. Gwin was staring hungrily at her, but Dustfinger shooed him away. Resa tried to peck his hands when he reached for her, but she had no strength left, and he carefully lifted her from the floor and stroked her feathers.

'What's the matter with your wing? Can you move it?'

The bird in her trusted him, as all wild creatures did, but her human heart remembered what the Piper had said. 'Why did you give Mo away?'

'Because that's what he wanted. Spit the seeds out, Resa! Have you forgotten that you're human?'

Perhaps I want to forget it, she thought, but she obediently spat the little seeds out into his hand. This time none were missing, but she still felt the bird growing stronger and stronger inside her. Small and large, large and small, skin with feathers, skin without feathers . . . she stroked her arms, felt fingers again, not claws, felt tears in her eyes, a woman's tears.

'Did you see where the White Book is hidden?'

She shook her head. Her heart was so glad that it could love him again.

'We have to find it, Resa,' Dustfinger whispered. 'Your husband is going to bind the Adder another book, remembering his old trade and forgetting the Bluejay, and in that way he will be safe from Orpheus's words. But that book must never be finished, do you understand?'

Yes, she understood. They looked everywhere by the light of the fire, groping among damp towels, clothes and boots, swords, pitchers, silver salvers and embroidered cushions. They even reached into the bloody water. When they heard footsteps outside Dustfinger dragged the unconscious servant with him, and they hid behind the wardrobe on which Resa had been perching. For a bird, the room had seemed as large as a whole world, but now it seemed too cramped to breathe in. Dustfinger placed himself in front of Resa to protect her, but the servants who came in were too busy emptying their master's bath of blood to notice anything. They cursed as they cleared the damp towels away, covering up for their disgust at the Adderhead's rotting flesh with mockery. Then they carried the tub out and left Dustfinger and Resa alone again.

Search . . . in every corner, in every chest, in and under the tumbled bed. Search for the Book.

70

Burning Words

It brewed in her as she eyed the pages full to the brims of
their bellies with paragraphs and words.
You bastards, she thought.
You lovely bastards.
Don't make me happy. Please, don't fill me up and let me
think that something good can come of any of this.

Markus Zusak, *The Book Thief*

Farid found Doria. When they carried him to the tree
Meggie thought at first that the giant had crushed him,
just as he had crushed the Milksop's men, who lay in the
frosty grass like broken dolls.

'No, it wasn't the giant,' said Roxane, as they put Doria
down with the other injured men: the Black Prince and
Woodenfoot, Silkworm and Hedgehog. 'This is the work of
humans.'

Roxane had made one of the lowest nests into a sickroom.
Luckily there were only two dead among the robbers, while the
Milksop had lost many men. Even fear of his brother-in-law

wasn't going to bring him back another time.

Sootbird too was dead. He lay on the grass with his neck broken, staring up at the sky with empty eyes. Wolves prowled among the trees, lured by the smell of blood. But they dared not come any closer, because the giant was curled up like a child under the tree with its nests, sleeping as deeply as if Roxane's singing had sent him into the realm of dreams for ever.

Doria did not come round when Minerva bandaged his bleeding head, and Meggie sat beside him as Roxane cared for the other wounded. Hedgehog was in a very bad way, but the other men's injuries would heal. Fortunately the Black Prince had only a couple of broken ribs. He wanted to go down to his bear, but Roxane had forbidden it, and Battista had to keep assuring him that the bear was already chasing snow hares again, now that Roxane had pulled out the arrow from his furry shoulder. But Doria didn't move. He just lay there, his brown hair full of blood.

'What do you think? Will he ever wake up again?' Meggie asked as Roxane bent over him.

'I don't know,' Roxane replied. 'Talk to him. Sometimes that calls them back.'

Talk to him. What should she tell Doria? He had asked her about the other world again and again, so in a soft voice Meggie began talking to him about horseless carriages and flying machines, ships without sails and devices that carried voices from one part of the world to another. Elinor came to see how she was. Fenoglio sat beside her for a while. Even Farid came and held her hand while she held Doria's, and for the first time Meggie felt as close to him as she had when the two of them followed her captured parents with Dustfinger.

Can one heart love two boys at once?

'Farid,' said Fenoglio quietly after a while, 'let's see what your fire can tell us about the Bluejay, and then this story will be brought to an end. A good end.'

'Maybe we ought to send the giant to the Bluejay!' said Silkworm. Roxane had cut an arrow out of his arm, and his tongue was heavy with the wine she had given him to dull the pain. The Milksop had left all sorts of things behind: wine and blankets, weapons, riderless horses.

'Have you forgotten where the Bluejay is?' asked the Black Prince. Meggie was so glad he was alive. 'No giant can wade through the Black Lake. Even if they did once like to look at their reflections in its water.'

No, it wouldn't be as simple as that.

'Come on, Meggie, let's ask the fire,' said Farid, but Meggie was reluctant to let go of Doria's hand.

'You go. I'll stay with him,' said Minerva, and Fenoglio whispered, 'Don't look so anxious! Of course the boy will wake up again! Have you forgotten what I told you? His story is only just beginning.'

But Doria's pale face made that hard to believe.

The branch that Farid knelt on to summon the fire was as broad as the road outside Elinor's garden gate. As Meggie crouched beside him, Fenoglio looked suspiciously up at the children sitting in the branches above them watching the sleeping giant.

'Don't you dare!' he called, pointing to the fir cones in their small hands. 'The first of you to throw one of those at the giant will go down after it. I promise you!'

'But they *will* throw one sometime, and then what?' asked Farid as he carefully sprinkled a little ash on the tree's wooden skin. There wasn't much left, even though he gathered it up again meticulously every time he'd used it. 'What will the giant do when he wakes up?'

'How would I know?' grumbled Fenoglio, casting a slightly worried look downwards. 'I just hope poor Roxane doesn't have to spend the rest of her life singing him to sleep.'

The Black Prince came over to them too. Battista had to support him. He sat down beside Meggie without a word. The fire was sleepy today. However hard Farid enticed and flattered it, it seemed forever before flames rose from the ashes. The giant began humming to himself in his sleep. Jink jumped up on to Farid's knees, a dead bird in his mouth, and suddenly the pictures came: Dustfinger in a courtyard, surrounded by large cages. There was a girl in one of them, weeping. Brianna. A black figure stood between her and her father.

'Night-Mare!' whispered Battista. Meggie looked at him in alarm. The picture dissolved into greyish smoke, and another appeared in the heart of the flames. Farid took Meggie's hand, and Battista uttered a soft curse. Mo. He was chained to a table. The Piper was with him. And the Adderhead, his swollen face looking even more terrible than Meggie had seen it in her worst dreams. Leather and blank sheets of paper lay on the table.

'He's binding him another White Book!' whispered Meggie. 'What does that mean?' In alarm, she looked at Fenoglio.

'Meggie!' Farid drew her attention to the fire again.

Letters were rising from the flames, burning letters that formed into words.

'What the devil is that!' Fenoglio uttered. 'Who wrote that?'

The words blew away and went out among the branches before anyone could read them. But the fire gave Fenoglio the answer to his question. A round, pale face appeared in the flames, its circular glasses looking like a second pair of eyes.

'Orpheus!' Farid whispered.

The flames burnt low, slipping back into the ashes as if returning to their nest, but a few fiery words still drifted through the air. *Bluejay . . . fear . . . broke ... die . . .*

'What does that mean?' asked the Black Prince.

'It's a long story, Prince,' Fenoglio replied wearily. 'And I'm afraid the wrong man has written the end of it.'

71

The Bookbinder

The real author was neither one of us: a fist is more than
the sum of its fingers.

Margaret Atwood, *The Blind Assassin*

Fold. Cut. The paper was good, better than last time. Mo's
fingertips felt the fibres on its pale white surface, ran
along the edges in search of memories. And they came, filling
his heart and mind with a thousand images, a thousand and
more forgotten days. The smell of the glue took him back to
all the places where he had been alone with a sick book, and
the familiar gestures made him feel his old satisfaction in giving new life and beauty to a book, saving it from time's sharp
teeth, at least for a while. He'd forgotten the peace that came
when his hands were doing their work. Fold, cut, pull a thread
through the paper. Mortimer was back again: Mortimer the
bookbinder, for whom a knife didn't have to be sharp because
a sharp blade killed better, and who wasn't threatened by the
words, because he was only making them new clothes.

'You're taking your time, Bluejay.'

The Piper's voice brought him back to the Hall of a Thousand Windows.

Don't let it happen, Mortimer, he told himself. Simply imagine that the silver-nosed man is still in his own book, is nothing but a voice coming out of the letters on the page. The Bluejay isn't here. Orpheus's words must look for him somewhere else.

'You know you're going to die when you've finished it. That's what makes you so slow, am I correct?' The Piper struck him so hard in the back with his gloved fist that Mo almost cut his own hands, and the Bluejay surfaced for a moment, thinking what it would be like to plunge the blade that cut the paper into the Piper's breast.

Mo forced himself to put the knife aside and picked up another sheet of paper, seeking peace in gluing all that whiteness together.

The Piper was right. He was taking his time, not because he was afraid of dying but because this book must never be finished, and the only reason for every move he made was to bring back Mortimer Folchart, the bookbinder who could not be bound by Orpheus's words. Mo hardly felt them any more. All the despair that had seeped into his heart in that dark cell, all the rage and hopelessness, had faded as if his hands had washed them out of his heart.

But what would happen if Dustfinger and Resa didn't find the other White Book? Suppose the Night-Mare devoured Brianna and her father? Would he stand in this hall for ever then, binding blank pages? Not for ever, Mo. You're not immortal. Luckily.

The Piper would kill him. He'd been waiting to do it ever since they first met in the Castle of Night. And, of course, the strolling players would sing about the death of the Bluejay, not Mortimer Folchart. But what would become of Resa and the unborn child? And what about Meggie? Don't think, Mortimer, he told himself. Cut, fold, stitch, win yourself some time, even if you don't yet know what for. When you're dead Resa can fly away and find Meggie. Meggie . . .

Please, his heart pleaded with the White Women, let my daughter live! I will go with you, but leave Meggie here. Her life is only just beginning, though she may not know yet which world she wants to live it in.

Cutting, folding, stitching – he thought he saw Meggie's face on the blank paper. He almost felt her beside him as he had in the Old Chamber in the Castle of Night, the room where Violante's mother had lived. Violante . . . they'd thrown her into one of the cells. Mo knew exactly what would frighten her most down there: she would be afraid of the darkness taking what little vision she had from her. The Adder's daughter still moved him, and he would gladly have helped her, but the Bluejay must sleep.

Four candles had been lit for him. They didn't give much light, but they were better than nothing. The chains didn't make working any easier either. Every time he moved, their clinking reminded him that he wasn't in his workshop in Elinor's garden.

The door opened.

'There you are!' Orpheus's voice echoed through the empty hall. 'This role suits you much better! What made that old fool Fenoglio think of turning a bookbinder into a robber?'

He stopped in front of Mo with a triumphant smile, just too far away for the knife to reach him. Yes, Orpheus would think of that kind of thing. As usual, his breath smelt sweetish.

'You ought to have known Dustfinger would betray you some time. He betrays everyone – and believe me, I know what I'm talking about. It's the part he plays best. But presumably you couldn't pick and choose who'd help you.'

Mo picked up the leather intended for the cover. It was red, like the cover of the first book.

'Ah, so you're not talking to me any more! Well, I can understand that.' Orpheus had never looked happier.

'Leave him to work, Four-Eyes! Or do you want me telling the Adderhead that he has to live in his itching skin a little longer, just because you felt like a nice chat?' The Piper's voice sounded even more strained than usual. Orpheus wasn't making himself many friends.

'Don't forget, your master will soon be rid of that skin, Piper, and he owes it all to me!' he replied in a supercilious tone. 'Your powers of persuasion haven't impressed our bookbinding friend much, if I remember rightly.'

So the two of them were competing to see who could be closest to the Adder. At the moment Orpheus seemed to hold the better cards, but perhaps that could be changed.

'What are you talking about, Orpheus?' said Mo, without looking up from his work. He tasted sweet revenge on his tongue. 'The Adderhead need feel grateful to no one but the Piper. I was careless. I ran straight into their arms. You had nothing at all to do with it.'

'What?' Piqued, Orpheus fiddled with his glasses.

'That's exactly how I'll tell the tale to the Adderhead. As soon as he's had a good sleep.' Mo cut through the leather and imagined that he was cutting the web Orpheus had spun around him.

The Piper narrowed his eyes, as if that would help him to see more clearly what game the Bluejay was playing. The Bluejay isn't here, Piper, thought Mo. But how could you understand that?

'Careful, bookbinder!' Orpheus took a clumsy step towards him. His voice was almost cracking. 'Use your silver tongue to spread lies about me and I'll have it cut out on the spot!'

'Oh yes? Who by?'

Mo looked directly at the Piper.

'I don't want to see my daughter in this castle,' he said softly. 'I don't want anyone looking for her after the Bluejay is dead.'

The Piper returned his glance – and smiled. 'That's a promise. The Bluejay has no daughter,' he said. 'And he'll keep his tongue too. So long as it speaks the right words.'

Orpheus bit his lips so hard that they turned as pale as his skin. Then he moved close to Mo's side.

'I'll write new words!' he hissed in his ear. 'Words that will make you writhe like a worm on the hook!'

'Write what you like,' replied Mo, cutting through the leather again.

The bookbinder wouldn't feel the words.

72

So Many Tears

. . . from the beginning of time,
in childhood, I thought
that pain meant
I was not loved.
It meant I loved.

Louise Glück, *Ararat*

She was crying! Jacopo had never heard his mother cry before. Not even when they brought his father back from the forest, dead. He hadn't cried then either, but that was different.

Should he call down to her? He knelt on the edge of the shaft and stared into the darkness. He couldn't see her, only hear her. The weeping sounded terrible. It scared him. His mother didn't cry. His mother was always strong, always proud. She didn't take him in her arms, like Brianna. Brianna hugged him even when he'd been cruel to her. 'It's because you look like your father!' the maids in the kitchen said. 'Brianna was in love with your father!' She was still in love

651

with him. She had a coin with his picture on it in the bag at her belt; she sometimes kissed it in secret, and she wrote his name on the walls. She wrote it in the air and in the dust. She was so stupid.

The sobbing down below grew even more violent, and Jacopo put his hands over his ears. It sounded as if his mother were breaking into small pieces, such tiny pieces that no one would ever be able to put her together again. But he wanted to keep her!

'Your grandfather will take you with him,' said the servants. 'Back to the Castle of Night, so that you can play with his son.' But Jacopo didn't want to go to the Castle of Night. He wanted to go back to Ombra. That was his castle. And he was frightened of his grandfather, who stank and gasped for air, and had skin so spongy you were scared you might dig holes in it with your fingers.

It must be all wet with her tears down there. She sounded as if she'd soon be drowning in them! No wonder she was so sad. She couldn't read any books in the darkness, and his mother wasn't happy without books. She loved nothing so much. She loved them far more than him, but never mind that. He didn't want her marrying Four-Eyes all the same. Jacopo hated Four-Eyes. His voice was like melted sugar on your skin.

He liked the Bluejay. And the Fire-Dancer. But soon they'd both be dead. Orpheus was going to feed the Fire-Dancer to the Night-Mare, and as soon as the Bluejay had finished the new Book they'd flay him. His grandfather had once made him watch a man being flayed alive. Jacopo had hidden away from the victim's screams in the furthest corner of his heart, but he had still heard them there.

It was quiet. His mother had stopped crying. Had she cried herself to death?

The guards took no notice of him as he bent far over the edge of the black shaft. 'Mother?'

The word didn't pass his lips easily. He never called her Mother. It was as Her Ugliness that he thought of her. But now she had been crying.

'Jacopo?'

She was still alive.

'Is the Bluejay dead?'

'Not yet. He's binding the book.'

'Where is Brianna?'

'In one of the cages.' He was jealous of Brianna. Violante liked Brianna better than him. She was allowed to sleep with his mother, who talked to her much more often than she talked to him, her son. But Brianna comforted him too when he'd hurt himself, or when the Milksop's men taunted him about his dead father. And she was very beautiful.

'Orpheus—' he began, but one of the guards grabbed him by the scruff of the neck and hauled him to his feet.

'That's enough chatter!' he said. 'Get out.'

Jacopo tried to wriggle free, but it was no good.

'Let her out!' he shouted, beating his fists against the man's armed chest. 'Let her out this minute!'

But the soldier only laughed.

'Hark at him, will you!' he said to the other guard. 'Mind you don't end up in that cell yourself, midget. Your grandfather has a son now. So his grandson doesn't count for much, specially when he's Cosimo's brat and his mother is thick as thieves with the Bluejay.'

He pushed Jacopo away so roughly that he fell over and

Jacopo wished he could make flames come out of his hands, like the Fire-Dancer, or kill them all with a sword, the way the Bluejay had killed so many men.

'Jacopo?' he heard his mother call from down below, but when he turned back to the edge of the shaft the soldiers barred his way.

'Get out, I tell you!' one of them snapped. 'Or I'll tell Four-Eyes to feed *you* to the Night-Mare. I bet you're not half as tough as the illuminator they're keeping in reserve for it.'

Jacopo kicked the man's knee as hard as he could, and escaped before the other guard could grab hold of him.

The passages down which he stumbled were so dark that he saw a thousand monsters in the shadows. It had been better when there was fire burning on all the walls, much better. Where was he to go? Back to the room where they'd locked him in with his mother? No, there were beetles there that crawled into your nose and ears. Orpheus had sent them. He'd told the boy so himself, laughing. Jacopo had changed his clothes three times already to get rid of the beetles, but he could still feel them everywhere.

Perhaps he ought to go to the cage where Brianna was? No, the Night-Mare was outside it. Jacopo crouched on the stone floor and buried his face in his hands. He wished them all to hell, Orpheus and the Piper and his grandfather. He wanted to be like the Bluejay and the Black Prince – and then he'd kill them all. Every last one of them. That'd soon stop them laughing. And then he'd sit on the throne of Ombra and attack the Castle of Night, just like his father. But he would conquer it and take all its silver to Ombra, and the strolling players would sing songs about him, and he'd make them put on a show at the castle every day, just for him, and the Fire-Dancer would write his name in the sky, and his mother would curtsey to him, and he'd marry a girl as beautiful as Brianna . . .

He saw it all so clearly in his mind's eye as he sat there, in the darkness that protected his grandfather's eyes. He saw it as clearly as the pictures that Balbulus had painted for him.

There would be a book about him. Jacopo. A book as magnificent as the one about the Bluejay. Not empty and mouldy like . . .

Jacopo raised his head.

. . . the White Book.

Yes. Why not? That'd certainly make them laugh on the other side of their faces!

Jacopo stood up. It would be easy. He must just make sure his grandfather didn't notice that it was gone at once. He'd better leave another book in its place. But which?

He rested his hands on his trembling knees.

Orpheus had had his books taken away, and his mother's were all gone too. But there were other books in this castle, sick books, as sick as his grandfather's. They were in the room where the Bluejay had been caught.

It was a long way there, and Jacopo got lost a couple of times, but finally the smell of decay guided him – the same smell that surrounded his grandfather – and so did the sooty trail, barely visible in the light of his torch, laid by the Fire-Dancer to give the Bluejay away. Why had he done it? For silver, like Sootbird? What would he buy with the silver? A castle? A woman? A horse?

'Trust your friends even less than your enemies, Jacopo.' That was what his grandfather had taught him. 'There are no such things as friends. Not for a prince.' At one time his grandfather often used to talk to him, but that was long ago.

He has a son now, Jacopo.

He chose a book that wasn't too big – the White Book was not very big either – and put it under his tunic.

There were two guards outside his grandfather's bedchamber. So he was back from seeing the Bluejay? Perhaps he'd killed him already? No, the new Book couldn't be finished yet. Such things took a long time, Balbulus had told him so. But when it *was* finished his grandfather was going to make the Bluejay scream, and either marry off his mother to Four-Eyes or leave her in that cell until she broke into tiny little pieces. And they would take Jacopo to the Castle of Night with them.

Jacopo straightened his clothes and wiped the tears from his eyes. He hadn't even noticed them. They blurred everything, the guards and the light of their torches. Stupid. Crying was stupid.

'I want to see my grandfather!'

How they grinned at each other! The Bluejay would kill them all. Every man of them.

'He's asleep. Get out.'

'He can't sleep, you idiot!' Jacopo's shrill voice rose. Only a few months ago he would have stamped his foot, but he'd learnt that that didn't work particularly well. 'Thumbling sent me. I'm to take him his sleeping medicine.'

The guards exchanged uncertain glances. Luckily he was cleverer than any of them. Much cleverer.

'Very well, in you go!' growled one of them. 'But mind you don't start carrying on about your mother to him, because if you do I'll chuck you into that cell with my own hands, understand?'

You're a dead man, thought Jacopo as he walked past the guard. Dead. Dead. Dead. Don't you know that yet? Oh, how good this felt!

'What do you want?' His grandfather was sitting on the bed with two servants beside him, wiping the fairy blood off his legs. His eyelids were heavy from the poppy-juice he took when he wanted to sleep. And why shouldn't he sleep now? The Bluejay was caught, and was binding Death in another book for him.

'What are you going to do to the Bluejay when he's finished?' Jacopo knew exactly what kinds of stories his grandfather liked to tell.

The Adderhead laughed and impatiently waved the servants away. Bowing and scraping, they made their way to the door.

'Maybe you do take after me, even if you look like your father.' The Adderhead let himself drop on his side, groaning. 'What would *you* do to him first?' His tongue was already as heavy as his eyelids.

'I don't know. Pull out his fingernails?'

Jacopo went over to the bed. There it was, the cushion that the Adderhead always had with him. To prop up his sick flesh, they said. But Jacopo knew better. He'd often seen his grandfather put his hand under the heavy fabric to feel the leather binding with his fingers. Once he had even caught a glimpse of the blood-soaked covers. No one paid any attention to what a child saw. Not even the Adderhead, who trusted no one but himself.

'His fingernails? Hm. Painful, yes. I hope my son will get ideas like that once he's your age. Although why does a man need a son when he's immortal? I ask myself that question more and more frequently. Why does a man need a wife? Or daughters . . .'

657

The last words were barely audible. The Adderhead opened his mouth, and a snore came out. The lizard-like eyelids closed, and his left hand clutched the cushion in which his death was hidden. But Jacopo had small, slender hands, not at all like his grandfather's. Very carefully, he undid the ribbons tying the fabric, put his fingers inside the cushion and took out the Book, the White Book – although it really should be called the Red Book now. His grandfather turned his head, and his breath rattled in his sleep. Jacopo reached under his tunic for the volume he had taken from the Lost Library, and exchanged it for its red twin.

'My grandfather's asleep,' he told the guards when he came out of the room. 'And you'd better not wake him or he'll pull your fingernails out.'

73

The Night-Mare

What should he fear who fears not death itself?
Friedrich Schiller, *The Robbers*

Resa had flown away to Silvertongue in the Hall of a Thousand Windows. 'The bird will never leave you again, Resa!' Dustfinger had warned her, but she had put the seeds into her mouth all the same.

He had had great difficulty in dragging her out of the bed-chamber before the Silver Prince came back. The despair in her face went to his heart. They had not found the White Book, and both of them knew what that meant: it wasn't the Adderhead who would die, but the Bluejay – by the hand of the Piper, Thumbling, or the White Women coming for him because he hadn't been able to pay the price Death demand-ed for his life.

Resa had flown to him so that Silvertongue would not be alone when he died. Or did she still hope for some miracle to save him? Perhaps. Dustfinger had not told her that Death was going to take him again too – and then her daughter.

'If you don't find the Book,' Silvertongue had whispered to him before sending him away to lay the fiery trail for the Piper, 'then at least let us try to save our daughters.'

Our daughters . . . Dustfinger knew where to find Brianna, but how was he to protect Meggie from the Piper, or the White Women themselves?

Of course the Piper's men had tried to hold him fast once he'd led them to the Bluejay, but it was easy to escape them. They were still looking for him, but the darkness in the castle hid the Adderhead's enemies as well as easing the pain in his eyes.

Orpheus seemed very sure that his black dog was enough to guard Brianna. Two torches burnt beside the cage where she sat, crouching like a captive bird. But there was no soldier on guard. The real guard lurked somewhere in the shadows, in a place that the torchlight didn't reach.

How in the world had Orpheus managed to tame it?

'Don't forget, he read it out of a book,' Silvertongue had said. 'A book for children too, although I'm not sure that Fenoglio made the Night-Mare any less dangerous because of that. But it's made of words, and I'm sure that Orpheus himself used words to make it obey him. Just a few rearranged words, a couple of slightly twisted sentences, and the terror in the night becomes an obedient dog.'

But Silvertongue, Dustfinger had thought, have you forgotten that everything in this world is made of words? He knew only that this Night-Mare was not less dangerous, but even more sinister, than those found in the Wayless Wood. It would not, like its fellows, be driven away by fairy dust and fire – it was woven of darker stuff. What a pity you didn't ask the White Women its name, he said to himself as he slowly made his way towards the cages. Don't the songs say that's the only way to kill a Night-Mare? For that was what he had to do: destroy the creature so that Orpheus could not call it back. Forget the songs, Dustfinger, he told himself as he looked around. Write your own, just as the Bluejay must write his now.

At the sound of his whispering the torches flared up as if to welcome him, weary of the darkness surrounding them. And Brianna raised her head.

How beautiful she was, as lovely as her mother.

Dustfinger looked around again, waiting for the darkness to start moving. Where was it?

He heard a snuffling sound, felt cold breath, panting like a large dog's. To his left the shadows grew and became blacker than black. His heart began to beat painfully fast. Ah. So the fear was still there, even though he so seldom felt it now.

Brianna got to her feet and stumbled away until her back was up against the bars. Behind her, a painted peacock spread its tail on the grey wall. 'Go away!' she whispered. 'Please! It will eat you!'

Go away. A tempting idea. But he had once had two daughters, now he had only one . . . and he would keep her, not for ever but perhaps for a few years yet. Precious time. Time – whatever that was.

All was cold behind him, dreadfully cold. Dustfinger called up the flames and wrapped himself in their warmth, but the cold made the fire burn low and go out, leaving him alone with the shadow.

'Please! Please go away!' Brianna's voice urged, and the love in it, that she usually hid so well, warmed him more than the fire ever could. He called on the flames again, more sternly this time, reminding them that he and they were brothers, inseparable. Hesitantly, they licked up from the ground, trembling as if a cold wind were blowing through them, but they burnt, and the Night-Mare retreated and stared at him.

Yes, what the songs said about him and his like was true. It must be true. The songs said Night-Mares were made entirely of the blackness of the soul, of evil that could not be forgotten or forgiven until they were snuffed out, consuming themselves and taking with them everything they had ever been.

The eyes transfixed him, red eyes in all that blackness, eyes both fierce and dull, lost in themselves, with no yesterday and no tomorrow, without light and warmth, caught in their own cold, the freezing entity of evil.

Dustfinger felt the fire around him like a warm fur. It almost burnt his skin, but it was his only protection against those dull eyes and the hungry mouth that opened, screaming so horribly that Brianna sank to her knees and put her hands over her ears.

The Night-Mare reached a black hand out to the fire. It hissed when he dipped it into the flames – and Dustfinger thought he recognized a face in all the blackness. A face he had never forgotten.

Was it possible? Had Orpheus seen it too, and so tamed his black dog by calling it by its forgotten name? Or had he given it that name himself, and brought back the man whom Silvertongue had sent to his death?'

Brianna was crying behind him. Dustfinger sensed her trembling through the bars, but he felt no fear now. He was just grateful. Grateful for this moment. Glad of this new encounter – which he hoped would be their last.

'Well, look! Who have we here?' he said softly, as Brianna's weeping died down on the other side of the bars. 'Do you remember yourself in all your darkness? Do you remember the knife, and the boy's thin, unprotected back? Do you remember the sound my heart made when it broke?'

The Night-Mare stared at him, and Dustfinger stepped towards it, still surrounded by flames – flames burning hotter and hotter, nourished by all the pain and despair he was bringing back to mind.

'Away with you, Basta!' he said, speaking the name loud enough to pierce the heart of all the darkness. 'Be gone for all eternity.'

The face showed more clearly – the narrow, foxy face that he had once feared so much – and Dustfinger made the flames bite into the cold, made them penetrate the blackness like swords, all of them writing Basta's name, and the Night-Mare screamed again, its eyes suddenly full of memories. It screamed and screamed, while its shape ran like ink, melting into the shadows, dispersing like smoke. Only the cold was left, but the fire ate that too, and Dustfinger fell on his knees and felt the pain leaving him – pain that had outlasted death itself. He wished Farid were here with him. He wished it so much that, for a few moments, he forgot where he was.

'Father?' Brianna's whisper reached him through the smoke.

Had she ever called him that before? Yes, long ago. But had he been the same man then?

The bars of the cage bent under the heat of his hands. He dared not touch Brianna because he felt the fire so strongly in them. Footsteps approached – heavy, rapid footsteps. The

Night-Mare's screams had brought them. But the darkness swallowed Dustfinger and Brianna up before the soldiers reached the cages, and they looked in vain for their black watchman.

74

The Other Side

She tore a page from the book and ripped it in half.
Then a chapter.
Soon, there was nothing but scraps of words littered
between her legs and all around her . . . What good were
the words?
She said it audibly now, to the orange-lit room. 'What good
are the words?'

Markus Zusak, *The Book Thief*

The Black Prince was still with Roxane. She was going to
splint his injured leg so that he could walk on it. Walk
to the Castle in the Lake. 'We have time,' Meggie had told
him, although her heart was in a hurry. Mo would certainly
need as long to bind this White Book as he had needed in the
Castle of Night.

The Black Prince intended to set out with almost all his
men to stand by the Bluejay. But without Elinor and without
Meggie. 'Your father made me promise that you and your
mother would stay in a safe place,' he had told her. 'With your

mother I wasn't able to keep my promise, but at least I'll keep it where you're concerned. Didn't you promise him the same thing?'

No, she had not. So she would go, even if it almost broke her heart to leave Doria behind. He still hadn't woken up, but Darius would talk to him. And Elinor. And she would come back – wouldn't she?

Farid was going with her. He would be able to call fire if the weather grew cold on their way, and she had stolen some dried meat and filled one of Battista's leather bottles with water. How could the Black Prince think she would stay after she had seen those fiery words? How could he think she'd leave her father to die as if this were some other, quite different story?

'Meggie, the Black Prince doesn't know about the words,' Fenoglio had pointed out. 'And he has no idea what Orpheus is up to either!' But Fenoglio did know, and all the same – just like the Prince – he didn't want her to go. 'Do you want what happened to your mother to happen to you too? No one knows where she is. No, you *must* stay. We'll help your father in our own way. I'll write day and night, I promise you. But what use is that if you don't stay here to read what I've written?'

Stay here. Wait. No, she was sorry, but she was going to steal away in secret like Resa, and she wouldn't get lost . . . she'd waited far too long already. If Fenoglio did indeed think of something – and he had certainly been able to write the giant here – then Darius could read it, and the children had Battista and Elinor, Roxane and Fenoglio to look after them. But Mo was alone, all alone. He needed her. He'd always needed her.

Elinor was snoring gently. Darius slept next to her, in between Minerva's children. Meggie moved as quietly as the woven structure of the nest allowed, picking up her jacket, her shoes, and the rucksack that still reminded her of the other world.

'Ready?' Farid was standing in the round doorway of the nest. 'It will soon be light.'

Meggie nodded – and turned as Farid stared past her, his eyes as wide as a child's.

A White Woman was standing beside the sleepers. She looked at Meggie.

She had a pencil in her hand, a short, worn-out chalk pencil, and with a look of invitation she was offering Farid one of the candles that Elinor had brought from Ombra. Farid went towards her like a sleepwalker, and with a whisper lit the wick. The White Woman dipped her pencil into the flame and began to write on a sheet of paper. Meggie had been trying to write a good end to her father's story on it after the giant took Fenoglio away. The White Woman wrote and wrote, while Minerva whispered her husband's name in her sleep, while Elinor turned over on to her other side, while Despina put her arm around her brother and the wind blew through the wickerwork of the nest, almost putting out the candle. Then the White Woman straightened up, looked at Meggie once more, and disappeared as if the wind had blown her away.

Farid breathed a sigh of relief when she had gone, and pressed his face into Meggie's hair. But Meggie gently moved him aside and bent over the paper on which the White Woman had written.

'Can you read it?' Farid whispered.

Meggie nodded.

'Go to the Black Prince and tell him he can spare his leg,' she said softly. 'We'll all stay here. The song of the Bluejay has been written.'

The Box

'Okay,' said the Lady, turning to Abby. 'Tomorrow bring
the book.'
'Which one?'
'There's more than one book?'

Alan Armstrong, *Whittington*

It wasn't easy to make your hands work slowly when they
loved what they were doing so much. Mo's eyes stung in
the bad light, his ankles were sore from the heavy chains, and
yet in the strangest way he felt happy. It was as if he were
binding not the Adderhead's death, but time itself into a book
– and with it all fears for the future, all the pain of the past
. . . until there was nothing left but *now*, this moment when
his hands caressed paper and leather.

'I'll bring fire to help you as soon as I've freed Brianna,'
Dustfinger had promised, before leaving him alone to go and
act the part of a traitor once more. 'And I'll bring the White
Book with me,' he had added.

However, it was not Dustfinger but Resa who came. Mo's

668

heart had almost stopped when the swift flew through the doorway. One of the guards had aimed his crossbow at her, but she darted away from the arrow, and Mo had plucked a brown feather from his shoulder. They haven't found the Book. That was his first thought as the swift settled on a beam above him. But whatever happened, he was glad she was there.

The Piper was leaning against a column, his eyes following every movement Mo made. Was he going to try doing without sleep for two whole weeks? Or did he think this book could be bound in a day?

Mo put down his knife and rubbed his tired eyes. The swift spread her wings as if she were waving to him, and Mo quickly bent his head so that the Piper's attention wouldn't be drawn to her. But he looked up again when the silver-nosed man uttered a curse.

Fire was licking from the walls.

It could mean only one thing: Brianna was free.

'Why are you smiling like that, Bluejay?' The Piper came up to him and drove his fist into Mo's stomach, doubling him up. The swift above their heads cried out.

'Do you think your fiery friend will come to make amends for betraying you?' the silver-nosed man whispered. 'Don't rejoice too soon! This time I'm going to chop his head off. We'll see if he can come back from the dead without *that*!'

The Bluejay would have liked to thrust the bookbinder's knife into that heartless breast, but once again Mo, the bookbinder, sent him away. What are you waiting for? asked the Jay. The White Book? No one's going to find it! Well then, Mo retorted, why should I fight any more? Without the Book I'm dead anyway, and so is my daughter.

Meggie. The bookbinder and the Bluejay were the same

man only in sharing their fears for her.

The door opened, and a small, thin figure made its way into the fire-lit hall. Jacopo.

He came towards Mo, taking small steps. Did he want to tell the Bluejay about his mother? Or had his grandfather sent him to find out how Mo was getting on with binding the new Book?

Violante's son stopped close to Mo, but he was looking at the Piper.

'Will it soon be ready?' he asked.

'If you don't keep him from his work,' replied the silver-nosed man.

Jacopo put a hand under his tunic and brought out a book. He had wrapped it in a brightly-coloured cloth. 'I want the Bluejay to cure this book for me. It's my favourite.'

He opened it, and Mo forgot to breathe. Pages soaked in blood.

Jacopo was looking at him.

'Your favourite book? There's only one book the Bluejay's supposed to bother with. So get out!' The Piper poured himself a goblet of wine. 'Go to the kitchen and tell them to send up more meat and wine.'

'I only want him to take a look at it!' Jacopo's voice sounded as defiant as ever. 'Grandfather said I could get him to do that. You can ask him if you like.' He was passing Mo a short, worn pencil that could easily be hidden in the hand. That was better than the knife – much, much better.

The Piper put a piece of meat in his mouth and washed it down with wine. 'You're lying,' he said. 'Has your grandfather told you what I do to liars?'

'No, what?' Jacopo thrust his chin out just as his mother

did and took a step towards the silver-nosed man.

The Piper wiped his greasy fingers on a snow-white napkin and smiled.

Mo clutched the pencil in his fingers and opened the White Book.

'First I cut their tongues out,' said the Piper.

Jacopo took another step towards him.

'Oh yes?'

Heart.

Mo's fingers shook as he traced each letter.

'Yes. After all, it's not easy to tell lies without a tongue. Although – wait, I did once know a mute beggar who told me shameless lies. He talked with his fingers.'

'So?'

The Piper laughed. 'So I cut them off, one by one.'

Keep looking up, Mo, or he'll realize that you're writing.

Spell.

Only one more word now. A single word.

The Piper glanced at him. He looked at the open book. Mo hid the pencil in his closed fist.

The swift spread her wings again. She wanted to help him. No, Resa! But the bird was already in the air, flying above the Piper's head.

'I saw that bird before!' said Jacopo. 'In my grandfather's bedchamber.'

'Did you indeed?' The Piper looked at the ledge where the swift had now settled. He snatched a crossbow from one of the soldiers.

No! Resa, fly away!

Just one more word, but all Mo saw was the little bird.

The Piper shot, and the swift fluttered upwards. The arrow

missed, and she flew straight into the Piper's face.

Write, Mo! He pressed the pencil down on to the blood-soaked paper.

The Piper's silver nose slipped when he struck out at the swift.

Death.

76

White Night

The poor Emperor could hardly breathe. It was as if something were sitting on his breast. He opened his eyes and then he saw that it was Death ... and strange heads were looking out from the folds of the great velvet hangings of his bed, some of them horrible, some divinely beautiful: they were all the Emperor's good and bad deeds looking down on him now that Death sat there on his breast.

Hans Christian Andersen, *The Nightingale*

The Adderhead was freezing. He was freezing even in his sleep, although he clutched the cushion to his sore chest, the cushion containing the Book that protected him from eternal cold. Even his dreams, heavy with poppy-juice, couldn't warm him any more. Dreams of the tortures he would inflict on the Bluejay. Once he had dreamt only of love in this castle. But wasn't that only right and proper? Hadn't the love he found here tormented him as much as his rotting flesh?

Oh, how cold he was. Even his dreams seemed to be covered with hoarfrost. Dreams of torture, dreams of love. He opened his eyes, and the painted walls stared at him with the eyes of Violante's mother. That damn poppy-juice. This damn castle. And why was the fire back? The Adderhead groaned and pressed his hands to his eyes, but the sparks seemed to burn even beneath his lids.

Red. Red and gold. Light as sharp as a knife-blade, and out of the fire came the whispering, the whispering he had feared ever since he first heard it at a dying man's side. Trembling, he peered through his swollen fingers. No. No, it couldn't be true. It was the poppy-juice making him imagine them. Nothing else. He saw four of them all standing round his bed, white as snow – no, whiter – and they were whispering the name he had been born with. Over and over again, as if to remind him that he hadn't always had the skin of a serpent.

It was the poppy-juice, only the poppy-juice.

The Adderhead thrust a trembling hand into the cushion to take out the Book, to hold it up and so ward them off, but their white fingers were already reaching into his breast.

How they were looking at him! With the eyes of all the dead he had sent to them.

And then they whispered his name again.

And his heart stood still.

77

Over

'I did it!' cried God. And he looked down at Sparrow and
pointed at the vanishing marvel. 'I did it! I made a Swift!'

Ted Hughes,
How Sparrow Saved the Birds, from *The Dreamfighter*

The White Woman appeared as soon as Mo closed the
blood-soaked Book again. At the sight of her the Piper
forgot the swift, and Violante's son hid under the table to
which Mo was chained. But this daughter of Death hadn't
come to take the Bluejay away. She was here to give him his
freedom, and Resa saw the relief on Mo's face.

At that moment he forgot everything. Resa saw that too.
Perhaps he hoped, for a split second, that the story had been
told to the end at last. But the Piper hadn't died with his master. For a few precious moments fear held him transfixed, but
when the White Woman disappeared she took his fear with
her, and Resa spread her wings once more. She spat out the
seeds as she flew at the Piper, so that she would get back
hands she could use to help, feet that could run. But the bird

was reluctant to leave her, and she still had claws as she landed on the flagstones right beside the two men.

Mo looked down at her in alarm, and before Resa could realize what danger she was putting him in, the Piper had taken the chains binding him to the table, to wind them around his own hand. Mo fell to his knees as the Piper tugged the chains. He was holding the knife he had been using to cut paper, but what good was a bookbinder's knife against a sword or a crossbow?

Desperately, Resa fluttered up on the table, retching in the frantic hope that there might be a seed still under her tongue, but her feathery prison would not let her go, and the Piper pulled at Mo's chains again.

'Your pale angel was in a hurry to leave this time!' he said scornfully. 'Why didn't she undo your chains for you? But don't worry, we'll leave you plenty of time to die, time enough for your white friends to come back again. Now, go on working.'

With difficulty, Mo straightened up. 'Why should I?' he asked, pushing the White Book over to the Piper. 'Your master won't be needing any second book now. That's why the White Woman came here. I've written the three words in this one. See for yourself. The Adderhead is dead.'

The Piper stared at the bloodstained binding. Then he looked under the table, where Jacopo was cowering like a small, frightened animal.

'Is he indeed?' he said, drawing his sword. 'Well, if that's so . . . I've no objection to immortality myself. So, as I said, go on working.'

His soldiers began to whisper.

'Quiet!' the Piper snapped, pointing to one of them with

his gloved hand. 'You. Go to the Adderhead and tell him the Bluejay claims he's dead.'

The soldier hurried away. The others watched him go with fear in their eyes. But the Piper put the point of his sword to Mo's chest. 'You're not working yet!'

Mo stepped as far back as the chains would allow, the knife in his hand. 'There won't be any other book. No book with white pages. Off you go, Jacopo! Run to your mother and tell her everything will be all right.'

Jacopo crawled out from under the table and ran for it. The Piper didn't even look at him as he disappeared. 'When the Adderhead's son was born I advised him to dispose of Cosimo's little bastard,' he said, looking at the White Book. 'But he wouldn't hear of it. Stupid of him.'

The soldier he had sent to the Adderhead came stumbling back into the dark hall, out of breath.

'The Jay's telling the truth!' he gasped. 'The Adderhead is dead, and the White Women are everywhere.'

The other soldiers lowered their crossbows.

'L-l-let's go back to Ombra, sir!' stammered one of them. 'This castle is bewitched. We can take the Bluejay with us!'

'A good idea,' said the Piper. And he smiled.

No.

Resa fluttered into his face once more, pecking the smile from his lips. It was the bird who did it – or was it the woman, the wife? She heard Mo cry out as the Piper struck at her with his sword. The blade cut deep into her wing. She fell, and suddenly she had human limbs again, as if the Piper had cut the bird out of her. The Piper stared at her in disbelief, but as he raised his sword Mo thrust the knife deep into his chest, right through his expensive clothes. And the Piper looked at him in astonishment as he died.

His soldiers, however, were still there. Mo snatched the Piper's sword and drove them back, away from his wife. But there were too many of them, and he was still chained to the table. Soon there was blood everywhere, on his chest, on his hands and arms. Was it his own?

They were going to kill him, and once again Resa could only watch, stand by and watch as she had done so often in the course of this story. But suddenly fire was consuming the chains and Dustfinger stood over her to protect her, with the marten on his shoulder. Beside him stood Jacopo.

'Is she dead too?' Resa heard him ask as the soldiers ran from the fire, screaming.

'No,' Dustfinger answered. 'It's only her arm that's wounded.'

'But she was a bird!' said Jacopo.

'Yes.' That was Mo's voice. 'Don't you think that sounds like a good story?'

It was suddenly so quiet in the great hall. No more fighting, no screams, only the crackling of the fire as it talked to Dustfinger.

Mo knelt down beside her. There was blood everywhere, but he was alive, and once again Resa had a human hand to take his. And all was well.

78

Staked on the Wrong Card

Like Orpheus I play
death on the strings of life.

Ingeborg Bachmann, *To Speak of the Dark*

Orpheus was reading frantically, he realized that himself.
He was reading in too loud a voice, and much too fast.
As if his tongue were trying to thrust the words through the
bookbinder's body like knives. He had written him the torments of hell in revenge for the Piper's mocking smile. That
smile still haunted him. How small it had made him, just
when he was feeling so full of grandeur! But at least there'd
soon be no more smiling for the Bluejay.

Ironstone stirred the ink and looked at him anxiously. His
fury obviously showed on his face, written there in small beads
of sweat.

Concentrate, Orpheus, he told himself – and tried again.
There were a few words that he could hardly decipher because
the letters ran together so unsteadily, drunk with his own rage.

Why did he feel as if he were reading the words into a void?
Why did they seem like pebbles being dropped down a well,
where their echo was lost in the darkness? Something was
wrong. He'd never felt like this before when he was reading
aloud.

'Ironstone!' he ordered the glass man. 'Run to the Hall of
a Thousand Windows and see how the Bluejay is doing. He
ought to be doubled up in agony like a poisoned dog by now.'

The glass man lowered the twig he was using to stir the ink
and looked at him in alarm. 'But . . . but master, I don't know
the way.'

'Don't make such a stupid fuss, or do you want me to ask
the Night-Mare if it fancies a glass man for a change? Turn
right outside this room and then go straight ahead. Ask the
guards the way!'

Unhappily, Ironstone set off. Silly creature! Fenoglio really
might have thought up a less ridiculous kind of assistant to
help scribes. But that was the trouble with this world – at
heart, it was childish. Why had he loved the book so much
when he was a child? Well, for that very reason! But now he
was grown up, and it was time this world grew up too.

Another sentence – and once again the strange feeling that
the words were dying away even before he spoke them. Damn
it!

Dizzy with rage, he was reaching for the inkwell to throw
it at the painted wall when he suddenly heard loud shouts outside. Orpheus put the inkwell back on the table and listened.
What was all this? He opened his door and looked down the
corridor. There were no guards outside the Adderhead's bedchamber any more, and two servants ran past him in a state
of great agitation. By all the devils in hell, what did this mean?

And why was Dustfinger's fire burning on the walls again?

Orpheus hurried out into the passage and stopped outside the Adderhead's door. It was open, and the Silver Prince lay dead on his bed, his eyes open so wide that it wasn't difficult to guess what his last sight had been.

Instinctively, Orpheus looked round before he went up to the bed, but of course the White Women had left long ago. They had what they'd been waiting so long for. But how? How had it happened?

'Yes, you'll have to look for a new master, Four-Eyes!' Thumbling came out from behind the hangings of the bed and gave him a hawkish smile. Orpheus saw the ring that the Adderhead had used to seal death sentences on his lean hand. Thumbling was also wearing the Silver Prince's sword.

'Let's hope the stink washes out!' he murmured to Orpheus in a confidential tone as he flung his master's heavy velvet coat over his shoulders. Then he strode away, down the corridor where Dustfinger's fire whispered along the walls.

But Orpheus stood there feeling the tears run down his nose. All was lost! He'd staked everything on the wrong card; he'd put up with the stench of the rotting prince, bowed low to him and wasted his time in this dark castle all for nothing! It wasn't he who had written the last song but Fenoglio, who else could it have been? And presumably the Bluejay featured as the hero again, while Orpheus was the villain. No, worse! He played the ridiculous part of the loser!

He spat in the Adderhead's rigid face and stumbled back to his room, where the useless words still lay on the table. Trembling with rage, he picked up the inkwell and poured its contents over what he had written.

'Master, master! Have you heard?' The glass man, out of

breath, was standing in the doorway. He was quick on his spidery legs, you had to give him that.

'Yes, I know, the Adderhead's dead! What about the Bluejay?'

'They're fighting! He and the Piper are fighting.'

'Aha. Well, perhaps Silver-Nose may run him through yet. That would at least be something.' Orpheus snatched up his things and stuffed them into the fine leather bag he had brought from Ombra: pens, parchment, even the empty inkwell, the silver candelabrum that the Adderhead had given him, and of course the three books – Jacopo's, and the two about the Bluejay. He wasn't giving yet, not he.

He picked up the glass man and put him in the pouch at his belt.

'What are you going to do, master?' asked Ironstone anxiously.

'We'll summon the Night-Mare and get out of this castle!'

'The Night-Mare's gone, master! They say the Fire-Dancer sent it up in smoke!'

Damn, damn, damn. Of course. That was why fire was burning on the walls again! Dustfinger had recognized the Night-Mare. He had seen who was breathing there in the heart of darkness! Well, Orpheus, you'll just have to read yourself another Night-Mare out of Jacopo's book, he thought. It wasn't all that difficult. Only this time he must give it a name that Dustfinger didn't know!

He listened for sounds in the corridor. Nothing. The rats had deserted the sinking ship. The Adderhead was alone in death. Orpheus went back into the bedchamber where his bloated corpse lay and stole what silver he could find, but Thumbling hadn't missed much. Then he hurried with the wailing glass man to the tunnel that had brought the Piper to the castle. Water was running down the stone walls as if the passage were sticking in the lake's moist flesh like a thorn.

The guards posted on the bank to keep watch on the way out were gone, but a few dead soldiers lay among the rocks. In the end they had clearly killed each other in their panic. Orpheus took a sword from one of the dead men, but threw it away again when he discovered how heavy it was. Instead he took a knife from another dead man's belt and put the soldier's coarse cloak over his shoulders. It might look ugly, but it was warm.

'Where are we going, master?' faltered Ironstone. 'Back to Ombra?'

'Why would we want to go back there?' was all that Orpheus replied, as he looked up at the dark slopes barring the way to the north.

To the north . . . he had no idea what to expect there. As with so much else in his book, Fenoglio had written nothing about it, and that was just why he would go north. The mountains looked far from inviting, with their snowy peaks and bleak slopes. But it was the best way to go now that Ombra, he supposed, would soon belong to Violante and the Bluejay. To hell with that wretched bookbinder, to the hottest hell the human mind can imagine, he thought. And may Dustfinger freeze in eternal ice until his treacherous fingers break off!

Orpheus looked back at the bridge one last time before making for the trees. There went the Silver Prince's soldiers, running away. And what were they running away from? Two men and their white guardian angels. And their lord's bloated body.

'Master, master, couldn't you put me on your shoulder?

Suppose I fall out of this pouch?' the glass man wailed.

'Then I'll need a new glass man!' Orpheus replied.

Northward into unwritten country. Yes, he thought as his feet, with difficulty, sought a way up the steep slope. Maybe that part of this world will obey my words.

79

Leaving

'Tell me a story,' says Alba, leaning against me like cold cooked pasta.
I put my arm around her. 'What kind of story?'
'A good story. A story about you and Mama . . .'
'Hmm. Okay. Once upon a time—'
'When was that?'
'All times at once. A long time ago, and right now.'

Audrey Niffenegger, *The Time Traveller's Wife*

The Piper's sword had cut deep into Resa's arm, but Brianna had learnt a good deal from her mother, even though she liked singing to Violante better than growing herbs in stony fields.

'The arm will heal,' she said as she bound up the wound. But the bird would never leave Resa now. Silvertongue knew that as well as Dustfinger.

The Piper had done his best to send the Bluejay after his master to his death. He had wounded him in the shoulder and on the left arm, but in the end he alone had followed the

Adderhead, and Dustfinger made the fire consume both his body and his master's.

Pale-faced, Violante stood at Silvertongue's side as the Adderhead and the Piper turned to ashes. She looked younger, as if she had shed a few years in the cell where her father had flung her – almost as forlorn as a child – yet when she turned away at last from the fire devouring her father, she put her arm around her son. Dustfinger had never seen her do a thing like that before. Everyone still disliked Jacopo, though he had saved them all. Even Silvertongue with his soft heart felt the same, though he was ashamed of it. Dustfinger saw it in his face.

There were still a dozen of Violante's child soldiers alive. They found them in the dungeon cells, but the Adderhead's soldiers had all gone, like the White Women. Only their abandoned tents still stood on the banks of the lake, with the black coach and a few riderless horses. Jacopo claimed that his great-grandfather's man-eating fish had come up from the lake and eaten some of the men as they ran for their lives over the bridge. Neither Silvertongue nor Violante believed him, but Dustfinger went out on to the bridge and found a few shimmering scales on the wet stones, as large as linden leaves. So they didn't take the bridge, but left the Castle in the Lake along the tunnel down which the Piper had come.

It was snowing when they stepped out into the open, and the castle disappeared behind them among the swirling snowflakes as if it were dissolving into the whiteness. The world around them was as still as if it had used up all words, as if all the tales there were to tell in this world had now been told. Dustfinger found Orpheus's tracks in the frozen mud of the bank, and Silvertongue looked at the trees into which they disappeared as if he could still hear Orpheus's voice inside him.

'I wish he were dead,' he said quietly.

'A clever wish,' replied Dustfinger. 'But I'm afraid it's too late to make it come true.' He had looked for Orpheus after the Piper was dead, but his room had been empty, like Thumbling's. The world looked so bright this cold morning. They were all so light at heart. But the darkness remained, and would go on telling its part of the story.

They caught some of the horses left behind by the Adderhead's men. Although weakened by his wounds, Silvertongue was in a hurry. *At least let's save our daughters.*

'The Black Prince will have been looking after Meggie,' Dustfinger told him, but the anxiety was still on his face as they rode further and further south.

They were a silent company, all caught up in their own thoughts and memories. Only Jacopo sometimes raised his clear voice, as demanding as ever. 'I'm hungry.' 'I'm thirsty.' 'When will we be there?' 'Do you think the Milksop has killed the children and the robbers?' His mother always answered him, although often abstractedly. The Castle in the Lake had spun a bond between them out of shared fear and dark memories, and perhaps the strongest strand of it was the fact that Jacopo had done what his mother intended to do when she rode to the castle. The Adderhead was dead. But Dustfinger felt sure that, all the same, Violante would feel her father behind her like a shadow all her life – and very likely Her Ugliness knew it herself by now.

Silvertongue took the Bluejay away with him too. It seemed as if the two of them were riding side by side, and not for the first time Dustfinger wondered whether they were only two sides of the same man. Whatever the answer was, the book-binder loved this world as much as the robber did.

On the first night, when they stopped to rest under a tree with furry yellow catkins falling from its bare branches, the swift came back, although Resa had thrown the last of the seeds into the lake. She changed shape in her sleep and flew up into the flowering branches, where moonlight painted her plumage silver. When Dustfinger saw her sitting there he woke Silvertongue, and they waited under the tree together until the swift flew down again at dawn and turned back into a woman there between them.

'What will become of the child?' she asked, full of dread.

'It will dream of flying,' Silvertongue replied. Just as the bookbinder dreamt of the robber, and the robber of the book-binder, and the Fire-Dancer dreamt of the flames and the minstrel woman who could dance like them. Perhaps, after all, this world was made of dreams, and an old man had merely found the words for them.

Resa wept when they came to the cave and found it empty, but Dustfinger discovered the Strong Man's sign out-side the entrance, drawn on the rocks in soot, and buried underneath it was a message obviously left by Doria for his big brother. Dustfinger had heard of the tree with the nests in it that Doria described, but he had never seen it with his own eyes.

It took them two days to find the tree, and Dustfinger was the first to see the giant. He took Silvertongue's reins, and Resa put her hand to her mouth in alarm. But Violante stared at the giant like an enchanted child.

He was holding Roxane in his hand as if she too were a bird. Brianna went pale at the sight of her mother between those mighty fingers, but Dustfinger dismounted and went up to the giant.

The Black Prince was standing between the giant's vast legs, with the bear beside him. He was limping as he went to meet Dustfinger, but he looked happier than he had for a long time.

'Where's Meggie?' asked Silvertongue as the Prince hugged him, and Battista pointed up into the tree. Dustfinger had never seen such a tree before, not even in the wild heart of the Wayless Wood, and he wanted to climb up to the nests at once and see the branches covered with frost-flowers where the women and children perched like birds.

Meggie's voice called her father's name, and Silvertongue went to meet her as she let herself down the trunk on a rope, as naturally as if she had always lived in the trees. But Dustfinger turned and looked up at Roxane. She whispered something to the giant, who put her down on the ground as carefully as if he believed she was made of glass. Roxane. He vowed never to forget her name again. He would ask the fire to write its letters in his heart so that not even the White Women could wash it away. Roxane. Dustfinger held her in his arms, and the giant looked down at them with eyes that seemed to reflect all the colours in the world.

'Look around,' Roxane whispered to him, and Dustfinger saw Silvertongue embracing his daughter and wiping the tears off her face. He saw the bookworm woman running to Resa – how in the name of all the fairies did she come to be here? – Tullio burying his furry face in Violante's skirt, the Strong Man almost smothering Silvertongue in his bear hug . . . and . . .

Farid.

He stood there digging his toes into the newly fallen snow. He still went barefoot, and surely he'd grown taller?

Dustfinger went up to him. 'I see you've taken good care of Roxane,' he said. 'Did the fire obey you while I was gone?'

'It always obeys me!' Yes, he had grown older. 'I fought Sootbird.'

'Imagine that!'

'My fire ate his fire.'

'Did it indeed?'

'Yes! I climbed up on the giant and made fire rain down on Sootbird. And then the giant broke his neck.'

Dustfinger couldn't help smiling, and Farid returned his smile. 'Do you . . . do you have to go away again?' He looked as anxious as if he feared the White Women were already waiting.

'No,' said Dustfinger, smiling again. 'No, not for a while, I think.'

Farid. He'd ask the fire to write that name in his heart as well. Roxane. Brianna. Farid. And Gwin, of course.

80

Ombra

What if this road, that has held no surprises
These many years, decided not to go
Home after all; what if it could turn
Left or right with no more ado
Than a kite-tail? What if its tarry skin
Were like a long, supple bolt of cloth,
that is shaken and rolled out, and takes
a new shape from the contours beneath?
And if it chose to lay itself down
In a new way; around a blind corner,
across hills you must climb without knowing
what's on the other side; who would not hanker
to be going, at all risks? Who wants to know
a story's end, or where a road will go.

Sheenagh Pugh, What If This Road

When the Black Prince took the children back to Ombra
snow lay on the battlements above the city wall, but
the women threw flowers they had made out of scraps of fabric cut from old clothes. The lion emblem waved from the city

towers again, but now his paw was laid on a book with blank pages, and his mane was made of fire. The Milksop had gone. He had fled from the giant, not to Ombra, but straight to the Castle of Night and his sister's arms, and Violante had returned to take possession of the city and prepare it for the return of its children.

Meggie was standing with Elinor, Darius and Fenoglio in the square outside the castle gates as the mothers hugged their sons and daughters, and Violante, speaking from the battlements, thanked the Black Prince and the Bluejay for saving them.

'You know what, Meggie?' Fenoglio whispered to her, as Violante had provisions from the castle kitchens distributed to the women. 'Maybe Her Ugliness will fall in love with the Black Prince some day. After all, he was the Bluejay before your father took the part, and Violante was more in love with the role than the man anyway!'

Oh, Fenoglio! He was just the same as ever. Although the giant had gone back to his mountains long ago, he had completely restored the old man's self-confidence.

The Bluejay had not come to Ombra. Mo and Resa had stayed behind at the farm where they had once lived. 'Let the Bluejay go back to where he came from,' he had told the Prince. 'Into the strolling players' songs.' They were singing them everywhere already: how the Jay and the Fire-Dancer, all by themselves, had defeated the Adderhead and the Piper with all their men . . .

'Please, Battista,' Mo had said, 'why don't *you*, at least, write a song telling the true story? About the people who helped the Jay and the Fire-Dancer. About the swift – and the boy!'

Battista had promised Mo to write a song like that, but

Fenoglio only shook his head. 'No one will sing it, Meggie. People don't like their heroes to need help, particularly not from women and children.'

No doubt he was right. Perhaps that meant Violante would have a hard time on the throne of Ombra, although all its people were cheering her today. Jacopo stood beside his mother. He looked more like a small copy of his father every day, but all the same he still reminded Meggie even more of his sinister grandfather. She shuddered to think how ready Jacopo had been to deliver the Adderhead up to Death – even though that had been the saving of Mo.

Another widow now ruled the country on the far side of the forest, and she too had a son and was taking care of the throne for him. Meggie knew that Violante expected war, but no one wanted to think of that today. This day belonged to the children who had come home. Not one of them was missing, and the strolling players sang about Farid's fire, the tree full of nests, and the giant who had so mysteriously come out of the mountains at just the right moment.

'I'll miss him,' Elinor had whispered as he disappeared among the trees, and Meggie felt the same. She would never forget how the Inkworld was reflected on his skin, or how light-footed he was when he strode away, so gentle in such a big body.

'Meggie!' Farid made his way through the women and children. 'Where's Silvertongue?'

'With my mother,' she replied – and was surprised to find that her heart beat no faster than usual at the sight of him. When had that changed?

Farid frowned. 'Yes, yes,' he said, 'and Dustfinger's with his minstrel woman again. He kisses her so often you might think her lips tasted of honey.'

Oh dear. Farid was still jealous of Roxane.

'I think I'll go away for a while,' he said.

'Go away? Where to?'

Behind Meggie, Elinor and Fenoglio began arguing over something Elinor didn't like about the look of the castle. Those two loved arguing with each other, and they had plenty of opportunity for arguments because they were neighbours now. The bag in which Elinor had packed all kinds of things that might come in useful in the Inkworld, including her silver cutlery, was still standing in her house in the other world ('Well, I was very excited, it's easy to forget such things then!'), but fortunately she had been wearing the Loredan family jewels when Darius read them both over, and Rosenquartz had sold them for her so cleverly ('Meggie, you've no idea what a shrewd businessman that glass man is!') that now she was the proud possessor of a house in the street where Minerva lived.

'Where to?' Farid made a fiery flower grow between his fingers and placed it on Meggie's dress. 'Oh, I think I'll just stroll from village to village the way Dustfinger used to.'

Meggie looked at the burning flower. The flames faded like real petals, and only a tiny spot of ash was left on her dress. Farid. His mere name used to quicken her pulse, but now she hardly listened as he told her about his plans, all the marketplaces where he would put on a show, the mountain villages, the far side of the Wayless Wood. Her heart leapt only when she suddenly saw the Strong Man standing there with the women. A few of the children had climbed on to his shoulders, just as they often used to in the cave, but she couldn't see the face she was looking for beside him. Disappointed, she let her eyes wander on, and blushed when Doria was suddenly standing there in front of her. Farid abruptly fell silent, and looked at the other boy in the same way as he so often looked at Roxane.

The scar on Doria's forehead was as long as Meggie's middle finger. 'A blow with a spiked mace, not particularly well aimed,' Roxane had said. 'Head wounds bleed a lot, so they probably thought he was dead.' Roxane had nursed him for many nights on end, but Fenoglio's opinion was still that Doria was alive thanks only to the story he had written long ago about the boy's future. 'And anyway, even if you want to believe it was Roxane who made him better, then who made up Roxane, may I ask?' He was certainly his old self again.

'Doria! How are you?' Meggie involuntarily put out her hand and caressed the scar on his forehead. Farid gave her a strange look.

'Fine. My head's as good as new.' Doria brought something out from behind his back. 'Is this what they're like?'

Meggie stared at the tiny wooden aeroplane he had made.

'That's how you described them, isn't it? The flying machines.'

'But you were unconscious!'

He smiled and put his hand to his head. 'The words are in here, all the same. But I don't know how the music thing is supposed to work. You know, the little box that plays music.'

Meggie had to smile. 'Oh yes, a radio. That wouldn't be any good here. I don't know just how to explain it to you . . .'

Farid was still looking at her. Then he abruptly took her hand. 'Excuse us,' he told Doria, and led Meggie into the nearest house entrance with him. 'Does Silvertongue know how you look at him?'

'Look at who?'

'Who!' He passed his finger over his forehead as if tracing Doria's scar. 'Listen,' he said, stroking her hair back. 'Why don't you come with me? We could go from village to village together. The way we did when we and Dustfinger were following your mother and father. Do you remember?'

How could he ask that?

Meggie looked over her shoulder. Doria was standing beside Fenoglio and Elinor. Fenoglio was looking at the aeroplane.

'I'm sorry, Farid,' she said, gently removing his hand from her shoulder. 'But I don't want to leave.'

'Why not?' He tried to kiss her, but Meggie turned her face away. Even though she felt tears coming to her eyes. *Do you remember?*

'I wish you luck,' she said, kissing him on the cheek. He still had the most beautiful eyes of any boy she'd ever seen. But now her heart beat so much faster for someone else.

81

Later

Almost five months later a baby will be born at the lonely farm where the Black Prince once hid the Bluejay. It will be a boy, dark-haired like his father, but with his mother's and sister's eyes. He will think that every wood is full of fairies, that a glass man sleeps on every table – so long as there's some parchment on it – that books are written by hand, and the most famous of illuminators paints with his left hand because his right hand is made of leather. He will think that strolling players breathe fire and perform comic plays in every market-place, that women always wear long dresses, and soldiers stand at every city gate.

And he will have an aunt called Elinor who tells him there's a world which is not like this one. A world with neither fairies nor glass men, but with animals who carry their young in a pouch in front of their bellies, and birds with wings that beat so fast it sounds like the humming of a bumblebee, with carriages that drive along without any horses, and pictures that move of their own accord. Elinor will tell him how, long ago, a horrible man called Orpheus brought his parents out of that world and into this one by magic, and how this Orpheus finally had to flee from his father and the Fire-Dancer to the northern mountains, where it's to be hoped he froze to death. She will tell him that even the most powerful men don't carry swords in the other world, but there are much, much more terrible weapons there. (His father owns a very fine sword, kept wrapped in a cloth in his workshop. He hides it from the child, but sometimes the boy will secretly unwrap it and runs his fingers over the shiny blade.) Elinor will tell him amazing things about that other world. She will even claim that the people there have built coaches that can fly, but he doesn't really believe that, although Doria has made wings for his sister, and Meggie really did fly from the city wall to the river wearing them. The boy laughed at her, all the same, for he knows more about flying than Meggie. That's because he sometimes grows wings at night, and he and his mother fly up into the trees. But perhaps he's just dreaming it. He dreams it almost every night, but he'd like to see the flying coaches all the same, and the animals with pouches, the moving pictures, and the house that Elinor is always talking about. A house full of books not written by any hand, and the books are sad, because they're waiting for Elinor.

'Some day we'll go and visit them together,' Elinor often says, and Darius nods. Darius can tell wonderful stories too, about flying carpets and genies in bottles. 'Some day the three of us will go back, and then I'll show you all these things.'

And the boy runs to the workshop where his father is making leather clothes for books that are often illustrated with pictures painted by the famous Balbulus himself, and says, 'Mo!' He always calls his father Mo, he doesn't know why, perhaps because that's what his sister calls him. 'When are we going to the other world, the one you came from?'

And his father puts him on his lap and runs his fingers through his dark hair, and says, like Elinor, 'I'm sure we will some day. But we'd need words for that, exactly the right words, because only the right words unlock the doors between worlds, and the only person who could write them for us is a lazy old man. What's more, I'm afraid he's getting more forgetful every day.'

Then he tells him about the Black Prince and his bear, the giants that they'll go and see someday, and the new tricks the Fire-Dancer has taught the flames. And the boy will see, in his father's eyes, that he is very happy and not at all homesick for the other world. Any more than his sister is. Or his mother.

So the boy will think that perhaps he'll have to go alone one day, if he wants to see that world. And he'll have to find out which old man his father means, because there are several in Ombra. Maybe he means the one who has two glass men and writes songs for the strolling players and for Violante whom everyone calls Her Kindliness, and who is much better liked than her son. Battista calls this old man Inkweaver, and Meggie sometimes goes to see him. Maybe he'll go with her next time, so that he can ask him for the words that open doors. Because it must be exciting in that other world, much more exciting than in his own . . .

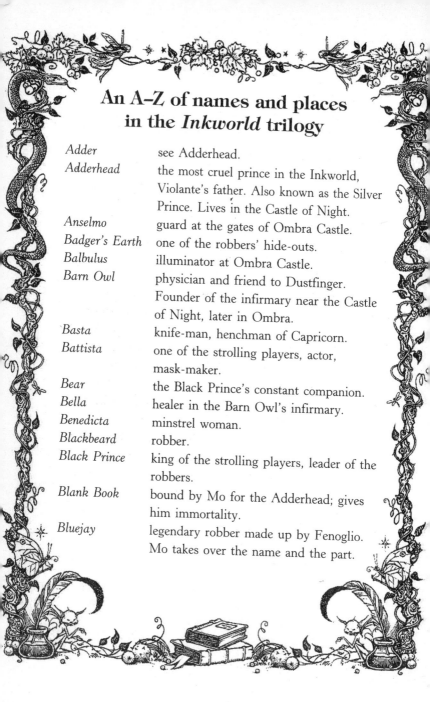

An A–Z of names and places in the *Inkworld* trilogy

Adder	see Adderhead.
Adderhead	the most cruel prince in the Inkworld, Violante's father. Also known as the Silver Prince. Lives in the Castle of Night.
Anselmo	guard at the gates of Ombra Castle.
Badger's Earth	one of the robbers' hide-outs.
Balbulus	illuminator at Ombra Castle.
Barn Owl	physician and friend to Dustfinger. Founder of the infirmary near the Castle of Night, later in Ombra.
Basta	knife-man, henchman of Capricorn.
Battista	one of the strolling players, actor, mask-maker.
Bear	the Black Prince's constant companion.
Bella	healer in the Barn Owl's infirmary.
Benedicta	minstrel woman.
Blackbeard	robber.
Black Prince	king of the strolling players, leader of the robbers.
Blank Book	bound by Mo for the Adderhead; gives him immortality.
Bluejay	legendary robber made up by Fenoglio. Mo takes over the name and the part.

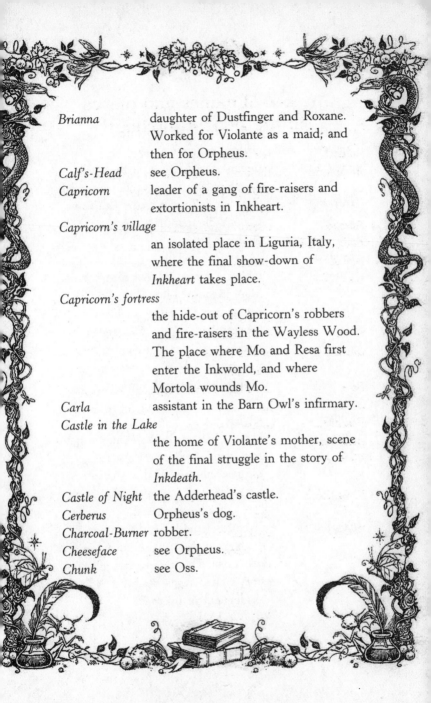

Brianna	daughter of Dustfinger and Roxane. Worked for Violante as a maid; and then for Orpheus.
Calf's-Head	see Orpheus.
Capricorn	leader of a gang of fire-raisers and extortionists in Inkheart.
Capricorn's village	an isolated place in Liguria, Italy, where the final show-down of *Inkheart* takes place.
Capricorn's fortress	the hide-out of Capricorn's robbers and fire-raisers in the Wayless Wood. The place where Mo and Resa first enter the Inkworld, and where Mortola wounds Mo.
Carla	assistant in the Barn Owl's infirmary.
Castle in the Lake	the home of Violante's mother, scene of the final struggle in the story of *Inkdeath*.
Castle of Night	the Adderhead's castle.
Cerberus	Orpheus's dog.
Charcoal-Burner	robber.
Cheeseface	see Orpheus.
Chunk	see Oss.

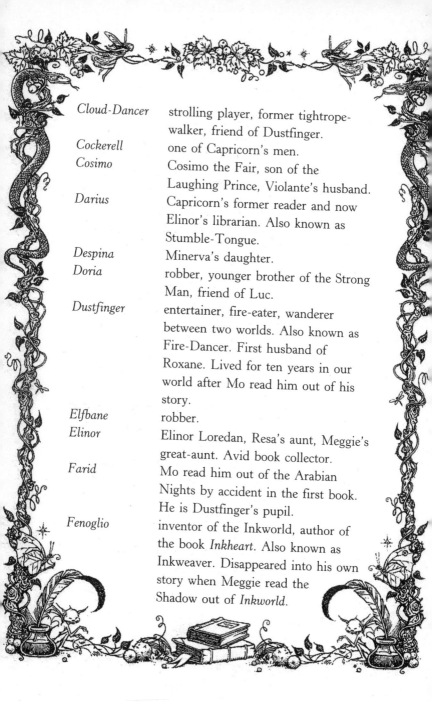

Cloud-Dancer	strolling player, former tightrope-walker, friend of Dustfinger.
Cockerell	one of Capricorn's men.
Cosimo	Cosimo the Fair, son of the Laughing Prince, Violante's husband.
Darius	Capricorn's former reader and now Elinor's librarian. Also known as Stumble-Tongue.
Despina	Minerva's daughter.
Doria	robber, younger brother of the Strong Man, friend of Luc.
Dustfinger	entertainer, fire-eater, wanderer between two worlds. Also known as Fire-Dancer. First husband of Roxane. Lived for ten years in our world after Mo read him out of his story.
Elfbane	robber.
Elinor	Elinor Loredan, Resa's aunt, Meggie's great-aunt. Avid book collector.
Farid	Mo read him out of the Arabian Nights by accident in the first book. He is Dustfinger's pupil.
Fenoglio	inventor of the Inkworld, author of the book *Inkheart*. Also known as Inkweaver. Disappeared into his own story when Meggie read the Shadow out of *Inkworld*.

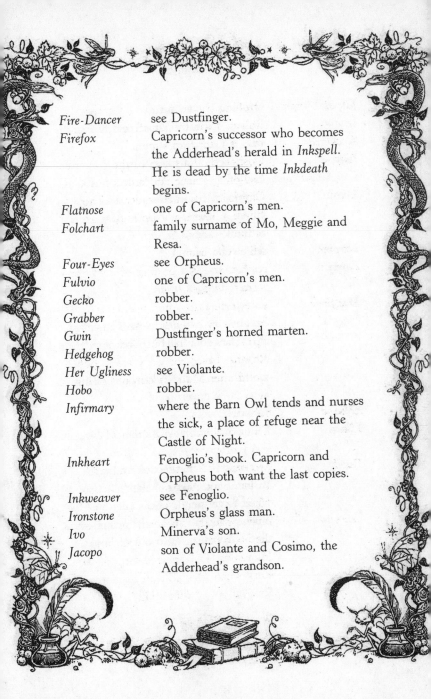

Fire-Dancer	see Dustfinger.
Firefox	Capricorn's successor who becomes the Adderhead's herald in *Inkspell*. He is dead by the time *Inkdeath* begins.
Flatnose	one of Capricorn's men.
Folchart	family surname of Mo, Meggie and Resa.
Four-Eyes	see Orpheus.
Fulvio	one of Capricorn's men.
Gecko	robber.
Grabber	robber.
Gwin	Dustfinger's horned marten.
Hedgehog	robber.
Her Ugliness	see Violante.
Hobo	robber.
Infirmary	where the Barn Owl tends and nurses the sick, a place of refuge near the Castle of Night.
Inkheart	Fenoglio's book. Capricorn and Orpheus both want the last copies.
Inkweaver	see Fenoglio.
Ironstone	Orpheus's glass man.
Ivo	Minerva's son.
Jacopo	son of Violante and Cosimo, the Adderhead's grandson.

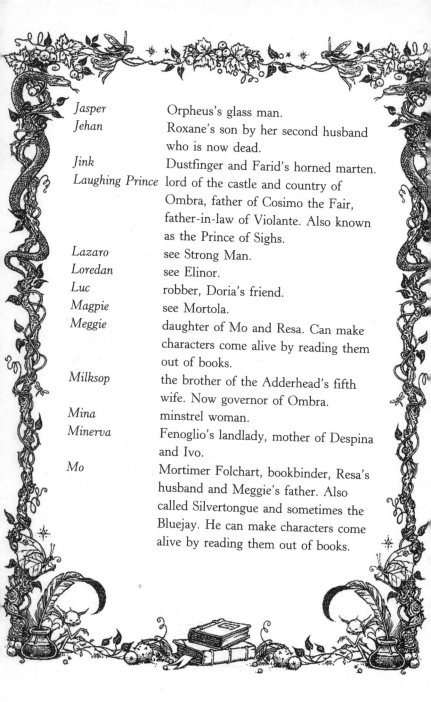

Jasper	Orpheus's glass man.
Jehan	Roxane's son by her second husband who is now dead.
Jink	Dustfinger and Farid's horned marten.
Laughing Prince	lord of the castle and country of Ombra, father of Cosimo the Fair, father-in-law of Violante. Also known as the Prince of Sighs.
Lazaro	see Strong Man.
Loredan	see Elinor.
Luc	robber, Doria's friend.
Magpie	see Mortola.
Meggie	daughter of Mo and Resa. Can make characters come alive by reading them out of books.
Milksop	the brother of the Adderhead's fifth wife. Now governor of Ombra.
Mina	minstrel woman.
Minerva	Fenoglio's landlady, mother of Despina and Ivo.
Mo	Mortimer Folchart, bookbinder, Resa's husband and Meggie's father. Also called Silvertongue and sometimes the Bluejay. He can make characters come alive by reading them out of books.

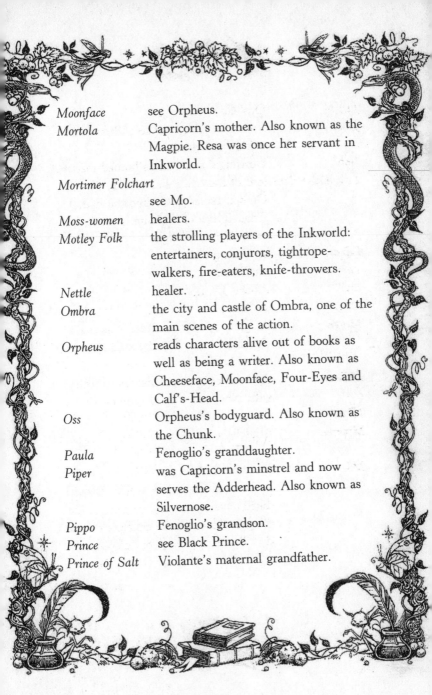

Moonface	see Orpheus.
Mortola	Capricorn's mother. Also known as the Magpie. Resa was once her servant in Inkworld.
Mortimer Folchart	see Mo.
Moss-women	healers.
Motley Folk	the strolling players of the Inkworld: entertainers, conjurors, tightrope-walkers, fire-eaters, knife-throwers.
Nettle	healer.
Ombra	the city and castle of Ombra, one of the main scenes of the action.
Orpheus	reads characters alive out of books as well as being a writer. Also known as Cheeseface, Moonface, Four-Eyes and Calf's-Head.
Oss	Orpheus's bodyguard. Also known as the Chunk.
Paula	Fenoglio's granddaughter.
Piper	was Capricorn's minstrel and now serves the Adderhead. Also known as Silvernose.
Pippo	Fenoglio's grandson.
Prince	see Black Prince.
Prince of Salt	Violante's maternal grandfather.

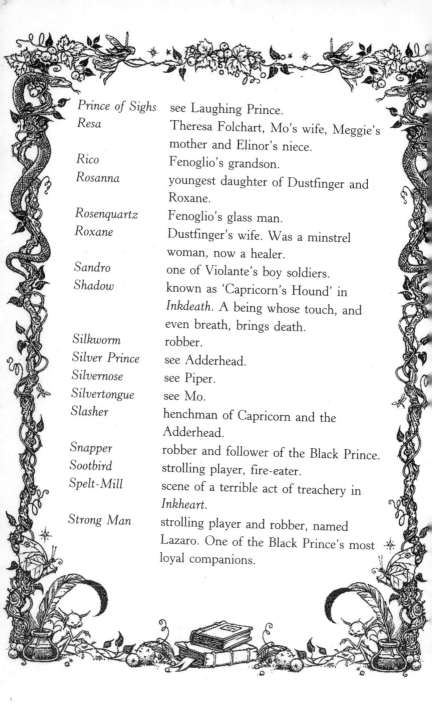

Prince of Sighs	see Laughing Prince.
Resa	Theresa Folchart, Mo's wife, Meggie's mother and Elinor's niece.
Rico	Fenoglio's grandson.
Rosanna	youngest daughter of Dustfinger and Roxane.
Rosenquartz	Fenoglio's glass man.
Roxane	Dustfinger's wife. Was a minstrel woman, now a healer.
Sandro	one of Violante's boy soldiers.
Shadow	known as 'Capricorn's Hound' in *Inkdeath*. A being whose touch, and even breath, brings death.
Silkworm	robber.
Silver Prince	see Adderhead.
Silvernose	see Piper.
Silvertongue	see Mo.
Slasher	henchman of Capricorn and the Adderhead.
Snapper	robber and follower of the Black Prince.
Sootbird	strolling player, fire-eater.
Spelt-Mill	scene of a terrible act of treachery in *Inkheart*.
Strong Man	strolling player and robber, named Lazaro. One of the Black Prince's most loyal companions.

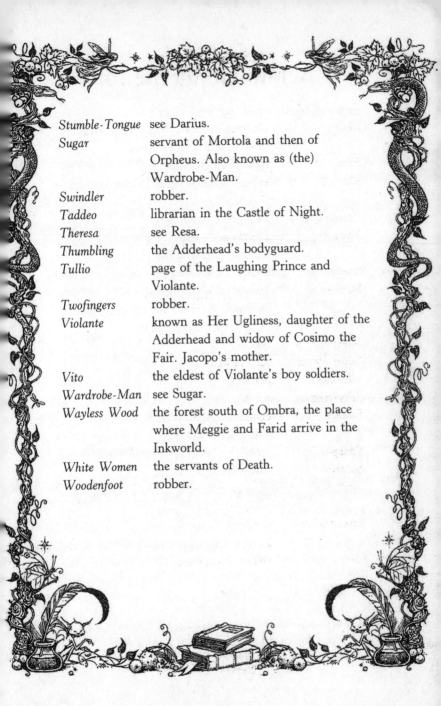

Stumble-Tongue	see Darius.
Sugar	servant of Mortola and then of Orpheus. Also known as (the) Wardrobe-Man.
Swindler	robber.
Taddeo	librarian in the Castle of Night.
Theresa	see Resa.
Thumbling	the Adderhead's bodyguard.
Tullio	page of the Laughing Prince and Violante.
Twofingers	robber.
Violante	known as Her Ugliness, daughter of the Adderhead and widow of Cosimo the Fair. Jacopo's mother.
Vito	the eldest of Violante's boy soldiers.
Wardrobe-Man	see Sugar.
Wayless Wood	the forest south of Ombra, the place where Meggie and Farid arrive in the Inkworld.
White Women	the servants of Death.
Woodenfoot	robber.

Acknowledgements

The Author and Publisher would like to thank the following for their permission to use copyrighted material:

Carlos Drummond de Andrade: from 'Looking for Poetry' from *Looking for Poetry: Poems by Carlos Drummond de Andrade and Rafael Alberti, with Songs from the Quechua*, translated by Mark Strand (Alfred A. Knopf, 2002).

Alan Armstrong: from *Whittington*, illustrated by Steven D. Schindler (Random House Children's Books, 2005), text copyright © 2005 by Alan Armstrong, reprinted by permission of Random House Inc.

Margaret Atwood: from *The Blind Assassin* (Bloomsbury, 2000), © 2000 O.W. Toad Ltd., reprinted by permission of Curtis Brown Group Ltd., London, McClelland & Stewart, and Random House Inc.

Ingeborg Bachman: from 'Darkness Spoken', translated by Peter Filkins, from *Darkness Spoken: The Collected Poems* (Zephyr Press, 2006), © 1978 by Piper Verlag GmbH, München; translation © 2006 by Peter Filkins, reprinted by permission of Zephyr Press, www.zephyrpress.org.

Saul Bellow: from *Henderson the Rain King* (The Viking Press, 1959), © 1958, 1959, renewed 1986, 1987 by Saul Bellow, used by permission of Viking Penguin, a division of Penguin Group (USA) Inc.

Wendell Berry: 'The Peace of Wild Things' from *The Collected Poems of Wendell Berry: 1957–1982* (North Point Press, 1987), © 1985 by Wendell Berry. Reprinted by permission of North Point Press, a division of Farrar, Straus & Giroux, LLC.

Ray Bradbury: from *The Martian Chronicles* (Doubleday, 1950). © 1950, renewed 1977 by Ray Bradbury, reprinted by permission of Don Congdon Associates Inc.

ACKNOWLEDGEMENTS

Bertolt Brecht: 'The Mask of Evil'/'Die Maske des Bösen' from *Deutsche Gedichte. Eine Anthologie* (Philipp Reclam jun., 2000); newly translated for *Inkdeath* by Anthea Bell.

Tor Age Bringsvaerd: from *Die wilden Götter* (Eichborn Verlag, 2001).

Charles Causley: 'I Am the Song' from *Collected Poems 1951–2000* (Picador, 2000), reprinted by permission of David Higham Associates.

Billy Collins: from 'On Turning Ten' from *The Art of Drowning* (University of Pittsburgh Press, 1995), © 1995, reprinted by permission of the publisher.

T.S. Eliot: from 'Little Gidding' Part V from *Collected Poems 1909–1962* (Faber & Faber, 1974), © this edition by T.S. Eliot 1963, reprinted by permission of Faber & Faber Ltd. and Harcourt Inc.

Michael Ende: from *Jim Knopf und die Wilde 13* (Thienemann, 1962), © 1962 by Thienemann Verlag, reprinted by permission of the publisher; newly translated for *Inkdeath* by Anthea Bell.

Louise Glück: from 'Whatever those cries meant' and 'First Memory' from *First Five Books of Poems* (Carcanet Press, 1997); from 'Lament' from *Vita Nova* (Carcanet Press, 2000), reprinted by permission of the publisher.

William Goldman: from *The Princess Bride. S. Morgenstern's Classic Tale of True Love and High Adventure* (Harcourt Brace Jovanovich, 1973), © 1973 by William Goldman, reprinted by permission of Harcourt Inc. and Bloomsbury Publishing.

Barbara Gowdy: from *The White Bone. A Novel* (Henry Holt, 1999), © 1999 by Barbara Gowdy Enterprises, Ltd, reprinted by permission of Henry Holt and Company and Westwood Creative Artists Ltd.

Graham Greene: from *Advice to Writers*, compiled and edited by Jon Winokur (Vintage, 1999), reprinted by permission of David Higham Associates.

Acknowledgements

Alfred Noyes: from 'The Highwayman' from *Forty Singing Seamen and Other Poems* (Blackwood, 1907), reprinted by permission of The Society of Authors as the Literary Representative of the Estate of Alfred Noyes.

Mervyn Peake: from *Titus Groan* (Vintage, 1998), reprinted by permission of The Random House Group Ltd. and David Higham Associates.

Sheenagh Pugh: 'What If This Road' from *Id's Hospit* (Seren, 1997), reprinted by permission of the publisher.

Philip Pullman: from *The Amber Spyglass*, copyright © Philip Pullman, 2000 the third and final volume of the *His Dark Materials* trilogy, published by Scholastic Children's Books. All rights reserved, reprinted by permission of Scholastic Ltd. and Random House Inc.

J.K. Rowling: from *Harry Potter & the Goblet of Fire* (Scholastic, 2000), © J.K. Rowling, 2000, reprinted by permission of Christopher Little Literary Agency.

Salman Rushdie: from *Midnight's Children. A Novel* (Jonathan Cape, 1981), © 1981 by Salman Rushdie, reprinted by permission of The Random House Group Ltd. and The Wylie Agency (UK); from *Haroun and the Sea of Stories* (Granta Books, in association with Penguin Books, 1990), © Salman Rushdie, 1990, reprinted by permission of Granta Books; from 'The Power of the Pen: Does Writing Change Anything?' from *PEN America: A Journal for Writers and Readers, Issue 7: World Voices (2006)*, reprinted by permission of The Wylie Agency (UK).

Norman H. Russell: 'The Message of the Rain' from *Songs from the Earth on Turtle's Back: Contemporary American Indian Poetry*, edited by Joseph Bruchac (The Greenfield Review Press, 1983).

Isaac Bashevis Singer: from *Advice to Writers*, compiled and edited by Jon Winokur (Vintage Books, 1999), © Isaac Bashevis Singer, reprinted by permission of A.M. Heath & Co. Ltd.

ACKNOWLEDGEMENTS

Markus Zusak: from *I Am the Messenger* (Alfred A. Knopf, 2005), © 2005 by Markus Zusak, reprinted by permission of Alfred A. Knopf, an imprint of Random House Children's Books, a division of Random House Inc., by Arrangement with the Licensor, Markus Zusak c/o Curtis Brown (Aust) Pty Ltd; from *The Book Thief* (Alfred A. Knopf, 2006), © 2006 by Markus Zusak, reprinted by permission of Alfred A. Knopf, an imprint of Random House Children's Books, a division of Random House Inc., by Arrangement with the Licensor, Markus Zusak, c/o Curtis Brown (Aust) Pty Ltd.

Every effort has been made to trace or contact all copyright holders. The publishers would be pleased to rectify any errors or omissions brought to their notice at the earliest opportunity.